IAN IRVINE

A SHADOW ON THE GLASS

ASPECT®

WARNER BOOKS

A Time Warner Company

WARNER BOOKS EDITION

Copyright © 1998 by Ian Irvine
Maps copyright © 1998 by Ian Irvine
All rights reserved. No part of this book may be reproduced in any form or by any electronic or mechanical means, including information storage and retrieval systems, without permission in writing from the publisher, except by a reviewer who may quote brief passages in a review.

Cover illustration by Mark Sofilas

This edition is published by arrangement with Penguin Books Australia, Ltd.

Aspect® name and logo are registered trademarks of Warner Books, Inc.

Warner Books, Inc.
1271 Avenue of the Americas
New York, NY 10020

Visit our Web site at www.twbookmark.com

For information on Time Warner Trade Publishing's online program, visit www.ipublish.com

 A Time Warner Company

Printed in the United States of America

First Warner Books Printing: July 2001

10 9 8 7 6 5 4 3 2 1

PAWNS OF THE NEW CLYSM

Karan of Gothryme: Her wild talents are born of a tragic, cursed heritage. They herald an unknown destiny—and give her an unexpected ability to stay alive . . .

Master Llian of the Zain: A brilliant prodigy, his voice is his magic, his memory is his strength—but his ambition is his doom . . .

Maigraith: An austere orphan raised by the uncanny Faellem, her distant coldness masks terrible pain—and a more terrible power . . .

The Whelm: Relentless and ghastly, they exist only to serve—but have long forgotten who their master is . . .

Lord Yggur of Fiz Gorgo: The conqueror/sorcerer may be a mad tyrant—or a hero cruelly wronged . . .

Magister Mendark of Thurkad: Paternal and petulant, compassionate and cruel, avuncular and egomaniacal, the most powerful mancer has ruled wicked Thurkad for millennia—and plans to hold on forever . . .

"A great find! Irvine writes beautifully . . . refreshing, complicated, and compelling."

—Kate Elliott, author of *King's Dragon*

To my legion of faithful readers,
companions on the long march,
who never faltered though having to
wait nine years for the ending.
But most especially to

Nancy and Eric

"*A grain in the balance will determine which individual shall live and which shall die — which variety or species shall increase in number, and which shall decrease, or finally become extinct.*"

DARWIN, *THE ORIGIN OF SPECIES*

CONTENTS

MAPS

PART ONE

PART TWO

PART THREE

ACKNOWLEDGEMENTS

Among the many people who have read drafts for me over the years and helped this novel to find its true home, I would particularly like to acknowledge the counsel and kindness of John Rummery, John Cohen, Van Ikin and Nancy Mortimer.

To all the warm-hearted people at Penguin Books, especially my publisher Erica Irving, thank you for your enthusiasm for the work and for providing the resources to make the series as good as it could possibly be. I would also like to thank Alex Skovron for meticulous proofreading, Barrie Frieden-Collins for cover-art concepts, Mark Sofilas for the wonderful covers, and Selwa Anthony, my agent.

To my editor Kay Ronai, it has been a privilege and a pleasure to work with you.

Most of all, I would like to thank Anne Irvine.

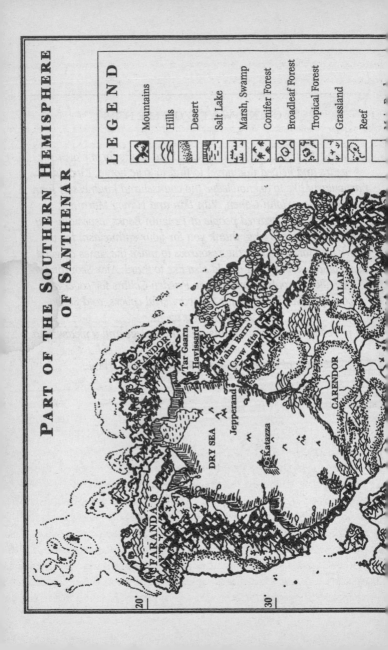

PART OF THE SOUTHERN HEMISPHERE OF SANTHENAR

LEGEND

- Mountains
- Hills
- Desert
- Salt Lake
- Marsh, Swamp
- Conifer Forest
- Broadleaf Forest
- Tropical Forest
- Grassland
- Reef

CRANDOR

Tar Gaarn

Havissard

Wahn Barre

Crow Mtn

Jepperand

Katazza

CARENDOR

KALAR

FARANDA

DRY SEA

STRADOMOR ISLAND

LUUMA NARTA

HA-DROW

MIRRILADELL

Burning
Mountain

FIZ GOLGO

LAURALIN

KARAMA MALAMA
(Sea of Mists)

OOLO

SHAZABBA

Steppe

SCALE

KILOMETERS

0 100 200 300 400 500 600 700 800 900 1000

LEAGUES

0   40   80   120   160   200

Maps by the author

50˚

60˚

70˚

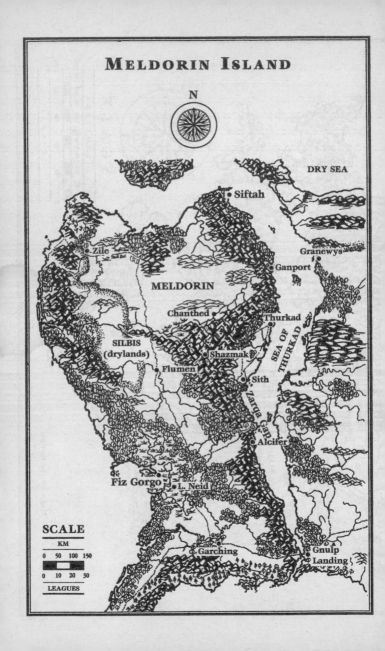

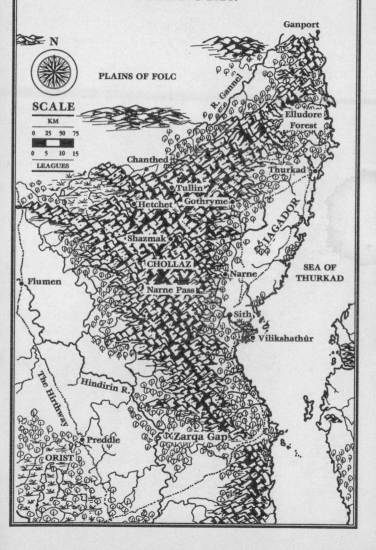

NORTH-EASTERN MELDORIN

N

PLAINS OF FOLC

SCALE

KM
0 25 50 75

0 5 10 15
LEAGUES

Ganport

R. Gannel

Elludore Forest

Chanthed

Thurkad

Tullin

Hetchet

Gothryme

IAGADOR

Shazmak

CHOLLAZ

Narne

SEA OF THURKAD

Narne Pass

Flumen

Sith

Vilikshathúr

The Hirlway

Hindirin R.

Preddle

Zarqa Gap

ORIST

PART ONE

1

THE TALE OF
THE FORBIDDING

It was the final night of the Graduation Telling, when the masters and students of the College of the Histories at Chanthed told the Great Tales that were the very essence of human life on Santhenar. To Llian had fallen the honor and the peril of telling the greatest tale of all—the *Tale of the Forbidding*. The tale of Shuthdar, the genius who made the golden flute but could not bear to give it up; who had changed the Three Worlds forever.

The telling was perilous because Llian was from an outcast race, the Zain, a scholarly people whose curiosity had led them into a treacherous alliance in ancient times. Though their subsequent decimation and exile was long ago, the Zain were still thought ill of. No Zain had been honored with a Graduation Telling in five hundred years. No Zain had even been admitted to the college in a hundred years, save Llian, and that was a curious affair in itself.

So, his tale must best them all, students and masters too.

Succeed and he would graduate master chronicler, a rare honor. No one had worked harder or agonized more to make his tale. But even a perfect telling would bring him as many enemies as admirers. Llian could sense them, willing him to fail. Well, let them try. No one knew what he knew. No one had ever told the tale this way before.

Once there were three worlds, Aachan, Tallallame and Santhenar, each with its own human species: Aachim, Faellem and us, old human. Then, fleeing out of the void between the worlds came a fourth people, the Charon. They were just a handful, desperate, on the precipice of extinction. They found a weakness in the Aachim, took their world from them and forever changed the balance between the worlds.

The Great Tales all began with that introduction, for it was the key to the Histories. Llian took a deep breath and began his tale.

In ancient times Shuthdar, a smith of genius, was summoned from Santhenar by Rulke, a mighty Charon prince of Aachan. And why had Rulke undertaken such a perilous working? He would move freely among the worlds, and perhaps the genius of Shuthdar could open the way. So Shuthdar labored and made that forbidden thing, an opening device, in the form of a golden flute. Its beauty and perfection surpassed even the dreams of its maker—the flute was more precious to him than anything he had ever made. He stole it, opened a gate and fled back to Santhenar. But Shuthdar made a fatal mistake. He broke open the Way between the Worlds . . .

The tale was familiar to everyone in the hall, but the crowd were silent and attentive. Llian did not relax for a moment. The story was hours long, and before it was done he would need every iota of his teller's *voice*, that almost magical ability of great talesmiths to move their audience to any emotion they desired. It was an art that could not be taught, though the masters tried hard enough.

Llian met the eyes of the assembly, one by one, as he told the tale. Everyone in the room knew that he spoke just to them.

The opening shocked Aachan, that frigid world of sulphur-colored snow, oily bogs and black luminous flowers, to its core. The Charon hunted Shuthdar to Santhenar, bringing with them a host of Aachim, that they had enslaved at the dawn of time. All came naked and empty-handed, for any object taken from one world to another might mutate in treacherous ways. The Charon must leave behind their constructs, mighty engines of transformation or destruction, and rely on older powers.

And Tallallame, its rain-drenched forests and towering mountains the antithesis of Aachan, was also threatened by the opening. The Faellem, a small, dour folk for whom the universe was but an illusion made by themselves, selected their best to put it right. Faelamor it was who led them so proudly to Santhenar. Neither did they bring any weapons. Their powers of the mind were such that on their own world they needed nothing more.

Shuthdar was hunted across the lands and down the grinding centuries, fleeing through gate after gate, and wherever he went he brought strife. But finally he was driven into a trap . . .

At last Llian came to the climax of his long, long tale, the part that would turn the Histories upside down. He took a deep breath, searching the faces for a sign that they were with him. The longing for their approval was a physical ache. But they were a true Chanthed audience, both reserved and highly critical. They would give nothing until they had judged the whole.

In his prime, using the stolen flute, Shuthdar could escape any enemy. But he had lived to a tremendous age, his very bones had shrunk and twisted, his once clever hands were no more use than paws. Now he was trapped and he knew it was the end. Sick with fear and self-loathing he huddled under a log in a scrap of forest, clawing out beetles and roaches and snapping them up, more a hyena than a man.

Only now as he looked back over his epic life did Shuthdar realize where he had gone wrong. It was not enough that he had been the greatest craftsman of his age, or any age. No, he must gloat over the priceless treasure that he had, that only he could have made, that had changed the face of the Three Worlds. There were times he would boast aloud, when there was no one to hear. But even the inanimate earth had ears for such a secret and his enemies always found him again. For half a millennium they had hunted him across Santhenar. Now they were all around and he had no will to defy them.

As he spoke Llian scanned the stolid figures, searching for a crack in their reserve, something to inspire him to that ultimate peak of the storyteller's art. He was sure that they approved of the telling so far; but would they accept the new ending? And then he found what he was looking for. At the back he made out a single pale face in the crowd, a young woman staring at him so hard that it burned. He had moved one person, at least. Llian used all the magic of his voice and spoke directly to her.

Shuthdar squinted out between the trees. Before him, on a promontory extending like a finger into the great lake, the rising sun illuminated a tower of yellow stone. As good a place as any to end it.

He crashed through an archway, terrifying a family eating at a square table. Shuthdar bared ragged iron teeth, corroded things that mocked his once exquisite craftsmanship. His mouth was stained rust-red. It looked as if he had dined on blood.

Children screamed. A meager man fell backwards off his chair. Shuthdar glared at them, his misshapen face twisted in a grimace of pain. Crab-like on writhen legs he scuttled past. Chairs, dishes, infants all went flying. A fat woman flung a tureen at his head, snatched a baby from the floor and the family fled, abandoning the crippled girl hidden away upstairs.

Shuthdar licked a spatter of soup from his hand, spat red saliva over the rail and dragged himself to the top of the tower.

At the sight of him the crippled girl put her hands up over her mouth. With yellow skin drum-tight over his cheeks, shrunken lips drawn back so that the rusty teeth and red-stained gums were vivid, he looked like the oldest, ugliest and most dissipated vampire that can ever be imagined. Pity the forsaken creature, if you will.

They faced each other, cripple and cripple. Black hair framed a pretty face, but her legs were so withered that she could barely walk. Time was when he would have despoiled her pitilessly, though that part of him had dried up long ago. Once he might have cast her off the tower, delighting in his power and her pain, but not even cruelty gave him pleasure any more.

"Poor man," she sighed. "You are in such pain. Who are you?" Her voice was gentle, concerned.

"Shuthdar!" he gasped. Red muck ran down his chin.

She paled, groping behind for the support of her chair. "Shuthdar! Do you come to plunder me?"

"No, but you will die with me nonetheless." He pointed

to the forest, now a semicircle of flame centered on the tower. "No one has more enemies than I do," he said, and knew how pathetic was his pride. "See, already they come, burning all before them. Are you afraid to die?"

"I am not, but I have so many dreams to live."

His laughter was a mocking howl. "I know the only dreams a cripple can have—misery and despair! Even your own family locked you away so you would not shame and disgust them."

She let go of the chair and drew herself up, like a queen in her dignity, but her cheeks were wet with tears. To his astonishment, Shuthdar the monster, the brute, was moved to compassion.

"What is your dream?" he asked tenderly, a new emotion for him. "I would grant you that before we die, should it be in my power."

"To dance," she replied. "I would dance for the lover of my dreams."

Without a word he snapped open the case that he carried and there was revealed the golden flute. No more perfect instrument was ever made.

He put it to his bloody lips and played. His ruined hands were in agony but his face showed none of it. His music was so haunting, so beautiful that her ancestors rattled their bones in the crypt below the tower.

The crippled girl took a step, looking up at Shuthdar, but he was staring into another world. She tottered forward in a mocking travesty of a dance, clubbing the stone with her feet. She began to think that he played the cruelest joke of all, that she would crash on her face to his brutal laughter. Then suddenly the music picked her up and bore her away, and the torment in her limbs was gone, and her feet went just where she wanted them to. She was as light in her slippers as any belle, and she danced and danced until she *could dance no more and fell to the floor in a cloud of skirts, all flushed and laughing, too exhausted to speak. And still Shuthdar played, till she was carried far off into her dreams and all her present life was forgotten.*

The music slowly died away. She came back to herself. Shuthdar seemed lit up from within, all his ugliness burned out. He lowered the flute and wiped the ruby stains lovingly from it.

"They come," he said gruffly. "Go down, wave a blue flag from the doorway. There is a chance they will let you pass."

"There is nothing out there for me," she replied. "Do what you must."

For an instant Shuthdar thought that he did not want to die after all, but it was far too late for that.

The audience sighed audibly—another sign! The Histories were vital to Santhenar, and no one, great or small, was untouched by them. The highest honor anyone could wish for was to be mentioned there. Llian knew what the masters and students were thinking. Where had he found this new part of the tale that turned Shuthdar's character inside out? The Great Tales were the very core of the Histories; tamper with them at your peril. He would have to prove every word of it tomorrow. And he would.

Llian looked down into the crowd, and out of the impassive hundreds his gaze was caught by that pale face again. She was concealed by cloak and hood, though from the front of the hood peeped hair as red as a plum. She was leaning forward, utterly rapt. Her name was Karan Elienor Fyrn and she was a sensitive, though no one in the hall knew it. She had come right across the mountains to hear the tales. Llian's eyes met her eyes and she started. Remarkably, she broke through his concentration and for a second their minds touched as though they were linked. Llian was moved by her impossible yearn-

ing but he wrenched away. He had worked four years for this
night and nothing was going to distract him.

He dropped his voice and saw the crowd inch forward in
their seats, straining to catch his every word. He felt reassured.

*Shuthdar's enemies crept closer. The great of the Three
Worlds were there, four human species. There were Charon
and Aachim and Faellem; the best of our kind too. Rulke
was at their head, desperate to recover the flute and to atone
for the crime of having had it made in the first place.*

*Shuthdar watched them with his blanched eyes. There
was no hope—his life was over at last. Soon the flute would
pass to another. Death he welcomed, had long wished for,
but he would not even think of the flute in another's hands.*

*And so, as they drew near, he stood up on the top of the
wall, outlined against the ghastly red moon, the deep lake
behind and below. The crippled girl cried out to him but
Shuthdar screamed, "Don't move!" He lifted the flute in one
claw of a hand, cursed his enemies and blew a despairing,
triumphant blast.*

*The flute glowed red. The air gleamed with luminosity.
Birds fell dead out of the sky. Rainbow waves fled out in all directions and flung the watchers into insensibility. The tower
fractured and Shuthdar toppled backward and smashed on the
hard dark water far below. The earth was rent and the waters
of the lake leapt up and broke over the ruins.*

*Some say that the glowing flute fell, faster than Shuthdar,
into the deep water, sending up a great cloud of steam and
boiling the water until at last it was quenched in the icy
depths and perhaps lies there still, buried in the slowly
deepening mud; preserved forever, lost forever. Others said
that they saw it melt and turn to smoke in the air and van-
ish, consumed by the forces trapped within it long ago.*

Others yet held that Shuthdar had tricked them again, es-

caping to some distant corner of Santhenar where no one knew of him; or even into the void between the worlds, out of which came the desperate Charon to take the world of Aachan in ancient times. But that is surely not so, for two days later the waters cast back his shattered corpse in all its hideousness onto the rocks not far from the tower.

The tale was well told but the audience had expected more. They began to fidget and murmur. But Llian was not yet finished.

Shuthdar was lost, the golden flute too. The broken tower was a nightmare of fumes and radiation, save for a protected space where the girl lay, unharmed. Specters walked the glowing walls, her heartless ancestors. The crippled girl wept, for her dreams were gone forever. Then she thought to tell the tale, to have a precious memento of this day, and to put a small white mark on the black stain that was Shuthdar's reputation; the most reviled man on Santhenar.

But as she finished her writing the world twisted inside out. Splinters of solid light seared her eyes. The sky began to shred itself into drifting flakes. The tower shivered; the rubble shifted like rubber blocks, then a gate burst open above the ruins with a flare like a purple sun, and she looked into the void between the worlds.

Shadows appeared in the brilliant blackness. An army swarmed behind the gate, creatures out of horror. The void teems with the strangest life imaginable, and existence there is desperate, brutal and fleeting. In the void even the fittest survive only by remaking themselves constantly, and every being there is consumed by a single urge—to escape!

Now the crippled girl saw that creatures out of legend did battle beyond the gate, struggling to get through. The whole world was in peril. Nothing could withstand this host.

Her legs were too painful to walk. Terrified, she dragged herself in among the rubble and hid. Then, as the sun stood nearly to noon, a cloaked specter separated out of the mass of ghosts that still swarmed over the tower. At first she thought it was her Shuthdar, restored to the flower of his youth, for the hooded figure was tall and dark.

The specter moved its arms over a fuming crater in the stone. Immediately it was attacked by carmine lightning that sizzled out of the gate. Ghost-fire outlined its cloak. Beneath its feet the stone suddenly flowed like water, dragging the specter down into the crater. The air reeked of brimstone, then it conjured a shimmering protection out of the turmoil, a cone of white radiance that hung the gate with a cobweb of icicles, a Forbidding! The gate boomed shut and vanished.

The crowd sat up in their seats. This was controversial, for the Histories told that the Forbidding came about by itself. If it had been *made,* it raised all sorts of possibilities. Yet Llian knew that it would take more than visions to convince this audience.

The audience began to stir uneasily. The tale was practically done but no proof had been offered. They felt let down. Llian drew out the moment.

And the girl? They found her too, when it was safe to go within, later that afternoon. A remarkably pretty young woman, she was crumpled up on the stone with the long skirt covering her sad legs. She was smiling as though she had just had the most wonderful day of her life. Strangely, among all that destruction the girl seemed to have taken no harm, but she was quite dead.

Anxious to mend Shuthdar's evil record, she had written down his tale, put it in her bodice, then thrust a long hat-pin right through her heart.

This caused a sensation! Llian held up his hand and showed two papers, one blotched with a rusty stain.

I have the proof right here, sealed with her own heart's blood.
So ends the Tale of the Forbidding—the first tale and the greatest.

The whole room was on its feet but no one made a sound. They were trying to work out the implications. Then the crowd took a collective breath—the black-robed masters were filing down the hall, two by two, and up the center steps to the stage. Llian's uncertain smile froze on his face. He had never wanted more than to be a chronicler and a teller. Had he failed so badly as to be publicly stripped of even his student's rank?

Wistan, the master of the college, a little man almost as ugly as Shuthdar himself, had always detested Llian. He stood right in front of him, yellow eyes bulging out of a face like a bowl.

"A remarkable story. But it was not in the *proofs* you gave me," he rasped.

"I kept these back," Llian replied, clutching his documents like a lifebelt.

Wistan held out a desiccated hand. Llian dared to hope. "The second paper certifies the girl's story," he added softly.

Wistan scanned the papers. The folds of the first were perforated through and through, the mark of the fatal pin. His face grew grayer and grayer. "So it is true," he sighed. "Even now such knowledge could be deadly. Say no more!"

Llian's knees were shaking so much that he almost fell down. Wistan was a study in indecision. The telling had been a marvelous one, but it threatened everything he had ever worked for. Then the assembled masters forced his hand. They gave a great cry as of one throat, surged forward, bore Llian up and carried him across the stage in triumph. The whole room was laughing and crying, cheering and throwing their hats in the air. Nothing like this had ever happened before. Wistan followed them reluctantly.

As they swayed across the room toward the exit, Llian caught sight of the red-haired woman again, staring at him. She tried to force her way through the crowd and once more he felt that extraordinary sensation, as though their minds were linked. Who was she? The Graduation Telling was closed to the public but she was not from the college—he had never seen her before.

She almost reached him, getting so close that he caught a whiff of her lime-blossom perfume, then the crowd forced them apart. Her lips moved and he heard in his head, "Who killed her?" then she disappeared in the mêlée and he was carried out of the hall to the celebrations.

But much later, rolling home down the cobbled street surrounded by friends as merry as he was, her words came back to trouble him. The apparent suicide had always puzzled him, but how could anyone else have gotten into the ruins unobserved? Nonetheless the question had been raised and it would not go away. What if someone had found something so important that the girl had to be silenced? That could be the key to an even better story—the first new Great Tale for hundreds of years, and if he were the one to write it, he would stand shoulder to shoulder with the greatest chroniclers of all time. Consumed by this thought, Llian forgot all about Wistan's caution.

"Look!" cried his friend Thandiwe, a tall handsome student. She and Llian had been friends for years, and occasionally lovers too. She was pointing toward the horizon. "A new star. That's an omen if ever I saw one. You're going to be famous, Llian."

Llian's gaze followed her finger. It was not a star at all, but a nebula, for it had a definite shape. A dark-red blotch that he had never seen before, like a tiny spider. Suddenly Llian felt cold though it was a warm summer's night.

"An omen. I wonder what kind of an omen? I'm going to bed."

"I'm coming too," said Thandiwe, embracing him and tossing the waterfall of her black hair so that it covered them both.

Before dawn a dreadful realization woke Llian so abruptly that he fell right out of bed. It was so obvious that he was amazed he hadn't thought of it himself. If the girl *had* been murdered, the record he had used for his tale might be false. And if it was, his career would be ruined beyond redemption. There was no more honored profession than chronicler, but no one would be more scorned than he who had debased the greatest of all tales.

Thandiwe sighed and snuggled down under the covers. Llian picked himself up off the floor and gathered a blanket round him, shivering and staring out the window. The nebula was high, seemingly bigger than before, and now that he saw it clearly Llian realized that it had not the form of a spider at all, but its more deadly relative, the scorpion.

Fame or oblivion? Either way he had to find the truth. Who had killed the crippled girl? And why? And how could he possibly find out, after all this time?

2

DECLINE OF
A CHRONICLER

While Llian slept, Wistan had been busy in his office. Now he stuck his head out the door. The captain of the college guard, a big merry old fellow with wooly hair and a grin as wide as a doorway, sat outside in an easy chair, whistling. He wore a scarlet kilt from which muscular legs stretched halfway across the hall. He was as opposite to Wistan in appearance, character and temperament as it was possible for any two people to be.

"Hey, Trusco, come in here. Shut the door behind you."

Trusco followed him inside. He had been the captain of the guard for as long as Wistan had been master, more than thirty years. The college was that sort of a place—tradition was everything. It was little changed from the institution of a century ago, or five centuries for that matter.

Wistan sat down at an ebony desk the size of a double bed, rummaging in its drawers. His hairless dome bobbed up and down as he stacked papers on the desktop. "We've got secret work to do tonight. I suppose you know what it is about."

"Llian's tale," said Trusco, looking down at the ugly little man with affection. "It set my mind wondering, I can tell you."

"More than you can know. The girl's story is true, beyond any doubt."

Trusco was not convinced. "Then how come it didn't come out at the time?"

"I've already checked that. There were so many dead that it took days to bury them all, and the girl's record wasn't discovered for some time. Then the chronicler who certified it drowned on the way home, crossing a flooded river, and though her bags were recovered, her papers lay forgotten in the archives."

"Documents can be faked," said Trusco sceptically.

"More often than not, but this one isn't."

He produced a stained sheet from behind the desk. "Look! Even after all this time the paper has a story to tell. It's good thick stock, and there wasn't much blood. It's mostly on one side, the side against the girl's breast. But see how the hat-pin pushed the torn paper out of the other side of the hole. The pin was coming out of her, not going in! She was stabbed in the back! And you know what that means!"

"Ghosts don't do murder," said Trusco.

"Someone got in secretly. Maybe someone did make the Forbidding."

Trusco furrowed his brow. He wasn't used to such complicated thoughts. "And maybe the golden flute wasn't destroyed after all."

"Don't even think that aloud! I don't know what happened. But what we have believed about Shuthdar for three thousand years is proven false; therefore everything else that happened then is open to question. A whole world of deadly possibilities is revealed."

"And you want me to take a message to the Council and put all this to Mendark?" Trusco teased, grinning his vast grin. His teeth were as big and square as tombstones. "Well, it's nice weather for a trip to Thurkad."

Thurkad was the largest city in Meldorin, weeks of travel to the east. It was ancient, powerful, wealthy, yet rife with beggars—a teeming, stinking cesspool of a place. Mendark, the cunning and devious Magister of the Council of Santhenar, had dwelt there for an age.

Wistan knew that he was being teased but he reacted anyway. "Mendark! It will be an icy day in the blackest pit of the void before I do that villain any more favors! It still rankles that I was forced to take Llian." He took a pinch of snuff from a *cloisonné* jar, applied it to his nostrils, went red in the face and sneezed mightily. Trusco passed over a green bandanna and Wistan mopped streaming eyes.

"But Llian has brought the college honor," said Trusco.

"So he has, and had he come to me in the proper way I probably would have admitted him, despite that he is an unworthy Zain. But not this way. Why did Mendark want to make a Zain into a chronicler anyway? And what does he want in return? I have a feeling that it won't do the college any good. Come on, we're going to the library."

"It's two in the morning," Trusco protested feebly. "Even Llian will be in bed by now." Trusco's protests were just for show; he knew that Wistan hardly slept at all and would not be put off.

"With one of my students, no doubt," snorted Wistan. "Here, carry this." He handed him the bundle of papers, then took a bracelet of woven silver out of a locked drawer and slid it on his wrist.

"You *are* serious," said Trusco. He knew that the bracelet was the key to the master's safe, but whatever was put inside could not be recovered in that master's lifetime.

"The proofs for Llian's tale. Four years' work by a genius—never to be seen again while I live."

He fell silent and Trusco asked no more questions. Wistan closed the door behind him and followed his captain down a wide hall paved with terracotta tiles. The walls were hung with portraits of famous chroniclers past and present. Trusco jerked his thumb at the last in the row.

"Has Llian sat for his portrait yet?" he asked cheerfully.

Wistan winced. "He may not have to."

They went out the side door. Trusco held up a lantern to light the winding path, though both could have trodden it blindfolded. They walked down between shoulder-high lavender and rosemary bushes to the Library of the Histories, an architectural extravagance of towers and spires, turrets and cupolas, with every surface so ornate that in places it was impossible to tell what was structure and what merest ornament.

At the library Wistan used his master key, opened the great carven double doors and signed the book out of habit.

"What a monstrosity this building is," he said, looking up at cornices decorated in at least a dozen colors, though the paint was peeling badly.

"But part of the history of the college, and therefore unassailable," Trusco said cheekily.

"A challenge! I would tear it down tomorrow if there was money to build a new one. A nice simple one, like a temple of antiquity."

"Then perhaps you should treat Llian better, since his sponsor Mendark has gold by the bucket."

"Bah! Come on, we're going down to the archives."

Trusco raised an interrogative eyebrow.

"We're going to put the proofs, and every other document about the time of the Forbidding, where no one can get them," Wistan said. "This secret could be deadly. I have to protect the college."

Trusco grunted.

"You disagree? Well, so be it. I don't want your agreement, just your strong back. In fact I wonder if I should not pile up all his proofs and put a torch to them."

That shocked Trusco out of his good-humored acquiescence. "You would burn the Histories? Without the Histories the college has no meaning. What has your life been lived for, master?"

"Yes, what has my life been lived for?" said Wistan heavily. "Once it was the Histories. Now, to my shame, just the college. I cannot risk it."

It took hours to move the shelves of documents down to the locked archives, a basement that contained documents forbidden, dangerous or obscene. In a corner of the basement was a safe large enough to walk into, with shelves piled high with old documents and scrolls. When the job was done, Wistan touched the silver bracelet to a niche on the back wall of the safe and a horizontal slot appeared below it. He reached in, dropped Llian's proofs through and whipped his hand back out again just as something slammed closed inside.

"That'll get you one day," Trusco said, smiling.

"Serve me right for putting off my problems to the future, I suppose." Wistan grimaced. "Well, let whoever succeeds me worry about it."

"Ah, but what about Llian? You can't lock him up, and he knows every word of his proofs."

"When he recites them it's not an original document. It's not *proof*. But I will deal with him too, just to be sure."

"Well, deal gently with him. I like Llian," said Trusco. "He has brought honor upon the college. And he has a rare mastery of the *voice*."

"Pah! Wretched Zain! He bothers me. He is too bound up in his work, and too curious. He would do anything to advance his art, to get his tale. He is Zain through and through."

"Yes he is, the good and the bad. Wistan—"

"I won't harm him as long as he cooperates!" snapped Wistan.

"And if he doesn't?"

"I will discredit him utterly and strip him of his honor."

It was midday when Llian rose. In the daylight his fears of the previous night had receded to a distant worry, one that could be put off. Fifteen years of toil at the college were over! He was a teller *and* a master chronicler at last, the youngest to have achieved either honor in more than a hundred years. He was just twenty-eight, the whole world was wonderful and it all lay at his feet. Whatever he wanted could be his, though all Llian really wanted was to be a chronicler, to fill in the gaps in the Histories; and a teller, one who searched out forgotten tales or made new ones. His dream was to make a new Great Tale, though a dream was surely all it could be. In four thousand years of keeping the Histories, only twenty-two tales had been judged worthy of being Great Tales.

Llian scratched himself, inspecting the damage of the previous night in a cracked mirror. His brown eyes were bloodshot and bleary, and his head throbbed. Llian might have been called handsome, save that his mouth was too wide and his chin lopsided, but when he smiled it lit up his whole face. He was of middle height and slimly built, though with strong shoulders. Llian was likeable and charming, though occasionally a little full of himself. Sometimes, because of his heritage, he tried too hard. His voice was soft and rich and mellow, touched with lights and shadows, utterly enchanting. Friends, enemies; all loved his voice. As did he.

Llian combed untidy brown hair, worn fashionably long, and was halfway through lunch with his friends when the expected summons came. It was Turlew, Wistan's detestable seneschal, a bitter failed chronicler who hated all students and, most of all, Llian.

"Wistan requires you in his office immediately," said Turlew, licking soft wet lips that looked as though they had been stung by a bee.

"Tell him I'll be along presently," said Llian, and belched. Everyone laughed.

Turlew's chubby cheeks grew red. "At once, Wistan said!"

"I'm not a student anymore," said Llian. "I'm a master now, you strutting peacock, though since you weren't invited to the telling last night I'll excuse you for not knowing that." Llian was not normally rude but he detested Turlew as much as Turlew resented him.

"A master, eh? You still have the manners of a student. Have you a position to go to?" Turlew looked as though he could spit venom. "Without Wistan's references you won't even get a clerk's post."

"Don't forget who my sponsor is," said Llian arrogantly. "Mendark himself! What does Mendark care for Wistan's references?"

"You might find that Mendark demands more than you care to repay."

That was something Llian had no answer for. Mendark was a mancer—a wielder of the Secret Art—of great power and subtlety, an uncertain friend, a deadly opponent. A perilous master, so the tales went. Mendark had extended his own life many times over, as mancers did, and now his tentacles reached across the known world. Why he had sponsored a Zain at the college no one knew. Suddenly the world outside seemed all too precarious.

Wistan was pacing the room when Llian entered. He did not smile.

"Good afternoon, *Master* Llian," he said.

"Good afternoon, Master Wistan," Llian replied politely.

He stared at Wistan, apprehension mingled with contempt, his teller's eye making a caricature of the ugly little man. The skin of Wistan's long and scrawny neck sagged in festoons like a curtain above a window and quivered with every forced-out word. On top of this column there tottered a head the like of which Llian could not look on without mingled mirth and horror. It was almost fleshless, small and flat at the top, flaring to a jaw so large that he appeared to be nothing but face. The lips were gray and bloodless, the nose a flattened, insignificant thing with large open nostrils of greenish hue. His head bulged at the back and the eyes protruded out of the concavity of his face like two peas resting on a saucer of lard. A few straps of dung-colored hair, hastily combed across the top of a blotchy skull, now hung limp and greasy about his ear.

"You will never tell that version of the tale again," said Wistan, pursing his slab lips.

"But . . ." said Llian. "I don't understand . . ." Did Wistan know what he suspected?

"Don't play the fool, Llian. The paper proves that she was stabbed from behind. You have uncovered a deadly secret. A brilliant piece of work, but it must be suppressed. I will not allow you to risk the college."

Llian could hardly control his face. So, murder *had* been done! There *was* a Great Tale here, and he was going to uncover it no matter what Wistan said. "But hundreds of people heard me last night—the whole college."

"And I will speak to every one of them. Everyone will swear, on pain of expulsion, never to mention it again."

Not everyone, Llian thought, remembering the small red-haired woman who had touched his mind. He could hardly remember what her face looked like, but the impression of her mind touching his was still vivid. She was not from the college. She might have told a dozen people by now.

"It's like trying to hold back the tide," he said. "You can't control two hundred people. The story will be all over town already."

"Chanthed is a town full of rumors. If you do not substantiate them they will die."

"How can I deny what I've already said? Anyway, it's traditional that the best tale of the graduation is told at the Festival of Chanthed next autumn. That is my right."

"Rights must be broken at need. If you wish to have what is your due, find another tale, or another way to tell that one. You have plenty in your armory."

"I demand my rights!" Llian said furiously. "I'm not a student anymore."

Wistan held onto his temper with an effort. "Grow up, Llian! You have a lot to offer, but a lot more to learn. You are about to go out into the world and seek a position, and for that you need my goodwill. Do you imagine that you can just write what you like, or tell what you like? If you do, then I assure you that your tenure will be very short indeed. *Good day!*"

Llian went out and wandered about the grounds. He climbed up a little knoll, a favorite thinking place, and lay down on his back in the grass. From here he could look out over the college and the winding streets of Chanthed further down the hill. The town was a lovely sight, a green and gold oasis nestled into the folds of the sun-browned hillside and extending its flanks to the clear waters of the Gannel. The yellow sandstone buildings positively glowed in the afternoon sun. The cobbled streets were like gray streams running down to the river.

If he looked the other way Llian could see the foothills of the mountain range that extended along the entire eastern side of the great island of Meldorin, a distance of three hundred leagues. Across the mountains were the fertile plains of Saboth and the ancient coastal city of Thurkad. Beyond that the long narrow gutter of the Sea of Thurkad separated Meldorin from the continent of Lauralin. The barren land where the Zain dwelt was on the other side of the continent, more than four hundred leagues away.

Time to consider his future. There would never be a post for him here while Wistan was master. Nor did he want one. After fifteen years Llian was chafing to get out into the world. In three months' time his stipend would expire, so he had to find a way to earn his living before that. He had no idea where to start. In truth Llian was naive about the world. Moreover he was clumsy and inept at most things save his art, telling, and his trade, the Histories.

The Histories were vital to the culture of Santhenar and permeated every aspect of life on it. Even the poorest families kept their family registers, taught orally to their children if they were illiterate and could not afford the services of a public scribe. But to have one's life told by a master chronicler, to actually play a part in the Histories of the world, was the greatest honor that anyone could long for. This longing supported a wolfpack of charlatans and false chroniclers, and it was a hunger that even the greatest were not immune to. Even Mendark, Llian's grotesquely rich sponsor, longed to be honored in his own Great Tale.

"Llian, I've been looking everywhere for you."

It was Thandiwe, her face flushed from running up the hill. She flopped down on the grass beside him.

"Is something the matter?" Llian asked.

"No, I just wanted to see you. I suppose you will be leaving Chanthed soon."

"I suppose so."

They sat in the grass for a long while, pursuing their own thoughts.

"So, what are you going to do with yourself, Llian?"

"I was just wondering that. For the last four years I've done what I wanted, working on my project. Now it's all over and I'm afraid. How am I to find a master? What if I end up with a coarse, stupid master who wants nothing but nursery tales?"

"What about your sponsor?"

"Mendark? I imagine that he will call me when he wants me. I'm . . . afraid to go to him. Afraid to presume."

"I would be afraid of what he wanted from me," Thandiwe said softly.

"That too!"

"How was it that he sponsored you? That's something you've never talked about."

"No, I haven't, because his name has earned me nothing but envy and blows. Mendark first came to our house when I was eight. We were a close family, though poor. We lived in Jepperand, a desert land next to the Dry Sea, my mother and father and my two sisters, and me."

"Two sisters," she sighed. "I have *five* older brothers."

"Llayis, my father, is a scribe. He looks like me, though taller, and he hasn't got much hair anymore. I suppose that's my fate too." Llian laughed somewhat tentatively and ruffled his fingers through his untidy locks. "Zophy, my mother, is little and round and cheerful. She is a letterer, an illuminator really, as are my sisters. My older sister Callam is tall and serious, with very dark hair; she takes after my father. My little sister Alyz . . . How I miss her! She is more like my mother, and the best worker of us all."

"How come they sent you so far away?" Thandiwe asked.

"I was too clever—I wrote a catalog of tales when I was eight. It amazed even our scholarly race, and I suppose that was how Mendark first heard about me. Anyway, when I was twelve, he appeared at the front gate. He bent down, inspecting me as though I was something he considered buying, then went into the house and closed the door. I was afraid."

"Mendark!" She gave a theatrical shudder. "I would have been too."

"As soon as Mendark had gone my parents called me inside. He had offered to sponsor me at the college, even to master chronicler if I could rise that high. An undreamed-of honor. I was shocked. The College of the Histories was famous even in Jepperand, but I knew it was on the other side of the world."

"You did not think to refuse?"

"I wanted to, but I wanted the honor too, and I did not want to let my family down. It is not uncommon for clever children to be sent away to learn, but no Zain child had come as far as Chanthed in a very long time. Such an opportunity would never come again. Though my parents were both learned, they were still poor. Almost everyone is, in Jepperand. I suppose they would have refused had they thought I really didn't want to go.

"I can still remember the look on my little sister's face as I joined that caravan of strangers. She was six; she couldn't possibly have understood. I was almost as bewildered myself. But we Zain endure what cannot be altered, so I bit my lip and clenched my fists to stop them trembling, and kissed my mother and father, and my older sister.

"Only little Alyz did not know how to behave. She

started to cry. 'Llian is never coming home again,' she wailed. 'Never, never, never!'

"That broke us all. Callam began to weep, and my mother cried, and even my father shed a tear. Then they all embraced me together, which made it much worse. I wept till my eyes could make tears no more, and then it was time to go, so dutifully I went.

"It was the worst time in all my life, that journey. I was the only child there and no one tried to comfort me. It took six months of heat and dust and flies and miserable food before we reached the Sea of Thurkad. On the other side Mendark appeared, examined me briefly and sent me straight on to Chanthed. All he said was, 'When the time comes, remember your debt.' "

"Is that all?"

"He spoke about posterity and his place in it. He was most concerned for his reputation."

"So, did the college live up to your dreams?"

"Not for a long time. Everyone knew I was Zain and that I was only here because my sponsor was too powerful to refuse. It was years before I made a friend, and my work became everything to me. You were my first friend, Thandiwe."

"I envied you," she said. "I thought you had everything. You seemed to do your work so easily. Your illuminated book of the Great Tales is as good as anything in the library."

"Not really! But I grew up with that art. I watched my mother do it every day."

"And your fees and board and stipend were paid for you. It has been such a struggle for my family to keep me here."

He made no comment.

"Are your family all still living?"

"Yes," Llian said. "They write, though a letter takes half

a year to get here, if it gets here at all, and my reply just as long to return. I would give anything to go home."

"Why haven't you?"

"I could not save enough from my stipend in fifty years, and they cannot afford to come all this way either. I want to go home as much as ever I wanted to be a chronicler and a teller. And now that I am one, if Mendark does not call me I may try to get passage on a ship, and work my way from port to port telling the Histories. But I'm afraid too. My parents are old now; even little Alyz is a grown woman. What if we have nothing to say to each other?"

Just then a bell rang far away. Thandiwe scrambled to her feet. "I have to go," she said. "I'll see you tonight."

Llian sat there after she had left, thinking over his options. Eventually roused by the rumbling in his stomach he turned his steps to the nearest stall, but on putting his hand in his pocket found it was empty. He headed down to the purser's office to draw his monthly stipend. It would go up substantially now that he was master. As he entered, Turlew came out smirking.

"Llian of Chanthed, *master chronicler,*" Llian said breezily to Old Sal, the tiny clerk behind the counter, who had been there even longer than Wistan had been master. No one knew what her real name was. Everything about Old Sal was bird-like—she had a small round head feathered with white hair, a long slender neck and stilt-like legs, and her arching nose had the look of a beak.

Old Sal knew every one of the students and none better than Llian, who had been a favorite of hers ever since he had entered the college a shy and terrified little boy of twelve.

"Master Llian," she said, but for the first time ever she did not smile.

"I've come for my stipend. It must have gone up now that I am master."

"I'm sorry," she said, consulting a register almost as tall as she was, although she knew every entry in it by heart. She angled her head to one side like an inquisitive bird. "I have nothing for you. Your allowance has finished."

"But it goes on for three months after graduation, and at the higher rate. How can it be cut off?"

"Turlew came down with the authority not long ago. You'll have to plead with Wistan. I'm sorry."

"But I just came . . ." He broke off and turned away.

As he put his hand on the door Old Sal called out. Her wrinkled old face looked genuinely concerned. "I have a little to spare, if you . . ."

Llian was touched, knowing how little a purser's clerk earned. "Thank you," he said bowing. "But I am not desperate yet."

"Then you will plead with Wistan?"

He laughed hollowly. "I won't give him the satisfaction. I shall sing for my supper."

That night he spread the story of his ill-treatment, though not the reason for it, and told a bawdy tale or two in a student's inn down by the river. Llian's treatment was unprecedented, arousing the sympathy of all but the most ardent Zain-haters. He passed his cap around at the end and it sagged most cheerfully when it came back, so Llian spent the better part of it buying drinks for all his new friends and mentally damning Wistan. The Histories were more than a profession to him—they were an obsession, and there was little that he would not do to feed that obsession; to track down the last fragment of a tale. When the festival came round in the autumn he would take his rightful place on stage on the final night and tell the *Tale of the Forbidding* just as he had done last night. Then he would leave Chanthed forever.

Llian arrived back at his room at midnight in a very jovial frame of mind, to find a stony-faced Thandiwe standing by the door. He stood there for a moment, admiring her lithe figure, her golden skin and black hair, her heaving bosom.

"What's the matter?" he asked, swaying just a little.

"I—I left something here last night," she said, avoiding his eye.

"Something's happened! Tell me!"

"Oh, Llian, I've been warned to keep away from you."

"What?"

"I've just spent the most unpleasant hour of my life with Wistan and that disgusting little worm of his, Turlew. If I'm seen with you again, I lose my place in the college."

"Well, damn them!"

"Damn you! Llian, I don't know what you've done, but you can please yourself now. I can't. I have a chance for the Graduation Telling next year. You know how much that means to me. If I'm thrown out, my life will be ruined and everything my family has sacrificed for me will have been wasted."

"I'm sorry," said Llian, though still he felt hurt. "Of course you must go."

"Llian, it doesn't mean that I don't care for you. I just can't see you for a while."

Her dark eyes pleaded with him to understand, and he did. But he also felt let down. "Goodbye," he said more coolly than he felt.

Tears streaming down her face, Thandiwe crashed down the steps and out the front door. Llian flopped onto his bed. His whole world was collapsing around him and there was nothing he could do about it.

He took out his book of tales and idly turned the leaves. The book had been his first major work, completed for his initial graduation four years ago, and its hundreds of pages contained short versions of all the Great Tales. There were enough blank pages at the end for another tale, a youthful fancy that amused him now. The book was indeed a beautiful object, gorgeously illuminated in lapis blue and scarlet, and here and there decorated with pilfered gold and silver leaf. The book was very precious to him, for all that he knew its every imperfection.

Llian put the book down and lay there for hours, staring at the dark ceiling, until the scorpion nebula rose and shone in through his window, red and black. What would the next disaster be?

He found out a few days later, when he signed himself into the library and went down to the archives to have another look at the documents from the time of the Forbidding. They were like old friends to him, these shelves full of tattered scrolls and parchments and codices falling apart from sheer age. He had spent four years of slavery here, teasing out the threads of his tale from the labyrinth of the Histories. Now the death of the crippled girl was preying on his mind and he wanted to see if there was anything he had overlooked.

Along the interminable shelves he went, to the furthest corner of the basement, and signed himself in again to the room where the oldest and most precious documents were kept. Llian turned the corner, luxuriating in the smell of books and the warm spicy odor of the rosewood bookcases. He stopped abruptly. The whole row of shelves was empty—every single document about the time of the Forbidding was gone.

It was like having a skewer thrust through his heart. Llian ran back out to the attendant on duty.

"I don't know anything about it," the attendant said, combing a magnificent black beard with his fingers. Crumbs rained down onto his polished boots. "You'll have to ask the librarian."

There was no point running but Llian did so anyway, all the way up to the top floor where the librarian sat in her solitary eyrie, a room packed with catalogs but lacking a single book. She folded her arms and listened to his plea. She was an overly pretty woman, save that she had a tiny prim hole of a mouth. She dressed like a princess, in a purple silk blouse with gold tassels on the shoulders and a full skirt of green silk-satin interwoven with golden threads.

"We can't have such precious old things lying around where anyone can misuse, or even steal them," she replied, arranging the pencils on her desk in military rows. "They were getting damaged, so they have been locked away."

"Libraries are for people," he said sarcastically.

"No—libraries are for books, and the fewer people in them the better for the books."

"Anyway, I'd like to see them," said Llian. "May I have the key, please?"

She consulted a catalog, pursing her lips. Purple lip paint extended beyond the edges of her mouth in a vain attempt to make it seem fuller. "For these documents you must have a permit."

"And how do I get such a permit?" But he already knew the answer to that.

"Only Wistan can give it!"

After a while Llian's life settled down into a new routine. He would get up late, somewhat the worse for wear, and after the best breakfast he could afford would go to the library to work at his quest. This was a frustrating and mostly fruitless exercise, since he was forbidden the documents he really needed, but he kept on until his eyes hurt from reading. Then he went to one inn or another, telling scurrilous yarns, often concerning Wistan, for the customers' entertainment and his profit. After he had gleaned enough coin for the morrow—or not, on one or two occasions—he wavered his way home to bed. Sometimes he saw Thandiwe in passing, but if anyone was looking she turned away, and after a while it became easier to avoid her.

One morning Llian was woken by thumping on his door. It was still dark when he opened it. Outside was a grim-faced bailiff.

"What's the matter?" asked Llian.

"Wistan, in his office, right now!" The bailiff seized him by the arm.

Wistan's office was cold and in the light of a single candle he looked positively malevolent. He looked up at Llian sharply, saggy jowls quivering with animosity. "Chanthed exists for the college," he began, his voice like bristles on canvas. "*My* college! Let me but say the word and you have no room, no library privileges, and not even the meanest water carrier will let you push his cart."

Llian blinked. "Turlew has told me of your performance in the taverns last night, and other nights," Wistan went on. "The office of the master will not be mocked."

Turlew sneered in the background.

"Last night he laughed as loudly as any," said Llian smiling. "Though he wouldn't have if he'd stayed for the second act."

"Be silent! Do not use the *voice* on *me*! What is your intention? No, tell me no more lies—I know it already. You seek to have my office, to so ridicule me that the college will cast me down and declare you master by acclamation."

Llian gave a bitter laugh. "A Zain, master of the College of the Histories? Not in my time." Llian cursed his ancestors for their folly, as he had often done. Though the Zain were no longer persecuted, they were still disliked and mistrusted.

And, arising out of their persecution, they had a great disdain for authority, though they were generally wise enough not to show it.

"Indeed not! Offend again and I throw you naked out of Chanthed. *Now get out!*"

I will not bow to your threats, thought Llian. I am not friendless. But he had no money, no references and nowhere to go. He set off down the street to a bar that opened at dawn, for it was almost dawn now. Halfway there he stopped.

I can't go on like this, he thought. I've been drinking every day this week.

He sat down on the curb with his feet in the gutter. He was broke, lucky if he had two copper grints. No one would pay for a yarn at this time of day. If he went in he'd have to buy his own, and though drink was cheap, two coppers would melt like camphor on a hotplate.

He went back up the hill to the library, but of course the doors were closed. He could wake up the porter, but the fellow would likely refuse. Llian's influence had evaporated of late.

He swore. Nowhere to go but back to bed. Then, down the street he caught sight of a pair of students weaving along, doubtless going home from an all-night session. He knew the girl but the fellow was a stranger. What the heck! If they could afford to drink all night they could buy him a few.

Pasting on a harlot's smile, Llian headed down to drown his miseries.

3

HAUNTED BY
THE PAST

The magical telling was over. Karan, the red-haired woman who had so discomforted Llian, was swept out of the hall with the departing audience. She loved the Great Tales with a passion, and to hear them told at the College of the Histories was one of the high points of her life. The tale still seethed in her brain—being a sensitive, it was as though she had actually been there in the tower with Shuthdar and the crippled girl.

Slowly the flames from the burning tower faded to a memory, and Karan found herself standing alone in the middle of a lawn surrounded by hedges of rosemary and lavender. For a moment she could not work out what she was doing there.

She looked around. Llian and his party had gone and the last of the crowd were disappearing down the path. She should go too, before the guards realized that she had no right to be here. The Graduation Telling was closed to the public; she might end up in the watchhouse if she were caught. Now her head began to ache, the inevitable result of what she had done. She had been incredibly foolish, but she shied away from thinking about that. Karan pulled the hood down over her face and headed off toward her inn, the cheapest that Chanthed offered.

Karan was small with a pale, round face, a warm open friendly face, framed by a tangled froth of hair as rich and red as sunset in a smoky sky. Her eyes were as green as malachite. She was twenty-three but looked much younger. In times of plenty her form was inclined to roundness, but after the long walk to Chanthed on short rations she was slender.

At dawn she rose, dressed in baggy green trousers and an oversized shirt that were of good quality but much repaired, splashed her face with water and forced a bone comb through her hair, though after it was done it looked much as it had before. She sprinkled a few drops of lime-blossom perfume on her fingers, rubbed it through her hair and her toilet was complete.

Breakfast was part of a loaf of hard bread and two apples, for money was so scarce that she begrudged even the copper grint they charged in the dining room. Still munching her apple Karan donned her pack and set off for home. She lived at Gothryme, an insignificant manor in the poor mountain province of Bannador. It was a week's journey east across the mountains (if the weather was kind), but one that she had done many times—as pleasant a trip now, at the end of summer, as it was miserable and dangerous in winter. Traveling alone did not bother her though; in spite of her small size she was well able to keep out of danger.

The wonderful tale came back as soon as she was through the town gates, and Karan began to tell it to herself from the beginning. It was a hard climb for the first few hours; the story helped to ease her into the journey. Mid-morning brought her to that point, just before the end of the telling, where Llian had paused and looked directly at her. Where stupidly she had made a link, her mind to his, putting him off balance for a second. Karan had avoided thinking about that quite uncharacteristic foolishness. She was normally so sensible.

She sat down on an outcrop of sandstone that looked over the valley, the winding track and, far below, the slate roofs of Chanthed shining in the sun. Why had she risked revealing herself as a sensitive to a stranger who might use her, or thoughtlessly give away her secret? People with her talents were rare and kept them quiet for good reason: such skills were priceless to those who wanted to spy or to dominate. In times of war, sensitives were bought and sold for their abilities, though thankfully war was a thing of the past. The lands of this part of Meldorin had been at peace for all of Karan's lifetime.

Fortunately her talents were not easily detected, as long as she was careful. It took another sensitive, or someone highly skilled in the Secret Art.

Where had her talents come from anyway? Karan was a blending, for while her mother had been old human, the original people of Santhenar, her father was half-Aachim.

About four thousand years ago, three other human species had come to Santhenar in the hunt for the golden flute. The mostly tall and mostly dark Aachim, like her father, were native to the world of Aachan. The Charon, also big dark people, were few but incredibly powerful, masters of the Secret Art and of machines too. The third species were the Faellem, a small, rose-skinned and golden-eyed people from the other of the Three Worlds, Tallallame. They were not physically strong, but skilled at deception and illusion. The three off-world species were much longer-lived than humans, and they had turned Santhenar upside down, but that time was past. Now only old humans were numerous on Santhenar. The Charon were all gone, one way or another, while the surviving Aachim and Faellem had long hidden themselves and concealed their differences.

Matings between the different species seldom resulted in children, and when they did, such blendings were often mad. But mad or not, they could have unusual talents.

Karan had not found *her* talents to be much use though, for they were not at all reliable. She could often sense people before she could see them, even sense what they were going to do or say before they did it, especially if she was in danger. She could sometimes make a sending to another person, though just a mish-mash of feelings and images, and it hardly ever worked when she wanted it to. Rarely, Karan could make a link to someone else and actually speak to them, mind to mind. She had only done that a few times in her lifetime. That was what was so shocking about the link to Llian; it had happened without her even thinking about it. Some expression of her innermost longings, she supposed.

But her talents had disadvantages too—she felt things more strongly than other people; sometimes so strongly that her emotions overwhelmed and paralyzed her. And using her talents always resulted in aftersickness, as little as a vague feeling of nausea or as much as a devastating migraine that could last all day. So Karan was normally careful.

Then why, at the end of Llian's telling, had she cried into his mind, "Who killed her?" Karan knew the answer to that. Because she was completely captivated by the tale and the teller.

She had heard Llian tell before; people came from all over Meldorin to hear the tales at the Festival of Chanthed. Llian had become well-known four years ago, after his very first public telling, and Karan had never forgotten it. That was part of the reason she had sneaked into the Graduation Telling, using the pass of a distant cousin who was a student at the college. Already she was planning her trip back for the autumn festival. It would be the highlight of her year, a whole fortnight of tales great and small.

Well, time to be going. Put away your foolish dreams, she told herself. What use is a teller to you? There is nothing for him at Gothryme. Karan took a swig from her water bottle, pulled her broad-brimmed felt hat down over her face and jumped up. She was anxious to get home now, where she had worries aplenty. If she traveled hard enough she might cut the journey by a day. Luckily Santhenar's huge moon was near full, its luminous yellow face lighting her way so that she could walk well into the evening.

But as the days passed the other, darker face of the moon rotated further into view, the yellow pocked with seas and craters of red and purple and black. The moon turned to its own more sluggish cycle, and the time when the dark face was showing was generally accounted to be unlucky; a time when decisions should be postponed and journeys put off. Thankfully she would be home by the time the waning moon was all dark.

On the fourth morning she passed through the tiny mountain hamlet of Tullin. It was just a straggle of houses and an inn, the only one between Chanthed and her home. She quenched her thirst at a well, then continued on—camping was free, and pleasant at this time of year. Behind the inn Karan saw an old man chopping wood vigorously. He raised one hand to her and she waved back. A group of children followed her up the track as far as the top of the hill. She smiled at them then disappeared over the crest.

Nearly there! Karan sighed, brushed the red coils out of her eyes and headed down the track toward Gothryme, her ancient and shabby manor. The inner glow from the telling had carried her almost all the way home. She was in such a hurry to get there that she avoided Tolryme town, splashing across the shrunken river Ryme half a league upstream and setting off across the meadows. The green slate roofs of Gothryme appeared over the brow of the hill, then the walls of pink granite, blushing in the afternoon sun. Beyond that was the sheer face of the Gothryme escarpment, a high cliff of granite that from here cut off the white tips of the mountains beyond.

Gothryme consisted of a squat oval keep, battered by time and by the periodic squabbles that had wracked Bannador, and two somewhat younger wings, two-storeyed with wide verandas, that ran out from the back. Beyond that was a sprawl of barns and out-houses, all in granite and slate. They were solid but very rustic.

It was hot and dry, the gray grass crunching underfoot. It didn't look as though there had been any rain since she left three weeks ago. All the problems of her rustic life came rushing back. The drought's relentless grip was slowly breaking Gothryme and ruining her. Even this brief trip had been an indulgence. If it did not rain soon, she would never afford the autumn festival.

Karan stopped for a moment and looked over her lands. Though she was heir to what at first glance seemed a sizeable estate—manor, land and forest—the land was barren, stony and drought-stricken, and the forest inaccessible by reason of the cliff. It provided a precarious livelihood for her and the people who worked it but there was nothing left over for luxuries. Yet it was hers, and after years of travel and turmoil she wanted nothing but to tend it and, when she could, to hear the tellers at the Festival of Chanthed.

Climbing the steep hill she lost sight of the house. At that point Karan turned off the track and circled round the back of the manor. She was tired and just wanted to get in the door without people making a fuss of her. She skirted a reed-fringed pond on which a family of gray ducks paddled. Karan waggled her fingers at the ducks. Where was Kar, the old black swan?

Just then there came a tremendous hissing and trumpeting from the far end of the pond. The swan's black wings flashed; the water was churned to foam. A thin brown arm let go of the swan's leg; a frightened boy scrambled up the bank and ran around the edge of the pond, skidding in the mud. It was the cook's youngest son, a good-natured rascal.

"What do you think you're doing, Benie?" she cried, pretending sternness.

The boy stopped dead. Even his hair was plastered with mud. "Fishin'," he lied with downcast eyes.

"Then do it in the river in future," she said. "Off you go now, and wash the mud off before you go inside."

He scooted off, shouting at the top of his voice, "Karan's back, mum. Karan's back!"

Karan watched him go, smiling. So much for a quiet homecoming.

"*Karan!*" cried Rachis, her steward, as she entered. "Welcome home." He embraced her.

She had known Rachis all her life. He was tall and thin with scanty white hair surrounding a pink crown like a tonsure. As she hugged him Karan realized that all the flesh was gone from his bones—he was an old man now. Rachis had managed the estate faithfully for many years after her mother died and left it to her. But he was now quite frail—even leaving him in charge for this brief trip made her feel guilty.

After the greetings were done and the news of the estate and the outside world exchanged, Karan got a bowl of stew from the black kettle hanging over the fire, sawed off a crust of bread and sat out on the veranda to enjoy the evening. It was good to be home, to enjoy simple home food and have all the old familiar things about her. She leaned back against the granite wall and took off her boots. Tomorrow a hundred chores demanded her attention. Tonight she would just sit back and relax.

She went to bed with the dark. Her bed was a vast box of black-stained timber that took up half the room. She curled up into a ball in the familiar hollow of the mattress, but later, as the scorpion nebula rose and shone in through her bedroom window, she was woken by a premonition so strong that it made her hair stand on end. Something had just changed in the world. She had no idea what, but after lying there for hours she realized that sleep would never come. Karan got up, caught sight of the dark, waning moon, and shivered. She made herself tea and was halfway through the miserable picture revealed by her book of accounts when dawn arrived.

Looking out the window down the track that led to Tolryme, she felt her hackles suddenly rise again. Someone was coming up through the fog, riding a big black horse and leading another. Nothing unusual in that, but this stranger burned in her mind like a flame. She put down her pen and went to the door.

It was Maigraith! Maigraith, who had rescued Karan from near-slavery after she had been robbed of everything in Almadin two years ago. They had not seen each other since, but Karan knew what Maigraith had come for. The obligation had to be repaid.

Though she tried as hard as she could to suppress them, the horrible memories of her servitude came flooding back as vividly as only a sensitive could make them. For a moment she was actually there again, chained to the tanning vats day and night, and beaten whenever she slackened her work. Even in memory the stench made her gag . . .

"Which way to Cadory, churl?"

Karan heaved a hide out of the vat. The skins had to be soaked until every scrap of flesh had rotted away and the hair could be rubbed off. The stench, even after a month of slavery, was unbearable. And she could feel the fever coming back worse than before. She knew that she was going to die of it. A shadow fell across her, giving blessed respite from the sun. She looked up dully.

"Yes, I'm talking to you," said a striking woman on a tall black horse. "My name is Maigraith. Which . . ."

Her arrogance and her freedom were infuriating. "I am Karan, a free woman of Bannador," Karan said angrily, hauling the hide onto the scrubbing rack. She rubbed her face with the back of her hand, smearing her cheek with green muck and knocking her hat off. Bright red hair sprang out in all directions.

"A free woman!" Maigraith repeated without even the hint of a smile.

"I was robbed of every grint I had. This was the only work I could get, but the stew and the water costs more than I earn. Each day I go further in debt."

She bent down for her hat. A rusty iron shackle circled her waist; a chain ran from it to the vat. Just then a stringy woman hobbled out of a shed and began beating Karan about the head with a bundle of switches. Karan fell down in the mud, protecting her face with her arms.

"Work, you lazy red-haired cow!" the woman screeched, a whack for each word. One side of her face was half-eaten away by sores that would not heal.

After a while the woman tired and limped away. Karan

hauled herself up on the side of the vat. Blood dripped from her nose onto the hides.

"I am on my way west, across the sea almost as far as Bannador," said Maigraith. "Perhaps I could take a message to your family."

"By the time they get it I will be dead," said Karan, sagging down into the mud again, sweating with the fever. "Please help me. I have assets in Bannador. I can pay whatever you ask."

The unfortunate were everywhere, but something in the girl's face moved Maigraith, for she too had borne cruelty in silence. "How much is your indenture?"

"Ten silver tars," said Karan.

Maigraith said nothing for such a long time that Karan began to wonder whether she begrudged her generous impulse, or even had the money.

Finally Maigraith spoke. "For a bit of gruel? You could eat it off gold plates for less. Very well, I will pay it. And in return, if I ever need help you will repay the obligation."

"I will do anything you ask," said Karan.

That night Karan was overcome by the fever and lay near death for days. Maigraith nursed her tirelessly, but finally, feeling that Karan was slipping away, she took her to her liege Faichand, a small woman with translucent skin and ageless eyes. Karan's memories of her illness were hazy, but she knew that there had been trouble between Maigraith and Faichand over her. As soon as Karan was well enough, Maigraith had taken her back to Thurkad, a month's journey, and made sure that she had a safe escort home to Gothryme . . .

Karan had returned home to find that, despite Rachis's best efforts, Gothryme was sinking under years of drought and bad seasons, and her four years of travel had used up all its reserves. In spite of her land and her manor, she was now a pauper. Only the most rigid economies had allowed her the trip to Chanthed, the only indulgence in the last two years. Unless a miracle occurred, the autumn festival would be beyond her. Now Maigraith was here. What did she want? The ten pieces of silver had been sent back long ago but the obligation was a tremendous one and could not be denied.

"Maigraith!" said Karan, suppressing the memories. "Welcome. Come down." She held the bridle while Maigraith dismounted.

Karan examined her enigmatic rescuer. Maigraith was of middle height and slender, with silky chestnut hair caressing her shoulders. Her oval face was striking, only the tenseness of jaw and the unhappy curve of mouth spoiling the perfection of her features. Her eyes were blue, but a strange blue that looked as though it was hiding something. Her clothes were somber, concealing; her only ornament an ebony bracelet, a plain, beautiful thing. Her every movement was deliberate, restrained.

"You took a lot of finding," Maigraith said. Her accent was flawless, yet she spoke with a certain formality that suggested it was not her native tongue.

"My family has dwelt here for a thousand years," said Karan, feeling as though Maigraith reproached her for living in such an out-of-the-way place. "Come in. I'll get you some cider."

"Water will do just as well," said Maigraith. "I like to keep my wits about me."

Karan recalled that Maigraith was abstemious and controlled in all her habits. She fetched a pitcher of water and two drinking bowls.

"Are you planning to stay long?" she asked, leading her guest through the keep and out into a yard enclosed by verandas on three sides. The posts were festooned with elderly vines, though this early in the season the grapes were like hard green peas. Karan offered Maigraith the best chair, an old cane seat that groaned embarrassingly under her slight weight.

Maigraith sat bolt upright with her knees together and her hands in her lap, inhibiting Karan from her normal careless posture. "No! I came to ask you to repay your obligation. Do you still hold to it?"

"Of course. Whatever is in my power."

"You are a sensitive!"

"How did you know that?" asked Karan, alarmed. If Maigraith could tell, maybe other people could too.

"Don't be afraid. Your secret is quite safe."

"How?" cried Karan. "I must know."

"In your fever two years ago you unconsciously made a link to me."

My first big mistake, Karan thought. And it tells me something about you too. Who *are* you, that you understand such things?

"Can you control it?" Maigraith continued.

"I beg your pardon?" Karan said.

"Can you deliberately link your mind to another, so as to send messages and receive them?"

"I have done it," she said in a tiny voice, "though my talent is seldom reliable."

"That is good," said Maigraith, ignoring the qualification. "I have a job to do and I need your support while I do it. That is how you will repay your obligation."

Will repay! Karan thought. You might at least do me the courtesy of framing it as a request. Already she felt dominated and overwhelmed. "What do you want me to do?"

"My liege Faichand requires me to recover something that she lost long ago. I cannot complete the task without the aid of a link," Maigraith said. "That is why I need you."

"Well, that seems simple enough," said Karan, and, having agreed, she wanted to get it done as soon as possible. "We can begin right after breakfast if you like. Where would you like to work?"

Maigraith laughed humorlessly. "It's not so simple. Nor can we do it here."

"That's all right. Wherever you want to go!" Surely it would take only a few days, or at most a week's trip to Thurkad and back.

"We have to go to Fiz Gorgo."

"*Fiz Gorgo!* But that's all the way across Meldorin—150 leagues at least!"

"At least," said Maigraith.

"I can't leave Gothryme for months at this time of year! Isn't Fiz Gorgo Yggur's stronghold?" She pronounced the name *Ig-ger.* "It would take an army to get past Yggur's guards."

Maigraith did not speak for a minute or two. She was deep in thought, remembering what had happened and sorting through which parts of it Karan could safely be told, if any.

Just a week ago Faichand had appeared in a dreadful flap and ordered her to go straight to Fiz Gorgo to recover a relic that she needed urgently. Maigraith had gone all cold inside. She knew enough about Fiz Gorgo and about Yggur to realize that without help the task was impossible. But Faichand did not accept excuses—if something had to be done it must be done. Even at the best of times she was impossible to satisfy.

Maigraith knew that she would need a sensitive, to get into such a well-guarded place and out again. She had mentioned Karan's name but her mistress had grown furiously angry. *Go alone! Whoever heard of a sensitive that could be relied upon?* Maigraith knew it too: sensitives jumped at shadows, broadcasting their every fear to the world.

She had been in despair. Without time to plan and spy out the defenses, without assistance, the task was impossible. Using a sensitive was a chancy business, but what choice did she have? And Karan was the only one nearby.

Karan cleared her throat, waking Maigraith from her reverie. Maigraith looked her in the eye. Little of that she could tell Karan.

"I have to take back a relic that Yggur has. It . . . belongs to my liege and she needs it urgently. Once we get to Fiz Gorgo you will make a link to support me, so that I can get inside the fortress, and find my way out again."

Karan could not believe it. "But Yggur is one of the most powerful warlords in Meldorin, and a mancer as well!"

"My liege is stronger yet," said Maigraith, "and I have a certain mastery of the Secret Art too. It will be difficult for me, but there will be no danger to you. You need not come within a league of the walls of Fiz Gorgo." She looked troubled. "Please, you can never know what it is like for me. Nothing I do is ever good enough for Faichand. Failure is unthinkable."

The plea touched Karan's soft heart in a way that Maigraith's arrogance could never have, but she resisted. The very idea was like a nightmare. "I have no stomach for spying and stealing," Karan said, "nor any skill at it. You'll have to find someone else."

"So!" Maigraith said coldly. "Honor and duty mean nothing to you. I had thought differently. Well, you have no choice. I don't know of anyone else."

"What you ask is out of proportion to the service you rendered me," Karan said desperately. "Name another task and I will render it faithfully, no matter what it takes."

"That's what you said before, as I recall."

"But all it took was silver, and that I have repaid. You ask me to risk my life."

"*All it took was silver!* I saved your life. I nursed you back from the grave at the risk of the fever. I carried you all the way to Thurkad. I put coin in your pocket and made sure you were escorted safely home. You paid back the *least* of the debt."

Karan felt trapped. She had not thought that her promise would be so taken advantage of. "I have to go to Chanthed at the end of autumn," she said, trying everything she could think of.

"Do you put pleasure before duty? What odd folk you are here in Bannador. Anyway, we will be back by then."

"I can't! I have a duty here."

Maigraith was relentless. "You have a steward—you had been traveling for years when I met you."

"He is old now. Besides, I don't have the money. We have had four years of drought and every grint is precious."

"You can afford Chanthed though! Of course, I will pay all your expenses, and a handsome fee, double the normal rate for a sensitive."

"A fee?" said Karan, feeling her last resort stripped away.

"Four silver tars a day for sixty days, to be paid in Sith on the way back. I repeat, do you honor your promise?"

Karan was amazed into silence. Money had always been scarce in her life. The figure mentioned was a fortune, enough to get her estate out of trouble, though she would rather have gone without and stayed at home.

After years of travel Karan had grown to love the tranquillity of her home, the solitude that she could find in the mountains at her back door, the knowing that she had no one to answer to. Maigraith was selfish and unfeeling. Even without the perils of Fiz Gorgo, months in her company would be almost unbearable. But she knew Maigraith would not give way, and fee or no fee, in the end it was impossible to refuse her. The debt was a duty, and duty was sacred.

"I will do it," Karan said, reluctantly and with a deep foreboding.

"Then swear, by what is most sacred to you, that you will serve me faithfully until it is done."

Her beloved father, Galliad, had been killed in the mountains when she was eight, beaten to death for a few coins. He was her most sacred image. "I swear by the memory of my father that I will do this for you," said Karan, feeling crushed.

So it was settled. Karan had a long talk to Rachis, who was not at all pleased. She put her affairs in order and the next morning they left Gothryme at dawn.

4

AN OMINOUS
REVELATION

The valley of the Ryme was a meandering line of fog as they set out. Maigraith skirted Tolryme town, heading south-east toward Sith. Karan followed her glumly. She was normally good-humored, but Maigraith intimidated and inhibited her. They rode in silence along the dusty lanes of Bannador, between hedges that afforded rare glimpses into stony paddocks where even the weeds were wilting in the drought.

At noon, with the sun blasting down on her old felt hat, they stopped briefly by a pebbly creek for a drink and a crust of bread. Karan headed down toward the water and began to take her boots off to soak her hot feet.

"No time for that," Maigraith said curtly. "We've got to be back in Sith in sixty days."

"Sixty days! Impossible!"

Maigraith had taken out a small map on parchment. "The roads are good for much of the way. A king's courier would do the distance in thirty days. Surely we can in twice that."

"A courier changes horses every day."

"And so will we, if we have to, but these were the best beasts in Thurkad. Come on."

Karan was left wondering just how much gold Maigraith carried in the wallet inside her shirt. Surely more than she, Karan, had seen in her life.

It was a long time since Karan had ridden a horse, and at the end of the day she was so bruised and sore that she could hardly walk. She sat by the fire, rubbing salve into her chafed thighs while Maigraith cooked dinner.

Maigraith handed her a bowl of something that looked like multi-colored gruel. "What's this?" Karan laughed. "Glue to stick me to my saddle?"

Maigraith frowned. She was quite lacking in a sense of humor. "It's your dinner."

It was horrible—mashed grain and dried-up bits of smoked meat and leathery dried vegetables boiled together into a gummy mass. Karan ate it without a word, then hobbled over to her sleeping pouch and pulled it over her head. This was worse than her worst imaginings, and it was only the first day.

They rode hard across the fertile meadows of Iagador onto the High Way, the main north–south road, and raced down that to Sith. Maigraith avoided everyone on the road and no one troubled them, for she gave off such an air of deadly competence that even the roughest villains kept their distance.

The city state of Sith was a trading nation built on an island in the middle of the mighty River Garr, and it was a clean, orderly place where law was law and life was devoted to business. Sith was a beautiful city built of yellow stone, entirely covering the slopes of the island. Here Maigraith bought supplies for the long trek south, exactly the same food as before. Karan's heart sank further. They had been six days on the road, and Maigraith's cooking was by now unbearably tedious, the same every night and cooked without any herb or spice or condiment. She did all the cooking.

"Can we at least have some wine?" Karan pleaded as they passed a wine seller, a prosperous-looking establishment whose front wall was faced with obsidian.

"I have no need of wine," said Maigraith.

Karan wasn't going to give in this time. "I have no *need* of it either, but I'd like to have some." She drew rein outside, feeling in her scrip for the few small coins she had brought. "I'll buy it with my own money, if you can't afford it," she said with a hint of sarcasm.

Maigraith made a face. "If it makes you happy," she said. "Wait here!"

Karan loved browsing and tasting in wine shops, but her companion had taken all the joy out of it. She sat fuming on the step while Maigraith went inside, to return almost instantly with a skin of wine the size of a watermelon. She tied it to Karan's saddle without a word and climbed onto her horse.

Before they left Sith, Maigraith took Karan to a nondescript doorway in a street of no particular distinction. "If anything goes wrong you will bring the relic to Faichand, here." Then they rode away, crossing the south branch of the Garr via a bridge with twenty stone arches and a soaring central arch of iron, painted red.

On the other side they headed south-east along the High Way that led first to the coast of the Sea of Thurkad at Vilikshathûr, a dingy coastal town that they bypassed, and thence south through more than twenty leagues of forest to the Zarqa Gap. Here they crossed the much-diminished mountains and turned west across unending grassy plains toward the forests of Orist.

Karan was almost screaming with frustration by this time, for Maigraith would answer none of her questions about the mission, or about the relic that they were going so far to recover, or even how she proposed to get into Fiz Gorgo under the noses of Yggur's ever-vigilant guards.

"But there are things I need to know," Karan said one evening, after they had been on the road for more than two weeks. She kicked a stick into the fire, sending hot coals showering out the other side.

Maigraith flicked an ember off her dinner plate. She was quite calm. "What you need to know I will tell you in good time."

"So far you have told me nothing."

"Therefore there is nothing that you need to know yet."

Her logic was infuriating. Karan felt totally controlled and there was nothing that she could do about it. The money that she had brought with her would not have taken her a quarter of the way home.

As they continued, Karan sank deeper into depression. She felt as though the unshed tears were dissolving her from the inside out.

Finally even Maigraith realized that Karan's misery was a problem for them both. "What is the matter with you?" she said the following night, after they had finished another tasteless dinner.

"I'm afraid and I'm lonely, and I'm unhappy too."

"Duty is happiness, if it is done," said Maigraith, as though she was reciting a formula.

Karan made no response to the absurd remark. Duty was just duty, one of the frames that held life together, and it broke as many people as it made. She turned her back on Maigraith, put her arms around her knees and stared into the dark forest, brooding about her out-of-control life. What was she to do about Gothryme? What about her own existence?

The fee would pay her debts, but there would be no money left to repair the manor or improve her drought-stricken holding. Though Karan was clever and capable and hardworking, it was not enough. If the drought went on until the winter, she would have to sell the contents of the manor just to survive. And then what would happen the following year? To lose Gothryme, where her family had dwelt for a thousand years, would be like losing a leg. *There is no way out!*

On the other side of the fire Maigraith suddenly jumped up. "What?" she cried, staring at Karan.

"I didn't say anything. Leave me alone!"

Maigraith leapt right over the fire and hauled Karan to her feet.

"You were *broadcasting,*" she accused.

"What are you talking about?" said Karan, trying vainly to get away.

"You were sending out your emotions in all directions. That is a very dangerous thing to do. I don't know how you have survived it."

"Oh!" Karan said, trying to work out what she had done.

"You should know better."

"I do! I learned to hide my nature before I could walk. I don't know why I let it slip here. Perhaps because you make me feel so unhappy."

Having said it, Karan felt even worse. She went over to her saddlebags and came back with the skin of wine purchased in Sith but not yet touched. She hoped that Maigraith had not bought rubbish.

It only took the tiniest sip to discover that she had not. It was a glorious wine, almost purple-black in color. Karan squeezed herself a mug full, since the skin was too heavy to hold up. She leaned back against a tree, sipping slowly.

"I make you unhappy?" Maigraith was amazed.

"This journey has been one of the most miserable times of my life. All you do is criticize and order me about, and treat me like an idiot."

"I'm sorry," said Maigraith. "That's what I'm used to."

Maigraith filled her own mug to the brim, hung the wineskin in the fork of the tree, and sat down beside Karan. She had realized that she must ease Karan out of this dangerous depression.

They sat together, not talking, just drinking, though shortly Karan felt tipsy and put her mug down. The wine, however, seemed to have no effect on Maigraith's rigid self-control.

Suddenly Karan's good nature reasserted itself. "Tell me about your life," she said. She knew virtually nothing about her companion, even after all this time.

"What is there to tell? I have no mother and no father. I don't know who I am or where I came from."

"I am an orphan too," said Karan. "My father was killed when I was eight. I ask myself why all the time. And soon after, my mother went mad and took her own life."

"At least you had eight years," Maigraith said bitterly. "At least you remember them! I might have been spawned in a pond for all I know." She refilled her mug, drank it down in one huge swallow and took another.

Karan went very still and Maigraith understood that she had been rudely dismissive of her tragedy. "Who were they, Karan?" she asked, as kindly as she was capable of.

"My mother was a Fyrn, who have lived at Gothryme for a thousand years. I got my name and my inheritance from her. My father was Aachim!"

Maigraith started. "Aachim!" She said it as though the name meant trouble.

"Well, half-Aachim actually. His mother was Aachim but his father was old human."

"You are a blending?"

"Don't shrink from me like that, I'm not a monster."

"I'm just surprised, that's all," said Maigraith.

"Where did you think my talent came from?"

"Talents come from all sorts of places."

Maigraith reached up for another mug. So that is what Faichand is afraid of, she said to herself. The unpredictable talents of the blending. Does Karan even know what she can do?

"Aachan has fascinated me since I first heard my father's tales," said Karan dreamily. She imitated his mournful mode of telling.

"Our world was Aachan, a dark, cold, barren place, but it was all we had, and we loved it. No people ever worked harder or wrought more cunningly, and in time we made it blossom. Every city, every structure, every garden, every device we made was a thing of beauty. Our art and our craft were our life. Then the Charon took our world; still we wrought but no more for ourselves.

"We never broke that slavery. Only those of us that came to Santhenar ever regained our freedom. Here came our renascence—we built our beautiful cities across the world, and our art was never more perfect.

"But we are destined to suffer. Again we were betrayed by the Charon and our cities and works destroyed. Now we live in the past, and for the past, and take no part in the affairs of Santhenar evermore.

"Such a sad life they had, on their own world and here," Karan added. "They see their destiny as beyond their control."

"So do I," said Maigraith, filling her mug again. She changed the subject. "About your broadcasting," she said gently. "I want you to think about what you were doing. Learn to control it. It is a great gift if you can use it well."

"I'm afraid," said Karan. "Who else knows that I am sensitive?" At least one other person did—Llian the chronicler. How many people had he told about her?

"Maybe no one. It just happens that I can tell people with your talents."

Karan sat up suddenly and took Maigraith's hand. "How so? Are you a sensitive too?" Karan knew no one who was like her. The prospect of a soul-mate was exhilarating, even if it was Maigraith.

Maigraith laughed. "More correct to say that I am an *insensitive*," she said, then looked momentarily surprised that she had made a joke. She drained her mug and got up to refill it. A trickle of blood-dark wine made its way down her chin unnoticed.

"You were telling me about your own life," Karan reminded her.

"Both my parents died when I was born, and I don't even know their names. All I know is that I was a terrible disgrace."

Her voice broke. Maigraith swayed, dropping the wineskin. Red wine spurted, forming a glowing arch in the firelight before hissing down on a hot stone. She giggled and fell off the log. Karan helped her up. The wine had suddenly hit Maigraith; she was quite drunk. She threw her arms around Karan. Tears flooded down her cheeks.

"Oh, Karan, you can't imagine how much I long to know who I am and where I came from. All I know is that, after my parents died, Faelamor took me in when no one else would have me."

Karan's hair stood on end.

Maigraith went on, oblivious to what she had said. "And I am not even her *species*. No one in the world cared for me, save for her. Despite my shame she raised me and gave me the best education that anyone ever had. I can never love her, for she is too harsh; too unyielding; too closed-off. Faelamor is an impossibly hard mistress. Nothing ever satisfies her. But how can I not try? I owe her more than I can ever repay."

Karan was so shaken by Maigraith's drunken revelation that she did not even hear the rest of the story. So Faichand was *Faelamor,* the mythical leader of the Faellem people! She was mentioned in all the tales, but there had been no word of her in hundreds of years.

Shortly after that Maigraith subsided gracefully onto the ground, closed her eyes and fell asleep. Karan threw a blanket over her and went to her own sleeping pouch, though sleep was a long time coming. She was caught up in the affairs of the mighty, Faelamor and Yggur, to whom ordinary people mattered no more than counters on a board. How could she protect herself? It got worse every time she thought about it.

Maigraith woke with the bright sun in her eyes. She jerked upright and such a pain speared through her temples that she cried out.

"What's the matter?" Karan said sleepily.

"I'm sick," Maigraith croaked. "Oh, my head."

"You got tremendously drunk last night," Karan said, amused.

"Are you all right?"

"I only drank a little and had lots of water after."

"Ohhh!" Maigraith groaned, coming to hands and knees. "I feel as though there's something I should remember."

Karan sat up, but she did not say anything.

"I remember! You are part-Aachim." Maigraith shook her head, then winced. The Aachim were inseparably bound up with the relic that she was planning to steal out of Fiz Gorgo. She had not told Karan what it was, but now realized that there would be trouble when she did. It was too late to do anything about it.

The mission had been doomed before it began. For all Karan's talents, her cleverness and capability, she was the wrong choice for the job; she was too much a sensitive. Better to cast her off and go alone. If only I could, Maigraith thought, but duty goes both ways.

"What's the matter?" Karan asked, breaking into her thoughts. "You seem worried."

"Worried!" Maigraith barked. "My life, my work, my impossible mission, who I am, what I am here for—it's all a disaster."

"I would help you if I could," said Karan tentatively, afraid of a rebuff. "We could—even be friends, if you did not keep pushing me away."

"I have never had a friend," said Maigraith. "Faichand never allowed it, lest it hinder me from serving her."

"How can she stop you?"

"Duty stops me. I owe her everything. My debt is so great that it can never be paid. She tells me so, constantly."

This gave Karan a new insight into her companion's obsessive nature. No longer did she feel so dominated by Maigraith. She pitied her, and longed to do something to help her.

"You must be so very lonely. I would be happy to be your friend."

Maigraith went quite still. She looked down at the ground then up at Karan. The offer made her afraid. "Thank you," she said. "You are kind and generous and warm-hearted; everything that I could wish for in a friend. Everything that

I am not. But it is futile to long for what I cannot have, and dangerous for us both." She got up and headed toward the forest.

"Maigraith!" Karan called.

Maigraith turned rather abruptly. "Yes?"

"I've got to tell you something."

"What is it?"

Karan's jaw was clenched. "Maigraith, last night when you were drunk—you gave your liege a different name."

Maigraith's honey-colored skin went as white as plaster. "What name?" she whispered.

"You called her Faelamor! Is she the same—?"

Maigraith swayed, looking as though she was going to faint. She screwed up her face, squeezing her temples between the heels of her hands, then forced back self-control.

"Never say that name again," she said in a voice that could have frozen molten lead. "My liege is Faichand. Faelamor died long ago."

Karan stared at her mutely.

"Faichand!" Maigraith cried, gripping Karan's head between her hands and screaming right into her face. "Faichand! Do you have it? *There is no Faelamor!*"

Karan nodded and with a wrench Maigraith released her and staggered off into the forest. She walked for an hour, feeling sicker with every step. Her self-disgust at having betrayed Faelamor's secret was much worse than the hangover. She stumbled into a forked tree, hung over the fork and was sick. She clung to the tree as though it was the mother she had never known, the hard bark cutting into her breasts, and heaved and heaved and heaved. But no matter how hard she tried, she could not bring up the clot of horror inside her. She had betrayed Faelamor, to a sensitive of all people, and great woe would come of it.

*   *   *

Maigraith was unusually distant after that, even for her. The business of Faelamor was not mentioned again, and Karan's tentative overtures were so coldly rebuffed that she withdrew as well. So while they rode across endless plains covered in tussock grass, Karan had plenty of time to fret about Maigraith's slip and what it could mean. If Faelamor's existence was so secret, she, Karan, was in danger just by knowing about it. She could see only two solutions: beg Maigraith not to tell Faelamor, or make sure that the whole world knew. Neither was appealing.

At other times on that interminable journey, she brooded about Gothryme, or dreamed about the Festival of Chanthed, or, as she did every day, wondered about the relic that Maigraith had come so far to recover. What could it be? Maigraith had not given her the least clue. Now the dark face of the moon, brooding ominously down at her, suggested that she probably did not want to find out.

They came to a huge river, the Hindirin, which was too wide and strong to swim, but downstream it was spanned by a stone bridge almost as long as the bridge across the Garr at Sith. Beyond that were other rivers, but the bridges were sound and they continued to make good time. After that they crossed plains and woodlands, following an old road that was sometimes there, more often not.

By the time the third week had passed, with the scorpion nebula glaring down at them each night from empty skies, and Karan's forebodings growing stronger every day, they had changed horses three times and ridden more than one hundred and fifty leagues. Now they were riding through tall trees, beyond which were the pathless bogs and swamp forests of Orist, that ran all the way to the walls of Fiz Gorgo and beyond.

At a small town without a name they left their horses, and Maigraith hired a guide to take them through the swamp forest. He was a ragged, toothless, leering fellow, a smuggler and out-and-out scoundrel whose eyes followed Karan everywhere she went. But he knew every pool and mire of the swamp and they ate fresh fish every night, a welcome change from the tasteless and unvarying fare that Maigraith prepared. And he provided some relief from Maigraith's dour company.

There was only one highlight of the trip as far as Karan was concerned. It happened on the day they arrived at Lake Neid, a cold clear lake about a league long. They camped on the northern shore among the half-submerged ruins of an old city. After nearly a week in the swamp, Karan was revelling in the clean water when she felt a stabbing pain on the ball of her right foot.

She sprang back and something black dropped into the water. Karan hopped to shore and sat down on a slab of marble to inspect the wound.

The guide, who called himself Walf, ambled over. "Something bit you?" he asked, revealing a toothless hole of a mouth. He took her small foot in a hand as gnarled as a mangrove root.

There was a triangular puncture in the ball of her foot, ebbing blood but blue around the edges. "This hurt?" He poked the wound with a hard finger.

"No, I can't feel a thing."

"You will," said Walf, holding her foot for rather longer than was necessary. Karan jerked it out of his grasp.

Maigraith came over to see what the trouble was. "Turret shell," said the guide. "Won't be able to walk on it today."

"Careless," said Maigraith, looking irritated. "What about tomorrow?"

"Should be better by then, as long as it don't get infected." Walf turned away to the fire.

"Well, we can't waste the day. You can show me the way to Fiz Gorgo. It's only a couple of days, isn't it?"

"Less."

"Good! We'll go as far as we can today and come back in the night. Karan, stay here and look after your foot. Expect us around midnight."

So Karan had the whole day to herself, an unexpected luxury. Her foot soon became too painful to put any weight on, but it was fine while she rested. She sat in the sun among the ruins, watching the birds wheeling and diving out over the water, and the little fish swimming around in clear pools among blocks of marble and broken columns. Neid must have been a beautiful place in its time.

For lunch she had half of a wonderful yellow-fleshed fish with wild onions and a sour lime, and as much sickly-sweet tea as she could drink. She had a great fondness for sweet things. She dreamed away the afternoon, thinking of tales and tellers. Her dinner was just as tasty, and the night was peaceful, no moon and the nebula veiled by thin cloud, all the menace taken away. Karan would have liked a fire but she wouldn't risk one so close to Fiz Gorgo. And she didn't think about *that* at all; all thoughts of what lay ahead she kept firmly out of the way, for one day at least.

They left Walf at Lake Neid, to wait for them and guide them back out of the swamp. Out of his sight they left their heavy packs too, for the last dash to Fiz Gorgo. Only now did Maigraith break her silence.

"I did not want to speak about this before, but now I must. There is a chance that I will be taken. If I am, and you are able to escape, go back to Neid. The guide will lead you out of the swamp. From Neid you must make your way back to Sith and give the relic to Faichand, at the place I showed you."

That did not bear thinking about. "I don't have enough money," Karan said tonelessly.

Maigraith handed over a small purse heavy with silver. "This is for your expenses. If you spend more, it will be reimbursed in Sith; and your fee, of course."

The weight was reassuring. Karan put it away safely. Finally they reached a creek that smelled of the sea. Maigraith tasted the water. She made a face and spat it out again.

"Salt! Fiz Gorgo is on an estuary. We must go carefully now—Yggur's guards may sweep this far out into the swamp."

They crept to the edge of the swamp and saw before them an expanse of cleared land, a road on the other side of it and, beyond, a fortress or possibly a fortified city. Fiz Gorgo! And only a day behind schedule. Even from where they crouched they could see guards patrolling the road, and others on top of the wall.

Fiz Gorgo was a huge fortified city partly recovered from swampy ruin by Yggur, the warlord and magus who had come out of nowhere to conquer the southern half of the great island of Meldorin. The city was ancient, built three thousand years ago, possibly by the Aachim. Later the south of Meldorin had fallen into barbarism and Fiz Gorgo into disrepair. The River Neid changed its course, creating a swamp of what was once fertile land. Swamp forest grew up around Fiz Gorgo and the city was forgotten.

Then Yggur came, fifty years ago or perhaps a hundred. He rebuilt the walls, drained the flooded lands nearby, restored some of the towers. But even Yggur had not made new all of that vast fortress, and the tunnels and labyrinths below remained untouched.

The night passed and the following day. There were guards everywhere and they were ever vigilant. The day was uneventful yet Karan felt uneasy, and the unease grew until it was a knot of dread in the bottom of her stomach. That was the problem with being a sensitive—she felt things much more keenly than other people. She *knew* that something was going to go wrong.

"Is anything the matter?" she asked Maigraith more than once. Nothing could be told from Maigraith's behavior save that her posture was even more rigid than usual.

"No, shush! Ah, here he comes."

A gate in the wall had opened and out rode a very tall man attended by six guards. They turned away and headed down the road in the direction of the estuary.

"That's Yggur! He often goes down to Carstain, I'm told. It's quite a distance. He surely won't be back until the morning."

They watched the company until they disappeared around a bend in the road, then sat in silence while the night fell. Lanterns sprang up all along the wall. Karan shivered. It was only the beginning of autumn but the nights were chilly this far south.

"The *link*!" said Maigraith. "Quickly!"

Karan was never sure how she made a link—it was just something that she could do. It didn't work with many people but she knew that it would with Maigraith. She thought about Maigraith, thought about speaking to her with her mind, and suddenly there it was, like a conduit from one to the other. She couldn't read Maigraith's mind, of course— she could only know what Maigraith gave her and what she sensed through the link.

Maigraith was so strong, so capable; and yet, Karan sensed, so vulnerable, for as a child she had been terribly hurt. And she was tormented by self-doubt, by the knowledge that nothing she did was ever good enough for her mistress. Maigraith had mastered every discipline she set herself, but she could not stem the pain inside her, so she closed everything off that made her human. She refused to feel. All the more surprising that she had felt pity for Karan two years ago, that she had actually got down from her horse and saved her. Or, Karan thought with unaccustomed cynicism, maybe it was because Maigraith had recognized her as a sensitive.

No, that was unworthy. Maigraith was so desperate to find out her own identity that it had colored her whole life. The rawness of the feelings that Karan sensed brought her closer to her companion than she had been since the night they drank together. Karan's gentle heart was touched. She wanted to help Maigraith and protect her. It quite took away her own worries.

Maigraith was speaking to her now, across the link. *Ah! That is good. I have never felt such a strong link.*

"What do you want me to do?" Karan said aloud. She did not like the feeling of Maigraith speaking into her mind, a very private place.

"Just maintain the link. Whatever you do, don't lose it while I am inside or I may never get out again. But if things go wrong I may need to draw on your strength a little. It won't hurt but you may feel a little . . . weak! Ready?"

"Yes," said Karan. She wasn't, but the sooner it was done the better.

Maintain the link, Maigraith repeated, then she just vanished. The leaves crackled under her feet as though she was walking away but after a few seconds silence fell. Karan looked up at the scorpion nebula and shuddered.

Just then Karan felt a shocking wrench in her head, as if the link had been torn out by the roots. For a minute she was blind and deaf, all her senses cut off. The feeling was intensely claustrophobic. She almost panicked, then her hearing came back, leaves crunched and Maigraith stood there.

"What happened?" she asked coldly, staring down at Karan lying on the ground.

"I've no idea," said Karan, holding her head. Her vision cleared. "The link was just ripped away. I couldn't even see for a minute."

"Then what's the matter *now*?

"It's the aftersickness. I always get it after I use my talent. I'll be better in a while; it's not too bad this time."

"I get it too, when I use the Secret Art," said Maigraith tersely. "Though not after such a little thing as this!"

When Karan felt better they tried again. This time the link was a fluttery, unstable thing that accentuated the pounding in Karan's head.

"I'm sorry," she said. "I'm doing my best. I told you my talent was unreliable. It doesn't like to be forced."

"It will have to do," said Maigraith, "Now *hold* it."

She disappeared like a candle snuffed out but this time Karan recognized that it was mere illusion. Within a minute the link was literally torn apart, although this time it was lost from Maigraith's end. Maigraith reappeared.

She looked alarmed. "Yggur must have some defense that interferes when we are too far away from each other. You will have to come with me. I can't possibly get in without the link."

"No!" Karan said. "*No, no, no!*" A searing pain tried to cleave the hemispheres of her brain apart. This was what she had been dreading ever since she had seen Maigraith riding up the track to Gothryme a month ago. The aftersickness blossomed in sympathy, forcing her to her knees.

"Do you think I want to take you, in this condition?" said Maigraith. "I have no choice. She handed Karan a powder in a rice-paper packet. "Swallow this. It'll help with the aftersickness. Don't break the packet."

Karan took it. The rice paper instantly stuck to the roof of her mouth and when she tried to dislodge it with her tongue the packet burst, flooding her mouth with a bitter and nauseating taste. She shuddered and gagged. Maigraith held the water bottle to her lips but nothing would wash the bitterness away.

"We'll never get out again," said Karan, knowing that it was useless. She could sense that something terrible was going to happen—a disaster, and there was nothing she could do about it.

5

THE FACE
IN THE MIRROR

K aran shrank down against the outer wall of Fiz Gorgo.
She felt quite alone, though Maigraith was only a few
steps away. Quite afraid. The paired tread of the sentries
above echoed her own heart's beat. There were guards
everywhere. The melancholy sounds of the night heightened
her despair.

*Why did I let her pressure me into this folly? Why did I
come?*

An elbow struck her in the ribs. Karan jumped.
Maigraith's strange eyes shone in the faint light. She
squeezed Karan's arm until it hurt. Maigraith's voice was
colder than the night.

"Damn you, Karan—you're broadcasting your feelings
to the whole fortress." She continued audibly, "You can
never rely on a sensitive. Why on earth did I bring her?"

The anger scalded Karan. The insult mortified her,
though she realized that Maigraith was right—she was

doing it again, sending her own terrors out in all directions, putting them both at risk. She took a deep breath, shuddered, touched the ancient, damp, yet somehow reassuring wall, and looked up.

A cloud drifted across the sky, concealing then emphasizing the nebula shaped like a scorpion, flaring white and crimson. Ominous, alarming. How it had grown since they set out a month ago. They watched it in their separate silences, waiting for the guard to change. Finally a bell clanked inside, gravel crunched at the top of the wall and the silence resumed.

Suddenly Karan felt a prickling between her shoulder blades. *Someone was watching!* She looked up, expecting to see a sentry glaring down at them, but no shadow broke the smooth line of the wall against the sky. How could anyone see her here, in the dark, veiled by Maigraith's illusions? Karan cursed her imagination and put it out of mind.

"Now!" said Maigraith.

Climbing was one of Karan's many skills. Even in the dark this venerable wall, with stone fretted and mortar crumbling, gave no more trouble than a ladder. She went up the first part quickly. Halfway up, her boot jammed in a crack. She jerked but it was stuck. Karan reached down with one hand to free it.

Then she heard a rhythmic tramping. She froze. Surely the perimeter guard couldn't be due yet? Lights appeared around a corner of the wall. The track went right past—impossible that Maigraith's illusions could conceal them at such short distance. She could see the guards now, two big men each carrying a storm lantern, directing their beams from side to side across the track. One ray swept the wall from top to bottom. The other passed over the cleared land between the track and the swamp forest. How thorough they were! Karan tried to merge with the wall, hiding her pale skin from the light.

The tramping grew louder, now accompanied by a patter-pat. What was *that* guarding the guards? A third figure, back a few paces. It was angular, almost stick-like, with a clumsy, jerking gait. Her skin crawled. The light moved along the wall, stopping just short of her. The beams flashed out to impale her. She felt an overwhelming urge to cry out, to jump out into the light. Through the link she could sense Maigraith's fears: that she was forced to rely on someone whose every emotion was sprayed to the wind's quarters; that her illusion would not hold.

"Haaiii!"

The stick-man whirled, leapt in the air and flung out an elongated arm. Karan started, her foot slipped free and she almost fell. The guards turned as one, spearing their lantern beams at a spot on the edge of the forest. Momentarily she sensed alarm, she heard splashing, frogs grumbled, then the feeling of being watched faded away. Guards crashed through the undergrowth, swinging their staves, the stick-man directing them with cries not unlike the call of the frog.

Karan went up as fast as she dared and peered over. The top of the wall was broad as a road, with a gravel base and hip-high parapets on either side. On her left, perhaps thirty paces away, a brazier glowed in an open watch-house. The sentries were beyond, leaning out and calling to their fellows in the forest. To her right the wall was empty. She went over. The forest was black against the night, save for two points of light among the trees, now well away to her left. Who could that spy have been, to penetrate Maigraith's webs of illusion so easily?

Now she sensed Maigraith's impatience. The rope tumbled down and her companion came up gingerly, anxious about the climb. They crept away and round a corner out of sight.

"What was that . . . *thing* with the guards?" asked Karan.

"Not now!"

Maigraith sought some objective among the chaos of walls, buildings and courtyards that was Fiz Gorgo. The inner fortress, squat, powerful and ugly, was surrounded by another wall. Unclimbable this one, too well guarded even for her; but there was a second way. She gestured. They passed down stone steps into shadow.

"Yggur has a personal guard—they call themselves Whelm. A strange, brutal, dogged folk. That was one of them. Being sensitive, you must be specially careful of the Whelm. I wonder why he came with the sentries? He must have sensed you."

"We were seen. I felt someone watching us from the forest," Karan said. "As likely he sensed the watcher."

Maigraith peered into the blackness, shook her head, then glared at the blur that was Karan's face. "Nonsense," she said. "My illusion is unbroken. It was just some forest animal. Come on!"

Karan coiled her rope with furious jerks. Maigraith wouldn't listen—but then, she never did.

Inside the wall were signs of hasty work: timber scaffolding and piles of stone and other materials forming a crude maze; at every turn another hindrance, another delay. And even here there were occasional guards, almost as vigilant as those outside.

Eventually, much later than their plan, in the corner of a neglected yard Maigraith found three large circular stone cisterns that collected water from the roofs and the yard. They were covered with rotting planks. She eased the planks of the first cistern apart.

"How do you know this is the one?" Karan whispered.

Maigraith looked at the stars. "The northernmost, according to my map, is connected underground to the cisterns of the inner fortress. That is how we will get in. How long can you hold your breath?"

Karan did not answer. They both knew she was the better swimmer. The wall of the inner fortress loomed over them, and the horned towers eclipsed the stars beyond. I don't want this, she thought.

"Where's the rope?"

Karan passed it to her. Maigraith checked Karan's knots, seated the hook over the coping and climbed down hand over hand. The water was a long way below. Her head went silently beneath. Karan waited, counting slowly under her breath.

At twenty the water swirled and Maigraith gasped, "Wrong one. Pull me up."

Karan heaved until her hands were blistered and her shoulder muscles burned. Maigraith was rather bigger than her. At last she reached the top. Karan flopped down on the rim, pressing her palms to the stone. The cold helped with the pain.

"I found a pipe but it just went to the next cistern. Ahhh! It's so cold." Maigraith shivered convulsively.

"Why don't you let me go?"

"I'll go. Quick!"

She ran to the second cistern while Karan put the planks in order. By the time she got there Maigraith was at the bottom of the rope and splashing into the water.

She seemed to be underwater for an age. Karan could see nothing, not even the reflection of the stars, then suddenly Maigraith surfaced, smashing the water with her fist and swearing horribly, something that Karan had never heard her do.

"Up! Up, damn it. Hurry."

Karan hauled. The coarse rope tore open her blisters; she almost wept with the pain. Maigraith perched on the coping for a moment. "Wrong again. Wrong, wrong, wrong! What fool made the map anyway?"

Just then a dog barked, not far away, and another answered it with a growl. Maigraith almost fell back down the cistern. Karan caught her and they stared at each other. "I can't beguile a *dog*," Maigraith said.

They ran to the third cistern. Maigraith heaved the planks aside with a great thrust of her arm and clapped the hook over the rim. One timber broke and fell with a splash. More dogs joined the chorus. She moaned, let go of the rope and jumped. Karan climbed inside the cistern and clung to the rope, peering out. The barking grew louder. There was not a sound from below. What was Maigraith doing?

A pack of dogs rounded the corner of the wall, howling furiously, and made for the first cistern. Suddenly they stopped and slowly separated into two packs. Karan's hackles rose. Between the packs came a larger, leaner dog, a gaunt thing the size of a calf, pacing jerkily like the Whelm guard. It stopped to sniff the air, ratcheting its emaciated muzzle from side to side, then pointed straight at Karan. *Hurry, Maigraith!*

The dog tensed, jumped one deliberate bound, then crouched. Karan stared into its eyes. The water gurgled. "Found it," Maigraith called through clattering teeth. "It's a long way down: count eleven blocks. The duct twists around and then goes up. Remember the rope." She sucked in three deep breaths and dived.

Karan looked down and the dog bounded forward. The starlight reduced it to eyes and teeth. She half-slid, half-fell down the rope. Her hands shrieked, then she struck the water. Black water closed over her head. It was frigid and it stank.

She surfaced and flicked the rope upwards. It hissed into the water beside her and the hook cracked her on the knuckles. She looked up to see the stars eclipsed by a soaring whippet shape that smashed into the water in front of her. Karan could not see it but she could tell where it was from the continuous back-of-the-throat growl. The dog snapped at her, clumsy in the water. She thrashed backwards. This was worse than any nightmare she could have imagined.

Something wrapped itself around her legs. Karan almost screamed, then realized it was the dangling rope. The dog snapped again, its breath rank in her face. She hauled up the hook and thumped it on the muzzle. It howled, Karan gasped a breath and dived. Even underwater she could hear the dog.

So cold was the water that it hurt her ears, so dark that she could not keep away a dread of nameless things, even worse than what was above. The blocks were slippery, the joins almost imperceptible to her numb fingers. Four, five, six, her toes aching; ten, eleven, twelve, already yearning for air. There came a sharp pain in one ear. Karan swallowed and the pain eased. Where was the opening? It should be right here.

She swam on, following the joins, and found it at last. The rope caught at her boot again. She kicked free, there wasn't time to coil it, and eased herself into the conduit. It was so narrow that even her slim shoulders touched the sides: confining; claustrophobic. Her calf began to cramp but she could not reach it; her lungs spasmed. A slimy curtain brushed her face and she struck it away, panicking. Karan thrashed, skinning her knuckles on the rock, clawed up a tight bend into open water, kicked with her good leg and heaved head and shoulders up into air.

Air! She gasped it down as though it was about to be snatched away again. A few strokes and her hand caught an edge, a low stone wall. She seemed to be in another underground cistern, much larger than the first. She pulled herself out and dropped an arm's length onto a floor, shivering and gasping and sucking her bloody hand. Her calf was a rigid, excruciating lump.

The dark was absolute; no sound but her own panting breath. "Maigraith!" she whispered hoarsely as she massaged the cramp away. No reply. Karan felt around her. The floor was stone, slabs of regular size and neatly fitted. The walls were of cut stone too. The air was cold and still. She called again, more loudly, "Maigraith!" The echoes taunted her.

Behind her, leather scraped on stone. She turned, her eyes straining against the black. "Maigraith?"

A glimmer of light appeared, revealing a curving wall and pipes running along the floor. Karan's eyes followed the pipes, more holes than metal, back to a dark device, evidently a pump, on the other side of the cistern. Beyond it a shadowy figure appeared, moving slowly. Karan edged back in against the wall.

"Do not be afraid, Karan. I wanted to be sure where we were. There are many tunnels. Rest a while, you must be worn out." The light came from a small globe in Maigraith's outstretched hand, reflected from her bleached blue eyes. Water still dripped from her hair.

Maigraith put her arm around Karan and hugged her for a second. The uncharacteristic kindness lifted Karan's spirits. She felt as though they were working as a team at last.

Maigraith sat down beside her and put the globe carefully on the floor. Everything she did was formal, restrained. She smoothed down her hair with deliberate strokes. Even the water of the cistern seemed not to have dulled its luster.

The light picked Karan's pale face and red hair out of the darkness. It was glorious hair, though requiring rather a lot of maintenance, and she had lost her brush weeks ago. The rest of her was just as messy. Once the shirt and trousers had matched her green eyes, but now the fine wool was travel-stained and worn, and her legs, arms and shoulders were smeared with brown muck from the sides of the tunnel. Her small feet and hands were blue with cold.

"What's that?" Karan asked, pointing to the glowing globe.

"A lightglass. Here, you might need it. I have another."

Karan inspected the globe. It was a polished egg of milky quartz, the base enclosed by five fronds of silver. Cool, but her touch left darker marks on the surface that took a minute or two to fade. "The Aachim have things like this. Where did you get it?"

"I made it."

"Made it!" That was beyond Karan's comprehension. "How?"

"There isn't time to explain," Maigraith said, wiping her face.

Karan coiled the rope and stowed it in her pack. "I hope *he* doesn't come back before we've gone," she said, rubbing vigorously at a smudge on her ankle with a wet sock.

"So do I," Maigraith began, though the sentiment was self-evident. Then, she asked suspiciously "Why?" Having no humor of her own, Karan's cheeky jokes were quite opaque to her.

"We're not dressed to go calling on one so exalted as the warlord of Fiz Gorgo," she replied with an almost straight face, giving Maigraith a sly sideways glance. "How could we face him? I would be mortified."

"Dry yourself! Get ready," said Maigraith crossly, rising, turning away. "How can you jest?" She leaned against the wall, pulling off first one boot, then the other, emptying them with a splash onto the floor, trying to steel herself.

Karan's eyes showed her secret delight, though that soon faded. "I joke because I'm so afraid," she said under her breath. "I know that Yggur will come." She thought of another jest, sillier than the first, but stifled it.

Maigraith separated her hair into thick strands, pulling each through her fingers until the water was gone. This seemed to calm her and she looked down at her companion. Karan's features had fallen back into their usual sunny expression; a smile quirked upwards the corners of her mouth as she wrung the water from her socks. Maigraith's severe, sad face relaxed momentarily; she almost smiled too. Then her burdens came on her again.

"Ready? Time is very short."

For Karan every passing minute rang like a gong but she said nothing. If it's this hard to get in, she thought, what's it going to be like getting out?

They walked a labyrinth of stone. Several times Maigraith referred to directions in her pocket, then finally they passed through a concealed door into a corridor so tall, dusty and narrow that it could only have lain within a wall.

As they walked Karan's apprehension swelled into alarm once more. She could think of nothing but the certainty that they would be discovered. She could not prevent herself from elaborating on what would happen to them, in this forbidden place.

Maigraith stopped suddenly and spun around, unable to conceal her anger. Karan was not broadcasting this time, but her panic flowed across the link, arousing Maigraith's own misgivings, weakening her. "Why ever did I bring you?" she hissed. "You will rouse the sentries. Control yourself."

Karan was stricken. She took a deep shivering breath. "You forced me," she replied in a small voice. "I didn't . . ."

"I did not realize that you were so soft, so weak," Maigraith said cruelly. Her head was splitting from the link, and she was beginning to feel that they were walking into a trap.

"Don't you understand what being a sensitive means?" Karan said, irritated. "Whatever you feel, I feel more!"

"Stop screeching and make yourself useful. Where is Yggur now? Do you know what he's thinking?"

"I'm not a mind-reader, Maigraith."

"What use are you? I wish I'd never brought you."

Karan was outraged. She grabbed Maigraith by the shirt and shook her. "Listen, I know my failings. Don't blame me for your own. You wouldn't have even got over the wall without me."

Maigraith had never learned how to deal with anger. She closed her eyes and rested her head on the wall.

"I'm sorry; I'm so afraid of failing. My mistress is unforgiving," she said, squeezing her temples between the heels of her hands. "My head!"

At Maigraith's distress, Karan's anger vanished. "Why on earth did she send you?"

"Since childhood she has schooled me for a great task, as she never fails to remind me. This is one of her tests." Maigraith looked irritable again. "Now, if we are caught leave everything to me. Don't try to defend me. You must get away."

"How could I get out alone?"

"You'd have to find a way. If the worst happens, wait three nights only, outside the ruins on Lake Neid. If I do not come, you must find your own path to Sith."

Karan nodded unhappily. She knew Maigraith's instructions by heart; she had heard them often enough. And there was her other worry.

"Maigraith . . ."

"Yes," she said tersely.

"Must you tell Faichand what you told me when you were drunk?"

Maigraith's hand gripped her globe until the knuckles went white. "I must," she whispered. "Don't mention it again."

On they went, up steps steep and narrow, down another corridor, then up a spiraling staircase of stone with no rail, to emerge on a landing facing a blank wall. Maigraith turned to the wall, holding her globe high. Placing one hand on the gray sandstone, and with her eyes closed, she seemed to sense what the stone concealed. Shortly she sighed and pressed gently. A door appeared; it was black and studded with brass nails.

Maigraith laughed in relief. "At last, Karan, this is the place! I can tell you now." She took her hand off the door. "We have to find the Mirror of Aachan, an ancient device that Yggur has."

"*The Mirror of Aachan!*" whispered Karan. Her face was bleached as white as paper. "But . . . you know my father was half-Aachim."

"When we set out, I didn't. Besides, you swore a binding oath to *me.*"

"I would not have, had I known! The Aachim brought me up after my parents died; they *never* give up such things. Is this why you wouldn't tell me before?"

Maigraith was defensive. "The Mirror was lost centuries ago. It belongs to whoever finds it."

"The Aachim will never agree," said Karan. "The Mirror is part of their heritage, brought secretly from Aachan; a reminder of their world when they had nothing else. Did Faichand not tell you how they lost it?"

"It was stolen by Yalkara, the Mistress of Deceits!"

"Another of the Charon, their nemesis. The Aachim are

an unforgiving people. Once they know that the Mirror is found they will move the heavens to get it back. And since I am part Aachim, that is where my duty lies. Please, release me from my oath."

Maigraith squeezed her temples again. She looked dreadful. "You swore!"

"You stretch the obligation to breaking point," Karan snapped. "The Aachim's ancient works are as precious to them as their art, their literature, their Histories."

"Do you now break your sacred oath *to me*? Here, where I have no other recourse? This is a deadly place for a debate," said Maigraith.

Karan banged her head on the wall. Either choice she was damned. How could she break her oath? That would be a betrayal of everything that her father had stood for. But if she took the Mirror and failed to give it to the Aachim, she would be betraying her father's people. Still, now that she knew about it, she could not leave it here either.

"I will keep my word, but ask nothing of me ever more. The debt is paid! Take no chances, then at least I can say I never touched it. I pray that I never have to."

Even as she spoke she could see Maigraith's liege in her mind's eye. Faichand was a small woman with deep feline eyes and smooth translucent skin, more like a living sculpture than a person. Then she fixed you with those ageless eyes and froze you from the inside out.

"Come on!" said Maigraith.

She put both palms on the door and pushed. It swung open. They stepped into the room—a library, dimly lit by a glowing flask to the right of the door. Two walls were lined with books from floor to ceiling, more than Karan had ever seen in one room before. Against a third wall was a massive desk scattered with papers and, above, a case divided into pigeonholes, most filled with rolled-up papers, charts and scrolls. A long workbench filled the center of the room. Next to their door was another, just the same, but it was closed. There were no tapestries, no pictures or decorations of any sort and the floor was bare stone. The remainder of the fourth wall was covered by two large charts, one showing the lands surrounding Fiz Gorgo, the other the central and southern parts of Meldorin—lands recently overrun by Yggur's armies.

Maigraith barely glanced at the maps. They were not what she had come so far for. She looked up at the high window, through which the stars shone faintly. "Quickly now. It's very late."

Karan needed no urging. They set to work. The pigeon-holes contained many scrolls, some in metal cases. Maigraith examined each carefully. Most were paper or parchment, though several were made from a silky brown material that looked like bark.

Karan lifted down the books, one by one. There were many languages, many scripts, but she could not read them. The books were heavy, the work tedious. One had pages of copper into which the writing had been pressed. She ran her fingers over the back of a page, feeling the shapes of the glyphs, wondering about the one who had made this book so long ago. Nothing came to her and now Maigraith was glaring. Karan slipped the book back in its place and took out the next, looking in the space behind as she did so.

Finally the bookshelves were done. Karan put back the last volume, wiping dusty fingers on her trousers. Maigraith was going through the drawers of the desk. Her face was haggard.

"Perhaps he has it with him," Karan muttered, relieved that it had not been found.

"I do not think so," said Maigraith, looking up at the stars again. "He would hardly take it out of the citadel. Check the bench. If it is not there we have failed. There is no more time."

Karan sorted through the papers and charts on the bench. Nothing. There was also a heavy scroll wrapped in cloth and three scroll cases. Unwrapping the scroll she found that it was made of verdigris-crusted copper. The coils were corroded together, so that when she tried to prise up a corner it broke off, a green flake with just a thread of copper at the core. Putting the flake hastily back in place Karan wrapped the scroll again and turned to the cases. They were made of lead; two were empty and the third contained a parchment scroll. She turned to Maigraith.

"Wait! There's a wrongness here."

"What do you mean?"

"Well," said Karan, examining one of the cases closely, "this one looks as though it's made of lead, but it's not heavy at all. And though the outside appears smooth, I can feel a pattern on it. Look!"

Maigraith snatched it from her hand and turned away. Karan suppressed her irritation, peering on tiptoe over Maigraith's shoulder. Maigraith weighed the case in her hand, stroked it with her fingertips.

"I see what he has done—a simple concealment. Unworthy of him."

Under the force of her gaze it changed slowly, dull lead becoming shiny black metal, chased with an intricate design. Maigraith shook out the contents and slowly it uncoiled to form a single brilliant leaf of black metal.

Turning it over she saw that on the other side the edge was raised, like a frame. Set inside the frame was something as clear as glass, though not brittle, that enclosed a shiny reflective stuff like gelatinous mercury. It shimmered and shivered, ghosting phosphorescent as though caressed by ripples and eddies of light. The border of the frame was scribed with the finest silver tracery, glyphs of an unknown language. The Mirror was otherwise featureless save for a symbol in silver and scarlet, impressed in the top right-hand corner. It was like three golden bubbles grown together, enclosed by touching crescent moons in scarlet that were set within a platinum circle, which was infilled with fine silver lines twining and intertwining.

Maigraith put a tentative fingertip to the symbol. Goosebumps broke out all over her arm. She bowed her head until her forehead touched the metal. Her hand trembled. She put the Mirror down on the bench, mouthing words to herself. The face of the Mirror went dark, then a line of silver letters appeared, as fine as wire, glowing bright against the black. Karan tried to see but again Maigraith put herself between, her lips moving. The script flowed.

Ice formed in Karan's belly. "He comes!" she said.

Maigraith did not attend: her whole quivering attention was on the Mirror. A minute passed. "Maigraith!" Karan called again, shaking her by the arm. Maigraith knocked her hand away without thinking. Another minute went by, and another, and another.

"Maigraith!" Karen cried frantically. "Are you bespelled? Is it a trap?"

Maigraith took an eternity to focus on Karan's frightened face. She spoke lethargically. "No. Not for me anyway. It's just—it calls to me, as though it were mine. It's—it's as though there's a lost world inside." Her eyes forgot Karan and snapped back to the Mirror.

Karan felt a momentary dizziness, Maigraith drawing on her strength through the link. What on earth was she doing? This was so unlike her. Karan's face was bloodless. "Maigraith. We must fly. I can *feel* him coming."

Maigraith tore herself away. "Let us go then," she said in a strained voice, but it was too late. There were footsteps outside the door, as loud as thunderclaps to Karan's heightened senses.

Maigraith pushed the Mirror into Karan's hands and thrust her below the level of the desk. Karan wanted to hurl the Mirror out the window. The metal was warm in her hands. Her gaze was pulled down; her life changed forever.

The writing scrolled across, then stopped. . . . *If you come to read this, I have for you a message, a warning and a task,* Karan read. Then the letters faded and the face of a woman appeared, looking down as if trying to work a device with her hands. Karan stared. The likeness to Maigraith was astonishing, though the face was older, the dark hair woven with silver and the eyes were of deepest indigo. The woman looked up and her lips moved.

"Take it," she seemed to say.

The door swung open. Karan touched the image with a fingertip. The Mirror went blank. She peered around the edge of the desk. A man stood in the doorway. They were in no doubt who he was, for he looked just like the magus of all the tales. Karan wondered if he used that illusion to bolster a more meager form. Remarkably tall he was, bleak of eye and the hair curving across his brow was black as the wing of a crow. He did not look old, but like all mancers he had extended his life many times over.

It was Yggur—the warlord who had overrun the southwest of the island of Meldorin. Yggur, whose strength and cunning were legend.

He tossed the hair from his eyes and the light caught the brittle planes of his face, the jutting black brows, the dark ovals around faded eyes—frost on slate. Into the room he stepped, all-powerful, all-knowing, confident in his terrible strength. His chest was broader than Maigraith's shoulders. She knew at once that there was no escape.

"Thieves!" he said, his voice as mellow as butter. "In my library!"

Maigraith exerted all her strength to oppose him. The illusion, if illusion it was, faded. He looked the same but now she saw that his right leg moved stiffly and he winced as if it hurt him, just a twitch of the cheek. Another surprise. He might be a mancer, as she was, but still he was just a man— very strong, but not more than human. Maigraith put herself between him and Karan's hiding place.

"Who are you?" He spoke haltingly now, packets of few words; even to form them seemed an effort. "Which of my ancient enemies has sent you?" His forehead corrugated, a muscle jumped in his lip. "Have you come from Thurkad, *from Mendark*?" Rage, but disquiet too.

"My name is Maigraith," she said boldly, though she was deathly afraid, "and my business is my own. I will tell you nothing."

Yggur took another step toward her and Maigraith quailed. His presence was overwhelming. The painful movements, the halting speech, the sense of overcoming great obstacles, only added to the potency. She felt confused, hesitant, for it seemed that he knew her weaknesses as well as she did. Faelamor had neglected, perhaps deliberately, that part of her training where will is matched against will, and the sheer force of him shocked her. Maigraith was trained to submit, she shrank from confrontation. Karan was right, she was not up to this job.

Yggur trembled, mastering himself with difficulty. Then, as if a window had opened, she saw directly into his mind, saw that he suffered too. It was extraordinary, for she seldom empathized with anyone, but she no longer wanted to defeat him. Her heart was battering at her ribs. She clutched at her breast.

He raised up his hand. His eyes might have been needles

of ice, so did they probe her, prick her. Her mouth was dry as sand. She fell back a pace, cowering, as though expecting him to strike her. At that he looked contemptuous, which struck her worse than any blow. She stepped back again. He had done nothing and already she was defeated.

"Speak," he whispered. Her lips began to make the words.

Karan, still crouched behind the desk, was outraged. She kicked Maigraith in the ankle, trying to rouse her.

Maigraith gasped. But I am strong, she thought, through the confusions. I have a duty here. She dashed the mist from her eyes. "No!" she cried, and drew herself up.

Their eyes locked and Yggur was shocked into stillness. Suddenly she showed her strength; the strength perhaps of an equal, if she had the will for it. And something in her eyes disconcerted him momentarily. He stooped and stared at her, both surprised and intrigued. For a long time his eyes searched her, then he turned away thoughtfully.

"Perhaps the weaker will serve," he said, looking toward Karan's hiding place. "Come forth. Look at me."

The pressure of his will was shocking. Karan looked as though the weight of a tree had fallen onto her shoulders, and she had no defense but her innate stubbornness. She staggered away from the desk. Her face was stark against the red confusion of her hair; her hand trembled so much that the Mirror fell to the carpet. Yggur looked from the Mirror to her to Maigraith.

"Ah," he said. "I begin to understand. Bring it to me."

Karan picked it up, backing away. "I will not," she said, her voice breaking.

"Go," said Maigraith. "Leave me, Karan. Do as I bade you."

Yggur held up his hand, saying, "Stay!" and she went

still, too afraid to move. He turned to Maigraith. "You *dare* defy me!"

Maigraith stepped forward. "I will have my will, even over you, Yggur. *Go no further!*" Her soft-spoken words disguised a power that shivered Yggur from top to toe. He struggled but could not move. Then, not looking at her, Maigraith whispered, "Karan, flee! I cannot escape."

Karan stood mesmerized. Maigraith was still draining her through the link. You're taking all my strength, she tried to say, but the words would not come. Yggur forced with all his will. Maigraith shrieked and he found he could move again. He took a painful step toward Karan, then another. He stooped over her.

Karan looked pleadingly at Maigraith. Maigraith could not help her. Yggur's huge hands gripped Karan's shoulders but still she would not look at him. Her back began to bow under the weight of him. His grip was cruel on her small shoulders. With one hand he turned her face toward him. His smoky eyes bored into her. She glared up at him—terror had not robbed her of dignity, nor resolution.

"Help me," she cried in a thick voice, but Maigraith could do nothing.

"I *command* you!" said Yggur. "*Who do you serve?*"

Karan resisted, though the very force of his gaze seared her. She felt strengthless, hot and cold, dizzy, faint. Maigraith was sucking the life out of her across the link. There came a dreadful clanging in her brain, and each toll was the name that she dared not name. Was she in greater danger if she kept Faelamor's secret, or if she revealed it?

At last Karan could resist no longer. A tremor passed through her from head to foot.

"Be silent," Maigraith cried.

Yggur shook Karan so hard that her teeth clacked together. "Was it *Mendark* that sent you?" He spat the name out, rage mixed with bitterness.

"Yes," cried Maigraith. "Mendark! Mendark sent us."

But it was too late. Karan's face crumpled. There was bright blood on her lip. She tried to stop her mouth with her fist, but it betrayed her. One single word, unwilling, whispered: "Faelamor!"

Yggur released her and she fell to her hands and knees, still clutching the Mirror in one hand. "Faelamor!" he breathed.

Maigraith cried out from behind, "Oh, Karan, you have ruined me."

Karan looked mortified, then her eyes sheered away and she broke the link. Maigraith reeled. Karan rose slowly to her feet and backed toward the door, still clutching the Mirror. Yggur shot out his long arm, but Karan sprang backwards out of reach, amazing him with her agility. A tiny hope flared within Maigraith—she did have the will after all. She reached beyond her despair to a deeper reserve of strength.

"Leave her!" she commanded, using the Secret Art as she had never used it before.

It struck him like a blow and he flung up a crooked arm, the way a bird might shield itself with its wing. A look of disbelief passed over his face. "I cannot move," he said in wonderment. The muscles of his jaw were like knots in granite.

"Go!" Maigraith screamed. "Do what you promised. I cannot hold him long."

Karan seemed smaller, her face rounder and paler, but there was a furious resolve, a determination to amend the failure. "I will take it," she said. Then, turning to Yggur with simple dignity, "Nothing will stop me!"

Yggur gave a single labored jeer. "Nothing? Let me tell

you about my Whelm, my terror-guard. They were lost in the southern wilderness for half a thousand years. I mastered them, brought them out of ice and fire, and they will do anything I say. How they beg me to set them on my enemies. The Whelm will deal with you." He made a curious gesture with one hand.

At the name, or perhaps the gesture, a shudder began at Karan's ankles and traveled upwards until her flesh crawled and her hair stood up around her head. The shadow outline of the stick-man outside the wall rang in her mind. She was almost overcome by nausea, by revulsion, as though a dead dog had put out its rotting tongue and licked the back of her neck, leaving a cold trail of muck up to her ear.

Yggur laughed coldly. "So!" he said. "Faelamor is alive, and she wants my Mirror. I will forestall her. My armies can march on the east within the week, if they have to."

Karan looked about to faint. Already her betrayal had begun to move the world. Maigraith put out her fist and squeezed it tight. Yggur went silent. Karan fled. The door banged and disappeared again.

Yggur turned slowly and painfully to face Maigraith. The right side of his face had set rigid. "Indeed you cannot hold me," he whispered. "In the end you will weaken. Then I will break you."

Maigraith stood straight, her fists clenched by her side, looking up at him. "I defy you. I *will* hold you till she gets away; what you do to me matters not."

6

FALL OF
A CHRONICLER

In Chanthed, Llian was dreaming the most delicious dream that any chronicler could have. After years of searching he had uncovered evidence of a terrible, breathtaking crime, a deed so bold and far-reaching that its perpetrator could almost be admired. Now he was putting the fragments together to make a new Great Tale, the first for two hundred and fifty years. His name would be forever linked with it—*Llian's Tale*. The deed would put him among the greatest chroniclers.

Someone shouted in the next room. Another voice joined in, then a third, in furious argument. Llian groaned and pushed back the bedclothes. His head ached abominably, reminding him of the previous night, erasing his glorious dreams.

The reality was not worth waking for. In the month since his famous telling, Llian's search for the killer of the crippled girl had become an obsession that consumed his whole life. He had scoured the library, read until his eyes would no longer focus, till even to look at a page made his head spin, but had found nothing.

All his other work was abandoned. He still did tellings, but despite constant requests Llian had never told the *Tale of the Forbidding* again. He didn't dare, in case Wistan heard about it. And at the same time Llian lived with the fear that his version of the Great Tale would be proven false, his career destroyed. His rivals were saying that he was burned out, a one-tale wonder. For someone who had never wanted more than to be a chronicler, that was the worst humiliation of all.

Llian had no money, for his stipend had not been reinstated. No one knew the Histories better than he did but he could get no living from them here. He existed by spinning scandalous yarns in the sleaziest drinking pits of Chanthed, and occasionally by writing pieces for students who were too lazy or stupid to do their own work.

His impossible fancy, to learn what had happened at the time of the Forbidding and to craft his own Great Tale from it, survived only in his dreams.

A few days later Llian got home well after midnight, after a night when he had not even earned enough to pay for his drinks, to find his door standing wide open. He threw his bag in the direction of the table and it crashed to the floor. Holding his candle high, Llian saw that there was no table, no chair, no clothing on the pegs, no books on the shelf. His room was completely empty save for his lumpy straw mattress. Everything he owned, even threadbare clothes and down-at-heel boots, was gone. Anti-Zain obscenities were scribbled on the walls.

The loss of clothes and possessions was not such a blow; they were easily replaced, had he any money. But also gone were all his books of tales, laboriously copied by hand over fifteen years, his personal journals, precious family histories, and all his notes for the new version of the *Tale of the Forbidding*. He had lost everything save his illuminated book of the Great Tales and a new journal that he had in his bag. Llian was devastated.

Then the rumors started. At first they were just drunken whispers in the inns or anonymous scrawls on the privy walls—that there was something strange about the way that he had become master; that his tale was a lie or a fraud. They could not take the honor from Llian, for that had been delivered by the unanimous acclamation of the masters, but they could fatally damage his name.

The less faithful of his friends fell away one by one. The ostracism had the opposite effect on Thandiwe, however. Though she did not dare to speak to him in public, she smiled at him and met him several times in secret. It was heartwarming to know that he still had one friend, though knowing that he endangered her, Llian stopped seeing her as well. But worst of all, worse even than the loss of respect from his fellows, was being cut off from the Histories that were his life.

Finally Llian had to admit that he was defeated. He sought audience with Wistan.

"I am beaten," he said. "What do you want of me?"

"No more than your word as a master chronicler that you will never tell this tale again, or even speak of it," Wistan said.

"Very well, I will give you my word. All I ask is that you give me back my rights to the archives." He tried to sound humble but was not entirely successful.

"Certainly." Wistan picked up a pen, a magnificent thing with plumes like peacock feathers that trailed over his shoulder and danced with every twitch of his wrist. He stabbed the nib at the ink bottle and drew a sheet of paper to him.

"And my proofs. I must have them back too."

Wistan paused with his nib in the air. "They were submitted for your mastership. I cannot return them. Besides, a true chronicler can read a thing once and remember it perfectly forever."

"So I can, but the papers are more than just words. I need to see the documents."

"Why?" asked Wistan.

"How can I not search for the truth? That is the essence of my training. Do you not see that there could be another Great Tale here? No one at *this* college has found a new Great Tale in a thousand years. Think of the honor, for the college as well as for me."

He had found Wistan's weak point and they both knew it. Wistan moved back and forth on his chair. Llian took a deep breath and continued, "I'm sure that the girl in the tower was murdered to cover something up."

Wistan started, dropping the pen. Blue ink spattered the paper. "Worse and worse," he said. "Anyway, you can't have the proofs. They are locked away and I can't recover them." He fingered a bracelet of woven silver on his scrawny wrist. "No one can, save the new master after my death."

"That might be sooner than you think," Llian cried in fury, thinking that Wistan was making excuses. "Those proofs are mine—four years of my life. How dare you take them!"

Wistan cleaned the ink from the table, icily calm. "The only part of them that is yours is what you carry in your head. You will never see them again."

"Damn you! Then give me my reference and what remains of my stipend and I will leave Chanthed forever."

Wistan smiled, a gruesome sight. "Certainly. As soon as you give your word to say no more about this matter."

"I can't! If you refuse, I'll go to Mendark!" A hollow threat and Llian knew it.

Wistan went so cold that Llian felt shivers of fear run up and down his back. "Mendark and I are on the Council together. If you did so, I would have to advise him how you recklessly endanger the college and the Council."

"The college has always stood for finding out the truth of the Histories, no matter what. You are a coward and a hypocrite."

Wistan had had enough. "You are banned from the library until after the festival. Give me any more trouble and you lose your telling. Now go away!"

Llian went.

Another week went by. It was festival time. People poured into Chanthed from all over the great island of Meldorin and even from beyond the Sea of Thurkad. Every bed in every inn was doubled up, and tent cities began to spring up in the park and on the common land.

Traditionally the festival began with minor tales given by the students of the college, building up to the Great Tales told by the masters on the last three nights of the second week. Of the twenty-two Great Tales only three were told at any festival. But the festival had grown so popular that there were now mini-tellings all over town, including less respectable tales from the romances, the tales of bawdry and the apocrypha—unproven tales from ancient times or unknown lands or the other of the Three Worlds. Some even told the frightful *Tales of the Void*. On the last night there was only one venue and everyone came to it. The final night was given to the master who had told the best Great Tale at the previous Graduation Telling. And that right was Llian's.

But this time not even the festival could cheer Llian up. He had lost everything except his name and even that was hanging by a hair. Impossible to continue here, nowhere to go. No money, no references, no friends. Well, if he was to go down, it might as well be for a major crime as for no crime at all.

*   *   *

The festival was well into the second week now. Llian decided to get into the library archives and take back his proofs, if he could find them. Then he would tell his tale and disappear from Chanthed forever. Without references his life as a chronicler was over, but no one could stop him being a teller. He knew that he was a good one. If he had to eke out his living as a miserable bard—what a come-down!—that is what he would do.

Wistan would be leaving any minute for the telling. Llian loitered down the corridor beyond the master's offices, and when it was nearly time he walked past and stuck a piece of card over the latch hole. The door was the kind that locked when it was closed.

Wistan was a slave to routine. At precisely ten to seven he came out of his room, shrugging on a cloak. To distract him Llian dropped a stack of books with a clatter. Wistan looked up, scowled, then banged the door and swept past with his cloak trailing behind him. He nodded curtly as he passed.

"Not going to the telling tonight? Better get moving if you are."

"I'll be there," Llian lied.

He busied himself with his books and when the corridor was empty again he pushed Wistan's door. It swung open, the piece of card fluttering to the floor. Llian retrieved it and closed the door behind him with a hand that was trembling.

What was he afraid of? What could Wistan do to him that he had not already done? Almost nothing. Nonetheless, with pounding heart he went across the polished floorboards to the old cupboard on the wall where the keys to the college were kept. It was locked.

He had expected that. Taking a chisel out of his pocket he prised at the door. It came open with a splintery groan but a strip of wood split off the side. Llian swore: the damage would be noticed instantly. He found a pot of glue in a cupboard and stuck the strip back on, but the damage was still obvious. Well, he'd just have to hope that Wistan did not come back after the telling.

Llian sorted through the keys—library, archives, office—and stuffed them in his pocket. Now I really am a criminal, he thought. He unlocked Wistan's private office and slipped inside.

He searched the room for his proofs but did not find them. The only other place they could be was in the archives.

It was airless in the archives, so Llian propped open the doors at either end to provide a draught, though as the library was locked up this did not help very much. He spent half the night there but found nothing that was of any help.

Finally, to relieve his aching eyes, he got out the books of engravings from the time of the Forbidding, and the racks that contained paintings of that event. There were hundreds of pictures, for the hunting down of Shuthdar had been one of the great quests of the age. Every important race and nation had been represented there, and a dozen generals and monarchs had brought their court and their official artists to ensure that every detail was recorded, not least their own part in the victory. There were pictures in watercolors and oils and crayons, most so faded and damaged by the centuries that they were barely legible. But there were also many engravings and these were in better condition.

Llian had seen these pictures many times but he never tired of looking at them. Here was a painting that captured the very moment that the flute was destroyed, the deranged Shuthdar capering on top of the tower while in the background a storm rolled toward him like a tidal wave. Every detail of Shuthdar's grotesque features could be seen—artistic license surely, since no one had dared to go within half a league of the tower while he was alive.

And here was a series of paintings in oil showing the aftermath of the destruction of the flute and the many foolish souls who went into the glowing ruins, each hoping to gain the flute for themselves. They got nothing; most died of a wasting sickness.

Here were the chief players of the age. Rulke the Charon, the architect of the flute and of the misfortunes of the Three Worlds ever after. He stood tall among the dozens jostling to get inside. By herself stood the enigmatic Yalkara, Mistress of Deceits, the other of the three Charon who came to Santhenar, and the only person ever to have escaped through the Forbidding. That was one of the greatest riddles in the Histories, but much later than the problem he was trying to solve here. This painting was in better condition than the others for most of the detail had survived, even to the gold on Yalkara's wrist and throat and brow.

Another painting showed her coming out again, empty-handed, her clothes smoking and her hands burned. A third, much of the picture flaked off long ago, revealed Yalkara stripped naked to be searched in front of all the others, as was everyone who entered the ruins that day. But the flute was never found. It was destroyed, utterly gone.

Although Llian had seen these scenes many times before, today he had a feeling that they had something more to tell him—that there was something yet to be revealed, if he could only find it. But time was wasting and there was a lot more to do. He put the paintings and engravings back carefully and untied the next packet.

This he had also looked at before, though only once. It contained the original sketches made in the field, hundreds of drawings by various artists, each numbered in order. Though the ink was faded to brown and the paper yellow and brittle, almost every detail could still be seen. All of the paintings and engravings were based on these drawings save for a few watercolors that were also made in the field, but they did not concern him.

Llian put the sketches in order and went through them one by one. Here was a series of sketches, quite clearly the source of the later painting, that showed the people going into the ruined tower. And here, another longer series as they came out.

As he stared at the two sets, riffling back and forward in time, Llian was struck by the realization that there was something wrong. Some inconsistency, though he couldn't put his finger on it. He was exhausted; it must be three in the morning at least. Or was it that the inconsistency was between the drawings and the paintings? He held one drawing up to the light, trying to extract truth out of the faded ink. Was that the trace of another number beneath the first? He examined it carefully. Yes, the number *had* been changed, almost perfectly. But what had it been changed from?

Just then he heard a door click somewhere across the library. Wistan! He must not be caught here. Llian thrust the drawings back in their box and put it on the shelf where it belonged. He snuffed his lantern and ducked across a couple of rows of shelves in case the light had been seen. Without it, it was pitch dark, but he could find his way out easily enough.

Thud! Someone cursed under their breath and a lantern appeared where he had been working. They were between him and the far door!

"He's gone!" It was Trusco's deep voice. "Spread out— guard the door!"

How many of them were there? Darting his head between the shelves he saw two lanterns, then a third. Llian ran silently back toward the entrance door but as he got there he realized that there was a fourth person waiting just beyond the door. He tried to slip through but the guard was too quick and grabbed him by the sleeve. He reeled Llian in effortlessly.

"Got him!" he shouted.

Llian made a desperate lunge and his head caught the guard under the chin. The guard gave a muffled cry and let go for a second, spitting blood from a badly bitten tongue.

It was just enough. Llian was out of his grasp like an eel and raced down the row for the back door that he had left propped open.

"Running your way, Wistan," gurgled the guard.

Llian ducked through the rows and cannoned into a small man holding a lantern. It was Wistan. He went flying and the lantern smashed against the base of a bookshelf, sending a trickle of burning oil across the floor.

Wistan shouted, "Fire!" and stamped at the little flame.

That gave Llian a second chance. He scrabbled down the row on all fours, sprang up and just beat Trusco to the door, knocking out the prop as he went past. The door slammed closed on his cloak. He tore it free, slipped the bolt and ran around the archives toward the front of the library.

Then he had a horrible thought. What if they hadn't put the fire out? Whatever the cost he couldn't risk the library burning. At the other door he looked in and saw that Trusco was beating out the last of the flames. Nothing had been damaged. He made for the front door, dropped the now useless keys and set off to his room. Within ten minutes he was wrapped in his blankets, though he could not sleep. The escapade had been a total failure and he knew they would come for him before the night was out.

7

THE SEWERS OF FIZ GORGO

She was cunning, the little one. The Whelm gave Karan grudging respect, that she had led them such a chase. But it would not be long now, and there would be a price, when they took her.

"Find her! Take her—alive or lifeless! Do not return without the Mirror!" So Yggur raged, when at last he broke Maigraith and freed himself.

Hours had passed, and Karan was lost somewhere in the labyrinth beneath Fiz Gorgo. "Flood the tunnels!" and Yggur's servants opened the floodgates, though the lower passages had been partly full of stagnant water for centuries. Eventually the waters went down. Then they searched all the traps and rusty gratings for a small pale creature flung up against the iron, the flesh flattened and protruding through the bars, the fire gone out of the limp hair, and all covered in rust and brown muck. But they did not find her.

*　　　*　　　*

Karan collapsed on the landing outside Yggur's library. Her shoulders throbbed; she could still feel the imprint of his fingers on her flesh. Such iron will she had never encountered. Her mind so burst with him that no thoughts came, save for the menace of the Whelm. Who were these Whelm, that just their name wrenched her so?

She lay in the dark, oblivious. To be sensitive could be a blessing or a curse. Eventually the screaming in her head subsided and Karan recalled the danger just a wall away. Blind fingers found the precious light Maigraith had given her, a globe of polished rock crystal the size of her eye, partly enclosed by five fronds of silver. A touch brought milky light welling out.

The light revealed her hazardous refuge. She had forgotten that the small landing had no rail; had not considered the long fall beside the spiraling stair. But Karan was bred to the mountains and the height did not bother her, just the realization that she might have run straight off in the darkness.

She got to her feet. The Mirror, coiled once more, was still clutched in her other hand. Momentarily she was tempted to drop it over the edge, but that was no answer; it would just be there when she got to the bottom. It fitted easily into the special pocket inside her shirt, under her arm. Karan fastened the opening securely and tried to put the Mirror out of her mind.

Down the staircase she went, along the corridors. It felt better to be walking. At last she emerged from the dusty secret corridor into the main passage. There she stalled. Her head had begun to throb and a sick pain suffused her belly. The aftersickness was beginning again, the penalty for using her talent. This would be a bad one. Even had she been well she was not sure that she could find the cistern again among this labyrinth of tunnels. And if she did, and somehow got out, the dogs were waiting, and the guards. She was trapped.

What confidence she had gained ebbed away. She walked slowly along, dragging her feet. How pathetic her boast seemed now. No, don't even think about that; the only goal that mattered was to get out of here. And as the aftersickness grew until it was like the worst migraine she had ever had, until her head boiled and her sight faded and her stomach felt as though it was filled with burning foam pushing back up her throat, even that goal was of no importance.

Afraid to use the light, she groped her way along the wall. At a crossway she squatted silently in the dark, clutching her stomach. No path offered more hope than any other. Then a lantern flared in the distance, shocking in its brightness and suddenness. Karan fell to hands and knees and almost cried out.

There was nowhere to hide, no crevice large enough to conceal a rat. Further on, another corridor went off to her left. Without thinking Karan scuttled up it, fleeing from the light. The movement made the pain worse; her head pulsed in time with her racing heartbeat. Crawling along in the dark she struck her temple on a fallen block of stone and had to bite her wrist to stop herself from shrieking. She lay on the floor, blind, totally disabled, oblivious.

Eventually the worst of the aftersickness was over, though her head and stomach would be tender for hours. Karan sat up, astounded that they had not found her. A distant rattling, as of great chains, echoed down the tunnel then. She took no mind of it, just wandered silently in the dark, arms out in front of her.

In her fear of the light she went further and further away from the passage she knew, walking randomly: up steps, along tunnels, down narrow adits, down and up again. She was hopelessly lost.

And many of the lower galleries were flooded. After the

first encounter she had kept the globe in her pocket, creeping along by feel, but that was as dangerous as using the light, for there were other openings in the floor. Once as she splashed along she fell into icy water. Not long after, passing the black mouth of another shaft, stale air rumbled out of it in a great flatulence, the water rose swiftly, overbrimmed the hole and made a dark stain as it crept away along the floor.

This brought all Karan's woes to the surface again and she sat down on stone with her feet in the water and wept. She wept for the dark and her hopeless situation. Wept for her foolishness in agreeing to help Maigraith in the first place. It took her back to her childhood, weeping alone in the dark, and she wept as well for her beloved father Galliad, who used to hold her hand in the night and smooth the bad dreams away. Then she was twelve again, her father four years dead (and her mother Vuula as well, taking her life in grief and madness), living in misery with her mother's family. The days were spent in drudgery and abuse, the nights in lonely tears. But one night, as she lay awake in her room under the roof, watching the moon and the stars, Karan remembered her father's people, the Aachim, and resolved to go to them.

Perhaps Galliad had foreseen her trials, for at his knee he had given her the secret of his people and where they could be found at need. Karan had no money and few possessions, for her inheritance was in the hands of a steward, but she sold a bracelet her mother had left her, bought the things she needed for that long journey and, one night, when the moon had set, she bundled up her clothes and treasures, climbed down the stone wall and set out to find the Aachim in their remote mountain fastness of Shazmak. She walked all that night, fearful on the road, terrified off it, and hid before dawn until the hunt had gone by. After a day or two the search shifted away from the mountains. What was up there for a girl of twelve?

Three weeks it took before she found Shazmak, long hidden from the world, over passes where the snow lay even in summer, after much searching and not a little terror. And somehow, incredibly, the Sentinels did not sound when she came across the pass; did not sound when she made her way along those interminable ledge paths with the Garr gnashing the rocks far below and the cliffs rising high above. She emerged from a tunnel and the sun touched the slender towers and gossamer walkways of Shazmak to silver and gold. Only when she crossed the last bridge and stood in the walled yard outside the gate did they sound, and then a single bright peal.

In her mind's eye she saw herself as the Aachim must have seen her at the doors of the city—a tiny dirty figure dwarfed by her mountain clothing; starving, exhausted, and her hair a flaming riot about her round face. Impossibly shy, but with a quiet dignity beyond her years. Suddenly afraid of these stern folk—terrified of being taken in by them, terrified of being rejected—she wanted to run away again. Then she saw that among the big-bodied, dark-haired people staring at her were one or two who were smaller, with pale skin and red hair like hers.

"I am Karan Elienor Melluselde Fyrn, of Bannador," she said, enunciating her names with care and pride. Fyrn was her mother's family name; Elienor a long-dead Aachim heroine of her father's line to whom Karan bore a singular likeness; Melluselde—another family name. "My father Galliad is dead. I have come home."

And she was so like her grandmother, beloved Mantille, tragically dead as well, that the Aachim wept for the sight of her. Yet unlike, too. They loved her for the echoes of her ancestors, even more for herself, and took her into Shazmak and into their hearts. And though the Aachim were a melancholy folk, wrapped up in a culture and a history that she could never understand, she was happy there for the first five years. Happier than she had ever been save when her father was alive. But the sixth year had changed all that. Unbearably harassed by the half-Aachim, Emmant, and feeling let down by the other Aachim, she had fled in her eighteenth year and never returned.

The memories gave Karan enough heart to think of ways of escape. Such a labyrinth of tunnels, built over centuries, built and rebuilt, might have many exits. She struggled to remember what she knew of Fiz Gorgo; what Maigraith had told her on the journey. But Maigraith had been closemouthed, even about things that Karan needed to know.

Think! The Aachim were incomparable engineers and they built to last forever. Shazmak had been a similar place and she knew every part of it. There would be huge water pumps below, and furnaces to heat the water, and a sewer to take it away again. Doubtless the pumps had failed and no one had the skill to repair them; the furnaces burned out long ago. But the sewer, the great cloaca of Fiz Gorgo, must still be there, if she could find it. It would empty into the estuary.

Karan followed the tunnel a little further but it ended in a wall of stone, and so did the other turnings that she took, as though that part of the labyrinth had been blocked off a long time ago. Finally she came to a crossways and a passage that led the way she sensed she should go. Twenty or thirty paces along she froze. A whisper echoed down the corridor and two figures, one tall and gaunt, the other squat, moved slowly by along the main tunnel. It seemed that the tall one turned its head in her direction as they passed, but the light of their lanterns did not reach her, crouched down in the blackness.

Then they were gone. The shock of them was less this

time. Perhaps these ones were not Whelm. Karan darted the other way. Down; she must get lower down.

Again that distant rattling. Now the cold, the tiredness, the hunger and the fear all combined to leave her mind a blank. She stumbled along in the dark, not caring where she was going as long as she went forward. When she came to a junction she turned one way or another without conscious thought, allowing her intuition to guide her and, hours later, long after dawn (though there was no dawn here), in a distant corner of the labyrinth at last she did find a way down, a simple hole in the floor. Once there had been a metal lid but now only the hinges remained.

The globe, just a brief flash, showed rungs leading down; below that, nothing. The rungs were badly rusted. Karan hesitated but a light in the distance took the choice from her. She put her foot on the first rung. Rust came off in thick flakes, and she went down swiftly and dropped about a span onto a slippery floor. Holding the globe out before her, she saw another shaft. Karan climbed down it until her eyes were at the level of the opening. A circular patch of light appeared, a lantern at the top of the upper shaft. But they could not have seen her. If she stayed still . . .

For a moment it seemed possible. Then a murmur from above, the light grew suddenly in the opening, feet on the rung, an arm thrust down holding a bright lantern; a harsh cry; a hand pointing. Her footprints were clear in the mud on the floor, but no one came down the shaft. Then Karan heard a hollow rasping and the light was shut out. She crept back and held up her globe. The opening was closed with a block of stone and she was trapped below.

Yggur's leg throbbed unbearably, and his back. The old injuries felt as though they were aflame, Maigraith had hurt him so. All he wanted was to lie down and take the weight off his bones, but he kept on, driving even the Whelm who needed no supervision. He could not show weakness before them.

The pain had made his speech even more halting than usual. "Lost her? How lost her, fool?"

The break-in, the insult, could not have come at a worse time for him, just as he was finalizing preparations for his next campaign, his march on the rich eastern states. How had they managed it? How could he have allowed the little one to get away with the Mirror, crucial to spying out the strengths and weaknesses of his enemies?

"There are twenty of you," he raged. "She is nothing; just a girl!" No, it was fatal to underestimate even the least of his enemies!

The Whelm at his side, whose name was Idlis, made no excuses. That was not his nature. Neither did he point out that she had escaped from Yggur himself. But the rigidity of his posture told that he felt the insult.

"We know not where she is." His voice was a glutinous roiling, the phrases coming out like bubbles rising through a vat of syrup. "But well where she is not, and that is most of the labyrinth now. She is isolated in the Skurrian quarter. All paths out of it are sealed save the main one. But it is a slow business. The water hinders us more than her. It goes where it wants and we cannot direct it; the workings are unfathomable."

Yggur smiled, though he knew the pun was unintended. The Whelm were utterly humorless. "What else is in that quarter?"

"Empty storerooms; empty cells. Beneath, the ancient sewage duct."

Yggur permitted himself another brief smile. "And that is sealed."

"Yes. The outlet gates are checked each month. They are sound."

Just then a runner burst in, a young woman dressed in drab; one of the toilers. Yggur saw a pinched face in a dark cowl, and sandals that were too big and flapped as she ran. She checked, then came the long way round, keeping well clear of the Whelm.

"What news, Dolodha?"

Saluting Yggur, Dolodha replied, "She has gone down into the sewer, by the shaft at the end of the Horthy passage."

"Ha! Then close the shaft."

"That was done at once."

"And the water shut off?"

Dolodha hesitated. Yggur noticed that she was watching Idlis out of the corner of her eye. "The mechanism broke. The gate is jammed wide open and we cannot free it."

"How long ago?"

Again the answer came slowly. "It took an hour to find you."

Yggur swore. He rounded on Idlis. "Get all the Whelm down there and find her. I make *you* responsible."

"I am least among the Whelm," said Idlis, his face showing expression for the first time, and uncertainty. "Vartila would be a better choice. Or Jark-un."

"I have chosen you," said Yggur. "Do not come back unless you have her. Even the least of the Whelm should be a match for her. But I want her alive."

"Earlier you said . . ."

"Maigraith was *linked* to her. She must be a sensitive. I have a use for her. Hasten. I will follow."

Karan went back to the lower shaft and sat there with her legs dangling down into the darkness. The air that came up was sour. Feeling in her pack she came upon a small wrinkled quince. She ate it with slow, nibbling bites, savoring every tart morsel, and though when it was finished she felt just as hungry as before, the simple act of eating gave her courage.

There was no way out save down. Karan turned and went backwards down the shaft. One, two, three rungs, then the fourth broke beneath her feet and she fell into the dark, into deep, still and icy water. The cold so shocked her that she dropped the little globe, the water closed over her head and she thrashed, on the edge of panic, in absolute darkness. Her boots pulled her down as though they were stone, but at last she came to the surface, spluttering and wiping slime out of her eyes. When the water was still again she saw the wavering light of her globe far below.

It was not that deep, as it turned out, but the cold water blurred her vision and the lightglass was embedded in the muck. It took five dives before she held it in her hand again and Karan was exhausted. She was a good swimmer, but now, fully dressed and bearing her little pack, it was all she could do to keep her head out of the water.

Treading water clumsily she held up the globe. Gray sludge ran down one sleeve to her armpit. The light showed an oval tunnel made of carefully laid stone, almost half full of water. The shaft above was a black circle, way beyond her reach. Further along Karan saw a narrow platform. She swam down to it and hauled herself up. Her fingers stank of ancient filth.

Karan leaned back against the stone and closed her eyes. Whatever the consequences, she must rest. She searched for some distraction, and it came at once, the tale that she had heard at the Graduation Telling and often thought about since. The threads of it wove together in her mind as though Llian was standing there, telling it just to her. He was magnificent. She could remember the least detail of his tale and every movement of his endearing, untidy features as he spoke. She smiled dreamily.

Just then the stone against her back shook and Karan realized that she had rested too long. She stripped down to her knickers, jumped back in and headed in the direction that intuition told her was downstream. At intervals there were brass rings let into the rock and, once, a long way downstream, another shelf—evidently a platform for the use of the sludge muckers. When she could swim no further Karan hauled herself up, rested as long as she could bear the cold, then swam on. But on the third of these rest stops she heard that sound again, unmistakeable now. A distant rattling, as of huge chains, and a reverberating thud like a big door being lowered. Her ears popped suddenly and a tremor passed across the surface of the water.

They were flooding the tunnels, one by one! She jumped up, holding out the globe and straining her eyes against the darkness. And, Karan realized, the outlet of the sewer must be blocked, for the water was still. But there was nowhere else to go, so without further thought she leapt into the water, which already showed a sensible rise from its former level, and swam on.

Her guess had been right, for after a few minutes she came to a grating, half-raised, and beyond that the sewer outlet was closed with a wall of sandstone into which had been let a set of metal doors wide enough for six people to pass through abreast. She could tell by the rustic design and the quality of the workmanship that this was a recent construction. The Aachim would never have built anything so prosaic, so out of harmony with the rest of Fiz Gorgo. Yet the metal was solid and the doors secured with an iron bar bigger than she could lift. The bar was clearly meant to keep out intruders, but as she came close she saw that it was fixed on the inside as well, by spikes driven through holes into the door.

The water rose steadily. She climbed onto the bar and tried to think. If she could prise the spikes out she might be able to open the door. After all, surely it was meant to keep people out, not in. They must need to open it at times to drain away floodwaters or seepage or king tides, otherwise they would have sealed it permanently. How long did she have? Two or three hours at most.

Karan caught the hook of her rope over the top of the door, ran out a long loop and tied it off again at the top. With her feet in the loop and the rope held in the crook of her arm, she could work with both hands. Using her knife she prised away at the first spike, but could not exert enough force for fear of breaking the blade. Was there any other way? She examined the door more carefully. The brackets that held the bar were bolted on; there was no way of removing them. The door hinges were massive brass, corroded but still strong. The frame through which the hinge bolts passed into the rock was rusted, though, and the edges of the sandstone blocks crumbly; had she a strong enough lever she might have prised the hinges off.

Karan went back to the bar, which was two-thirds of the way up the door. The water was already lapping at it. Back at the last platform stone had fallen from the roof. She fetched a piece, climbed back up and thumped the spikes with it, one by one. Now she tried the first again. To her joy it moved slightly and by cautious exertion she managed to free it. It was round, as long as her forearm, tapering to a blunt point, and clearly designed to slide in and out. The next came out easily, and the one after, but the fourth and fifth were as difficult as the first and by the time she had freed the last the water had risen to her waist.

As she worked, her thoughts went home to Gothryme.

Though it was poor and barren, it was all she wanted. How far away it seemed. How had she come to this, alone at the end of a foul sewer and, for all her angry words earlier, her debt still to repay?

The second task was more difficult than the first because now she was working underwater, but finally she levered the bar up over the brackets and it fell away.

Karan leapt up and clung to her rope, expecting the doors to burst outward under the weight of water. They shuddered and groaned. Nothing else happened. She beat her fists against them in frustration. What was holding them now? And looking closely at the part of the door that was still above the water, she saw a line of small rivets where the two doors closed against one another. Rivets! She could do nothing against rivets.

Utter hopelessness overcame her then—all Karan could do was cling to her rope and watch the water rise up the door. Drowning was no worse a way than any other. The water was rising quickly now.

But she was not ready to die, would do anything to postpone the end, even for just an hour. She flopped into the water again, looking back up the tunnel. At intervals there had been inspection traps in the roof, small circular shafts with rungs leading down, but they were all sealed at the top. The last of these was beside the grating, just a few spans away. Karan climbed up into it and clung there, shivering. The sewer was almost full and, now and again, long bubbles of air would be pinched off and go wobbling past, tickling her toes, to disappear up the tunnel.

Then, as she clung there, Karan heard a distant clang. Metal striking against metal! Time passed. The water rose. Another clang, less distant.

The water level began moving up inside her little refuge;

more slowly now, yet visibly rising. Her ears popped again. Only minutes remained. Still her mind would not let go. She needed some kind of pointed tool to lever away that rusted frame.

Clang-bang! Right above her head. So loud and ringing that she fell off her perch into the water. With a shocking horror she realized that they—the Whelm—were breaking open the inspection shaft. This was the end.

8

THE WATCHER
IN THE FOREST

Suddenly the answer leapt into Karan's mind—the hook on the end of her rope was made of best Thurkad steel; she could not even bend it. But the air was almost gone now. Karan took several deep panting breaths, filling and emptying her lungs until she felt dizzy and her lips tingled, and stroked underwater to the doors. A little air was trapped in a recess above them. She came up to it slowly, the globe in her hand, and saw that from underneath the trapped air made a perfect mirror, a surface as smooth and reflective as quicksilver.

Gulping the air, she went down again. The doors were distinctly bowed in the middle, along the line of rivets, and when she thumped them with her fist they quivered. Yet they held.

Karan caught her hook on the eroded frame around the uppermost hinge, which had pulled away from the stone under the weight of water, braced her feet against the door and heaved. The metal tore a little. She strained again, it tore a little more, exposing the gap beneath the hinge. Her lungs were spasming.

She drifted up, took another breath of the precious air and swam down again. Easing her hook beneath the hinge she worked it back and forth, holding the globe between her teeth. One of the split bolts that secured the hinge in the soft sandstone came out in a little puff of grit. She levered over and over. Another bolt came out, then the others pulled free all at once, the hinge sagged away from the wall and the door made a grinding sound. But the other hinges held.

There was a muffled clang above, and Karan saw yellow light through the murky water. The light waxed and waned. Now it was blotted out by a moving shadow. She attacked the second hinge furiously. It was harder than the first, because the frame had warped, but at last these bolts came out as well. Up she went for another breath, down again. The last hinge moved, the door groaned, but the bolts refused to budge.

With the last of her breath Karan swam across to inspect the doors again. The globe was fading but the yellow light was so bright now that she didn't need it. Her head throbbed, her vision had begun to blur from the cold, but she saw clearly that the door was buckled in the middle. Some of the rivets had popped and little streams of bubbles were whirling in through the gap. She put her lips to the stream, greedy for air. It smelled of the sea.

Then the shadow was above her, swimming lazily, its long arms spread. Karan reacted violently. Gripping the right bracket she brought her feet up against the other door and pushed with all her strength.

Flat fingers clamped on the back of her neck and squeezed. Karan jerked free and, still clinging to the bracket, twisted and kicked out blindly. She struck something yielding and the Whelm jackknifed, clutching at himself. Momentarily his face almost touched hers: eyes screwed tight in his agony, gaping mouth gushing air, filed teeth.

With a shriek that hurt her ears the doors gave, the left one torn completely off by the vast weight of water. The face was snatched away. Her fingers were ripped from the bracket and she was flung through the door in a maelstrom of water and mud and the putrid sludge of aeons.

That would surely have been her death, for there was another grating on the outside, but the great door smashed it to one side, tumbling over and over down the main and eventually out into the estuary where it sank in the deep water.

And Karan came after, the breath driven from her lungs, in her head a roaring and a flashing of black and white and red, tossed and tumbling, bruised and battered and fighting for air. Yet somehow she survived, undrowned, unbroken and with a secret fierce exhilaration at having beaten Yggur and Fiz Gorgo too.

When the current was dead Karan found herself more than a hundred spans offshore, with just the strength to swim back to shore in the darkness. She waded up a creek into the swamp forest but as she splashed along she sensed, just for a moment, the watcher that she had felt the previous night.

She had spent all day underground. Up above, the scorpion nebula was reduced by mist to a formless red blur. She waded through swamps, swam up streams so shallow that her belly touched the mud, but at last, after midnight, confident that she had concealed her trail, Karan crept into the rushes. Even as the Whelm swarmed out of a dozen hidden grubholes and Yggur himself limped to the sewer exit, she rolled herself in her wet cloak and slept, and dreamed of a festival far away.

*   *   *

Karan had been right about the watcher in the forest. Maigraith's illusion *had* been broken and it was the same spy this time. Her name was Tallia and she was chief lieutenant of Mendark, the Magister in far-off Thurkad, he whom Yggur so feared and hated, and Llian so fretted about. Tallia was spying out Yggur's defenses, though it was not coincidence that she was watching when Maigraith and Karan came. There had been word of them from the smugglers.

Tallia was a dark, striking woman, though she did not look it, for she had plastered herself with mud and her black hair was matted with twigs and water weed. For three days she had lain hidden there. She had seen Yggur's departure, Karan and Maigraith's entry, Yggur's furious return. And even from outside Fiz Gorgo she had felt the ripples from Maigraith's profligate use of power. That made her very thoughtful indeed.

Just as she prepared to depart there came a roar on the seaward side of the fortress, not far from her hiding place. Tallia found a flood still gushing down an obscure channel into the sea. She picked her way along the shore and was hidden when Karan struggled out of the water and disappeared into the forest.

Soon after, she heard a fitful thrashing and, creeping down, Tallia saw a Whelm staggering in the shallows. Tallia was not afraid—she was highly skilled in combat with and without weapons and had other powers to call upon at need. They weren't necessary—the fellow was dazed and bleeding from a dozen lacerations. She dragged him into the scrub.

"Who are you following, Whelm?"

He struggled but did not answer. She had not expected that he would. A Whelm would die rather than betray his master. She had other ways, not always effective, especially with these, but the man was half-dead. The simplest of tricks might be enough.

"Who is your master?" she asked.

"We serve Yggur," he replied in a monotonous gurgle.

She sent him into a trance with her voice and her fingers, and put her hand over his eyes. The feeling of his skin was horrible. "I am Yggur," she said, imitating Yggur's voice imperfectly. It had been months since their only encounter.

"You are not my master."

She tried again, got it right this time.

"I am Yggur. What are you doing here?"

"The woman escaped from the sewer. I, Idlis, hunt her until she is found, and the Mirror recovered."

"Do you remember her name, and the name of the other thief?"

The Whelm gave their names. Further questioning revealed what little he knew: that Maigraith was imprisoned, that the relic was the Mirror of Aachan. Tantalizing but unsatisfactory.

"Sleep now; forget that we met."

He fell face-down in the mud. Although Tallia tried to follow Karan she could find no trace of her in the swamps. It was essential that she get this information back to Mendark.

A couple of leagues from Fiz Gorgo she came to a creek that rushed over stony ground into the estuary. Tallia washed the mud away, donned fresh clothes and dozed fitfully in a vase-shaped tree until dusk. During her waking moments she wrestled with the problem of these intruders. Their strength argued for an important new power, or a resurgent old one, but the Whelm had not been able to tell her anything useful about them or the Mirror, whatever *that* was.

Where had Yggur got the Mirror from? He had been at Fiz Gorgo for many years now, but only recently had he begun his campaigns against the lands of the south. She recalled Mendark's reaction after the last victory.

"How does he do it?" Mendark had said, fretting and worrying his beard into rat's tails. "It's as though he knows his rivals better than they know themselves." Mendark, formerly so commanding, seemed to have trouble coping with this colleague of times long past who had now reappeared as a foe.

As dark descended, dogs began to bay in the forest beyond the creek. Tallia was shocked, thinking that she'd covered her trail better than that. It sounded like a whole pack, too many for her to deal with. She waded into the creek and went like a wraith down the braided channels into the sea. There were islands out in the bay, half a league away, a long cold swim, but she had no other recourse. She set off for the nearest. By the time the dogs howled and leapt around the foot of her tree she was well out into the bay and it was so dark that the islands could not be seen. Treading water, she listened for the sound of waves breaking on rock and stroked silently in that direction.

Shivering in wet clothes all that night she barely slept. The scorpion nebula shone in and out of the mist. In her far-off homeland of Crandor the appearance of a nebula was an evil portent. This one, this scorpion, was as ill an omen as she could imagine.

Days later she boarded a smuggler's boat and, in the foggy night, traveled up the River Or to an island among many in a vast lake. At a manor concealed in the forest she wrote a note that went by carrier bird, or skeet, all the way north and east to distant Thurkad.

Pulin 3

Mendark,

You were right—Yggur *had* found something. A relic of the ancient past called the Mirror of Aachan. But it is gone, stolen. One of the thieves was taken. Her name is Maigraith. The other escaped. Karan of Bannador she is called. There is a dangerous new power here. I'll try to learn more. Send orders to me in Preddle.

Tallia

"She's gone!" Yggur's voice fell to a deadly calm. "Whelm sealed the sewer. Whelm checked the sewer. Idiot Whelm assured me they had her. How gone?"

He had been waiting above the shaft while Idlis went in to get Karan. Then the water roared and Idlis did not come back.

Another Whelm stuck her head out of the shaft. "The sewer is breached. She got the bar off the doors and the water burst them open. Certainly she's drowned."

"No. This woman is a formidable foe. Find her! What about the wretched Idlis?"

"He is . . . not as capable as some. Surely dead as well."

"A fool among fools! Find him too. He has a job to finish, if he lives."

A ladder was fetched and Yggur climbed down to see for himself. The sewer was almost empty. The great bar lay in the sludge. There were fresh scratches on the stone where the hinges had been.

He'd had no sleep and his leg was so painful that he had to hold onto the ladder. Any other man would have ranted. Suddenly, to the astonishment of the Whelm, he chuckled.

"What a woman! She is unarmed, has no powers, just a bit of a talent, yet she's got away. When all this is over I could enjoy—" Seeing the Whelm's expressions he kept the rest to himself. They could never be generous to an enemy—he knew they wanted to torment and crush Karan, to utterly expunge this defeat. Something close to contempt for him showed on their faces. How much longer could he rely on them?

"Help me back up," Yggur said. "Bring my boat."

It was already dark outside. They searched the estuary from boats and the shoreline for half a league east and west of the place where the sewer came out. Not a trace did they find of Karan. Some went back underground, others down the shore to the fishing villages, or hunted down and searched the fishing boats and the smuggler's vessels.

Now it was late and there was still Maigraith to question. Yggur signed for the boat to turn back. They rowed up into a creek that was close to the perimeter path.

"Stop! What's that?" said Yggur, pointing up the creek to what looked like a gray log on the mud. "Hold the lantern higher."

Two Whelm loped up. Yggur limped after them. The log turned out to be Idlis, clad only in a loincloth.

Yggur looked down at Idlis. The sight of the Whelm unclad disgusted him—the anorexic thick-jointed limbs, the protruding ribs, the spatulate fingers and toes, the fish-belly skin that burned even in the weakest morning sun. The black eyes that must also be shielded. At times he hated himself for keeping them, would not have but that they were so obedient, so dogged, so frightening.

Someone turned Idlis over. He groaned and heaved up mouthfuls of black mud and mucus. A grid pattern of bruises and lacerations covered his torso and one leg; his hatchet nose was bloody. He had hit the grating outside the sewer doors very hard.

A hatful of water was flung at his face. Idlis moaned and tried to get up.

"What happened to Karan?" asked Yggur coldly.

"Followed her, far as I could," Idlis choked. "Already I told—" His eyes crossed, tongue clove to the roof of his mouth and he flopped back down.

"I haven't—" Yggur began. His mind raced. "A *compul-*

sion! Search this place," he cried. "Vartila, find out what happened here."

A bony woman with gray hair to her shoulders knelt in the mud and put her hands on Idlis's head.

"Master!" a shout from down the creek.

Yggur hobbled down.

"See, bootprints," said the Whelm. "Someone dragged him up from the water. Spoke to him here, then went that way. Then Idlis crawled up there."

Shortly Yggur knew how Idlis had been questioned and what he had said. An outside accomplice was his first thought, but an accomplice would not have asked those questions. This had the mark of Mendark.

Idlis was beginning to recover. "Fix his injuries," barked Yggur. "Give him some robes and go after Karan. You three, after the spy. I'll come with you a little way. Vartila, you begin with Maigraith." Then in afterthought, wondering why as soon as he had spoken: "I would not have her harmed."

Was it coincidence that the two parties had arrived here at the same time; and the guards were distracted just in time for the intruders to go over the wall? Possible but unlikely. Could Faelamor and Mendark be in league? Also improbable, but the Histories told of stranger alliances. And it would be a difficult one for him to combat.

This spy intrigued and bothered him too. It must be Tallia, the best of Mendark's lieutenants and the only one who had heard the sound of his voice. What a blow it would be if he could take her. He sent one of his guards running back for the dogs.

Yggur followed the tracks for some time but learned little new. Finally he turned back to the estuary and sought out the Whelm who were searching for Karan. They found nothing until the early morning. Near the mouth of a tiny creek less than a thousand paces from the sewer they came upon a single small footprint in the mud, where in her weariness Karan had wandered out of the stream and the sluggish tide had not come in far enough to wash the mark away.

Yggur inspected the print. It was quite distinct, a small foot, of a small woman or a child. It need not have been Karan but he knew it was, for the people of the villages had wide feet with splayed toes. Even the children had broader feet than these and they did not go barefoot at this time of year.

"It is Karan," he said, calmly now. "She has gone into the forest."

He gave the rest of the hunt their instructions and turned back to Fiz Gorgo to interrogate Maigraith. Another mystery, another challenge.

Clouds came up and rolled away again. The sun came out. The Whelm donned their eye shields of carved bone against the glare, adjusted the slits so they could see, pulled their hoods low over their faces and pressed on with the hunt.

9

LOST IN
THE SWAMP

Karan woke, warm for the first time in days. She
stretched and thought of breakfast, but all she had in
her little pack was wet bread and muddy, moldy cheese. The
bread was horrible, a soggy pulp. She cut off a piece of
cheese and, scraping off the mud with the edge of her knife,
regarded it warily. The cheese had a strange flavor, the pun-
gency of crushed ants mixed with the stench of sweaty
boots. Even before Fiz Gorgo she had found it barely edible,
but it was all they could get in Orist.

She chewed the mess, considering. Maigraith had carried
most of the food. No way of getting more here, where no
one lived. Wild food was scarce anywhere at the end of autumn, save nuts, but there were no nuts in the swamp forest.
Doubtless there were edible plants, but the country and the
flora were foreign to her, and after an experiment on the way
in that had left her lips and tongue numb for half a day she
was reluctant to try again. She had nothing to fish with ei-

ther. What food she had was enough for two mean days, but
Neid was at least three days away. There was food there,
where they'd left their heavy packs, though it was scarcely
better than what she had. But what if Yggur had learned of
Neid? She shivered.

Black eyes glared through the slitted bone. The sun made
dazzling reflections on the water, hurting Idlis's eyes despite
the shields. His battered body throbbed, though that was
easier to endure than the shame of his failure. He dipped a
leaf-shaped blade, thrust, and the prow of the canvas boat
parted the reeds and glided into the adjacent channel with
the barest rustle. Indeed she was cunning—but not cunning
enough. There were signs. A handprint on the bank; a V-
shape through the rushes. Soon he would redeem himself.

Karan repacked her pack. In spite of what was behind and
what lay ahead she felt good-humored today. Yesterday had
done a lot for her. So good it was to be alive, to have beaten
such an enemy, that she felt positively cheerful in the sun;
not discouraged by the hard hungry days ahead, not really
daunted by the filth of the mire.

Then she looked down at herself and laughed wryly. Her
trousers were caked with dried mud that flaked off with
every movement. Her feet were gray with mud, there was
mud under her nails, in her hair, up her nose. She stank, the
sulphurous odor of swamp mud and the foulness of sewer
water. She had not changed her clothes in a week. Disgusting!

Catching sight of her face in the Mirror, Karan quickly
put it back in its inner pocket and buttoned the flap down.
She was not ready to tackle that problem yet. Humming
softly to herself, she settled the pack on her back and set off.

But she'd only taken a few steps before a shiver went up

her spine; a chill, even though she was standing in bright sunlight. Karan stopped but her talent told her nothing. It might have been nothing. The talent could be unreliable, sometimes capricious, as it had often been in her mother's family.

Brilliant or mad are the house of Fyrn. How often had she heard that in her childhood? Not least about her mother Vuula, a lyrist of genius who had abandoned her instrument for that disgraceful liaison with Karan's father. After Galliad's death Vuula had lost her mind completely. And of Basunez too, her grandsire of twenty-odd generations back. He had been brilliant and mad too, first making the fortune of his house, then squandering it on a succession of conceits, not least the absurdity of Carcharon, that extraordinary, extravagant construction, half-fastness, half-folly, set on the highest pinnacle of a barren, frigid and windswept ridge in the mountains beyond Gothryme. All the necessities for existence had to be carried there on the backs of laborers. There he had lived and there he had died: mad; lonely; alone.

The sun came though the trees on her face, as she crossed through a patch of reeds and found firm mud beside the channel. What was that? The note died on her lips. She froze.

The long head turned slowly. Reeds rushed across his lens-shaped field of vision and there she was, a smear against the white of a dead tree. A momentary surprise—surely this filthy wretch could not be the thief he had pursued for so long? She barely came up to his shoulder. She was trembling, mesmerized by him. Her curly red hair, bright as a flame, stood on end and stirred in the breeze, a sight he found unpleasant. Her knees were small, her ankles slender, her fingers long and tapering; her bones could not be seen through the skin. Hideous creature!

Idlis got out of the boat, not taking his eyes off her, as though his will was enough to keep her there. He stepped carefully onto the shore; his limbs moved in jerky arcs. There was a long-handled battle axe in his belt—broad curving blades and a spike between.

"Who are you?" She spoke in a dismal voice.

"I am Whelm," the man replied. "Idlis is my name." His speech might have been filtered through a mouthful of tar. His face was like his axe: arching sharp nose, narrow chin, hard slit of a mouth, black eyes.

Karan trembled. Terror has taken away her courage, he thought. His long arms reached out, the bony fingers spread to grip the pathetic thing.

But she was no longer there. She moved more quickly than his blinkered eyes could follow, easily avoided the flailing arms, and catching at his gray cold shanks, wrenched his legs from under him. Idlis felt terror for the first time in his life—she could have held him down till he suffocated. But she did not. While he cleared the mud from his eyes, supporting himself on the prow of the boat, she leapt into the channel and swam with violent strokes beyond his sight.

Idlis waded out into the channel, washed clean the eye shields and called to the other Whelm. His planar face showed nothing, but a student of the Whelm would have noted that his movements were more fluid, as though fury had lubricated his rough joints, and every aspect of his motion showed his rage, his humiliation and his malice.

That was just the beginning of her nightmare. Wading through mud and reeds, every touch reminded her of the texture of his skin. It had been rubbery, like something dead. And over and again her talent revisited the image that Yggur had threatened her with: the tongue of a dead dog sliding up her backbone. Her earlier optimism was revealed to be foolish pride, her previous successes just blind good fortune. Her fortune had turned now. The day dragged on and with every hour she felt more driven, more inadequate, more hopeless.

On she fled, through a swamp forest that was endless, ever the same. It consisted solely of sard trees, giants with bulbous bases sprouting multiple trunks. The pale layered bark, soft as a child's skin, hung down in sheets long enough to form a writing scroll. There had been several bark scrolls in Yggur's library, she recalled. Far above, the strap leaves filtered sunlight to silver.

If she could just get to Lake Neid, food, clean clothing and the guide awaited her. In her mind she made the rancid cheese and stale bread into a banquet; the depraved smuggler became a savior. Maybe, against hope, Maigraith would be there as well. Even Maigraith could be forgiven for so manipulating her, if only she were waiting.

Karan still couldn't believe that Maigraith had allowed herself to be taken. She was normally so strong and single-minded. But as soon as she had looked at the Mirror she was captivated, as if what she saw there outweighed her duty to her mistress, or even her own safety. Even more staggering was how she had reacted to Yggur. Maigraith, who to Karan's knowledge had never looked at any man, seemed to have felt empathy for him.

Three days to Neid. But that was from Fiz Gorgo. Since then the Whelm had driven her the other way, deeper into their environment. It must be further now. Water and mud had been her existence for more than a week. Her feet seemed to be rotting in her boots.

Sometimes the Whelm were closer, sometimes further

back, but always there. She could not rid herself of them, no matter how she tried.

She took off her boots and trousers, the better to swim. She swam up tiny creeks and across bottomless lakes; across still ponds the color of tea, leaving no trace. They soon found her again.

She crawled through bogs, parting each rush with care, replacing it carefully once she had passed. In clinging mud she stood still as a shag, then moved a few lean spans before stopping still again. The mud was thick and sticky, clinging to her boots in layers that made it difficult to walk, though several times she stepped without warning into mire as soft and slippery as jelly and sank instantly to her hips. This muck sucked so powerfully that it could take ten minutes to get free; once she lost her boots in it and it took half an hour to dig them out again. And all day she watched the snakes skimming across the surface of the marsh, admiring their economical grace and their venom.

Now she stirred. The ooze sucked at her feet. Every movement sent tickling bubbles up her legs, bubbles that popped on the surface, releasing a gas foul as rotting eggs.

Suddenly she felt weak: dizzy and sick. Something was wrong; the water moved strangely about her legs; her feet were numb. She slipped and fell; brown water washed over her face. It took an effort of will just to come to her feet again, and her heart was pounding. She dragged herself out of the water onto an island of mud, looked down and almost vomited with disgust.

Her legs were thickly clustered with leeches. Dozens of them dangled from the soft skin at the back of her knees, as many again on her feet and ankles; they clung to her thighs, her calves, even between her toes. Already they were purple and swollen, many as big as her thumb. Threads of blood ran down her legs from a myriad of little punctures. She gripped the largest, revolted by the pulpy feel, and tried to pull it off. It would not come—it was surprisingly tough, but eventually broke in an explosion of blood and hung down behind her knee like a burst balloon.

Salt or fire would make them let go. But she had no salt and could not risk fire. So many bites, they were sure to get infected. Her sensitive side explored that possibility, dragging herself on gangrenous legs, black and bloated . . .

There was a shout across the channel, an answering shout behind. Karan slid off the bank into the water. The marsh whirled; even in the cold water her skin burned. The leeches wavered back and forth as she moved, tugging gently at her skin, then she was inside a pocket of reeds. Looking back she saw her marks on the shore, and blood as well.

That day was the worst that she could imagine. The Whelm quartered the area, calling to one another all around. Too dizzy to stand, Karan clung to the reeds for support while the leeches bled her life away. The blood in the water brought more of them—one time she ran her hand down her thigh and felt hundreds, and then she was sick, retching silently and miserably into the water.

The air was thick with mud flies, tiny green flies that bit like a hot wire and left welts on the skin that throbbed for days. They crept into her ears, her nose, beneath tightly buttoned cuffs and even into her thick and mud-caked hair. In desperation she smeared her face and neck with stinking mud, but still they burrowed through her hair and clothing until no part of her remained unbitten.

Then *they* were near again. She could see the Whelm across the channel, searching the mud islands one by one. As she watched them she felt, with indescribable horror, something big slide across her foot. Its skin had a slippery texture; it undulated around her ankle, over the toes of her other foot. Thick as her calf it seemed, as long as her leg.

Idlis was only a few paces away. She dared not move. Was it an eel, or a snake? It touched her toes, a gentle tugging of the skin. It was between her ankles, tugging again, the slippery skin caressing her calves, her knees, tweaking, nibbling; then with a flick of its tail, prickling the back of her knee, it was gone.

The sun went down. The mud flies disappeared and the Whelm, by some miracle, were moving away. Or were they just waiting for her to move? How did they track her anyway? She recalled Maigraith's warning: *being sensitive, you must be specially careful of the Whelm*. There had not been time to find out what she had meant. Could they find her because of her talent? She might shut it off, if she knew how, but that would be cutting off the only thing that kept her ahead of them. Karan resolved to wring all emotion out of her life, to feel nothing, to care about nothing but getting to Neid. Let them try and track her then!

Maybe it was not her they tracked but the Mirror. The temptation to drop it into the mire was very strong. No, surely it could not be enchanted, else they would not have lost her again. Anyway, she would not take the easy way out.

The twilight lingered. Mosquitoes came out. They were not as bad as the mud flies, but it added to the torment. She stood in the water and tried to practice stoicism. Something stung her on the eyelid, a pain like a needle prick. Don't react! she told herself as her eyelid swelled. Endure the pain!

When it was nearly dark Karan came cautiously out of the swamp and inspected herself. All the leeches were gone and most of their bites had stopped bleeding. She took the eel as an omen; not everything was against her. Don't feel that too deeply either!

Two days had gone by, since fleeing Yggur's library. She was further away from Lake Neid than she had been this morning. There was no possibility of making the rendezvous with Maigraith, even if she had escaped.

With a twinge of guilt Karan realized that she had given no thought to Maigraith's plight. From this distance she could not remake the link to find out if she had escaped, but Karan knew in her heart that Maigraith had not.

In her pack was a little soapstone jar of ointment she'd brought all the way from Gothryme. It eased the pain of the bites and the stings but still they became infected, and all that interminable night she huddled in the rushes, burning, then freezing, then burning again. She could feel the thin blood rushing through her veins and it roared in her ears like a waterfall.

Eventually morning came, but it brought only more torment. The exhilaration of her escape was erased from her mind. Now she kept on her boots and socks even when swimming, and bound her trousers tightly at the ankles, yet still the leeches found a way in.

The Whelm drove her east into the deep slough, a slower and more perilous path than the way she'd gone to Fiz Gorgo. They were more at home than she in this country, and the cold did not bother them, nor the leeches. It took all her bushcraft and all her cunning, and what assistance her talent gave her, to keep ahead of them.

The next day was like the one before, and so was the day after, and the day after that. If it was not the cold or the foul of the swamp, it was the mud flies, the leeches, the mosquitoes, or the other biting, sucking or creeping things; or all of them together. In the brief moments that nothing else troubled her it was the utter weariness, the hunger, the filth, and being wet day and night.

The infected leech bites spread some slow toxin and on the third morning she woke to find her legs as swollen and shapeless as sausages. Moving was agony, yet walk she must (or rather, wade and swim), almost a league that day, and her mind retreated from the pain and the pursuit into a little bright knot at the back of her head. Her food was gone, so she cut channels through the bark of a sard tree and caught the sweet sap in her mug. It did not ease her hunger but it kept her going, though after drinking it she felt slightly dizzy, mildly intoxicated.

Karan dared not sleep. Several times a day she dozed, where she could find a secure hiding place, and once while standing up. She was so weary that she could not tell where the dreams left off and the waking began, save that her dreams were more vivid and more real. Once she dreamed of the Whelm, four of them sitting together on a log. She could not see their faces, just the thin heads under their cowls, but they all sat as if listening to something. The dream shivered her awake. Listening for her? Could they sense her from her dream emotions?

The chase had become a long hallucination with no beginning and only one possible end. She was so terrified that she could no longer weep. Her self had contracted to a single urge—she must get to Neid (though she could scarcely remember why)—and to a single fear, even greater than her fear of the Whelm: that madness was taking her as it had her mother.

Yet somehow her bushcraft or her carefully managed talent was just enough. At last she emerged from the swamps into dense forest. She did not see the Whelm after that, for she could move faster here, but she knew they still followed.

Four nights after the affair of the leeches she crept out of the forest, a filthy, bedraggled creature, her tender skin covered in welts and wounds, across gray grass and into the clean water of Lake Neid. Gentle rain pattered on the still surface.

She walked east along the shoreline for half the night, staying in calf-deep water all the time, weed catching at her ankles.

Midnight. Without warning something clutched at her coat, she thrashed, tripped and landed head down in the water with her pack banging against the back of her neck. Karan tried to come to her feet but she was held down. How had they come upon her here, in the dark? The more she struggled the harder she was pushed. Red sparks danced against her eyelids. Water burned in her nose, her chest. Her strength gave out; Karan went still.

No! Not even the Whelm could have tracked her here. Even the Whelm must sleep some time. Her hand caught a twiggy branch—she was tangled in a fallen tree. She clawed her way along the bottom, pushed through a slippery nest of twigs and floated free. Her feet did not touch the bottom. Karan was too cold and tired to swim. She simply turned on her back and floated, exhausted and lethargic, onto a gravelly shore.

After a few minutes she found the strength to turn over, coughed up water and crawled up the gravel until her head struck something solid—the trunk of the tree. There was a little hollow underneath. She would just lie here for a minute until her strength came back.

How lovely and warm it was. *Warm?* Karan rolled over and the high sun dazzled her. It was midday. She looked around cautiously. The shoreline was bare as far as she could see, and she was lying in full view of anyone to come along. The realization paralyzed her. She peered over the trunk. In the distance she saw a broken wall and, beyond, a pair of standing columns—the ruins of the town of Neid, where she and Maigraith had hidden their large packs, spare clothing and food.

The thought of food became a screaming need but she was too afraid to go on. The force that had driven her had dissipated. There had been plenty of time for the Whelm to catch up; they probably knew her destination anyway.

Where the roots of the tree had been torn from the ground was a small crater, a meager and obvious hiding place. That was where she spent the rest of the day, ravenous, but with not even a stalk of grass to chew on. The only consolation was that a thin sun shone all day, her stained clothes dried and she actually felt warm.

As soon as it was dark she slipped back into the water and swam to the nearest part of the ruins, a small stone jetty. Nearby were the broken walls of a small building, the place where the packs were hidden, but the town proper was perhaps half an hour's walk to the west.

Karan huddled among the stone blocks, eating small portions of the revolting food, bathing over and over again in the cold water; enjoying the luxury of soap until she was clean all over and the ordeals of the past days were washed away with the muck of the swamps. She perfumed her hair with the lime-blossom essence that so reminded her of her mother, and immediately felt whole again.

Early the following morning she crept through the forest to the place where they had arranged to meet the guide, Walf. She expected nothing, neither Maigraith nor Walf, for she was four days late, but as she stood on the crest of a small hill, looking east toward the ruins, their meeting place, she saw a thread of smoke near the water. A campfire, *here*! Such carelessness—or the mark of a man very much at his ease, as perhaps a smuggler might be when he had nothing to hide.

Walf was little more than a beast, though a cunning and dangerous one. And yet how she yearned to go to the fire, to warm herself by it, to eat hot food and drink sweet tea. After the past days even his animal company would be welcome.

She approached with caution and found the campfire in the angle of a wall, sheltered from the cool breeze off the lake. Another ruined building, marked only by standing columns, lay behind. The guide sat on a rock beside the fire, massive but shapeless in a coat like a bag. Fish were frying in a pan and a pot was bubbling. He seemed to know she was out there, for as she came across the grass he was already forking fish out of the pan onto a metal plate, hooking out onion rings and pouring tea into a mug.

Her stomach contracted at the sight of the food. He did not look so brutish now—his big ugly face was friendly and Karan was glad to see him. He smiled, showing bare gums, and held out the plate. How she ached for the food.

"Thank you, Walf," she croaked.

"Where is the dark-haired one?" His voice was indistinct, his lips barely moving. He did not look at her as he spoke and she felt a vague unease.

"Taken," she replied, putting down her heavy pack but keeping the small one on, just in case.

She sipped her tea. It was wonderfully hot and sweet, just as she'd imagined it would be. She took a mouthful of the fish. Slightly oily, beautifully firm and pink, delicious. So grateful was she, so hungry for good food that tears sprang to her eyes. She swallowed the first mouthful, selected another piece with the point of her knife. Her eyes met the smuggler's across the fire. His eyes slid away and she paused, the fish halfway to her mouth. He was looking behind her, to one side, and there was a shifty look in his eyes. *No!* her talent screamed; she leapt sideways and in the same movement flung the scalding tea in his face. A two-bladed axe whirred through the space she had just vacated and buried itself in the turf. The smuggler clutched at his eyes, then she was past him, dodging around the end of the wall and away through the rubble and broken columns. There she paused and looked back.

Idlis stood where she had been, his foot upon her plate, retrieving his axe from the lawn. He stared after her, black eyes glittering. Two other Whelm were running jerkily past him, spreading out, axes in their hands. Idlis lifted the weapon and flung it again. She twisted away and it struck a column behind her. Stone chips stung her cheek, the blade rang out, then she was sprinting along the shore of the lake and into the trees with the Whelm in close pursuit. The treacherous guide had already disappeared.

Though she was small, Karan was agile and very fleet, and in the trees she soon put a good distance between her and the Whelm. She felt a moment's regret for the beautiful fish trodden into the ground but the brutal attack soon put it out of mind. She imagined, as only she could, the axe tearing through her back, the agony blossoming, the futile attempts to pull out the intruding blade, her blood pumping onto the grass, then the light fading, and the pain, and quick death.

More than once that afternoon the Whelm almost had her, for the forest was open here. They spread out, calling to each other in their muddy voices. Each time she took a new direction the nearest Whelm would cut across the angle. They were tireless and they hunted her like a pack of dogs, first one taking the lead then another, so that she could never rest.

Now she was sobbing with weariness, the little pack thudding against her back with every step, her will fading. And darkness was hours away, though it offered little protection against the Whelm, who covered their eyes against even the light of this cloudy autumn day.

Several times they came close enough to fling their weapons, and finally it was only a storm that saved her, the kind that was common in Orist in autumn, coming in suddenly from the sea in the afternoon. Dark clouds grew in the west, and with them came a squall of wind, then a downpour. The light faded, the air was full of concealing mist. Karan reacted instantly, turning and running diagonally away up the hill, over the crest and down into the thick forest to the east, running and running through the rain until it was dark and she knew that she had lost them. She kept walking in a northerly direction all that night. Just before dawn Karan hid in dense scrub and slept fitfully until dusk.

Now the nights were overcast and Karan traveled quickly, seeing no further sign of her pursuers. Hunger was her worst enemy, for her heavy pack was left behind and all she could find to supplement her rations were fallen nuts, but they were old, shriveled and moldy. Then on the third day she came to a village in the forest and for a few coppers bought food enough to fill her pack.

The way to Sith lay east by north, across the Hindirin River then east through the Zarqa Gap, the tiny break in the mountains that ran up the eastern side of Mcldorin, and finally up the wooded eastern coast of Iagador to Sith. That journey would take a month if she could get back to where they'd left the horses. But Karan found that all the roads east were watched by troops in the livery of Yggur, and the bridges guarded. She was cut off, for the Hindirin and other big rivers could only be crossed by bridge or ferry. There was no way to get to the horses either, for the village where they were stabled was occupied.

She sat for a day among the trees, watching the road, wondering what to do. She had vowed to take the Mirror to Faelamor in Sith. But there was no way to get to Sith—the whole of the south was alerted. Yggur must have broken Maigraith.

Her only chance was to go due north, away from Sith, though that would more than double the distance. But in the north there was help, for that was country she knew. Chanthed, home to the College of the Histories, she had often been to. It was not long until the autumn festival.

And the Histories were the key to her dilemma—the legends of Faelamor and her people, the Histories of the Aachim, the *Tale of the Forbidding*. Great events of the past were bound up with this Mirror, and what she chose to do with it could set the direction of the future. How could she decide where to bestow it, which oath to break, whom to betray?

Chanthed was a long march north, but achievable if she could afford to buy a horse. It would be her next destination. And after that, across the mountains to Bannador and home. From there it was not so far to Sith but she would worry about that later.

Karan went cautiously north and joined the Hirthway near the walled city of Preddle. There she found cheerful hospitality and good hot food for the first time in weeks and, most glorious of all, a hot bath and a clean bed.

The next morning, in the market square, twice within an hour she noticed a tall figure staring at her. Her talent did not tell her of any threat so probably it was not a Whelm. Doubtless just an innocent encounter but she dared not take the risk, her talent being unreliable. She walked casually between two booths and ducked underneath a long cloth-covered trestle on which were displayed the wares of a rug-seller: bright tribal rugs in coarse yak wool, red and yellow saddle cloths, towels, gray blankets and, up the further end, under the tireless eye of the merchant, hand-knotted carpets and hangings in lamb's wool and silk. The rugs and cloths hung down on either side to the paving stones.

Karan sat on her pack and waited. Feet came and went. Abruptly a corner of the cloth was flung aside and a tanned face, hollow cheeks and hawk nose, glared at her from only a handspan away, so close that she could smell his cardamom-scented breath.

"Get out," he said, with a jerk of his chin and a flash of yellow teeth. "The next time you kids . . ."

Karan turned her face to his.

"Oh," he said.

"Please," she said. "I'm being followed. The tall dark fellow in the hood. I'm terribly afraid."

He stared at her. "No business of mine," he said, then stood up suddenly and dropped the cloth, leaving her wondering.

A minute passed, then a wiry brown arm thrust in with a glass of cold sweet lime juice. She took the glass with a soft "Thank you," and drained it. A few minutes passed, then the hawk was back.

"You're safe now."

Karan threw a cloak over her shoulders and tucked her hair up under her hat. For the moment that was all the disguise she could manage. No more bed, no more bath; she would not stay a moment longer than necessary. She slid out, scanned the market and bowed to the carpet merchant.

"I have daughters," he said, showing his teeth again, then turned to a customer.

Down a miserable alley near the eastern gate she found a stable. Karan went in despite her misgivings, for it was a dingy place. The straw was moldy and there was manure all over the floor. Two men and an old woman were playing dominoes on a filthy table. Karan felt at once that there was something wrong. She wanted to run straight out again, but she had not seen any other stables and there wasn't time to start searching now.

"Yeah?" said the old woman. There was not a single tooth in her head. Dirty gray hair straggled down to her waist. The low-cut gown revealed sights that Karan preferred not to contemplate.

"I'd like to buy a horse, please," said Karan, advancing to the table. The old woman cackled and scratched a draggled armpit.

"You don't look old enough, stranger!" She turned to the man on her left, a big fellow hideously deformed by the scar of a burn that seamed and puckered him from mouth to ear. The whole side of his head was scarred and bald save for a few bristly clumps of white hair. He was grimy with ingrained dirt. "Does she look old enough to you, Qwelt?"

Qwelt's mouth flopped open in a leer so grotesque that Karan wanted to scream and run. He had some horrible disease of the mouth—his gums were black and festering, shrunken away from teeth that jutted in all directions like stones in an ancient graveyard.

"She looks old enough," he said in a rumble like a belching cow. He heaved a vast belly out of the way and stood up.

Karan felt sick. I must have a horse, she thought. After Fiz Gorgo, after the Whelm, what can these people do to me in the broad daylight?

The old woman's eyes flickered. Karan turned to bolt. The stable door banged shut and a third big man, a giant compared to her, slammed the bar across.

"Bring me the purse," said the old woman through her gums. "You can have her."

10

THE GATE
OF HETCHET

The men moved toward her with their arms out. They might have been brothers. Karan's knife flashed, and instantly the fellow near the door snatched up a long-handled shovel. They'd done this before, she realized. Karan waved her knife in the air, turning and turning, waiting for them to come closer. Her talent was most reliable in desperate times. He was going to strike . . . *now!* The shovel swung viciously at her head, Karan dropped flat and the edge crunched the second man right over the heart. He fell without a sound.

She clawed her way under the table, crouched, then snapped upright. The edge of the table caught the old woman under the chin and she toppled back into the manure.

"Mama!" screamed the scarred Qwelt.

Karan shouldered the table into his path, jumped over the old woman and ran into the back of the stable, past the stalls. They were all empty anyway. The man with the shovel lumbered after her. There was a back door but it was bolted. She

spun around just as he speared the shovel at her. She
dropped, rolled under the half-door of a stall and kept
rolling, scrambled up the frame, leapt, caught a roof truss,
hopped across to the next and heaved herself up into an open
loft above the middle of the stables.

At the other end was a ladder. She tried to throw it down
but found that it was nailed in place. The loft was partly full
of hay, bales of straw and bags of moldy grain, as well as
broken packing cases, pots of olives, onions, hanging hams
and other foodstuffs. Odd that such things would be kept
above a filthy, smelly stable. The roof was of leaky thatch.

The ladder creaked. Karan ran across and looked down.
Qwelt was on the third rung, leering up at her, the other man
just below him.

She heaved a bag of grain over the edge. It tore on a nail
and moldy grain cascaded down. Qwelt swore, clawed at his
eyes, fell on his brother and they both crashed to the floor.
She shook the last few lumps down and rained down crocks
and boxes at them until Qwelt fled and the other man lay
motionless. The air stank of vinegar and pickled onions.

Now she clambered up onto the bales and started to hack
away at the thatch where it was black. The dust tickled her
nose. It was hard work but shortly blessed daylight was visible through a small hole. The ladder creaked again but she
did not hear it. The hideous head edged up. Karan hacked
with all her might; still the hole wasn't big enough.

Qwelt was in the loft now, advancing on her with a
wicked pitchfork in his hand and a lunatic glower in his
eyes. Karan started and fell down. Qwelt lunged at her with
the pitchfork, she rolled and the tines speared into a rafter
with a crash that shook the whole building. While he tried to
jerk it out, she smashed a crock of olives over his head.

She crept across to the ladder and as the battered head of the
second man appeared she clouted him in the face with a leg of

ham. Rotten ham splattered far and wide and there was a tremendous stench. He slipped, fell through the ladder, hung by his chin for a moment then plummeted to the floor. For good measure she dropped the putrid remains on him, flung another jar at Qwelt then hurtled back to her hole. Finally it was big enough to get through. Karan sheathed her knife and sprang up, but the bales toppled, revealing a hideaway stuffed with boxes of silver and goldware and other precious things. No wonder there weren't any horses for sale!

Karan frantically restacked the bales so she could reach the hole. Already the scarred man was stirring. She sprang upwards, forcing head and shoulders through into open air, but something stopped her from going any higher. The forgotten pack was caught in the thatch! Her legs kicked uselessly in the air. She heaved until her shoulders creaked and at last the pack popped free.

Just then someone caught her by the foot and wrenched. Karan screamed, kicked and felt an impact. She heaved again with her arms, the boot came off and she was free and scrabbling up the thatch.

Qwelt bellowed and the pitchfork shot up through the hole, so close that the tines went through her trousers. She tripped, rolling back toward the hole just as he burst through. Karan thrust the pitchfork at him but he wrenched it out of her hands. He was on the roof now, astonishingly quick despite his bulk and his belly. Karan snatched out her knife, but realizing that it was useless against his weapon, she leapt sideways, bounced on the thatch and slid off the edge.

The eaves hung low and the fall was not as bad as she expected. Karan landed hard on her bottom, yelped and hobbled down the alley, still clutching the knife.

At the corner she ran full tilt into a tall figure in robes and hood. Fingers the color of chocolate clamped her wrists so tightly that there was no possibility of getting free. Karan looked up at her captor in dismay.

"Karan of Bannador, I presume," said a cheerful voice in a Crandor accent. "I am Tallia bel Soon. I have been looking for you. Here, give me that knife; you won't need that again today."

Tallia pushed back her hood. She was very tall, with beautiful skin and a flashing smile. There was something familiar about the sense of her. What was it? Fiz Gorgo! *The watcher!* Karan tried to fling herself out of Tallia's arms but was held effortlessly.

"Hold on! I mean you no harm. I want to talk to you. Come with me—there's an inn here that has rather good tea."

Karan jerked in her arms, trying to look down the alley. She was sure that Qwelt would plunge the pitchfork right through them both. Tallia looked over her shoulder. "Whoever you were running from, they've gone," she said.

Karan could not get the scene out of her mind. She shuddered, then for the first time in weeks she allowed herself to give way to her feelings. Tallia let her weep, and when the worst was over she led her along the street to a brightly painted inn. At the door Karan resisted; she did not want to go inside.

"As you wish," said Tallia. "We can sit here."

She ordered hot drinks from a menu of fifty kinds, licorice tea for herself and hot sweet tea, spicy with nutmeg, for Karan, who was shivering.

Karan sat down with her back to the wall. She laid her head on her arms. She had given up. She had no more strength.

"Would you like something to eat?"

Karan nodded without lifting her head. She was ravenous. Tallia signaled to the waitress again.

"What happened back there?

Karan sat mute, then the whole ghastly story flooded out

of her. "All I wanted was a horse," she ended, and burst into tears again.

Tallia was horrified. "That can be fixed," she said, waving to a street boy. He came running, anxious to earn a copper.

"Go to the street of the silversmiths and bid Yehudit come to me here. Give him this sign." She found a fragment of sard bark in a pocket and inscribed a glyph on it. The boy scampered off. "I have no power here, you understand, but I know those that do. These people will be brought to justice."

Karan suddenly slumped down on the bench, in shock. Tallia lifted her back up. Her skin was clammy, her head wobbled. Tallia took a paper-wrapped slab out of her pocket, broke it in half, cracked off a brown corner and pressed it into Karan's mouth. Karan jumped. She spat it back into her hand and examined the substance suspiciously.

"What is it?"

Tallia broke off another corner and ate it with relish. "In my country, Crandor, which is on the other side of the world, it is called chocolate. Eat it. It'll make you feel better."

Karan nibbled the tiniest corner off. "Oh!" she said, her face lighting up. "It's wonderful—the nicest thing I've ever tasted." She ate it all and felt better.

Tallia folded the waxed paper over carefully and put the rest of the chocolate in Karan's pocket. "For later," she said.

Shortly a platter of meat and cheese and vegetables appeared. Karan consumed the lot without once looking at Tallia. She was too afraid. "What do you want from me?" she said with her mouth full.

Tallia sat back and stared at Karan as though weighing her. Finally it seemed that she had passed the test. "I lie only when I must," she said.

What an odd thing to say! Karan examined Tallia with renewed interest.

"I judge that you are honest too, despite what you have

done. I will not lie to you," Tallia continued. "I am chief lieutenant of Mendark, though I am here under another name."

Karan looked startled. "Mendark! But I sensed you at Fiz Gorgo."

"And I saw you. Why did you steal the Mirror of Aachan?"

Karan was profoundly shocked. Was the secret out already? A map of the future began to unroll in her mind's eye. This woman was diabolically clever and capable, for all her play-acting at kindness. Tallia would carry her in chains to Thurkad or, more likely, take the Mirror from her and leave her dead in a ditch.

"I saw you come out of the water," said Tallia. "Who did you steal the Mirror for?"

"Myself," said Karan sullenly.

Tallia laughed with genuine amusement. "You could use one!"

Karan was stung, so striking a woman criticizing her looks.

"What do you want it for, Karan?"

"I'm giving it back to its rightful owners." It was not necessarily a lie: she might yet do that.

"And who are they?"

"Find out for yourself! What are you going to do with me?"

"Nothing. Until you threaten Mendark I obey the rule of law. You are free to go once we have finished our chat."

"I've finished already," said Karan, draining her tea. "The matter has nothing to do with Mendark. Nothing I will *ever* tell you, either. May I have my knife?"

She was astonished when Tallia put it on the table in front of her. "I can go?"

Tallia waved a hand. "Go," she said.

Karan stood up, very suspicious, slammed the knife into its pouch, backed away and, when she was well beyond Tallia's reach, said, "Thank you for lunch," and disappeared into the throng.

On the other side of the city she found an entirely respectable stable. Karan bought a horse, the best she could afford, though it was a bony creature and much scarred along the spur line. At a nearby market she purchased boots, food, soap, salve and warm clothes for the mountains, measuring out the coins reluctantly. The horse had cost half her money. As soon as it was dark she reclaimed the nag, bought a large bag of oats, another coin begrudged, and slipped quietly out the Sunrise Gate.

Four torches flared on the wall outside the gate. The light drew her eyes up. Beside each torch a corpse swung from a gibbet—three big men; a woman with streaming gray hair. Swift justice in Preddle. She dug in her heels and fled north along the Hirthway.

Tallia had spent more than a week in Preddle, for Mendark had a factor there and she had other business with him. She had not specifically been waiting for Karan, though she was not surprised to see her, for Preddle was the only town of substance in these thinly populated lands.

Tallia, weighing the possibility of learning more from Karan, decided that without forcing her she would get nothing. There had been no reply to her earlier message to Mendark. This Mirror might be worthless, like most ancient things that people thought to profit by. Had it been war she would have acted differently, but she did not have the inclination to take the Mirror by force without good reason, even assuming that Karan still had it.

Four days later Tallia's skeet reappeared, bloody and missing the feathers of its right breast.

Tallia,

I must have this Mirror. Leave everything else and find her. If she does not come willingly, take her and bring her to me. Beware the Whelm.

M.

Tallia was furious with herself. She took two horses, the best in town, and rode them day and night, but somehow knew that she would not catch Karan. She took the skeet as well, in a basket. Karan's destination appeared to be Hetchet, a village at the foot of the mountains, a long way to the north.

At the dismal halfway hamlet of Flumen, where the inn was made of warped logs through which a cold wind rushed, she sent another message to Mendark, advising him to contact his people in Hetchet, Chanthed and other possible destinations and have them search for Karan. Later she came upon Karan's horse on the road, but it had been dead for days and in the stony hills she lost all trace of her.

Karan rode most of the night, stopping off the road before dawn for a few hours' rest, all she dared in this open land. She rested again in the afternoon by a creek that was nearly dry, just a few shallow waterholes in a cobbly channel.

The horse, whom she had named Thrix, had a congestion of the throat that made him cough and snort constantly. You will be no use if ever we have to go secretly, she thought. She dozed while the hobbled Thrix tore at the dry grass.

At dusk she rose, took her mount to water, rewarded him with a hug and a double handful of oats which he snorted all over her, then climbed into the hard saddle and rode till after midnight. By the time they stopped, with the glaring nebula already starting its descent, she was so sore that she could barely stand. Most of the night she lay awake, picking oats out of her hair, counting her bruises, watching the stars and the standing shadow of Thrix, who snorted even in his sleep.

Before dawn she woke suddenly from a troubled sleep, from dreams of faces in the Mirror, faces glaring out at her, accusing her, demanding that she do her duty. The dreams faded as she was still trying to remember who the faces were. Maigraith was there, or was it the older woman she had seen in the Mirror in Fiz Gorgo?

And now there was this new complication. Mendark would know as soon as Tallia could get a message to him. This Mirror was drawing all the powerful to it, sucking the whole of Santhenar into its whirlpool. She did not know much about the Magister, but rumor did not make him a kind man. Karan had no wish to have any dealings with *him*.

Karan rode on, still troubled by the dream. For days she had been worrying about her duty to the Aachim. She owed them so much, much more than her debt to Maigraith. Breaking *that* oath now seemed the lesser crime. After all, the Aachim had held the Mirror for thousands of years and did no harm with it. And Karan knew that the making of the Forbidding had been a time of great upheaval. What would happen if Faelamor broke it?

Karan still had friends among the Aachim of Shazmak. One of them, Rael of the red hair and the wistful smile, could have been more than a friend once. She lost herself in memories of growing up in Shazmak among the towering mountains, the roar of the furiously rushing Garr never out of her ears. It was Rael who had taught her how to climb. She still missed him. If only Tensor hadn't . . .

Tensor! Leader, if they could be said to have one, of the Aachim of Shazmak. A mighty man with a mighty presence; a hero in the struggles of the Aachim with their enemies, the Charon, in ancient times. One of the original Aachim whom Rulke had brought to Santh from Aachan. Tensor was a stern proud man who had never given up the struggle, who was full of bitterness at their loss and who talked constantly of the renascence of his people. A man with an implacable hatred for their ancient enemy Rulke, the Charon responsible for all their troubles.

She could see him now, black locks flying, beard bristling, great fist upraised. "Just give me the power," he had raged.

Karan's respect for Tensor bordered on awe, as was due to him, but she had never felt comfortable in his presence, had always felt that he had something against her, as though he had judged her and found her wanting; or perhaps had found her father wanting for *going outside*. Tensor had tutored her in the development of her talent in her early days in Shazmak, though the experience had been uncomfortable and she felt as though she had lost something because of it. And later when he had sent Rael away to the eastern cities, Karan had known that it was because of her.

Perhaps I *should* give the Mirror to Tensor. After all, I owe the Aachim more than I can ever repay. But, they failed to support me when Emmant harassed me. That cancels a good part of the debt. What would Tensor do with it anyway? Perhaps it would just be fuel to his hate.

Faelamor or Tensor? The Faellem or the Aachim? Was one option better than the other? Was either better than Yggur who, for all his imperial ambitions, was reputed to be a just man, a law-bringer?

Well, I took the Mirror, she thought. I set all this in motion and now I have a duty to make the right choice.

Agonizing over her decision, Karan traveled the Hirthway north to Flumen, through country that became increasingly barren, and then to the hills of Sundor, a distance of a hundred leagues, in only eight days. In all that time there was no sign of any pursuit and she relaxed a little. That was when it all began to go wrong again.

Climbing into the arid and desolate hills of Sundor, riding too hard, Thrix slipped on the rough ground, fell and shattered his foreleg. Her heart went out to the great beast as it lay on the road, looking at her with its moist brown eyes, but there was only one thing to be done. She gave Thrix a last hug, her arms not meeting around his sweaty neck, covered his eye with her hand and cut his throat with one deep cut. The hot blood sprayed all over her arm and her clothes and the big head slowly sank to the road.

She turned away, tears watering her dusty face. It was a long time before she forgot the killing of her horse, and the smell of his blood stayed with her for days. And, in her distress, she relaxed the control of her talent and her emotions that she had been exercising since the swamps.

In the hills of Sundor the hallucinatory dreams came back. Once more she dreamed that the hooded Whelm were listening for her. But this time it was worse, for a big wasted hound crouched beside them, the firelight reflected in its staring eyes. For two nights she had these dreams. On the third morning Karan woke in terror and saw the Whelm far below, and so she fled once more. Soon the chase blurred into that hunt in the swamps, and though that was weeks ago the interval now seemed like a minute's waking in a day-long nightmare.

That night, as she dozed upright with her back against a stone, a single howl came on the wind. A low-pitched, ragged-at-the-edges note, endlessly drawn out. Karan jumped. It cut off suddenly and was not repeated, but she knew what it was—the hound from the cistern, or another just like it. She had been expecting it even before the dream. She could sense it, could imagine the gaunt thing perfectly, if she closed her eyes. She was more afraid of this Whelp— that was a good name for it!—than even of the Whelm.

She looked around her camp. It wasn't much to defend—

a pouch of coarse grass with upthrust rocks above and below, halfway up a stony hill, and a couple of scrubby conifers on her right. She was protected only from above. Karan was tempted to light a fire even though it would draw the Whelm. They would find her soon enough in this country, with dogs. There was no hope even if there was only one Whelm, one dog! The panic built up until the urge to scream was irresistible. She put her fingers in her mouth and bit down hard and kept biting until the pain brought her to her senses.

Karan realized that she was broadcasting her panic again, drawing them to her. She forced herself to breathe slowly, to slow her racing heart, to make some defense.

Fire was not a good idea. Up among the rocks with her back to a bit of an overhang was the best she could manage. Her only weapon was her small knife. Not enough! She gathered a pile of rocks for the sake of doing something. What a stupid idea: rocks were useless in the dark. She wrenched a small branch down off a tree, hacking the tough bark away from the trunk. It wasn't big enough to do serious damage though it felt good in her hands. Now she waited, wanting sleep but not game to doze for an instant, staring into the night until her imagination began to make Whelm stick-figures out of the shadows.

The night dragged to a close. Monochrome shades gave way to the faintest colors. Pink dawn touched the east. The wind died down momentarily. She had survived another night. Her neck ached. Time to go. No, just a little bit longer. She closed her eyes.

The sun leapt above the horizon. Karan slept, a few blessed moments of peace. Her breast rose and fell. Sunlight crept up her outflung arm, her slender throat, struck gold in her lashes and brows, bronze in her hair.

The hound crept closer, taking advantage of every

shadow, every hide, to get within springing distance of Karan, crouching on its belly, then swinging its gaunt body up and forward on anchored feet; springing forward one bound then crouching down again. Now it was just a leap away. It opened its long mouth in a grinning yawn.

Karan dreamed that she was lying in a lovely soapy bath, luxuriating, warm and clean. Suddenly the bath dream drained away and she was naked, unprotected. The wind blew on her throat, shivering her awake, shocking her with the realization that for the second time she had slept on watch.

But the sun was just up. She had not slept long at all, and she had survived the night. A fragment of another dream came to her, a child's birthday party. *It's my birthday!* Not much to celebrate. Nonetheless the thought was a little bit cheering. She rubbed the sleep out of her eyes, massaged her scalp with her fingertips, ran fingers through tangled hair and automatically looked around.

The biggest, gauntest dog she had ever seen crouched just a few paces below her. It wavered its muzzle from side to side but the yellow eyes did not leave her face. Karan felt for her knife—it was by her side—and grasped her stick. She rose to her feet, sliding back into the rocks so that it could only come at her one way. She flicked her eyes around but there was no one in sight. Did the dog plan to attack or just bail her up here until its master came?

She lifted the stick with both hands. The dog quivered. "Get away!" Her voice sounded unconvincing. The hound grinned then leapt at her.

Karan swung her stick and struck it on the shoulder, knocking it to one side in a jumble of legs.

The dog was up again at once, unhurt, gray claws scrabbling on the rocks. It snapped at her thigh. She swung the stick again but it struck the overhanging rock and jarred out of her hands. Karan snatched the knife with her right hand.

The dog sprang and hit her in the stomach, knocking her back on the stone. It straddled her, snapped, and caught her knife arm halfway up to her elbow. Then it looked her deliberately in the eye, sank its teeth in and held her.

Blood ran down her arm; saliva dripped from the huge jaws onto her chest. She let her arm go limp and the knife clattered on rock. One crunch of those great jaws could probably bite her hand off. She stared up at the dog, trying to find a chink in its armor. It wore an iron collar. The front teeth were broken stumps though most of the side ones, the bone crunchers, were good.

Karan moaned. The dog flicked up its ears. She moaned again, putting all of her pain and weariness and fear into her voice, trying with all her talent to reach the dog, to convince it she was harmless, to make it let go for an instant. But even if she could reach it, put it off-guard for a second, what could she do? Her reflexes were lightning fast but hardly as fast as a dog's. Unless the dog was slow and awkward like the master . . .

Karan gave a little sigh, rolled back her eyes and closed her lids to the merest slit. Her body went limp. The dog held on, standing patiently. She gave a low shivery groan, then a shudder that rippled her from head to foot.

The hound lowered its head and sniffed at her face. She shuddered again. The dog let go her wrist and instantly her left hand flashed up, grabbed the iron collar and twisted with every ounce of strength she had. It jerked back, choking. She balled up her right fist, punched it through the open jaws and jammed it hard into the dog's throat, at the same time pulling it onto her fist by the collar.

The dog convulsed, jerked its head and fell sideways, almost tearing her hand from the collar. It snapped its jaws, the rotten teeth lacerating her wrist and forearm. Sure that she was going to lose her hand, Karan thrust harder down its throat, thrusting and thrusting while its claws scratched frantically at the rock.

Just then someone whistled, a low creepy sound not far away. The dog flung up its head, trying to bark, its eyes rolling, and Karan's wrist snapped with a shocking pain. She wanted to shriek, to scream out her agony, but instead thrust against the pain until the dog went still, and even after that until she was sure that it was dead.

She withdrew her hand. Her forearm was rent by dozens of gouges and punctures and there were strips of skin hanging off. Blood poured down her wrist. Karan sat down suddenly, feeling that she was going to faint beside the emaciated hound. Though it had been her life or the dog's, still this corpse was almost as bitter to her as the horse she had left up the road.

The whistle came again, off to one side, shocking her. Karan wiped cold sweat from her brow with a hand that shook, found her knife and climbed awkwardly up into the rocks. The slightest movement was an excruciation.

On a rock she perched, washed and salved the wounds and tried to bind her wrist. Though she was left-handed, her efforts would have been comical if the situation had not been so dire, the pain so awful. She found some knobbly sticks for splints, but could not fix them tightly enough to make any difference and finally gave up, just binding her arm and wrist and hand as tightly as she could bear, knowing that it was a hopeless job and would have to be redone today if her wrist was to heal properly. Happy birthday!

"Droik! Droi-ik!" called Idlis in his burbling voice, looking this way and that as he came closer. It would be *his* dog! If she looked down Karan could still see the dead thing, gray tongue flopping out. She started to clamber up between the stones. She did not want to be here when Idlis found it.

"*Droiiik!*" A moan of utter despair. "Droik, little puppy."

Don't look down. She looked down and beheld Idlis cradling the giant hound in his arms and weeping as though it was his own child. Then he looked up and saw her staring at him. His face showed no recognition. His agony moved her soft heart, but she wanted to be well away when his grieving was done. She eased her way between the rocks and ran.

It was nearly midday when next she saw him. Idlis, the tireless one. It was as if they had been running together for weeks, for all of her life, some thread of common purpose holding them together. Karan was empty inside now, sucked dry, an exhaustion of the spirit, her wrist and arm a killing pain. Why did she run? She no longer knew. Why did he follow? She couldn't even imagine what drove him.

Now he was close behind, so close that she could hear the grit squeaking beneath his feet. It was a hot day for late autumn, with clear skies and a dry wind blowing. Now she fell, cutting her knee open on a rock, scrambled up; but it was all over—Idlis was on her. Disgusting creature! Desperation lent her a last strength. She flailed at his face, tore at his robes, leapt backwards. The fabric tangled about her good arm and, rotten from sun and sweat and wear, tore right off his back.

Idlis gave a strangled cry and snatched at the cloth. Karan jerked the other way and fell backwards, carrying his robes with her, hood and all. All he had left was a rag in his fist and a short underskirt that fell from a band around his hips and was looped back up. His flesh was the pallid gray of a fish, his limbs bony and thick-jointed, the ribs raised bands around his chest.

Karan scrambled to her feet and limped away, unwinding the cloth from her arm as she went. The fall had badly jarred her wrist and the least movement was agonizing. Then she was struck by the distress on Idlis's normally blank face. He ignored her and ran jerkily toward his habit, one arm shielding his anemic face from the sun. She scooped the rank garments up in her good hand and hobbled on.

For more than two hours the chase went on, on that barren plain, but Idlis became slower and slower, his motion more palsied, and at last was lost to sight. What kind of trick was this? A blatant one perhaps but Karan was bothered by it and so she went creeping back. She found him collapsed on the red soil. Even from a distance she could see that his limbs were contorted, his bare torso and shoulders burnt bright orange over the gray.

Closer she crept, her curiosity aroused now. Did they have a weakness after all? The Whelm had lost his eye shields in his last travail, and as the long head lifted sluggishly all Karan could see were his eyes, and they were red, weeping wounds.

Once she would have pitied Idlis but not any more. Not after Lake Neid. Then she looked in those eyes and that gave her pause, for she saw what she had seen in her horse's eyes as she cut its throat.

"What can I do with you?" she said.

The Whelm gave what passed for a painful shrug, a curious oscillation of the shoulder blades. "Do what you will," he said, blinking fluid out of his eyes. "I expect no mercy, nor would give any."

"Why do you hunt me this way? What have I done to you?"

"The master's shame is ours. We cannot rest until we have you."

Karan could not understand. "What evil creatures you are."

Now the Whelm did not comprehend. "You stole our master's mirror, you killed my pup—*and you call us evil?* Did we serve you, you would know none more faithful."

In spite of herself Karan was fascinated. She crept closer, though not too close. She had never met anyone like him. "Who are you?"

"I am Idlis the Healer."

"Healer!"

"Why not? We hurt, we get ill, we die. *We feel.*"

His words struck Karan strangely. Somehow she had not thought of him as being human. "But what *are* you, Whelm?"

"*We* are just Whelm. We came from the wilderness of ice. Before that——" he was momentarily confused "——too long ago. We have lost what we once had—a perfect partnership of servant and master. We cannot even remember our true master, so long is he gone." He seemed a little sad, a little wistful. Then his face changed and his voice went cold with rage and self-disgust. "So Yggur is our master now, though he hates us. 'The contemptible Whelm,' he calls us. And we serve him, to our shame."

"Then why do you serve?"

"We are Whelm!" Idlis said vehemently, as though that explained all. Then, seeing that it did not, "Without a master and a purpose we were nothing. We cannot go back to nothing; so we serve Yggur. Do you kill me then?"

"I do not."

He writhed. Karan leapt back, then realized that he was trying to put himself in her shadow. The very skin of his face seemed to be dissolving. He wrapped his long arms around his torso. "How the sun burns."

Karan said nothing, only looked down at his blistering face. His eyes wept thick yellow tears but he could not ask.

"I pity you," Karan said. "That is my weakness." The Whelm flinched. The eye shields were lying about twenty paces away. She walked over and picked them up. They were carved from a single piece of flexible, yellow bone. Idlis watched her without expression. She should do for him as she did for her horse. But he was in torment. She feared him still but could no longer hate him.

She came back and threw the eye shields down on the dirt before him. He showed surprising dignity—reaching across, he touched the bone, then slowly and painfully forced himself to his feet, the yellow tears flooding his cheeks, and bowed to her. She looked at him in astonishment. He bent down, picked up the shields and put them over his eyes.

"Your weakness is your strength," Idlis said, "your pity my humiliation, the worst torment you could put me to. No one has ever done me a *kindness* before." He said the word in a shuddering way, as if it was an insult or an offense, and his upper lip twisted back to show the gray gums and the dog teeth. "What can I do? To let you get away is treason. Yet honor demands that I repay even an enemy her gift. Come, let me attend your wrist. I can see how it hurts you. You are quite safe—I do not avenge my dog today."

Her wrist was now so swollen and painful that she had to hold it rigid with her other hand. The knee, by comparison, was a minor wound. Karan was no stranger to the dictates of honor and duty but his kind was beyond her understanding. How could he offer aid one day while planning her demise for the next? She could never trust him, this alien Whelm. The thought of his touch, his rubbery cold fingers on her wrist, his nearness, was worse than the pain. "No!" she said with a shiver.

"Then go. I give you half a day, though it cost me dear."

Karan stepped back half a step. Idlis's skin had grown redder even as they spoke, and huge blisters were forming on his shoulders, his arms, his chest. He must be in agony, though he showed it only by a shuddering.

She put her hand in her pocket to take the weight off her wrist and encountered something long forgotten, the slab of chocolate that Tallia had put there in Preddle. Instantly her mouth filled with saliva and longing. She unwrapped it, still staring at Idlis, and broke it in half.

"It is my birthday today," she said, offering him one half.

Idlis's face twisted and a yellow tear leaked out of one eye. "I am your enemy still," he said, bowing his head. "But I wish you joy this day."

They ate their chocolate in silence. Karan had never in her life eaten anything that tasted so delicious, so intensely sweet. She was glad she had shared it.

"My brother Whelm are coming," said Idlis. "My torment is their shame, which they must amend. Go at once."

His eyes blinked behind the bone covers and what she saw there frightened her badly. She looked back. Half a league away a small patch of dust clung to the stony plain. Karan walked away without another glance, but rather more hastily than her own dignity would have liked, and when she was beyond his sight she ran and ran and ran.

There was no pursuit for hours, but after that their presence, and his face, were always in her mind. She set her wrist clumsily, so that it ached constantly and the hand was almost useless. Several times she crossed the hills of Sundor, back and forth, working her way east toward Hetchet and the mountains beyond, feeling that they were driving her and knowing that she would be trapped there.

There were five of them now and they were mounted again. She often saw them in the distance, far apart, and though she managed to keep away from them in this rough country she could not find a way past; there was no way to go but the way they allowed. At last the Gate of Hetchet appeared at the end of the road, the slot in the hills that framed the once great city of the same name.

She had grown hard and humorless during the past month. Cold and obsessed. Emotionally closed off—the most difficult thing of all for her. The Whelm were not far behind. Where to now?

She still longed to go to Chanthed, to seek out someone

to tell her the Histories, what she needed to choose the fate of the Mirror. She knew people in Chanthed but they were not chroniclers. Who had she met there that would know? Only the master of the college, a withered little man called Wistan, at a meeting with her father when she was a child. Wistan was still there, or at least had been a few months ago. He could surely tell her what she needed if she had the courage to approach him.

But she sensed that the Whelm were too close, possibly between her and Chanthed. Even with the crowds there for the festival it was too small a place for hiding, unless she sat in a cellar for weeks. Not Chanthed then. How she longed to hear the Great Tales again. How she wished that she'd said no to Maigraith, that she'd never met her. But Maigraith was in Yggur's cells and she was here.

With heavy heart Karan turned away and took the eastern path to Tullin and Bannador, miserable, exhausted in body and soul, trapped. The moon was in its first quarter, and all of it was dark—a miserable omen. The terrible dreams kept coming back. Looking up at the mountains she saw that already they were white with snow. Even uninjured it would be a hard crossing. She was more tired than she had ever been. How her wrist pained her. If only it would end.

The Whelm came to Hetchet close behind her. It was little more than a village where once a city stood, but every step told of its former greatness: the wide streets, curbed and guttered and paved with flat stones that were as neat and even as the day they were laid; the magnificent temples and columns and empty villas on either hand. And its people seemed to have the same air about them, an air of pride, antiquity, dignity.

"They are the proudest goat-herders in all of Meldorin," said the Whelm leader with contempt. He was quite unlike the others, being short and stout. They rode up to the great gate, so broad that ten could ride abreast between its carved stone flanks.

"We seek a young woman with red hair," said the tall man with the face like a hatchet. The gray skin was scarred and flaking as though it had been burned, and the whites of his black eyes were stained yellow.

"Such a one was here recently," replied the guard.

"And where is she now?" The Whelm moved forward in their saddles.

The guard had spoken to Karan more than once, and liked her. He would help her as long as there was no risk to himself.

"She asked for the road to Chanthed, and she went that way," the guard lied, moving backwards into his box.

"Chanthed! You are sure of this, guard?" The hard eyes probed him.

The guard looked away. "People come and go every day, and I speak to them all. She said Chanthed. That's all I know."

The Whelm rode away. "Why would she go to Chanthed?" one asked, a woman who looked rather like Idlis. "What is there, save the College of the Histories? The guard must be lying."

"Doubtless he is, Gaisch," said the stout one. "But nothing can be left to fortune. There are those in Chanthed who might have an interest in the Mirror, even though the other thief said Sith. Two will go to Chanthed. Another two will come with me: you, Idlis, where I can watch you, and you, Gaisch. It is more likely that she goes to Bannador, that being her home, but she will find no refuge in the mountains in winter. To go off the main way means death. But if you do find her in Chanthed, bring her back here. Away!"

*   *   *

Karan was high in the mountains now. One night, after worrying herself to sleep in her refuge, a cave that stank of bats, she had a quite different dream. She dreamed she was in Chanthed again, walking through the sun-drenched streets, past neat houses of yellow sandstone up to the college at the top of the hill, her hand in her father's hand, seeking out the master of the college. Now they were in Wistan's office, her father talking to the balding little man about things she did not understand. The scene changed, her father was gone and she was pouring out her tale to Wistan, who looked ridiculous in nightcap and gown, a gnome in a bed made for a giant. He sat up suddenly, the dream Wistan, as though he had just found the solution to an old problem. He did not respond to her pleas though, just stared past her and faded away.

Her last memory was of that marvelous telling and the young chronicler, Llian, who had the entire hall on its feet. She recalled how their minds had touched briefly during his tale. That was normally like finding the path through a maze, but the way to him was marked at every turn. Momentarily he seemed like the hero of one of his Great Tales, and in her desperation Karan reached out to him.

11

A SECOND CHANCE

Once more Llian's wonderful dreams were interrupted by someone belting at the door. It was so loud that they might have been trying to smash it in. He had a premonition that he was not going to get off so lightly this time.

"All right," he screamed.

The crashing continued, louder than before, and the latch was rattled furiously. Llian searched the floor by feel, found a cloak and wrapped it around him as he stumbled to the door.

"I'm coming," he shouted over the racket, but the noise continued. He slipped the bolt and wrenched the door open. "What do you want," he began angrily, then stopped, recognizing the visitor. "Turlew!" he stammered. "There's something wrong?" He knew what it was though. They had found out who had raided the library in the night.

The seneschal of the Master of Chanthed held the lantern up, eyeing the young man with disfavor. The yellow light fell on Llian's pleasant, untidy face, the mess of brown hair and the tawny eyes.

"Stop pretending!" Turlew said, prim voice oozing from thick, pink, moist lips. "Get dressed. Last night has finished you. Wistan would have words with you before you go."

"Go?" Llian said, pulling the cloak tightly about him. "I'm not going anywhere. I've got to do my telling."

"Ha!" Turlew spat. "You've had your last chance." He glanced around the room. "What a disgusting hovel you live in."

"It's all I can afford since I have no stipend. Anyway, my friends don't seem to mind."

Turlew sniffed. "Well, that's no wonder. Get packing. You have an hour."

"Where would he have me go?"

Turlew smiled a malicious smile. "You are expelled and banished from Chanthed."

Shortly Turlew rapped at the door to Wistan's chamber. A thin voice called, "Enter." Turlew stepped inside and dragged Llian blinking into the light.

Wistan wore slippers and a dark-blue cloak over his nightgown. He was talking to his captain, Trusco, who was waving his hands in the air, flat hairy slabs the size of Wistan's head.

Llian hesitated in the doorway, awaiting the notice of the master. Banished! What would he do?

"Master Wistan," said Llian, after a long silence. "You sent for me?"

"Of course I did, you fool. Shut the damned door."

"What do you want with me?"

"Breaking, entering, stealing; entering the library and the archives when they are banned to you; resisting the lawful authority of the college guard; causing bodily harm. These are crimes enough, though were you of good character I might have overlooked them in view of your previous contributions."

"But . . ." Llian began.

"Don't bother to deny it. Trusco!"

Trusco held up a torn corner of red fabric edged with black. With his other hand he lifted Llian's cloak, revealing the rent edge where it had been caught in the door. Llian slumped. He was ruined.

"But the crime that I cannot overlook is that you knocked over my lantern in our most precious archives and did not stop to put the fire out. That speaks a want of care that is unforgivable."

"I checked a minute later," said Llian. "The fire was out."

"But it might not have been! A minute is a long time in a burning library." He paused, giving Llian time to dwell on what his punishment would be.

Llian sat silently, sure that he would be stripped of his master's honor. Finally Wistan began again, in a more moderate tone. "You're finished! Dozens clamor for your place here, and I will waste no more time on you. However, something has come up during the night that I must address urgently. I have an offer for you—an urgent mission to Thurkad. Take it and I will give you money enough, and references, to make your life elsewhere."

"What!" cried Turlew from the corner. "You would *reward* him?"

"Shut up, Turlew," Wistan snapped. "I've had about enough of you too."

Turlew looked shocked. "An offer, Llian," Wistan repeated. "A second chance. You still have a lot to contribute if you will only grow up. Refuse, and you are out with nothing." He was not looking at Llian, just staring into the ashes of the fire.

Autumn was passing. Llian wondered what message could be so urgent as to require crossing the mountains at this time of year.

"But what about my telling! People will wonder . . ."

"You've lost it! Anyway, a skeet came last night with a message. Mendark has begged this favor in the name of the Council and I cannot refuse. You know Mendark, and you have a debt to him." Mendark would never have requested Llian for this task, but Wistan did not mention that. "Will you do it?"

"What is the job?"

Wistan's eyes seemed to protrude even further, as though outraged that Llian should question him, and, getting up painfully from his chair, he hobbled over to the window. The casement crashed open and he stood there, leaning on the sill, looking out. A blast of cold air sent the candles dancing. Llian moved closer to the embers. The light of dawn outlined the hilltops to the east, and in the street below, the first of the *tudos* was already setting up his little stall on the footpath, lighting the charcoal stove, mixing batter. A bird trilled from a nearby ledge. There was a long silence. Wistan turned back.

"Someone has stolen a relic from Yggur. The thief has been hunted all the way from Orist and tries to cross from Hetchet into Bannador by the Tullin pass. Her name is Karan. She must be found and escorted to Mendark."

A tiny memory woke in the back of Llian's mind; his glorious dreams unfolded again. Suddenly he was interested in what Wistan was saying. "What is the relic?"

"It's called the Mirror of Aachan and about it I cannot speak, save that it contains records, or memories of ancient times. *We* do not keep our secrets lightly."

Pompous old fool, thought Llian.

"As to the woman, I know nothing of her. That is why I send you. You have a certain ability to gain the confidence of others," Wistan smiled mirthlessly. "Mostly ill-used by recent accounts."

Llian did not respond immediately. Wistan always carried out his threats. That was how he'd remained master so long, though it was his only quality. It turned his stomach to submit to the odious little man, but what other choice was there? And it sounded as if the mission had a minor tale in it. That was all he really cared about anyway. He would have left Chanthed long ago if he'd had money and references.

"How will I find her?" he asked.

"She left Hetchet more than a week ago, heading to Tullin. She's young, red-haired; she won't be hard to find. You'll have to go at once if you're to catch her. Well?"

"I will do it," said Llian; then, with a half-hearted attempt at defiance, "though not because of your threats."

Wistan smiled, his slab-like lips peeling apart to reveal yellow teeth angling from gray, eroded gums. "The reasons for your choice do not concern me. Go now, before the town is stirring."

"I'll need gear for the mountains," said Llian.

"All here," said Wistan. He snapped his fingers and Turlew brought forth a bulging pack.

Wistan handed Llian a small purse tied with a drawstring. "This will suffice for your expenses, I trust? And here, your references." A small scroll case.

Llian weighed the purse in his hand. It was heavy enough. His thoughts strayed. If he did it well it would gain him favor, but all the same, he wasn't sure he was ready. And what would Mendark require of him when he got to Thurkad? He turned away. Turlew's eyes watched the purse all the way to his pocket.

"And Llian," called Wistan, as he reached the door. "Never come back to Chanthed."

*		*		*

After he had gone Trusco said, "Why him? I have many who could better serve you. Llian is a dreamer. It's not an easy crossing at this time of year."

"He's as happy to be going as I am to be rid of him," snapped Wistan. "And he is well provided for, the best down-filled coat and sleeping pouch to be had, the stoutest boots, waterproof cloak, to say nothing of the money. No one can accuse me of skimping."

"I can't believe that you rewarded him after last night's crimes," said Turlew petulantly.

"They are mere misdemeanors," Wistan replied, "despite what I said." How I have sunk, he thought, to condemn a chronicler for doing what we trained him for. But there are some secrets that should remain buried. He endangers everything I have ever worked for, but I cannot tell these louts that. "The Zain are always trouble. After his tales in the taverns, half of Chanthed is laughing at the office of master. I have tolerated it for too long."

"All know how tolerant, how flexible you are," murmured Turlew.

"But it has gone too far. I could not allow him another festival, another triumph. Since the last one, the masters have spoken of nothing but his telling. The mob is a curious thing—before today they have used the festival to acclaim a new master."

"And they will speak ill of you if they hear of this," said Turlew.

"That I must accept. My time as master draws to a close but the thought of him in my place is unendurable. He knows nothing, save the Histories, and he would do *any-thing* if it would advance his knowledge or his art. He thinks me just an ugly old fool, as perhaps you do too."

Turlew's lips moved in a pretense of demurral, but Wistan no longer cared.

"As perhaps I am. But I love the college and he would destroy it. He is better gone. Genius untempered by ethics is a deadly commodity."

They stood together then: master, seneschal, captain, each thinking his own very different thoughts. At last Wistan spoke and the anger was back in his voice.

"No, I would be rid of him, and this way has a certain symmetry. I dreamed about this Mirror and immediately thought of him. Let him go where his talents can be used. Mendark pressed me to take him, many years ago. Now I send him back. The irony amuses me."

"He is no more trouble than some, and cleverer than most," said Trusco, "though he be a dreamer. He has brought honor upon Chanthed."

Wistan made a slashing motion with his hand. "Enough. Escort him to the gate."

"I'll go," said Turlew, licking his lips. "They think they're so clever, these young chroniclers. It'll be a pleasure to hound him out of Chanthed."

Wistan fixed him with a keen stare. "They are our past and our future, whatever their sins. Trusco, go at once."

Llian began his exile in shock, bewilderment and loss. Chanthed had been his home for more than half his life, and there his needs had been attended to by others. Now he must look out for himself. What would he do when his purse ran out? More immediately, where would he sleep tonight? There was no inn between Chanthed and Tullin, four days away, and he had never walked alone across the mountains. In fact he barely knew how to make a campfire. His beloved Histories and his books of tales were lost, stolen. All he had was his journal and the book of the Great Tales that he had made himself.

By mid-morning the fog had lifted. Chanthed was gone

from sight. It was a glorious sunny day, a perfect walking day with just the gentlest of breezes, over everything a sense of winter holding its breath, waiting while autumn lingered. Llian felt as though a great weight had been taken off him. He should have left Chanthed years ago to make his own way in the world. In this mood even the magical dreams of last night could be achieved.

Once or twice he thought he heard the clack of horse-shoes behind him as he walked, but no other traveler appeared. That bothered him for barely a moment, such was his humor.

At first the road was well kept and broad, with low stone walls on either side, but by the end of the first day it had dwindled to a potholed track. Still, this was country he knew well. Every fragment of wall, each ruined bridge or standing column had a label for him, and he could read the label and tell its story. There—a cluster of gellon trees, the black bark deeply fissured, the limbs tormented as they became in great age. Pellban, fifth master of Chanthed and everything that Wistan was not, in Llian's eyes, had sat beneath those very trees and composed *The Lay of the Silver Lake,* the most bittersweet of all the epic romances. It was a Great Tale, and a very moving one, and Llian felt a special kinship with the ages-dead Pellban when he told it.

Damn Wistan! Flinging his pack down on the path he went across into the trees. The fruit of the gellon, over-ripe, lay on the ground all around, and its luscious peach-mango fragrance hung heavy in the air, like a sleeping potion. Llian sat in the afternoon sun, eating gellon and dreaming again, the smooth brown flank of the mountain framed between the black trunks, Chanthed a smear far below, and beyond the plains of Folc fading into the haze. The landscape slowly went out of focus, a misty background for the tragedy that had unfolded here, pure and bright as a jewel, from Pell-ban's genius.

The Lay of the Silver Lake: the tale of the subjection, and ultimately the desolation, of the tiny state of Saludith. He opened his book of tales to the place, the rice paper silky under his fingers, but did not read. He could recite it word for word. The ending was in his mind now, the tragedy of Narcies and Tiriel. Narcies, in despair at the thraldom of her family and her people, went to the victory celebrations, on the mountain above the Silver Lake, in the guise of a con-cubine. Wrapping her arms around the Autarch she flung them both off the cliff into the lake. When the word was brought to her lover, Tiriel, he hurled himself over at the same place and was smashed on the rocks. Narcies, who had miraculously survived, came upon his broken body as she was borne back in triumph. She took her own life then, but all was in vain, for the vacuum was filled by a worse tyrant and her name became synonymous with futile sacrifice.

Llian walked a little further, but suddenly his legs ached, and his back, so he looked around for a place to camp. Even that was easier than he'd imagined, for here was another patch of ancient trees. These had no story to tell him, only an invitation. There was fuel in plenty, and he made camp among the trees. After much striking of sparks into damp kindling he got a fire going and burnt bread and cheese and fatty strips of cured meat together in a pan. Llian was a com-petent cook but this night he was too tired to care. He wolfed the greasy mess down, then discovered that there was no water left and that his perfect camping place was a long way from any. He swore, licked the last drops out of the water-skin, threw it on the ground and climbed into his sleeping pouch. All thought of the quest was put off until the morn-ing.

Llian went to sleep almost at once but woke soon after,

freezing cold, having slid halfway out of his bed. Just then he heard the clack-clack of hooves—that horse again. He peered uneasily out of the trees. The road was clear as far as the first bend, not far away, but he could not get back to sleep, on the stony ground, and lay watching the stars and the winking embers. Now he was really thirsty. Llian found his waterskin and his boots and trudged off downhill through the forest. The filtered moon was just enough to see by.

Twice he got lost on the way back. The second time, Llian sat down on a log, thinking he would have to wait until morning; then he caught a whiff of smoke and, walking on, stumbled out onto the road not far below his camp.

A horse whinnied not far away. That was strange, someone on this road so late at night. There were no houses up here, no farms; not even the woodcutters came this high. Only a desperate man would ride that track in the dark. Or, cursing himself for being so slow on the uptake, someone who was hunting him!

Llian had no weapon save a knife so blunt he'd had trouble preparing his dinner with it, nor any training with weapons. He'd never needed any, in his profession. Anyway, the knife was back at the camp. Seized by the thought that he was being watched, he gripped his waterbag, slid back into the forest and looked for the campfire.

Leaves rustled behind him. He jumped but it was just the wind on the road. A stone rattled on the other side of the fire; a shadow blotted out the firelit trunks. The shadow disappeared then reappeared near his bedroll. Violence was done to his pillow, then it was flung aside with a curse.

Llian stole back to the road, coming out right next to a horse tied to a sapling. As he approached the horse whinnied, flung up its head, pulled the reins off the branch and cantered off through the forest. Someone shouted, a voice he knew well. Turlew! Llian wrenched off the branch and followed carefully. Not far from the fire the horse pranced and pawed at the air while Turlew clung to the reins trying to calm it.

A stick cracked under Llian's foot. Turlew spun around, seeming to know exactly where Llian was, and rushed him with his knife out. Llian swatted at his assailant with the pathetic weapon, stumbled, and before he knew what was happening he was face-down in the leaves. Turlew's arm went around his neck and the knife pressed into his throat.

"Why?" screamed Llian.

Turlew flung Llian on his back and banged his head on the ground. "I hate you, treacherous Zain that you are," he spat, so vehemently that flecks of spit showered Llian's face. "Always showing off your lovely voice and boasting of your honors. I've worked for years to bring you down. Ha, that surprises you!"

Llian twitched but the knife was directly over his heart. "I thought it was Wistan!" he said in dazed tones.

"That old fool! I thought I'd convinced him, then he gives you a bag of gold and sends you off to Mendark! *Mendark!* Any chronicler in Chanthed would give his hand for a post with the Magister."

"But—I've never done anything to you. I hardly know you."

"No? I well remember when you first came to Chanthed, a sniveling, snot-crusted brat. That was my class, and I was the best, until you came. Pushed out by a filthy Zain."

"I don't remember you at all," Llian dissembled, knowing that would hurt him the more, though he recalled the obsequious little worm well enough. The child had truly fathered the man. "The best? You are a clerk, not a chronicler."

"You made me fail. You destroyed my career. And now I do for you."

"With a voice like that you would never have made a teller anyway."

Turlew struck him in the face. Then he laughed, a chilling sound. "Here's a fine idea, much better than killing you," he said with venom enough to choke a horse. "Let's see how pretty you are with your nose gone, how well you tell with your tongue off, *how much a man when your manhood sizzles in the fire.*"

He put the knife to Llian's mouth and tried to prise his teeth apart. "Open up," he said coaxingly.

12

THE INN
AT TULLIN

Llian had never felt so terrified. His fingers, scrabbling on the ground, came upon the neck of his waterskin. He swung it hard, Turlew turned at the movement and it struck him full on the nose and burst, drenching them both. Turlew was momentarily blinded. Llian smacked the knife out of Turlew's hand, knocked him down and heaved a great log across his chest, pinning him to the ground. Turlew sucked asthmatically at the air, straining to fill his lungs against the weight, while Llian bound his hands with the cord from the waterskin.

Suddenly Turlew began to scream and kick his legs. "Get it off me!"

Llian put one foot on the log to keep it in place, then threw wood onto the fire so that it blazed up. "What is it?" he enquired, inspecting his enemy with all the interest of a teller in search of new material.

The flickering light revealed a huge and fuzzy-looking

black spider that had emerged from the log and was now crawling up Turlew's throat toward his chin.

"Don't panic, it's just an *enormous* spider," said Llian, as the creature hesitated next to Turlew's plump wet lips.

"Kill it," Turlew screamed, flinging his head from side to side.

"A few minutes ago you were going to kill me," said Llian, taking a malicious pleasure in the reversal. "I'd stay still if I were you. One bite from a black huntsman . . ."

Turlew went utterly still. Llian fetched a brand from the fire. Holding it close he saw that the fuzziness was due to hundreds of baby spiders clinging to every part of the mother. The spider darted across Turlew's cheek, sat up on its back legs just below his eye, waving its forelegs in the air, then darted again and straddled his glossy eyeball. Llian shuddered; he didn't like spiders much either. Turlew shrank visibly.

He convulsed, then as the spider ran across Turlew's forehead Llian killed it with a blow from his burst waterskin. Baby spiders fled in all directions across Turlew's face, taking refuge in his hair, his ear, up his nose. He screamed and screamed and did not stop even after Llian poured the remaining water over his head, washing off the splattered remains.

Llian was not cruel by nature, but he could bear it no longer. He dragged Turlew across to his horse, heaved him head down over the saddle and tied him on. Despite the bonds, Turlew thrashed and tried to claw at his ear, tickled agonizingly by the little spiders hiding inside. Llian smacked the horse hard on the flank. It kicked backwards, almost braining him, and cantered off down the track, the screams taking a long time to die away.

Llian watched it out of sight in the moonlight and turned back to his fire. His knees would barely support him. He was

astonished at his victory though already the events seemed
unreal, impossible. His only fights had been in the school-
yard, and he had seldom won.

He moved his camp across two hills, well away from the
road and the fire, went to make a brew of tea, recalled that
his water bottle was burst and turned to his sleeping pouch
in disgust. More than once that night, as he tossed on the
rocky ground, he thought of his warm bed in Chanthed. And
for the whole night his skin crawled at the memory of the
spider on Turlew's eyeball.

Eventually he slept and dreamed, and his dreams were a
curious blending of the fight, fragments of the Histories and
his own romantic fancy. He was a hero, a protector, brave,
cunning, always doing the unexpected, daring impossible
dangers. And when he finally got to Thurkad they shouted
his name in the streets.

Llian had been so occupied with his troubles that it was not
until he woke at dawn, remembering with amusement and
yet with a tinge of yearning his dream, that he gave any real
consideration to his own task. He went to the creek with his
cooking pot, then sat with his journal and his tea, as was his
daily habit. Only now, as the previous day's events were
recorded, did he give serious thought to what Wistan had
said.

Llian hardly knew whether to take the quest seriously or
not. Why had he been chosen? Llian was not blind to his
failings; he knew that outside his world of learning and
telling he was awkward and ignorant. No, whatever the mission really was, he was here because of the malice of Wistan. Maybe there was no thief, no Mirror. Certainly he had
never read of such a thing in the Histories.

Seized by a sudden fear he pulled out the purse and
spilled the contents on the ground. It was real enough: good

gold and silver, a small fortune. And Wistan's references, he found, described his qualities and accomplishments fairly, though without warmth. The master's faults were legion, but evidently meanness was not one of them.

So the quest was real; though why did someone clever enough to bring the Mirror all this way need him for an escort? It didn't make sense. It did not occur to Llian that Karan had stolen the Mirror for someone other than Mendark.

Still, any young chronicler needed a rich and powerful patron, lest he end up that despised thing, a wandering teller: a mere jongleur, or *jangler* as he had often joked. Mendark was very old, very rich, very powerful. Who better to help him with his search? And Mendark must have interesting work for a chronicler. For a Zain such as he, cast out into the uncertain world, the chance of such employment was worth any sacrifice.

The only thing that interested him in the whole affair was this Mirror. An ancient relic that had inspired such larcenous feats was interesting enough, but one that was not even mentioned in the Histories, that was intriguing. To learn its history, to write its tale, he would tramp from one end of Santhenar to the other.

Llian suddenly realized that the sun was well up, and he had been writing his daydream for an hour. If Turlew had freed himself and ridden all night he could be back in Chanthed collecting a gang of ruffians right now. And, importantly for Llian's own future, what if he got to Tullin and Karan was already gone? He hurried on up the mountain and did not stop, save for a breather or two, until it was truly dark.

The two Whelm that had gone to Chanthed to look for Karan were worn out, iron-hard though they were. They had ridden long days, asking everyone they encountered about her, but there had been no sign. More days they spent in Chanthed, asking their monotonous questions to no avail.

"She never came this way," said the woman. She was almost pretty for a Whelm, in a dark gaunt way, all black hair and black eyes, though her lips were meager, fleshless.

"No," the man agreed. "That guard lied for her. He will suffer, if I go back that direction."

"On to Tullin then. Perhaps Jark-un has had better luck."

They sold their horses that afternoon, since the upper part of the road to Tullin was presently passable only on foot. The next morning they came upon a curious sight: a man with arms and legs bound, lying in the mud of the track. The woman turned him over with her boot. Turlew was battered and bruised from his fall, but when she gave him water he gasped and was able to sit up.

"Do you know of Karan of Bannador?" she asked, as she had dozens of times.

"I know of her," groaned Turlew, scratching furiously at his ear. "What will you pay?"

"A gold tell," said the man, hiding his eagerness. "If your news is any help. Where is she?"

"Give me meat and drink first."

The woman hauled him upright. "First the news, then the payment."

Turlew croaked out the story of the message from Mendark.

"Mendark!" said the woman.

The man took her arm, the way a lover might, and drew her out of hearing. "Mendark is our master's enemy," he whispered. "This is bad news."

"Indeed! If he gets the Mirror our master's business will be exposed. The Magister is a fierce enemy."

"All the more urgent to get it back then."

They went back to Turlew. "What other news do you have about this matter?"

He told how Llian came to be sent after Karan.

"Who is he?" asked the man, touching her arm tenderly. "We heard this name in Chanthed, did we not, Yetchah?"

She frowned. "A chronicler who had gone missing."

"A Zain, a fool and a scoundrel," said Turlew bitterly.

"It was he who left you this way," guessed Yetchah. "Not quite the fool you make out." She gave him another drink from her bottle, wiping it fastidiously afterward.

The man cut off a greeny-black lump of some unidentifiable substance and put it in Turlew's hand, then counted out the worth of a tell in silver tars, twenty of them. The two Whelm turned together and loped off up the road.

"Hey, what about my bonds," cried Turlew, holding up his hands.

"That was not part of the bargain," she said over her shoulder, then they disappeared around the bend.

"This is a strange thing," said the male Whelm.

"Scarcely credible," she replied, "but I believe him. I say we shadow this Llian until he finds her. Let him lead us to her. I sense that he will."

"Good. We will go secretly."

"Even from Jark-un and Idlis?"

He spat in the road. "They've had enough chances. Time to think of our own favor."

In the afternoon of the third day Llian passed the ruins of Benbow. Even the scars of the dreadful fire had faded into the grass, and the scorched and blackened beams of the hall were hung with pale-gray lichen. The ruined walls might have been that way for a thousand years, the way the vines crept around and over them. Llian had told the *Tale of Benbow,* a minor tragedy, only months before, and he was disinclined to linger there; so evident was the truth of it that he could yet hear the screams, see the flames leap up. But no aid had ever come.

It was late on the fourth day that, squelching around a high shoulder of rock, he came in sight of the old village of Tullin. From where he stood the main road from Hetchet to Bannador could be seen winding its way up the steep mountainside. There had been snow the previous night and it still crusted the ground in shady places, but as he looked down to the west he saw that the snow lay thickly on the steep slopes, and dark clouds threatening more were already sweeping in.

He found the village in a dimple near the top of a long steep hill. It comprised a straggle of small stone houses, some ruined, on the downhill side of the inn. The inn was a massive structure of gray stone, with a slate roof and small windows fitted with shutters of weathered timber. The front door was painted dark-blue and reinforced with iron bolts. A pole above the door protruded across the street but it was bare of any pennant. Smoke came from several cottages and the chimneys of the inn but there was no one to be seen.

He pushed open the front door. Before him was a long hall with doors opening off to right and left. The left door was open, and through it was a large, high-ceilinged room with an open fireplace occupying half of the far wall. A few embers smoldered there. The room was chilly and empty. He turned down the hall, passing a narrow stair that ran steeply up to his left. It seemed too small and mean for such a large building. The far end of the hall opened onto the kitchen, where a vast stove glowed. The back door was open and from outside came the sound of wood being chopped.

"Hello, is anyone about?" Llian called from the door.

The chopping stopped. A gray head emerged from behind

a woodheap. "Come and give me a hand," sang out an old man. The head disappeared and the chopping resumed.

Llian sat down on a stump beside the pile and ostentatiously took off a boot. "Be glad to help you," he murmured, rubbing his blisters, "just as soon as I get this bound up."

"Get off, Llian," said the axeman, turning toward him with a smile. "You tried that one on me the last time you were here. I'll not fall for it twice." Dark-green eyes were twinkling in a face deeply tanned, a mountain dweller's tan. He rubbed square hands through iron-gray hair that was sparse at the front though falling to his shoulders at the back. The woodchopper was shorter than Llian but well built, despite his age, and must have been a handsome man when young.

"Shand!" Llian grinned. "I'm surprised you're still alive, old man. It's five years since I was last in Tullin." He leaned back on his seat, looking around cheerfully, making himself comfortable.

"I'm alive," grunted Shand. "I can't afford to die with all this wood to carry *by myself.*"

"Where is everybody?"

"Tullin dwindles. Those that remain are down the Hetchet road a way, looking for a lost traveler. They'll be back soon, wanting a fire and a hot dinner." Shand looked west, at the road winding its way down the mountain.

Llian, bowing to the pressure, squatted down and loaded his right arm. "A traveler?"

"Stupid thing to be doing, this time of year, traveling alone across the mountains. Hurt too—broken arm or something. You going to squat there all evening?"

Llian trudged inside and dumped the wood in a recess next to the stove. When he came back out again, the first flakes of snow were falling.

"How did you hear of her?" he asked, picking up another piece.

"That's what's so odd," old Shand replied, laying down the axe and hefting a log rather bigger than Llian would have attempted. "Some other travelers came searching for her; three foreigners from over Orist way, on their way east. Or so they say. And in a right hurry too. Funny thing was, they weren't in a hurry at all this morning. Went out searching for her, down the mountain." He settled the log on his shoulder and disappeared up the path.

Llian sat down on the woodheap with half an armload. A chill went through him. Wistan had said that Karan was being hunted . . .

Shand was back, staring down at him with a half-amused, half-irritated expression. "It's snowing, Llian," was all he said, and Llian leapt up and hurried inside with his small load of wood.

"Did they happen to say what her name was?" asked Llian, as he passed Shand on the path again.

"Karan, of Bannador," said Shand thoughtfully.

By the time they had carried all the wood in and set the fires blazing, it was dark. Llian sat at a table near the fire with a mug of hot wine while Shand passed back and forth, lighting lamps and bearing mugs, plates and cutlery from the kitchen.

The searchers arrived back noisily just after dark, brushing powdery snow from their cloaks in front of the fire and calling loudly to Shand for food and drink. Llian hung back, content to observe for the moment. The landlord, a big bony man with sandy hair and a flat nose, saw the stranger sitting quietly there and came across to him.

"I'm Torgen—your landlord. My wife, Maya."

She was little and plump, a remarkably attractive woman

of middle age with black eyes, round rosy cheeks and a sparkling smile. Her tiny wrists were layered with silver bands that rang together as she moved.

Torgen went the rounds of the little group: an old man wearing a soldier's cap, returning to the west from Thurkad; two messengers, traveling east; a couple recently wed, or so their total self-absorption proclaimed, but they were so alike they might have been brother and sister. They were on their way from Bannador to Hetchet. Last of the travelers was a priest with watery eyes. There were five or six villagers too, though they quickly went to their accustomed table and became immersed in a game of dice.

"Rather a lot for this time of year. I see you've met Shand already. We have three more, from Orist." Torgen paused. "They keep to themselves. Haven't come in yet. If you'll excuse us, dinner's already late. It's been a long day."

He continued over his shoulder, in answer to Shand's question: "No, we didn't find her. I expect she's in a drift somewhere—there's a lot of snow on the road."

The soldier, Jared, and the priest joined Llian at his table. Llian and the priest shared a jar of hot spiced wine, while Jared called for tea. "What's this about a lost traveler?" Llian wondered.

The priest and Jared looked at each other. Jared had the sad, droopy face of a bloodhound. He stroked his jowl with broad, flat fingers, took off his cap to reveal a blotched dome, slowly rubbed his scalp, the skin mounding under his fingers, put his hat back on again and mutely sipped his tea. There was a long pause, then the priest began, "Well, so *they* say. But it seems mighty queer to me." He stopped.

"What do you mean?"

The priest squinted at him across the table. "Why is the miserable girl traveling alone at this time of year? And what do those scrawny wretches from Orist want her for? Making us risk our lives at a time like this." His tone was peevish. He took more wine from the jar greedily, slopping it on the table, and drank the whole bowl down with a gulp and a gasped breath. He reached for the jar again, then pushed it away, heaved his chair back as if to go but just slumped there, wet lips gleaming, and stared morosely at the fire. Maya tinkled across with a cloth to mop the table.

"I'm not sure I understand you," said Llian.

"Can you not feel it? The past sweeps toward us, renews itself in the present. At night my bones ache with the imminence of it. The cycle of death, the cycle of ruin." He shivered. His eyes seemed to be watering more than before and he dashed the wet away with his sleeve.

The old soldier gave Llian a thoughtful glance. He wore thick woolen trousers and a heavy brown cloak, caught at the neck with a copper pin. He rubbed his pouched eyes.

"Your creed and mine are very different, priest," he said in a slow, low voice, the r's rolled into a *prrr*. "I'm a pr-rractical man, but there are signs enough for me too. Something is building such as Santhenar has not seen in an age. Where is the will to combat it? I don't have it."

Their sentiments made Llian shiver. What did they see that he did not? At that point the front door banged, and, twisting around in his chair, Llian saw three people enter in a flurry of snow. The better to observe them he stood up and leaned on the mantelpiece with his back to the fire. He sipped the wine, which had gone cold and developed an oily taste.

The three were dressed alike, in robes of dark-green wool gathered at the waist with cord. Two were tall, with sharp gray faces—the man with scarred cheeks; a woman, lanky though large-breasted. Each bore a short wooden staff but they were otherwise unarmed. The third was shorter and heavily built, almost stout, with thick graying hair. A wallet hung at his hip from a narrow belt. His legs were bowed so that he walked with a rolling gait, and his skin was as gray as steel.

He spoke briefly to the landlord, whose darting eyes betrayed his nervousness, then glanced around the room. His gaze rested for a moment on Llian, who did his best to look rustic, then he gestured to his companions and they walked off toward the stairs.

Llian was struck by something familiar about them, some image from a tale of long ago, but when he tried to pursue it, it was not there. He sat down again but the priest had moved to a table by himself and the soldier was gone. Llian signaled for food and another flask of spiced wine. Suddenly the benefits of this mission seemed outweighed by the risks.

Shand brought Llian his dinner, a large bowl of soup and some dark bread. The soup was thick, full of vegetables and beans and black, smoked meat. Llian sipped it from the bowl, as was the custom. It was very hot. He put it to one side and tore a strip from the loaf, dipping it in the soup while he resumed his deliberations.

Had Karan slipped by her pursuers, or had she hidden and let them overtake her? Or was she lying injured or dead somewhere off the path?

Just then Shand came back bearing a steaming bowl and mug. Llian gestured him over. Shand sat down, pulled a knife out of one pocket and a hunk of bread from the other and cut the bread into cubes which he dropped into the soup, pushing them under with his spoon.

"Who are they?" asked Llian.

Shand lowered his voice. "Yggur's trusted servants. Whelm, they are named. The squat one is in charge, called Jark-un, and the woman's name is Gaisch. They arrived yesterday evening. Took their meal in their room. They called me up there a few times—more blankets, more wood for the fire, that sort of thing. Shouldn't have thought they'd feel the cold, coming from Orist. The last time I went up, the fellow with the scarred face, name of Idlis, called me in and asked when the red-haired woman had left. Not secretively, he asked me straight out, but he made me uneasy.

" 'Been no one traveling alone these last weeks, and don't expect none, what with winter closing in,' I told him. 'Unusual even the few that we have. Generally it's a big party or none.' The other two looked surprised. 'Are you absolutely sure?' he asked. As though he thought I was hiding her, but that was my story and it was true.

"Anyway, enough of them. What are you doing here? I've heard you're something of a master now. I should have thought you'd be doing a telling at the festival."

"I was going to," Llian said, looking down at the remains of his soup, unsure how much to reveal. "To tell you the truth, I'm in a bit of trouble back in Chanthed. I've been satirizing old Wistan in the taverns these past months. The patrons thought it most amusing, and it was profitable for the innkeepers too, I dare say, but Wistan has banished me."

"Hmn," said Shand. "Seems to me there's more than you're letting on."

He was disturbingly well-informed. Llian changed the subject, ordered a new flask of spiced wine and began spinning ever more outrageous yarns with each bowl. Shand listened in silence, though once or twice he laughed, and each time the flow dried up he asked Llian something that set him going again.

Llian couldn't work out whether Shand was enjoying his tale-spinning, tolerating it or secretly laughing at him. Then, when Shand came back from the bar with yet another flask, suddenly he didn't care. He held out his bowl in an unsteady hand, and as he watched the red liquid rise his quest floated to the top of his mind. He felt a vague unease; there must be some good reason for not talking about it, but he couldn't remember what it was. How would he ever learn if he was too afraid to ask?

"Shand—did you hear about my Great Tale?" The words slurred together and Llian realized that he was drunk.

"What tale? The one from your telling of four years ago? *The Loneliness of Faelamor?*"

"No, the *Tale of the Forbidding* I made for the Graduation Telling last summer."

"Oh yes—strange tale, that. I heard it on the road a while ago."

"Well . . ." Llian hesitated. "There's something bothers me about the ending."

"Oh?"

"An insignificant thing. You probably wouldn't recall it."

"If there is something you want to ask me," Shand said rather testily, "then ask it. I remember the tale well enough."

"Well, recall that the crippled girl did not seem to have been harmed by the Forbidding, but she was found dead. That's what's wrong."

"Didn't she kill herself?"

"She stabbed herself from behind?"

"What are you trying to say, Llian?"

"I think a great secret was discovered there and the crippled girl was killed to silence her."

"What does it matter after all this time?"

"Is my tale right or wrong? Is there a greater tale to be found? If the record is false, I am ruined."

Shand screwed up his lips, as though he had just found something unpleasant in the bottom of his bowl. "Look, Llian, why ask me? I chop wood for a living. But if something was discovered there, and has been hidden ever since, don't you think that raving about it when you've had a few drinks might be rather dangerous?"

"I just needed to talk to someone."

"Well, I can't help you. I suggest you leave it lie. Where are you off to, anyway?"

"Thurkad. I think perhaps I might see Mendark there."

"The Magister! This is worse than the other! You overreach yourself, Llian. What does a lowly chronicler want with the Magister?"

"He was my . . ." He broke off. "I know him," he stammered. "We spent weeks together once, on the road to Zile."

Shand looked sceptical. "No one who wasn't in a desperate hurry would take this way to Thurkad, not at the beginning of winter. Unless there was another reason to come to Tullin. To meet someone, for example. Take care with your alliances, Llian. Haven't you Zain learned that lesson yet? Mendark is a dangerous friend."

He rose heavily and left Llian there with his thoughts.

Llian woke suddenly to find his room cold and dark. He had dozed off in the chair in front of the fire, the lamp had gone out and the room was lit only by the coals in the fireplace. He stumbled across to the window, sluggish from the wine, pushed the sash up and thrust the shutters out. Outside it was black as a tomb, and large flakes of snow began to settle on his forearms as he leaned on the sill. What was he to do with his life?

Llian considered his options. The sensible thing would be to forget all about the crippled girl. No matter how he searched, after all this time he would probably never find the answer, or his new Great Tale. But on the other hand, it was unlikely that anyone would ever prove his *Tale of the Forbidding* wrong. Yes, the sensible thing was to put it all behind him and get on with rebuilding his life and his career.

Then there was Karan and the Mirror. That was a knottier problem, because her life was at stake, and his own word.

Even so, to go out searching for her with the Whelm here was a deadly and immediate peril. Just the way they looked at him downstairs had sent an icicle melting down his back.

And Mendark—a dangerous friend maybe, but a magnificent patron. No better opportunity could ever be offered Llian. But Mendark was an exacting taskmaster. To win his favor Llian must get Karan and the Mirror safely to Thurkad. Anything less was failure. How could he find her in this weather? How could he get her there against such potent foes?

A gust sent the snow flurrying into his face and Llian came to himself abruptly. His hands were aching from the cold. He pulled the shutters to and closed the window. He warmed his fingers over the embers, built the fire up again, locked the door and, removing only his boots, crawled into the cold bed.

For what seemed an eternity he lay drifting in and out of sleep, fretting about Karan's plight and wondering about the Mirror, but there were too many questions and no answers. A wind sprang up; somewhere it found a loose shutter, which every so often would crash open against the wall of the inn, then slowly creak shut on its hinges. Llian ran through one wild scheme after another, but none seemed to offer any hope. Who could blame him if he did not find her, in this!

In the end he had virtually decided to give it away; to give up his dreams and become a pathetic jongleur or, worse yet, a drudging scribe.

In the night the snow turned to rain, heavy drops pattering on the slates and splashing in the gutters. The downpour found a gap in the roof and Llian was awakened by water dripping on the hearth. He rubbed the sleep from his eyes. Suddenly he was wide awake, sensing some other presence nearby. What was it? It was so faint, this stirring inside, that he could not tell if it was malevolent or benign. Was it Karan, laid up in a cave or retreat nearby? Or some potency of the Whelm, stirring when the world was at its weakest?

As he lay in the dark, listening to the slow drip on the hearth, he became aware of a complex rhythmical beating in his head. The pattern rose and fell, rose and fell, then died away. Shortly it began again. Llian suddenly realized that it had been running through his subconscious while he was asleep. He closed his eyes and lay back, trying to make sense of it, for there seemed a meaning. But as he concentrated on the pattern it blurred and retreated, becoming a distant, meaningless burr, and eventually fading to nothing.

The fire had gone out again. Feeling around in the wood box in the dark he found some kindling, which he used to excavate hot coals from the mound of ash. He sat on the warm hob and fed the coals with little pieces of kindling until the fire drove him out onto the hearth. Sitting on the hearth, staring into the flames, his mind drifted back to Chanthed and the festival. Tonight was the final night, and it was he who should be telling the final tale, the greatest of all the Histories, the *Tale of the Forbidding*. If only he could!

The tale unrolled in his mind, an insoluble puzzle, as always. Immersed in his reverie, in the highest achievement of his art, it was a while before he realized that the message, if message it was, had started to come through again. It was as if someone had been listening in to the tale.

Suddenly a recognition, or a yearning, pulled it into focus. It became urgent, panicky. The emotions grew in him. Was it a cry for help? In his mind's eye he could see her, for Karan it must be, huddled in the snow, so terribly cold and her wrist throbbing unbearably. Now there was nothing but the pain, the cold and the burden she could not relinquish.

The image was so real and clear that Llian felt he knew

her better than anyone. It was strangely familiar too, as though he had met her before. He cried aloud, "Where are you?" but she could not hear him.

Help me, came the cry in his head.

"Where, where?" he cried silently in reply. Everything stopped, as though she had not expected to be answered. His mind went blank, something sighed inside his head, then urgently, *Oh, hurry. I am . . .*

A shattering discord erupted in Llian's head and images flashed through his mind more quickly than thought: a steep, snow-covered hill, with a bony crown of rocks and someone huddling over a tiny fire; a dim tunnel, a small figure wading through knee-deep water; a tall man in robes, one hand outraised. Then the face of Idlis the Whelm, twisted in rage. The after-image of that face hung long in his mind.

But another image canceled it, forming slowly this time—a Nightland, a void with drifting banners of mist, a shadowy keep rising above, a somber hall flanked by obsidian pillars. A figure dwarfing its carved stone chair, but bound about with adamantine chains. Slowly the figure drew itself up to its enormous height, raising its arms, shattering the chains effortlessly. It took a step forward, then another, reaching out its mighty hand. A ribbon of mist swirled, obscuring it, only the eyes showing, carmine whirlpools, drawing him . . . Llian's mind revolved with sickening slowness, and darkness enfolded him all around.

Someone shouted down the hall, shocking him back to his senses. It was answered, a cry that pierced the night like a beacon flaring from a stony hilltop. Doors crashed open and shut, there was more yelling, then Llian's door burst open and Gaisch and Idlis hurtled in. Idlis picked Llian up and held him high, shaking him as a dog might shake a rat, then just as suddenly he was flung down again. Gaisch's face almost touched his. Her voice was iron squealing on glass.

"Where is she, chronicler?"

This was like a horror out of one of his tales. Llian was still groggy, but there was no doubt that these were deadly enemies to Karan. *His Karan!* That fleeting touch had brought him closer to her than to anyone he had ever known. He babbled some nonsense, a fragment of a tale that popped into his head, anything to distract them while he gathered his thoughts. Gaisch shook him and a knife as long as her forearm touched Llian's throat. She pressed the knife against his larynx until he gagged and tears sprang to his eyes.

"A teller who cannot speak is no teller at all," she said. Her breath had the smell of metal.

"Glmpf," said Llian, paddling his hands weakly against the air. The knife eased back a trifle. "I don't know," he gasped.

"You dreamed her, chronicler. Tell your dream."

"Nothing. Just . . . *Aaaahhhhhhh!*"

Gaisch slammed the back of the knife hard against Llian's throat. Llian thought his throat was cut; his eyes nearly started from their sockets.

"Make up your mind, chronicler," she said, holding the knife out and reversing it slowly. The blade moved toward his throat again.

Llian had had enough. "I just—"

At that moment the light grew brighter and Shand spoke from the doorway.

"Leave him," he said softly.

The Whelm stood up slowly. Idlis's voice made Llian's skin creep.

"Go away, old man, lest you be next."

"Leave him, I said!" Shand's voice was a whip-crack.

The lantern flared and thunder roared in Llian's ears. It felt as if the inn had rocked on its foundations.

Gaisch let go of Llian, the two Whelm backed away and disappeared through the door. Flat feet flapped down the stairs. Shortly hooves clattered on the stone outside. Shand offered Llian his hand. Llian sat down on the bed, feeling his throat, while the old man flung the shutters apart and watched the Whelm ride through a puddle of light and off into the darkness.

"Come and see me at dawn," said Shand. "Outside!"

He went out, closing the door behind him. Clearly he was more than he seemed, but Llian was too shocked and sore to think about it. Twice in three days he had nearly had his throat cut. Whatever Mendark had to offer, it was not worth it.

13

THE ROAD TO THE RUINS

Sometime later Llian picked himself up, crawled to the window, pushed it open and vomited on the snow below. The sun was rising. He wiped his face on his sleeve, staggered back to the bed and fell onto it. There he lay, alternately hot and cold, a piercing pain in his temple. He was more afraid than ever, but he could no longer think of giving up, not after touching minds—that strangely familiar feeling—with Karan.

Come at dawn! Shand had said. Already the sun was flooding into the room. The inn was empty in this early hour, but he found Shand sitting on a cushion on the stone steps leading from the kitchen to the woodheap. The old man had a gellon in his hand and a steaming bowl of chard beside him on the step. He was staring across the valley at the shadowy bulk of the mountains and the low sun beyond. Llian poured a bowl from the pot on the stove, helped himself to a chunk of black bread and sat down beside Shand. His head still throbbed.

"Any news of the Whelm?" Llian asked.

"No, but the rest of the inn are astir," Shand replied.

"The two messengers went at first light. Though they were most unusual messengers, and until now traveling without haste. Even the priest is out of bed, the lovers too. Jared went out a while ago, but he walks every morning." Shand took a bite of the gellon. The straw-colored juice ran down his wrist unnoticed. "They're very good this year," he said appreciatively. "Though we lost most of the crop to hail. Still, it's usually that way."

"Are the Whelm coming back?"

"I'd say that would depend on what they find out there, wouldn't you?"

"Last night we talked about Mendark," said Llian obliquely. He hesitated. Shand gazed at him unblinking. "You said he was a dangerous friend."

"The powerful are always a danger, Llian. Their motives are more complex, their gaze more far-reaching. And they use even their friends if the need arises. Mendark has been Magister for a very long time, but now the world is changing. This is a deadly time for him, if he cannot adapt. I knew him well, once. Beware, I say."

Shand put the seed of the gellon down carefully on the step and wiped his hands on his trousers. He fixed Llian with his own far-sighted gaze.

"Let's talk about this business. Normally at this time of year there'd be no one on the roads up here, yet all of a sudden we have a whole circus. I can't help wondering if you're not all here for the same purpose." Shand looked sideways at Llian, who stared straight ahead, wordless.

"If you mean to do something for her you'd better be quick," Shand went on, a glint in his green eyes.

Llian took a deep breath. "I don't know where to look, or what to do."

"Then you'd better get after the Whelm—*they* seem not to be in any doubt."

"I'm no thick-skulled warrior. What can I do against them?"

"Thick-skulled, but definitely no warrior," said Shand. "Maybe you should ask *her*. If she has come all this way with something Yggur wants so badly, she must have resources to supplement your remarkably meager skills."

"Where did they go?" Llian asked.

"East, on the road to the pass and to Bannador. I watched them. But on the other side of the hill they turned south and followed an old track running toward Mount Tintinnuin. That's the tallest mountain hereabouts, to the south of the twin peaks. There," he pointed. "The tip is just visible over the ridge. Do you see it? There's a ruin about four hours away, up the path. An old fortress. That's where she'll be."

"How can you know that?"

"I too had a strange dream."

"But they'll be halfway there by now—I couldn't possibly catch them on foot. I'm sure I'll get lost, anyway."

Shand sighed, and his look said: why on earth did they send *you*? "Come upstairs."

Llian followed up to Shand's room. It was like Llian's, but with a smaller bed, and the walls were completely covered in maps of all kinds. "So many maps," Llian sighed.

"My hobby," said Shand. "I've been collecting maps, and making them, all my life. Look here." He pointed to a small chart to one side of the window. "This is Tullin. The old bridge to the fortress has been broken these last fifteen years. They'll have to climb down the ravine and up the further side. They won't get to the ruins before dark. If you take the hidden path on this side of the ridge, and after an hour follow the right fork of the ridge—they will have taken the left—you'll come to a place where you can cross easily.

Well, perhaps not easily, but it is possible—not afraid of heights are you?—and approach the ruins from the other side. You'll be there in the mid-afternoon. They won't go that way because from the east it looks unclimbable. Go now, there's a storm coming."

He ushered Llian out and they went back to the steps. But Llian had lost confidence, and he was terrified of heights. The reality was very different from his tales. "Will you come with me, Shand?" he asked suddenly.

The old man was taken aback. "Me? I'm a worn-out old hack!"

"The Whelm didn't seem to think so a few hours ago."

"Bluff, Llian. It was all bluff. What powers I had are long gone."

"But you know the mountains. You know them. What can I do alone?"

Shand was silent for a long time. Almost, Llian thought, he was ready to agree, then a cloud, or a memory, crossed his face and he spoke as though giving an overused speech. "No, I won't go with you. The world has passed to another generation and what is going to be will be. Once I wandered Santh meddling, thinking I was doing right, though in truth I just wallowed in the power and self-importance. More than once have I raged against fortune. I raved, I swore, I vowed to stop time itself, even to fling it backwards. It broke me anyway and took away everything I cared for. Oh Aeolior!"

He turned toward Llian, but his eyes were unfocussed, his thoughts far away, or lost in some unimaginable sadness.

"If all is chance then what use striving?" said Llian. "I was taught that there is always a way; we have but to find it. Our fortunes are not fixed. We cannot stop fate, nor turn it back, but by our great labors we can sometimes move it from its path, even direct its course, though we know not where it will run to. Why did you come to my aid earlier if you do not think the same?"

"I used to think like that," Shand said as though to himself. "The fruits of my labors were rich indeed, but they are all gone now. Fortune did not take them, only time and my own folly. I will not go with you. Seldom have I touched a thing and made it better. Go, and remember your honor."

"Who was Aeolior?" asked Llian.

Shand got up hastily. There were tears on his cheeks. "Someone I lost long ago." He gripped Llian's shoulder tightly and then went heavily back into the inn, forgetting his cushion and his bowl.

Llian's head buzzed with unanswered questions. He rose as well, left a note and a coin behind the counter, shouldered his pack and set out up the road.

Halfway up the hill he trudged past two hidden Whelm, the ones that had questioned Turlew days before. They had reached Tullin just before dawn, barely missing their fellow Whelm, and concealed themselves in a patch of scrub beside the road, watching the inn, watching for Llian. Only after he had turned into the forest near the top of the ridge did they move after him, and then very slowly and silently.

On the evening of the following day Shand, once more at the woodheap, saw another traveler coming slowly up the road from Hetchet. It was a tall, black-haired woman, leading a horse that favored the off hind-leg. By the time she reached the inn it was almost dark. She saw her horse attended to, went inside, laved her face and hands at the trough and sat down near the fire. The big room was almost empty now. Shand went across to her.

"Shand is my name," he said. "What will you have?"

She stood up. She was much taller than he. She held out a slim hand. Her skin was as rich and fine as chocolate. "I am Tallia," she said. "I will be direct. Mendark has sent me. I am looking for Karan of Bannador. Do you know of her?"

Shand regarded her with a smile, liking her instantly. Here is one worthy of trust, he thought. More so than the one who sent her. Should he tell her what he knew? Why not? Better that Mendark have Karan's secret, whatever it was, than the Whelm. Mendark, for all his failings, at least had the interests of Meldorin at heart.

"I know Mendark," he said.

"Yes. I've heard him speak of you."

"Doubtless. The fool who turned aside from duty. Still, that is not what you came for. Yes, I know of her, but it's a tale made up of several fragments, and will take time. First, let me bring you meat and drink."

Tallia ate in silence, then Shand came back with tea and green wine. She drank the wine with considerable relish, and poured another glass. "Tell," she said.

"I rather think that Llian will have got a rude surprise when he met her," said Shand at the end of his tale, smiling.

She raised an eyebrow.

"I knew her father well," said Shand. "He died when she was a child, and her mother soon after. I last saw Karan at the burying. A small, quiet, clever girl, very strong-willed; utterly determined."

"So she has shown. But you don't feel the need to help her?"

Shand looked uncomfortable. "I have already. But if you mean, why don't I go up there and defend her from the Whelm, and get mixed up in whatever business it is between her and Yggur—no, I don't!"

She probed a bit deeper. "Despite your friendship with her father?"

"You are thinking that I am a faithless friend. But she's a

grown, capable woman, and I am an old old man. There is no more that I can do."

They sat with their drinks and their thoughts for a long time. Finally Shand broke the silence. "What will she make of him, I wonder?"

"He is a great teller, I am told."

"Indeed. A marvelous teller, and a master chronicler as well—a rare amalgam. Charming he is, and generous, and good-natured. But too obsessed with the Histories. Too curious. A dangerous preoccupation, and a danger. There is something about him that bothers me. Though perhaps it is just that he is Zain."

Tallia's eyes reflected some surprise at the prejudice, but she said nothing.

He shook his head, came back to himself. "Yet, he is charming. Also proud, vain, boastful and indolent. And as awkward outside his little world as he is clever within it." He laughed again. "I wish I could have seen their meeting."

"I'll go after them at first light," said Tallia. "You will show me the way?"

He nodded. "But I don't think you'll find them, in all this snow. Karan knows the mountains very well; she will know where to hide."

Most of the snow had melted in the early-morning rain, but the air held no warmth and the low sun gave little heat. At the top of the hill Llian cast around in the undergrowth before coming on a faint path running along the western side of the ridge. At one time the path must have been wide enough to take a cart, but it had long since fallen into disrepair and was so overgrown that it was hard to follow.

As he progressed the country became more rugged, the way broken by a succession of rocky gullies. Once these had been spanned by stone culverts, of beautiful workmanship, but now mostly undermined and falling into ruin. Here and there was a fragment of wall or an overturned stone idol beside the path, artifacts that brought forgotten fragments of the Histories from his subconscious.

As he walked along with the sun on his back his earlier doubts fell away. Once again he gave way to romantic fancies and one compartment of his mind began composing his own tale, the tale of Llian and the Mirror, that would be told at future festivals, while another part looked on mockingly at the indulgence.

After he had been walking for about an hour the path forked, one way turning abruptly west, the other seeming to go straight on. This contingency was not covered by Shand's instructions. Llian scrambled up to the top of the ridge but all he could see through the trees were other ridges, and no clue as to which way to take. He pressed on the straight way. Soon the path plunged steeply down into a narrow valley cleared of trees. The valley bottom was smooth under its cloak of snow, but the further end was concealed by a huge buttress of slick gray rock. Surely this could not be the right way.

He slipped and skidded to the bottom and was plodding along through slush and mud, longing for a good night's sleep, when a violent cry echoed across the valley. Llian jumped, staring all around, but could see nothing. The cry came again and a stone whizzed past his ear. Outside a cave in the buttress a wild-maned figure capered, brandishing fists as big as pumpkins. He was clad in a loincloth and was gaunt to the point of emaciation.

The lunatic, or hermit, bent for another stone. Llian turned to flee and the stone struck him painfully on the backside, knocking him to the ground. He scrambled to his feet and fled back the way he had come, pursued by crashing rocks and wild hoots. Up the steep path he raced, heart threatening to push his ribs apart, and did not stop until he was back at the fork.

Here, as he caught his breath, he had an uneasy feeling that he had been followed. Llian stood for a long time, staring back in the direction of Tullin. He saw nothing, for the Whelm, alerted by his crashing return, had plenty of time to slip away into the forest.

Llian followed the other track and took the right fork of the ridge as Shand had advised. Eventually he found himself on the rocky crest of a steep-sided spur, barely wide enough for three people to walk abreast. The ground fell away steeply on his left and almost sheer to the right. For a painful moment he hesitated there, staring numbly up, but it was too late to stop now. The crest was broken with sharp outcrops of slate which he was forced to clamber over or around, sometimes with barely room to put his feet side by side, clinging fearfully to the rock.

West ran the ridge, then south in a great curve. To the west he looked down on a tangle of steep hills and deep rocky gullies. Ahead the path climbed sharply to a cliff-bound plateau, the upper cliffs being a dark red rock. On a promontory he saw the ruins he was making for. This side of them a stream plunged over the cliff and, far below, flowed away to the east.

His gaze followed the waterfall down. He was looking into a steep-sided bowl some leagues across. The second ridge, the way the Whelm must have taken, completed the rim of the bowl by joining the plateau on the other side of the ruins. From where he stood the slot cut by the stream in the rim of the bowl, and the remains of the bridge over it, were clearly visible. It was so far down that it made his head spin. Llian started, feeling as though he was going to fall, and stepped back abruptly.

A cold wind had sprung up, bringing dark snow clouds

with it. It was past noon and already the warmth had gone out of the day. The trip was taking a lot longer than Shand had said. Icy snow patches lay behind every boulder; wiry grass cut his fingers and stabbed his calves through his trousers.

He stopped for a respite: a swig from his water bottle and a hard piece of bread. Squatting out of the wind behind a tall plate of rock he stared down. From this angle he could see the slot plainly as a thin dark line in the ridge, but there was no sign of the Whelm.

Or was there? Those faint specks on the snow at the base of the cliff—were they people? He stared until the tears ran from his eyes. He was sure they were, at least two of them. The sky was black behind him now, the storm coming on so quickly that he grew afraid. He shouldered his pack and hurried on.

As he neared the edge of the plateau Llian saw why the road had not followed this ridge. The crest narrowed—in places he might have straddled it like a horse—and rose up so steeply that he could only climb the last five hundred paces on hands and knees. He would have gone back, only he was so afraid of falling that he dared not turn around. The rock here was sharp and brittle and glazed with ice, the western side of the ridge a smooth gray ramp of slate completely bare of soil or bush. The eastern side fell to the bottom of the bowl in a series of steps like the teeth of a saw.

A flurry of tiny hailstones stung his cheeks as he neared the plateau, and then a wild gust of wind almost flung him off. His fingers clung to the rock as he squinted down into the bowl, but the air was full of swirling rain and the bottom no longer visible. The ruins could not be far away though he could not pick them out. Mid-afternoon should see him there.

He struggled up the last few paces and stood on the edge

of the plateau. There was a brief respite from the wind, then it resumed in fury, flinging icy stinging drops at his face. Llian staggered and fell to his knees, crawling blindly away from the cliff. He got out cloak and hood and squatted down with his back to the storm. Shortly the wind squall passed and the rain teemed down. Llian set out, squelching through the saturated grass in what he thought was the direction of the ruins.

There was one consolation, he realized, as chilly threads trickled down his back: the Whelm could not climb the cliff in this, and after dark the wet would freeze to ice. Surely he was safe until the morning.

The waterfall stream lay in a channel cut deeply into the plateau, with steep rocky banks. It was only ten paces across but rising visibly, and soon would be impassable. Upstream the river narrowed between two rocky shoulders and a scatter of boulders in the stream might serve as stepping stones. He plodded along the bank and stood there, uncertainly. From the shore the first three stones looked secure, but the last two were small and already awash. If he fell in, the current might carry him over the precipice. But Llian could see no other crossing place.

He jumped—a long stretch to the first boulder, then two short steps to the second and third. As he leapt to the fourth he knew that he had misjudged the distance—his outstretched foot overshot and skidded off the far side. He flailed and crashed into the water. The torrent whirled him away, rolling him over and over. Llian panicked, unable to tell which way was up.

He thrashed and the race flung him against rock with a thud that drove the breath from his lungs. It felt as though his ribs had given way. He lay there for a moment, the river tugging at him, the weight of the pack pulling him ever so slowly down in the water. Llian clawed his way up, groaning and grunting. A fingernail tore half off and he did not notice. Blood was running down his face from a cut above his eye and the whole of his left side was raw. Each breath, each movement stabbed through him from front to back.

Llian ripped off a rent sleeve and tried to bind it round his forehead. His fingers were grated and hurt abominably. He bit off the torn nail, warmed his fingers in his mouth and wavered off again. The bandage kept slipping off, and just to tie it back up was too difficult, too wearying. How he longed for Chanthed. Wistan did not seem such a bad fellow after all.

Then Llian was reminded of how Karan had touched him last night. Something in him had responded to her call for help, her loneliness, her pain . . . She was no longer an anonymous stranger. He had to find her, to meet her, to hear her tale. Before all, he was a chronicler.

His mind began to wander. The Mirror, the Whelm, the enigma of Shand and the mystery of Karan, all began to blur together into a horrible dream. Llian had just enough wit to realize that if he did not find shelter he would die of exposure. He staggered off, falling down every few paces, each time getting up and dragging himself a little further, his only goal to take the next step.

An eternity of cold and wind and pain, but at last the mass of the ruins loomed up before him. Their shape reminded him of a tale, a grim one too, but he was too weary to care. He climbed over a pile of rubble and flopped at the base of a wall, squatting there until his head steadied. There was a faint smell of smoke in the air but no light and no sound save the sleet hissing down.

Before him were the ruins of many buildings: a corner of a wall here, and there a standing chimney. To his right was a tall keep, to the left the hulk of a tower loomed. The rain must have come less heavily here, for there were still icy drifts in sheltered places. It was late afternoon, the light fading, the sleet turning to snow. Llian was utterly exhausted, saturated and freezing, the cold creeping into the core of him, filling him with lethargy. He sat down for a while in the snow and it did not feel cold any more. Blood was trickling into his eye again, the bandage lost somewhere in the rain. He pressed his hand to the wound and stumbled off toward the tower.

Adjoining was a hall with part of its roof still standing, but the rain had streamed in through holes of every shape and size, so that it was scarcely more sheltered than outside. The smoke smell was stronger here. As he dragged himself down the hall he spied an anteroom on his right, at the end. A faint glow came from inside, and a welcoming aroma of stew. He reached up to the doorway and saw that a door still swung on brass hinges. Llian brushed the blood from his eye and pushed the door. The hinges whined and the door swung open. A small woman leapt up from beside the fire, feeling at her hip. Her hand came up empty, then she sprang sideways, snatched a knife from the hearth and held it out in front of her.

"My name's Llian." Her eyes widened in disbelief and the knife fell to her side. "I've come to save you." He caught his foot on a broken step, stumbled and crashed to the floor at her feet. His head struck stone and the lights went out.

PART TWO

14

THE CELLS OF FIZ GORGO

The guard flung Maigraith into the cell. She skidded across a slimy floor, cracking her knee painfully against a bench of stone. The door crashed closed. She clung to the bench in the darkness, trying to will away the pain and the fear. She was prisoner in Fiz Gorgo, prisoner of Yggur. Karan had fled with the Mirror hours before; she was utterly alone.

Holding Yggur was the hardest thing that she had ever done. Maigraith still did not understand how she had held him all those hours. With Karan's link supporting her it had just been bearable; without, it had nearly broken her. But the greater the power used, the worse the aftersickness. The pain in her head was so bad now that she wanted to shriek, to batter her head against the stone until something broke. It felt as though crystals as long and sharp as needles were growing behind her eyes, needle balls spreading out from each of those points, impaling, interlocking.

All at once she felt dizzy. Then her head whirled violently, the needles behind her eyes grew as hot as candle flames, her stomach roiled and she slipped forward underneath the bench and retched, over and over again, into the dank moldy space until her throat burned and she could retch no more. The aftersickness had never been this bad before.

Maigraith roused. She was thirsty, and so cold. They had taken her pack but she still had the water bottle. Her fingers were so weak that just to prise the stopper out made her heart pound, and her shaking hand slopped water down her front. There was enough left for a good draught, and a little remained to wash her face.

Maigraith measured the bench with her fingers. It was long but narrow, the stone rough on the sides but smooth on top, as if it had been waxed. That was a grim thought—how many years or centuries had other prisoners huddled here, for the grease of their bodies to bring the stone to this silky state? She put the thought away, levered herself onto the bench and sat down. Her eyes could now make out the bare details of the room: four walls, the outer one slightly curved, her bench and a tiny high slit of a window. It was dawn.

She lay down on the bench, shivering, willing her mind to become blank, the way she had been taught, but she could not. One scene played over and over again—Yggur stooping down, Karan's pale terrified face, herself trying to help but failing. Then Yggur's *command,* and Karan's choked whisper, *"Faelamor."* Then Karan had broken the link and fled.

Over and again Maigraith saw the agony on Karan's face. Over and over she saw the potency of Yggur, the fury that bent Karan like a sapling in a tempest. Yet underneath, most curious, the puzzled way he looked at her. Maigraith groped for a meaning, but could not find one.

Maigraith stared at the dim, stained ceiling of her cell,

sick with her failure and fearful for Karan. How badly she had treated her. What could Karan do alone? Perhaps she had already been taken; perhaps she was already dead. She imagined them dragging her, heaving her broken onto a great pile of filth for the vermin to scuttle over . . . Her mind shied away from the images.

Maigraith looked back on the long journey from the east, the difficult way through the swamps to Fiz Gorgo, to her last brief meeting with Faelamor.

"Go alone into Fiz Gorgo," Faelamor had said. "And tell no one of me. No one!"

But Faelamor's secret had been revealed to Yggur, and because of it his armies would soon march on the east. What other disasters would flow from the betrayal? How could she tell Faelamor?

If only she had not delayed. Why *had* she stood there staring at the Mirror for so long? It had called to her so powerfully that nothing else mattered. She knew, as soon as she held it in her hands, that it would change her life. Why her? But the Mirror was gone as well.

The light grew in the room, seeping from a slit near the ceiling. Presently a rectangular patch of sunlight appeared on the opposite wall. It showed a small room with bare stone walls, a stone floor and a thick door of aged wood reinforced with iron. There was nothing else; not even a water jug, toilet bucket or blanket. Everything was damp and covered in mold, save for a patch around the window where the mold was replaced by a green growth.

Maigraith took off her sodden boots and lay down on the bench again. She was freezing. Her clothes were still damp from the cistern, though that was ten hours ago. She had not eaten for almost a day, nor slept for two. Her head throbbed abominably. She was filled with a sick feeling of failure. Her mission was in tatters. Much worse, Faelamor's long-kept secret was betrayed. In her mind's eye she saw the cold, mask-like beauty of Faelamor, the look in her eyes worse than any anger; the look that told Maigraith of her own worthlessness.

She was right about me—I do not deserve her. If I had set out to ruin all her long-laid plans I could not have hoped to achieve so much, she thought, and abandoned herself to misery.

The day passed and night fell; still there had been no sign that anyone cared about her existence. Each moment she expected a thump on the door: Yggur coming to interrogate her. Did he prolong the waiting just to torment her? But Yggur was far away, directing the search of the tunnels and, later, along the shores of the estuary. Maigraith could wait.

Maigraith was unable to sleep. She had hardly slept since leaving Lake Neid, and though exhausted would not sleep now. She paced the cell, four steps across, four steps back, four steps and four and four. When the shivering stopped she lay down again, but her feet were still icy and the cold soon seeped back up her legs. So she had passed the day, and now the evening. Within her was a vast emptiness.

In the middle of the night, without warning, the door banged open. The man standing there was extremely gaunt, with an angular face and long graying hair—a Whelm. He beckoned. Maigraith sat up slowly, shielding her eyes from the glare.

"I am Japhit," he said, in a voice that was like sand rubbing against steel. "Come!"

Maigraith reached for her boots.

"You will not need them," rasped Japhit, gripping her arm just above the elbow. His bony fingers were hard and cold. He led her down many flights of steps and into a large room without windows but brightly lit by lamps on the walls. The room was as cold as hers had been and smelled of damp. There was wood in a large fireplace but the fire was not lit.

Inside were two more Whelm, a man and a woman, both with sharp faces like the first. In the center of the room three short benches were arranged to form a square open at one end. The woman led Maigraith to the center of the square.

"Sit!" she said.

Maigraith sat down on the cold floor. The three Whelm sat on the benches, staring down at her. The woman was thin and bony like Japhit, with a narrow prominent nose as sharp and curving as the blade of an axe, and long gray hair. All had skin of a pallid gray, akin to the skin of a fish. In spite of the cold the woman wore sandals, the straps criss-crossing up her legs, and Maigraith saw that she had narrow ugly feet, the bones visible beneath the skin and the veins. Her toes were long and thin but fleshy at the tips. Just to look at her put Maigraith on edge, as though something about her, about *them,* was not quite right.

Finally their gaze became unendurable, and she looked down. The woman spoke. "Your name is Maigraith?" Her voice grated, like Japhit's voice, but her face was harder still.

She nodded.

"Why have you come here?"

Maigraith did not answer; the question was repeated. Again she said nothing. The three Whelm moved as one along their benches, their collective will enveloping her, cutting off all her senses, stifling her. Her heart was thudding wildly. Her mouth was dry.

"Water, please," Maigraith said hoarsely.

"When you have answered our questions you may drink," said the woman.

"Who was your accomplice?" asked Japhit. "What is her destination?"

Maigraith did not respond. She felt that if she once began to speak to them she would not be able to stop.

"How did you get into Fiz Gorgo?" asked another. No answer.

"Who sent you?" It was the woman again.

"Why does your master want the Glass?"

"Glass?" Maigraith asked.

"The Mirror of Aachan," cried the woman. "Why does your master want it?"

Maigraith sat mute while their questions beat against her. Already she feared them more than Yggur. She sensed a little humanity in him, but here there was none.

"Who are you? What is your business with me?" Maigraith gasped. She felt she was choking.

"We are Whelm. I am Vartila. Yggur is our master. We do his will in all things."

The stifling blanket of their will, which had given slightly, returned stronger than before, and with it came a feeling that they were probing her mind, that their questions were only part of the interrogation. An icy pulse came and went in her temples.

The questioning continued for a long time, and though she did not yield, to Maigraith it seemed that the Whelm were growing, while she was shrinking into the hard floor. They were tireless. She was so thirsty that she could barely speak. She could scarcely think, for the menace of the Whelm filled her whole mind: images of torment, and their delight in it. No, not delight, satisfaction! That was what struck her so oddly. As though they knew not right or wrong, only how best to do their master's will. As though they took no pleasure in torment, save where it advanced their master's purpose. Their faces might have been cut from agate, so little did they show.

As the hours passed the probing pressure intensified until her whole head was a network of pain, leaving no room for thought. And yet, no one had so much as touched her.

Sometime after noon of the second day since her capture, another Whelm came into the room. For a moment they all drew away. She did not hear the message but it was evident that the news was bad, for once the messenger had gone she heard them speaking among themselves.

"It is a dangerously weak master that we have," said Japhit, looking gaunter and older than before.

"Yes, but what can we do? Without a master we are nothing," replied another.

"We must be strong," said Vartila. "We can delay no longer with this one," and they came back to her and resumed their positions on the benches.

Japhit reached across and put the flat of his hand on her throat. He drew his fingers slowly downwards. The touch left trails of fire and ice that spread in all directions and faded but slowly. The pressure, the probing, swelled again, and now there began inside her an awful, diseased chuckling. The Whelm did not so much as glance at each other. Her skin shivered, as though some parasite was feeding on her, its pulpy body bloating within her. She retched, so powerful was the sense of loathsomeness that came upon her, but her stomach was empty.

In a submerged corner of herself smoldered an anger at the abuse; it began to grow, slowly in the beginning, then with a rush, swelling until she could no longer contain it.

Without warning—without even thought—it burst forth: Maigraith thrust her hand at Japhit, her fingers spreading like the petals of a flower, and abandoning the warnings and checks that had been part of her long training, she directed the full force of her pain-sharpened mind at him.

The Whelm stopped in the middle of a word, went still as a statue, then red blotches sprang out all over his face and he toppled backwards onto the floor. His face was wracked by his agony, and his arms wrapped and unwrapped themselves around his body, over and over again.

Too much strength, too late, thought Maigraith. Another of my failings.

The other two did not move. The man was pale, his knuckles white where he gripped the bench. Vartila had risen in a half-crouch, smiling a phantom smile. Maigraith found it profoundly disturbing.

"Jark-un must know of this," said Vartila to the man. "Ask him to come here, if he will."

"He is not back yet."

"Then call him as soon as he returns. This one bothers me—she is too strong. We must know who sent her. It may be easier to break the other."

Just then the door slammed. Yggur stood there, dominating the room, impossibly tall. He wore a heavy cloak, a tall gray hat, to the edge of which still clung a few drops of moisture, and high boots thick with black mud.

"I will . . . take her now," he said softly, in his halting way. "Bring her to my workroom."

"But master . . ." Vartila began, then stopped and turned away.

Maigraith stumbled into the room, exhausted from the long climb, the aftersickness full on her again. Yggur spoke to her but she could barely hear him, could not even see him until he came close. She huddled on the floor, swaying, looking up at the towering blur, aware only of her thirst and the terrible pain in her head.

"Water," she croaked. "Please give me some water."

Yggur squatted painfully, examining her face. He flushed and she flinched away, afraid that he was going to strike her. He heaved himself up with a groan and limped over to the doorway, pulling the cord that hung there.

A servant appeared almost immediately. Yggur said something to him that Maigraith did not hear and pulled the cord again. A second servant appeared as quickly as the first and the two bore her away to a set of chambers nearby. There they bathed her in glorious hot water, took her filthy clothes and brought clean ones.

Afterwards, they led her back to the main room and served her food and drink at a small table with black carved legs, beside a fire. The food was the simplest of fare: pickled fish, steamed vegetables and coarse bread, with lasee, the weak yellow brewed drink that was served with every meal in Orist. Maigraith was so thirsty that she drank two bowls. The two servants stood by the door as she ate, watching her all the while. When she was finished they took her back to Yggur's chambers and sat her down on a couch drawn up to one side of a freshly lit fire, another bowl at her elbow. Yggur was not there. Beside the fire she felt clean and warm for the first time since they had entered the swamps of Orist, and she was more afraid than ever. The lasee, weak though it was, had made her drowsy, but she sat bolt upright on the couch.

Shortly Yggur returned, now wearing a long woolen shirt and thick trousers over gray boots. The servants withdrew. He pulled up a chair on the other side of the fire. The fury was gone now, or hidden, and Yggur's long, strong face was calm, almost amiable. Maigraith did not know how to deal with this. For all her strength, she had little skill in reading people or understanding them, and could not see how to unravel this new complexity.

"You are a little better now?"

"Thank you," she responded, unsettled by the appearance of kindness.

"The Whelm are overzealous. I was occupied with the hunt."

Maigraith could scarcely believe what she was hearing. He was apologizing to her?

"What have you done with Karan?" she asked.

Yggur drew his chair closer to hers, looking into her eyes. He seemed to be looking for something, and once again seemed puzzled by what he saw there. She shivered and drew back.

Yggur spoke quickly now, his impediment barely evident. "I have no more time. Who is Karan, and where has she taken the Mirror?"

Could Karan have escaped? It was barely credible. Maigraith averted her gaze. The cunning of Yggur was legendary, but rumor had never made him considerate or kind. He was capable of any sort of trickery, and her best defense was to say nothing at all.

"I will tell you nothing," she said.

He asked his questions again and again, patiently, even tried his will on her, as he had done before, but not a word would she say. Once only did a rage take him, and he raised his fist and dashed her cup off its little table. Yellow liquid ran down the wall. "Speak," he shouted, raising his fist again, but yet her eyes defied him. And somehow she knew that the rage was a calculated rage, an assumed rage, even a good-humored one, so different from the blind fury of before. What had changed him so?

Finally Maigraith was too weary even to sit up. Yggur called the servants, who carried her back to a small room with a bed. They took off her clothes while she stood silently, her eyes already closed, then Maigraith crept between the cold sheets.

The door opened without a sound and Yggur came in, carrying a hooded lantern. She was right to mistrust him. It was rage that impelled him down the corridor to Maigraith's room, though he did not show it. Fury at the loss of the Mirror, so central to his long-term plans, and the thought that in her utter weariness he might find a way to break her. He had long used the Mirror to spy out his enemies' defenses. But, hidden within it, Yggur was sure, was a much more crucial secret, a way to overcome the limitations of distance that bound the overlords of Santhenar within their petty kingdoms. A way to right the great wrong that had been done to him. Yggur was motivated not only by lust for revenge, a lesser and a greater, but also by a vision—to unite all Meldorin, even all Santhenar, in the knowledge that he was fittest to do so. The lesser revenge was the first stepping stone. Uniting Santhenar would permit the greater revenge—for that he might need all that the world could provide.

But Yggur was impelled by more than just rage—curiosity too, and puzzlement. Something had passed between them during the long hours that they had striven against each other, before she had been beaten down. Perhaps something of Maigraith's loneliness and pain found an echo in his own. Or perhaps it was a half-recognition of what she was, or might become, that made him want to know more.

He set the lantern down on the floor beside the bed and perched himself on a chair, just looking at her. In repose Maigraith was relaxed as she never was when awake, and he felt a compelling urge to reach out and stroke her cheek, though he did not.

Maigraith stirred, forcing her unwilling eyes open against the glare of the lantern. So tired was she that it was almost a minute before she realized where she was, then instantly the tension pulled her face into its familiar desolate expression.

What has Faelamor done to you? he wondered. Why has she so tormented you? Maigraith aroused strange feelings in him—feelings that he had not felt before in all his long life. Who was she? Why did she have this sudden hold over him? What guile did she use?

Maigraith sat up. Pulling a blanket around her shoulders against the cold, she retreated to the far side of the narrow bed. She forced herself to meet his gaze, her thoughts viscous from sleep. The yellow lantern light flickered, giving his face a look of added menace. His eyes were pools of darkness from which only a stray gleam escaped.

When he spoke his voice seemed overloud in the silent night, echoing off the hard walls. "Why does Faelamor want the Mirror?"

"Read the Histories," she snapped.

"I do," said Yggur mildly. "But Faelamor is thought dead these hundreds of years, and the Faellem vanished. Where has she come from? Why now? And where do you spring from with such great strength and unknown purpose?"

"I merely serve her. I have no purpose, only duty."

Yggur gave her an odd look. "I can scarcely believe you. Your way is not her way—you are not Faellem."

His words made Maigraith uncomfortable; he had touched on a taboo. "I will not speak about her."

"Then what of your friend? Karan, was it?"

So you *haven't* found her. Maigraith permitted herself the ghost of a smile. "She is of the house of Fyrn, in Bannador."

"Ah," said Yggur. "Fyrn? A most unstable family; cursed

with madness. And she is so young. This could break her mind. Do you not fear for your friend?"

Maigraith looked away, afraid to speak. How did he know so much? "You do not know her," she said wistfully. "She looks young, and she makes a joke of what she cares about, but there is steel in her. She knows the wrinkles of the world. You will never catch her." Even to herself the boast sounded thin. Why was she talking like this to him, her enemy? How had he so disarmed her?

In spite of himself Yggur was touched by her distress, her defense of Karan. He reached across the bed and took her face between his hands. His touch was surprisingly gentle, but she could not forget his earlier rage.

Neither saw the door move fractionally, or the watcher. It was Vartila. Her agate face flowed, showed a furious anger, recrystalized to agate and she was gone.

Yggur looked into Maigraith's eyes. "Which way did she go? To the sea? East, toward Lake Neid? Ah, I see it in your eyes. She has gone to Neid. She is meeting someone there, perhaps?"

Again Maigraith's eyes betrayed her—could she conceal nothing from him? She was too tired. She sank her head on her arms, trying to shut him out, dreading the next question.

"One last question. Where is Karan to meet Faelamor?" Maigraith did not answer. She willed herself not to answer, not to even think of Sith. But Yggur was suddenly behind her, at the head of the bed, his long fingers covering her face, her eyes.

"Where?" he whispered again; again his will scorched her. She thought that she would faint. His fingers were gentle but his strength was as a rod of iron, smashing her down. "Let me guess." His voice was barely audible, though his thin lips were at her ear. "Always the Faellem dwelt in the far south-east. But it would be too risky to carry it all that way. She will be in Meldorin, but near to the sea. Thurkad perhaps?

Maigraith could not prevent an involuntary relaxation.

"Not Thurkad. Vilikshathûr? Alcifer—hardly! Gnulp? No, too far away. Of course—not on the sea, but close to it, and on the great River Garr!" Her eyelids flickered slightly, silkily against his fingers. "Ahhh! Sith! You can sleep now. That is all I need to know."

Yggur gazed at her a moment longer, at her bare shoulders, the dark hair covering her beautiful sad face, then abruptly he rose, collected his lantern and went out, the door clicking softly behind.

She sank slowly down into the bed, pulling the covers tightly around her, shivering. She would sleep no more tonight. All her efforts had been for nothing, and all her training. The lack of sleep had broken her.

There was but one consolation: two days had passed since Karan had fled into the tunnels. But when Yggur came in last night his boots had been covered in mud from the estuary, for she had smelled the sea on him. So Karan had got out of Fiz Gorgo. She must do something to help her. She must make some diversion, little though it might be.

Maigraith dressed herself quietly in the dark, eased open the door and looked out. Across the room, in the far doorway, there was a shadow. She crept nearer, praying that it was not a Whelm. It was not, merely a servant. The man had his back to her. Now he stirred, scratched his back and went into the other room. She withdrew into the darkest corner. Shortly the man returned to his post. Her bare feet made no noise. She struck him on the nape of the neck and dragged him to a corner. Was there another? Not in the room; perhaps outside. She put her ear to the door, but could hear nothing. She tensed, jerked the door open, ready to strike the guard down, but there was no one there.

Maigraith hesitated, knowing she did not yet have the strength to get away. Not yet. She made her way to Yggur's rooms nearby. They were lit only by a glimmer from the grate. She ghosted in, surveying the room carefully. He was not there, though his presence lingered. The long table attracted her attention, covered as it was with maps and papers. She took up the topmost map, which showed the lands of eastern Meldorin, from the mountains to the Sea of Thurkad. The map was marked in many places. She held it up to catch the light, and a cold hand caught her wrist from behind and held her. Her flesh crawled again, and she almost screamed in fear and disgust.

"This time we will finish our little talk," said Vartila, and led her away.

15

NOT WHAT HE HAD EXPECTED

The shabby, battered figure at Karan's feet *was* Llian, though much diminished from the great teller she had admired before. Yet his voice, even the preposterous statement, was like a caress. How had he got here without her sensing him? How did he come to be here at all? Could her formless dreams and longings have really fetched him so far from his comfortable teller's life? It was not possible—she had never had power of that sort. It must be coincidence, but what coincidence could bring him all the way up here? What an honor for her!

Llian groaned and shivered. Blood welled out of his forehead. She heaved him over on his back with one arm, for her other wrist still throbbed at the slightest exertion. Llian's skin was freezing. He was battered and bruised and drenched. He might die of the cold, and it would be her fault.

Karan built up the fire till it roared, exhausting her whole stock of wood, then stripped him down to his underpants. She felt as though she was handling a sacred object. His skin was almost as smooth and pale as hers, she noticed with admiration, though badly bruised and lacerated from chest to hip. She rubbed him dry with one of her shirts, chafed his limbs with her hands until he was warm and she was sweating, and wrapped him in a blanket by the fire. The color began to come back into his face.

Karan looked in his pack for dry clothing but everything was saturated. She strung a bit of rope in front of the fire and hung his garments there, so close that they steamed and scorched, the only way to get them dry tonight.

She tried to work out how this had come about. The last week had been one of her worst, climbing the steep path in the snow. Her broken wrist had knitted badly and ached constantly. She had kept herself going with a fantasy about the great chronicler, when she'd been able to think. No romantic nonsense—just someone she could talk over her dilemma with, one to tell her the Histories of Faelamor and Yggur, Mendark and even Tensor, to give her what she needed to make the right decision about the Mirror. She was obsessed with that decision. It had to be right—that was more important than any duty to Maigraith, or to the Aachim.

But what had she expected, when her sending touched someone last night? She had sensed that help was near, but not *how* near, not *where*; certainly not *who* it was. What had she been thinking of, those times she'd called him? She tried to remember. The first sending, more than a week ago, had been just something her dreams made out of inner longings. But in the second, the one that had fetched him here from Tullin last night, she *had* called for help, *had* begged him to hurry, and here he was. What was she to do with him now? He might have a wonderful talent but clearly he couldn't take care of himself. *I've come to save you,* indeed!

*   *   *

Llian groaned and opened his eyes. He was on the floor in front of the fire. The red-haired woman squatted beside him with a mug of hot water and a rag, dabbing at the cut over his eye. Llian flinched and moaned. His head ached. Every breath sent a sharp pain through his side. She got up abruptly, rummaged in a pack beside the bench and returned with a little soapstone jar. Opening it awkwardly, she smeared brown salve on the cut, stuck a pad of cloth to it and tied a fresh bandage around his head, using one hand and her teeth to pull the knot tight. She made no attempt to be gentle. Then she sat back on her haunches, staring at him.

Aching head and bleary eyes reduced her to the sketch of a face—red pen squiggles her tangled hair, eyes a splash of jade. No, richer and deeper than jade—her eyes were green as the malachite columns in the hall of his college. He tried to sit up. It hurt. He blinked away the tears. She bent down and wiped smears of blood from his cheek. Her features were so neat they might have been engraved, quite unlike his own untidy face. Curves of cheek and brow in single strokes, delightfully rounded, the whole set off by a small scar above her eyebrow. Her hair had a faint familiar perfume, like crushed lime leaves. Jacket and trousers gray-green; right wrist bandaged, the bandage weather-stained, arm in a sling. She fitted the description, but seemed too young. And there was something else vaguely familiar about her. What was it?

She was quite charming in a funny sort of way, he thought, and had she been a bit older and a bit taller and her hair any color but that awful red he might have found her attractive. What accident of fate had mixed her up in such a business? She looked so young that no one could take her seriously. "Karan?" he asked doubtfully.

She stared at his face. One word, but it showed the magic

of his voice. "What am I to do with him?" she enquired of the ceiling in a voice that was gentle and low, and to his discomfort just a little bit amused. "If *this* is the fruit of my sending it is a most unripe one."

She chuckled, a mellow gurgling sound. The past month and more of flight, pursuit, dreams and nightmares, had changed her: here was a leaner, harder Karan than the one who had crept into Fiz Gorgo so timidly. Her small round face was pale as ever, for she did not tan, but her nose and cheeks were chapped from wind and sun, and she looked worn and weary. Yet she had not entirely lost her sense of humor.

She spoke with a Thurkad accent, that broad and slightly nasal intonation that was really no accent at all, since Iagador and indeed the whole of the island of Meldorin revolved around that great city. But in her speech the accent was modified—less broad, less nasal; traveled, schooled. Enriched with something of the speech of the alps of Bannador, as in the lengthened vowels: "most" that came out as "moost". This Llian knew after a few words, master of accents and dialects that he was. Yet her speech was overlaid with another accent, another pattern, a lilt that hinted of speaking verse. He could not identify where it came from, and it vexed him. Her apparent lack of appreciation, her disrespectful amusement, were further irritants.

"Are you really Karan? I was expecting . . . I thought you'd be older."

The grin disappeared. Karan looked hurt and insulted, that someone she so looked up to could not take her seriously. "I'm twenty-four," she said in a defensive voice, and immediately regretted it.

"Have we met before?"

"No, we haven't *met.*"

She had not expected that he would remember her. Why

should he, among the thousands that had heard his tellings? Nonetheless it hurt a little bit.

"Well, I've come to take you to Thurkad."

Karan was amazed. He struggled to his feet, then a shocking pain came, like a spike being hammered into his side, and he would have fallen had she not caught him across her good shoulder. The scorn on her face faded momentarily, for he was in great pain, helpless and more lost even than she. She made allowances. What manner of creature is this, she marveled. Maybe his hurts make him say such silly things!

Llian's face suddenly went as gray as parchment. He pressed his hand to his side. Swaying under his weight she pushed him backwards until his knees came up against the bench, then let him down with a thump.

"Aahhh!" he cried, lifting himself off the seat.

"What's the matter?"

"It's . . . my bottom."

She raised an eyebrow.

"Some lunatic threw a rock at me," he muttered. "I went the wrong way and this half-naked madman—"

Karan burst out laughing. "A fine comedy. The great chronicler's dignity wounded by Alus the hermit. I presume you don't want me to check . . . No? Let's have another look at your side."

She drew the blanket apart and probed his side with her fingertips, picking out a few small pieces of slate embedded there. "You've broken a few ribs. I'll try to ease them back in place, but it'll hurt—I'm no healer." She took her hand out of the sling, using her fingers awkwardly. He caught the enchanting lime aroma again.

It was a painful operation, and after that there was the wound to clean, the bits of cloth and grit to be picked out. He flinched at every touch, and by the end of it her pity was turning to irritation, so loud and frequent were his groans. Now it was dark. She banged the door closed and wedged it, and pushed the fire sticks together. From a small black pot she filled two mugs and handed one to Llian, saying, "Have some soup. It's hot, if nothing else." She sat back and looked at him, feeling a little sorry for him, a little amused by him, but guilty at whatever she had done to bring him here.

Llian, although ravenous, regarded the offering dubiously. It was green, with an oily scum on the surface. A sip confirmed his suspicions. The soup appeared to be based on dried peas and rancid fat, flavored with bitter herbs. "Delicious!" he murmured, trying not to gag. But it was hot, and nothing else really mattered.

"It's all I have left," she said.

Llian indicated his pack. "I brought food for the journey."

Again she stared at him, as though he were a great incongruity.

Llian suddenly remembered why he was here. "There are Whelm down in the ravine. I saw them just before the storm."

"I know. I can sense them now, when they're near. They won't get up tonight—the path will be too icy. Still, I must be gone before dawn. But where can I go?" She looked away, trying to hide her uncertainty. "And what to do with *you* I cannot imagine." She scowled. "What can *you* do?"

Llian was disconcerted. This was not going as he had planned. "I know the Histories rather well," he began foolishly.

Karan laughed, her mouth crinkling up at the corners in a most engaging way. There was magic in his voice even when his words were empty, and she had to force herself to resist it. "What will you do when the Whelm come?" she snorted. "Tell them a tale?"

He sat up a bit straighter. He spoke more boldly than he

really felt, using a little bit of the *voice*. "You're safe now," he said soothingly, as one would speak to a child. "I'm going to take you across the pass to Bannador, and then to the Magister."

Her green eyes narrowed to hard slits. Was he less of a fool than he looked, or more? Her voice was still gentle but there was no warmth in it anymore. "I do not go to Thurkad. Anyway they're between us and the pass. How did you plan to get there?" Perhaps he knew some way that she did not.

The vain hope was dashed. "South through the mountains, I suppose, then east."

"Have you ever been up here before?"

"Not this high," he replied. "But . . ."

"It's coming winter. So far the big snows have held back, but they'll come any day. The next pass is thirty leagues and more to the south, the way the track winds; in snow and ice that could take fifteen days—or fifty. You couldn't even carry enough food."

"We could go back to Chanthed."

"And what would the Whelm be doing?"

"We could hide until they went away."

"Perhaps if you were to instruct me in the making of wings I could fly to safety."

"I was trying to help."

"I haven't got the strength for this," she said irritably. "Go back where you came from." She stood up abruptly and walked away to the fire.

He ignored her. "I think we should—" he said, reflecting.

Not only was he a fool—he didn't even listen! Karan turned back bitterly disappointed. Her foolish dreams of him were humiliating to recall.

"You live in a dream world," she said deliberately. "Your Histories were made to entertain the toothless while they swill their slops. Romantic tales are all they are, and your help is just as worthless."

Llian looked bewildered. This was nothing like he had imagined, or was used to. "The Histories are truth!" he cried. "The best truth that we can recover from the past, and the foundations of our culture."

"Go away," she shouted. "I don't want you. You're useless." The message sank in at last. Llian cried out and covered his face with his hands. Then he got up and wavered his way to the door in his blanket. Karan could scarcely believe what she was seeing. "Not now, you imbecile—tomorrow, or the next day, when you are better."

Llian turned at the new order and staggered back to his seat. His progress was too painful to watch. Karan went outside to calm herself, torn between laughter and despair. How to manage such a one? A few minutes later she peeped around the door and saw that he was sitting on the bench, staring down at the floor. He looked absolutely miserable and Karan's soft heart was moved. She should not have been so rude; after all, she had called him here. She marched back in and took him in hand.

"*You* are going back to Tullin, and I am going on alone. Come now, lie down and get some rest." She took the pot from the fire and rinsed it out, flinching at the pain in her wrist, filled it with water from a cracked stone jar on the hearth and put it on to boil.

Shortly Llian was slumped before the fire, wrapped in his blanket again. Karan turned his clothes, which were scorching. She made tea with a pinch of herb, tapped the side to settle the leaves and poured the green liquid into mugs. Llian wrapped his fingers gratefully around the hot metal, perhaps thinking that the offer of tea signaled a truce. A thought came to him.

"Last night you seemed so desperate. I really felt for you. Yet today . . ."

Karan weakened a little. "It's nearly two months since I fled Fiz Gorgo, and I've been hunted all the way. Every time I lose them something leads them back to me. Yesterday I hid in the snow, without a fire, and my enemies were so close I could sense them, when the pain was very strong. Finally they gave up for the night but it was a terrible one; one of the worst I've had. I gave way to my weakness. My call was a fantasy, a dream. I did not imagine for an instant that you were close by, that you would come."

Llian regarded her through the steam from his cup. There had seemed more than Karan in that dream sending, more even than the Whelm. Who was that other, greater figure? Yggur, trying to get back his Mirror? He sipped his tea. It tasted of the bitter herb in the soup. Karan sat cross-legged in front of the fire, staring into the flames, rocking slowly back and forth. In her left hand she still held the stick and was drawing absently on the stone with the burnt end.

"What happened in Fiz Gorgo?"

"Yggur came back too soon. Maigraith had the strength to hold him, but not to escape herself. I did what I was told; I fled."

"I didn't know there were two of you. Who do you serve?"

"You are too curious. You appear out of nowhere and expect me to trust you. I don't. I did not ask for your help. You're arrogant and I don't think I like you very much. I'm going on, and I go alone. The stream will have fallen in a day and you can go back to Tullin."

Llian went red with mortification. Perhaps he had thought she would change her mind. Karan felt the tiniest morsel of pity for him then, for his face was so open that he must be genuine. And after all, he had come all this way to help her, whatever his motives.

"What can I do?" she said as kindly as she could. "You are hurt worse than I am, and you don't know the mountains. You are kind and soft. I was like that myself once. You don't belong up here."

"But you have no food, and you are hurt as well. You cried out for help."

"I did, but not yours," she said. "I'll pay you for what spare food you have. You won't need it, save for tomorrow. Rest now. You can best help me by delaying them. Even an hour will help." She lapsed into silence, staring into the fire again.

Llian turned onto his good side on the stone bench and pondered his situation. Why should he go on? He couldn't force her, nor wanted to. He would have to pay his debt to Mendark some other way. But he wanted to see the Mirror very badly. And learn the tale of it, and her tale too.

Lost in these thoughts, it was a while before he noticed that Karan had quietly gone out, leaving the door ajar. Outside the wind whistled in the ruined roof. Every now and then a gust swept in, sending the fire leaping and scurries of sparks across the room. Llian looked around. Her small pack lay in a corner. Perhaps that was where she kept the Mirror. Temptation beckoned. He sat up too hastily; pain stabbed through his side, so sharp that he cried out. Now was not the time.

That was a good decision for, a minute later, the door was kicked wide and Karan lurched in backwards, dragging a large branch. She heaved it through the door and dropped it in the middle of the floor. There was snow in her hair.

She hacked off several smaller branches with a hatchet, broke them into pieces and cast them onto the fire. She poked the thick end of the branch in for good measure, the remainder extending across the hearth into the middle of the room.

Llian slumped on the bench. He felt utterly demoralized and useless. Not since he was sent away as a child from home and family had he felt such emptiness and despair. Had she not been staring at him he might have burst into tears.

It was snowing heavily outside now. Llian lay in an exhausted sleep. He was wrapped in a gray blanket, one bare foot sticking out the end, and Karan's coat under his head for a pillow. Karan sat on her pack in front of the fire, watching the patterns of light and shadow on the wall. Every so often she got up and pushed the thick end of the branch further into the fire, then sat down and resumed her deliberations.

If she could just cross the pass into Bannador she would feel safe, but one way to the pass was cut off by the Whelm and the other by the flooded stream. How, after all this time, had she allowed them to drive her into this trap? And what were they planning now? Would they try and catch her unawares in the dawn, or lie in wait as she made her way back down to the pass? Was there a way to make use of this gift that had come so unexpectedly?

Llian rolled over in his sleep and groaned. Even in his sleep he looked lost and miserable. Why had someone with so little to offer spent so much of himself to find her? Or was it another trap? What would he do, if she slept?

The wind began to howl in the roof. Karan slipped out and walked down the ruined hall. The storm had passed and the sky above was clear, though more heavy cloud was coming up from the west. Inside the ruins the wind had piled the snow in deep drifts, fantastically shaped in the starlight. She waded through a shadowed drift and walked down to where a low stone wall ran along the cliffed edge of the plateau. The wind hissed through the dead grass, flinging gritty snow against her cheeks.

She sat behind the stone wall, partly sheltered from the wind. It was very cold. Llian of Chanthed. Llian the Zain. They say your voice is like the singing of angels. So it was when I heard you in Chanthed. When you tell the Great Tales, Rulke himself would weep; as I did, once. I was needlessly cruel to you tonight, but what else could I do? Your voice will not get me home. She could feel his charm working on her again, and tried to harden her heart the more.

The stars showed the tenth hour now. There was no sound save the hissing of the wind and the rustling leaves of a bush on the precipice. If I leave him it might delay them for half a day. Damn him! I didn't ask him to come. No, I'm being dishonest. That other night, and last night, I did call him. He answered and I was glad of it, so glad that it colored my whole day. Surely the Whelm will see how harmless he is.

No, they will tear him apart in case I told him something. Perhaps they would do it anyway, out of malice, thinking that he is my friend. I must take him under my protection. The thought made her snort. An ironic reversal that should amuse him too, since it is one of the tools of his trade. Oh, how am I become such a fool, to so burden myself? But how can I leave him to *their* mercy?

A rustle behind Karan made her jump and she cracked her injured wrist against the stone wall. She cried out, but it was only the wind scraping a twig against the rock face. She sat down again, cradling her wrist. The tears began to freeze on her cheek. It's no good. I must have help. But there is no one, only him.

Far below, in the vast bowl, the starlight caught a stretch of the river in a glittering ribbon of silver. Patches of snow and ice shone whitely, and here and there was a dark rumor of forest. The ridges leading back to Tullin were a broken, shadowy mass. The plateau stretched out of sight to east and west. Her gaze was caught by the towering bulk of Mount Tintinnuin, sheathed in snow and ice and with a banner of cloud breaking from its eastern tip.

She stared down into the bowl, trying to compose herself. The wrist began to throb. It had been healing, but now she felt the bones grate. As she looked down the cliff face she realized that something was moving below. But surely no one could climb this crag at night, in snow and ice?

Yes, there it was again, unmistakeable this time. Fifty spans below, no, less! Methodically, purposefully, a figure was scaling the precipice. Were there others? She scanned the cliff, but only the one was to be seen. As soon as he reached the top the smoke would give them away. No time to get away, with Llian not even dressed. But there was no good hiding place in the ruins either.

Karan made as though to run back to Llian, then stopped. Dropping to her knees she peered over the edge again. The figure was baffled by a smooth, projecting rock surface. It moved to left and right, indecisively; then, evidently finding a handhold, it resumed its steady progress. Now and again she saw the starlight glitter on its upturned eyes. She leaned out over the cliff. Karan was an excellent climber but she would not have attempted this climb without ropes and irons. She watched in admiration, astounded by his technique. The wind had died a little, although the climber's cape flapped behind him still, and she fancied she could hear his harsh breathing. He was scarcely a dozen spans below her now; she saw clearly his pale face and his bared teeth. Idlis!

She drew back suddenly from the edge, inadvertently putting her whole weight on her wrist. The pain galvanized her and she leapt up, looking around wildly for a weapon, not even thinking what she did. There was no branch or log nearby. Stones there were in plenty, fitted into the wall and lying on the ground in little heaps. She heaved wildly at first one, then another until her fingers bled, but it was no use. Even if she'd had the use of both hands, the blocks were too large. No, there was a broken one. She hefted up the smaller piece, about the size of her head, and hobbled over to the cliff, holding the rock awkwardly between arm and hip.

Idlis was scarcely three spans below. She remembered his skin blistering in the sun, and hesitated. He was terrifying, but human. She stood frozen into immobility while he climbed steadily. The light struck his eyes again, and they were cold.

Then he saw her and grinned, wolfishly. That shocked her. Human he was, and her enemy. Karan swung her body around, releasing the stone from her hip. The throw was true, but at the last moment Idlis twisted away to one side. The stone skimmed the side of his head, glanced off his shoulder and fell into the night. He swayed away from the cliff, holding on by a hand and a foot, his face twisted with pain.

For a moment Karan thought he would fall, could not believe that he clung there still after that blow; then he mastered himself, brushed his hand over his eyes as though to clear them, and resumed the climb. She stood there, appalled at what she had done, shocked at its lack of success. She fled.

After a minute or two she looked back, but the edge of the cliff was hidden. Now she climbed the ruined inner wall and scurried along it, bending low. Across the yard, a few hundred paces away, the wall was broken where it joined the hall. She made for that point and dropped noiselessly to the ground at the partly roofed end. The door of the anteroom was ajar, as she had left it. The room was lit only by a faint glow from the fireplace, but still was warmer than outside. The branch had gone out, leaving a scatter of ash and charcoal on the stone floor. Her pack was untouched and Llian lay as she had left him. She felt his forehead; he was slightly feverish. At her touch he flung his arm out and mumbled a few disconnected words. She stepped away and he went back to sleep.

Karan wedged the door with fragments of slate and roused the fire. The flames leapt up. She took up her little hatchet, settled back into a recess beside the door and waited. The wind moaned in the ruins. The fire crackled for a while, then grew silent. The night wore on.

16

FEAR OF HEIGHTS

Llian began to toss in his sleep, crying out in a strange voice. Karan laid her cool hand on his hot forehead until he grew still. The wind died away to a whisper. Only a faint glow now came from the fire. For a time there was absolute silence.

Then from outside there came a faint but unmistakable crunch, as of a piece of slate breaking underfoot. A pause. Then a scrape. He was at the door. He tested it. It yielded a little. Karan tensed.

A rush, a thud. The door smashed open. Idlis hurtled into the dimly lit room and crashed down the steps, struggling to keep his balance.

Llian leapt up with a cry of terror, became tangled with his sleeping pouch, and fell. Idlis threw himself on top of him in a frenzy and the two rolled over and over, striking blindly at each other. Llian cried out in pain.

Karan crept out from her recess and struck Idlis behind

the ear with the back of the hatchet. He fell on top of Llian without a sound. Karan threw wood on the fire and in its light bound the Whelm's hands and feet behind his back with cord. She stuffed bark in his mouth and awkwardly dragged him off the half-suffocated Llian to a corner. Her fingers cringed from the texture of the Whelm's skin.

Llian sat up, stunned by the violence of his awakening. Karan was standing over him, breathing heavily, with a wild look in her eyes. He tried to heave himself to his feet but his legs failed him. She held out her hand. He pulled himself up, walked unsteadily back to the bench and fell down again.

"You saved my life! I must have been asleep. Where did he come from?" He still had no idea what had happened.

"Up the cliff. He thought you were me."

Llian stared at her. "Why didn't you wake me?"

"I didn't think you could help. Now we've got to go. If he can scale the cliff in darkness and ice, the others might be close behind. You'll have to come with me."

Llian subsided.

"We can't talk here," she went on. "They might be able to get our speech from him." As she spoke she was repacking her bag. "How are you feeling?" she asked, looking over at him. "Better, I hope."

Llian tried a tentative smile. He felt awful. And yet, he wanted to go with her. "I'm much better now," he said as steadily as he could. "Something hot to eat and I'll be ready to walk all night."

Karan gave him a searching stare. She retrieved the pot from the fireplace, unwrapped something from her pack, cut off a lump and threw it in the pot. Water sizzled on the fire.

Llian dressed. The clothes were warm but still damp. His side was hurting terribly and there was a large bruise on his cheek. Karan had gone down on one knee beside Idlis and was feeling his head. Even in repose the Whelm's mouth had a brutal curve to it. He stared at the scarred face. The back of the head was bruised and bloody, and there was a large lump, rudely bound, on the side of his head above his eye. "How did he get that?" Llian wondered aloud.

"I dropped a rock on him while he was climbing the cliff," said Karan, with a curious expression. "He was lucky. Though perhaps he'll wish he hadn't been when the others get here. Here, drink this." She handed him a full mug.

Llian did not know what to think. All this had happened while he was asleep?

There was enough soup left over for another mug each. Llian picked bits of charcoal out of his mug, slurped the residue, wiped his mouth. Karan had her hand on the door.

"Are you just going to leave him there, to follow us again?"

"Would you kill a helpless man, even a Whelm? I cannot. What I did to him on the cliff was shameful enough." Three times now I've spared this one, she mused. In Bannador we would consider that an omen; and even for an enemy, a debt. Having had Idlis's life in her keeping, she felt a certain bond, a certain responsibility. As indeed she felt for Llian. Her life had suddenly become complicated and confining.

The wind had died. The rising moon in its last crescent shed barely any light. But it was still hours short of dawn. She turned to the west.

"Where are we going?"

"Back to the waterfall stream. Sometimes these mountain creeks fall as quickly as they rise."

But long before they got to it they could hear it roaring and grinding the stones of its bed. They found a sheltered place among the rocks for the short wait till sunrise, just to be sure. When it came, dawn was a steely-gray affair, for thick clouds racing in from the west had covered the whole sky. The river was still a black torrent.

"It's much higher than when I crossed," Llian said.

"Wait a bit; it must fall during the day."

Karan was trying to doze, cocooned in cloak and hat, while Llian kept watch. The light grew slowly, then suddenly came that indefinable moment when the world was more light than dark. He looked absently back toward the stream and was shocked to see two figures on the other side, not far upstream.

"Karan!" He shook her awake.

"Mmmm."

"There's two people on the other side, and they look like Whelm."

She was awake in a flash, rolling over and peering through the gap in the rocks. Her scalp crawled. They *were* Whelm, though not the ones hunting her lately. A man and a woman, both young. There had been five before Hetchet and now there were five again.

"They must have tracked me here," Llian fretted. "Several times I felt as though I was followed."

"It doesn't matter how they got here—they've found me plenty of times without you."

"It looks like he's going to cross."

The two Whelm clasped arms and then the man leapt high and landed on an outcrop that stuck up out of the water. Two more huge, awkward, scissoring leaps followed and he was halfway across. The river was twice as wide as when Llian had crossed. The woman called to him; he raised a hand, then sprang out. He churned the water to foam with clumsy but powerful wheeling strokes, both arms striking the water together, then was snatched under. Llian watched with mouth agape, reliving his own experience. An arm briefly cut the surface then was gone again. The woman stared at the water; a long way downstream the Whelm reappeared, still thrashing, and ran aground on rock. Soon he was out of the water. He lay on the shore for a moment, got up on shaky legs, waved to the woman once more and set off in the direction of the ruins.

She raised her arm to him and went unhurriedly back in the direction of the ridge.

"What a feat!" said Llian in admiration. "What a sight for a teller! Already I am putting it into a tale."

"Don't forget that he is our deadly enemy," said Karan coldly. "And she's gone to guard the way down."

"We wouldn't have got across today anyway."

"Not here," she agreed, "but we might have further up-stream. Now our only hope is to try and get past the other Whelm and go down the eastern way. And I don't have much hope there either."

"They will surely guard it too."

"Doubtless, though there is a second way down. At least there once was. It won't be easy to get to, though."

Light snow began to fall as they turned back, Karan aiming to pass the ruins well to the south, for fear that the Whelm were searching there already. So it proved to be, for they heard a hollow rumbling cry, like the cries that Karan had heard at Fiz Gorgo and in the swamps, as they went past in the concealing snowfall. Shortly it was answered by a more high-pitched, squealing call that put Llian's nerves on edge, for it reminded him of Gaisch and the knife at his throat.

"They must be looking for Idlis," he said with a shiver.

"Or else they've found him, and now they're after us."

They wallowed on through thickening snow, veering over to the very edge of the escarpment.

"What are we trying to do?" Llian muttered. "Whatever it is I don't like it."

Karan gave him a quick verbal sketch. "The ridge runs down off the plateau not far ahead, and along it a little way there is a gorge, just a slot really, where the waterfall stream cuts through. That's where the bridge used to be."

"I saw the gap on the way here."

"A path goes all the way down to the stream. You can cross there, when the river is not in flood. But there's also a very old track, made long before the bridge was built, I suppose, that runs up the other side of the ridge. I saw it yesterday but it was too late to start down. The Whelm may not know it's there. Here we are now."

Karan led Llian out onto the ridge, which ran steeply down in the general direction of Tullin. It was much wider than the one Llian had come up yesterday, for the top had been leveled to make the road to the bridge, in the time when the climate had been warmer and the lands around the ruins populous. The road was overgrown but blown almost free of snow and they made good progress. Like the escarpment below the ruins, the ridge was bounded by a cliff of red rock. Light snow drifted down. Out of the gloom two black stone piers loomed, squatting at the end of the ridge like ominous sentinels. They were all that remained of the stone bridge that had once spanned the gorge.

"The path goes down there, just beside the pillar," she said, pointing to the right one, "then winds its way down. We're in luck; they've left it unguarded."

Even as she spoke a tall Whelm stepped out from behind the pillar. It was Idlis, his head swathed in bloody bandages.

"Back," she cried. She whirled and ran back the other way, and Llian stumbled after, clutching his side. Looking back, Llian saw that Idlis had not moved. He remained, guarding the way down, evidently having strict orders not to leave his post. The snow whirled, blotting him out, then a great cry boomed out, echoing across the slopes and cliff faces of the valley. Karan snapped a leafy branch off a bush and brushed out their tracks.

"That won't gain us much," said Llian irritably, for the pain in his ribs was intense.

"He's calling them back," she replied, continuing on, and when they were well away from Idlis she turned into the windswept scrub and headed down the ridge toward the red cliff.

The old path was hard to find under its blanket of snow. Eventually Karan picked up what seemed to be the trail, a treacherous ledge cut into the red rock, covered in snow, ice and fallen stones. They crept carefully along the slippery track, Llian's fear of heights overwhelming the pain of his injuries. Now a long straight stretch of ledge lay ahead of them. It was narrow and sloped outwards. Idlis's call echoed around them once again. If he were to come to the edge and look down he would see them, for the snow had almost stopped.

"Come on," she cried, pulling Llian by the arm. "They can't be far away."

Llian started and tried to go a bit faster. He was increasingly afraid of falling. Ahead the ledge was glazed by an icy gel.

"Hurry," she called.

He stepped gingerly on the ice, his foot slipped, he put the other down hastily and his feet went from under him. Llian landed flat on his back, put his left arm out to brace himself and it flapped uselessly over the edge. He cried out, almost a scream of terror.

The fall pulled Karan to her knees, nearly wrenching Llian's wrist out of her hand. She slipped toward him. Afraid that she was going to knock him over, Llian cried out. Then she got the toe of her boot in a crack and it held. Karan reached back to the crack with her free hand, the weak one, and slowly pulled them to safety.

"I'm sorry, I'm sorry," cried Llian.

He flung his arms around her. After a moment she pushed him away, squeezing her bad wrist with her other hand, grimacing.

"Not your fault," she said. "I shouldn't have tried to hurry you. This path is more treacherous than I thought."

She checked the way ahead once more. The icy patch went for three or four paces and covered the whole of the ledge. Dangerous for her, but deadly for Llian.

"What if I go ahead and run the rope from here to there?"

Llian still didn't like it, but neither did he want to be a hindrance. "I suppose so," he said very tentatively.

"Good. Stay here." She tied the rope to a sturdy tree root, knotted the other end around her waist, then went forward slowly, making little cuts in the ice with her hatchet to improve her footholds. She reached the opposite side and tied the rope there too. "Can you manage it now?"

"I think so."

He gripped the rope like a lifeline and took a first shuffling step. Just then Idlis shouted again, loud and urgent, right above. Llian looked up and saw the Whelm staring down at them. Idlis looked back along the track, then down again. Karan's eyes followed the direction of his stare. The call was not answered, though that did not mean that no one was coming. Suddenly Idlis came to a decision—he put his shoulder to a boulder, one of a number near the edge. It wobbled.

"Llian," Karan called frantically, afraid to hurry him but knowing that he had only seconds to get across.

Llian took another couple of uncertain steps, then stopped with his foot outstretched. His eyes were locked on the boulder. Idlis strained, grunted and the boulder slowly revolved. Llian was frozen, sure that the rock was aimed directly at him. Had he run he would have got through but he just shuffled forward. The boulder began to topple.

"Go back," Karan screamed at the last moment and he flung himself backward just in time.

The boulder smashed down on the ledge right where he had been standing. Gravel stung his face and hands, the rock bounced away and fell. Eventually it struck far below and set off a landslide that rattled away for ages.

Llian was too shocked to stand; he crumbled to his knees, looking through the dust at Karan. The rope was gone and the ledge in front of him broken away for a couple of spans, revealing the raw irregular rock beneath. The wind swirled around the end of the ridge, chilling him. Snow began to fall, then a heavy flurry blotted out everything but the blood-colored rock.

Karan measured the gap. There was no chance of him getting across now, even if she went back and helped him. Why had he just stood there like a fool?

"Well, that's that," said Llian. "I'm stuck here, and nothing can be done about it. You'll have to go on without me!"

Karan's choice was agonizing. If she fled now they'd probably never catch her. In a few days she could be home in Bannador. Home! The temptation was overwhelming.

"Go on, I'll be all right. There's nothing you can do anyway."

She did not move.

Llian could not bear it. "Fare well," he called with a cheerfulness that he did not feel. Then, turning back to her, "Hey! I'll come to Bannador to see you and find the ending of the tale. Don't forget the least detail." And his beautiful voice cracked just a trifle. "I'll miss you, Karan," he said. "Be careful." He turned his back to her deliberately and started walking back the way they had come.

Karan was laughing and crying. Without that she might, just possibly, have gone on by herself. But she could not abandon Llian when his back was turned. Anyway, leaving him was as good as betraying him to his death. Even as she watched, his foot slipped and he almost fell. She clutched her breast, noticed that her heart was pounding. Llian steadied himself and went on without looking back.

"Come back," she cried through the snow. "I won't leave you. I think I can get across if I go down a bit, but I'll need a hand back up."

He turned and crept back, clinging onto every handhold. The freshly broken rock was not so difficult a climb for her, being rough and free from ice. With two hands it would not have bothered her at all, save for the precipice below. She limp-wristedly spidered her way down and across, wavered her hand up to Llian's, missed, then he found the outstretched arm and pulled her up. His hand was warm. She was glad of his strength. It was her turn to embrace him and he didn't push away.

"What are we going to do now?" he said miserably. "I've ruined . . ."

She put cold fingers across his lips. "Shhh! I have a last resort," Karan whispered in his ear. "There is a track that goes further up into the mountains."

"But you said . . ."

"We might be overheard. It really is a last resort, but better than the alternative."

They hurried back along the path, Karan brushing away the tracks again. Once they had to take refuge in the scrub as the other Whelm pelted past just above. They continued on and eventually regained the plateau not far from the ruins. The snow continued to fall as they set out toward Mount Tintinnuin, but it was not heavy enough to conceal them completely.

"The path is supposed to begin east of Tintinnuin. I hope I can find it. It's a long and hard trek, and a very dangerous one in winter. It leads south, into the high mountains. An ancient way, no longer used. If we can conceal our tracks, or the snow falls, we may just disappear. How are you feeling now?"

"Terrible."

Later in the morning it stopped snowing and they saw that three Whelm were on their trail, though they were a couple of hours behind. By midday the Whelm had cut the distance by half, their long legs and big feet a distinct advantage in the snow. Llian gasped as he caught up to Karan. Every movement was like a beak tearing at his side, and his face was gray. "Does the path go to Bannador?"

"You can get to Bannador this way," she said, giving a half-truth.

"Last night you said we couldn't carry enough food."

"I'm thinking on it." She said no more, knowing that her evasiveness, and the contradictions, were vexing Llian. I'm doing just what Maigraith did to me, she realized. There were two possible destinations on this path—Bannador and Shazmak, the hidden mountain city of the Aachim. But Shazmak was a secret she was forbidden to reveal, and she would not betray that secret unless they were in mortal peril. Even then, to take an outsider there would be a terrible gamble. She would not do so if there was *any* alternative.

By mid-afternoon the distance between them and the Whelm was halved again. Now Karan led them into hilly, heathy country, an unpleasant place to walk, full of spiky, scratching leaves and thorns, and they lost sight of their pursuers. Again Karan brushed out their tracks. She was beginning to get very worried about Llian, who had long ago ceased complaining, was clearly exhausted and in considerable pain. At any moment she expected him to collapse, but somehow he kept on.

They were now quite close to a tributary of the waterfall stream. Karan turned along the rocky ground beside the stream, where the falling water had left the ground bare of snow. Then they went across, splashing in the icy water, up the other side, crossing and recrossing the branching tributaries, leaping from outcrop to outcrop, leaving no tracks, until not even a dog could have tracked them. They kept on until dark, the streams taking them further and further west, away from the path they were seeking, around the wrong side of the mountain.

At dusk they camped in the lee of a boulder, one of many strewn across the landscape, and gathered prickly heath for their beds. Dinner was bread, cheese and cold meat from Llian's store, and water. They did not dare make a fire. As soon as the meal was ended Karan repaired to her bed, pulled her sleeping pouch around her and lay down, though she did not sleep.

She was too tired, too angry with herself and with Llian, though she tried not to show it. She went back over the scene at the ledge. If only Llian hadn't been so clumsy, so useless! If only she had acted more quickly. Since then he had tried to be as inconspicuous and as helpful as possible, but she had ignored every overture. He had upset the equilibrium that she had achieved with so much effort—and the command of her talent and her emotions that had allowed her to get ahead of the Whelm. But really it was all her fault, for going so far off the path in the first place, days ago, for getting lost and having to take refuge in a place where her escape options were so limited.

Llian too slept badly, and each time he woke he sensed that Karan was awake as well, tense, observing him. Perhaps she was afraid to sleep, for fear of what he might do.

They rose at dawn, gnawed a little of Llian's cold food, the stringy meat gone tooth-breakingly hard in the night, and drank tepid water from Karan's bottle which she had kept in her bed. Llian had left his on the ground and it was frozen solid. Her toilet consisted of a futile struggle with a comb that left her hair as tangled as before, and a few dabs of the lime perfume.

"There's no need to go to any trouble on my account," said Llian, jamming his hat on his head. He had had a bad night because of his injuries, and the cold which he was quite unused to.

Karan threw the comb down on the ground. "I do nothing on your account," she said in a voice that was like the grinding of ice floes, "save curse myself for bringing you. And scatter that pile of heath away, or they'll know we slept here."

Not even his banishment by Wistan had felt so cold, so cruel. Llian scurried off, his face blanched. Karan swept away the marks of the camp and they set off.

They struggled along a valley, through deep snow. The weather was much worse on this side of the mountain, and it snowed all day, wet gritty granules that matted their hair to icy strands and froze in lumps on Llian's week-old beard like wax at the base of a candle. The snow clung to their boots till each step was like lifting a brick and they constantly had to stamp the excess away. Karan grew more tired and more cross as the time passed, more withdrawn and wrapped up in her own troubles. How would she ever find the path from here, leagues away from anywhere she knew?

Next morning Karan woke to find that the weather had turned. The snow had stopped and the cloud was breaking up. Llian followed her up the valley without complaint, though he hurt all over.

Now they were confronted by an escarpment, an irregular cliff of rotten schist perhaps five or six spans high, covered in brown lichen. Though the layers of rock slanted out of the cliff like shallow steps they looked none too safe.

"Lesson one," said Karan. "Follow the ridge, not the valley. Have you any rope?"

Llian shook his head. "Over there looks easiest," pointing to a place where the slope was gentler and the steps a little wider.

"Yes. If we fell there we wouldn't be in too much danger."

The climb was more difficult than it looked because the rock was wet and crumbly. Once or twice Karan was glad of Llian's assistance: a steadying hand as she strained above her head for the next hold, a lift when her pack caught on a thorn bush, a leg up over the last sheer face to the edge of the escarpment. She noticed that Llian was sweating as she helped him over the edge with her good hand.

"I've always been afraid of heights," he said, sitting down on a rock and wiping his hands on his trousers.

Karan turned away, looking south across a sloping expanse of snow and the flank of the mountain rising steeply to her left. Evidently he was not without courage. It would be severely tested by the end of this journey.

By the afternoon of that third day they had skirted the lower slopes of Mount Tintinnuin on the western side and were scrambling in the broken country to the south. This was an inhospitable and secret land; even Llian knew no tales about it. There was no sign of pursuit and Karan began to think that they had lost the Whelm. Now in the afternoon the sun came out, the wind turned around to the north-west, a warm wind, and soon they were sweating in their heavy clothing.

"Rain, sleet, snow and now this," said Llian. "Winter's late in coming this year."

"A late winter is a hard winter. Don't call it down on us now."

The land was crusted with congealed rock boiled out of the mountain, bare outcrops thrust into heaps and billows like frozen foam, and riven with deep rents. Walking was extremely troublesome. They had sought the path to the south for most of the day but Karan could not find the signs she was looking for and grew ever more irritable.

"Shouldn't we go this way?" said Llian, pointing back toward the north. His sense of direction was hopeless.

Karan ignored him. How stupid he was. She had scarcely slept the past three nights, and she was so tired that she could no longer think coherently. She plodded on dully. Just her boots were visible below the hem of Llian's coat, so that she looked like a walking tent with a red tassel on top. He smiled every time he looked at her and, though it was not an unkind smile, it fuelled her ill-temper.

The wind died away. The air was humid and still. "We'd better find a camp," he called, a little later. "There's a change coming."

She looked around. They were advancing across the south-facing flank of the mountain. Before them an island of trees separated the twisting flows, but the center of the island was smashed down by a black boulder the size of a house. Here and there the flowing rock had drawn out of its dark cocoon, leaving behind an empty tunnel that pretended to offer refuge, though they found most had collapsed and were choked with rubble and ash. The sky to the north was clear, but from the southwest a wall of olive-black clouds was advancing. The light from the setting sun was a pallid green. Lightning played continuously on the underside of the cloudbank.

"Here's something," Llian called, pointing toward the

small dark hole of a tunnel nearby. It was partly concealed with bushes and he had almost walked right past.

"Get some wood. I'll start the fire," she shouted, over the rumble of thunder. She gathered dry grass and twigs with her good arm. Llian ran to the patch of trees and began wrenching off dead branches. The advancing storm clouds overtook the setting sun. A gloomy twilight descended.

The tunnel was about ten spans broad and two high on the inside, although the mouth, being largely blocked with broken rock, was much smaller. Its length she could not tell. Karan kindled a smoky fire in an embayment a few paces inside the entrance. She no longer used her lightglass, for fear that it might draw the Whelm to her. Instead she bound twigs together to make a torch and, holding it high, carefully checked the lower end of the tunnel. The walls were like tortured glass. The passage sloped upwards, sometimes steeply, sometimes gently, twisting and turning, but empty save for scatters of rock. Halfway along, the roots of a tree grew through the roof, making a fibrous curtain across the tunnel. White spiders and other small blind things scurried away from the light. After a hundred paces the air was stale, the floor littered with bat droppings. Further on the way was blocked by fallen rock. Karan turned back and opened Llian's pack to see what there was to eat.

Many packets spilled out, wrapped in waxed cloth, and most still dry. Perhaps among all this bounty he had real tea too. She rifled through the packages, opened one, sniffed. Yes! Proper tea grown in the foothills above Chanthed; the aroma was unmistakable. The horrible stuff she had got in Hetchet, hard curled-up leaves of some desert saltbush, full of twigs and cobweb and red mites, was intensely bitter.

Already the storm was overhead and it was almost dark. Llian was still outside and there was no wood. Karan climbed up out of the entrance, looking across to the patch of dead trees where he had been working. Lightning flashed and she saw him. He had chopped down a small tree with her hatchet and was struggling to drag it across the rubble and broken ground to their refuge. He looked over his shoulder at the sky. Karan followed his gaze.

"Leave it," she shouted, suddenly afraid for him, but her voice was drowned by the thunder.

There was a sudden, tearing gust of wind and the storm struck with a fusillade of hail and a single flash of lightning, so close that her hair glowed and crackled. A whip-crack of thunder and the storm was all around them, all over them, the lightning striking everywhere and hailstones falling as though they had been flung from a bucket, bouncing, shattering on the rocks until the air smoked with chips of ice.

Llian dropped his burden and fell to one knee, holding his head. He stayed that way for half a minute then got up and ran toward her, weaving, protecting his head with his arms. Lightning struck the patch of dead trees, shattering the tallest and sending splinters as tall as Karan in all directions. One fell on the roof of the tunnel behind her. He gained the entrance and leapt through in a scatter of hail.

"That was stupid," said Karan coldly. "We could have collected more wood after the storm had passed. Now we have none. And why a tree? There are plenty of dead branches. If the lightning had been a little nearer . . . Truly, you are a fool, Llian."

She turned away and sat by the fire, her straight back communicating her anger more clearly than any words.

Llian remained where he was, head sunk in his arms. He had set out with such high expectations, but nothing had turned out the way he thought it would. It had not been like this in Chanthed. He felt keenly that he was stupid, even contemptible, and it was more than he could bear.

17

A COMPANION
ON THE ROAD

Eventually Llian noticed that the storm was passing and the hail had stopped. Climbing the rubble pile he looked out on a white world that glittered with each lightning flash. The hail was piled calf-deep as far as he could see. As he watched, the first soft flakes of snow came ghosting down through the still air, falling more and more heavily until even the nearest trees were lost. The fire had gone out for lack of fuel. He crunched through the hailstones, fetched as much wood as he could drag, set the fire blazing again, put the pot on to boil for tea and sat down beside Karan.

"I'm sorry," he said. "I don't even know what I'm doing here."

Karan turned her face to his, empathizing with his misery (though the back of her mind told her that he might be playing on her soft heart), and weakened a little more. Her feelings had come around in a circle. She had begun to realize that she liked him after all, ridiculous though he was.

She put her arm across his shoulder, saying, "I'm sorry too; I also got into this affair unwillingly. But I swore a binding oath; an unbreakable oath."

"I would be happy to tell you a tale—any tale at all."

"I don't think I could stay awake long enough to hear it. Tell me about yourself. How is it that *you* came after me?"

"Wistan dragged me out of bed and told me I was banished. I'll tell you why another time. Then he offered me money and references to seek you out and escort you to Thurkad. He always wanted to be rid of me, and this was a good excuse."

Karan sat up, thinking furiously. That must have been about the time she had pleaded with Wistan in her dream, and dreamed about Llian. Had she put the idea into their heads? At least that was better than thinking that she had dragged him here all by herself. "You might have refused."

"No chronicler can make a life without references." He hesitated, took a deep breath: "I am also Zain."

"I know. Why should I care? But why did you stay at the college?"

"A chronicler is what I really am, even more than a teller of tales. I love the Histories, and where better to study them?"

"Why did they send *you,* of all people."

Llian was not insulted. "Wistan believed that I intrigued against him, that I would be Master of Chanthed in his place."

"And would you?"

"If I wanted that, *then I would have it,*" he said with a sudden flash of fire, and for the first time Karan saw the iron beneath. Then it was gone and he was smiling at her. "Though not in such a way. There's no intrigue in me. I never wanted to be master, yet I did make fun of him in the taverns. It pleased me to mock him in heroic songs and sagas, for he is a scheming, miserable, sour wretch who loves no one, not even himself, and thinks everyone else the same. The folk of Chanthed flocked to the taverns to laugh, and so he feared for himself."

"Not without cause," said Karan.

"I almost gave you up in Tullin, you know. I would have, had it not been for your sending. After that I felt that I knew you, so to speak. You seemed so desperate. I couldn't abandon you then."

Once more he surprised her. He had felt that way after their minds had touched for just a few seconds? What would he have thought of her if she *had* abandoned him back at the ledge?

"I still think that I've met you somewhere before."

He turned her face to his with his fingertips.

"Yes!" he said, suddenly realizing. "You were the red-haired woman in the audience when I first told the *Tale of the Forbidding*. Back there at the ruins you said we hadn't met."

Karan felt embarrassed. "Well, you were very irritating. Anyway, we didn't *meet*. You had no idea who I was."

"But you touched me with your mind! No one ever did that before. And then—you asked the question that turned my life upside down."

"What are you talking about?"

"*Who killed her?* The crippled girl. I have been searching for the answer ever since. That was the other reason why I was thrown out. Wistan was afraid of what I would uncover."

"So, what have you found?"

"I thought that there was a great mystery to be uncovered, a Great Tale to be written. You have no idea how I yearn for that—to be the chronicler who discovers a new

Great Tale." He looked into the distance and his eyes grew misty. "But I found nothing.

"And what if the truth I uncover shows that my telling was false? Once broken, a chronicler's reputation cannot be remade. Even if it is a new Great Tale, the credit will go to someone else. Even more perilous—whatever secret was uncovered back there where Shuthdar fell, there are people even now that would kill for it. All my alternatives are bad."

"Save one," said Karan, putting her arm across his shoulders again.

"What's that?" he asked, without hope or interest.

"Find out the truth, make the tale yourself and broadcast it far and wide, so that, whatever secrets you uncover, hundreds of people will know as much as you do. Then you will be in no danger."

"But I don't even know where to start," Llian said morosely.

"Then put it aside until something comes up. I'm sure you can make some sort of tale out of our troubles."

"I've thought about that already. I will tell you honestly, there was something else that brought me here—the Mirror! Few in these times know more about the Histories than I do, though perhaps you think me boastful."

"I do," she murmured slyly, "but then, you are a teller. Tell on."

"But there is nothing in the Histories about the Mirror, not by that name, or other names that I can think of. Why not, if it is such an ancient thing? Why is it not recorded? I must know. I cannot get it out of my mind."

"Perhaps those who wrote the Histories had reason not to speak of it."

"Perhaps, though many other curious, remarkable, even perilous things are recorded."

Karan changed the subject. "How came you to Chanthed? The Zain no longer dwell in Meldorin, I had heard."

"That is so, though our heart remains here. We mostly live in Jepperand, a poor land far to the east. You would not know of it."

"I do know it," she said quietly.

He continued as though he had not heard. "It is north of the *Wahn Barre,* the Crow Mountains, and west of the land of Crandor. We still do not think of Jepperand as our home, though we have dwelt there for near a thousand years. It is a barren, thorny place, and the withering salt winds blow unceasing up from the Dry Sea. But we have no other home, any more."

Karan sat back and closed her eyes, fascinated. What a beautiful rich warm voice he had. She could have listened to him all night. Just then he looked across at her with a smile, saw that her eyes were closed, and went silent. "Don't stop," she said. "Tell me the story of the Zain."

"The Zain!" said Llian. "A month would not be long enough. You need to sleep. I'll give you just the barest bones of our history.

"In centuries long past we dwelt in the imperial lands of Zile, at a time when that kingdom was not a declining city in a barren land, as it is now. The whole of Meldorin was Zile! The Zain were a minor people, a scholarly, clever, inward-looking folk, as indeed we still are. That has always been our weakness, as it is my own."

"Inward-looking, you? You strike me as a lecherous dog! I imagine no maiden in Chanthed was safe from you, if the way you use the *voice* on me is anything to go by." Karan laughed, though not unkindly.

Llian looked slightly abashed. "Scholars have a great tradition of lechery, according to some tales, though generally it is not we who tell them." His thoughts touched on

Thandiwe, the doe-eyed friend that he had left behind in Chanthed. What would she be doing now? Studying in the library, he supposed. He could scarcely picture her face anymore, though their friendship had been a long one. "But I meant inward-looking in the political sense. Anyhow, it was the Zain who established the Great Library at Zile, which still remains, though the empire be dust. They grew too fond of learning and were corrupted by Rulke in the wars of the Clysm. They paid dearly for that alliance, for when Rulke was imprisoned in the Nightland the Zain were exiled, those few that escaped the slaughter. We are from that remnant, and still we are but few. We wandered for many years, and everywhere we were hated and reviled. Those days are long gone now, but still the memories linger."

"What was the pact?" asked Karan sleepily.

"I cannot tell you that, save that the Charon were warring with the Aachim. The Aachim had made a defense against the Charon, a mind-breaking potency. The Charon could not, within themselves, contrive a defense against it, but they found that we Zain, of all the peoples of Santhenar, had a degree of immunity. So they made a pact with my people and helped them to develop their talent. The Zain cared nothing for the immunity but they craved the knowledge that only the Charon had. The Gift of Rulke, the talent was called then, but later the Curse of Rulke, for it left the stigmata that identified us as Zain. Such have always been the gifts of the Charon. But even that is of no importance now, for over the centuries the talent has decayed and the stigmata with it, and few even know that they have it anymore."

"How do the Zain tell?" she asked, looking at him wonderingly, curiously. "Perhaps you?"

"I don't think so," he said, laughing. "There is a test, and those who pass it are not sent into the world, as a rule. They are too much at risk, even in these times.

"Eventually we came to Jepperand, an arid place of thorny plants and venomous animals where no one dwelt. There we took refuge, for we were tired of wandering, and by our wits and great efforts made a new home there. But the lesson was learned—no longer did we make allegiances. We Zain have no ambitions anymore, outside ourselves. But some of us live secretly in other lands and keep watch, that we never be taken by surprise again. So we have gained a reputation for spying and for deviousness."

"And you are one such?" asked Karan, with the hint of a smile.

Llian laughed again. "There are others among the Zain who are clever but have no talent for spying, and they are sent abroad to study, for we have a great reverence for the arts and for learning. That's how I ended up at the college. Mendark selected me, and sponsored me too. I suffered there for a long time."

Her eyes narrowed at the mention of Mendark. "Then why did you stay," she said after a long pause, "when you could have left with honor these past years?"

"Often I wondered myself. Perhaps I was afraid to leave: more than half my life was spent there."

"Then you have never been away from Chanthed?"

"Oh yes; several times. I have been across the mountains, though not as far as Thurkad. And to the north and west. Twice to the Great Library. For a student of the Histories Zile is a magnet irresistible. But I have never been home, though I long to. My stipend would not cover that."

"I knew who *you* were," she said, thinking back to his arrival at the ruins. "As soon as you opened your mouth I knew you, even before you fell down the steps so foolishly. Even when I touched you with my sending in Tullin I was thinking about you, though I never really imagined that you could be there. I had seen you twice before. Once at the Festival of Chanthed four years ago, and again at the Graduation Telling, when you had your triumph."

Her eyes shone at the memory, then she went on slowly, "I couldn't understand why you had come. I admired your tellings much more than the deeds of any hero. I needed help but all I got was you; I was bitterly disappointed."

Llian laughed aloud, the criticism bothering him not at all. He put all obligations out of his mind; for once he would do what he wanted. "That is so," he said, "but I have stepped on the path and now I must tread it. I cannot go back."

"What will you do then?" Looking up at him with her soft green eyes, knowing already.

"I will follow you, if you will have me," he said. "And I will learn all about the Mirror that can be learned. When that is done I will amend the Histories and write the *Tale of the Mirror*. I don't think it will be the Great Tale that I have always dreamed about, but it will be well worth the listening. Will you have me?"

"You have picked a hard road," she said, "and if you could see what is to come, you might choose differently. You will find that, as a companion on the road, I can be as foul as any."

It was his turn to smile slyly. "I knew that as soon as I met you," he said, and, getting up, discovered that the pot of water was completely boiled away. He threw wood on the fire and went outside for more.

She looks so pale and tired, Llian thought, as he came back with the pot full of snow and hail, and put it in a corner of the fire. Karan sat with her arms folded across her knees and her head on her arms. Her eyes followed him as he moved about but he could tell that her thoughts were elsewhere. What strength she must have, what iron will. What a tale it was going to be!

He sorted through the wrapped packages of food—vegetables, still relatively fresh, onions, slightly moldy on the outside, a small piece of meat wrapped in oiled cloth, and spices in twists of paper, somewhat damp. Taking the pan he chopped the onions into it, whistling as he carried out the mundane tasks, poured in a little packet of spice and fried the lot gently with a little oil and the meat. He went back to the tunnel entrance and gathered hailstones and snow in the front of his coat, poured the lot into the pan and set it back on the fire. When the hailstones were reduced to the size of peas he threw in the chopped vegetables and a handful of dried grain and put it to one side to cook.

The pot was boiling merrily. He stirred tea herbs into it. "It's ready," he said. There was no answer. He turned to Karan. She was sitting exactly as before, smiling still, but she was fast asleep.

Between the fire and the far wall the floor was relatively flat. Llian made a bed with their sleeping pouches. He called her name, shook her gently by the shoulder, but she did not stir. Llian picked her up in his arms, his ribs hurting more than a little, carried her across and laid her down carefully on her side with her injured wrist supported on his pack. He arranged the cloak beneath her head, eased off her boots and stood them near the fire to dry, and tucked the covers around her chin. She was at peace for the first time since he had met her.

The night dragged. Outside the storm had passed but the snow continued to fall. Llian poured himself another cup of tea and carried it over to the mouth of the tunnel. The wind had swung around to the south-west and built a drift across the entrance, so that from inside it was no longer possible to see out. He climbed up on top of the boulders and peered over the drift. There was nothing to be seen but snowflakes appearing out of the darkness above, in the dim light from the fire, and fluttering down to settle at his feet.

Llian shivered and drew his cloak more tightly about him, sipping the last of the tea and longing for sleep. He threw the dregs onto the snow and turned back to the fire, which had burned low. The last of the wood thudded onto the coals, sending out a shower of sparks that drifted slowly up the tunnel. Karan stirred and began to whimper softly in her sleep, then turned onto her side and was still.

Llian went out for more wood. The hail and snow had filled the broken ground, but every so often, as he struggled back with his haul, his foot plunged through an icy crust into a crack or crevice and once he skinned his ankle on a sharp face of stone. When he clambered down Karan was sleeping soundly. He threw a branch onto the fire. The twigs were thick with dead leaves and blazed up with a crackle and a roar.

The sudden noise seemed to amplify some aspect of Karan's dream for she cried out "No!" in a tortured way. "No!" she cried again, jerking herself upright, her arms crooked in front of her face to ward something off. "I can not. I will not." The whole side of her face was twisted as though gripped by huge fingers, and her eyes were glazed.

He called her name, softly. "Karan," he said more loudly. "It's me, Llian. You're safe now."

"Away! No! Away!" she moaned. Her eyes flicked from place to place, as if seeking a certain face in a crowd. "Away! Oh, help me. Don't . . ."

Her voice faded out and she went completely rigid. Her face was the color of sleet. Llian knelt beside her for a minute, holding her in distressed indecision, then without warning she went slack and he barely caught her before her head struck the stone. With the contact an image flashed briefly into his mind, the face of a woman seen side-on in a mirror. He adjusted the cloak beneath her head and pulled the covers up. Karan was still breathing heavily but now she slept. He picked up another stick and put it carefully on the fire.

That was more than just a bad dream. As though she had relived something terrible from the past. Or, *as though something had tried to reach her in her dream*. And who was the woman? No ordinary face that. Staring obliquely from the mirror that way, it reminded him of a bas-relief he had once seen on a wall in the Great Library. Was that *the Mirror?*

From the instant Wistan had mentioned that the Mirror contained memories of ancient times, Llian had burned to see it. Now he was almost consumed with desire for it. But not to possess it—even to see or touch it was just the minor part of his need. His lust, now growing unbearable, was to see the Histories through the Mirror, as they had happened. To actually see the past, as it had occurred, was more than any chronicler's dream. Who *had* held the Mirror over the centuries? What records did it contain? There could be no end to them.

And Karan was sleeping the sleep of utter exhaustion— he could look at it and she need never know. He bent down over her. She opened her eyes, smiled dreamily up at him, sighed and snuggled the covers up under her chin, fast asleep.

No! Llian was moved by her faith in him, her trust. He put the pot on for more tea and took out his journal, which he had not touched since before Tullin. Forcing all thoughts of the Mirror away, he immersed himself in his writing, setting down every detail.

The long night wore away. At last, when he was beginning to think that dawn would never come, a pale light began to spread across the sky outside the cave. As he went toward the entrance to look at the dawn he felt a feather-soft presence behind him. Karan was lying as he had left her, on her side with the blanket up beneath her chin and her red hair fallen across her cheek. Her eyes were open and she was looking at him with a serene expression that made her seem ageless and at the same time very young.

Llian was unsure of himself in the morning light. "Would you like some tea?" he asked blandly.

"Please," she smiled, raising herself up on her elbow. Her eyes followed him as he climbed up to the entrance and packed snow into the pot. "I was so tired. You looked after me." A fleeting shadow on her face. "Thank you."

"I made dinner for us last night," Llian said as they waited for the pot to boil. "But I'm afraid it will be rather a stew by now."

"Put it back on the fire. After what I'm used to, I won't complain."

Llian, remembering the evil substance they had eaten that first night, could only agree.

18

MOUNTAIN SICKNESS

The sun had only just risen when they prepared to set off. Llian climbed up, looked out, then stopped. "There's someone out there," he hissed to Karan, who was waiting below with the packs. "It's them—Idlis, I think, and the fat one."

"What are they doing?" she asked, jumping up beside him.

"They're standing over by that tree: the one the lightning struck."

"Right next to the one you chopped down—a little signpost." Llian flinched, but she wasn't angry. "Get down. They may not realize there's a tunnel here."

Faint hope, thought Llian, if they've tracked us this far. "I don't understand how they found us, in all this snow."

"How have they ever found me? There have been times when I've gone for a week without seeing them, then they appear as though out of the air. Last night was the first time

I've dreamed for days and, suddenly, here they are. It is as though they reach out and touch me in my dreams."

It was their fortune that the wind had drawn the smoke up the tunnel to seep out unseen through a myriad of little fissures and be dispersed across the mountainside. That would not protect them against a determined search though. Karan tramped snow onto the coals to be sure.

They huddled inside, away from the entrance, scarcely moving all day. Without the fire it was miserable and Llian got into his sleeping pouch and tried to sleep while Karan stood guard, but the thought of their pursuers so near would not permit any rest; he gave up the struggle and got up again. The Whelm appeared and disappeared, quartering the mountainside, then around midday, unaccountably, they turned in haste, as though they had seen something, and went diagonally away from them up the slope of the mountain.

"That's strange," said Llian. "They're going away."

Karan was beside him in a flash, standing on tiptoe to see. "Where can they be going?"

"It looks like they're following someone."

They learned no more about this strange circumstance. Late in the afternoon they caught a last glimpse of the Whelm, a smudge on the snow far to the west, and then they were gone.

When it was dark Karan and Llian crept out into the cold. An icy wind still blew from the south and the snow swirled about them. They were thankful for it at first, but it soon became a nightmare night of wading through drifts, struggling over rocky ridges and suddenly plunging to the neck in soft, damp snow. Within half an hour they were soaked and bitterly cold. As the night went on the snow became thicker and by midnight they could go no further, even had they known where they were going. They found shelter of a sort under an overhanging rock, though it was on the steep side of a south-facing ridge and exposed to the full force of the wind. But this was not one of the fleeting snowstorms of autumn. The wind was hard from the south, the wind that turned ice to iron, the wind of a long and bitter winter. And they were lost in the mountains.

Llian felt the cold terribly, much more so than Karan. He thought that they were going to die that night. They could not generate enough warmth to dry their clothes. Their wet fingers and toes kept freezing, so that they had to rub them constantly to keep the blood flowing. Finally they made a cocoon of their sleeping pouches and cloaks and crept inside, clinging together like lovers, and made enough warmth between them for survival. At last the morning came.

"Never again," said Karan, as she cracked the ice from their covers. "I will face the Whelm first. I will hunt them as they have hunted me."

Her round cheeks were sunken so that the knotted muscles of her jaw were clearly visible. Her green eyes were bloodshot and contracted to mere slits, and such fury in them he had never experienced. He put his hand on her shoulder but she slapped it away, and the enforced intimacy of the night with it. Llian was suddenly alone, and afraid of her, and for her—there were depths to her that were beyond his comprehension.

During the night they had climbed across a steep spur and now found themselves looking into a long, straight, broad valley that ran due south for several leagues. A frozen stream meandered across the bottom of the valley, which was covered in thick forest. There was no sign of habitation, or even of life, save for the hunting birds that hung in the middle air over the stream. Tall mountains lay all around. The wind was keen in their faces. They hurried down the slope into the shelter of the forest.

*   *   *

Night again, the fifth since they left the ruins. They sat, nestling together for warmth, in a shallow cave, no more than an embayment at the base of a low cliff. There had been no more sign of the Whelm, though they were haunted by the fear that they would suddenly appear. It had taken them all day and most of the evening to force their way through the snow and forest to the southern end of the valley. The sky was clear behind them but the south promised more snow.

"Are you *sure* you know where you're going?" asked Llian, not for the first time. "We've eaten nearly half the food already."

Karan gave him a bleak look. She was beginning to think that even Bannador was beyond them.

"Why did we have to come this way?" he continued irritably.

"I chose to come *this* way," Karan said icily, "because there was no *other* way. I didn't ask you to come. I brought you only out of pity."

She got up and stalked away into the night. Llian sat there in the darkness, cold and miserable. The camaraderie of two days past seemed gone forever.

Hours later she returned silently from another direction. Llian had dozed off and the fire was no more than a bed of coals. "Wake up," she said, cheerful now, brushing his face with something soft and wet. Llian woke sluggishly from a fitful sleep. It was the tail of a small plump fish, and four others dangled from a string.

"Where did . . . ?"

"I was sitting above a pool and the scorpion shone so brightly that I saw a shadow move under the ice, so I broke it and there they were, all fat for the winter, so tame that I caught them with my hands."

She roused the fire to a fierce blaze and began to clean the

fish. "I'm sorry I was so rude. I was worried, but I think I
know where we are now. When we went around the wrong
side of the mountain we ended up much too far west. Now
we must follow the ridge and cross over at that saddle we
saw earlier."

"Will this give us enough food to get to Bannador?"

"Almost. If the weather holds."

On the morning of the sixth day they set out as soon as it
was light. The path now left the valley and skirted the edge
of the eastern mountains. The lower slopes were rounded
and they crunched through prickly heath and dry grasses
that stuck up through the snow. They went this way for two
days, traveling slowly in thick snow, before the track began
to climb.

For three days they climbed. The track wound its way
into the high mountains, but always to the south; yet even as
it climbed the peaks rose ever higher, so that their task
seemed to grow more difficult the further they went. And the
mountains were highest and most steep to the south and the
west, and it seemed that in their shadow the steep northern
slopes were left rocky and barren. No longer did they wade
through soft snow, and that was a blessing, yet the higher
they climbed the harder it became, till every step was an effort that made them gasp, and the burden of their packs,
even half-empty as they were, was almost too much to lift
onto their backs each morning.

Finding water was another chore, for every trickle was
frozen, and now there was seldom any wood for a fire. They
had to pack their water bottles with snow, or sometimes
chips of ice, and carry them under their clothes so that their
warmth would make a little water, but never quite enough.
They were always thirsty now; always cold, even when they
huddled together at night. But there was one consolation—

Karan dreamed no more, and there had been no more sight of the Whelm. If Llian's presence had anything to do with that she was grateful for it.

Llian was particularly slow now, so that Karan found herself constantly waiting for him, and fretting about their lack of progress. At this rate their food would run out long before Bannador, and that left only one alternative, one that Karan did not want to think about . . .

On the eleventh day, Llian woke exhausted from a night of tossing and turning, with a headache that became worse as the day dragged on. Twice during their trek he was sick without warning, and even during rest breaks he panted like a dog in the desert sun.

The path dwindled to a track that was indistinguishable from all the other animal trails. Karan had difficulty finding her way, and many times they plodded to the top of a ragged hill only to look down into a pathless wilderness of rocky ravines, and knew that they must go all the way back down again. The ground was bare and stony, littered with flat sheets of slate that cracked and slipped underfoot, and off which the low sun reflected silver. The path zig-zagged up a steep ridge and the way forward was hidden.

Suddenly Llian flung himself down on a boulder. His face was red and blotchy. "I'm so thirsty," he panted. "How much longer is it going to be?"

Karan passed him her water bottle and pointed up the hill without saying anything.

"What does that mean?" he asked frettishly.

She glared at him. She was worn out as well, but she didn't make a constant fuss about it. "Once we cross this ridge we'll be able to see the top of the pass. What's the matter with you anyway?"

Llian did not answer. Shortly they reached the top of the

ridge. Before them the mountains ran, steep and snow-
tipped, in an unbroken line from east to west. The distance
was obscured by haze.

"Look! There's the pass!" said Karan, pointing toward
the middle of the line of mountains.

Llian could see nothing that looked remotely like a crossing place, and said so in a morose tone.

Karan pointed again. "There, a little to the east of south.
It's as plain as day." Llian still could not see it. "Don't trouble yourself," she said in vexation. "Just follow."

They woke early the next morning, eating a frugal breakfast
of preserved fruit and moldy cheese while the sun rose.
Hunger and headache had left Llian sullen and Karan was
still angry and worried.

It was late in the afternoon when they finally reached the
top of the pass. There had been no sign of a path since they
had crossed the ridge and Llian, now staggering like a
drunkard in Karan's footsteps as they passed back and forth
across the steep northern flank of the mountain, had long
since abandoned hope of finding a way across. They crested
the ridge and looked across a sea of white-tipped peaks and
bottomless, shadowy defiles. Llian was dismayed. He
dropped his pack and flopped across it as though he was
dead, and might have been, save for the rasping breathing
that Karan could hear from ten paces away.

"What is this place?" he asked listlessly. "I thought we'd
see Bannador from here."

"If only!" Karan said, with a mirthless laugh. "This is the
land of Chollaz," indicating the mountains ahead with a
sweep of her arm. "All you see within the ring of mountains.
Bannador is still more than a week away. We'll camp now.
Look, there's a way station!"

Llian looked around him. The mountains to right and left

towered above the pass. They continued in a chain of peaks making a ragged semicircle that enclosed Chollaz on the northern side. The mountains within the semicircle were only marginally smaller. The southern extent of the land was lost in a mist that rose even as they watched. Within minutes the shafts of sunlight that spilled through the gaps in the western range were gone, the blue seeped out of the sky and in the thin mountain air they were chilled to the bone.

The way station was just below the crest of the pass, a tiny spherical building of stone with a curving roof and a small entrance-way. There had once been a sliding door, a slab of stone, but it lay on the ground in pieces. The shelter kept out the wind but inside it Karan felt claustrophobic so they sat outside for their meal. The only fuel was a few windswept bushes. Karan chopped them and made a meager and temporary blaze just outside the door.

Llian was so miserable and depressing that she could not bear to be with him and after they ate she pulled her coat around her and walked down the path. She did not go far, only away from sight of the fire, where she sat down on a cold boulder and stared into the mist. The night was very dark, just the brightest stars visible, swimming in white haloes. She clutched the thick coat more tightly around her. Somehow she seemed to have lost her direction, her purpose, since she had taken on the burden of Llian. How would she get out of it now? She could hear him coughing from here. It just went on and on.

After a while the cold became disheartening and she walked back to the dying fire, warmed her hands and sat down beside Llian, who was bent down with his head in his hands. He broke out in another coughing fit, sat up suddenly and Karan was horrified to see that there was blood all over his mouth.

"How long has this been going on?" she cried, tilting back his head so that she could see his eyes. They were red as well.

"Just this afternoon. I feel like I'm going to die. What's the matter with me?"

Karan had seen it before. "Mountain sickness," she said, a chill going down her back.

"How bad is that?"

"It's a common thing, this high up. You *could* drop dead of it, although most people don't. But the only remedy is to go back down the mountain again."

Llian almost wept. "I can't!"

She thought he was talking about the descent, but he went on, "I can't. There is a tale here and I have to write it. *I will not die.*"

His face was so twisted with passion, his eyes so red, so liquid that it looked as though he was weeping blood.

"I won't let you die," she said, holding his head in her arms. "But we are in desperate trouble, even were you well. There isn't the food to go back, nor to get to Gothryme anymore; we've been so slow these last few days. I miss my home terribly."

"I'm sorry," he said miserably. "If it wasn't for me you'd be nearly there." He broke into another fit of coughing that left him so weak he just lay on the ground.

Karan heaved him up again and wiped pink foam from his lip with a handful of snow. "There's only one thing we can do—keep going."

"Tonight?"

"As soon as it's light. This is the highest point on the path. Tomorrow we go down a bit. You should get better then." Karan hoped so, though she knew that mountain sickness did not always go away so easily.

"Where can we go? What's the point, if we're going to starve anyway?"

She hesitated. It was prohibited to speak of Shazmak, but he had to know now. "There is a city. A forbidden place, but it is our only hope." She paused for a moment, listening, still looking down. A solitary howl came on the still air. Llian looked uneasy. "It was far away," she said, then continued. "A city of the Aachim. A city in size though no longer in numbers, I should say. But a stronghold still. Few know of this place, for the Aachim require little of the outside world. They seldom go abroad, and in disguise, and secretly."

"I know something of the Aachim," said Llian, "from the Histories; but not of such a place."

"It is called Shazmak."

"Shazmak! Then I do know it, of course I do! But Shazmak was abandoned long ago."

"Not abandoned. Hidden; withdrawn from the memory of the world. I lived there for six years, after my parents died. My Aachim friends will help me."

"And me?"

There was a long pause.

"Aachim. The Mirror of Aachan," said Llian, puzzling over the possibilities inherent in the names. "I have a tale of the Aachim, though the Mirror is not mentioned. Oh, how I wish I could see it!"

"You can't." Karan got up before he could harass her further and walked away from the fire again, out of sight down the slope. She came to a withered old tree and rested her cheek against the corrugated bark, looking down into the mist. The matter was not finished and she knew it. Just above her head a dead branch still had a cluster of cones on the end. She snapped it off and walked back up to the fire, plucking off the cones as she went. She sat down beside

Llian and threw a cone onto the coals. Eventually it blazed up with red and blue fire.

"Did the Mirror belong to the Aachim?"

"Once," she said. "Long ago."

"You are returning it to them?"

A perceptible pause before she answered. "I did not say that." Karan hesitated again. "I don't know. I just don't know what to do."

"Surely the Aachim will want it back."

Karan did not answer. She could hardly stop thinking about Shazmak, now that they were going there. It was the most beautiful place she had ever been, though its was a harsh, uncompromising beauty. Most of the happy memories of her life were there.

Llian was staring at her. "Give me your confidence," he cried in passion. "If you demand trust you must also give it."

Yes, she thought, gazing at his red, ardent face. I must. But why is it so difficult to trust you? Can *I* be guilty of prejudice against the Zain?

Or is it because of the look in your eyes when you are thinking about the Mirror? The more you learn the more you will want.

"I will tell you what little I may, and in return you will protect me," said Karan. "Say nothing about the Mirror in Shazmak, even if they ask you. You know nothing about it."

Her thoughts went back to Shazmak. Perhaps Rael would be there. Rael, so different from the other Aachim, and once her closest friend. So gentle, so patient, so sad. She could see his face as clearly as on the day he had been sent away to the east—the curling red hair, the sad green eyes. She could hear, even now, the music that he had played so often for her, melancholy despite his attempts to cheer her.

Karan realized that her heart was beating wildly, just at the thought of seeing him again. She trusted Rael utterly.

She could give up the Mirror to him and know that she had done the right thing. For a long time now Karan had deliberately not thought of the Mirror, as though by ignoring the problem it would disappear. But she could ignore it no longer. Suddenly the decision she had agonized over for so long was made. She *would* give back the Mirror to the Aachim, to Rael.

Llian hunched over the coals, coughing and spitting blood. The Histories flowed in his mind, the faces of the great whirling and spiraling like the flames in the wind, calling to him, whispering their secrets in voices that he could not quite hear, laughing at him, jeering and insulting him. A bas-relief high on a stone wall became a face on the Mirror, dissolved into other faces. Llian crawled to the doorway and put his face in the snow to cut through the hallucinations, desperately trying to think straight.

The Aachim came into the most ancient tales, even the first, the tale of Shuthdar and the flute that he had made for Rulke the Charon. Then after the Forbidding the Aachim grew strong in their own right, and fought the endless wars, now called the Clysm, against the Charon.

"But the Aachim were destroyed in the Clysm," said Llian, speaking his thoughts aloud. "The Histories no longer tell of them."

"Some survived," said Karan, who had come back without his hearing, "but they retreated from the world. The high mountains were most like Aachan, and there they went, building their iron cities. To Tirthrax they went, in the Great Mountains; to Stassor, eight hundred leagues east of us; and to other cold remote places. And here. Shazmak was once their stronghold in Meldorin, but with the waning of the years they have allowed it to dwindle to an outpost. Yet they guard it still, and ward away any who wander near." She dragged him back inside and brushed the snow off his face.

Llian was silent, shaken by the realization that the Aachim existed still, though the Histories no longer spoke of them. Why had these things not been mentioned? Were the Histories corrupt? He lay down on the floor. The cold seared his cheek but he was too sick to move.

"How can *you* go there, then?" he rasped.

"My family has had a long alliance with the Aachim, and my grandmother was one of them."

"What about me? The Zain conspired with Rulke, remember. The Aachim were enemies."

Karan said nothing. She knew that too, and worried about it just as much as Llian did.

Llian drifted away into a delirium of names and faces, all jumbled together, and then into a troubled sleep where the delirium became a dream that was no different.

19

CONFESSIONS

Maigraith struggled furiously but without avail. Vartila was incredibly strong and tenacious—nothing would make her let go. She dragged Maigraith toward a small door in the far corner of the room, a place to question in secret. Maigraith grew frantic. She opened her mouth to shout and a cold hand instantly clamped shut her mouth and nose. She felt nauseated. She was choking. She slid her foot down Vartila's shin, then stamped her heel down on the instep with all the strength she could manage. Had she been wearing boots Vartila might have been crippled, her instep crushed.

Vartila stifled her scream into a shrill yelp. She hopped on one foot for a moment, then snatched up a heavy ruler from the table and cracked Maigraith over the side of the head with it. The blow was unexpected and incredibly painful. Maigraith fell to her knees in a daze. The metal edge had cut her; red blood glistened in her hair.

Vartila raised the ruler again. "Get up," she panted. "Go into the room. Do not make another sound."

Maigraith felt utterly cowed. She put her hand up to the side of her head, then brought it slowly round in front of her face, looking at the bright blood. She bowed her head in submission, then reached up and, gripping the table edge, laboriously pulled herself to her feet. She swayed, took a step toward the door, and bumped seemingly by accident against a pedestal on which stood a tall porcelain urn. Though Vartila leapt forward she was too late to stop it smashing on the floor. Maigraith swung her arms, and other vessels flew through the air and broke with satisfying crashes. Then Vartila knocked her down, put her hands about her throat, and her questions were spat with cold fury.

"You have one minute, and then I choke you," she gritted. "Who are you? Where did you come from. What is—"

The door smashed open. Yggur's deep-set gray eyes took in the scene at once. He turned to Vartila, his voice dangerously soft, no trace of impediment now.

"What do you do with my prisoner? I gave no orders for you to touch her."

Vartila was unmoved—it was clear that the conflict was to her liking, that she had been expecting it. Her voice was cold and arrogant. "*You* lost the Mirror, *master*. Our duty is to get it back. We warned you about this one, yet you play games with her, games that affect your judgment."

Yggur was incredulous. "What is this?" he cried in a great voice. "The contemptible Whelm rebel? The worthless Whelm accuse *me* of failure? Where is the Mirror, Whelm? One small human, barely a woman—untrained, unskilled, with no talent worthy of the name—has humiliated the mighty Whelm. Give back your warrant; you are not fit to serve mash to swine."

Vartila faced him unmoving, but her eyes showed her

outrage and humiliation. "We are Whelm—we serve! But the master also has a duty to the servant, *and you have failed this duty.* You make faces with the slukk. You should have broken her at once. We would have done it, if you could not. You kept the Mirror from us and you lost it. Information vital to the hunt you keep from us. You are the unworthy one."

For a moment Maigraith thought Yggur had lost control; he did not seem to know what to do. She looked from one to the other and was dreadfully afraid.

"Yours is to serve, never to question. You . . . will . . . serve," said Yggur again, forcing the words through his teeth. They faced each other for a long minute, then Vartila bowed, but a little too low, and when she smiled, her teeth were pointed like the teeth of a dog.

Yggur appeared to relax. "She is mine. Return her to my chamber," he said and withdrew.

Vartila hurried her along the corridors, the grip cruelly tight on her arm.

"Your master is not pleased with you," croaked Maigraith, as they mounted the stairs.

"He knows not how to be master," she said with contempt.

"Yet you serve him."

"Only until we find a better."

After Maigraith's escape Yggur made a special cell for her, by walling off a corner of his workroom with bars stretching from floor to high ceiling. Why he did not throw her into a cell far below Fiz Gorgo to rot she did not know. Perhaps it was the enigma of her, that which still seemed to startle him when he looked at her. But there she was and there she stayed, watching him all day through the bars. And in his turn he watched her. A tiny space against the stone of the main wall was curtained for her toilet, otherwise the cell was open to his gaze.

The days flowed into weeks. His routine was almost unvarying. Each morning he appeared before it was light, went straight to a small table set in an angle between two shelves of books and sat down to read for an hour. At dawn a servant came with two baskets—Yggur's breakfast and Maigraith's. The servant, an old retainer, was fearful and would not look at her, but placed the basket outside her cell until Yggur should notice and bring it in. At first Yggur simply opened the door, handed Maigraith the basket and closed it again, but as the days and weeks passed it seemed that he sought her company; or perhaps this was another facet of his plan. He would bring the basket carefully into the cell, keeping one eye on her while he relocked it, then sit down on the bed and watch her as she ate. At first this angered her but in the end she grew used to it, even, in spite of her mistrust, came to look forward to it. The breakfast over, he would spend another hour, sometimes more, consulting the maps and papers on the large table, and writing in a journal.

After this there was a continual stream of people. Messengers came, or spies, from all the lands around. Yggur sat impassively while they spoke or read from documents. Next, the Whelm appeared but such was the tension between them and Maigraith that after only a few days they came no more, and Yggur would leave the chamber to speak to them, his guards waiting silently in his place. But several times the Whelm arrived unexpectedly and Yggur always put himself between her and them, even though she was locked in her cell. The Whelm would stare at her with a disturbing intensity, and at these times Yggur struggled to maintain control of himself.

His troubles could not be disguised from Maigraith's cool gaze. She saw the strangeness that Yggur hid from others, and his pain; and surprisingly she found that she felt for him. Normally the feelings of other people were a blank page to her.

She often thought about the Whelm after that. What was it about her that disturbed them so? In their first questioning they were concerned for the Mirror and how to recover it, but after her attempt to escape it was she that they wanted to know about. Who was she? Where had she come from? She told them nothing and they watched her constantly.

By the time Yggur returned from his daily meeting with the Whelm the morning was gone. At noon they ate a frugal lunch together: unleavened bread; a salad made from the green leaves of plants that she did not know; pastes of the flesh of nuts, pounded, soaked in thickened milk, and spiced; lasee. Yggur rarely ate meat. Lunch was a brief affair, and no sooner were the remnants taken away than his generals came. For hours they would discuss the reports of messengers and spies, the disposition of armies, the state of the weather, the disrepair of roads and bridges, or the quality of the crops and livestock of all the surrounding lands. Great charts were brought out, old maps of leather and canvas so large and heavy that it took two to carry them. They were spread over the floor of the chamber while Yggur crawled over them like a schoolboy, examining them in the minutest detail, his generals following like ducklings after their mother. And often the master map-maker was called to fill in a new detail or to amend an old one.

Maigraith listened in wonder and turmoil. Yggur knew more about the countries around him than their own rulers, and she saw why they feared him so. It was not the dread power that rumor attributed him, though perhaps he had that too. It was the cool intellect, the genius for strategy and the attention to every detail. And doubtless, the Mirror too, his tireless spy.

After that it was time for the management of his own land. Yggur spoke with his seneschal and his bailiffs, and sometimes two parties with a grievance were brought before him. He listened to their claims and resolved them. But this was rare. It was clear that his realm was well-ordered, that his lieutenants knew his wishes and carried them out exactly to his will.

The evening meal came late, long after dark. Again it was frugal, though occasionally he seemed to feel the need of richer fare, and then would come a basket of pastries stuffed with meats or ground nuts or meal, flavored with diverse spices aromatic, pungent or bitingly hot; dark meats that were dried, smoked, steeped in herbal solutions or done in subtle, unusual sauces; vegetables pickled in brine or oil; salt fish; lastly, more pastries, scented with citrus-blossom water or rose oil and filled with fruit. Then Yggur would talk to her, or sit by himself, reading or writing in his journals again. Often he questioned her about Faelamor, and Karan, and the Mirror, though after a while he realized that she would tell no more, and his examination turned to herself.

After that first night she found the strength to resist him, though still each time they spoke she was afraid that she would give something more away, and watched him warily. To distract him she would ask him about himself—his past, his people, his fears and his desires, and though he smiled, knowing what she was about, he always answered her.

"How did you come to this, Yggur?" she asked him one day.

"Surely you've heard?"

"I know the stories that others tell," she said.

"What stories?" His smoky eyes grew dark.

"That you were the youngest and most brilliant mancer

ever to be invited to the Council. That you set to work on the great project—the banishing of the Charon from Santhenar. That in your wickedness and youthful folly you tried the sorcery of the Proscribed Experiments and were snared by Rulke, leader of the Charon. That even then you would not call for aid, but strove alone until Rulke almost escaped. That it drove you beyond madness."

"The lies of the Council no longer even anger me, just weary me," said Yggur, though his eyes showed wrath. "Lies put about to cover their own misdeeds, their own follies, and not youthful ones, but the follies of those who are grown greedy and wicked through power unfettered. Long the Council sought to banish the Charon—a noble aim—and they tried the Proscribed Experiments not once, but many times; they failed each time. So they *begged* me, and my folly lay in agreeing.

"I succeeded too, but when Rulke attacked their courage failed them and they abandoned me. No man or woman of Santhenar could have held him alone, and I could not. He took my mind, was near to freeing himself, yet still I struggled to contain him. At last the Council feared for their own safety, and rightly, for had he gone free his first act would have been against them. They joined together and drove him into the shadow world in which they hold him still, the Nightland, and sealed the gate once more.

"Then did they protect and heal me?" Yggur's voice became venomous. "They left me to die, made me to be the fool responsible for all the woe that they had caused, and that was much; made themselves once more the saviors of Santhenar. But I would not die. I lived, regained my strength, and eventually my wits returned. For years I endured the taunts of humankind, both as fool and madman. Do you wonder that I threaten them, now that I am strong and they are weak?"

He had been sitting on the bed, across the little table from her. Now he rose so abruptly that the bed skidded backwards across the floor, its legs scraping against the stone. "Should I tell you? Why not? That was long ago, and all that Council is dead now, *save Mendark*! But he will pay, and the new Council, for the crimes of the old. That is only my lesser revenge. The greater—surely that is clear to you. I will finish what I began so long ago. I will finish Rulke forever."

He turned to go, but Maigraith put out her hand and caught his wrist. "There is more. Tell me. I have seen how you struggle with yourself."

Yggur looked down at her, then at the hand on his wrist, then back at her face. To her surprise, and his own, he sat down again.

"It is the memory of . . . Rulke," he said in halting words, his mouth twisting down on the left side. "I can still feel the way he clawed at my mind." With an effort he gained control of his speech. "It will be with me as long as I live. The fear of him consumes me, as though he were a great scorpion on my back, and its sting already curving into my throat." A shudder wracked him from black hair to long gray boots, and he covered his face with his hands.

"But is he not securely held?"

"While the lookout is maintained he cannot escape. But he can be freed, if the watch fails; *or released*, if someone should find the key. And you have thrown such a key, the Mirror, out where any lunatic can find it. I have bided my time, trained and disciplined myself; found the Mirror and almost broken it. Yes, I was close to having its secrets."

"It called to me too," she said, remembering how she had been fascinated by it.

"Then beware. It is a twisted, lying thing and it will do its best to entice you and trap you."

"Oh!" she said soberly.

"Now all my plans are overturned. The Mirror is abroad and might fall into the hands of anyone. The Faelamor I knew long ago was cautious; she would have done nothing foolish, but who knows what changes the centuries have wrought? What if Mendark gets it? Or worse yet, his challenger Thyllan?

"These last weeks," Yggur continued after a pause, "I've had to revise the strategy for my campaign—turn it on itself. What I might have done at will with the secrets of the Mirror I now must do with armies and bloodshed. My armies await my command, but they cannot be kept on alert forever. Do I give the order, or do I wait and hope that the Mirror will be found?"

He recovered his composure, giving Maigraith a fierce glare. She withdrew her hand from his wrist. "And what am I to do with you? The Whelm pursue Karan, but again and again she escapes them." Maigraith's eyes widened. "Ah, I see that she surprises even you. Clearly there is more to her than I saw. She is now far to the north, near Hetchet, my spies last told me. But the Mirror might be anywhere. Perhaps Faclamor has it already, and Karan was only a decoy. The Whelm have failed with her."

He walked away, ruminating to himself. I must know more, but how? It seems Maigraith knows nothing of Faelamor's plans. But perhaps her subconscious mind can give me a clue. The Whelm have a way, but can I trust them with her? I care for her now and would not have her harmed. And can I trust them with what she might reveal? For the Whelm, whom I thought I had schooled to myself, suddenly rebel. They would direct me, and not the other way. My carefully constructed world begins to unravel and I am come to a dreadful realization: that I have embraced the sting, put it to my own throat.

Yggur turned back to Maigraith, admiring her for her

courage, hating himself. He rose heavily to his feet and went out. Once he was gone, her confidence crumbled. She felt sure that he was going to hand her over to the Whelm. But he did not.

After that Maigraith saw little of Yggur. Her guard was doubled, for he was busy elsewhere with the training of his armies, the making of strategies and contingencies, the rehearsal of tactics. She was lonely and afraid, and with nothing to do she brooded more and more on the Whelm, and on what would happen to her when she finally fell into their hands.

Then one day, after she had not seen Yggur for a week, he came to her. He was different, she saw at once—something had changed. He said abruptly, "What will Faelamor do about you?"

Maigraith marveled that in all the time of her captivity she had not considered that question. She had no idea what Faelamor would do. Perhaps she would just abandon this failure and begin anew.

He stood leaning over her for a moment, then sat down right in front of her. "How did you come to serve her?"

Faelamor? Maigraith dragged her thoughts back, but could see no harm in the question.

"My mother and father both died soon after I was born; I have no memory of them. I was looked after by another family for the first few years, though I have no idea how I came to be in their care. Then Faelamor appeared. I was very young, perhaps three years old, when I first remember meeting her. I recall it well; she frightened me. She still does. She came every so often, taking me for weeks at a time, and giving me instruction. I thought of her as a strange kind of aunt, though I do not believe that there is any blood relationship. Certainly there is no resemblance between us. Then when I was five she took me with her to Mirrilladell, where the Faellem dwell. That place is south of the Great Mountains, a cold land of lakes and forests. But of course you would know that."

Yggur nodded but said nothing, not wanting to break the flow.

"I lived with her all my life, and that was a long time, for I am far older than I appear. I had the finest tutors, and Faelamor herself took charge of my instruction. I worked and studied unceasingly. Her syllabus was curious, her methods remarkable. I learned things that none but the Faellem know. As you felt before," she said absently, referring to their initial struggle.

"But I was never a part of them, never one of the Faellem. They treated me coldly, though they are a kind people as a rule. When I was still a child they shunned me completely. I often wonder what shameful thing my mother and father did, that carried on through the generations, for one day Faelamor and I left the Faellem very suddenly and went into exile. Even Faelamor was tainted by her association with me. I think the exile hurt her badly."

After a while she looked across at him and smiled, a curious sad pensive smile, as though she was only now learning how to. "It's funny," she said, smiling still. "You are the first person I've ever felt I understood. Perhaps it is like to like, for both of us are prisoners—you of the torment of Rulke, I of the will of Faelamor."

"You have Karan."

"I care for her, but I will never know her."

Maigraith fell silent, drawn back into the period of her growing up. Her long chestnut hair hung across her face. His gaze rested lightly on her features: her skin smooth as marble and the color of honey, the oval face and long straight nose, and the sad eyes, much darker than before, that hinted at her secret.

At last he spoke. "Tell me where I can find Faelamor and why she wants the Mirror, and I will tell you who your parents were, what happened to them, and why it brought such shame upon the Faellem."

Maigraith looked up suddenly and there was such child-like eagerness on her face that even Yggur's heart was touched. Twice she almost spoke, then her face clouded over and she lowered her head so that he would not see the tears in her eyes.

"I cannot," she whispered.

Yggur struggled with himself. Maigraith saw that he was torn and now she grew really afraid.

"My people recently intercepted a skeet far to the north. Mendark has learned about the Mirror and is moving the earth to get it. I *will not* allow him to have it," he said, the agony visible on his face. He stood up. "I must have it back, even if it means giving you to the Whelm. I must take the risk. You have until the morning."

He went out and she did not see him again that day. She sat there in her cell the rest of the afternoon, dreading the night and even more the dawn, but when they came for her it was barely dark, and she was unprepared. Two Whelm seized her roughly from her bed and took her away.

20

THE TALE OF
TAR GAARN

In the night Llian coughed himself awake again and could not sleep. He was still weak and feverish from the mountain sickness. He looked up and saw Karan staring at him in the feeble light of the fire.

"I know a tale of the Aachim," said Llian.

"So you keep saying." She sighed heavily. "I'm sorry, I'm too tired."

Llian was hurt. "I thought . . ."

The silence stretched out. Karan lay back suddenly on the ground and closed her eyes, trying to think, but all she could see in her mind was his wracked figure propped up against the wall.

"You thought what?"

"I thought you might like to hear it. It's . . . it seems the only thing I can offer you."

Karan felt a twinge of remorse. "Tell it then."

"It's the *Tale of Tar Gaarn*. Perhaps you know it, having lived among the Aachim."

"I know of the treachery, but not the tale. That is not something they speak of in Shazmak."

"It is quite a long tale, as we tell it in Chanthed. One of the longest."

"Not a long tale, Llian. Not tonight."

The irony struck her then, that for most of her life her greatest wish had been to hear the tellers in Chanthed, and now that she had the best of them all to herself, she was begging him not to tell. "No, tell it as you will. Perhaps it will help after all." All I know about the Aachim is what they told me, thought Karan. Doubtless the chroniclers have a different insight.

Llian gave a wan smile. "It won't be a long one tonight, I assure you," he whispered, coughing and dabbing at his mouth with a rag. His beautiful voice was quite hoarse.

"After the Forbidding, the Aachim realized that there was no return to Aachan, and turned their minds to making their way on Santhenar. Because they were strong in their own right, and tireless when they had a goal, they quickly grew to a great nation. At this time it was their will to make a city that would rival any on Santhenar, even those of the Charon, and be an emblem of their pride and their strength.

"So Pitlis was chosen, for as an architect and builder he had no equal, and the city that he raised was incomparable. It was a place of domes and towers and soaring arcs of stone that seemed to hang unsupported in the crystalline air—a fusion of air and water, metal and stone. None saw it without a gasp, or left it without a tear. A place of music and poetry. A place of community, yet a place of solitude. That was Tar Gaarn, until Rulke came."

He broke off in another fit of coughing that left him so weak he had to support himself with his arms.

Karan opened her eyes and looked up at the veiled stars. A shiver went up her spine. The seeping cold came right through coat and cloak and blankets, numbing her flesh but making the bones ache.

When he began again Llian's voice was like gravel rattling in a bucket. "But Tar Gaarn was also raised for a purpose, for the Aachim knew that war with the Charon, *with Rulke,* was inevitable. Tar Gaarn was their greatest fortress, and their final refuge, if others failed, and in it rested their hope as well as their pride. And shortly came the Clysm, the terrible wars between the Charon and the Aachim that lasted for centuries and devastated Santhenar. But wars that could never be won, for Rulke, greatest of the Charon, was impossibly strong. Yet Tar Gaarn was impregnable—so cunningly designed that the countless assaults scarcely marred its timeless beauty; so vast that its storehouses could stand the longest siege.

"But at last it seemed even Rulke tired of the endless conflict, and one day he met secretly with Pitlis and craved peace with him. 'Let us end this fruitless war,' he said. 'I would find an answer to the great problem of the age—*the breaking of the Forbidding.* This project is in your interest too, and I need your aid, for I must go back to my people.'

"Pitlis was old, seasoned, wary. He knew Rulke's reputation for treachery too well. He would not risk Tar Gaarn or his people. Yet how he yearned for his own world. *Aachan is ours,* he thought, all we ever wanted. If we break the Forbidding it is we who will be going back. And once home, with the strength we have gained here, we will wrest Aachan back and cast the Hundred (for that was the number of the Charon when they took Aachan—so few!) into the void from whence they came. I will go along with Rulke's plan until my own is ripe.

"So Pitlis agreed, but he also made a secret alliance with

the Council of Santhenar, against Rulke. The head of the Council, then as now, was Mendark, and he was balanced by the brilliant Yggur, who was so young that he had never needed to use his mancer powers to lengthen his life.

"The Clysm ended at last. And for a long time it seemed that Rulke had indeed changed, for the truce lengthened into an uneasy peace and, after many years, as memories dimmed, to an alliance of equals. The Aachim knew peace, prosperity and serenity such as they had never known. And Pitlis was revered by all.

"Then Rulke came to him again. 'I would raise a city in my own lands,' said Rulke. Then looking almost abashed, if such an expression can be imagined on the face of a Charon, he asked, 'Would the Aachim, would Pitlis conceive, even design such a city for me?'

"'What would you do with so great a city?' Pitlis asked suspiciously.

"'A monument, and a symbol. But more! To break the Forbidding I will need an army of scholars and engineers; alchemists and all the sciences. And to shape such tools I must have the right forge, and the right anvil. Will you do it?'

"How can the Forbidding be broken? thought Pitlis. Only with a device like the flute, and if Rulke could have made it himself he would not have needed Shuthdar. Perhaps I will. I see an opportunity. But I will watch him like a skeet.

"'Rulke can never be trusted, not in a thousand years, or a thousand thousand,' the other Aachim cried. 'Do not make this contract.'

"Now the great weakness of the Aachim was hubris, and in their overweening pride and arrogance they were prone to folly, to the making of foolish alliances and the pursuit of hopeless ends. Once having taken a certain course they would not be advised, and continued headlong even when it could lead only to destruction. So it was with Pitlis, who had grown proud and remote. He was sure that Rulke was lying with truths, but could not decipher his purpose, and so he agreed, for his own plan was developing. To subtly misdirect, to thwart, or if the chance came, to seize Rulke's new weapon, whatever it might be, and turn it against him."

Llian broke off abruptly. "Perhaps he used the Mirror to spy on Rulke," he croaked his sudden, excited thought. "What secrets . . . ?" There was a long silence, then he flushed as red as a boil. "I would have failed an apprentice for such an interjection," he said.

"Pitlis swore at the other Aachim and drove them away, and went forthwith to Rulke. 'I will make you such a city as has never been seen on the Three Worlds,' he said."

Karan shivered again. His folly was inevitable, and tragic beyond any description.

"For years the two worked together on the plans, for there was much work in the designing of a city and Pitlis would share it with none. Rulke knew exactly what he wanted, and what he wanted was strange and beautiful. Many things he insisted on had no conceivable purpose, yet each must be just right.

"Whenever he was wrestling with a problem, Rulke worked unceasingly with his hands. He constantly made strange devices, never saying what they were for, and casting most of them aside as soon as they were done. And Pitlis spent each night with the cast-offs of the day, feverishly examining them to conceive Rulke's true plan.

"Picture the two of them together. Rulke was a giant, a great black-bearded bear of a man, his hair so dark that it gleamed blue. He would have been head and shoulders above me and twice my weight. He was inhumanly handsome, and charming too. You could not but like him and want to be in his company.

"And Pitlis was a big man too, his thigh the equal of your waist. Long and lean in the face he was, with a broad nose and a square chin. Not handsome, not in the least, but he had a will of iron. A brilliant man but not a likeable one.

"But even yet his caution prevailed. Pitlis watched Rulke for the smallest slip, and tested him in various ways, but Rulke made no mistakes and took no advantages. For tens of years they worked, for time was of no moment to either, and Pitlis became obsessed with his creation—a work more subtle, more harmonious, more magnificent even than Tar Gaarn. A city utterly different, the epitome of the Charon. He knew it was his greatest work.

"Pitlis often met with the Council, yet no one could fathom what Rulke was up to. But in the times when Rulke had to go away, Pitlis took a petty revenge. He made tiny changes to the plans—changes that twisted Rulke's conception ever so slightly, though always ones that made it more harmonious, more hauntingly beautiful, more complete. And at last the design was done.

"But somehow it was not quite right. Some detail was lacking for its perfection, though neither could tell what it was. Rulke was visibly distressed. 'In the past I've walked in the cities of the Aachim,' he said, 'and each had about it a fusion, a coherence that is missing here, that I must have. If only I could see what it was.'

" 'How was it solved in Tar Gaarn?' was always his final question. 'If only I could see Tar Gaarn. But I do not ask that.' And he turned to other matters and never mentioned it again.

"As the days passed Rulke became more and more distressed at the failure. And at last Pitlis—"

"No!" cried Karan involuntarily.

Llian gasped a breath and wiped the carmine gloss off his

mouth. "I don't think I can finish it," he croaked, and there were tears of shame in his eyes.

"No matter," said Karan, unsuccessfully trying to hide her disappointment. Though it had been years since he had told a tale so badly, it meant everything to her.

Llian struggled on. " 'I would not have you betray your people so,' said Rulke, and Pitlis was shamed and relieved. Then came the blow! 'Besides, I have *learned you* so well that yesterday I took your shape and went right through Tar Gaarn undetected.'

"Pitlis was struck with horror at his folly, and Rulke's arrogance, and the genius that could allow him to do such an impossible thing. Yet the work had become a drug that he could not give up. Soon Pitlis went back and worked anew on the plans, effecting subtle changes that enhanced the beauty and perfection of the work.

"Months went by, and Pitlis slowly realized that Rulke was still not happy, that something still troubled him. 'It is here and here and here,' he said, pointing to certain subterranean structures. 'Such tiny details that I scarce dare mention, only that I know you strive for perfection in all things.'

"Pitlis looked where he indicated, on all the dozens and hundreds of plans of the great city, and indeed saw tiny imperfections there, insignificant asymmetries and disharmonies, though only in structures that would never be seen. Now he began to think Rulke's criticisms trivial, knew that they were of no moment, yet so humbly were they offered and such was his pursuit of perfection that he set to and came to alternative, more harmonious solutions.

"Now Pitlis was exhausted, but he knew that the city was the most perfect thing he had ever designed, or could. 'I am weary in body and soul,' he said. 'I can do no more.'

"Rulke thanked him, proclaiming the work perfect, and looked through the plans one by one. But then he frowned.

'What is this,' he cried, pointing to one. 'This spoils the whole. I cannot accept it.'

"Pitlis proposed alternatives. Rulke rejected all angrily, as though Pitlis sought to cheat him. Pitlis was desperate, intimidated. Would nothing satisfy him? 'Show me the plans of Tar Gaarn,' Rulke demanded. 'I would see how the problem was solved there.' And by now Pitlis was so weary of the project that he could think of nothing but a way to end it, and so cowed by the sudden imperiousness of Rulke that he agreed."

Karan jumped. Her mouth was round as an O.

"'So!' said Rulke, and stared at him for a full minute. 'You *would* betray your people after all. I thought as much. That is the defect that allowed the Hundred to take your world from you. But I do not need the plans after all. There is no more harmonious solution.'

"Then he thanked Pitlis with great courtesy and went away to his own lands. But after he was gone Pitlis, aimless now that the project was completed, came across a small chart fallen (or perhaps deliberately left) behind a cupboard. It was a detailed drawing, in Rulke's hand, of one of the most secret defenses of Tar Gaarn. Rulke had learned Pitlis's mind so well that he had been able to deduce the secrets of Tar Gaarn without ever having seen the plans.

"Now the veil was snatched away from Pitlis's eyes and his folly became clear to him. Rulke had been playing with him—the city, the devices, the excuse of the Forbidding, all had been just a ruse. All along his plan had been to break Tar Gaarn. How foolish Pitlis's petty revenges seemed, the tiny changes to the plans that Rulke had never noticed. And all through that brutal and interminable winter he lived in dread, tormented by a negligence so great that he could not bear to speak it.

"And in the spring his fears were realized, for a great army came out of the south and besieged Tar Gaarn. The Aachim called on their revered leader, but Pitlis was paralyzed by shame and dread, and told them what he had done. And though they resisted valiantly, Tar Gaarn was doomed, for despair had fallen on them like a shadow, and Rulke knew their secret defenses. Within a matter of weeks the city was taken and the Aachim put to the sword. Only a remnant escaped, fleeing into the high mountains. Pitlis followed behind them, a tormented husk of a man, reviled, abandoned. After that he lived alone, never having a home, wandering through other lands, longing for death but unable to find it.

"Years later, as he wandered even in the lands of Rulke, a beggar on the roads, he heard rumor of a great new city. Alcifer it was called, the most magnificent in all Santhenar. A sick horror tore at his insides, but he must see it, and he made his weary way there. He came into the city, and there was confronted by Rulke.

" 'See what you have created,' Rulke said with a smile. 'Never was the character of the Charon more perfectly realized. Soon I will put my hands to the levers and hurl the power of Alcifer at the Forbidding, and it will shatter like window glass. No more will the Hundred be paralyzed by the dread of extinction. Our seed will flower across the Three Worlds.'

"Pitlis understood at last. Alcifer was magnificent: a city vain and proud; cruel and predatory; majestic; perfect. So he had made it. But it was also a *construct*—and all its alchemists and engineers, scholars and toilers, and Rulke himself, made up a single living machine dedicated to a single end, the breaking of the Forbidding. Rulke had deceived him with the only story that he could never have believed—the truth!

"Never had he hated anything more, or anyone, and he staggered at Rulke in a rage. But Pitlis had aged and withered since Tar Gaarn. Rulke defended himself with his scepter and Pitlis fell broken on the road.

" 'So dies the greatest of the Aachim,' said Rulke, 'and their dreams with him. Such genius, such folly. Their fatal flaw.'

" 'Put your hands to the levers then,' gasped Pitlis, and what might have been a smile of triumph broke through his death rictus.

"And so ended the hopes of the Aachim. They withdrew into the mountains and the past, nursing their hopeless revenge, and took no further part in the affairs of Santhenar. Just one of Rulke's many betrayals, though possibly the most subtle; so he was known as the Great Betrayer. Thus the tale ends."

The worst I have ever told, he said to himself.

Karan was silent. That story is the Aachim, she thought. Magnificent. Tragic. Doomed. She opened her eyes again to find the mist gone and the sky teeming with stars. "Some of them came and built Shazmak after that," was all she said, wrapping the cold covers around her.

"And yet," rasped Llian, "it leads inevitably to the next tale. One day Rulke did grasp the levers, compelled Alcifer to his will, and directed all its force against the shimmering wall of the Forbidding. At once the wall bulged outward, a great tumor pressing into the void. And if it were not for those tiny changes Pitlis had made long ago, he would have broken through. But at the last moment the tumor turned inside out and pinched off a fragment of the void. Then the Council of Santhenar, who had long bided their time, struck, using the Proscribed Experiments."

"The what?" said Karan.

"Sorcerous procedures that were forbidden long ago because of the risk that they would get out of control. They forced Rulke inside, severing his control of Alcifer. The tumor collapsed to a bubble, the unbreakable prison of the Nightland, that touches everything and nothing equally. A thousand years later Rulke is still trapped there. So Pitlis had his revenge after all.

"And that is where the great enmity arose between Mendark and Yggur. But that is yet another tale."

Coughing woke her soon after from a dream of Rulke and his great city. Karan was almost overcome by the magnificence and malevolence of the Charon, and afraid to sleep again, for fear of her dreams.

Then, brooding about the tale, she was struck by a horrible thought. Tensor is just like Pitlis, she realized in the bell-like clarity of the night. Suddenly all that she had ever known about Tensor turned inside out. The dour, obdurate face that she had always seen was just a mask. Underneath was a vengeful, implacable, impossibly proud man; not reserved but calculating, not so much a leader as a manipulator.

She must never let Tensor get the Mirror—it would only fuel his hate and rage, give him the chance of power that he had never dared reach for. Llian had solved her dilemma after all.

Llian was sleeping now, breathing rapidly, almost panting, but as she listened his breathing slowed right down and suddenly stopped. She waited, holding her own breath, but he did not breathe again.

He's dying! she thought, and it felt like a fish-hook had been dragged right through her belly. She flung her covers out of the way, crying, "Llian, wake up!" but just then he started breathing again and soon was gasping, as fast as before. There was frost in his scrubby beard. She stroked the hair off his brow tenderly, and he turned, smiling up at her, but the smile was ripped off his face by another fit of coughing that left him limp as a rag and his lips red. Then he turned over and drifted back to sleep.

Between her fear that Llian would die, and this sudden new terror of Tensor, Karan could sleep no more. But Tensor was not in Shazmak, she realized, for he had come through Bannador early in the summer. He was going all the way to Stassor, in the far east, and would be away for a year.

By the time the morning came, Karan had managed to convince herself that it would all be right after all, that Rael and her other friends would be there in Shazmak, and that anyway Tensor could not be as bad as she had painted him. I know he cares for me, she thought in the lassitude of her weariness, unable to cast away the loyalty that she had always owed to the great Aachim. If Rael is there, and Tensor is not, I will give the Mirror to them. But if by some chance Tensor has returned, I will take it with me.

Llian was no better in the morning, and so weak that he could barely stand. His throat was so inflamed that he could not eat. Terribly thirsty, he drank half a bottle of water and promptly heaved it up again.

In the cold, clear air they saw how the land of Chollaz was outlined by the range of mountains on which they stood. They ran in a straggling oval to the south, the far end of the oval being completed by a rampart of jagged and unclimbable peaks. The land was cut across by a chasm whose path was traced out by the early-morning mist—the gorge of the River Garr, which looped its way from below them south-east and through the encircling mountains into Bannador. There was no sign of life—not a village, bird or bush.

"Where do we go now?" Llian croaked.

"This way. Come!"

Llian took her arm, and she led him down the pass along well-made and cunningly concealed paths that drew them eventually into the gorge of the Garr, which at this point was a scant forty spans across. Down, down they plunged. Now the way was a narrow shelf carved from the living rock, hardly wide enough for one person. At intervals a passing bay was cut into the cliff. The shelf bore neither handhold nor rail, and fell away to dark, unguessable depths on his right, where the sun penetrated only at midday, and in the winter not at all. Llian's fear of falling was numbed by his illness, otherwise he would never have made it.

"I can't," he said, as Karan tried to lead him onto the shelf. "I'll fall."

"You must. There's no other way. Hold my hand and walk behind me. Think of nothing but the next step. Look neither down nor up."

Llian stood up and took her hand. The warmth helped, and her presence reassured him a little. She squeezed his hand, smiled and, still holding him tightly, took a step backwards. He shuffled forward one step. She took another but he did not.

"What is it?" she asked gently.

"I'm afraid for you now."

"You needn't be. I lived here for six years. I'm used to these paths."

"Turn around. I can't bear to watch you walking backwards."

She laughed. "Oh. All right!" and she did so, still holding his hand.

The ledge wound back and forth down into the ravine until, reaching a level, it flattened out and followed the meandering course of the river downstream. The frequent spurs were cut through by narrow tunnels, their walls like polished

glass, but undecorated apart from carvings, so weathered
that they were unidentifiable, over the entrance and exit of
each. Llian looked around him. There was nothing to see but
the smooth dark walls of the cliff looming above and the
river foaming far below.

"Surely we must be near now?" he asked in the mid-
afternoon.

"We've gone perhaps two leagues as the river winds, but
less than one in a direct line. We won't reach Shazmak until
tomorrow afternoon."

Karan had expected Llian to get better as they went
down, but he coughed up bloody froth until the front of his
coat was stained red with it. She felt as though she was
marching him to his doom.

And when she thought about Tensor, it might have been
her doom too. If Tensor was in Shazmak after all, she would
not be able to hold out against him. He was overwhelming.
He had always seemed to know when she had done something wrong. She would never be able to keep such a secret
from him.

If only Llian wasn't with her, she would have been two
or three days further on by now, and only days away from
food. She would have crawled all the way on her belly, eating snow and stones, just to be home again.

They now found the path to be in poor repair, the edges
crumbling. Several times their way was blocked by heaps of
broken rock, one of which they were unable to scramble
over and had to clear laboriously by hand, in spells, for there
was room for only one to work at a time. Water flowed down
the cliff, showering on their heads; the stone under their feet
was slick with pink slime. Further along, the path had broken away and they had to creep across the raw rock on their
bellies. Llian was like a zombie, stepping where Karan told
him to step, waiting when she told him to wait, allowing her

to place his hands on the right handholds. He knew with a certainty that was absolute that the next step, or the one after, would fail, the next handhold would crumble within his grip and he would fall silently into the chasm. So the day passed.

The light had begun to fade when they came around a gentle curve in the gorge and looked down on a straight stretch running toward the south. Not far ahead, where the gorge narrowed, the path was joined to another from the east by a slender bridge built of metal and wires; a strange, delicate thing.

"That way leads to Bannador and Gothryme, my family home," said Karan.

"Why do we not go that way then?" Llian gasped.

"We'd never get there. Gothryme is at least a week away, at your pace."

As they drew near, the sight of the bridge raised Llian from his torpor. "I've never seen anything like it," he said. "It is built the way a spider would build—so delicate, so beautiful, so irregular. No engineer of Iagador would ever make such a thing."

"That is the way the Aachim have always built," said Karan, looking at it with a kind of satisfaction. "Many times have I stood here and gazed at it, the link between my two lives."

"The road is better here."

"Yes. Of the three paths into Shazmak, this is the only way still used."

Across the gorge the path continued downstream for fifty paces or so before sweeping east along the side of a tributary gorge. The ravine was sufficiently broad and open here that, though they were well below the rim, they could see the tips of the eastern ranges in the distance.

They camped near the end of the bridge, where the cliff had been cut back from the ledge, leaving an open space perhaps five paces across. In one corner a jumble of boulders, where part of the cliff had collapsed, offered shelter from the wind. And shelter they needed, for with nightfall the breeze had intensified to a frigid gale that howled in the structure of the bridge and chilled them even through their thick clothing.

"It's going to be a grim night," said Karan, as she struggled to make a shelter with their cloaks. There was nothing to make a fire with.

All that remained of the food was a small quantity of damp oatmeal. Llian made a slurry of the stuff in luke-warm water from his bottle and they sat in their makeshift shelter shoulder to shoulder eating the unsatisfying mess. It had a moldy taste. The roof was made from their oiled cloaks, stretched across a cluster of boulders and weighted down with stones. The edges flapped in the wind and Karan had to constantly adjust the structure to ensure that it did not blow away. Inside it was dark, but not as dark as the gorge below, up from which the misty air spiraled and the river roared.

After dinner Llian was a little better. He still breathed heavily but the cough was gone. "Please tell me about the Mirror," he begged, speaking what had been on his mind for days. "I think about it all day and at night I dream of it. Where did it come from? May I not see it?"

A faint glow appeared in the east, outlining the tips of the mountains from behind. The moon was rising. Karan stared at the spot until it came up, almost full and mostly the yellow side showing.

"I can't show it," she said. "But I will tell you what I know—that is no secret. Though doubtless it will only whet your curiosity and cause me trouble later. All I know is from a story told by my father. This is how I remember it." She felt self-conscious, telling the Histories to Llian, and she began stiffly.

"The Mirror of Aachan is old—very old. It was made in Aachan in ages long past, as a thing to look from one place to another. Such devices were common there. It was smuggled into Santhenar when our ancestors were brought here as slaves to Rulke. But here on Santhenar it was difficult to use and did not always show true. Perhaps its essence rebelled against the fabric of the world. And it changed with time and with use, as such things are wont to do, taking on a shadow of the life and color of their owners. The Mirror became capricious, showing things that never were; things that might never be. Sometimes, if the user was unskilled, or careless, it concealed or deceived. Eventually it grew so strange and entangled that it was perilous to use and it was laid aside by the Aachim. It was lost in the Clysm, some say, along with much else."

A gust of wind swirled into the shelter, sending one corner flapping loose in a shower of little stones. She paused while Llian adjusted it, then said, "My father used words that I didn't understand, but I can recite every one of his tales from memory. Others say that Yalkara, the Mistress of Deceits, the third of the Charon to come here, stole the Mirror at the fall of Tar Gaarn and took it on her long march to the *Wahn Barre*, the Crow Mountains. For she knew how to control it, and had learned its other secret. On Santh it had acquired (or had been given) a memory. It retained the imprints of the scenes that it had reflected, and though the remembrances were confused and cloudy they could be read by one who was skilled. Yalkara forced the Mirror to her will; she used it to see across the world, to pry into the secrets of the past, and she grew powerful, and cruel. But at last she found what she had sought for so long, a warp in the Forbidding, and escaped back to Aachan."

"How did she escape? How did she get through the Forbidding?"

"I don't know. That wasn't part of the tale. Let me finish my father's story. After that the Mirror was lost, or hidden. That is what the Recorder told him."

"The Recorder?" The name had aroused Llian's professional interest.

"Someone my father mentioned a few times. He knew a lot of the old tales."

Llian suddenly looked much better; alive again.

"Tell me about the Recorder," he said eagerly.

"I don't know anything more about him."

"So, the Mirror is a *seeing* device too—maybe that explains Yggur's successes!" said Llian.

"And everyone thinks that they will be the one to master it, and read its secrets . . ." Her voice trailed away. She stared at the moon unblinking, her face pinched in the cold gray light. The wind buffeted the shelter, ruffling her hair. The oilskin quivered. "I'm dreadfully afraid." She shivered and retreated into the shadows.

"That's all over now," said Llian, thinking of the Whelm. "We've lost them."

"No! It'll never be over until I can be rid of it. I don't know what to do, who to trust." Karan's voice came melancholy from behind. "I had thought to give the Mirror back to the Aachim, but how can I, after your tale?"

A sudden thought came to Llian. "The other night, in the tunnel," he said, "I caught a fragment of your nightmare. It was as though I looked down at a surface of polished metal, on which there appeared fleetingly the face of a woman.

Dark were her eyes, and her hair was dark too, save where it had turned to silver. Who is she?"

"I often think of her. Perhaps that's why she came to you. I saw her on the Mirror just as Yggur appeared. She is the very image of Maigraith, but much older. Perhaps it *is* Maigraith in some distant time and place, perhaps someone else. Perhaps just a deceit of the Mirror."

"Have you seen anything else?" he asked breathlessly.

"No. I tried it once or twice, but nothing came. And why should it? I've no training in the use of such things."

He sat there, hugging his knees, staring out across the gorge. The bridge hung like a web in the night, swaying gently and touched with moonlit silver. The wind wailed in the wires, moaned around the boulders, flapped the roof of the shelter, roared in the ravine below. Ice gripped his heart. Karan, too, was a pawn. What drew the powerful together around her? Was it only chance? Or was it a tide that swept through the vast sea of the Histories, casting them all together on this cold shore?

The names washed across his subconscious: Shuthdar the smith; Rulke the Great Betrayer; Yalkara, or the Mistress of Deceits; Mendark; Yggur; Maigraith; the Recorder . . . So many names, so many people. And one of them he knew.

Llian thought back on the time. It was when he was still a student; to prove his skill he had been set the solving of the riddle in the *Lay of the Wanderers,* a saga from the time of the Zurean Empire. Traveling west to Zile to consult the librarian, he had fallen in with a shabby man of middle age, and they found a common interest in the sagas, or so it had seemed at the time. Llian had enjoyed the companionship, and it was not until much later that he realized that the man was Mendark, watching him in disguise.

A desperate fear crept through him, driven by the cold seeping into his bones. These were not mere happenings.

Something brooded in the abysses of the world; something moved with slow patience toward a long-awaited consummation. The malevolence was almost palpable in the frigid night. Who was shifting the pieces? Llian shuddered involuntarily. He crept closer to Karan and they huddled together for warmth and comfort all the long night.

21

OLD FRIENDS
FALL OUT

A s Karan and Llian dozed in their frigid shelter a crucial meeting was about to take place in distant Thurkad, almost fifty leagues to the north-east, as the skeet flies. Mendark, longtime Magister of the High Council, sat by his fire in the citadel, scowling, afraid. Even the servants knew of the intrigues building against him—and their eyes no longer met his as they passed. Llian would scarcely have recognized the man he had traveled to Zile with five years ago. At that time Mendark had had dark hair, bright blue eyes and laughter wrinkles about his mouth, and he had drunk great quantities of wine and laughed at everything.

Now his long hair was lank and flecked with gray, his eyes were dull, his fingers had worried his beard into ratty coils, and the wrinkles were almost obliterated by scowl marks that curved down from mouth to chin. And still Tallia sent no message. She was his only comfort now, the one that he could rely on. It seemed an age since she had left for the east. Word had come that she went to Tullin, then nothing.

The door was thrust open without knocking and an orderly sauntered in. "A man below says he must see you, Magis," he said, using the familiar mode. "He would not give his name, only said to show you this." The servant passed Mendark a bracelet made of interwoven strands of black silver. It was remarkably heavy for such a fine thing.

"This man, is he big and dark, with black hair?"

The orderly nodded. "Then send him up. And when next you come, knock first, and wait until I bid you enter."

The orderly withdrew, crashing the door behind.

"Tensor, my old friend," said Mendark, when the huge frame filled the doorway. "It is overlong since we last saw you in Thurkad."

They clasped hands and Mendark drew the Aachim over to the fire, calling the servant back. They took chairs facing each other, close to the warmth. Tensor sat in his heavy coat, oblivious to the heat. There was ice on his bushy black beard and his eyebrows, and snow in his thick black hair.

The characteristics that identified him as Aachim, a different human species, were carefully concealed: the small ears that were as round as a circle; the unusual way that his hair grew to a peak on his forehead; the ridge that crested his head; the extra sensory glands in his nose; the vestigial tail. There was only one characteristic that he could not conceal—his fingers were remarkably long, almost twice the length of his hand. But he used his hands in ways that minimized that. Not that the Aachim were persecuted—in these times they were almost forgotten, but it was better not to stand out.

Beside him, Mendark looked pale and ineffectual, and his

tangled beard scanty. Eventually the servant came with tepid drinks and congealed food.

"I had not expected to see you in Thurkad this winter," said Mendark, smiling, delighted to meet his old friend again. "Were you not away in the east?"

Tensor did not smile. "I was on my way to Stassor and did not plan to return until the year after the coming one." His voice was deep, so deep that it might have been a purr or a growl, but there was no mistaking his mood this time. "But events have brought me hurrying back. Events of some importance to the Aachim."

He fell silent then, waiting for Mendark to respond, obviously hoping the rumors were not true, but Mendark did not reply. The fire crackled. A log fell apart, exposing the white coals inside. The flames leapt up briefly, the coals turning red, then black with a tracework of orange. Tensor stared at the fire, his big hands clasped together.

"What do you know of these things?" he asked at last. "You have your spies in the east."

Mendark seemed to find the term indelicate. "I have people there, but it is very difficult," he hedged. "Orist's boundaries are closed; Yggur has occupied the surrounding lands. It is hard to get people there, harder to get them out again."

"That may be so," said Tensor, "but you will have found a way."

"My people have brought me some information, but it is obscure and contradictory."

As are you, my friend, thought Tensor. You are failing and this chance is too much to pass up, as it is for me. But it sunders us. He approached the subject from a different angle.

"I have also heard that Yggur is marching, that already his armies are camped in Quilsin and Galardil, that he is preparing to move on Iagador from the south. What has made him act so suddenly?"

At the mention of Yggur Mendark started, as though reminded of something he preferred not to think about. When he spoke his voice was curiously flat. "The roads are good in Galardil, he can move there in the winter."

There was another long pause. Tensor stared at Mendark, but Mendark would not meet his eye. He got up and prodded the fire, sending a shower of sparks up the chimney; filled their glasses; sat down again. Tensor changed the subject.

"How is it with you? I hear that there is trouble in the Council."

Mendark was suddenly eager to talk. "Your information is good. My hold over them grows ever more tenuous. It is said openly that I have been Magister too long, that I am declining. Few care anymore for our great project, the final banishment of Rulke, or even the watch; but what other purpose have we ever had? Thyllan would be Magister. He is greedy for power, but he would turn the Council to a new design. How did you learn of this?"

"By chance I met Hennia across the sea, at Larnat. We spoke briefly. She told me of the doings of the Council since our last meeting, and of your troubles."

"They will soon be *our* troubles. I have tried to call a meeting, but time and distance are against us. Nadiril refuses to come—I fear he will never leave Zile or his Great Library again."

"He is very old now, for a human," said Tensor softly.

"Yes, so there is only you, myself, Nelissa (though we have never agreed on anything), Thyllan of course, he won't miss the opportunity to take me down," Mendark said bitterly, "and Hennia the Zain. And she will stand aloof, as always. I doubt if Wistan can get here, over the mountains. Orstand is over the sea, and the others so far off that they are no use to us. We have fallen back into our old folly, of warring cities and petty states, and once more comes a tyrant to crush us."

"Yggur is more than just another warlord. Do not underestimate him, for your own sake. That was one reason for going east. I needed the counsel of my brother Aachim, even their aid, though they had little to give, so far away as they are. But I dallied when I should have hastened and the opportunity is gone. Even across the sea a messenger found me, bearing the news that you, *old friend,* are so reluctant to tell. You would first learn what I knew, so you could decide what to tell me."

Mendark looked uncomfortable, and at such times was inclined to take refuge in pomposity. "In this matter our interests may not fully coincide," he said at last, "but at such an hour we should look to strengthening the bonds of our friendship, not fall upon each other like dogs over some trifle."

"Do not speak to me in the language of embassies, Mendark! The Mirror of Aachan is no trifle. It is ours, stolen from us long ages ago. Well you know how hard we searched for it, and how long. We have never given up our right to it. The Mirror will free us. The thought of the Great Betrayer is what saps us of will. Only when Rulke is utterly extinguished can we flourish, as we did before the Clysm."

Oh, Tensor, what a fool you are, Mendark thought. I may be waning, but at least I know it. Your pride leads the Aachim to the abyss, and you draw all Santhenar with you. Give up your hopeless dreams. The Twisted Mirror it was called, a deceitful, perilous thing. But he said nothing, and Tensor took his silence for assent.

"We Aachim will not compromise. If you thwart me in this you are my enemy." Then he paused, deep in thought. When he resumed his tone was more personal. "Why do you want it anyway? How can you hope to use it?"

"Yalkara did. And did what none thought possible— found a way through the Forbidding."

"Surely you don't compare yourself to her? That evil is gone forever."

"Yggur marches," said Mendark, "and who does he march against? He is a tyrant, a warlord, but he has a greater purpose. It is me he wants, and revenge for the Council's ancient blunder that crippled him for so long. He is strong, but my tide is running out. I'm afraid, Tensor. Does that not shock you? Do you not wonder that I seize upon any weapon? I, *Mendark,* am afraid. A great upheaval approaches, and Santhenar will be reshaped. But who will do the shaping?"

Tensor smiled, a dreaming look in his eyes. "Yes, a conjuncture, a climacteric, and it will be ours."

Then he came to himself. "What do you know of the thieves?"

"What have you heard?"

"That someone broke into Fiz Gorgo and stole something of great value to Yggur. That it is thought to be the Mirror of Aachan. That the one who took it was pursued across half of Meldorin, but had come into the care of one of your people."

"That is mostly correct. There were two of them. One was taken. The other escaped *after they were discovered by Yggur.*"

"Incredible. What more?"

"I have a name for the one who escaped. Perhaps you may know of her, for she comes from Bannador—Karan is her name. A small young woman with red hair."

Tensor was shocked. "Are you absolutely sure? It cannot be!"

"Tallia said it, therefore it is so. You know her?"

"If it is indeed her, I know her well. Her grandmother—beloved, tragic Mantille—was Aachim. It is exceedingly rare for us to marry outside our own, as you know. The blending usually has unhappy consequences, as it has had in her family, though it has given her a talent. Her family has bonds with us that go back a thousand years, and for a time she lived in Shazmak. No! It is impossible! In any case, the task is beyond her.

Karan is not one to match power with Yggur, within his stronghold or out of it. Her strength is not of that kind."

"So," breathed Mendark. "She is a *blending*! That explains much. She could be useful to me here. You are sure that she is the lesser of the two thieves?"

"As though she were my own." Tensor's stern face softened and a wistful tone crept into his voice. "She is clever, and if you set her a task she will find a way to do it. She has a talent of seeing, sending, perhaps even linking. It is very strong, though she is poorly educated in its use. Deliberately so, for she can never be one of us. No one can predict how the talents of a blending will develop. Dangerous for us, but more so for her, should the world learn what she is. But why would she do this? Why would she act against us?"

"Perhaps she was just a helper, taken along for her talent. She may not know that it is the Mirror. They who seek it would want the secret kept."

"Possibly, though I do not believe it. Even so, it is a dark day for the Aachim, for we love her dearly; she is so like Mantille. Where is she now? Do you truly have her?"

"Alas not, and we do not know where she is. More than two months have passed since she fled Fiz Gorgo. Yggur's Whelm hunted her north, at least as far as Hetchet, but were unable to take her. Learning that she was near Hetchet and fleeing east into the mountains, I sent a skeet to Wistan at Chanthed. I asked him to send someone to Tullin, find her and bring her here."

"This was done?"

"Unfortunately Wistan chose to settle an old score with me; the one he sent has neither skill-at-arms nor knowledge of the mountains. Wistan would be rid of him, I believe, for he is Zain. His name is Llian, a young chronicler."

"I have heard of him," said Tensor slowly. "He is your protégé, is he not?"

"I sponsored him at the college."

"Why so? You're not usually altruistic."

"Am I not? He's not the first. I've always thought it important to encourage talent that would not develop by itself. But now that he has fulfilled his promise, I will certainly use it. Chroniclers hear everything and understand what they hear. They make excellent spies. Being a Zain though, Llian would never have got into the college without me, so he is greatly in my debt."

"Did he not do a great telling at the Festival of Chanthed four years ago?"

"Yes, and an even greater one last summer, I hear, though I haven't seen it written. Wistan promised, but I haven't got it. Anyway, I was in despair to hear that Wistan had sent Llian, but he did better than anyone expected. He found her near Tullin and they fled into the mountains, pursued by the Whelm. That was a couple of weeks ago. One of my people brought the news yesterday."

"Karan knows the mountains. There was an old path that led to Shazmak once, though we've not used it for many years."

"I believe I have a map showing it," said Mendark.

"Perhaps she has taken the Mirror to Shazmak, to us."

"Perhaps," conceded Mendark, though he did not think it likely. "If she is still alive; if the Whelm don't find her first."

"I will send people out for her," said Tensor, talking half to himself. "But who would watch her carefully enough, if she is brought to Shazmak?" His handsome face twisted, as though he had thought of something loathsome. "Yes, there is one, though it dishonors me to use him. But the Mirror! I never thought that such a chance would come. What is my honor beside this chance." Then to Mendark, "You have a skeet?"

Mendark shook his head, not meeting Tensor's eye. "There are but three remaining, and none here. The past weeks have taken a toll of them. I expect one from Tallia at any time. It is a strong beast, but still it would need to rest a day; and then be schooled to the new destination. You may have it when it comes. Will you stay?"

"I cannot. It is a hard road to Shazmak at this time of year. Even for me it will take seven days and nights, perhaps longer, and time is precious. I will write a note and you must send it when you can."

Mendark got paper, pen and ink and Tensor wrote a careful note. He sealed it with wax from a candle, and wrote one word on the outside: *Emmant.* Then he wrote another note, sealed the first inside it and reached out to hand the package to Mendark—but hesitated, drawing back his hand. "No, there are other skeets in Thurkad," and he put it in his pocket.

"Now, the Mirror! If it comes to Shazmak, it is ours. If it comes to you, pledge that you will not use it or give it to another, but hold it until I come. Then we will discuss terms."

"That I can promise," said Mendark, and they shook hands.

"We come to your own problem—Thyllan! I have spoken with Hennia, as you know, and will meet Nelissa before I leave. And Thyllan, too, if he will see me. I think you are secure until Yggur marches on Iagador. I doubt that he will come until the spring."

"I'm not sure Thyllan will wait. As soon as he learns that the Mirror is for the taking, he will act. This business has come at the worst of times for me."

"Then what will you do?"

"I have prepared myself. My villa here in Thurkad is made safe for the present. But eventually I must leave the city, for a more secure refuge. You know where it is?"

Tensor nodded. "Then be watchful, and keep my warnings to heart. All of them."

I do, thought Mendark, as he watched him go. You have aroused fears worse than I ever imagined. I will never let you have the Mirror, whatever the cost to myself. You were wise not to give me the letter.

He went along the corridor to his map room, searching through the old charts of the mountains. Then he sat down and wrote a hasty note to Tallia, and sent it by skeet to Tullin that very night.

> The Citadel,
> Thurkad
> Sord 8

Tallia,

I write in urgency and despair! Thyllan moves openly against me and I am friendless. But there is worse. Tensor came today, and he also knows about the Mirror. Long have I kept his secret, but now you must know. He is Aachim, the leader of the few that remain in Meldorin, and dwells in their secret mountain city of Shazmak.

The Mirror belonged to the Aachim an age ago—Tensor himself held it for a time. He would use it to raise them up again, for his pride is overweening, but his folly matches his pride and the result will be our ruin.

Tensor knows Karan: indeed there is a bond between them, as she dwelt in Shazmak once. He thinks that she follows an abandoned path to the city. I enclose a fragment of map that may help you to find it. Use it as a guide but do not rely on it. Find Karan at all costs and turn her back. Do whatever is needful. I will try to strengthen my position here. If you need aid, Shand can probably be trusted.

Mendark

22

SHAZMAK

The next day dawned cold but sunny. Llian was much better, the mountain sickness almost gone. They left as soon as there was light to see, for walking was preferable to huddling in the cold and there was no breakfast to delay them. The ledge was well kept and broad and now they went along at a great pace, Karan leading, Llian following steadily, experiencing none of the horrors of the previous day. Neither spoke, nor wanted to, so immersed were they in their own concerns. It was almost noon when they came around a last bend in the gorge and Karan stopped.

"Look!" she said, gesturing ahead with one arm. "There is Shazmak."

Llian looked. Before and below them the brown walls of the gorge plunged almost sheer for more than three hundred spans to the white foam of the Garr. The cliffs rose equally sheer above. Half a league away the river parted around a pinnacle of rock. Out of the pinnacle grew the city. Llian stared at it in wonder.

Shazmak was a profusion of towers, breathtakingly slender, of aerial walkways and looping, helical stairways, all intertwined and connected to each other with an organic irregularity and complexity by threads of metal the color of old iron. It looked as though it had grown there. The city was joined to the cliffs on either side of the river by two bridges of gossamer, similar to the one they had camped by the previous night, though larger and more intricate, more web-like.

It was like a song. Even from where they stood they could see the mindless violence with which the Garr flung itself at the base of the pinnacle. They saw, too, the way the gorge-funnelled gales tormented the towers and made them quiver; and the shriek of the wind in the wires and around the spires even from this far away plucked at Llian's nerves. Shazmak! Ethereal above, but with the solidity of stone below: such a coalescence of delicacy and strength was almost too much to be imagined. The two materials so different, yet the fusion so perfect that none could have told where stone failed and metal took over.

"Shazmak was built by the Aachim after the Clysm," said Karan. "It has never been taken, and in these times has faded from the memory of the world. I love it more than even my first home in Bannador. It is very beautiful, is it not?"

Llian did not answer her. How was it that there were no tales of such a place? It was beautiful, incomparable, and it filled him with dread. How would the Aachim treat *him*?

They made their way toward the city. Llian's stomach throbbed as if his entrails were knotted together, not solely from hunger, and his legs were unaccountably tired. What would their reception be? Shazmak was in decline and the Aachim looked forever inward. He sought in his mind for other stories of them but only fragments, mostly of betrayal or despair, came. He shuddered. The Aachim had passed out of the Histories aeons ago. All that he knew of them was from the Great Tales. Doubtless there was more, but not in the library at Chanthed.

The path went into a tunnel. Karan walked beside him but he could not see her in the dark. Since they crossed the pass into Chollaz she had grown increasingly edgy; now, within sight of the city, her anxiety was intense.

"Why are there no guards or fortifications?" Llian wondered. "Are the Aachim grown so tired and so few that they no longer watch?"

"Their defense is not based on guards, except at the last. They would have known we were coming hours ago. If they wished to keep us away they would have done so."

The lighted oval of the tunnel mouth grew in front of them and shortly they emerged on a wide platform, off which other tunnels issued. Ahead of them the bridge was a single, unbroken span no more than two paces wide, without wall or railing. The abutments were of black metal decorated in silver tracework.

Llian stared at the bridge in horror.

Karan gave him a look of amused tolerance. "After what you have been through? Come." She stepped out onto the span.

Llian wished she were holding his hand, but she was already moving away. He followed, slowly at first, then more quickly. The surface yielded slightly beneath his feet, and though in the middle it swayed alarmingly in the wind he did not feel insecure, and that was strange. At the city end a great gate opened onto a roofed passageway. They passed along it and into a wide courtyard paved with black and amber flagstones and surrounded with slender polygonal, helically coiled towers decorated with silver tracery, surmounted by jade-topped domes. A small black fountain played, slightly off the center; in the opposite corner there was a stone table and bench. The courtyard was empty and the air still, though the wind shrieked above them.

"Here we must wait," said Karan in a low voice, gesturing to the seat. "It may be some time before they come. And remember your bargain." She put her lips to his ear. "You know nothing about the Mirror."

"I remember," said Llian. He felt awful, terrified. They sat down. "Where are all the Aachim?"

"They are a people governed by ritual, order and habit," she replied. "When the tasks of the hour are completed, they will come. You will need much patience in Shazmak."

It was not long, however, before they appeared. There were three of them, a young woman followed by two men: one with hair the color of brown earth, the other's closer to the color of a carrot, orange-brown, and his skin pale rather than brown. Llian examined these Aachim with interest bordering on fever, recording them in his memory so that he could bring the Aachim to life in his *Tale of the Mirror*.

At first it wasn't easy to distinguish them from the people of his own world. The older man was huge, but the others were not remarkably big. They wore their hair to the shoulder in ringlets and their eyes were yellow, with oval pupils, or green with flecks of yellow.

"Rael!" Karan whispered. She stared at the man with the orange hair with such intensity that she shook.

Rael stared back, then recovered himself with a shiver and a shake of his head that sent his ringlets dancing. He bowed low then embraced her formally and stepped back. The others did the same. They held out their hands to Karan. She grasped each of their hands in turn, then bowed till her forehead touched the ground. Llian stood to one side, feeling foolish. The Aachim had not so much as glanced at him.

He was almost afraid to stare at them, evidently having no status whatsoever.

The woman spoke, using the common speech of Meldorin in a lilting melodic way, as though she was used to speaking in verse. Here was the source of Karan's unusual accent that had so puzzled Llian.

"We bid you welcome, cousin Karan. Six years have passed since that bitter day when you left us."

"Sunias," Karan replied, "I dreaded to come back. Only when I was far across the sea did I realize how much I wanted to return, but I went home to Gothryme and found that I'd neglected my obligations."

The greeting continued in a formal and obscure manner for so long that Llian ceased to follow it, and his thoughts wandered along paths of their own. Suddenly he realized that they were talking about him.

"But Karan," Rael went on, "what is this—" (here he made an unpronounceable noise in his throat, but the meaning was clear) "that you have brought? It is not even of your family. It cannot be permitted. No one could trust such a thing." Large oval eyes, emerald and honey, pierced Llian.

The vague unease that had lain in Llian's stomach ever since he had seen the city sharpened suddenly into a pang of fear. The Zain had conspired with Rulke against the Aachim long ago. What would they do to him? His eyes pleaded with Karan, but she was smiling at Rael.

"Come, Rael. For a thousand years my family has kept the secrets of the Aachim. I would not have brought him here if he could not be trusted."

She turned and held out her hand to Llian, drawing him to her. "This is Llian, the famous chronicler from Chanthed. He is my road companion and dear friend. Long he has served and guided me." Llian stared at her. "He will swear to serve the Aachim and keep the secrets."

The discussion went back into prolonged formalities. Normally Llian would have noted every detail, but he was too tired, too hungry, too afraid. The negotiations seemed not to require his participation so he sat down on the bench again and leaned back with his eyes closed. The sun was shining and in the shelter of the courtyard he was warm for the first time in days. The privations of the journey retreated a little. His thoughts touched on Chanthed, his adopted home that he would see no more; on the honey-colored stone houses and halls, the narrow twisting streets on the hillside, the crags and boulder-strewn fields above, the ruins in the valleys below. The winter months when it seemed the rain would never stop, the mountain meadows bright with flowers in the spring. How he wished that he was there now.

A furious gust struck the nearby towers, sending a tremor through the stone beneath his feet. The wail rose to a shriek and Chanthed was gone. He opened his eyes and looked up at the spiraling towers of iron, the lacework of pathways and platforms, the curves and angles that were somehow wrong. They have made a little piece of Aachan here on Santh, he thought. They have twisted the fabric of the land and made it their own. But it could not be home for me.

The others had moved across the courtyard, nearer the fountain, still talking in low voices. Just then they turned as one and advanced toward him. Rael held out both hands to him, smiling. Llian gripped Rael's hands as he had seen Karan do, smiling uncertainly, unsure of the protocol. The grip felt strange, because of the Aachim's remarkably long fingers.

"We have discussed your problem," Rael said in a deep resonant voice. "We do not permit strangers to enter our land, as Karan Elienor has told you. Nor do we permit those who have entered illegally—" here he frowned "—to live."

Llian directed a furious entreaty to Karan, but she looked away blandly.

"On the other hand, Karan has spoken for you. She says that you are neither practical nor resourceful, but your heart is pure."

Did she smile? Did Karan mock him?

"What to do?" Rael paused, looked to the woman, who nodded, and then to the older man, and continued. "In order to resolve this difficulty to our satisfaction, as well as your own, we have taken the unusual step of confirming you as Aachim-ning, that is to say, a friend of the Aachim. You are permitted to enter Shazmak, and to leave again, provided that you are accompanied while you are in the city. Karan and I have agreed to perform this office. Will you assent to the condition?"

Llian agreed, the Aachim each gripped his hands once more and, to his surprise, the ritual was over.

"I thought that we would be there another hour," he said to Karan as they picked up their packs.

"It is only the unimportant things that they surround with ritual," she replied. "What is urgent or vital, they do without fuss."

Rael led their way from the courtyard into the city. They parted from the other Aachim and followed him through a labyrinth of passages, up and down stairways numberless and once across a gossamer bridge between two slender towers. In a paradox of dimensions each part of the city seemed to be connected to every other part. Passages twisted endlessly and often turned back on themselves. Every ceiling, wall, architrave and panel was decorated with intricate, alien designs and scenes.

The floors of the halls were pale marble and slate, much worn. Every chamber and hall was decorated with murals showing different scenes of a gloomy, stormy land. A world of huge mountains, crusted with sulphur-colored snow and trickling lava. A land of icy rifts and furiously rushing rivers; of still, oily bogs and blue-black luminous flowers.

Between the mountains were plateaus covered in gray grass, and the kidney-shaped mounds and ruins of ancient cities. The hilltops were crowned with fibrous iron towers, leaning at improbable angles. The halo of a small red sun was sometimes seen through the storm clouds. More often the sky was dominated by a huge orange moon, hanging sullenly a little above the horizon and bathing all in its dreary light. When the Aachim were shown in these murals, which was seldom, they appeared as groups of small, toiling figures.

They passed many empty chambers, their doors standing open, but met few other Aachim on the way. Eventually Rael stopped outside one door and showed them in.

"Your old chambers," he said to Karan. "They have not been used since last you were here. They are sufficient?"

Karan nodded and thanked him. All the fear had gone from her, and she was happier than Llian had ever seen her.

"We will speak later of your plans. The city is yours."

Llian thanked him too. "I dreaded to come here," he said.

Rael's eyes softened, as though he knew how Llian felt, and he spoke kindly to him. "When I said that none could trust such a one, I meant it, for that is the way we look on all outsiders. But Karan has spoken for you and that is enough. We knew that you were Zain, but our grievance against the Zain is long ended, that alliance paid for many times over. Remain in Shazmak without fear." He bowed and withdrew.

The chamber in which they stood was large, simply decorated and dimly lit by glowing flasks set on brackets around the walls. It was cold, as was the whole of Shazmak. The walls bore somber murals of an alien worldscape, similar to those outside, which he took to represent Aachan. Llian was too weary to look at them closely. The only furniture was a small table set against one wall and two large couches in the middle of the room. Four rooms opened off the main chamber. One was a cooking and eating area, the second a bathing room with extravagant plumbing, the third a room with a pallet along one wall, chests for storage, a table, chairs and something resembling an armchair. Karan touched the flask over the table and it began to glow more brightly.

"This will be yours," she said to Llian.

He eased the pack off his shoulders and let it fall onto the pallet. It rolled off the end and the contents spilled on the floor. Llian left it where it lay and trudged after Karan.

The last room was smaller than the others, though still spacious, and brightly lit by a large window let into the far wall. The furnishings in the room were similar to those in Llian's. The weariness seemed to have been lifted from her; Karan moved as though she was dancing on air. Llian, by contrast, was so exhausted that he felt like a great slug.

"This was my room when I lived in Shazmak—they made it so for me," she said, gesturing. "It is the only apartment in Shazmak with a window."

"How can they bear to be shut up in this gloomy place?"

"They rather look on it as shutting our world out, the better to remember their own. Now, there are things you will need to know," she continued, "but later. I plan a bath, a long soaking tub—at least an hour to remove the grime of the past month, and another hour just for me. Then, since you made our last meal, it is only fair that I cook tonight. I hope I can outdo you." She laughed at her own humor, and Llian laughed too, reminded of the moldy slurry that they had endured last night. "I'll cook Aachim-style, for I see the kitchen is well stocked. Go away now, I need to be alone."

Llian went out. Karan walked around the room once or twice then sat down on the end of the pallet, looking out the window at the spires and towers. There were so many memories here. This had been her room from her first night in Shazmak, this apartment her home for six years. She closed her eyes and lay back. The wind howled outside, and that too was a comforting, familiar thing. The memories were so clear that her first night here might have been last night.

How kindly they had treated her at that time. They had bathed her, taken away her ruined clothes and burned them, and brought her garments newly made. They had given a small banquet in honor of her and her dead father. They had done everything they could to make her feel at home: shown her the whole of the city and the land of Chollaz, taken charge of her education. And everywhere, helping and guiding her, comforting her when she was lonely or unhappy, asking nothing in return, had been Rael. Dear Rael. The instant she saw him again she realized how much she had missed him.

Llian lay dozing on his pallet. Through the open doorway came the sound of splashing and a high clear voice was singing a carefree, silly child's song. He hadn't heard Karan sing before. Her voice was not well-schooled, but very charming. He closed his eyes again. The next he knew she was standing over him, wrapped in a large towel, water dripping from her red curls.

"Wake up, sleepy," she said gaily, smiling down at him and shaking her head so that a shower of drops fell on his face. "You need a bath: I can smell you from the kitchen. Hurry now."

He stared at the apparatus in the bathing room for ten minutes before deciding that he had absolutely no idea how to make it work, but after her previous insults he was loath to admit his inability. When she finally came to investigate the noises the room was full of steam and water was spraying at the ceiling while Llian sat, naked and incredibly grubby, in the bathtub, trying to wash himself in a trickle of icy-cold water.

"Don't stand there laughing," he said in a surly voice. "Help me. I'm neither practical nor resourceful enough to make a bath for myself, it seems."

"I *am* sorry," she said, with a total lack of sincerity, dashing the tears from her eyes. "You look so ridiculous, so dirty. I can't help myself. I'm sorry," she repeated, more soberly. "You should have asked for instructions. What I said to Rael today, that was but a joke. Please forgive me."

She leaned over him, shut off the steam and the spray and with a few quick flicks the bath began to fill with warm water. "To turn the water off you do this," she demonstrated, "and to let it out again, this." She maintained a contrite expression as far as the door, then turning around for a last look, exploded with laughter again and danced out, slamming it behind her as a misdirected boot crashed into the lintel.

Half an hour later Llian crept out again, realizing only after he had washed his filthy clothes that he had nothing left to wear. However, in one of the chests in his room he found a robe in the style of the Aachim which, although much too large for him, at least kept the cold out. He simmered in his chair but, in a little while, hunger, curiosity and the smells from the kitchen combined to draw him out of his room and his anger evaporated.

Karan was rummaging under a bench when he entered the cooking area. She looked up sideways at him with a soft expression, apologizing with her eyes, but seeing that he was no longer angry her mouth twitched again and she gave a muffled snort. She, too, was wearing an Aachim robe in cream with devices in maroon and black. The robe was too small and did not reach to her knees. Her feet were bare. She had pretty feet, he noticed. Her ankles and calves were shapely too—not at all what he had expected under the baggy trousers. His gaze moved slowly upwards.

"I often wore this when I was young," she said. "Everything I left behind is still here, but this especially reminds me of those times. Go away now, I can't think with you staring at me so. Here, open this if you can." She handed him a large squat bottle made of glass, with a glass stopper sealed with hard blue wax.

"What is it?"

"Wine, of course. Hurry up."

Llian had not seen wine kept in glass before, but where drink was concerned he was prepared to experiment. He chiseled the hard wax from around the stopper and got the bottle open with no more damage than a cut finger, then Karan poured him a large goblet and put him out of the kitchen.

The food of the Aachim was like nothing he had tasted before. There were many small dishes—pickled nuts, large and small, wrinkled and smooth, and some in thick sweet sauces with the fire of ginger, or the aroma of unknown spices. Meats there were of all kinds, in tiny portions: some dried, hard and black as coal, others smoked or pickled sour or spicy; vegetables and fruits raw, preserved, smoked or served with extraordinary sauces, or crystalized in honey; dried cheeses, shaved or sculpted into unusual shapes, sometimes with a single shred of fiery herb inside, or corn of pepper; flavored mushrooms and other fungi, the ones that grew on long-fallen trees in the forest, as well as pale long-stalked kinds from dark caverns, and some that looked like tangled skeins of cotton. And there were other foods so strange that he could not guess what they were made from, or whence they came. The wine was familiar, though it was of an excellence beyond his experience.

Within their tower the howling of the wind was barely audible, save near Karan's window, and, well-fed, clean and comfortable, Llian could find nothing to complain about, except that it was cold. But even that could be solved. Karan went to a cupboard and came back with two thick, silvery-gray blankets. They each wrapped one about themselves and sat sipping their wine, feeling no need for speech. Karan looked as though a great burden had been lifted from her.

"I think I am safe here," she said. "Safe at last."

She had not slept in a bed for months, and since they had entered Shazmak could scarcely think of anything else. She laid her glass aside, sat back and looked at her companion. Llian's cheeks were red and his eyes bright from the wine, for which his appetite was prodigious. He was smiling and happy. And he was talking, *telling,* and though she loved his tales, and this was a marvelous one, her bed had more appeal. After a while she got up quietly and went into her room, lying down on her pallet in the darkness. The magic of his voice came softly through the half-open door and carried her off to a sweet and dreamless sleep. Llian watched her go, and happy for her. He needed no audience but himself for the perfecting of his art.

The inn at Tullin was empty now, save for the landlord and his family, and old Shand, and a solitary guest: Tallia. And Tallia grew restless. She had done everything that could be done, searched everywhere that could be searched, but all traces of Karan and Llian were gone. Now she sat watching the snow falling gently outside and fretting. All at once she got up, tore a half page from her little journal and wrote the following note.

The Inn, Tullin
Sord 10

Mendark,

Your message came yesterday, but I have no news to comfort you. I searched for more than ten days but could not find them, only traces. Llian met Karan and they fled into the desolation south of Tintinnuin. I caught up with the Whelm there, hunting in a place of caves and tunnels, and drove them to the west; but I dared not return at once for fear that they would follow. More than a day it was, and though by chance I found the place where Karan and Llian had sheltered, they were gone and the snow so thick that there was no chance of finding them. After that the weather drove me back to Tullin. This is no country to be alone in at this time of year. Now that I have your map I see where they might have gone, but it is too long ago. If they have survived they must be far away. I spoke long with Shand, and searched all around in case they turned back, but no trace could I find. I will remain another week, then if there is no word I will return to Thurkad. Even the Whelm have given up. They went back toward Hetchet a few days ago, at a great pace.

Send back the skeet.

Tallia

Tallia went downstairs, encountering Shand on the doorstep. He smiled at her request and turned into the grain store next to the stables. Shortly he returned, carrying a bowl with a large brown rat in it, freshly dead. They went together to a lean-to shed at the back of the inn, where Tallia's courier bird was housed. Even for a skeet it looked miserable, clinging to its perch in the half-light, though when they came near it snapped at their faces viciously, shifting its weight from one foot to the other, the gray claws grasping the pole. Its large black eyes were dull, not even reflecting the light from the doorway, and the dark skin of its breast was visible where it had plucked away the down in its distress.

Shand snapped his fingers before the skeet, keeping well out of the way of the lunging, spitting, croaking beak, while Tallia stole behind it and with a swift movement slipped the snool, a leather bag on a long handle, over its head. Instantly the skeet became docile and Shand held it, stroking its soft neck feathers while Tallia put on the string harness with the message pouch. When this was done Shand stepped back, put the bowl with the still-warm rodent on the platform beside the perch, and Tallia eased the snool free of the head and the long curved beak.

The skeet struck once at Shand in a half-hearted way, then turned and noisily tore the animal apart and swallowed it in large dripping chunks. The metallic smell of warm blood filled the lean-to. The skeet walked sideways along the perch, wiped its beak on the straw, took a long drink, then another, its throat undulating, then abruptly spread its wings with a crack and lunged forward eagerly, bright-eyed now.

They went carefully to the door, opened it a fraction and slipped through and behind. Shand flung the door wide. Nothing happened for so long that Tallia moved to peer around the door. Shand caught her arm and pulled her roughly back, and as he did so the big wings cracked again, like a whip, and the bird flashed through the doorway into the open, slashing at Tallia's face with one long claw as it passed. Free of the shed it sailed, hung in the air a moment, glaring evilly at her, then the cold wind rushed across its wings and it shot up into the sky and turned toward Thurkad.

They watched it go in silence. When it was a speck blurring into the dark sky they went back to the warmth of the inn.

"I should have known better," she said, her hand on the door. "Had you not caught me . . ."

"You can never relax with them. Not for an instant. I saw a man die once, his throat gone. But as long as messages must be sent . . ."

Two days later another skeet came. This time the message was not on the Magister's parchment but on a soiled scrap of brown paper.

Tallia,

My worst fears have come about, and I am overthrown with violence. They came in the night. Some of my poor servants are dead, but I was ready and fled the secret way. I think they would have killed me too, could they have done it in darkness, but now my villa is made secure and I am safe for a time.

No point searching anymore; come back to Thurkad, but come carefully. I will try to maintain my factors for as long as I can, for information is all, but without the resources of the Magister it will be difficult. We must make contingencies against the finding of it.

Yggur marches on the south.

Send no more skeets.

M.

Tallia showed Shand the letter, wordlessly.

"You are going?"

"I will, in spite of the snow. He needs me now. As long as I've known him he has lived in dread of this time, of Yggur. But to have the world go crazy at the same time . . ."

"Yes," said Shand. "It even begins to worry me, here in Tullin. Though I swore it, I can no longer remain aloof. If I had helped Llian when he asked me . . . But no use, that. I too will go to Thurkad, though not with you. I'll come later, when the snows have hardened. There are things I must do here first."

23

TALES OF
THE AACHIM

The next day Karan rose at dawn, prepared her breakfast and took a tray into the other room. She shook Llian awake.

"What?" he cried, screwing his eyes closed. "Is it an earthquake?"

"Wake up, you slug."

He rubbed his eyes and pushed himself up in the bed. "What's the matter?"

"Breakfast," she said, putting the laden tray in his lap.

He shook his head, which throbbed to remind him of the wine.

"I'm going to see Rael. Would you like to come?"

"I need another ten hours' sleep," he said grumpily.

She touched him on the forehead and danced out of the room. Llian picked at the tray, but as soon as the door banged he put it down on the floor and was fast asleep in an instant.

Rael was eating alone when Karan appeared at his door. He embraced her in the doorway. "Come and breakfast with me," he said. "I've just begun."

"I've eaten, but I'll take some tea, if you have my favorite."

She took a cushion and sat down on the other side of the table, holding the bowl out in the correct manner while he poured cold ginger tea. Shards of ice rang together in the bowl.

"It's so good to be back in Shazmak. So good to see you again."

"I missed you," said Rael, "from the moment I left; and the whole year that I spent in Stassor. When I came back you were gone and I couldn't find you."

"That year after you left was one of the worst," she said. "Emmant tried to fill your place, as though anyone would do for me. Vile, depraved beast. Shazmak became unbearable." She shuddered. "I tried to leave no trace, for fear that he would follow me, and I kept traveling for four years. Why *did* you go?"

"Tensor required that I do so."

The name struck her like a blow in the face. "Tensor! Is he . . . here now?"

"Does it matter?" He was looking puzzled. "No, he went east months ago, and won't be back for a year."

Karan tried to suppress her relief. "When you left I was devastated," she said. "I had thought . . . thought that we might—"

"I had thought that too," he said, his big sad eyes fixed on her. "I came back ready to ask you, and if you said yes, to break with my people and go into exile. But it was not possible."

"I thought that Malien cared for me," she whispered, staring just as hard at him.

"My mother loves you dearly, but Tensor would not allow it."

"What does he have against me?"

"*Blood,* and the consequences of mixing it."

"There have been cases . . ."

"I know. I quoted them, but he was inflexible. There is something about your heritage, but he would not even whisper it."

Karan sagged down as though her bones had dissolved. "Perhaps he is right. There is much madness in my family. *Brilliant or mad are the house of Fyrn.* That saying goes back more than five hundred years."

"It wasn't that. In Aachan we valued madness for the genius that came with it. It was something else."

"Well, you could not have gone against him."

"I would have, seven years ago," Rael replied. "Karan, I . . ." He choked; began again. "I am so sorry. It can never be."

Karan drank her iced tea in silence, watching Rael while he tried to eat his breakfast. Finally he pushed it aside, as though it was bitter in his mouth.

"Well, as you say, that was seven years ago," said Karan in a flat voice. "I've gone a long way since then. Perhaps it was for the best."

"Perhaps." He seemed to take that as a sign that the subject was closed. "You've certainly come here the long way. Where did you come from?"

"Tullin."

"Why on earth did you take that path, or is it something I should not ask?"

"I . . . I would not want to lie to you, Rael. I am mixed up in strange business. I used my talent to help a friend into Fiz Gorgo, and to steal something from Yggur. She was caught and I took on the burden of the rest of the mission. I have been hunted these past two months."

She had never seen Rael look so surprised. "Truly the girl I knew back then is gone. What was it that you stole?"

"I am sworn to secrecy."

"No matter. What do we care for the intrigues of Santhenar? Tell me the rest of it, whatever you can."

The morning fled as she told Rael the rest of her tale. Several times she almost unburdened herself to him about the Mirror, was on the point of taking it out and offering it to him, but the reserve that had arisen between them held the impulse back. Suddenly she realized that it was midday.

"Oh!" she cried. "I have left poor Llian all alone, in a strange city. What must he think of my manners?" She jumped up.

"Karan!" cried Rael. "The world is at a crossroads. Blendings will soon be more at risk than ever. Tell no one of your heritage."

"I won't," she replied, kissed him on the cheek and ran out.

Back at her chambers she found Llian to be amply catered for, for a number of the Aachim had come to visit her and had stayed to talk with the Aachimning, the stranger. Needing to digest what Rael had told her, she went out again, wandering the corridors of Shazmak, dreaming and remembering, and greeting old friends wherever she went, sometimes bringing them back to meet Llian, to explain him to them, though they all knew about him already.

Everyone treated Llian with great courtesy, and some even asked him about himself, and what his talents were, and he was delighted to hear that they too kept the Histories and knew of the Festival of Chanthed, though he was secretly chagrined to learn that they had not heard of him or his tellings.

*   *   *

In the late afternoon Karan and Llian were drinking tea when Rael came in through the open door of the apartment, smiling.

"I have some news that will delight you," he said. "Tensor will be here in a few days, a week at most."

Karan dropped her bowl, which smashed on the table, sending a flood of yellow tea toward Llian's book of the Great Tales. He snatched it away and wiped the cover on his shirt. By the time the mess was cleaned up, she had regained her composure and her voice did not betray her further.

"Tensor! I thought that he was across the Sea of Thurkad."

"He was, but events called him back, apparently. A message has just come from Thurkad, dated two days ago, and he will be nearly to Bannador by now. He will be glad to see you."

"I hope so," she said in an odd way, as Rael withdrew.

When he had gone Karan sat there as still as stone, and did not speak again. Shortly she got up, went into her room and closed the door. Climbing up onto the broad windowsill, wide as a seat, she sat for hours with her shoulder against the thick glass, watching the light fade, even after it was dark and the window had become a mirror showing only her face.

Tensor! What was she to do? She could think of nothing. The chance to give the Mirror away had passed; now she was trapped here with it. And she had brought Llian into the trap as well.

Llian respected her need for privacy for as long as his curiosity would let him, then knocked at her door. She did not answer but he came in anyway, bearing fresh tea and a platter of food left over from the previous night. Karan indicated the pallet and he sat down, looking up at her and then away again.

Suddenly she jumped down from the window. "I have to get away," she cried, and rushed out of the room.

It was not clear whether she wanted to get away from him or from Shazmak. Llian sat there, moodily eating the food and drinking the tea, then picked up the platter and went back to the main room. The rest of the evening he spent writing in his journal, conscious that it had lain unopened in its bag for more than a week. He quickly became immersed in the writing and all other concerns disappeared.

It was quite late when Karan returned. She came in softly, looking weary and unhappy, and flopped down on the couch opposite. Her eyes met his.

"Tea?"

"Please." She sounded exhausted.

She sipped the hot tea, warming her hands on the cup, and nibbled at a piece of dried fruit.

"It's Tensor," she said. "I knew I should not have come here."

"Tell me. Maybe I can help."

"You can't." Then, after the silence had drawn out uncomfortably long, she said, "Thank you, Llian. It's good to have you with me, but there's nothing you can do. Leave it alone."

In the middle of the night Karan woke from a horrible, terrifying dream. She had dreamed that Shazmak had been betrayed, that it had fallen without any opposition, her friends slaughtered like unresisting sheep. Everything she knew and loved about Shazmak was utterly destroyed and violated, and it was all her fault, for it all came from her bringing the Mirror here.

When she woke her dilemma was worse than ever, as she could not recall whether the cataclysm came from giving the Aachim the Mirror or keeping it from them, only that she had caused it all.

*   *   *

In the morning Karan was morose and as time passed she became increasingly sullen and withdrawn, almost furtive in her movements. Llian did his best to help her, but she kept him away; he saw little of her after that morning. She rose early and often did not return to their chambers until after he had retired, and he was left alone.

Their rooms were cold and he spent little time there, preferring to wander the halls and corridors of the great city, sometimes with Rael, more often by himself, for Rael had described an area within which he might move freely. Everywhere he was treated with restrained courtesy, his questions answered with unfailing patience. Not by the flicker of an eyelid did his hosts show irritation at his inquisitiveness. And he learned much about the Aachim, fitting their story into the greater pattern of the Histories in his mind, and making notes for his *Tale of the Mirror,* though he did not ask about that and they did not speak of it. And how much greater his *Tale of Tar Gaarn* would be now, after living in Shazmak.

By the second day Llian had tired of wandering. Though the buildings and murals were everywhere different, the somber world they symbolized was the same. He sought Karan in vain; she had risen early and left her chamber before he woke, and Rael was nowhere to be found. In the morning he practiced his art, but this only reminded him of the Mirror, and his craving to see it, *know* it. He wrote in his journal for a while, but today that did not satisfy him either.

Then a thought occurred to him. Shazmak must have a library; indeed, he remembered that yesterday it had been mentioned as they passed the stair to a certain tower. What a coup for a chronicler, if they would allow him there! Perhaps he might even learn something about the Forbidding. With that delicious thought he set off. A short time later he was hopelessly lost, standing at the foot of a long stair with his hand on the railing, wondering which direction to take, and if he was beyond the area where he could go alone, when he caught sight of Rael above. Rael came down and Llian explained where he wanted to go.

Rael gave a half-smile. "You are well off the path this time, Llian. The library is up, not down; in the Tower of Sind. But you cannot go there by yourself. Do you know the way home?"

Llian did not. Rael gave directions, but on seeing Llian's doubtful frown offered to escort him.

"I was looking for Karan," Rael said, "but she is not to be found, and next I must go that way. Have you seen her? She was to meet me early this morning. It is strange that she has not come."

"No," Llian replied. "Perhaps she forgot."

Rael gave him a keen glance but Llian did not notice; his thoughts had already wandered. Who was Tensor, that she so feared? He was reluctant to ask Rael, but the question led on to the Mirror itself, never far from his thoughts. Particularly here in Shazmak, surrounded by scenes of Aachan whence it came, and the Aachim who made it in the first place. Llian lost himself in these thoughts as they walked along, and it was a while before he realized that Rael had spoken.

"I beg your pardon," Llian said. "My thoughts were deep in the Histories. Why am I interested in the library? In olden times it was the duty of the chroniclers to recover and set down the Histories lost during the Clysm. So I look wherever I go, whether I be in the great cities of the ancients or the taverns of my own country. The libraries of the Aachim must be a treasure-store of lost tales."

"Doubtless they are," replied Rael, "though I do not imagine that you will be able to read them. These days we mostly use the common speech in Shazmak, as you do, but when we write it is in the script of Aachan, which even you would find perplexing. However, I will take you there one day, if you wish. The librarian may be able to help you."

Llian must have looked disappointed, for Rael then smiled and said, "Wait! If you are not busy, come with me to my chambers and share food with me. Then there are some things which duty, or habit, require me to do, but after that I will be free to take you to the library."

They went to Rael's rooms, talking cheerfully all the way. The food was simple compared to what Karan had given him, but superb, for all its strangeness. Afterwards Llian sat for a time, sipping from his bowl and leafing through one or other of Rael's books, though he could not read a word. Rael wrote in a journal for half an hour, then took out an instrument not unlike a flute, but with several tubes and a complexity of levers and stops. It was a beautiful instrument that Llian knew was distinctively Aachim in design, made of silver and ebony.

The music was slow and strange to Llian's ears—a lament. At the end of it he felt melancholy and lethargic, and cold. He wanted his warm bed, and a bowl of thick hot soup, and blankets clutched about his neck. The idea of the library seemed foolish, even a little menacing.

"I'm sorry," said Rael. "We can be a dismal folk. The past is everything to us, and we forget that Santhenar is different. What can I tell you that will amuse? Would you like to hear about Karan?"

The trip to the library took half an hour, during which Rael entertained Llian with tales of Karan's girlhood, her numerous pranks and practical jokes on the Aachim, and escapades that were downright dangerous, including one time when she had climbed the outside of the tall Tower of Sind, after Rael had said that it could not be done.

"She is a remarkable woman," Rael said, sighing. "She is clever in so many ways. You are a lucky man, Llian."

Llian misunderstood him. "She has given me so much. I am beginning to think that this might be a Great Tale after all."

After that they were so busy talking that Llian scarcely noticed where they were going, save that they climbed a lot of stairs.

"Rael," said Llian, already thinking of him as a friend, someone who could be trusted. He explained about the ending of the *Tale of the Forbidding,* and what he was searching for.

"I do not know, Llian. That was long, long before my time, before any of us here, except Tensor. And Llian, bold chronicler that you are, I hope that not even you would be so foolhardy as to ask *him* about it."

"Why not?"

"We look back to that time with shame. The Aachim fled in fear when Shuthdar brought down the Forbidding. Even Tensor ran. He is a proud man, and cannot bear to be reminded. And because we owe him so much, we keep silent. Never mention it, I beg you."

Llian did not care a fig for the dignity of this Aachim who Karan was so afraid of. If there came an opportunity he would not spare Tensor's feelings.

The library was not at all as Llian had anticipated. The room they entered was light and airy, with curving walls, and unexpectedly, lit by tall windows. But the windows let in the incessant shrieking of the wind and put him on edge; a feeling that he had not felt in a library before. The room contained a number of compartmented scroll cupboards and many shelves, but there were far fewer books than Llian had imagined, and he said so.

"There are several other levels," Rael explained. "Most of the books and scrolls are kept there, for they are little used in these times. But this is only a cadet library, suitable for an outpost as Shazmak now is. The greater is at Stassor, in the far east. As an Aachimning you may enter, if you are ever there, though it is a journey of two hundred days, and in these times a perilous one. I will fetch the librarian. His name is Emmant."

Rael disappeared and Llian examined the books and scrolls on the nearby shelf while he waited. Few were illustrated and the tiny, convoluted script in which they were written was unreadable. He was looking at a small book illuminated in the style of the murals in his chamber when another man came silently in, as one used to creeping. Llian was shocked to find the Aachim suddenly beside him.

"Oh!" he said, and looked up into black eyes sunk deep in lightless caverns of bone. The hostility in the eyes was shockingly intense. Llian knew that his voice would work no magic here.

Emmant was short for an Aachim, though still taller than Llian, and massively built with a large head and a thick powerful neck, but in spite of his bulk he moved with a subtle, dangerous grace. His dense black beard was cut by twin scars curving from his right ear to the corner of his mouth.

"Emmant, here is Llian. He is Aachimning. Take care not to show him any secrets," Rael added cheerily. "Llian is a lore master of Chanthed. Let him read a thing once and he will never forget it."

"I know the training of the master chroniclers," said Emmant sourly. "What do you want?"

Llian explained his interest in the old tales, but even to his ears his story sounded childish and irrelevant.

"We do not concern ourselves overmuch with such things," said Emmant, "though we have kept the Histories since we came from Aachan, and that was long ago. I have copies of many books, though I do not think you will find what you are looking for. There are thousands of volumes and none are in your language, or indeed in any of the tongues of Santhenar. You will not be able to read them. Even if you could, it would take more than a lifetime."

"I have studied the *Tale of the Forbidding*," said Llian. "I would know the Aachim's story of that time."

"I've heard," said Emmant with a knowing smile. "You are a hundred years too late. Our records from that time went to Stassor long ago. If that is all you came for . . ."

Llian was beginning to despair. Whoever he asked, no one knew anything. "Is there no one in Shazmak who can tell me about that time?"

Emmant gripped his arm with overlong fingers, so hard that the bones hurt. "Ask the only one who was alive then, who was there," he said in tones that dripped malice. "*Ask Tensor,* if you dare."

He turned away, but Rael laid a hand on his arm and said in a low voice, "Emmant, he is Aachimning. Karan brought him to us."

"Karan! I heard that *darsh* was back," Emmant said in an ugly voice, and his face was twisted.

Rael winced at the insult. Llian too was shocked, though he did not know what the word meant; shocked also because he had encountered only politeness from the Aachim. This man was a great danger. He looked at him more closely. Emmant's features were pocked with little marks and he had a thick accent that Llian did not recognize.

"Emmant!" Rael said again. "All that is over now. You gave your pledge. And Tensor would wish him made welcome."

"Indeed," said Emmant. "He sent word to me about Karan." They faced each other for a moment, then Emmant shrugged and turned back to Llian.

"Is there any other tale that you seek?" he enquired in an

ambiguous manner, his features now composed. "I can see that you came here with something in mind. What is it?"

Llian started. *The Mirror!* he thought. Mirror, mirror, mirror. The words reflected back and forth endlessly in his mind.

The librarian was staring at him. Mirror, mirror. Llian looked down at his boots, closed his eyes. He saw Karan's face. "Never tell anyone," he heard her say.

They were standing beside one of the large windows. Outside, the windsong rose from a wail to a shriek. Even with his eyes closed he could feel the smoldering presence of Emmant before him. Llian looked up slowly; looked into the eyes of Emmant. The intensity burned him.

"What tale?" Emmant asked softly.

"The Mirror of Aachan," he gasped, as though short of air.

"Ah!" Emmant said, searching his face. "Why that one? The Mirror is long lost, and the secret well kept. Where did you hear the story?" His eyes glittered.

Llian tried to look away but Emmant laid a hand on his hand. A thrill ran through him and he could not stay his tongue.

"The Mirror is found."

Rael almost fell down in shock. His face showed that he had added Llian's and Karan's stories instantly, and the conclusion was anguishing. He reached out and gripped Llian's shoulder, and he could breathe again, could think again.

Emmant stared at Rael. "Found? What does Karan know of it?" His thick voice became shrill.

The enormity of his folly began to come home to Llian. He tore his gaze away. What had Emmant done to him? "Nothing! I heard it in Chanthed," he said, struggling to keep the tremor out of his voice.

Emmant looked at him with curious satisfaction, then

turned and walked off down the rows of cabinets on the left side of the room. He beckoned to Llian and stooped to open a small black cupboard. Llian came slowly, his feet dragging.

"There was little ever written about the Mirror," he said, his manner now almost jovial, "for it was such a trivial thing; used only for seeing. Later it was different; it changed, or was remade, and once it was our salvation. Yalkara stole it and profaned it but what happened to it in the end no one can say. Nothing was written about *that,* that you can read."

"Outside Shazmak I have heard other accounts," Llian observed.

"Doubtless," said Emmant. "And they are lies. But there was a book of our history in your tongue." He was pulling books, papers and scrolls from the cabinet as he spoke and placing them on a table nearby. "Ah! Here it is." He bent down in front of the cupboard, seeming to take a long time. "It's a copy of the *Nazhak tel Mardux,* an early history of the Aachim from their coming to Santhenar to the end of the Clysm. You might call the book *Tales of the Aachim.* It was prepared in one of the scripts of Santhenar, for it was meant as a gift to an ally, though it was never given. It is a most beautiful book and very old. There is nothing in it that you may not know."

Emmant placed the book on Llian's palm. The writing was in a fine hand and there were hundreds of thin, silky-soft pages. Llian knew the script. It was a variant of one once used in southern parts of Meldorin, but the language was unfamiliar to him, although here and there he could make out a word. Given time he might be able to decipher parts of it.

But he was puzzled. Emmant clearly had some terrible grievance against Karan, and therefore against Llian too, so why the sudden change? *Unless it was a trick or a trap.* What could he do, save put the book back and go away? But the Mirror had become an obsession. Llian stayed, and Emmant stood watching him, while Rael watched them both.

He turned the pages slowly, lovingly. Such a beautiful book, such a fine hand. The frontispiece was an illumination of Shazmak as it must have been when first built. He compared it with his own mental picture of the city. If anything it had grown more beautiful with time. There were other illuminations, though not many. Some he recognized, great cities of the past; others he did not. And one he knew instantly, though he had not seen this likeness before. It was utterly unlike any other, the city conceived and designed by Pitlis for Rulke—*Alcifer!*

But how, in this long and incomprehensible book, could he find a small reference to the Mirror? He turned the pages; the next, and the next. Emmant walked down between the shelves, and as soon as he was out of sight Rael gripped Llian's wrist in a grip as hard as metal.

"Come with me," he said.

Llian resisted, still under the spell of the book.

"*Now!*" cracked Rael in a low voice that could not be resisted. "And don't ever mention the Mirror again."

Llian closed the book and followed Rael back to his room in silence. It was late in the evening. Karan was still not there, and after a sketchy meal he went to bed and was soon asleep.

Sometime later he was awakened from a dream, a wonderful, tantalizing dream for a chronicler, by the sound of voices in a heated argument. One of the voices belonged to Karan; the other he did not recognize. The argument had evidently been going on for some while.

"Do you tell me that I cannot leave Shazmak until Tensor returns?"

"Karan, Karan. We do not hold you against your will," came the unknown voice. "Never would we so disgrace you. But great changes are afoot in the world and we must protect ourselves. Tensor has sent word that you know something of the Mirror. He wishes to speak with you ere you leave us. The request is reasonable, surely? We have long been friends, your house and the Aachim, and you owe us this. We ask you to wait."

"I acknowledge the friendship and the debt," replied Karan, "but wait I cannot. Already I'm long overdue. I would be happy to meet Tensor on my way, perhaps in Narne, for I am hurrying to Sith. I know nothing of any Mirror."

"Karan, Rael was in the library today and heard the Aachimning tell Emmant that it is found. Do you tell me you know nothing about this?"

"Emmant!" he heard Karan cry in a rage. "What has he done to Llian? I should never had left him alone."

"The Zain is unharmed," the voice said, then there was a sound as though a chair had been knocked over. "Karan, you must not . . ." The outside door banged.

Llian sat up in bed, his face hot with embarrassment and self-disgust. In spite of her troubles, despite that he had broken his promise at the worst possible time for her, her first thought had been for his safety. What a fool he was.

He wished that he had never heard of the wretched Mirror. Just then his dream came flooding back. He wished that Karan would come back, and at the same time dreaded the meeting with her. The Mirror—always the Mirror. Even in his sleep he dreamed of it; just then he had been dreaming about it. In his mind's eye he could see it now, just like that image he had caught from Karan's dream a couple of weeks ago, the mirror with the woman's face glimpsed fleetingly.

But in *his* dream there had been more. Something had

dissolved into it, *or out of it*. What was it? The more he tried to reach it the further it receded. Then it flashed whole into his mind and was gone again just as quickly. But it had been there long enough for recognition. It was a stone tablet showing four distinct scripts in its four quarters. Two he knew from the shapes of the letters, even in that fleeting glimpse. Ancient scripts of Santhenar that he had studied years ago. The third was a syllabary from eastern lands. He did not know it.

But the fourth he recognized instantly, as any student of the Histories would have. It was the complex, convoluted, beautiful formal script of the Charon, whose secret they had guarded for millennia. Not even the Aachim, long their toilers, knew it, and it had never been deciphered. A shiver went up his spine. He had dreamed about the Renderer's Tablet—the mythical key to the script of the Charon. In modern times scholars scoffed at its existence. Most of the ancient chroniclers (and Llian had read them all) had been sceptical. But to others it had seemed necessary that such a thing exist, like the supposed Great Northern Land that was needful for the balance of the world. The script of the Charon had never been broken, so somewhere must be a key to it—the Tablet must exist.

With such a key, archives full of undeciphered Charon manuscripts would lie open to him. Alcifer alone had filled libraries, after Rulke was put in the Nightland. And the killer of the crippled girl could have been a Charon.

As though in a dream, an enchanted euphoria, he rose and went out into the main chamber. It was empty. Karan's room was dark; only a handful of stars glittered in the black night. His dreamlike logic sought an answer. Where, but on the Mirror itself? He reached up and touched the flask above the door to a dim light.

The chamber was simply furnished, with just a small

table and three chairs beneath the window. They were made of metal, blue almost to the color of black, and intricately wrought. Against the left wall were two chests bound with iron and a cupboard with many small drawers. Karan's pack sat between the cupboard and the further chest. Halfway down the right side of the room was her broad pallet, also framed in metal, with a powdery blue coverlet. A book lay on the coverlet, a slim volume bound in leather, light but with many pages.

Llian picked up the book. The first part contained handwriting in a spidery, intricate hand. The latter part was blank. He had not known that she kept a journal. He replaced the book as he had found it.

The cupboard was empty. He opened the first of the chests. It held only folded bed coverings. The second, a small pile of clothing and Karan's traveling gear—the oiled cloak and hood in drab green, travel-stained and worn; rolled-up blankets; cooking and eating utensils; hatchet; her boots and other small items. Llian bent down and felt under the pile of clothing. His hand, moist and shaking, touched something hard.

Just then there was a noise at the door. He spun around, guiltily. Karan stood in the doorway, her eyes desolate.

24

NO WAY OUT

"What a fool I am," Karan said bitterly, biting off each word. "You have shown the worth of your promises. Get out of my room."

"But you don't understand," said Llian desperately. "All I wanted was to *see* it. I . . ." Even as he spoke he knew how feeble he sounded.

Karan's lip curled, on her face a fury beyond his imagining. She took a step toward him. There were two red spots on her cheekbones. "Get out," she said, in a voice barely audible. "I trusted you. I could admire an enemy if he was cunning and clever, even though I hated him. But you promised, and you broke your promise, and now you make pathetic excuses. You are beneath contempt."

Llian laid his hand on her arm. "It's not as you think. Emmant had a power over me . . ."

The next moment he received a stunning blow to the face and Llian found himself lying on the floor. He scrambled to his hands and knees, looking up at her in amazement. A brilliant pain extended the whole length of his jaw. "You *hit* me."

Karan was holding her wrist with her other hand. As he watched all the color drained from her face and she sat down abruptly where she stood. The fingers of her left hand clung to her other wrist. "It's broken again," she said.

She lay down on her side, cradling her wrist. Llian soon saw that he was in no further danger. She was pale, near to fainting, and her eyes were closed, though a tear or two escaped. He bent down and gently touched her wrist. Already it was swollen and through the swelling he could feel the break, a very bad one. A tiny moan escaped her. He looked around for something to splint it. Her voice was a feeble whisper. "Go into the kitchen. The basket with the fruit. Take the stand to pieces."

Llian ran out. The stand was intricately made, in the manner of the Aachim, but based on a tripod of long metal tubes connected by shorter ones. There was a smash and a thump, as though Llian had jumped on it. He came back looking foolishly at the wreckage in his hand.

"It unscrews, you idiot," said Karan, and shortly he managed to obtain two short slender pieces of tubing, much engraved, that would serve. With these and a length of cord he fashioned a clumsy splint. She opened her eyes and sat up, gripping his shoulder tightly as he straightened the bones and bound her wrist, but made no further sound.

When he was finished he carried her to the pallet. She lay down on the cover, closing her eyes, while he looked down anxiously. Her eyes opened. "Get Rael," she said, and closed her eyes again. He went at once, shutting the door gently behind.

*   *   *

After a long search he found Rael, who came directly with an assistant, and plaster. He made to dismantle Llian's contraption of tubes and strings but Karan was fractious and shouted at him. Rael compressed his lips in a thin line as he worked, but made a cast with the plaster over the splint and went out again. Karan slept, woke and slept again, while Llian sat on the floor at the end of her bed, guilty and confused. Eventually she stirred, looked around, saw Llian sitting there and sat up. She was still angry.

"Why did you tell him about the Mirror?" she asked. "Why *Emmant,* of all people in Shazmak? You could not have chosen more ill if you had been my enemy."

"I don't know!" he whispered. "The whole incident is muddy in my mind. I can remember Emmant pulling out books and showing them to me. There was one special book, a history of the Aachim, and I could read the script, though I didn't know what the words meant. The book was so beautiful it was like the sun coming up when I opened it. No!" He paused, looking confused. "It was before I saw the book. It was almost as if he knew about you."

"He did," she replied, and suddenly her anger was gone. "Tensor sent word to Emmant to keep me here. He already knew about the Mirror, luckily for you."

Llian rambled a little, straining to remember what had happened. "I suppose I was already thinking about it—I do all the time. Once it came into my mind it seemed that he knew it. Can the Aachim read minds?"

"No, but Emmant sometimes seems to sense what people are thinking," she said, "as I well knew. Oh, this is all my fault. I should have warned you, though I never imagined that Tensor would betray me to *him.*"

"He touched me and then I couldn't stop myself. It was as if he bewitched me; as if some dark thing crouched on my back, prodding me. But I didn't tell him you knew anything about it," he added defensively.

"If you had, you'd be swimming in the Garr now," she said fiercely. But then she put her splinted arm across his shoulder to show that it was all in the past.

"Oh, Karan, I wasn't trying to steal it, *just to see it.* Can't you understand how much it means to me, to be a chronicler in the midst of such a tale, without ever seeing the Mirror?" He said nothing about the Tablet. With hindsight, that was altogether too much a dream.

For a moment Karan was tempted. If only she could, she would gladly offer him that triumph. But would he be satisfied, or would he want more? And then, why should he get that favor so easily? Let him earn it.

"How can you ask such a thing? The Mirror would not give up its secrets so casually anyway. And even if you could use it, you know its nature—the *Twisted Mirror.* Besides, I swore. It takes a lot before I break *my* promises."

Llian squirmed. In truth he had expected nothing else.

"What was there between you and him?" he asked sometime later, as Karan was preparing for bed.

She looked down at her blanket, smoothing the wrinkles mechanically with the side of her good hand. "It's a bitter story for us both. When I lived here I was just a girl. Emmant loved me, or claimed he did, though his actions told otherwise. I endured him for too long, out of kindness, for I knew not how to tell him otherwise, and I was good-natured then. And I pitied him, for he is a blending, half-Aachim and half-human. But he cannot come to terms with it. He is an outcast, though it is only he himself that makes it so. Finally his attentions grew unbearable and I spurned him. Then he became hateful and vindictive, and spread deceits about me, and crept about, hoping to catch me unawares.

"Finally he did." She shivered at the memory. "I struggled with him and he gave me this," she said, touching the scar above her eye. "I cut him with my knife, humiliated him, for he is mean and sneaking, and at best a coward. Thereafter the Aachim kept him away from me. But the violence I did to him only made him worse. It scarred him inside as well as out, and corrupted me as well, so now I'm torn between sympathy and loathing—perhaps he senses it. How I hate myself for the violence. Shazmak was intolerable after that, and I was shamed. What would my father have thought? Galliad was a big, powerful man, but very gentle." Tears welled in her eyes. "He would have stopped Emmant without raising a finger."

"Big men don't have to," said Llian. "But you are entitled to defend yourself."

"Doubtless. It did not save my father, anyway. He was set upon in the mountains and killed for a few miserable coins." She wiped the tears away abruptly.

"The violence has become easier; it hardly shames me at all, now." She put her fingers to the great bruise on his cheek, a mute apology. He took her hand in his and squeezed it tight.

There was a long silence, finally broken by Llian. "They won't let us go, will they?"

"They can't, though it offends against their honor to hold me. They take the shame of Emmant's abuse upon themselves; so they are slow to judge me. But all along I knew it was a mistake to come here. I thought that Tensor was across the sea; I would not have come otherwise."

"Then I didn't . . . ?" His voice was unwontedly timid.

"No," she said softly. "But you might have. What am I going to do with you?"

"What will they do to us?"

"Nothing, until *he* comes," she replied. "They won't dishonor themselves, or me. But if I am proven traitor," she added, "no dishonor could be greater than my own. The penalty is death."

"You are no traitor," said Llian. "I will not believe it."

"You know nothing of the Aachim."

"That is because you have told me nothing."

"Think back to your own tale. They can never forget their ruin, though that be an aeon ago. Treachery has a special stench to them, and revenge a special spice. For even a blending such as I to block that revenge is treason."

"Then why don't you give it back?"

"Your tale told me the answer to that, too. I dreamed that Shazmak lay in ruins, and all because of me."

Karan lay back on her pallet, staring at the ceiling. Llian's hands writhed in his lap.

"What will they do to me?"

"The same, though it does no good to dwell on it," she replied absently.

"They will search you, and then—torture and death!"

"You're being melodramatic now; this is not one of your tales. They will not dishonor themselves by searching me; *they* do not suspect me, only Tensor does."

"You know this place. Let's steal away tonight. There must be many ways out of Shazmak."

"There aren't. We're on an island. There are only two bridges, and both are guarded. Besides, there are Sentinels inside as well as out, and they have already been alerted to watch for us. Go one step past where you are permitted and they will sound. I'm sorry, Llian. It seems that I have brought you to your death."

"What can we do?" cried Llian.

"I'm afraid to even talk to him," said Karan, speaking half to herself. "How can I conceal my mind from him?"

"Who is he anyway?"

"He is the greatest of them now, and leader of Shazmak. He sees his destiny as to rouse the Aachim from their long languor. He is like a stern father, unforgiving of failures or other viewpoints, and he will look into my heart and see what I try to conceal."

Llian groaned. "Then we're doomed. This isn't how the tale is supposed to end."

His doleful tones seemed to put the courage back into her. She reached out and hugged him about the neck, and when she spoke it was with the fond sarcasm that she reserved for his most exasperating moments. "The tale goes on, no matter what. When I thought you had betrayed me I felt I had a chance, alone. Now that I find you merely confirmed as an idiot, and must still protect you, I fear that there is no hope."

"Don't mock me. I'm terribly afraid."

"That all can see. But do not the Zain say that there is always a way?"

"You're right, there always is."

"I have thought long on it," said Karan, "but I cannot find one."

Several days passed. As the time neared for Tensor to return Karan became impossibly moody. She was tormented by guilt, sure that she had brought Llian here to his death, but there was nothing she could do about it. There was no way to get out of Shazmak, not even if she gave up the Mirror. It was too late for that now. When she was in their chamber she kept to her room, either staring out the window at the river far below or writing in her book.

Llian, as before, was treated with reserved courtesy by the Aachim. He was now allowed to go to the library, and though he realized that the permission might be a trap, he could not keep away. He went back more than once, against

Karan's wishes. At first he wandered the shelves, pulling out books, manuscripts and scrolls at random, looking over his shoulder in case the librarian should come creeping up behind him, but Emmant was not in evidence.

Llian soon tired of this occupation for, as Rael had said, the books were all in the Aachan script, which he did not know. He returned time and again to *Tales of the Aachim*, staring at the unfamiliar words, or just thinking about the Mirror, and dreaming. He had come to a fatalistic acceptance that he might never leave Shazmak, that he might even die here. The matter was out of his hands, and nothing he could do would make any difference, so he might as well go on with his work.

It was the afternoon of the seventh day since their coming to Shazmak. Llian sat alone at the table, nursing bowl after bowl of tea in his hands, enjoying the seeping warmth in the cold room. His thoughts kept coming back to the book. It would take months to translate. But I *can* read the script, he thought excitedly. I'll read it, and commit it to memory, and later on, I will write it all down again and translate it. What an addition to the Histories that will be! He suppressed the thought that there would probably be no later on.

He got up at once and hurried back to the library. Though Llian was accustomed to reading and remembering perfectly—that was one of the chief skills of the chroniclers—he did not underestimate this task. To read and remember so much, and in a language he barely knew, would require a very great effort. Perhaps more than any test he had ever done.

At first he struggled; then as his eyes grew accustomed to the crabbed script and the cadences of the language, he read more quickly. Though he could understand few of the words, the sense came across. He became caught up in the remote, musical language and the images that it conjured. A story began to unfold, of the Aachim, their coming to Santhenar and their trials and triumphs. The story was different from the Histories that Llian knew, and contradictions were many. A picture of the Aachim emerged: a people proud and strong but never secure; noble and steadfast allies but too often betrayed; the makers of great but ill-judged alliances; artists and builders of the greatest skill yet looking always to the past; finally retreating into isolation. And always, always plotting revenge on Rulke, he who had brought them to Santhenar, the architect of all their misfortune.

Time passed swiftly; outside it grew dark and still he read. The nebula swung across the sky and the light came in through the tall window, bright enough to cast faint shadows on the floor, shadows with red-tinged edges. The wind shrieked and moaned. Llian sat at his table, the book lit by the tiny flask on the wall beside him. Higher rose the nebula. Its radiance washed back toward the eastern window and seeped out again, leaving the room in darkness. The moon in its last quarter rose, its pale light filtering in through the window as he finished the book and realized where he was, who he was. He was cold, hungry and shaking with tiredness.

Dawn had broken by the time he got back. Karan's door was open and though her bed had been slept in she was already gone. Llian paused only long enough to throw off his clothes before falling into his bed.

Sometime later he wakened to the sound of an argument in the main room. It was Karan and Rael; Karan shouting angrily, Rael replying in his soft, reasonable voice. Doors slammed, there was silence again and he went back to sleep. Karan came into his room and sat down heavily on the pallet beside him. He looked up at her drowsily and put his arm around her back, quickly drifting back into his dreams. She sat there for a while then disengaged his arm and went out.

Llian woke in the mid-afternoon. He ate hurriedly and went straight back to the library, again finding the room empty. *Tales of the Aachim* was not where he had left it, and for a moment he feared that Emmant had taken it, but he soon found it on another shelf of the cabinet. Now the book took on a new light. The sense came off the pages, seemingly independent of the words he was reading, though if he stopped to think it blurred back into a mass of empty syllables.

As he turned the first page, the spaces of the library receded and Llian felt himself drawn into the world of the Aachim. He was there when they followed Rulke through the portal. He stepped naked onto the grass and smelled the warm rich spicy air of Santhenar for the first time. He looked out on the steep green hills and the blue forested mountains in the distance. He felt the joy and freedom of the Aachim in their new world, their vigor and youthful strength as they shook off the shackles of Aachan and made another life. The centuries fleeted by and he saw their delight as they built and grew strong.

He saw too the response of the Charon, their resentment turning eventually to fear, and how they worked unceasingly to frustrate the Aachim, to thwart their alliances and destroy their works. The Aachim fought back and the horror of the Clysm spread like a plague across all the lands. Then a tale he knew: the Aachim betrayed by Rulke. In despair, their hopes shattered, they withdrew into the mountains and the past.

Llian came back to the present, the tears coursing down his cheeks, suddenly aware of a presence in the darkness nearby. He stood up abruptly, knocking the chair over and, peering fearfully around him, saw Emmant standing in the shadows. The librarian stepped forward and Llian shrank back.

"*What has she done with it?*" Emmant rasped. "I must have it." The eyes flamed, the voice throbbed with passion.

"Why?" cried Llian wildly. "You are not Aachim. What can it mean to you?"

The next second Emmant had him by the throat, squeezing him till the room faded in a blur of red, shaking him till his teeth rattled like bones in a coffin. Yet even through the blur he could see those eyes.

"*I am Aachim!*" Emmant shouted. "*I am more Aachim than they are!* No one has ever cared for their books as I do. No one knows their Histories as I do. Their revenge is just a pretense. They weep and wail about lost Aachan, but do nothing to get it back, just hide in the past and dwindle away to nothing. Once I give them the Mirror there will be no 'half-Aachim this, half-Aachim that.' They will beg me to lead them, and I will, I will. They will have their revenge, too, *and I mine*! *What has she done with it, the darsh?*" he screamed. He shook Llian again, thrusting his face into Llian's until all he could see were those ghastly eyes.

He made a horrible gurgling sound and Emmant's grip moved suddenly from his throat to his shoulders. Llian sucked a deep, shuddering breath, his windpipe throbbing from the crushing fingers. His will to resist was weeping away. Then an image came into his mind, Karan helping him in his mountain sickness, and he clung to it, but it soon fell into tatters and was stripped away. The eyes impaled him.

"Tell me!" screamed Emmant through foam-flecked lips, shaking Llian by the shoulders.

"I . . . will . . ." Llian croaked.

The grip relaxed a little but the eyes still burned.

Something clicked at the far end of the room. Emmant turned his head, but Llian could not. Emmant began to speak, then the fire died in his eyes, his hands left Llian's shoulders and he turned away to face the intruder. Llian turned too. It was Karan. She was advancing slowly down the room, bearing a look so murderous that Emmant took a step backwards.

Karan came up to Llian, took him by the hand and jerked him toward her. "I was right to treat you as I did," she said to Emmant with glacial ferocity. Though she was only half his bulk, and a head shorter, Emmant cringed away from her fury. "You are *hundiss,* without honor. Never will there be a place for you among the Aachim. You are nothing."

It was clear that her words meant everything to Emmant. His face went white, then red, and he tried to step toward her, even raised his great fist as though he would strike her, a blow that would have smashed her to the floor; but his courage failed him. Karan spat at his feet, turned her back on him quite deliberately and stalked away, dragging Llian behind. Emmant's deranged, hate-filled glare followed them to the door.

Back at their chamber she thrust Llian inside and kicked the door shut. He continued across the room in a daze. She caught him as he was about to walk into the wall, whirling him around. "What did you tell him *this time*?"

To Llian it was as though he had escaped one tyrant only to fall into the hands of another, and he saw not Karan's face but another set of mesmerizing eyes.

"I-will-not-speak. I-will-not-speak," came his pitiful croak.

She raised her cast at him then thought better of it and struck him across the face with her good hand. He sank to his knees, looking dazed. The book was still clutched in his hand. He broke out into a long speech in an unfamiliar tongue, punctuated with wailing and weeping, while Karan stared at him in amazement. Suddenly she seemed to understand, for she slipped out of the room, locking it carefully behind her.

She returned with Rael, who came up to Llian and examined him carefully, and then the book. Rael took the book from Llian's fingers and spoke two syllables in the tongue of the Aachim; then he took Llian by the hand and repeated them. Llian jerked, closed his eyes, then slowly opened them again, and looked blankly at Karan.

"What happened?" he said dazedly. "I was in the library reading. It's dark." He looked around the room. "Where's the book?"

Rael brought out *Tales of the Aachim,* which he had been holding behind his back. "There was a charm on it for you, though only a shabby little thing."

With difficulty Llian forced his mind back. "I started reading it in the library," he said in a painful whisper. "At first I could barely make it out, the language is so strange. But today it called to me, and though I didn't know the words somehow I knew the story it was telling. I was there! I became as one of the Aachim; I knew their hopes and their fears, and their secret plans of long ago. Then Emmant came. I tried to resist him, but I could not. All my will was gone." He stared at Karan, coming back to himself. "It's fading now. Ah! My head! How it aches. And my throat. I thought he was going to choke me to death."

Karan sat down in front of him, stroking his bruised throat with her fingertips. "Oh, Llian, forgive me!" she exclaimed.

Llian closed his eyes, and saw again the look on Emmant's face—such hate as he had never seen. "You have a deadly enemy there," he said, clutching her small hand. "Promise you won't go out alone."

Karan almost laughed aloud at the thought of him protecting her, but she saw how afraid he was for her, how much he cared, and was touched. She dismissed Emmant with a wave of her hand, concealing her disquiet.

"He is nothing," she said, "a craven. But I will be careful." Then she turned to Rael. "This is a very great dishonor. To use a charm on Llian, who knows nothing of this matter, and has no talent, was cowardly and unworthy."

"The charm was such a little thing. No Aachim would have succumbed to it. Yet it was ill done and not of our doing. We have cautioned Emmant before, as you know. For his error we beg your leave."

"It was not his error alone. He had instructions from Tensor." Karan was so angry she could barely speak.

Rael looked ashamed. "The letter to Emmant was sealed. We did not know what it said, at the time. But Karan, we know that you had the Mirror once. Please tell us where it is. You know what the penalty is, for you and Llian both, if you keep it from us."

"I cannot tell you what happened to it. More than that I will not say, save that I do not act against the Aachim. Your own honor is at stake. Will you at least support me?"

"That I do already, though it may cost me dear. No more can I do. Tensor is expected in the morning." Rael turned and left the chamber.

Karan paced the room. She sat down, chewing her fingertips, then got up abruptly and paced again. "What can I do? I can't face Tensor."

"Give it to him then. Maybe nothing will ever come of it. Maybe the Mirror will be impossible to use. The Aachim did not misuse it before, remember."

"But it was not so valuable then. Each time the Mirror is used it grows greater, for the print of what it is employed for remains within it. They know that Yalkara used it to escape from Santhenar. That is a very powerful secret. And remember this: the Aachim made the Mirror. If anyone can extract the secret from it, they can."

"Why don't you throw it into the Garr and let the rocks grind it to powder?"

Karan walked away from him and put her face on the wall. She did not speak for a very long time.

"Llian," she said, "have you not wondered that, among my few possessions, you never actually saw the Mirror?"

"No," said Llian. "I knew it was a small thing, easily hid."

"Maigraith planned that if we were pursued she would take the Mirror and I would decoy the Whelm by pretending to have it." She looked away. She could not look at him, just sat down again with her head in her hands, looking as though she wanted to cry. "I . . . I do not . . ." One little ear, peeping out of the tangles, was almost as red as her hair.

What was she trying to say? That she did not have it after all? The faintest germ of a doubt crept into his mind, a mind that was trained to weigh the smallest nuances for their truth and to set down the truth whatever the consequences. But he had come to a turning point in his life: the chronicler was in conflict with the man. Karan had shown him such loyalty, such kindness, such trust. He could be just as loyal, just as trusting. Llian put the scales up over his eyes. Whatever she did, he would not question it, would not even entertain the thought of disbelief. Would not put her in the position of having to lie to him.

He knelt down before her and put his finger across her lips. "Tell me nothing," said Llian. "I ask you nothing."

"Oh Llian," she cried, putting her arms around his neck and wetting his shoulder with her tears. "I do not deserve . . ."

"Shhhh!" he replied, squeezing her face into his neck.

After a while she raised her head and gave him a sad little smile. She brushed the untidy hair off his forehead. "I have got you into desperate trouble. They *will* kill us both, you know."

Llian had been trying not to think about that. "Well, we'll have to think of a way to trick them."

He got up and went into the kitchen, returning shortly with a steaming flask and two bowls. He poured the tea. Karan lifted her bowl with both hands and sipped it, eyes closed. Llian stared at his own bowl, and the patterns of the steam rising from it, but did not drink. His words had been hollow; he was completely out of his depth here. After a while he lay on the pallet in his room, in the darkness, rejecting scheme after scheme until at last he drifted into a restless sleep.

25

INHUMAN BONDAGE

I will not cry out this time, Maigraith told herself, as the old one came back with his instruments. I will not let them hear me scream this time. She watched him from the corner of her eye. He approached. The instruments clinked in his hand. She gripped the metal frame, clinging to it so tightly that specks of blood welled out from beneath her nails. Not this time. The tools were applied. She screamed.

It was a long time later that she realized that the screaming had stopped. Why, I've stopped screaming, she thought in a detached way, momentarily divorced from her body. Maigraith opened her puffy eyes. The pain hit her again, but it was old pain, the pain of a hundred little wounds. The old man was moving away, crossing out of the field of her vision, gone. She slumped against the frame, hanging limply by her wrists. Someone flung water over her from a bucket, cold water that stung her wounds. A trickle ran down her forehead, her nose. She licked it from her lips, grateful for its coolness, though it was briny and did not ease her thirst. Someone, perhaps the same person, retightened the thongs at her wrists and ankles. The hands were bony, with sparse clumps of yellow hair between the thickened knuckles. Then Vartila returned.

Maigraith recalled her words as the Whelm had borne her here, bound and her mouth stopped. "Allow her no respite. The body, then the mind, then the body again. She is very strong, and the pain will magnify her strength, focus her will. Allow her to use it at your peril; always keep the bonds tight; check her constantly."

Vartila had underestimated Maigraith. Already two of the Whelm lay unmoving, but it did not aid her. Every resistance was matched by an increase in their cold ferocity.

Vartila had questioned her about herself. "Who are you, that have so weakened our master? Who are you, that bring us to defiance? We are Whelm, and do our master's will." Her voice rose then, shaking with a passion that Maigraith had not heard before. *"Who are you, that have so corrupted us?"*

The torment began again, but redoubled. And they questioned her about Karan, over and over again. "Who is she?" their voices rasped. "Who is she, that even the Whelm cannot take her? How can she, a petty human, make a link? We have tested you, and you are barren of that talent."

What harm can it do to tell them, Maigraith thought, through a delirium of pain. "That is no secret. She is human, but her grandmother was Mantille, an Aachim."

The reaction of the Whelm was unexpected, and shocking. "A *blending*!" Vartila cried. "Now I know what to use against her." She called the others in a loud voice and they came running. A flurry of orders, then two Whelm ran out the door.

Vartila came back smiling, showing her teeth. "You have

given us power over your friend. No more will she run. She will wait for us to come, unable to resist, her limbs numb and her mind paralyzed, able to feel nothing but terror. But do not stop with that; there is much more you can tell us, now you have begun."

Maigraith had no time to wonder at their reaction, or what she had done to Karan. Soon all thoughts were overwhelmed in her own nightmare.

Vartila laid her hand on Maigraith's bare shoulder. The crawling of mind and body began again, a sensation so hideous and shameful that only death could wash away the memory of it. But death did not come. She clung to the memory of the pain, using it to anchor her whimpering mind in her failing body. Bring back the pain, she wept, let me only have the pain, but not this. Oh, Yggur, how could you do this to me? And in between that she agonized about what she had done to Karan.

"*I will tell you. I will tell you,*" she screamed, no longer knowing who she was, or what she was.

Again and again she cried out, until she was reduced to a whimper, to a whisper. But only when she could no longer even whisper did the torment stop. There was absolute silence then, in that damp cavern of a room. Maigraith opened her mouth but no sound emerged. She tensed, remembering the old man. This time he did not appear. Then, a choking sound from the entrance. She twisted on the frame, turning her head, opening her eyes. Closing and opening them again, but the hallucination was still there.

Maigraith saw a woman with a restless cloud of pale luminous hair. She was as small as Karan but slight, and moving so lightly that she seemed to float. A bleached radiance streamed out from between her clenched fingers; the flesh glowed pinkly translucent, and the slender shadows of the bones. She turned her hand this way and that; the light

bathing first one of the Whelm, then another. They struggled
toward her, dismayed, and as the light caught each in turn
they flung out their arms as though trying to grip the air, and
fell to the floor. She saw Vartila fold over in the middle, sliding forward like someone diving into shallow water and
striking the floor with her face.

The light fell briefly on Maigraith and she was surrounded by red whirling darkness. A wave caught her, flung
her away, then the black folded in on itself and she could see
again. The hallucination drifted toward her, behind her, her
bonds fell away and she was caught about the waist as she
fell, and lowered to the floor. Maigraith closed her eyes. A
hand touched her shoulder. She tensed, then a voice, cool
but not at all like the Whelm, said, "Drink this," and helped
her to a sitting position.

She held out her hands to take the cup, but they were
numb. The cup was held to her lips. She sipped the thick
aromatic fluid, and it warmed her. After a few sips she
pushed the cup away, opening her eyes a fraction. "*Faelamor!*" she whispered, smiling weakly. "How came you
here so quickly?"

Faelamor did not smile back. "I came from Sith to meet
you, and heard that you were prisoner here." The corners of
her mouth were tight with strain. She had a small hoarse
voice, the only aspect of her that was not, at this time, utterly
controlled. She must indeed have been exhausted, to allow
the illusion to slip, even in front of Maigraith. "But we will
talk of that in a moment. We must go at once. Can you
walk?"

"I do not think so, not yet."

Faelamor rubbed her feet and legs until the circulation
began to come back, while Maigraith lay staring up at her.
Faelamor's eyes were deep-sunk, with a golden, almost feline liquidity. Her skin was smooth as waxed rosewood, and

translucent; the pink tint of flesh showed through and the blue webs of veins. That was just the most visible difference between Faellem and human, though they usually covered their skin, or dyed it. Her features were as delicate and precisely formed as a sculpture, but it was the smoothness and delicacy of a mask, and Maigraith had no idea what she might be thinking. Only once did her face betray anything, when she examined Maigraith's scourgings.

"Why did they do this to you? Had I seen this first, what I used on them would have been no illusion."

"I don't know." Maigraith was weeping softly with the pain. "They seemed to hate me as soon as they saw me."

Faelamor examined the still forms of the Whelm. She bent down and began stripping the clothing off the smallest. She came back with her arm laden with boots, robes and undergarments. Maigraith looked at them with distaste.

"I will not wear the underclothes," she said, but allowed Faelamor to help her with the robes, noticing for the first time that Faelamor's hands were old, and they shook a little. The boots were too long and narrow, hurting her feet as soon as she put them on. The coarse fabric rubbed against her injured back and thighs.

"How did you do that?" she asked, looking at the still forms of the Whelm scattered so casually about the room. "What was that in your hand?"

"Each has their weakness, as I taught you. For the Whelm our mind-twisting illusions are enough, though to quell this many was a great trial. The device? Nothing at all, just an image to strengthen my illusion. Drink the rest of the cup now, it will ease the pain. I can do nothing for your wounds until we are safely away." She offered Maigraith her arm.

Maigraith felt confused and uneasy. Faelamor in the role of protector was strange to her, though it was good to have someone to lean on, to follow rather than to lead, to not have to decide. But it did not last.

"Did you get as far as the library? Was the Mirror there?"

Maigraith stopped dead. "You do not *know*? The Mirror is gone. Karan escaped weeks ago, to bring it to you in Sith. How is it that you have not heard?"

"*Karan the sensitive!* You utter fool! I warned you to go alone. Far better that you had not come at all."

The coldness, the feeling that she was of little value, this was what she was used to. How thankless to be Faelamor's protégée; how impossible to prove her worth. But there was worse to come, for as she spoke the light from a lamp beside the door fell on Maigraith's face. "Your eyes!" Faelamor said, in a whisper. "Your eyes have changed. You have not taken the *kalash,* as I bade you. Why do you not take the drug?"

"They took everything from me," said Maigraith. "What has happened? I have not seen my face since I was taken."

"The color is changing. Your eyes are deepest indigo now. Oh, this is unimaginable. And to let *him* see it." Faelamor turned and walked back to the center of the room, staring at the frame, holding the bars, her head hanging down.

Maigraith's eyes followed her. The tenseness, the strain, now the genuine anguish—this was not the Faelamor she had known so long. All her emotions were normally so controlled, so useful to her.

"There is another thing I must tell you," said Maigraith trembling. "Perhaps the worst of all. When Yggur caught us—caught us," she repeated hesitantly, "he questioned us about you."

Faelamor went deathly still, her lips a thin white line. "You could not tell him. You could not betray my secret."

Maigraith was so mortified and afraid that she could

barely speak, but the awful words must be spoken. "I did not," she whispered, "even when he put a *command* on us. Karan resisted too, as long as she was able. But he was too strong for her. She spoke your name."

Faelamor was icy calm. "*How did she know my name?*"

Maigraith choked. "One night on the way here—she was so unhappy—she began to broadcast. I—we drank together, to comfort her, and I had too much and said your name. I am so sorry."

She cringed away, expecting Faelamor's awful rage to strike her dead, but nothing happened. She did nothing at all, just stood there, staring absently, until Maigraith wondered if Faelamor had even heard. At last she spoke, very quietly.

"Nearly three hundred years have I concealed my name, my life. All the world thinks me dead, and I am forgotten, since that terrible struggle with Yalkara when I drove her from Santhenar. All this time I have protected my secret, telling only one soul, the one I *made*, chose, protected, schooled. And you betray me like a tavern slattern, as though my name were valueless."

She turned to Maigraith, and there was grief in her eyes, not anger. "We are weak. All my plans, for all those years, have depended on none knowing that I lived. None knew but my people, and you. Nothing could make the Faellem tell. Nothing could keep you to your pledge."

"I trusted her. I needed her. He was too strong!" cried Maigraith. Had a chasm opened up before her she would have gladly thrown herself within, anything to escape this.

"What need for friendship? You had your duty. The doing of it would have been a greater comfort than any friend. I warned you not to bring her into my affairs. *If I find Karan, she is dead.*" A sudden thought struck her. "The Whelm, do they know as well?"

"They do not, I swear it," Maigraith said frantically.

"Twice they tortured me, but I said nothing about you. Yggur tells them nothing—my coming seems to have opened a rift between them. They have an implacable hatred of me, or an instinctive fear. I see it in their faces."

The calmness of Faelamor's rage was terrifying. "Your value is diminished, but there is no time to start again. Tallallame cries out for us—our own world begs us to come home. I *must* break the Forbidding. I *will* find a way. But first I must have the Mirror. This duty is my torment, my nightmare—my betrayer. No," she said softly. "I have chosen. I will take the Faellem home. Whatever the cost I will pay it. I *am* the Faellem."

She came back, walking quickly to where Maigraith supported herself against the doorway. Faelamor's voice changed, becoming businesslike, as though all that had been said was done with.

"What is done cannot be changed, though now all my plans must be recast, and there is so little time. We must leave at once. I would be well into the swamps before dawn. When we reach the boat I'll give you more of the *kalash*. Until then, look down. Let no one see your eyes; though I fear it's too late for that. Take my arm. Hurry. Even I cannot conceal you in the full daylight."

Maigraith never knew what miracles Faelamor wrought to bring them safely and undetected out of Fiz Gorgo that night, consumed as she was with her guilt and shame, her weakness and failure, and the torment of her injuries. Before they had gone a hundred paces she was staggering, her whole body a mass of pain. At last they reached the forest. A half league into the trees they came to the edge of the marshes. Faelamor waded in and returned pulling a small flat-bottomed boat. She heaved the comatose Maigraith over the side, stepped in herself and poled off into the swamps.

*   *   *

Dawn came, and Yggur went later than usual to his chamber. His eyes were hollow from lack of sleep and his face was haunted. Whatever the cost to his ambitions, he could not do it to her. Not the Whelm. What a fool he was. In a month and a half she had turned the plans of decades on their heads.

At the door he froze. Where were the guards? Inside he saw two bodies; no, they were sleeping! No, drugged; he could smell it from here. He lurched across to Maigraith's cell, saw the half-opened door, the table and chair knocked over. Her clothes still hung neatly on the other chair, where she had left them. Her boots were beside the bed. His heart turned over.

They *had* come for her. Why had he not checked her this night? Yggur ran down the stairs, faster than he had run in fifty years, to the quarters of the Whelm. She was not there. He began the long search of the caverns beneath, finding the room at last.

He took in the scene from the doorway: the frame in the middle of the room, the thongs hanging down, the floor red beneath. The old one lay beneath the frame, surrounded by his scattered instruments. The other Whelm were strewn about the floor. He squatted down beside the nearest. The man was conscious but incapable of movement.

A small clump of hair was caught on the frame, the long strands a deep chestnut color. Yggur untangled them, absently putting them in his pouch. He caught sight of the cup on the floor, sniffed it and tasted the residue with a finger. An age-old memory stirred.

She is gone, he thought. Faelamor has come for her! He closed the door and walked slowly back up the stairs to his chamber. It seemed empty now. Strange that he had not noticed it before.

He sat for a long minute at his workbench. How he

missed her. He had never felt this way for anyone before. What should he do? The Whelm had failed against Karan; failed against Faelamor as well. There was no one here who could hope to follow her through the swamps of Orist, save himself. And even he might not be *her* match out there.

No, Maigraith is gone. Forget her. How had she so bewitched him that he had lost sight of his own purpose? Besides, he knew that Karan was headed to Sith, however tortuous the route she took. *They* must go there as well. He leapt up, pulled the bell. By the time the servant came he was already deep in the maps and papers on his bench.

"Call my generals together," he cried, writing orders furiously. "We march on the east. And call the Whelm; they can yet redeem themselves."

But still Maigraith would not go from his mind.

26

THE TRIAL

Karan stirred. A plan had come to her, so risky that her knees went soft at the thought of it. She crept to the door and peeped into Llian's chamber. He was lying on his side. The light from the open door shone on his face and she saw that he slept. She touched his forehead with her fingers but he did not stir. She looked around the room. What could she use? The book, *Tales of the Aachim*? No, that was the worst thing she could possibly choose, like trying to get a true reading from the Twisted Mirror. It had to be something that he kept with him always.

Around his neck, beneath his shirt, Llian wore a silver chain from which hung a small jade amulet. Karan opened his shirt carefully. His skin was very smooth under her hands. She wanted to stroke it. She unclasped the catch and drew the amulet out. Llian turned over, drowsily, but did not wake. She held the chain up to the light, then let it fall into her cupped palm, where it made a little silvery pool.

Then she glided out of the room and pulled the door to behind her.

In her own chamber she barred the door, took off her boots and sat on the floor with her legs crossed, an elbow resting on each knee, the amulet in her cupped hands. She clenched her hands around the amulet, became lethargic, lowering her head slowly onto the triangle of her arms, resting there, the amulet warm in her fingers, the chain cool on her forehead. A stray image floated into her mind: a storm over the ruins; Llian bursting through the door with bloody face, to fall down the steps at her feet. She brushed the image away. Others followed: Llian tortured by his fear of falling as they followed the path along the gorge; there looking foolish as they were received in the courtyard by Rael; here dazed and mumbling from Emmant's charm. All these memories she suppressed.

Then nothing, save the droning of the wind outside her window. Nothing at all, and she grew anxious. She forced her mind to calmness. Finally it came, the faintest tickle at the very fringe of her senses. The amulet became hot in her hands; she gripped it more tightly. The tickle swelled into a pinpoint of light, drifting this way and that, growing into an image of now. It was Llian, and he lay dreaming in his chamber, dreaming the Histories of the Aachim.

Karan left him to his dream. She thought on the morrow. Truly did she fear Tensor. He would break her if he believed she knew anything about the Mirror. Then he would take it and use it. The terrible dream, the destruction of Shazmak, touched her. But long before that she would be dead, and Llian, *her Llian,* too. Karan allowed the terror to seep through her until she was clawed by echoing, silent screams.

She turned back to Llian. Now his dreams had drifted and he too was at judgment with Tensor, and afraid, though his was a strong, healthy fear, not the nameless terror that she had made. She wafted this image of herself toward him until their senses overlapped and Llian dreamed of her. Then she wove into her terror a story, and the story was true save for one tiny lie.

Maigraith took me to Fiz Gorgo, she wove, for she needed a sensitive, a link. I went with her without knowing what she was seeking, only that it was a relic from the past, and even when I saw it I knew not what it was and she did not say. I escaped, she was taken. At Lake Neid I gave the Mirror to another and fled north as a decoy. It was only weeks later that I learned that it was the Mirror of Aachan.

As she wove the dream Llian dreamed it. He was with her on that icy swim through the cistern into Fiz Gorgo. He saw, with wonder, Maigraith's defiance of Yggur. He was beside Karan as she fled in terror through the swamps of Orist. Then the lie: he saw her give the Mirror to another, beneath the crumbling jetty on Lake Neid. He saw the betrayal; the relentless pursuit of the Whelm; he felt again her night-sending at Tullin. All this Llian dreamed, and his own failures and follies too.

On the story went, pace by pace. They stood before the bridge into Shazmak. They were made welcome. Llian dreamed it all, and at the end knew that Karan had been led and did not know why; had given up the Mirror to another without knowing what it was, and now was afraid and shamed.

The tale was ended; she could do no more. Llian drifted into other dreams and Karan allowed her sense of him to contract to a point that she put away in an obscure compartment of her subconscious. Slowly she raised her head, her face still wet with tears. Her hands and feet were cold and numb; she could barely stand up. She hobbled over to the window and as she did so the chain and its little amulet slipped from her fingers and fell down beside the table.

Karan leaned on the sill. The outside of the pane was crusted with ice. The aftersickness was rising in her throat and there were needles of pain behind her eyes. Then the stars began to dance; she fell unconscious beside her pallet.

Llian woke early the next morning from an unusually deep sleep, to face the problem that he had been unable to solve the previous night. He made breakfast, coffee and sweet-cake, and knocked on Karan's door. There was no answer and the door was locked. That had never happened before. He took the tray back to the table and was going through their options on a blank page of his journal, for he always thought better with a pen in his hand, when there came an imperious knocking at the outer door. Llian laid the bowl aside and opened the door. Outside was a tall, strongly built man with black wavy hair, a full dark beard and the self-contained presence of an Aachim. He was clad all in gray, with a gray cloak and high boots.

"I am Tensor," he said. "I have returned from the east and convened the Syndics. You are Llian, master chronicler of Chanthed?"

Tensor's presence was quite overpowering. Llian indicated that he was.

"I call upon you to speak at the trial of Karan of Bannador. The charge is treason. Will you speak?"

Llian choked. "I will," he said, suddenly needing the support of the door handle.

"Good. Depending on the result of her trial you may also be charged. Karan is within?"

Llian nodded. He felt completely numb.

"May we enter?"

Llian knew that the request was just a meaningless politeness. He was seized by an irrational urge to spit on Tensor's polished boots, but he stood aside.

Tensor strode across the antechamber, followed by Emmant and five other Aachim. Rael, whose face was as pale as paper, rapped at Karan's door. There was no answer. He rapped again and tried the door. It did not budge.

"May we break it?" Tensor asked Llian.

"Yes," he replied in barely more than a whisper.

The door was broken and pushed aside. Karan lay on the floor where she had fallen. Llian ran to her. As he did so she lifted her head and looked around. A shadow crossed her face as she caught sight of Tensor, then she sank down again wretchedly.

Tensor bent down beside her and stroked her forehead gently, brushing aside the red locks. "Karan, Karan, why have you so shamed yourself?" he said in a voice thick with sorrow. "You who were our joy and our life. This is a grievous day."

"Why Emmant?" she cried in an angry croak. "How could you so betray me?"

Tensor's face went rigid, but for a moment his eyes skidded away from hers. "I am shamed," he said, "but I *will* have it."

He stooped there for a moment longer, in silence, then stood erect, saying in formal tones:

"Karan Elienor Melluselde Fyrn of Gothryme, I call upon you to defend yourself before the Syndics against the charge that you betrayed the sacred trust and great purpose of the Aachim by stealing that great heirloom—long lost, long sought—the Mirror of Aachan, from Yggur of Fiz Gorgo and taking it for Mendark, Magister of the Great Council. Will you defend yourself and the honor of your family?"

Karan was bemused. "Mendark?" she said in a whisper. "Mendark has nothing to do with it."

"So you say! Then how come you are accompanied by his protégé?"

She did not answer.

"Will you defend your family's honor?"

"I will," Karan said weakly.

"Then come," said Tensor brusquely. "The world turns. We must begin at once."

He signed to two of the Aachim and they came forward and gave Karan their arms. She moved slowly off; her feet still bare and her right arm, in its cast, hanging limply. Behind her went Rael, like a corpse reanimated; then Llian, so afraid for her that his stomach heaved and he almost disgraced himself. The others followed slowly, all save Emmant.

He remained for a moment after they departed. His sharp eyes caught something shining on the floor beside the window, and he bent down and picked up the chain and amulet. Emmant thrust it in his pouch and hurried after.

In spite of Tensor's haste it was not until the mid-afternoon that the trial got underway. It was held in a cavernous hall, the roof an oval dome supported by curving walls on either side. Great iron doors stood open at each end. The walls were painted to represent the landscape of Aachan: iron towers on crags sculpted as though from ice; mountains crusted with sulphur, yellow and red; vine forests, black-leaved, tangled and tortured. The dome showed an alien sky of greenish hue, the swollen orange moon brooding from the further end. Yellow globes suspended below the dome gave out a dim light.

Llian had entered the room from the rear. The floor sloped downwards in a series of benches but without seats except at the lower levels. At the far end of the room was a platform, slightly raised, on which stood a semicircle of high-backed iron chairs, intricately wrought in the fashion of the Aachim. Just off the center of the semicircle was a pedestal of stone, around which spiraled a black iron stairway of twenty steps. The pedestal was topped by a dock of iron lace, surmounted by a railing of veined red marble. Karan stood limply in the dock, supporting herself on the rail. Somehow the height of the dock diminished her: she looked small, afraid and guilty.

Llian sat down among the Aachim, while Rael, in robes, went onto the platform and took a seat among the Syndics. The room became still. Then Tensor strode in from a side door and stood at one end of the semicircle of seats.

The trial began with an exchange of courtesies which, even though they were made in his tongue, Llian found difficult to understand. He watched Karan, who was required to respond at intervals. Her responses became progressively more absent—she felt in her pockets, searching her wallet again and again for the lost amulet, but without success, and eventually gave up and sank her head on her arms.

The courtesies ended and there was a long silence. Karan raised her head and looked around the hall. Llian knew she was looking for him, that for some reason she needed him. He stood up. Their eyes locked. For a moment he felt his mind begin to drift, as when Emmant had charmed him, then someone nudged him and he sat down again. Karan bowed her head.

Tensor spoke. His normally rich deep voice, stripped of all color, was utterly neutral, as all save the defendant must be before the Syndics.

"Karan Elienor Melluselde Fyrn of Gothryme in Bannador, scion of Elienor, most ancient house of Aachan. Elienor, greatest of heroines! The only one to stand against Rulke when the Charon came, when the scourging of Aachan began! Your house has always been ally to the Elders of Shazmak. Karan Elienor, granddaughter of beloved Mantille, Mantille remade; esteemed cousin. You are arraigned on the charge of treason. I, Tensor, your accuser, contend that you, the recipient of the gifts and secrets of the Aachim, betrayed our sacred trust and great purpose. I contend that you stole the Mirror of Aachan from Yggur the Mancer. I contend that you took the Mirror to give to Mendark, Magister of the Great Council of Iagador, to use for projects inimical to our great purpose. I will call the witnesses against you. Then you will plead your argument to the Syndics, that you may be judged."

Melluselde! thought Llian. What a curious, ancient name. Who was it had that name in ancient times, and how did it come down to her? The name that came before it was much more ancient, and greater yet, but Llian knew nothing of the early history of the Aachim. Then the trial was underway and he had no time to think about it.

The witnesses came forth, and each of them spoke as blandly, as simply and as neutrally as Tensor had. Each presentation was fair, measured, unhurried. There was no drama, and the tension in the room was all the greater for its lack.

First spoke Tensor of a messenger coming to him when he was across the Sea of Thurkad, bearing news that the Mirror had been found. He had returned at once, and in Thurkad had learned from Mendark that the Mirror had been stolen from Yggur, that Karan knew about it and that Mendark had sent Llian to escort her from Tullin to Thurkad. Mendark, he told, was evasive and would not admit all he knew in spite of their long friendship. Tensor guessed that Karan was trying to cross the mountains via Shazmak and had sent messages to keep her there.

The Syndics considered his testimony, conferring among themselves in voices that did not carry. They questioned him about the message that he had sent to Emmant, and it was evident from the form of their interrogation that what he had done was, at the least, distasteful. There was another brief consultation and Selial, the leader of the Syndics, rose. Cool and dignified, she had thick silvery hair that stood out from her head in waves. Llian was comforted by the air she gave out, of impartial justice.

"None can lie to the Syndics," she said. "We have weighed the evidence of this witness, and it is truth, as he knows it." Tensor bowed to the Syndics and to the audience, and even to Karan, and resumed his seat.

Rael was called down from his seat among the Syndics. He told of the coming of Karan and Llian, of the debate about Llian and his eventual confirmation as Aachimning, of Karan's strange behavior after she heard that Tensor was returning. He retold what Llian had said to Emmant in the library, and his subsequent conversations with Karan about that. Rael stood rigid, and his voice was wooden with the effort of suppressing his feelings.

Again the Syndics spoke among themselves, then Selial stood. "There are no questions. We have weighed the evidence of this witness, and it is truth, as he knows it."

After that other witnesses spoke: the two Aachim who, with Rael, had met Karan and Llian at the gates of Shazmak, the man with whom she had had that late-night argument, other Aachim that Llian had never met. Also called were the ones who had searched her, and her apartment, and every place that she had gone to and might have hidden the Mirror, though they had no evidence to report on that. Each spoke briefly, simply. Some were questioned by the Syndics, most were not, and after each testimony was completed it was accepted.

Last of all, Emmant was called. Emmant spoke, unemotionally, of the message he had received from Tensor. *Karan of Bannador returns to Shazmak. Watch her, secretly. Find out what she knows of the Mirror of Aachan and you will be well rewarded*. He told that he had shadowed Karan, but had learned nothing. He recreated the scene in the library where Llian had mentioned the Mirror, and told how later he had questioned Llian again and Llian had seemed to be on the verge of telling more when Karan intervened.

The Syndics conferred for a long time. Then the leader stood. "This witness has told truth, but it is not all the truth. You will tell how Llian came to make this admission."

"I used a charm against him," Emmant said, showing for the first time a trace of pride. "I put it on the book so that whenever he touched it, it would sap his will and I would be able to force the truth from him."

The Syndics stirred. "And the second time?"

"The same charm, though it worked less well. I had to use other methods."

"You almost choked him to death."

"Pah!" Emmant sneered at Llian. "Look at the pathetic creature: he is so paltry. That charm would not have worked on the smallest of our children. Even so, he is not harmed."

The Syndics conferred for a long time. Eventually Selial stood again. "We have weighed the evidence of this witness, and it is truth, as he knows it. But the evidence is tainted; it would dishonor us to admit it. We do not."

Emmant's face showed his shock and disbelief, but he said nothing, merely returning to his seat.

It was Llian's turn. He told his tale, beginning with his interview with Wistan, and all his adventures on the way to Shazmak. The Syndics questioned him closely about everything Karan had said relating to the Mirror, but when it came down to it she had told him virtually nothing. Selial stood, and Llian's evidence too was accepted as truth.

*   *   *

"Karan of Bannador," said Tensor, "you have heard the evidence against you. Plead now your case, that the Syndics may judge."

Karan, standing in the dock, made a pale figure against the huge orange moon. How alone she looked, and how afraid. The silence grew so long that the Syndics began to glance at one another.

She has nothing to tell them, Llian thought. They will condemn her unheard. The same conclusion showed on Rael's anguished face.

At last she broke the silence, speaking randomly, incoherently at first, knowing not what to say or how to say it, knowing only that she must speak and that she could tell no lie to that synod. She started with Maigraith demanding her aid in Gothryme, and forcing her to swear that sacred oath by her father's memory. That caused a stir, the oath that would betray his memory whether she kept it or broke it.

After that Karan lost the thread of the story, jumping back and forth between Gothryme and Fiz Gorgo and the swamps of Orlst, stumbling over her words, stammering and even shouting snatches of remembered conversations from that time.

Karan was trying to raise that sense of Llian that she had secreted away so carefully, but in her confusion and terror she could not find it. She had lost the amulet and did not know how to retrieve the link without it.

Her voice grew wilder, her speech more incoherent. The Syndics began to whisper to one another. Tensor bent to the woman opposite, speaking urgently in a low voice. Karan knew what they were thinking—that she was mad. No more time, else they would *read* her. She must risk the direct way.

She stopped short, lifted up her head and stared directly at Llian. Their eyes meshed. A spark leapt between them. An itch began in the back of Llian's head. An anxiety grew in him, a compound of all his sorrows. It swelled, becoming a blind, unreasoning terror, a terror of the Aachim and of his fate. Abruptly it was dashed away, calm descended, then in a blink he was with Karan and Maigraith as they stole into Fiz Gorgo, the fortress of Yggur the Mancer.

He was wide awake and dreaming.

Karan stood motionless and spoke at last.

The dream that she had planted welled up in Llian's mind as truth, and as truth she read it back from him and spoke it aloud to the Syndics. It was so real that they trembled with her at the power of Yggur, the strength of Maigraith, the malice of the Whelm; they squatted with her in the stinking mud beneath the wharf at Lake Neid as she gave the Mirror to her accomplice; they struggled with her to lift one-handed a block of stone and fling it down the cliff at Idlis in the dead of night; they tasted the bitter, oily gruel in the ruins. The Syndics paced each pace of that cold, hungry, fearful journey, until at last she stood in the courtyard at Shazmak. When her story was finished they wept with her at her shame and dishonor, for they saw that she knew not what it was that she had done. Llian wept also.

The Syndics wept but Tensor did not. He stared at her, greatly puzzled, for he had expected lies, denials, the rejection of her evidence by the Syndics, ultimately her condemnation and a truth reading. Anything but such a tale.

The Syndics went into conclave, but it was interrupted by Tensor. "There is a wrongness in this story," Tensor cried. "The prisoner must be *read*. I will do it, if you will allow."

"Be silent!" thundered Selial. "It is for the Syndics to judge, as you know better than any." Tensor bowed his head and sat down again. The conclave resumed. Eventually they had agreement, and Selial stood.

"Karan Elienor Melluselde Fyrn."

Karan, who had been supporting herself on the railing,

looking utterly exhausted, pushed herself away and stood up straight. She looked directly at Selial. Llian's heart went out to her.

"You have been charged with treason. You know the penalty, and it is death. Are you prepared for our verdict?"

"I am." Her voice barely carried to where Llian sat.

"We have weighed your evidence, as we have the evidence of all the witnesses." Selial looked down at her hands. Llian found it difficult to breathe. "We judge that your evidence is truth, as you know it. The charge is dismissed. You are free."

Karan gave a great sigh and slumped forward on the rail with her head in her hands. It seemed that she was weeping.

"*No!*" cried Tensor. "She lies. She must be *read*."

"I sense no wrong," said one of the Syndics, looking at her with compassion; then another. "Karan cannot be *read*. That would shame us, and her. Can you not recall how she came to us, what joy she brought us, and the debt we owe her because of Emmant's behavior when she lived with us before? There is no crime. She has behaved with honor and must be freed."

"I do not wish it," said Tensor grimly. "She lies. She knows where the Mirror is. Perhaps her contempt for us is so great that she even brought it here. She stands between us and our great destiny. Will you not allow me to reach out and bring it to you?"

The Syndics were united against him. "The price is too high," one said.

"You let this need cloud your judgment," said another.

"We no longer have a destiny," said a third. "We are content just to be."

"To be is to wither," said Tensor. "I am not content. The search may not have been sufficient."

"It was, Tensor," said another. "All she brought has been checked and checked again."

"Her arm?"

"The cast was made here; I made it," said Rael, and the one who had helped him verified it.

"Can she have hidden it in the city?"

"We do not believe so. They were both watched when they left their chamber."

"The search must be made anew. I will not consent to freeing her. I say we hold her another day, for there is a wrongness here, whether you see it or nay. We must swallow our shame. What say the Syndics?"

The Syndics consulted among themselves. "Very well," said Selial. "We sense no lie, but we will allow you one more day. Then if you find no firm evidence she must be allowed to go. Karan, you are released into Rael's protection."

Tensor bowed his head. "It will be as you wish. We will talk further this night." He turned to lead the way out, then Selial called to him again.

"There is another matter to be dealt with—the matter of Emmant. To spy on them was wrong, but to use the Secret Art against the helpless Zain was unforgivable. We are Aachim, nobler than any, but only while we so act. We have no need of base devices."

"The error was mine," said Tensor with bowed head. "I cared too much for the glory of the Aachim."

"Our honor is too great a price to pay for future glory," Selial said. "Never again. But the greater error was Emmant's. Too great for one who seeks to be Aachim; for one who has already been warned." She turned to him.

But Emmant was on his feet, shouting, "She has it! I know she has it!" He held out his hands to the Syndics. "Give her to me; give *me* leave. I will find it for you, never doubt me. My ways are sure. I will flay her, layer by layer, and peel back the layers of deceit as well. And when her weeping flesh is laid bare I will reach into her still-beating heart and pluck out the truth for you. Then you will know my worth . . ."

Even on the impassive faces of the Syndics their horror and contempt was evident. Even to Emmant. Selial spoke with cold formality and her words cut through his self-delusion like a blade through a veil.

"Say no more! You are stripped of all duties and responsibilities to the Aachim. You may go or remain, as you wish, but you are worth nothing to us now."

Emmant let out a tortured wail. He had expected to be praised and rewarded, not the loss of all he had ever striven for. He was shattered, shaking so much that he had to be led from the hall. At the door he turned and looked back at Karan, his face in torment, his eyes just the surface expression of a malignancy with its roots in his soul. Llian felt a twisted pity for him then, pity mixed with a terrible dread of this driven man. But Emmant opened his mouth and vomited forth a torrent of abuse so vile that Llian, who was no stranger to uncouthness, was almost sick. Then as suddenly the flow was cut off and he allowed the Aachim to lead him away.

"Hold," said Selial, as Tensor turned to go. "There is yet another matter."

Tensor turned back to her.

"Do you still wish to charge the chronicler?"

Tensor was silent for a long time. Finally, "I will hold that in abeyance until the other issue is resolved."

"Then, Llian of Chanthed, you are free to do as you wish, save that you may not yet leave Shazmak."

As they spoke Karan limped down the spiral stair. Near the bottom she stumbled, slipped and cracked her cast against the iron. Screwing her eyes shut she stood still as

death, supporting her arm. Then she threw her shoulders
back and, head in the air, walked across to where Llian sat.
But once there she could keep it up no longer, and slumped
on the chair as though the marrow had been withdrawn from
her bones.

Llian had never hated anyone more than he hated Tensor
at that moment. The urge to strike back, though he knew it
was foolhardy, was overwhelming. "In that case I have a
question of my own, if the Syndics will allow it," he said.

Tensor jerked upright. The audience murmured.

"Truly a presumptuous chronicler!" said Selial. "You
have no right to examine any of us, unless you have been
charged."

"You said I was free to do as I wished. I wish to have an
answer to one question at this Syndic."

"Very well. If I must err it will be on the side of courtesy," Selial replied. "Who would you question, and what
would you ask?"

"My question is to Tensor, and it is this—"

Karan looked up at Llian in amazement. Surely he didn't
have the temerity?

Llian did. "Tell me what happened at Huling's Tower
after Shuthdar destroyed the golden flute and the Forbidding
was made."

Tensor's head jerked around. His eyes glowed golden, his
whole body gone rigid in his shame and fury.

"Insolent dog of a Zain, I will crucify you for this! You
shall be tried right now. Charge him!"

Selial stood up. She was small for an Aachim. She bent
before Tensor's fury, then snapped back.

"Do not! Would you bring the Syndic into disrepute to
cover up your own failings?" She looked to each of her fellows, nodded, then spoke again.

"In the circumstances the Zain has a right. We do not see

the relevance of this question, but since it is the only one he asks, we allow it. You must answer Llian, and be sure that we will judge the truth of it. To the dock, if you will."

Tensor's flesh seemed to run before the white heat of his fury, but he climbed the stairs and stood in the iron dock. He gripped the rail so hard that Llian expected the marble to crumble in his fingers.

Llian felt Karan's hand slip into his. She was shivering.

Tensor shook his head, forcing himself to calmness. If he must confess his shame, he would do it with dignity.

Then he looked Llian in the eye. "The destruction of the flute," he said softly. "Why *did* it unman us so?

"It was not the very air glowing red, yellow, blue and violet, battering past us like a solid rainbow, a painted cyclone. It was not the waves that rolled head-high through the ground, throwing men, women, horses and even wagons, up in the air. Not the unseen force that flattened every tree outwards for a league, nor the lightnings that streamed from sword and chain mail and helmet, nor the birds that fell dead with brains boiling out their beaks. It was none of those, nor the hundred other strangenesses not seen before or since.

"What made me run like a craven? I'll tell you, chronicler. I'll tell you, and pray that you never see it, lest your entrails liquify and dribble out your backside."

Selial stiffened at the vulgarity, then coldly motioned for Tensor to go on.

He nodded an apology to the Syndics. "The flute struck down every creature save us Aachim. Death or unconsciousness spared them what we saw, chronicler!

"The flute opened the Way between the Worlds, and for an instant we saw right into the void. Know you what dwells there, chronicler? Not even a teller such as you could imagine it.

"In the void, life is more desperate, more brutal, more

fleeting than anywhere. Every race and every creature is armored, toothed, clawed, and deadly cunning. Every weapon, every protection, every unearthly power and talent must be bettered daily, as, in the desperation required for survival there, every other race and creature does the same. To fail once is to be extinguished. To stay the same is to be extinguished. In the void none but the fittest survive, and only by remaking themselves constantly.

"The Charon were cast into the void in their millions, chronicler, and fled from it reduced to hundreds, on the precipice of extinction. The void was too violent, too brutal, too clever even for the Charon. That is what we saw, and that is why we fled, but then the Forbidding came down and could not be undone. Have I satisfied you?"

Llian's skin crawled. The answer raised a dozen other questions, but he would not get them answered here. "You have not. I asked what happened at the tower *after* the Forbidding."

"I do not understand."

"There was a lame girl in the tower. She was murdered shortly after Shuthdar's death. I would know who killed her, and why."

"You think that someone entered in secret?" Something glowed in his golden eyes, as though he saw a new hope, or a new fear.

"Yes," said Llian.

"I cannot say. I was . . . not there."

"Then who can I ask? Where can I look?" cried Llian, despairing again.

"I have answered your question. I will say nothing more, save this. Who was the first to enter the tower? I always thought that it was a Charon, perhaps Rulke, but the whole history of that time is bound up with deceit. Only three Charon ever came to Santhenar. If Rulke, go to Alcifer. If

Yalkara, to Havissard, far to the east. If Kandor, who once had the fabulous Empire of Perion, before the sea went dry, seek the lost city of Katazza, in the center of the Dry Sea. That trek will test you, chronicler, to the last sinew of your feeble bag of bones. Had I the Mirror, I might find a better answer. Without it, I can tell you no more. I did not see." His resolve broke, his shame overflowed. "*I was not there!*"

Selial rose. "That is the key to the mystery, chronicler. No one knows who got in, or what they found there, and that is all we can tell you. We have heard the evidence of this witness, and it is truth, as he knows it. This trial is ended."

Tensor, despite his bulk, came down the steps like a panther. His yellow eyes were fixed on Llian.

"You will pay for this a hundredfold," he said, then turned his back and strode away.

"Thank you for standing up for me," said Karan, holding onto Llian's arm, "though I would rather you hadn't. You have made yourself an enemy who will never forget, or forgive."

Rael escorted Karan and Llian back to their chambers. Karan's aftersickness was worse than it had ever been. She could do no more than lie on the couch with her eyes closed. Llian was restless, exhilarated in spite of her peril and his own, and Tensor's unsatisfactory response.

"What are they doing now?" he asked, as he paced back and forth.

"Arguing about me," she replied weakly. "We have had a victory, but not enough. Tensor will never give in. He will convince them, if it goes long enough. But the Syndics have judged and they do not change their mind easily. Go away now."

He went into the other room and sat in the gloom, thinking about what he had learned. That the first person into the tower was probably a Charon. That the Mirror might hold the answer. That if it was a Charon, the answer could lie somewhere in one of their great cities, each a long trek away; each abandoned long ago.

Tempting, if he knew where the Mirror was, to make a bargain with Tensor. The Mirror in exchange for whatever secret it held about the Forbidding. He might have done it too, a few weeks ago, but not now. Not even for a Great Tale.

The debate had been going back and forth for a long time now, and even Tensor was weary, but at last he began to sway them.

"I do not ask you to betray the honor of the Aachim," he said softly, "only to relax the rigidity of our code, this once. The time has come when we must go forward and grow, or disappear. An opportunity has come that we did not even hope for; may we not reach out for it?" He looked eagerly at each of the Syndics, in the long silence that followed.

Finally Selial spoke, sadly and with prescience. "We have followed you, Tensor, through all the emptiness since the Clysm. You have served us faithfully and with honor all that interminable time, thinking only of the glory of the Aachim, never of yourself. Were it not for you we might have dwindled to nothing. We owe you this chance, and will not deny it—though not without dread. And we give you this warning: beware your pride. Do not let yourself be led into folly. You are given leave to present us your arguments one final time."

Then Rael, alone of the Syndics, rose and drew apart from the others. "All this evening I have kept silent, but I can sit here no longer. Do not do this thing, I beg you. Remember Pitlis. Your folly is our damnation, and this time it will be beyond redemption."

Tensor spoke kindly to him. "Your honor is great, Rael,

but you are so close to her that you cannot see the other side. This choice must be made without passion."

"Or pride," said Rael. "Then let me go from this Syndic. I will not be a party to our wrack."

"Then go with our blessing. Do not violate our trust."

Rael stood for a moment, a tortured look on his young face, then he bowed and turned away from the Aachim. Before he had left the room Tensor began the final presentation of his arguments.

It was after midnight and Llian was dozing, when he heard the knock. Rael had a lumpy sack in one hand and a pack in the other.

"I must speak with Karan at once," he said urgently, dropping his pack at the door. "The resolve of the Syndics is wavering. Take me to her."

"She is exhausted and sleeping. Must it be now?"

"It must," said Rael. "The choice has come down to one—flee or die."

Karan proved difficult to wake. Once roused she was confused and fractious.

"Go away!" she snapped. "Let me sleep."

"Get up!" said Rael, pulling her bodily out of her bed. "Tensor has prevailed against the Syndics. Soon they will agree to let him *read* you. When that happens you are done."

"This is monstrous; a travesty," said Karan angrily. "None can lie to the Syndics."

"Tensor says that you have lied, that you used some magic or trickery."

"I have no capacity for the Secret Art—all know that."

"That defense will not avail you, Karan, though it be true. I know you better than any."

"Then you must help me, Rael."

"I cannot, yet I must," said Rael, twisting the sack in his

hands. "If I aid you, I betray the Aachim and my treason is even greater than yours. If I do not, I betray family, friendship and . . ."

"Rael, you must choose. Choose wisely. Betray me and you aid the Aachim in their revenge, but if you give Tensor the Mirror the downfall of the Aachim will be beyond recovery. Aid me and you betray your people, but you also offer them hope."

"Do you swear to me, on the honor of your family and our own long . . . friendship, that you do not act against us?"

She grasped his hand in hers and looked him in the eye. "I swear it, Rael, by everything we ever felt for each other."

"Very well, I will aid you. I feared it would come to this, when first Llian spoke of the Mirror. Alas! You have your other house and your unspoken purpose to comfort you. For me there will be no return." Rael sank his head against the wall where he was standing. "Karan. Answer me truly. Have you deceived the Syndics?"

"I have."

"And what happened to the Mirror?"

"I have it with me. Do you wish to see it?"

"No. Not now or ever."

"That is as well," said Karan. "And now, if we are to go, let us go at once."

27

FLIGHT

While they were talking, Llian had packed their few belongings and as much food from the kitchen as he
could carry, and now he was standing by the doorway listening. Karan looked quickly around the room, heaved the
pack awkwardly onto her shoulder and they went out. At the
door Llian turned and looked back. *Tales of the Aachim* still
lay beneath a chair where it had fallen the previous day.

"Leave it," she said, catching his arm. "We've committed
crimes enough."

Still he looked toward the book, longing for it.

"You are still Aachimning," she said quietly, and Llian
turned away.

"You said before that there was no way of escape," he
began, as they caught Rael up.

"I have disabled the Sentinels," Rael responded. "Whatever the vote, the Syndics will not come for Karan until the
morning. It will take time for them to discover our way in

the labyrinths of old Shazmak below. With luck we will get that far. But first we must negotiate these corridors, and any chance meeting will undo us."

"If there are but two ways out of Shazmak," Llian thought aloud, "and each many days' journey, how can we possibly escape? Karan is ill. She cannot walk any distance."

Karan interrupted in a weary voice, "There is a third way out of Shazmak, Llian. It leads not over the bridges but down the River Garr. For us it is the only path."

At first Karan led the way, but as they moved down into the deeper levels she became tired and unsure; she fell back and allowed Rael to lead. So the remainder of the night passed in an endless maze of corridors, stairways and long, dark tunnels. Llian stumbled along, a dim globe in one outstretched hand, aware only of the figure in front and the motion of the shadows before him. At last he called a halt.

"It's no use," he said. "We must rest. Karan is exhausted and I am too weary."

Karan had been walking along in a daze. She continued for a while after they stopped before suddenly subsiding on the floor. They rested a scant ten minutes, then Rael urged them on, picking up Karan's pack where she had dropped it and throwing it over his shoulder. Karan was asleep, but when Llian took her hand she roused without complaint and followed him like a sleepwalker.

After another two hours, as far as Llian could judge, they began to descend into an older, unused part of the city, where the walls were of native rock polished to an oily smoothness, and decorated not with the somber landscapes of Aachan but with delicate, time-worn carvings of the plants and animals of Santhenar. Llian ransacked the Histories to recall who had been here before the Aachim, but nothing came to mind. The air was warmer and more moist; water trickled down the walls and here and there collected in depressions on the floor. They were well into this lower city when Rael allowed another rest.

"It will be dawning outside now," he said. "Soon they will discover that we are gone. Rest briefly. They will be swift on our trail, once they have found it."

Hardly had he finished speaking when the corridor around them vibrated. Less than a minute later came a hollow boom. "The Sentinels are sounding," said Karan. "They know our path."

On they fled along endless corridors, down steep stone stairs, finally reaching, at the end of a narrow, damp-smelling passage, a circular staircase terminating in a well, sealed by a broad metal lid. The lid could be opened by a lever connected to a chain that was attached by a ring to the top of the lid. They worked the mechanism and descended into the tunnel below. A chain hung through a small hole beside the underside of the lid. Rael tugged the chain and the lid crashed down.

"Can we not bar the way from this side to buy a little time?" Llian wondered.

"There is nothing to bar it with," Rael replied tersely. "Come."

Llian looked down the tunnel. It was empty, save for a trickle of water. Then inspiration seized him and he leapt up, heaving at the thick, heavy chain until he had formed a knot.

"That will hinder them a moment when they try to lift the lid," he said with an air of satisfaction.

"Not long," Karan responded dreamily. "The Aachim have a power over metal and stone."

They hurried on, eventually coming to a huge set of flood doors that closed across the tunnel. "These we can bar from either side," said Rael. They had just pressed the doors shut when there came a distant crash.

"Run on," cried Rael. "I will bar the doors and catch you. They are close behind."

Llian set off down the tunnel, pulling Karan by the arm. She was almost unconscious and in great distress; twice she fell. The second time he caught her up, threw her over his shoulder and staggered on. Shortly they came to another set of doors: Rael barred these also. Now Llian too was staggering from side to side, his eyes wide and staring.

"I must rest," he gasped. "I can go no further—not if all the hordes of the Aachim are behind us."

"They are," shouted Rael, his face a rigid mask. "You must keep going; it is not far now. Around the bend ahead is a final set of doors and, beyond those, a landing. A boat is kept there. Unless our fortune is very bad it will be there today. If it is not, we should fling ourselves into the river. We will be treated more kindly there than in Shazmak."

They ran. Soon daylight was visible around the bend. Karan had recovered a little and jogged beside Llian momentarily, but by the time they reached the last set of doors she had fallen again. Once more Llian turned back and hoisted her up. Beyond the doors, as Rael had said, the tunnel opened out into a wide, high-roofed cave, lit by daylight. On the left the floor of the cave continued as a gently sloping rock platform into calm, shallow water. A ridge of rock ran out into the river on the upstream side for perhaps a distance of ten spans, creating a natural breakwater. Beyond this point the Garr foamed and raged. There were two small boats upon the platform.

A dull boom came from up the tunnel. Llian hoisted Karan and his pack into the boat nearest the water and ran back to where Rael was struggling with the last door.

"Take the packs and get the boat ready. I will follow," shouted Rael.

"There are two boats."

"Then push the other out or they will follow us."

Llian grabbed the packs and ran back to Karan's boat. He tied the painter to an iron ring on the landing, paid out a little rope and heaved. The boat slid smoothly in and glided out across the calm water toward the torrent beyond. Too much rope, he thought, his heart thudding, as the current caught the stern of the boat and flung it downstream, shuddering wildly. He jerked on the painter and drew the boat back into calmer water, then tied it off again.

Llian looked anxiously back toward the tunnel but Rael had not yet appeared. He ran to the second boat, which was further up the landing, and heaved wildly. It did not budge. He slammed his shoulder against it. Not a shiver! He scanned the landing for something to use as a lever. The landing was bare. He ran back to the flood door. Rael had closed it and was struggling with the bar but could not get it over the racks. The door was slowly being forced from the other side. Llian threw his weight at it and the bar slid home.

"There must be few of them yet, or we would never have closed it," Rael shouted, as they ran back to the landing.

"I can't move the other boat," Llian cried.

They heaved, time and again, but it was stuck fast. Rael hauled in Karan's boat and snatched the hatchet that hung below Karan's pack.

"Get it ready," he screamed to Llian, running back to the second boat and chopping frantically at the stern post.

Llian pushed Karan's boat out to the limit of the rope and stood there, in the freezing water. Karan was sitting up in the stern, her hand on the steering arm. There came a shattering roar from the tunnel and a cloud of dust billowed forth. Rael continued to chop. Two Aachim rushed out, followed by a third, then others.

Rael screamed, "Flee!" but continued his work, concealed from view by the bulk of the boat. Llian hesitated as the Aachim swarmed out. Rael looked over his shoulder, gave a last mighty hack, then flung himself across the landing and slashed at the painter of Karan's boat. It parted and the boat began to move out slowly into the current. Llian leapt in. Rael splashed through the water, sprang up onto the breakwater and ran, pursued by a host of Aachim.

Someone caught the dragging painter but Llian whipped out his knife and cut it free. The boat was moving quickly now. Rael reached the end of the breakwater, threw the hatchet in and dived. He soared through the air, just missed the side of the boat and before Llian could drag him aboard the torrent seized the boat and flung it downstream.

Rael's head bobbed above the foam for a moment, then he was gone. Karan stared at the spot in disbelief, letting go the steering arm and rising to her feet to scan the water. The boat lurched wildly and water poured in. She yanked the steering arm across the other way without looking, trying to pick Rael out in the foam and the dark water. Water gushed over the other side, the boat almost capsizing. The river opened its jaws and flashed toothed rocks at them. Llian shrieked. Karan, realizing what was happening, jerked the steering arm across and back, and steered an unsteady course downstream.

A number of the Aachim slid the other boat into the water and set off after them, controling the little vessel expertly in the flood and gaining swiftly until they were but a few boat lengths away. They cried out to Karan, all together. The man at the front could almost have reached out and plucked her over the stern.

Karan was staring at them as the two boats raced together. She put her hand on the gunwale, half-rising, and for a moment Llian thought she was going to fling herself into the water; then there were cries of fear from the Aachim, the boat spun wildly as the helmsman stared at the ruins of the steering arm, went sideways on to the current, rolled over and over and smashed to pieces on a rock in midstream.

Karan and Llian stared at one another, shocked at the suddenness of the tragedy, then the current whipped them around a bend in the gorge and Shazmak was lost to sight.

Ahead of them the gorge opened out and the current slackened a little, although it was still desperately fast. The straight stretched before them for perhaps a league. Llian, who was sitting in the bow of the boat, looked back at Karan. She made a small, pale, upright figure at the stern, holding the steering arm with her left hand.

"He always loved me," she cried, the tears streaming down her cheeks. "From childhood he was my dearest friend. They were all my friends, once. How I have repaid them. Tensor is right—I have become a monster, incapable of trust. I should have let them take me."

Llian rose and began to waver down to her. The boat rocked dangerously.

"Sit down," she snapped.

The boat sped on down the swift-flowing river. The channel was wide but here and there choked with broken rock around which the water swirled crazily or rushed over in staircase rapids. The cliffs fell sheer to the river on either side and the low winter sun did not reach the water. Karan remained at the stern, refusing all offers of food, though several times she took small sips of water. Once Llian offered to spell her, but she only said, "There is rough water ahead, beyond your skill. The Aachim taught me to sail the Garr. How they must rue it!"

* * *

All that day they sailed the river, Karan's face a white mask and her hand a claw on the steering arm. At last the sun passed beyond the mountains, though the light lingered.

"Are you going to keep on in the darkness?" Llian asked as the sun went down. Karan had been like a statue for hours.

"No!"

Shortly they passed out of the gorge into hilly country. They had to find a place to land and abandon the boat, for already they could hear the roar of the great falls, where the river plunged over the cliffs into the land of Bannador.

There was but a little light remaining when Karan turned the boat out of the stream toward a rocky bay on the right. They glided across the still, dark water and the keel grated on stone. Llian jumped out and pulled the bow onto the shore. He carried his pack up the beach and found a place to camp, a patch of coarse gray sand among the boulders. Then he went back for the remaining gear, but Karan shouted, "Leave it. Go away!"

He walked downstream over the boulders and rock ledges, the coarse sand and flood-wedged nests of debris that formed the shoreline. From ahead came a continuous roar. He clambered onto a spire of rock to see if he could see the falls, but the light was too dim to make out the farther course of the river. He looked back at the boat. Karan was taking things, unidentifiable in the failing light, out of Rael's pack, one by one, looking at them and placing them carefully to one side. Finally she put a few things back, fastened the pack and, wading out until the water was up to her waist, pushed it out into the current. She stood there for a moment, staring at the place where it had disappeared, then splashed her way back to shore and walked up to the campsite.

"Will they follow us?" Llian wondered a little later.

"Not tonight. Their other boats are hours from that place.

They dare not sail the river in darkness; there is no landing place between the city and here. The Aachim are few, and life is precious. The loss of the five in the other boat, and Rael, will be a bitter blow to Tensor. As to me; they were my friends." She got up abruptly.

"Then they cannot reach here until this time tomorrow."

"Earlier—after midday."

"In that case let's make our camp and dry ourselves. May we risk a fire?"

"If you can find any wood. Now leave me alone." She walked away.

Llian set up a camp among the rocks a short distance from the river, and after some clumsy work with the hatchet in the darkness he had obtained enough splinters from the boat to start a fire, as well as some larger pieces. Returning to the fire with another armload he found Karan sitting on a stone in her wet clothes, staring into the flames and shivering fitfully.

He spoke to her but she gave no sign of having heard him. He went back to the boat, bringing back what remained of Rael's gear: the bag of food, a small tent, a sleeping pouch. Karan had not moved. He took his cloak and placed it around her shoulders to break the wind, which, out of the shelter of the gorge, blew strongly. He took off her boots and stockings and dried her feet. What beautiful feet you have, he thought oddly, holding them in his hands, but so cold. He toweled her feet until the pink warmth came back, then removed her outer garments, dried her, replaced them one by one with dry clothing, finally putting her feet in the sleeping pouch and pulling it up around her. Apart from lifting her arms or her feet when necessary she gave no sign that she noticed what he was doing.

Karan sat unmoving while Llian put the tent up in the darkness. He gave her hot, sweet tea; she sipped it absently.

He cooked food; she ate it without a word. He built up the fire and retired to his own pouch, lying there in the darkness surrounded by the rushing of the river, the crackling of the fire, the sighing of the wind. He closed his eyes and tried to sleep, but the past days were so full in his head that sleep would not come. The night grew cold under the clear sky and the stars wheeled. Only now did it occur to him to wonder about the Mirror, and what she had done at the trial. Did she really have it? How had she smuggled it out of Shazmak?

A long, shuddering ululation smashed him awake. Llian leapt out of the tent. Karan was flinging her head from side to side, crying and tearing at her clothes. Now she went still and pressed her palms to her temples as though trying to squeeze something out of her head. Her staring eyes passed over him without recognition. Had her grief driven her mad?

He touched her hand and the nightmare rushed out of her like air out of a bladder. Karan flopped onto the sand, sound asleep. He picked her up in his arms, the pouch still around her, and placed her carefully in the shelter. The bitter frost seared his bare feet. She did not stir. Hours more he lay awake, watching the stars swinging across the sky, going over and over their escape, wondering if there was any way that Rael might have been saved. And dreading that he might wake in the morning to find Karan gone mad. And if she had he could not save them, for he had no idea where to go from here.

28

IN THE CAVERNS
OF BANNADOR

Llian woke, still weary, to the crackling of the fire. Where was he? Then he saw the ruined boat on the sand and the memories came back. The winter sun, rising, told how little sleep he'd had.

Karan was already up, making tea, the pot balanced on a small nest of kindling. Her eyes were red, and when he spoke she did not answer. She walked across to the boat and attacked it furiously with the hatchet. Llian groaned and closed his eyes. Shortly he was woken again, this time by Karan shaking his shoulder insistently.

"Get up, you've slept too long already. Here!"

A mug of ginger tea was thrust under his nose. The pungent aroma went up his nostrils, he jerked and bumped her hand, and a few drops spilled on his bare chest. He swore. Karan banged the mug down on the sand, stalked across to the tent and began to pull it down. Considering her arm she was surprisingly adept.

When she had finished, and all was packed save Llian's few things, she called out crossly, "Are you ready yet?"

Llian gulped down the remains of the tea, which was still too hot, quickly dressed and threw his gear into the pack. They ate well, onions and eggs, a little piece of meat and a mound of vegetables and pounded grains all cooked together in a pan and piled onto a slab of dark bread, with the remains of the tea. It was very strong; the ginger seared his throat and cleared away the slightly dizzy lack-of-sleep feeling. He felt better.

She picked up a sliver of wood and smoothed the sand in front of her, and began to answer the question that he had not asked. Her voice was dreary.

The stick etched a wavy line that extended in a south-easterly direction. "The River Garr. We are here. The mountains here; here the falls. Then the river runs through the hills of Bannador and Sable." Each time she said "here" she made a dot in the sand with her stick.

"North of Sable, here, the river marks the boundary between Crayde and Plendur. There is a loop in the river here, then it turns south and splits into two channels around the island of Sith—the free city. That is my destination. Until we reach Sith we're in danger; maybe even then. We will go down the cliffs here and follow the river. There are towns along the eastern side—perhaps we can hire a boat to take us to Sith. That journey would take four or five days. On foot, it would be weeks."

"I thought you were going to Bannador?"

"My final destination was always Sith, and from here it's closer than home, by river."

"You didn't tell me about this way before," said Llian.

"Nor would I now, if there was any other choice. It's an escape route for the Aachim, but it could be used to enter Shazmak secretly, and so they keep it hidden."

"You are . . . all right today?"

"Of course I'm all right," she said sharply. "What did you expect, that I had gone mad?"

He looked away.

"Six Aachim drowned yesterday because of me." She walked off and stood staring at the river. By the time she came back Llian was ready to go.

"What about the Whelm?"

"The Sentinels around Shazmak reported no sign of them."

"Then we are safe from them?"

Karan was silent. Three times before she'd shaken them, and suddenly they came from nowhere, each time after a dream. They touched her in her sleep and drew a thread back to them. Last night's nightmares were the strongest she'd ever had. She shuddered. They will come again. They want me, as much as the Mirror, but you are nothing to them. They would smash you down without a thought. Oh Llian, I can't lose you as well!

"They'll find me again. Let us go, quickly." Some of the color had come back into her voice, the urgency of today's problems distracting her from the disaster of yesterday. She smoothed out the sand with her stick and they departed. There was no path, but the way was easier along the river bank and they took that route.

"Shouldn't we try to hide our tracks?" asked Llian, as they crossed from a boulder field to a broad expanse of coarse gray sand, leaving deep marks.

"Why?" Karan responded. "Tensor knows the way we take. There is no other. When we obtain the river again, below the cliffs, will be soon enough."

Now they turned away from the river, which was on their left, and made their way through a meadow of hummocks and boulders, bogs and little rocky pools, still rimed with ice. They paused at the top of a round hillock. Ahead a few hundred paces the land disappeared on a gentle curve as though it had slid downwards, leaving a line of cliffs sweeping away out of sight both to right and left. Immediately to their left the river rushed over the precipice and thundered down, obscuring all before them in spray and mist which the uprushing wind whirled about, before running away through the steep hills to the southeast, where its course was eventually lost in the haze. Behind them the mountains of Chollaz loomed up, an impenetrable snow-clad wall with the great gorge of the Garr a black slot cutting through it.

"I don't see a way down," Llian murmured.

Karan glanced at him. She had a preoccupied air. Eventually she spoke. "There! In front of you. That crack."

Immediately to the north-east the meadow was cut by a fissure which ran parallel to the cliff line and joined up with it several hundred paces away. They walked across to it and Llian peered down into the dimness. The walls were almost sheer, of crumbling limestone, and the bottom beyond sight. His stomach turned over.

"I can't climb down there," he said wanly, turning a shade of gray. "Does it go all the way to the bottom?"

"Of course not. The cliff is more than three hundred spans high. That little crevice is scarcely fifty. The base of the fissure leads into the caves. Perhaps I should send you first. If you're going to fall anyway, there's no point in you knocking me down as well."

"That's not funny," he said. "You know how I hate heights."

"I'm sorry, I hate the world today. I'll lead the way. It won't be so bad now, the ginger will steady your stomach. Just put your hands and feet exactly where I put mine. This path is very old and the rock could be rotten."

Karan adjusted her pack, eased the cast on her wrist and

climbed awkwardly down into the fissure. The first few paces were steeply sloping broken rock. At the bottom of this incline she paused, groping with first one foot and then the other. She looked doubtfully up at Llian.

"Just here where it falls sheer there should be metal rungs let into the rock," she said.

"Perhaps they've rusted and fallen away; perhaps you're in the wrong place."

"They would not use *iron* for such a purpose," Karan said, still feeling about with her foot. She looked carefully about her. "No, this is the place, I'm quite sure of it."

"How long is it since you came this way? Perhaps part of the cliff has fallen."

"I've never been this way. As I told you, the path is secret. Since the Aachim sealed themselves away from the world it has been used only in great need, lest the way be discovered. But it is known to all the Aachim and to those they trust. And even to me." The last was said bitterly.

She began to climb back up. "The first few rungs are gone. Perhaps there's been a rockfall. There's a short piece of rope in my pack. Can you get it?"

Llian found the rope and handed it to her. It was about four spans long. She tied one end around his chest, checking the knots with care, then the other around her waist. "Brace yourself behind that rock and when I call lower me carefully."

Llian got behind the outcrop at the cliff edge. Karan disappeared down the cleft. Pebbles rattled down the cliff and the rope tightened sharply. "Let out a little rope," she called.

Llian paid out it out carefully. There was only an arm's length left when she called out again, "That's enough. Pull me up again."

He pulled her up slowly. Though she was small it was

hard work, and his knees were trembling by the time the strain came off. Her head reappeared.

"It's no use," she said. "Part of the cliff has fallen, carrying ten or twelve rungs with it. Below that most of them seem to be there."

"What can we do? There's nothing up here to tie the rope to. I can get you down, but not myself."

Karan looked along the edge. He was right. The outcropping limestone formed smooth, rounded masses, too large to loop a rope around, too gently curving for it to take a grip anyway.

"Down there I can see a few cracks. Perhaps we could wedge a knife in one of them and tie the rope to it," Llian suggested.

Karan considered the idea, frowning. "The rock's too weak, and I wouldn't care to hang from my little knife over such a drop. Besides, we'll need the rope later, so we'll have to use it double, looped over something."

"It isn't long enough. I was almost out of rope when you called."

"You were up on the cliff edge. Suppose we could wedge something in that crack down there, that would save a little. If we looped it around, it might just do."

Karan measured the length carefully with her eyes, her head on one side, whistling tonelessly through pursed lips. "No, even then we would be short by so much." She spread her arms apart three times. She climbed out and sat down on the ground, pulling everything out of her pack. "We could cut up a blanket and tie the strips together, but that still leaves us with nothing to anchor it to. What do you have?"

Llian went through his pack. "Nothing I would trust my life to."

Karan sank her head in her arms, rocking her body back and forth. She looked up at the sky. "Already I can sense them. They're only a few hours away." She began to despair that they had left too late.

Llian paced back and forth. "What can we use to anchor the rope?" he wondered aloud. "There isn't even any wood, save at the boat." Then, he said, "Anchor the rope! Of course."

Karan stared at him. "There was an anchor in the boat," he said excitedly. "A two-fluked anchor under the transom. Just what we need."

"Was there any rope?"

"I can't remember. There was also a painter, though I cut it short as we escaped. Shall I go back and get it?"

"Yes, but go quickly, and carefully. Time is precious now."

He ran off. With a leaden feeling growing inside her, Karan lay down on the rocky ground, staring up at the sky. Surely all this wouldn't come to naught for the want of a piece of rope. That should have been the first thing to pack.

She closed her eyes and allowed the contents of her mind to seep away, even the tiny image of Llian, always present since the trial, now jogging over the hummocks and hollows toward the ruined boat. She cast around for other presences and soon caught them; a roaring, a thundering of Aachim coming down the river, foremost among them a storm cloud speeding out of the north, out of the mountains, billowing up and spreading out over all with its tempestuous winds, its darkness and its lightnings: Tensor! Karan shrank back before the storm and wrenched her eyelids apart. What a curse to be sensitive. The sun still shone in a pale blue sky, but a chill had gone through her and she was more afraid than ever.

I will not be taken again, she thought. I will never let Tensor have the Mirror, even if I have to leave Llian behind. Though that would end it all; that would break me now.

*   *   *

She heard the thud of Llian's footsteps long before she could see him. Poor Llian; he must be exhausted. She climbed onto an outcrop and watched him all the way back.

"I saw them," Llian burst out as soon as he saw her, "just then, from that tall hill back there. A boat is coming down the gorge." He was red in the face but he had the anchor and the rope.

"How far back was it?"

"It had just come into sight."

"Then they'll soon reach the campsite. The search will take a while, but still they can be here in hours. Oh, Llian, they are so strong, and I'm afraid. Quickly, the anchor."

She hammered the flukes more or less parallel to the shaft with her hatchet, until the anchor resembled a badly made arrowhead. Then Karan went down and bashed it deep into a crack in the rock just above the sheer part of the fissure. She tied the two pieces of rope together and passed one end through the eye of the anchor until the rope hung down in two equal lengths.

"I don't think I can climb down that," he said, his stomach turning.

"Then tie some knots in it. Make sure they'll slide through the eye though. Or better still, tie them in only one length so that we can pull it out after. Keep calm; it's not that far."

Llian tied several knots in the rope, trying not to think of what lay ahead. "It's ready," he said.

Karan nodded. She took off her boots and socks and thrust them in her pack. Taking the ropes confidently, she eased herself feet first over the edge and made her way down, clinging with her toes and one hand, the other holding the ropes as tightly as her plastered wrist would allow. Llian could scarcely bear to watch, but at last she reached the rungs and he saw her clinging to the cliff face while the ropes swung free. She looked up at him with a pained expression, shaking her wrist, then moved slowly, hand over hand, down the rungs.

He hung over the precipice, gripped the rope firmly in both hands and tried to climb down. His palms were too sweaty to get a good grip. The rope slipped across his hand, he squeezed with all his might, stopped in mid-air, then his weight pulled him down again, faster and faster, and he could do nothing to stop it. Llian was almost paralyzed with terror, then his hands hit the first knot and he stopped with a jerk. He hung there, slowly revolving on the rope, the strength ebbing from his fingers, sure that the next slide would finish him.

"Hurry up," came an impatient call from below.

The shout startled him and he slid down to the next knot before realizing it. He stayed there only a second before continuing, a shocking pain in the palms of his hands. He reached the last knot and took a death grip on the rungs. He was shaking and his knees were weak. "The rope," she called. He gave a clumsy jerk and it fell past them to the bottom. Karan scowled up at him, then turned and continued down. Llian followed grimly.

The rungs had originally been two handspans apart, but some were missing and others broken, or moved alarmingly when his weight came on them. On one section, where the cliff face bulged outwards, all the rungs for more than twice his height were smashed down against the rock, apparently when part of the cliff above had fallen, and offered the most meager of holds.

Eventually they reached the bottom. Llian sat down on a boulder. Karan touched his shoulder gently. "You did well," she said.

"It wasn't quite as bad as I expected," he lied.

"Of course not. You've learned a lot. Though you have an amazing way of going down a rope. Show me your hands."

Llian held them out, palms upward. Huge welts were burned across them. "You shouldn't have held it so tightly," she scolded, smearing the marks with ointment from her soapstone jar. It was nearly empty. The ointment burned; his palms throbbed. She bent down for the rope and replaced it carefully in her pack. They picked their way over the jumble of boulders filling the narrow space at the bottom of the defile. Shortly they came to a low ragged opening in the limestone, leading away from the cliff in the direction of the river.

Inside the cave it was pitch dark. Karan stopped and pulled a small globe from a special pocket; she held it out between thumb and fingers so that it lighted the way ahead.

"What's that. Did you get it in Shazmak?"

"No, Maigraith gave it to me. It's a lightglass. I once thought that if I used it the Whelm might sense me, so I put it away."

"Can I see?"

She passed it to him. Following its dim luminance they set off down the passage ahead.

As their vessel shot out from the enclosing gorge, Tensor caught sight of the ruined boat. He pointed; the helmsman directed the craft toward the bank and the Aachim came ashore. They examined the boat carefully then followed the footprints to the campsite. Tensor stood on a rock overlooking the campsite, the Aachim gathered behind him, silently observing. Finally he gestured and they fanned out around the area, while he stepped down onto the sand. At last a small patch of smooth sand caught his eye. Beside it were the deep impressions of two pairs of boots.

"They squatted here for a while," he said. "Why, I wonder."

He stood there for a moment, then held his hand out, palm downwards over the smooth patch. He murmured a word. The Aachim watched, impassive. For almost a minute nothing happened, then, ever so slowly, the grains began to rearrange themselves. In a few minutes, when the movement had stopped, Tensor withdrew his hand.

"It's a map, of course," he said to nobody in particular. "But how to read it? Ah! I see. This line must be the River Garr. Of course it is, for there is the island of Sith lying within its two branches. This line represents the mountains of Shazmak behind us. Then this dot must show our present location and—" here his voice rose a little "—this beside the city of Sith must be their destination. So! In that at least she spoke the truth. The closest place for a downriver ferry is Narne, two days' march below the falls. They stayed the night here: the ashes are still warm. They can't be more than half a day ahead."

"Perhaps this map is a trick. This Karan, she is *szdorny*, both clever and cunning. We must doubt everything she does," said one of the Aachim standing near.

"We must!" agreed Tensor, grim of face. He had taken the death of Rael very hard. "If we don't take them in the tunnels we will split our party, sending half directly to Narne, the remainder to follow them wherever they lead. Away!"

They set off toward the edge of the cliff, but before they had gone far across the boggy ground Tensor halted abruptly. "Most curious," he said, looking down at the tracks. "One of them, the vile Zain I would say—yes, definitely—returned to the boat for something. And not long ago, for see this print—" He pointed to a single set of footmarks, and nearby the tracks of two people. "The water still seeps slowly in, while the others are near to full."

"The anchor was gone from the boat, Tensor," called one. "And all the rope. They must be having trouble with the climb."

"We are within hours of them, then. We'll take them in the tunnels. She doesn't know the way. All speed now!" he shouted, and they set off at a great pace, Tensor running slightly ahead with loping, tireless strides. The Aachim followed close behind, twenty in number. They were heavily armed and grim of face, men and women both.

The cave developed into a labyrinth, though at first the way was clear to Karan and they made good speed. As time went on she grew more and more uncertain; yet still, after each choice was made, she walked so fast, almost running, that Llian could barely keep up with her. The globe gave out only enough light to see the floor of the cave a few paces ahead. The way gradually became humpy and broken, full of dark crevices to trap the unwary foot, and deep icy pools, some they could splash through, others they must wade across. Moisture dripped continually from the roof. Once they passed through a curtain of water spraying with great force from a crack in the side of the cave. Soon they were saturated and cold.

They had been going along at this pace for about an hour when Llian called a halt. He grabbed Karan by the shoulder and cried, "I can't go on. I'm exhausted."

Karan stopped dead and dashed his arm away. She swung around to face him. "You want to *rest*?" she demanded, her voice stone grating on stone. "They're close behind and gaining fast. They may know a shorter way. Don't you have any idea what Tensor will do to you? Come on!"

She stared up at him for a moment longer, her breast heaving. Her hair was plastered to her head and moisture dripped from her forehead. In the bluish light from the globe she looked ghastly, and far too fierce for Llian to dispute. He mumbled something incomprehensible and she turned and made off with redoubled energy. Llian was glad to be out of her withering glance. He ran after her.

Shortly afterwards they came to a fork in the tunnel and Karan, after a moment's hesitation, chose the right-hand way, which sloped slightly downwards. Before long, however, it petered out into a narrow rift which no Aachim could ever have squeezed through, and they were forced to go back. Karan began to fret.

"By now they will have reached the top of the cleft," she said. "They're only hours behind us and already I'm losing my way. Oh, Llian, I'm afraid that I've led us into a trap."

Llian had become infected by her disquiet and found himself looking continually over his shoulder for a light. This was no good. If she lost confidence in herself they had no chance.

"A few hours," he said. "They'd have to travel very quickly to make up that time before we get out of the caves."

Karan stopped and searched his face for a moment, though for what Llian could not tell. She turned and made off again. I take the lesson, she thought, though I know you to be wrong. They will travel much more quickly than us, and if I make one wrong turning we are finished.

The left-hand tunnel ran along level for a while then plunged abruptly down. Water trickled along the slope beneath their feet. The smooth rock floor was slippery and the path became so steep that they were forced to cling to each other to maintain their balance.

"We'd better use the rope now," said Llian, after one slip had nearly dragged them both down. Karan stopped and he took the little coil from her pack and tied them together. The path continued steeply below, down and down and down. Shortly they came to a place where steps had been cut in the rock, though there was no rail. A breeze moved up steadily past them, suggesting a straight passage of considerable length, but in the dim light of the globe its dimensions could not be guessed.

The steps were greatly encrusted with a deposit from the flowing water, smooth and slippery. The cautious descent seemed interminable. Finally they reached the bottom. Karan immediately sat down on a stone, talking to herself.

"The passage takes four or five hours, I was told. We've been going for three hours and more. We may yet escape, though from here the way is difficult to remember. Let me think for a moment—the sequence of turns is complex. It was so long ago and I never thought to come this way. I believe I remembered it only for the romance of it."

Suddenly, as they sat there, a pale distant light appeared behind and above. "Tensor!" said Karan, dismayed. "Already he reaches the slope above the stair. They're barely half an hour behind. There's no escape." She leapt to her feet, running this way and that.

Llian caught her arm, hissing urgently in her ear. "Quick; we don't want them to know that they're close." He dragged her around the bend out of sight. "Can they have seen your light?"

Karan came to herself. "I don't know," she said, more soberly, though her voice still had an edge to it. "It's quite dim, and I had it in front of me. But their senses are keen." There was a pause while she thought. "We've no hope of outrunning them now, for I'm uncertain of the way. He won't be."

"Then if speed will not suffice, we must use cunning," said Llian. "Can we hide from them?"

"No," said Karan, shaking her head as she walked along. "This close he would sense our presence. They might even be able to smell us."

"We can't fight them, reason with them, hide or outrun them," said Llian slowly. "Then there's nothing left to do but go somewhere that they can't."

"If we found a cave that we could creep through, but was too small for them, that would serve," said Karan. "There have been lots of small fissures and caves leading away from the path, but whether they go anywhere or just end in blind tunnels, who can say? Still, we must take any chance, no matter how fragile."

They hurried on, passing the mouths of many other tunnels. Each time Karan took the lower way. The path was steep and winding now and they did not see the light behind them again. In half an hour they came to a larger cavern with a deep pool of water on its floor. The cavern was cut across diagonally by a crevasse that intersected the floor at the water level. Beyond the pool, caves large and small went off in several directions.

"That's the way the path goes," said Karan, pointing along the larger tunnel that ran ahead. "Let's try these others." They scrambled into several tunnels but all turned out to be caves that ended no great distance away or narrowed to conduits too small for even Karan to slip through. She sat down at the end of the last and squeezed her head between her hands in frustration and despair. "This is the end," she whispered. "Oh, Llian, I tried, and it wasn't good enough. I'm so sorry."

For the first time since the trial Llian realized just what danger he was in. "What will they do to us?"

"I don't know. Probably flay us alive, for starters!"

"But . . ."

"But the Aachim are so civilized, you think. Not when they see themselves betrayed, Llian. If they catch us it is the end, and a nasty one it will be."

Then Llian saw what had been staring him in the face.

"No! You saw it! Water was running down into the crevasse from the pool. It must lead somewhere or it would have filled up. Quickly."

They leapt up and ran back to the main chamber, splashing across the pool to the crevasse. Karan took off her pack and, holding it sideways in front of her, slipped into the crack. As she did so they heard the rattle of a dislodged stone from up the tunnel. Llian thrust himself in after and followed as closely as he could. It was a tight fit, and many times he forced his way past projections of rock until his ribs were scored and bruised, and though he favored the side that he had damaged, the healing ribs pained him terribly. The crevasse meandered down steeply, and soon they knew that their tiny light could no longer be seen from the chamber. They pressed on.

It was only a few minutes later that they heard the echo of voices and the splashing of feet. Llian tapped Karan on the shoulder. She thrust the globe into a pocket, just to be sure, and stopped at once. Let them go past, Llian prayed, squeezing her hand. The noise died away to a rustling in the distance.

"They must be searching all the tunnels," he whispered in Karan's ear.

They crept on, silently. The crevasse shrank down and widened out, finally becoming a low-roofed tunnel down which the water still flowed.

They crawled along steadily, dragging their packs behind them. Suddenly, without warning, a vast roar seemed to come from up the tunnel and at the same time from within themselves. For a moment Llian's thoughts were paralyzed. He looked around at Karan, who was behind him now, his eyes staring. She touched him on the cheek with two fingers and tried to smile.

"Be still," she said softly. "Tensor has retraced his path

and discovered how we made our escape. He tries to bewilder and confound us, and thereby make us come back to him." This time she managed a wan smile. "It shows his desperation; if we stay calm we just might be able to get away now. Either he doesn't know where the crevasse comes out, or he knows but cannot reach it. The compulsion won't work at such a distance. If he continues it'll only tire and confuse him. Let's hope that he does."

The roars continued for a while, then all grew silent again. Absolutely silent. Even the trickle of water made no sound, as they crouched there in the embrace of the indifferent rock. They crept away.

The tunnel continued to slope down, though the going became easier now. The trickle became a flood that tried to overbalance them. Then it split and became a trickle again, and eventually fell over a ledge into a pool, four or five paces wide and extending before them beyond the light shed by Karan's globe. The pool was waist-deep and cold.

"Now we can rest for a few moments," said Karan.

Llian said nothing, but he took her hand again and held it tightly. They sat together on the driest part of the ledge with their feet dangling over the pool and ate bread and preserved fruits from his pack. "What will they do now?" he wondered.

"They won't give us up. Some will search all the springs and caves around the base of the cliff. Others will wait along the main path to Narne, in case we've found a way back to it. We've earned ourselves a little breathing-space, but once we get out of the caves our perils begin again."

They waded out into the pool. After thirty paces or so the roof began to decrease in height, so that they had to walk bent over, and shortly it plunged beneath the water. Llian turned to Karan. "What now?"

"It may not extend very far. I'll go and see."

She stripped down to singlet and knickers and packed her clothes carefully in a bag made of waxed cloth. With the globe in one hand, Karan pushed past Llian, dived into the water and disappeared. Llian waited anxiously, but very soon the water swirled in front of him and she reappeared, water cascading from her hair, her face mottled blue and red from the cold.

"Had you waited for a moment I would have volunteered . . ." he began in a dubious and unconvincing tone.

"That's why I didn't," she interrupted rudely, her teeth chattering. "I didn't want to have to find you under there. Besides, I've done this kind of thing before."

"It's a long swim—almost a minute," she went on, after she had wrung the water from her hair. "And longer with our packs. Can you do it?"

He nodded. He had always been a good swimmer; it was the cold that he found hardest to bear.

They swam the tunnel. It was, as Karan had said, a long swim, though not a difficult one. Llian was not greatly troubled by it, except when he caught his pack on a projection and struggled for what seemed an age before wrenching it free. Once on the other side the floor sloped gradually upwards, and all at once the roof was higher and they could walk upright again. They pressed on, and ten minutes later, to their great surprise, daylight appeared at the end of the tunnel. They crept closer. Karan turned to Llian in puzzlement.

"That's strange," she said. "I can't sense them at all. It's as though there's no one there." They walked cautiously through the entrance, blinking in the light of the setting sun. Suddenly Karan laughed out aloud and threw her arms around him. There on their right was the waterfall and the River Garr, flowing away to the south-east.

"I don't understand," said Llian, holding her tightly.

"Somewhere underground we passed right under the river and now we've come out on the other side," she replied. "The stair of the Aachim opens on the eastern side, but we're on the west. *We're free!* There's no crossing the river before Narne and that's more than two hard days' walk downstream. No wonder Tensor despaired, if he knew. We don't deserve such good fortune. Perhaps my luck turns at last."

"Won't they be waiting for us at Narne? You said so yourself."

"Undoubtedly, but that's a long way away, and much can happen. Besides, we're in Bannador now. Let's get clear of the falls; then we shall eat and rest and make our plans."

They had come out right at the base of the cliff and the ground was a vast pile of broken and shattered rock which they must negotiate before they could find their way free to the south. Eventually they passed beyond the scree and as it grew dark found themselves in a hilly country, thickly forested and shrouded in drifting mist from the falls. They were still high up but the hard cold of the mountains had gone; the air was moist and spicy between the trees.

"A forest," said Llian. "I thought there were no trees left in the world, after Shazmak." He sat down on a mossy log and gave himself over to contemplation.

They spent two more days in that country, making their way slowly through the dense forests, and it was hard going. The land was corrugated by steep valleys, tributary to the Garr, that cut directly across their path. They started off near the river bank, but shortly the country became so rugged that they had to climb up into the foothills of the mountains to find a clearer way. At last they came across a narrow path that led more or less in the direction of Narne. Here the land was broken into small ridges like ripples on a beach, and as the path led across them they were forever trudging up the gentle slope and peering uneasily along the ridge line before plunging down the steep side and splashing through the creeks that trickled in every gully.

It was late on the second afternoon now. Llian labored along behind, following Karan without thought, hoping that the top of each succeeding ridge would show the town of Narne below. The trip had become an ordeal. How he hated traveling, if this was what it was all about. How could he ever have thought that there was romance in tales such as this? But at least they had lost their pursuers; there had been no sign of them since the caverns.

Just then Karan stopped. "This is close enough. Let's find a place to camp. It'll be dark shortly."

"Can't we go on to Narne?" Llian pleaded. "It's so close. I'm so sick of walking. I want to sit in an inn beside a fire with a great bowl of wine in front of me and a hundred other people doing the same."

"You'll have to wait until Sith!" Karan replied. "Narne is across the river and late at night we'd have to signal for a ferry. We know Tensor will go to Narne, and he will be watching all the ways. It's too small a town for us to hide. Even in the daytime, in a crowd, it will be difficult. Anyway, Narne is not a friendly place."

They came to a spot where the path crossed a brook, the clear water running silently in its stony bed, and Karan turned upstream. Shortly they found a grassy mound where the forest drew back from the water; there they made camp. The grass was soft, green and welcoming. The tall trees made a wall around the clearing that seemed somehow protective. Fragrant herbs grew in the damp soil at the edge of the water. The atmosphere was so soothing that Llian, sitting beside the pile of twigs he had collected for the fire, put his head in his hands and fell fast asleep.

In a while he was awakened by Karan, who had gone into the bush with her hatchet and now returned, whistling and dancing, with an armload of wood. He began to get up guiltily, but she put her hand on his forehead and pushed him down again. "You have not done badly," she said fondly.

He sat there, enjoying the stillness as the light slowly faded. Karan crossed back and forth in front of him with her quick, graceful step, now cutting out a circle of turf and the soil beneath, now lining the hollow with stones from the river, building a little nest of shredded bark and twigs. Expertly she set it smoldering with a single spark, blowing the spark into red fire and feeding it with larger sticks until it blazed up. She looked up and caught his eyes on her.

"What is it?" she asked.

"I was just thinking how little your wrist hinders you. There seems to be nothing you can't do for yourself."

"The first time I broke it I was fleeing for my life. I had to do everything, and so I learned to. It healed quickly, but it troubled me even after I met you, for I'd set it badly. You and Rael did a better job—already the bones are knitting. There's no pain anymore unless I jar it. But there's no strength in it either. Go and bathe if you want to—I'll cook tonight. Here," she threw something at him. "Use my soap."

Llian caught it and went downstream a little way, where he took off his clothes and stepped into the water. The stream was only a couple of paces wide and no deeper than his ankles. He squatted among the coarse pebbles and scrubbed himself with soap and handfuls of sand. The water was cold on his toes, but nothing like the Garr had been. It was invigoratingly cold, and his scoured skin tingled.

She glanced down at him once or twice as she cooked.

He'd lost weight on their trek and his shoulders seemed disproportionately broad, his ribs bony; yet he still had a careless, boyish charm. And he seemed to have gained something—he was more confident, less awkward.

Just then Llian looked up from drying himself with his shirt. He caught her gaze on him and, suddenly self-conscious, dropped the shirt into the water. He let out a yelp and darted after it, and Karan turned away with a smile.

"Only you would stand in the river to dry yourself," she said as he came up.

"And where would you stand?" he asked with mock surliness.

"By the fire of course. Where else?"

She served the food with a flourish, with some of the dark granular Aachim bread and small sprigs of a minty herb that grew beside the stream. They ate silently, their only accompaniment the snapping and popping of the fire and the placid gurgle of the stream. Llian rinsed the plates in the river and stood them against a cobble to dry. Karan took a generous pinch of tiny pods from a bag, crushed them between two stones and brewed a special kind of coffee from them. While it was simmering she went down to the river and rejoiced in the cold water too. There had been so few opportunities before Shazmak. How she hated to be dirty.

"The coffee's ready," Llian called, and she wrung the water from her hair and came quickly up to the fire. She revolved slowly, bathing in the warmth, the firelight turning the drops on her pale skin into rubies, and her tangled hair to polished copper. Llian was watching her without expression, though she noticed that his hand shook as he poured the coffee, spilling it on his foot. She dried herself quickly on a clean shirt and wrapped her coat around her. She combed her tangles as best she could, dabbed lime perfume on the back of her neck and ran her fingers through her hair.

"I can't remember when I last had such a cup," she sighed, making a bowl around the mug with her hands and breathing the rich aroma. "I wonder where Rael . . . came by it. It doesn't grow in Bannador anymore—the frosts are too hard. What a pity we have no wine."

"No, but I've something that will serve," said Llian, remembering the little silver flask that had lain in the bottom of his pack all the weeks since he left Chanthed. "It's a liquor that we make in Chanthed in the winter. We drink it to celebrate an unexpected good fortune, or the return of a loved one."

He unscrewed the cap on its silver chain and passed the flask to Karan. She sniffed cautiously then took a small sip. The liquor was thick and sweet, with a pungent aftertaste of wild herbs, and it burned her lips and throat. She took another small sip then passed the flask, with a smile, back to Llian.

There they sat in silence, on opposite sides of the fire, with their coffee and their thoughts. Karan looked serene in the flickering light, but Llian's thoughts went back to the trial and the Mirror, and the entrancing possibility that the information he sought might lie within it. Dare he ask her again to see it? He hesitated to.

"We're in my country now," she said. "How I love it."

"I didn't know that Narne was in Bannador."

"Narne isn't. Horrible, ugly place, full of unpleasant people. The river marks the border here. Bannador is a long narrow land, right against the mountains." She breathed a great sigh.

"You're in good spirits tonight. Are you no longer afraid of Tensor?"

"I am. He will never give up. By morning they may even have crossed the river."

"And after you've given the Mirror away?"

"He will pursue it rather than me. If he gets it, perhaps there will be an amnesty. Perhaps not. Who knows?"

"Could they have taken the ferry tonight?" Llian asked, suddenly afraid that the Aachim might even now be creeping toward them. He looked around him. The light from the fire flickered, throwing long shadows on the grass, turning the enveloping forest into a hard dark wall.

"I don't think so. I've thought about it all day. How could they have reached Narne in time? They might hire a ferry during the night, but how would they find us up here, in all the forest? No, they'll wait."

"So, what are you going to do with the Mirror now?"

She looked into his brown eyes. "I've made so many plans, and broken them all. At least, every option has been closed off, save the first. I will keep my oath to Maigraith after all, and take it to her liege in Sith. And pray that no evil comes of it. If we get up early, and get the first ferry across to Narne, we can hire a boat and be in Sith in four days."

"What then?"

"I get rid of the Mirror and go straight home to Gothryme. I've been gone much longer than I said I would."

"How far is that from here?"

"It's at the other end of Bannador. A week or two. So what will you do? Continue on to Thurkad?"

Karan held her breath, and Llian did too. They had only been together for a month, but it could have been years, so shocking was the realization that they might soon part and never see each other again.

"Well, that was my destination. I don't know. I suppose I will head in that direction."

Karan's knuckles were white, so tightly were her fists clenched.

"And then, I've never spent time in Bannador." He gave her a sly glance from under his lashes. "What is it like at

Gothryme this time of year? Would I be bored, do you imagine, if I went there for a day or two?"

"It is the most wonderful place on Santhenar, at any time of the year," she said, laughing. "At least, if that is what you think. Here is an idea—what say you walk that far with me, and I will show you some of the special places that I know, and then, when the rains have eased and the snow is hard, and you have read all the Histories in our library, and told me all your tales, and we are heartily sick of one another, you can go on to wherever you want to."

"Then it is settled. Who knows what I might find in your library. I *will* walk to Gothryme with you."

She settled back with her eyes closed. Llian drifted away in his own thoughts. What could he make of the clue that Tensor had given him? Even if Tensor's guess was right, it could have been any of the three Charon who had come to Santhenar after the flute. Three cities to search. What did he know of them?

Alcifer, Rulke's great city and the closest of the three, was still inhabited. It lay on the coast less than a hundred leagues south of Sith. But doubtless Rulke's records were long gone. Mendark would know, but would he tell?

Havissard, Yalkara's fortress, lay far to the east, in the mountains of Crandor, not that far from Llian's homeland, Jepperand. He knew nothing about Havissard.

Katazza, the island city of Kandor's empire, was in the middle of the once beautiful Sea of Perion. But the sea had dried up long ago, and Katazza was abandoned after Kandor's death. That was also a long way off, and no longer shown on current maps, which depicted the Dry Sea as a vast desolation. And if Tensor was wrong, Llian's quest was no further advanced than when he'd left Chanthed.

* * *

"What did you do to the Syndics, Karan?" asked Llian a while later.

"It's not easy to explain," she said, thinking back on it. "I'm not sure that I understand it myself. I don't even know where it comes from, that talent of mine: perhaps from my grandmother, Mantille, though it's not a gift that is common among the Aachim. Perhaps from my own family. My talent allows me, sometimes, to sense the feelings or moods of certain people, even when they are far away. If the need is dire and the temper takes me, sometimes I can make a sending, even a link, though at cost of much pain and aftersickness."

"That night, when I was in Tullin?"

"That was one such time," she replied, "though I was not sending to you, specifically. There was no one for me to focus on, just a vague sense that help might be near."

"I think you woke everyone in Tullin that night," Llian murmured.

"Such sendings are difficult, and very dangerous. Often they go astray. But I did not do anything to the Syndics," she said with a twisted smile. "I did it to you—that's why you can scarcely remember." She paused. "No one can lie to the Syndics. That was my salvation, a formal trial, and why I made such a fuss about my honor. More than was necessary for someone who stands revealed in high hypocrisy, you might think," she said, looking away. "But if Tensor had been able to question me directly, you and I would both be dead now.

"Think back to the night before. When you were asleep I made another sending to you. It was easier that time: you were still weak from Emmant's charm. I took the little amulet you wore around your neck, to bind you to me. Doubtless you've missed it; I lost it afterwards. I put my tale into your mind: the taking of the Mirror and how I eventually came to Shazmak. Most of the story you knew, and everything was true except for what happened after Fiz Gorgo. I put one lie into your dream, that I had given away the Mirror at Lake Neid; that ever since I had been just a decoy. I could not risk a greater deceit; they knew too much. But a small lie might pass.

"In the trial I rewoke your dream memory and, as you relived my story, I took it back and told it to the Syndics. That was a hazardous thing," she said, making a profound understatement. "I don't think anyone has ever done that before. But the Syndics believed it. Better, they *knew* it to be true because for you it *was* true and I told it as you knew it. Only Tensor did not believe; I was acting strangely and he was sure of his own information. Besides, he did not want to believe. He could not go against the Syndics in open court, but as the bringer of the charges he had the right to persuade them in secret council. Then it became only a matter of time before all the oddnesses were piled together and sent my story crashing down. I'm sorry for using you, but there was no other way."

"I'm not. You should have been a teller—no tale was ever told more convincingly."

Karan had been smiling as she told her story, a soft slow sad smile, but all of a sudden she seemed struck by a pain, or perhaps a premonition, and as she finished speaking she put her hands over her face.

"Oh!" she cried once, her voice muffled. "Oh!" she said again. "Such pain. No, I cannot. Oh!"

"Karan, what is it?" he whispered.

Then she looked up at Llian, slowly taking her hands away, and so great was the change in her that he could scarcely comprehend it. The warmth was gone from her voice, and the quirky way that her mouth curled up at the corners when she smiled was no more. Her cheeks were sunken, her voice cold and distant and full of bitterness, so

that it frightened him, and it came haltingly, as though even
to speak took more strength than she had.

"Be warned! I am a great danger to my friends. Some I
betray, some I lead to their deaths, some I twist their minds.
Why do you linger, Llian? Get away while you can."

Llian sat there, confused and shocked, staring into the
fire, hardly daring to look up lest she caught his eye. What
had happened just then? Just when he thought he knew her,
she had turned everything upside down again.

A long time went by. Karan sat utterly still. The fit, or
whatever had possessed her, had passed, leaving her bereft.
She had opened up a gulf between them and Llian knew not
how to bridge it.

"What did you really do with the Mirror?" he began at
last, haltingly. "You told Rael that you had it. Was that another lie?"

She winced as though he'd struck her, and all at once she
looked terribly sad. "No, I have it," she said. "But I will not
speak of it, tonight of all nights," and she gathered her coat
around her and disappeared into the tent.

29

IN THE HILLS
OF BANNADOR

Llian remained by the fire for a long while, alone with his doubts, angry and miserable. Then suddenly all his confusion and anger evaporated, as he realized how clever she'd been, how she'd found the only way out, how hard she'd worked to save him, and how much it had cost her. What was this new attack? Was it Tensor, trying some new weapon of the mind against her, or was it her other enemies trying to find her again?

After the cold of the mountains the night seemed balmy. Llian threw off his clothes and crept into the shelter, afraid to disturb her. He lay down on top of his sleeping pouch and pulled his cloak over him, lying on his side and staring out the opening at the fire. A single star winked in the triangle between the roof and the tips of the trees. The fire crackled. Something scurried through the leaves on the edge of the clearing. Silence.

Her small hand touched his wrist and gripped it tightly.

"Oh, Llian," she said. "Come and comfort me. I'm so afraid."

And Llian reached over and took her in his arms, and she pressed her cheek against his throat. Her breast moved slightly against his chest and her breath was like the touch of velvet upon his shoulder.

"What was it, Karan?"

"Something reached out and touched me, worse than my dreams; but it's all right—it's gone now . . . Tell me a tale, Llian my love," she said then, dreamily.

"What tale would you like to hear?"

"Any tale." It's the sound of your voice that I need, she thought. The words don't matter now.

Llian thought for a moment. "It is a very sad little tale that I have," he said.

"No matter," she murmured.

"It is the tale of two lovers, Jenulka and Hengist." He paused. Karan burrowed her face into his neck. "A very old tale. A slight tale, excessively romantic, to my mind—no more than a diversion, really."

"Tell it."

"Jenulka was the wife of Feddil the Cruel, the Tyrant of Almadin, in ages long past. And Feddil was a beast of a man, big and fat, old and gross in his habits. Yet he was strong, stronger than any, and wickeder, and more cunning. His chief delight was in making war, his greatest pleasure in tormenting his people; and especially Jenulka, the youngest, smallest and most beautiful of his three wives."

"Naturally," came Karan's voice smugly in his ear. The familiar forms were the best.

"Who knows why he had taken her to wife, for he had sons and daughters aplenty to carry on his line, and some were older than she was, and all had their father's beastliness. And Jenulka could scarcely bear the thought of sharing his bed, because he never washed; his feet were black, his breath foul and his belly huge. But she never did, for Feddil had developed grosser tastes. But that was almost as bad, for all the court, the sons and daughters and the other wives, sneered at her, so little a wife that even Feddil would not bring her to his bed, and Jenulka was mocked by everyone. Her life was a misery and she was more unhappy than the lowest pig girl in all Almadin."

Llian stopped then, for Karan's breathing was so faint that he was sure she slept in his arms. The slight aroma of lime blossom came yet from her hair. As long as he lived that perfume would bring her to mind.

"Pig girl," she murmured appreciatively, her lips almost brushing his ear. "Tell on."

"Jenulka took to wandering down to the River Alm in the early morning, before her chaperone was awake. There was thick forest along the river in those times, and meadows where the tyrant grazed his flocks. There she would sit on the grass, or on a log or a rock, and dream of a lover who was young and handsome and lusty. For though she was shy and quiet she was also passionate, and she longed to give pleasure and be pleasured."

Karan gave a throaty chuckle.

"Now it so happened that there was a young man came sometimes to those meadows by the river, to sit, to watch the water and the flight of the diving birds, and to think. Hengist was his name. He was an apprentice to the master silversmith, and the least in years though the greatest in talent. A soulful, sensitive young man, fond of music and reading and beautiful things, and he had no interest in the company or the vulgar pleasures of the other apprentices. He often crept off to be by himself. And sometimes, if he saw something that was especially beautiful, he would go back to his master's workshop and model it in silver. He was a handsome, dark-haired lad; not tall, but well built, *and clean.*"

"But foolish, no doubt," Karan said.

"Hush! Hengist came down to the river early one morning and there, sitting on a rock near the shore, was the most beautiful girl that he had ever seen. The rising sun was fire in her hair, dazzling his eyes so that he did not recognize her. If he had he would have fled at once—even to speak to the tyrant's wife was to court death. But the sun was in his eyes and he crept closer. She turned her face to him and he was smitten.

"Now each of them was shyer than the other, and would never have approached a stranger, but their eyes met and both knew that they had found their undying love, that they were made for each other and for no other. And Hengist crept closer, as in a daze, and his eyes never left hers, though the few paces that separated them seemed like the gulf between the stars. And she half-rose from the rock on which she sat, reaching out her arms to him.

"Hengist took her two hands in his, kissing her fingers, and a delicious shiver passed through her. He looked up at her face, and she was soft and gentle and beautiful; so beautiful that his heart almost broke. Then the splash of a heron nearby broke the spell and he knew her for the wife of the tyrant. To touch her hand was death. He sprang back with a cry and was gone, not even daring to look back.

"Hengist went back to the workshop. He worked at his smithing day after day and night after night, oblivious to the taunts of the other apprentices, and the work that he did, the herons, the meadow flowers, the silver fish in the River Alm, were never more beautiful. How he longed to go back to the river and take her in his arms, but he never dared.

"Jenulka went down to the river still, every morning, to the place where they had first met, and when he did not return her heart was broken. But Jenulka was strong-willed; she knew that he was too afraid to come—that she must go to him. She went into the town to search for her lover, staring into the faces of the people in the street with such intensity that the townsfolk began to talk about her: that the wife not worthy of love grew mad. Many days she went into the town with her chaperone, until she was quite run out of reasons to go there, and she despaired of ever finding her love.

"Then one day, as she turned back toward the castle of the beast (so she thought of her husband), she chanced to pass the shop of the master silversmith. There, in the window, her eye was caught by a sculpture in silver, a heron splashing in the river. So lifelike was it, so beautifully realized that she knew it—among all the herons on that stretch of the river she recognized it, for it was the one whose splashing took her lover away. She knew at once that only Hengist could have made it, though before that she had not known what he did. She went into the shop and bought it, so praising its beauty that the fawning silversmith brought out his apprentice to meet the wife of the tyrant; for even the *least* wife must have influence. So Jenulka and Hengist met again, and their fate was sealed.

"The next morning Jenulka went again to the river, before her chaperone was awake. She knew Hengist would be there, and he was, and before they knew it they were in each other's arms. And there, while the river gurgled and the waders browsed stiff-legged in the shallow water, they made their union of love. And each morning after, they went there, and in those brief minutes at dawn their happiness was perfect.

"It could not last, of course, but it might have lasted longer than it did were it not for Hengist's foolishness. For in the nights, when he had finished the tasks his master had given him, and the other apprentices sweated and snorted in the houses that no one spoke of, at the wicked end of town, he set to work on a secret project. It was a statue in silver, a naked girl sitting on a rock by the water, dreaming of her lover. An entirely suitable project, then as now, save that Hengist gave it the face and form of his beloved.

"You would have wept if you could have seen it, for she had skin as soft as satin, as rich as cream and as smooth as marble. Her eyes were as green as jade, as large and moist as the eyes of a cow. Ahh!" he said. "That hurt!" for Karan had jabbed him in the ribs with a knuckle. "I'm sorry. As soft and liquid as the eye of a dove. And her hair was as red as the flesh of a plum."

Llian warmed to his task. "Her form was as sweet and lovely as you can imagine, for she was slender in such places where it is womanly to be slender, and full and rich and rounded in those other places. Her throat was soft and pale, her shoulders slim and beautiful, and her breasts were firm and round, with such a pearly shimmer to the skin that . . ."

"Enough," cried Karan, and even in the darkness he could tell that she smiled. "Where do you get such inspiration? Remember you are describing a statue."

"Oh yes, a statue. A most beautiful piece, and he worked on it carefully, secretly, and hid it away betimes. But his master, a mean and avaricious man who knew how much silver he had to the dram, grew alarmed at the loss of it and, spying on Hengist, discovered what he had done. Here was a chance for favor, for all knew that Feddil's youngest wife was cold as well as barren . . ."

"*Cold?*" said Karan imperiously in his ear.

"Hush! It's just a tale, remember. Please, no more interruptions.

"Doubtless Feddil would be glad of the chance to be rid of her, and the silversmith had a daughter who could take her place. He sought audience with the tyrant and showed him the statue, though the reward he gained was not what he expected. Feddil slashed off his head with a single sweep of his sword, but the rage passed as quickly as it had come, and he watched Jenulka. Before dawn of the next day he saw her creep from her bed and followed her, with a delicious thrill for the torments that were to come.

"All unknowing they came together in their glade by the river, and lay naked in each other's arms as the sun rose. But Jenulka was stricken by an inexplicable sadness, as though their love was the echo of a dream that was gone, and she wept hot tears on Hengist's throat. She would not be consoled, but only wept, and then Feddil came.

"Each saw their death approaching, and wept for the other, but Feddil was not called the Cruel for nothing. He put them naked in a big cell, chained by the ankles on opposite sides of the room. They could see each other, but could neither touch nor speak, for if one spoke the other was whipped. And Feddil's wicked heart saw at once the best torment for each of them: Hengist to see his weeping lover, but not able to comfort her; Jenulka to see her lover tortured before her eyes.

"But Feddil had another project in mind, and in between the scourgings he brought to Hengist the equipment from the silversmith's workshop—the furnaces, crucibles, hammers and tongs; the clay and sand for molding and all the other things that he might need. For though he was a coarse and brutal man, Feddil knew Hengist to be a great artisan, and he would have him make a statue of the two lovers in solid silver, to remind him of his power over them, and to *scathe* them. And it amused him that their final embrace should be at his command.

"For Hengist this was the greatest agony of all, to make his beloved in silver, but if he refused she would be beaten and put upon the rack. So each day he took up his tools, gazed at her longingly, and began to work. He knew every curve and contour of her body as only a great artisan could, and could have made the statue even if he were blind.

"Months went by. At last the work was finished, perfect, and Hengist threw down his tools and wept. Jenulka was but a shadow of herself, thin and pale—a waif with huge dark eyes. Her ankles were chafed to running sores from the chains, and her belly, on which he had once delighted to lay his head, was shrunken and wasted from hunger. And Jenulka looked at Hengist and saw how faded he was. Once he had been slim and handsome, but now the flesh seemed to have dissolved from the bones and the taut skin clung to his skull like a mask. But in their despair they loved each other more than ever.

"Then, it seemed, a miracle, for as they reached for each other as they had many times, stretching, straining to the utmost but unable to touch; perhaps because her bones had shrunk from hunger, no matter what, the fetter slipped down over her slender ankle and she was free, and for once the guard had neglected his duty and was not there to whip them apart.

"'Oh Hengist!' 'Oh Jenulka!' and they were in each other's arms at last, and theirs was an ecstasy for which there are no words.

"Presently Feddil came in, to view his statue and gloat, and finding the lovers together he thrust his sword through them in a single furious thrust. But Jenulka smiled, looking at the statue that showed what they once had, and had again.

"'Our love will endure forever, while ever there are people on Santhenar, and that is its symbol,' she said. 'But you and your children will be cursed and forgotten.' And then she died, and Hengist too, still locked together.

"Now the statue was valueless to Feddil, a symbol of his

humiliation, and in a rage he ordered it destroycd, melted, even taking hold of the ropes himself to heave it into the furnace. But it toppled and crushed him flat. The people rejoiced at the death of the tyrant, and destroyed all his works; and the statue they put in the great hall of the people, where it remains to this day, the symbol of a perfect and undying love."

"Oh, Llian," she said, stroking his lips. "I take back everything I ever thought about you."

"As I said, perhaps excessively romantic," replied Llian, smiling at her in the darkness.

Neither spoke then, for their cares had retreated far away and each was content just to lie there, unified by the warmth of their contact and the rhythm of their breathing.

Then Karan gasped, a tiny, disturbing sound, as though she was in pain.

"What is it?" holding her tightly.

Her voice came slowly, as if she brought it from a long way away. "I'm all right now. I had a terrible pain, like a hot wire behind my eyes, but it's gone already." She clung to him a moment longer, then gave his hand a hard squeeze and rolled away. "Llian, promise me something?"

"I promise."

"Promise that whatever happens tonight you will do exactly what I tell you to, however I tell you."

"What a strange thing to ask."

"Just promise; no, swear."

He took her hand in his and held it to his lips. "I promise. I swear. Whatever you ask, however you ask, I will do it."

"Even if it seems utterly wrong to you."

A shiver went all the way down his back, a foreboding. He could not speak. He could sense her whole body rigid beside him. "What is going to happen tonight?"

"Maybe nothing. Maybe another night. Maybe never! *Llian!* You must swear. You *must*. Trust me!"

"I swear," he said.

"I'll never forget you, Llian."

"You speak as though you were going away," he said softly, suddenly afraid, but Karan did not answer. She was already asleep. He lay awake for a long time, uneasy now, but at last his weariness overcame his fears and he, too, drifted into sleep.

That morning, as Karan and Llian found their way onto the path, Tensor, on the other side of the river, had stopped abruptly. The Aachim had lost much time in the caverns, clearing a fall of rock, and since that time had not dared to sleep. He divided his party: half he sent hurrying to Narne along the track that followed the eastern side of the Garr; the rest he called to him.

"They're not far away across the river," he said, "for I can sense them now; within three leagues, I think. They'll be off their guard. They will never believe that we could cross here."

"Nor can we," said one. "It is deep and too fast for swimming. And we have no boat."

"Then let us find one. There are folk living along the river."

"It would have to be a most superior boat to carry us all across that flood."

They separated and searched all day along the high bank. There were several dwellings along the rind of fertile land on this side of the river, but the local people were farmers, not fisherfolk. At last, long after dark, they found boats, two of them. The first was large but ruinous, the planking rotted and holed and the rudder broken. Tensor considered it carefully, finally shaking his head. "It is not worth the chance," he said. "I might be able to hold it together, but it would be a great trial. If the river were less wide . . . No! Show me the other."

The second boat was in better condition but tiny, just a dinghy. They found the owner and hired it from him, though at a price that was more than its value.

"If we can get five in we need only make two trips," said Tensor, and they piled in, but even with four the water was at the gunwale. He shook his head in frustration. "Not even I can keep the water out with five," he said. "It must be three journeys. Hurry now or they will be gone."

They were wild, alarming night rides, even for the Aachim, and those who had seen the boat destroyed three days past could not rid themselves of the memory of it smashing against the rocks. Eventually the last were across, but it was already morning and they were far downstream, for the strength of the current was such that it was easier for them to walk down to the boat on each return journey than to row it upstream to their starting point.

Tensor had lost the grim euphoria of the previous day; now he was puzzled and uncertain. "Yesterday I sensed her that way," pointing to the west. "But last night her image disappeared from my mind, as though she was no longer there. Let's begin. There is much forest to search."

Llian slept for a time and drifted into strange dreams, neither waking nor sleeping, so it seemed. On the other side of the shelter Karan stirred and flung out an arm, then lay still. The night was dark and very quiet. A thrill of fear breathed against the back of his neck and he shuddered in his sleep. At the same time Karan began to make a low, keening sound that filled him with dread. He reached out blindly in the darkness and caught her cold hand in his. As he did so a shock leapt up his arm and the image of a man, dark-bearded, massive, piercing eyes gleaming, seared into his brain. It was the face he'd seen before, that night in Tullin, in the dream woven into Karan's sending. A demon rising and flinging off its chains!

The man was speaking softly and with terrible menace, but Llian could not make out the words. Then the face turned toward Llian, its gaze resting lightly on him, and Llian felt that the beam of a great lighthouse shone on him. His heart thudded wildly in his chest and he cried out with terror and anguish for he saw death in those eyes.

Get away, away, anywhere! The dream had become agonizingly real. Did he dream or was he awake? It was so black that he could not tell.

Go now, said a soft voice in his head, *while she is asleep. You've always been a burden to her. She no longer needs you; she will be in Narne tomorrow.*

The voice stopped and the face flashed back, then the voice and face alternated. Something inside him rebelled. He would not be dominated. Get out of my mind, he screamed silently, willing up the face to scream his defiance.

Oh, you fool! came the voice in his head, as the face turned to him once more. The eyes struck him, etching him away layer by layer, his defiance less than nothing.

"Go now! Just go, you fool!" He wanted to go, but he could not leave her. Then it struck him with the force of a hammer blow. It was Karan's voice, Karan was telling him to go, screaming at him to go. *"Go! Get away now! You promised. Don't break this one."* Her fists were pounding his shoulder, his chest, his face.

All at once the dam burst, Llian leapt to his feet, flung on his clothes, caught up his boots in one hand and his pack in the other.

"Karan," he cried, putting his arms around her. "I won't go without you."

"Go!" she screamed, so loudly in his face that his hair stood on end. "You'll kill us both!"

"Where shall I go?"

"Away, anywhere. Go to Narne." Llian backed slowly out of the tent, looking down at her shadow in the starlight; then, at her final screamed "Go!" he turned and fled down the rivulet toward the forest path.

Karan sat up in her covers, looking after him, holding her head. When he was gone from sight, she fell back on her blankets and wailed in grief and despair.

The night was cloudless and lit only by the ribbon of bright stars known as the Chain of the Tychid, and the bright nebula, for it was the time of the new moon. It took only a few minutes to reach the path and turn left toward Narne. A light mist hugged the ground, making all the land a dreamscape. Infected by Karan's panic Llian ran and ran, squelching through bogs, crashing into thickets in the darkness, falling over, getting up again, heedless of the mud on his face, the scratching, catching branches and the clinging grasses.

He was walking now through open forest, and ahead was a glade surrounded by shadowy spreading trees. Llian stopped at the edge of the clearing and leaned against the rugose bark of an ancient trunk while he put on his boots. He still felt as if he was in a dream, intoxicated or driven, lacking all will to wonder or to question. The night held its breath for a moment, then a soft "peep-peep" sounded beside him, a clicking noise began away on his left, and out in the open space there came a sharp metallic tapping from several places at once.

Without warning there was a scrabbling sound beside his foot and a small rodent streaked away into the dry grass. A silent glide, a sudden crack of wings, a shrill squeal cut short; the night bird rose from the grass with the limp thing in its beak and flapped heavily into the trees. The night noises resumed. Llian shivered, the menace from behind reawakening. He eased the pack on his shoulders and swiftly crossed the patch of cleared land, the dry grass rustling about his ankles. The ribbon of stars blazed out strongly; he fancied that his shadow followed him for a moment, then he was within the trees on the other side and the gloom descended.

He walked for another hour, or perhaps two, following the faint trail through the trees, the rich moist misty air all about, splashing through little streams and struggling up slippery gullies, and as he went the fear and horror dwindled to a memory, and he was overcome by a sweet melancholy, a sense of something lost and gone beyond recovery.

Finally he saw that he stood on the top of a steep, treeless ridge. Below to the right was the shadow of the river and, beyond, the yellow lights of Narne. Downstream the hills were lower and rounder, and the forest was cleared back to the mountains. Here and there was a point of light, a farmhouse perhaps, and that cluster of lights in the distance must be a village.

As he stood there, staring down, the veil still before his eyes, a chill wind struck him in the face and roused him enough to realize that there was no way to get to Narne before the morning. To his left the crest of the hill broadened until it was twenty or thirty paces across, dotted with small windswept trees. He crept between two boulders into the shelter of a patch of trees, made a bed on the flattest piece of ground he could find and the dream that he had never fully woken from dragged him back under. Llian fell instantly asleep.

*   *   *

Llian was gone at last. Karan fell back on the ground. The pain behind her eyes began once more, swelling like a carbuncle, her whole head throbbing. And then the visions, the dreams, the nightmares came back. The eyes. Where had she seen those flaming eyes, those black and carmine eyes before? Now they were gone and there was nothing; and she was paralyzed. Never before had she known such terror; never had her own resources of self been so stripped from her. Directly above the trees the scorpion nebula glowed, bigger and brighter than she had ever seen it.

The dog again. The dead thing from long ago, its rotting tongue cold and slimy between her shoulder blades. Uggh! Never had she felt so befouled, but it broke the bewitchment that paralyzed her and Karan bethought herself of her nakedness. She leapt up, thrust legs into trousers, fastened her shirt, threw wood on the fire until it blazed up. She took out her little knife and waited. She would flee, only there was no place to go, no place where they would not find her. No way to escape those who crept upon her, who knew her.

The eyes. The face. Vast, unbearably handsome; treacherous and cruel. Many times now she had dreamed that face, and each time it was stronger, more potent, more demanding. Yet it was prisoned, tormented too. It wanted, but it could not have. Then the dog. The eyes. The pressure. The pain. The eyes. The paralysis. The dog.

She gasped for breath. She panted; her eyes flicked back and forth like mad things. The world grew dark, flamed red and black, dark again. A wind sprang up from nowhere and the limbs of the trees rasped together like scaly hands. Then all was still again.

Now a shiver began on her scalp, running down her neck to the small of her back. Sweat prickled in her armpits, the paralysis again and suddenly she knew that they were all around. Dark shadows crept through the trees. Their sandals rustled in the grass. The Whelm had come! And she could not move for they knew her, knew all of her; *knew what to use against her.*

A hand appeared at the opening of the tent. Her heart turned over. She could do nothing!

But in a tiny corner of her being, hope prevailed. There was a remote part of her that they did not know, that no one knew. A fierce determination dwelt there, and it reached out and spoke to her. No one was invincible, not even the Whelm, and she knew it more than any. Had she not seen Idlis in torment? The paralysis lifted, a fury took her, and as the Whelm reached its thick-knuckled hands toward her she slashed at it. It fell back with a howl.

But these were not Idlis's band—there was a colder intelligence at work here. And the pain was back, swelling, glowing, her head bursting with pain. Though she was wide awake, the handsome, cruel face of her dreams was back. *Would she do it? Could he force her?* The tent torn apart, the Whelm reaching for her, her head pulsing with fire and pain and burning eyes, her knife parting flesh, the Whelm falling but another behind, the knife struck from her hand, then a nightmare, a maelstrom, a fury, her tormented mind seeking out for solace, *sending*; unbelievably, finding it nearby. But what a price for that solace!

Maigraith! she cried, a golden light in her eyes, and drew a link between them.

It was as though the very depths of the abyss sighed, a vast exhalation, relief beyond hope. But the stars wept crystalline tears; tears that were shattered as they fell into glittering shards that scored her eyes with fire. The link was snatched from her, twisted back on itself and into dimensions beyond. Then, an explosion of fire and pain, the touch of the Whelm, the dead dog at her throat, then all pain gone, all pressure gone, consciousness fading, sliding down into a dark well of oblivion, the last thing she knew a sense of inexpressible relief in the eyes, a catharsis of exhilaration in the Whelm.

"Oh, perfect master," the Whelm cried. "At last! At last!"

"*Oh faithful servants,*" it boomed. Vast, forbidding, foreboding. "*The crisis approaches, and so much to do. Listen, and obey. Already the link fades. Do you remember yourselves?*"

"Now we remember. We are Ghâshâd, master."

"*I have an enemy, Ghâshâd!*"

"We know him, now."

"*Torment him. Goad him. Drive him to folly. But do not harm him. Call together the Ghâshâd, and when the opportunity comes,* seize it!"

Llian woke the next morning more tired than when he'd lain down to rest: the whole night, it seemed, he had been a fugitive in a shadow land. Always he fled, always he was pursued. His colossal enemy grew more powerful and more baleful as he came closer, and he could do nothing to save himself, for there was another presence in his mind that tormented him and frustrated his every way of escape.

Now a light shone on his face and a stake was in his back. He prised open his puffy lids. It was morning, and the sun shone in his eyes. He leapt up, rubbing his back. At first he struggled to remember the chain of folly that had led him to this spot, alone in the bright morning on a bare hilltop. Memory of the previous night came stealthily, then flooded back.

Karan! What madness of the night had led him to this place? Call it by its true name: what cowardice? How could he have abandoned her, been held to such a ridiculous promise?

He flung the pack over his shoulder, glanced at the sun. It

was after seven o'clock. He had to find her. She might be at the ferry already. He ran down to the path and looked over toward the river. There was Narne, a clutter of buildings and jetties on the far side. And there was the ferry now, inching its way directly across. His gaze followed its path. On his side of the river was a smaller wharf of wooden piles, partly hidden by a grove of trees, and an open shed housing the huge cable wheel. It was half a league away. If he ran he could be there in twenty minutes. Surely it would not be gone.

He set off with bounding strides, but the path was little more than a stony gully; with each bound the pack crashed into his back, unbalancing him. After falling twice and nearly breaking an ankle he dropped back to a fast walk until he reached the bottom of the ridge. Then he ran again but it was almost half an hour later that, weak-kneed and dripping sweat, he staggered onto the wharf, past a straggle of rustics who looked at him without curiosity.

The ferry was a hundred spans out into the stream on its return journey and, despite his wild caperings and beseeching cries, it continued steadily on, grinding on its cable, the upstream gunwale pushed down to water level by the force of the river. Ten people were visible on the deck, though none resembled Karan with her bright hair and pale face.

Llian ran back to the group of laborers, who by now were making their way up the hill, and called out to the nearest, a tall uncouth-looking fellow in baggy green shirt and brown pantaloons, carrying a hoe over one shoulder. The group kept walking as he ran beside them.

"Hey!" he cried. The fellow turned and looked at him but did not stop. He was unshaven, with several days of stubble on his cheeks and a bulbous nose.

"Did you see a woman, red hair, green eyes, about this

tall, get on the ferry?" he asked, holding his palm out level with his nose and running backwards to keep up.

"Eh?" said bulbous nose thickly.

Llian repeated the question, slowly, loudly.

The man's rubbery lips parted in a leer, revealing a crater full of black stumps. "Woman, red hair, beautiful!" He sounded as though he was talking with a mouthful of molasses. He grinned broadly. The vision of decay was so horrible that Llian was forced to look away.

"Beautiful? No, I didn't say that," he began, then realized that the man was talking to himself.

"Did you see her?" Llian asked urgently, still running backwards. He caught his foot in a pothole and fell sprawling.

"No, no girl, no red hair, no girl," the man said, his voice trailing off, then looked away and lengthened his stride.

Llian sat on the ground where he had fallen, looking after the little group of laborers. "No girl! No girl!" came drifting back to him, then they disappeared over a rise, heading downstream.

Llian calculated. Last night he'd walked for at least two hours. She'd have to have left well before dawn to have caught the ferry. He ran back down to the wharf and stood there, unable to decide what to do. He took his pack off and sat down beneath a tree, alternately looking across the river to Narne and back up the path. No one came. Time passed; he grew uneasy. He paced the wharf.

Where *was* she? She should have come long since. Suddenly he came to a decision. He'd leave the pack here and go back up the path a little, just to the top of the ridge, to see if he could see her coming. Llian thrust it into a tangle of berry bushes down below the end of the jetty and set off back up the path.

From the crest of the hill he looked back. The ferry was

almost across to Narne. The stony soil showed no footprints, not even his own. Forward the path disappeared in the thick forest that began part-way down the ridge.

A feeling of woe grew in him. Something had happened to her—Tensor must have found a way across and used another of his potencies on her. That was why she had sent him away. He, Llian, should have been there to help her. What a fool, a cowardly wretch he was.

Without any conscious decision he found himself jogging back to the camp. The further he went the more his disquiet grew; the jog turned to a run, the run to a sprint, he must not stop, not for the agony in his side or the throb of his head, down valley, across stream, up hill, across clearing he ran, on and on, gasping down each breath. At last, here was the brook cutting across the path. He dashed up, into the clearing, and stopped.

There was no sound but his hacking breath. The grassy mound was shady, cold, damp, and the tall trees seemed to hang back from it. The tent was still there. The unease drained from him in a wave of relief. She must have decided to stay another day.

"Karan," he called. There was no answer.

A shiver began to make its way up the back of his neck. He walked across and saw that the tent was torn open. Karan's pack lay half inside. It had been ripped apart, the frame smashed beyond repair. The contents were strewn about and broken. Inside the tent the blankets were in disarray. Llian picked one up. It was slashed and covered in blood. The others were the same. He dragged them out of the shelter. The ground beneath was also wet with blood, a great deal of it. More than one person could lose and still be alive. He threw himself on the ground and wept.

PART THREE

30

THE LINK

When Faelamor finally poled the boat out of the channel into the reed thicket, it was near to sunset. Ten hours had gone by since she had stolen Maigraith out of Fiz Gorgo. Maigraith was slumped against the side, feverish and only semiconscious, her blistered feet in a black, foul-smelling slurry of mud and swamp water that washed back and forth with every lurch of the boat. They grounded suddenly on an island of mud. Maigraith gave a low moan and opened her eyes. They were sunken, the whites yellowed.

Faelamor stepped out into the brown water and pulled the boat up onto the bank, though with the tall reeds all around there was no chance that it would drift away. Then she backtracked, teasing the bent reeds back to their former positions until there was no sign that anything had passed that way. She climbed onto the shelf of mud, exploring the island. The mud was soft on the surface but firm beneath and clung to her boots in sticky layers, so that it took an effort just to heave each foot forward. She forced her way through the reeds to the other side, then back again and across the other way. There was no dry land anywhere, just cold gray mud and the reeds and a single spindly tree, long dead. With sunset the mist began to rise.

When she returned to the boat Maigraith was sitting up, retching over the side. She looked up as the boat rocked, then another spasm caught her and she clung to the side again. Faelamor watched her impassively.

"We'll make camp in the boat," she said, when Maigraith was better again. "There's nothing but mud here. Let me attend you now, while there remains some light."

Faelamor eased the stiff fabric from her back and examined the wounds carefully. "You've taken in some poison here, and here," she said, frowning. "I would guess that they had it on one of the instruments. I've a liniment that will help."

She took three steps to the other end of the boat to rummage in her pack. The wind cut into Maigraith's back. Her coarse garments were already dank from the mist. The night was bleak. Faelamor returned and smeared her wounds with the ointment. The touch of her fingers was painful but the salve brought a relieving numbness.

"I've nothing to dress your injuries with; they are too many, though they'll heal quickly now. Put this on." Faelamor took a long loose shirt out of her sack; it sighed over Maigraith's shoulders and down her back like silk. Maigraith held it back up while Faelamor treated her remaining wounds.

Maigraith woke late the next morning to find the boat sliding through an endless swamp forest. The water was dark, the color of tea, and speckled on the surface with yellowing leaves of the sard tree. The trees were tall, at least twenty spans, with enormous boles and multiple trunks; soft bark the color and texture of parchment hung down in banners or floated on the water in rafts. The boat was heading almost due north; the low sun struck at them through a gap in the trees.

"Good morning," she called out to Faelamor, who was poling the boat from the stern.

Faelamor, who had evidently spent the night brooding about Maigraith's failures, stared at her briefly, scowled and turned away without answering. All the morning they continued in the same direction; after every temporary detour Faelamor turned the boat due north. At midday Maigraith tried again.

"Where are we going? Why north?"

"Be silent!" she shouted at her. "I no longer trust you with my business. Ask no questions. You failed me, after all I taught you."

Faelamor turned away and resumed her poling, heaving the boat along with furious thrusts.

Maigraith closed her eyes, laid her head on the side and tried to sleep. And sleep she did; that day and the next she spent more time asleep than awake, the boat rocking gently under her. And surprisingly, her dreams were gentle too, most of the time. Once only she dreamed of the Whelm and woke screaming. Faelamor was beside her at once, stroking her damp brow and murmuring to her in the language of the Faellem. As she drifted back to sleep she thought she saw a tinge of pity in Faelamor's eyes, that she had never seen before. Pity—or sorrow. Something that Faelamor had never allowed herself to show.

Whenever she woke the picture was the same: Faelamor standing at the stern, pole in hand, staring straight ahead with a face of stone. Twice a day she stopped briefly while they ate a silent meal of bread, smoked fish and dried fruits, washed down with the cold brown water from the swamp.

On the fourth day Maigraith stirred well after midnight. The crescent of the rising moon slanted through the thin leaves, the white trunks stretching away in all directions like the columns of a temple. The boat was still, Faelamor taking a brief rest at the stern. Maigraith came softly up to her, laying a hand on her shoulder.

"I am sorry," she said. "I failed you badly. But everything is not lost. Karan still has the Mirror. She will bring it to you. She swore a binding oath."

Faelamor woke up suddenly, dashing Maigraith's hand away. Her ageless face suddenly cracked. "You wretched fool," she said. "Don't beg. I can never forgive you. I told you to go alone."

Maigraith took an involuntary step backwards, caught her heel on a rib of the boat and fell heavily against the side. Faelamor stared down at her with a bitterness rooted in the age-long frustration of the Faellem.

"I had to have her help; I could not do it alone."

"Pah! This upstart Yggur is no match for you, for what I made of you."

"That may be so. Sometimes even *I* feel that I am strong. But there is one thing you neglected in my training, one vital thing. The will, the urge to dominate. I did my duty by you, sent away with Karan that thing which you want so badly; even overmastered Yggur for a time. I took no pleasure from that, and soon my will failed me. Later, when I knew him and what troubles him, I came to pity him. I learned that in Fiz Gorgo."

"Pity him!" Faelamor was incredulous, realizing for the first time that the instrument was flawed, and it was of her making. "After what he did to you? You must live to hate him, *burn* to destroy him. He showed no pity."

"I do not believe that he sent *them* for me. His control of the Whelm is failing; they serve him only so long as it suits them. And he is not the only one to have used me ill. Many times I have asked myself what vile crime my mother and father did, *or was done to them*. Why did you take me? To what end do you instruct me? Why must I hide the color of my eyes?" Her voice rose until she almost screamed: *"Who am I?"* Then her tones became soft, pleading. "Why me? You have shown how easy it would have been for you, a master of illusion such as you are, to take the Mirror. Why did you not?"

Faelamor was momentarily disconcerted by the attack and the unaccustomed display of emotion. By the knowledge that there were parts of Maigraith about which she knew nothing, over which she had no control. What had happened in Fiz Gorgo to transform her so?

"Think what you will. It wasn't easy, even for me. With the working of illusions the hard work is done before."

"You wanted to test me, test my training! To what purpose would you put me? The Faellem knew, for when I was a child they cast you into exile over it. Why will you not trust me? I have always been loyal. I think of nothing but my duty to you." Her tones were plaintive now.

Faelamor came close, looked into Maigraith's eyes and laid a hand upon her brow. "Maigraith, Maigraith," she said soothingly. "The fever burns in you and sends you wild imaginings. Come, you must rest now."

Almost at once Maigraith felt calmness descend upon her, the torturing emotions draining away. She struggled for a moment, but already the effort was too great and she allowed Faelamor to sit her down. A blanket was placed around her shoulders and she gripped it and pulled it tight, suddenly very cold. She sat with her back against the side, shivering, staring with unfocused eyes into the swamp. Faelamor was busy down the other end, then she came back with a small bowl in her hand.

"Drink this," she said. "It will ease the pain and the fever and help you to sleep."

But the pain is gone and there is no fever, thought Maigraith drowsily, looking into the bowl. A small quantity of a thick, metallic-looking liquid lay there, moving sluggishly, like quicksilver in the thin moonlight.

"Drink," said Faelamor, and she drank. Faelamor watched her carefully, noted her swallow, then took the bowl and put it away.

As she did so Maigraith sank her head down on her arms, and under their cover allowed the remaining liquid to dribble out of the corner of her mouth onto the side of the boat, where it ran down into the muddy bilge and disappeared. Even as she did she was overcome by weariness. She slumped against the side and was instantly asleep.

Faelamor looked down at Maigraith. In her robes she made a dark shapeless lump, with one bare slender arm stretched along the gunwale. I am not barren of pity, she mused, but pity does not benefit my quest. I will not give it up, or you, but I must be more careful with you.

She eased herself out of the boat onto a small, reedy island. There she found a clearing among the reeds where some low herbs grew, and sat down, trailing her fingers through the aromatic leaves. How did I come to this?

To lead the Faellem to Santhenar—how I strove for that honor in Tallallame, uncounted ages ago. How I burned for it. How eagerly I reached for the glory; how carelessly I assumed the duty. Did I know then that there would be no respite from that duty, save in death? I can no longer remember. Happy are the Faellem to put their burdens on their leader.

Yet so reluctantly did the congress send us here. Duty drove us, and fear. Once the Charon broke free of Aachan we had to follow. The Three Worlds are linked. We had to oppose them for the sake of the balance, for everything touches everything else. But how we hated Santhenar. Oh, there is beauty here, of a sort, but nothing as to Tallallame. So lonely we were. So lonely am I. How I long to have my people about me, enfolding me. This remnant I brought here are corrupted, as I am . . .

I led the Faellem here, and I must take them back. But no one was made for such an impossible task. The Forbidding was seamless, impenetrable. Duty bound me to find a way, but there was no way. The conflict almost drove me beyond my wits, and my loneliness became unbearable. Then my enemy Yalkara, cunning beyond belief, found with the Twisted Mirror a warp in the Forbidding; but she closed it behind her when she fled. Utter despair followed swiftly upon that brief hope, and it was then that my corruption began. Brooding, searching, spying, at last a hope came to me, and an opportunity.

Perhaps if you knew us better, Maigraith, you would understand how, seeing at last a way home, I did this terrible wrong to make it so. Little wonder that I hate you so. I made you, and when I look at you, all I see is my own debasement.

The soliloquy became a vigil, and Faelamor sat silently on the grass, staring up at the stars until they faded with the dawn.

Maigraith woke late, with a dry mouth and a dull feeling in her temple. The events of the previous evening were curiously distant, though she knew with an awful urgency that she must remember. She forced her dull mind back. As she did so she looked up and caught Faelamor's gaze on her, a gaze of particular intentness.

"How my head aches this morning," she said, wrinkling her forehead and turning away so that Faelamor would not see the sudden remembrance in her eyes.

"But the fever is gone, I see. My medicine was effective then."

"I suppose so, though I have no memory of it. What day is it?"

"It's the morning of the fourth since I brought you out of Fiz Gorgo. What do you remember?"

"The chamber of the Whelm. I could never forget that. You came for me," she said in a dreaming tone. "Stone corridors. My feet paining me, and my back. All of me hurting. You lifted me into a boat. This boat," she said looking around her. "For a long time we seemed to be drifting through a forest of great white trees, though that could have been a dream. No, unless we are still in it, for such trees are all about. I knew you would come for me," she said smiling at Faelamor, and Faelamor smiled back at her and touched her on the shoulder, though there was still a wary look in her eye.

Later she questioned Maigraith at length about the stealing of the Mirror, the Whelm, and Yggur, but especially about Karan. Maigraith did not know what to say, torn between loyalty and duty. The Whelm had been curious about Karan as well. What was it about her? That she was sensitive? Why were they so exultant when she'd betrayed Karan's ancestry? What had Vartila said? *Now I know what to use against her.*

I warned Karan to conceal her heritage. I should have warned her about me. Never to trust me. What have I betrayed her to? Death, or slavery?

"Curious," said Faelamor. "There are depths to Karan that I had not imagined. This talent of linking—where can it have come from? I must know more about her. Her family seat is near Tolryme, you once said. One of the Faellem dwelt there in ages past, and it was rumored that he fathered a daughter, though of course she never came to us. Perhaps something remains in the line."

But Maigraith was not listening. She was consumed by guilt and shame; terribly afraid for Karan. She said no more about her.

In the middle of that day they poled through a band of rushes into a small lake. Across the lake they abandoned the boat, walking for another day through forest before coming into a village beside a river that flowed east rather than west. There Faelamor bought a canoe for a few pieces of silver.

"This stream flows into the Hindirin River," she said. They traveled day and night after that, as best they could, for there was no moon. Faelamor was desperate to find Karan, even though such a long time had gone by that she knew the hope of her still having the Mirror was faint indeed.

One day, when they had stopped so that Maigraith could climb the high banks and find out where they were, she saw that the forest was gone save for a narrow band along the river. Grassy plains extended as far as she could see.

"Good progress," said Faelamor when she climbed back into the canoe.

"We should come to a city downriver," said Maigraith. "Preddle it is called. If we are to go openly I must have other clothing, and boots in any case."

"I see only two choices," said Faelamor, "assuming that Karan is still going to Sith. We can go south-east, cross the Hindirin at Galardil, go through the Zarqa Gap and enter Iagador from the south, or we can go north-east and cross into Iagador over the mountains. The southern way is longer; on the other hand the passes may all be blocked if there has been heavy snow."

"There are two passes that might be open," said Maigraith. "There is the one from Hetchet to Bannador, through Tullin. But that is too far from here. The other is the old road across the mountains from Preddle to Narne and Sith. I came that way only a year ago. It is the most direct way from here to Iagador, though still a month's journey. From Narne we can go down the river to Sith, or north to Bannador and Thurkad. Those are the places she will head for."

"Let me go to Preddle and buy the things you need, and food. I will seek information while I am there. Then I will decide."

They paddled on until they came to the hovels that signaled the outskirts of the city. Faelamor put a different appearance upon herself and went to Preddle. Maigraith paddled back upstream, hid the canoe in the trees and slept, but only for a little while. She was restive now that Faelamor was not there, and there was a great deal to think about.

What would Yggur do? Would he send after her? For a while it had seemed that what she could tell him was secondary to the planning of his campaign, his struggle with the Whelm and his own nightmare. As though he did not know what to do with her. No, he would not pursue—she'd been a diversion, something that had intrigued him, but now he would carry on with his own campaign. What would happen then? And what of the Whelm?

And she began to understand the nature of her own conflict. She was growing out of Faelamor's shadow; there must be more for her than simply duty. There *must* be.

*   *   *

It was mid-afternoon when Faelamor returned. "We must go over the mountains," she said, as Maigraith threw off the robes she had worn for the past days and donned her new clothes. "There was no talk but of the marching of Yggur's armies from Orist, and from the south. They are advancing on Iagador through the Zarqa Gap and all the bridges are under guard. We cannot go that way."

Maigraith listened eagerly to the news of him, perhaps too eagerly, for she saw that Faelamor was looking at her curiously. I must be on my guard, she thought, allowing her face to relax, the smile to fade imperceptibly. This is one secret that she must never learn. And thereafter, whenever they had news on the way, she was careful not to show too much interest in the doings of Yggur, or too little.

As soon as she had cast off the clothes of the Whelm Maigraith felt a weight leave her, and she went along cheerfully and at a faster pace. They paddled down to the Hindirin, going hard for a week and more, and finally abandoned the canoe at a town called Gessoe. There they bought horses and raced north for another week under a bright moon. Finally they came onto the track that led to the Narne pass, reaching the mountains without incident in another four days.

They were climbing steadily when they crossed onto a spur that gave them an uninterrupted view down to the plains below. There, converging on their path, was a band of riders. Faelamor stared at the distant specks, shading her eyes with her hand.

"Whelm," she said at last. "I'm almost sure of it. A large band riding fast. They're making no effort to hide themselves, and why should they? We are but two, though two that they have found redoubtable. Our horses are weary. We must prepare to defend ourselves."

Whelm! Maigraith could not conceal her fear.

"Take hold of yourself, craven! Have you forgotten all

your lessons?" Faelamor was contemptuous. "You know this place—what choices do we have?"

"Higher up," Maigraith said, her voice fluttering, "a track runs away from the path. Among the rocks there is a little basin; cliffs lie all around. I camped a night there, once. It would be easy to defend, though there is no way out. But what use is defense against so many?"

"The will indeed burns feebly in you," said Faelamor with disgust. "We defend because we must not submit, because death is preferable to being taken, because while we are at large there is hope." She seemed to grow a little, her voice rising. "I defend because I am the hope of Tallallame, and Tallallame cries out for me. No Whelm can take me, be there ten or fifty, for their will is the will of servants—paltry, pallid weak things. I am the Faellem, and I have wrestled with Rulke himself. Talk not to me of will."

The riders came on so fast that before they reached their refuge they were clearly visible on the turns of the road below them, less than an hour behind.

"Look," said Faelamor. "Do you recognize them?"

"Whelm, no doubt."

They established their defenses as best they could. Night fell and a gentle snow began to cover their tracks, but later the wind came up and the snow ceased. They huddled in a rude shelter out of the wind, prepared to defend themselves, but though they waited all night long the Whelm did not come.

In the cold dawn they crept back down to the path. Their tracks of the previous day were still visible, where they had veered off the way. The tracks of the Whelm were also clear. They had not even stopped. When, a little while later, the two reached the crest, they saw the band high above, riding at a great pace.

"Whatever they seek must be more important than us.

Probably they go to stir up trouble in advance of Yggur's army."

"I have an evil feeling about them," replied Maigraith.

They mounted again and traveled warily along steep mountain paths for another week, still half-expecting an ambush. At last they crossed the last pass and came down into the forest. There among the tall trees they made camp.

"Tomorrow evening we can be in Narne, with luck," said Maigraith, as they huddled close to the fire after eating. "There will be news of the war there."

Maigraith lay on her back in her bedroll, head propped on a log, uneasy, unable to sleep. Once she got up quietly and walked into the forest until the light of the fire was no longer visible. There was a still, silent, brooding quality to the night. What was it that troubled her? She could not say, but the Whelm were at the heart of it. They were not going to the war—theirs was a more careful purpose.

It was past midnight, a cold clear night, the brittle stars gleaming through the treetops. Faelamor was sleeping a long way from the fire, just the top of her head extending from the sleeping sack. Maigraith came back and lay down in her cold blankets. The fire had died down to a bed of orange coals. She looked at the dark sky. A wisp of high cloud eclipsed the star she was staring at. Her eyes closed, and then she dreamed.

A shadow passed in front of the leaping flames, then another, then many shadows. She trembled but did not cry out. There was none to aid her. A cloaked figure appeared outside the tent, stooped and tore open the entrance. She held up the little dagger. The figure pushed inside, groping for her in the darkness. She slashed at it. It fell back with a wail. Then others came, and though she cut them, they overwhelmed her. "Maigraith!" she cried out, then the link turned in on itself, a fist crashed into her temple and there was nothing more.

Maigraith sat bolt upright, crying out, "Karan, where are you?" but there was nothing to be seen save the faint glow from the coals and the tall trees around.

Faelamor leapt up, instantly alert. "What is it? What did you see?"

"Karan! They came for her; the Whelm. For a moment the link was alive again, between us. So that was why they were hurrying so. She must be nearby."

"Then get a move on, before they get away with it."

Maigraith almost smacked her in the face. "Curse the Mirror, and curse you, too! I have been in their hands. I know what they will do to her."

"Where was she? Did she tell you?"

"No!" Maigraith said angrily. "Perhaps she didn't even know it was me, at first. I saw what she saw, then she cried out, then nothing."

They packed up the camp in haste, put out the fire, and left.

"Then what did you see? What was the land like?"

Maigraith tried to think. "It was quite light there, with starlight, and the fire still burning, but I saw little; she was in a tent or shelter, until the end. A clearing; grass underfoot, the trees taller than here and the ground flat. There was no snow, but there must have been a creek nearby—I could hear it trickling past, right near the tent. That is all."

"Not much there to guide us. Some little way from here though, down out of the mountains; nearer the river, perhaps. You know the country hereabouts; try to think. But how comes she here? You said you heard of her near Hetchet: that is a long way to the north."

"And a long time ago. Maybe she doubled back and crossed the pass as we have done. One of Yggur's spies saw her and sent the Whelm a message, no doubt. How else would they have known where to find her? Ah! I remember this country now. There is a path leading toward Narne, to the ferry of course. But that is a big area to search."

"Let us assume that she camped near the path. A flat area, with a stream, near the path. Make haste."

All night they searched, but it was not until dawn that they saw the prints of many people, along a stream that crossed the path. They came up into the clearing and there was the tent on the grassy mound, the little stream running cold beside, her few possessions broken and trampled, the blanket soaked with blood.

"She was here," said Maigraith. "These are her boots, and here the cup and plate that she carried. Oh, Karan! My weakness, my *need* it was betrayed you to this end."

"They have it then," said Faelamor bitterly. "It's all been for nothing."

"Not yet. It cannot be more than six hours since they took her. But where would they go? To Narne? Hardly, in daylight. They may be hiding somewhere in the forest, waiting for night. Let us follow them."

They set off cautiously down the stream but soon lost the trail in the forest. It was too dense to ride, so they tied the horses on long leads by the water. After more than two hours of searching, during which time Faelamor became increasingly agitated, she said quietly: "This is wrong; some kind of trick. She no longer has the Mirror, and they haven't found it either. She must have hidden it."

"Then go and find the cursed thing," said Maigraith in a sudden fury, filled with despair and horror and contempt for herself. "But I do not go with you." So saying, she turned and faced Faelamor squarely. Faelamor came toward her, her hand outstretched.

"Stay!" said Maigraith. "*I have the will,* if you force me."

They confronted each other for a long moment, then Fae-lamor turned on her heel and made off at once, leaving the water and heading directly up into the forest. Maigraith's eyes followed her until she could no longer be seen. She felt as though she had put aside a great burden. She turned and continued down the stream.

31

FAELAMOR'S STORY

F aelamor went uphill through the forest and back to the clearing, drawn by the feeling that something still lay undiscovered there. So intent was she that she gave only passing thought to Maigraith and her peculiar show of wilfulness. She would come back in time—duty would drive her back. It was past midday when she finally reached the clearing again, but as she drew near she was warned by the sound of voices. She used illusion to disguise herself and took advantage of the concealment of the forest. Almost immediately a troop of the Aachim entered the clearing. She recognized the leader, whom she had known of old. It was Tensor.

He strode forward, examined the remnants of Karan's tent and the items scattered and broken around the campsite, shaking his head. He took a few steps across to the stream, stepping carefully to avoid disturbing the footprints, and stood there for a moment, looking downstream. Then he gestured to the Aachim, who were standing at the entrance to the clearing in a group, as though waiting for him. At once they fanned out across the open space, scanning the ground. The drizzle began to turn to heavy rain.

After a few minutes one called to the others in a low voice, holding something white in each hand. The man was standing on the far side of the clearing, and through the rain Faelamor could not make out what he held, or hear what was said. The Aachim gathered around, examining the objects carefully. After a minute the gathering broke up, the objects were tossed to the ground and the search resumed.

Tensor and one other, a smaller man, stood on the edge of the clearing, talking, then the man pointed to the forest and they walked that way, slowly, heads down, occasionally bending to examine some marking on the ground, and disappeared from view. That was what saved them.

Almost as soon as they were gone a band of Whelm began to assemble silently on the other two sides of the clearing. Without warning they attacked the Aachim with arrows. Three fell on the first volley without making a sound, then one on the next, and the Whelm rushed the clearing. One Aachim who still stood, a tall handsome woman, was cut down in seconds. The three that remained, seeing that the situation was hopeless, fought their way into the forest and vanished. Of the ten Whelm, two had fallen. Two stayed and six followed the fleeing Aachim. Faelamor looked on in horror. The battle was over in less than a minute and there was nothing she could have done.

Soon after that, another Whelm came running out of the forest, a tall woman, and all three ran back the way she had come. The others did not return.

Faelamor rose up on tiptoe, staring out over the bushes, her acute senses strained to the fullest. Yet the ones who crept up on her were more cunning still, and the attack came completely by surprise. A heavy arm went around her throat and a sharp point pricked between her ribs. The arm tightened until she was unable to breathe.

She gave a little cry and allowed her legs to give slightly, hanging limply off the arm, awaiting an opportunity, but the knife dug into her and forced her up again. Then someone tied her hands swiftly, jerking the cord tight before each knot, and she was flung sprawling among the wet leaves. She lay there for a moment, her cloak over her face, then heaved herself awkwardly onto her back and stared up at her attackers. Tensor! At first she was not afraid, for they had been allies once.

Tensor stared at her for a minute, evidently wondering who she was, then he penetrated her disguise and it faded away.

"Fay-el-amor!" he said slowly. "You did not die then? What are you doing here?"

"I might ask the same of you," she said, struggling to her feet. "Take off my bonds."

But Tensor continued to stare at her through narrowed eyes, a slow realization coming. Not Mendark at all. Mendark had said that it was not he, but Tensor had not believed his friend. Faelamor had as much reason as any to want the Mirror, and had he known she lived he would have suspected her at once. Yes, this was much more plausible. And in his despair he allowed himself to believe that she would want the Aachim gone—the more of them dead, the better it would suit her. So she hid here while others did the deed, and gloated.

"*You!*" he said at last, with a gathering fury, in his grief and his grandeur, inflamed by the nearness of the Mirror and the loss of it once more. "I understand now. All this comes down to you. You seduced Karan into betraying us, with your Faellem deceits. It was for you that Karan took the

Mirror. Because of you my people lie dead and the Whelm hunt us like dogs."

He turned to one of his people. "Bind her securely and stop her mouth. Take her back to Shazmak; hold her until I return. Blase, you go with them across the river, then to Narne and tell the others all that has happened. I will follow the Whelm where Iennis and Thel have led them. Meet me by the Garr, two leagues upstream of Narne. Wait there at dawn, and again at dusk."

He turned to Faelamor. "You will be held in Shazmak as hostage for the Mirror. When it is returned you will be freed."

When Faelamor spoke there was a chill in her voice to make even Tensor quail, for she saw in this accidental meeting the unraveling of all her plans. "The treachery of Karan is not of my doing. I ordered Maigraith to go alone. Karan betrayed my name to Yggur, just as she betrays you. Neither blame me for the deeds of the Whelm; it grieves me to see the precious blood of the Aachim spilt here.

Her voice dropped below freezing point. "But I warn you, the very survival of the Aachim rests on a blade. Now is your time of choice; and it is now, whether you know it or nay. We should pursue the Whelm, not each other. Hold me and you bring about the doom of Shazmak, for *nothing* will shake me from my path."

"You must listen to her, Tensor," said Blase, a lanky man with a bloody shoulder wound. "This is madness. We should look to making friends, not turning our friends into deadly foes."

Tensor looked into Faelamor's eyes and saw his fate writ there. For a moment he wavered, but such was his fury, despair and folly that every entreaty only further strengthened his resolve. He drew himself up, and even Faelamor was struck by the grandeur of him.

"We are Aachim! Your friendship would aid us, but we do not beg. You could have saved them," he said coldly. "Take her. Treat her well but watch her always. Beware her talents. Never allow her to be free."

The Aachim seized her, though she resisted them for a moment, bound as she already was. She glowered at Tensor and he stepped back a pace, suddenly disconcerted. Her will, her pride was no less than his own, and her strength, and only one of them could come out of it.

"Scatter this seed upon the wind and the storm will bring it back a hundredfold," she said. "You will know again that fear that you have not felt for fifty generations of humankind. Already your enemies stir."

She turned away, but a shiver went through the two Aachim. They tightened her bonds and stopped her mouth and eyes, and led her away without further words in the direction of the boat. Tensor stood there, alone in his agony of choice then, casting her out of his mind, set off in the tracks of the Whelm.

For Faelamor that march back to Shazmak was like a never-ending nightmare. She was dragged blindly through thickets and icy streams. Once they came to the shore of the river and her captors helped her into a small boat for a wild, rocking, rushing ride, all the more frightening because she could see nothing. Then they were across, the keel rattling on pebbles. On the other side of the river Blase left them and they went upstream in great haste. Not once did the Aachim stop, and he spoke only to offer food or drink.

A long journey underground, through caves filled with the still, chill dampness of the earth. Up slippery stairs and long ladders, then another forced march, to the towers of Shazmak and the unceasing wail of the wind.

*   *   *

The first day of her captivity in Shazmak passed at last, and Faelamor was so weary that even her bones ached; so desperate that she could not sleep. And in that half-mad state of sleeplessness Faelamor brooded on her captivity, the injustice done to her by Tensor, and her need for freedom. How had she let them take her, when the Mirror had been so near? She *must* be free.

She looked around and discovered the dimensions and quality of her prison—no chance for freedom there, in that cell within a cell; and outside, too distant for her to work on them, the guards patrolled, six to a watch. Even if she could somehow thrall all the guards, the Sentinels could not be fooled. The second day passed and she was rabid with exhaustion and desperation. There must be a way; any way. Then a chance came unlooked for . . .

The Aachim had been ordered to treat her with the courtesy due to her station. One time Emmant, who had stayed in Shazmak after Karan's trial, came to see if she would lighten her imprisonment with books. She would not, but when that hulking, brooding, scarred figure entered it took her little time to see the torment that lay on him, and its source—his alienness, his obsession with Karan, and his rejection and humiliation by her and the Aachim.

She questioned Emmant about Karan, trying to identify that illusory quality about her that had bothered her so much at their only meeting. But the picture was one full of hate and bitterness—he made Karan detestable, treacherous.

Everywhere I go I find her deceptions and betrayals, she thought. She and Emmant deserve each other. For she saw clearly the weakness in Emmant; the violence and the dangerous, crazy cunning; the obsession. And she saw something that she could use, and pursued it, drawing out of him his weaknesses until he was driven into a frenzy of hate and despair.

And suddenly he said something that struck her like a bolt of fire.

"Karan is a cross, like me, but a lesser one, only a quarter. Why the Aachim . . ."

"No, *she* is a blending of . . ." she began, then realized suddenly that he could not possibly know what she suspected, that Karan had blood of the Faellem in her. She was almost afraid to listen. "What did you say?"

"Her grandmother was full-Aachim, a distant cousin to Tensor. Mantille was her name."

"Already a blending!"

Faelamor was so shocked that she could barely retain control of her face. This was much, much worse. Perhaps she was a *triune,* one with the blood of all the Three Worlds. No wonder Maigraith was drawn to her. An accident of history, unrecognized, uncontrolled; and so vile, so treacherous. Faelamor had been right to fear her. And Karan had the Mirror now, or at least had it not long ago. How had such a one come to be uncontrolled, this blending of a blending, this wild triune?

Fear struck deep into her heart—her own quest was also on a blade. What might this triune be capable of? What chain of events might she set off; perhaps had already begun? How might she divert the order that Faelamor had spent so long shaping? No room for sentiment here, or honor, the danger was too great to let her live. And what finer weapon than this wretch before her? He might be made to serve both purposes at once.

And yet she must confirm it, must go to Gothryme. There might be sisters, brothers just as deadly. More important than even the Mirror, this.

Faelamor had tried to tempt Emmant to give her her freedom, but not for himself would he betray the Aachim, or for her. Not for me, no, and why should he? But for *Karan*—if

I could give *her* to him, I believe he would do it. And it would serve my own purpose, for he is full of such lust and hatred that he would destroy her in the end. Once set upon the task nothing would divert him, neither hunger nor exhaustion nor fear of death.

And Emmant, sensing that she could give him what he most desired, came back again.

"The woman that you lust after," she said to him. "I will tell you how you can have her."

Emmant's eyes glittered but his face remained sour, the curving scars white through his beard. "She will never submit."

"I will show you the way."

He sat there unmoving, staring through the bars, his eyes never leaving her face, hating her more than anyone. "Tell me," he said at last.

"She has a talent of linking. It can be used to take control of her will. I see that you too have a small talent to sense the minds of others. That is not uncommon among the crosses of the Aachim," she said, making little effort to conceal her contempt. "I will show you how to make a link that she can never break. Then you may do with her as you wish. But of course if you truly love her . . ."

Emmant was impatient now. "And what must I do in return?" he said angrily. "I cannot free you. There are too many guards now, too many checks. I have already thought on it."

"You will leave Shazmak by the secret way. You will go to Bannador and there seek out the Whelm near Narne. Show them the secret way into Shazmak, and the disabling of the Sentinels. Tell them that Karan hid the Mirror here. That will bring them."

"The Whelm! I cannot do it."

"They are not your enemies," said Faelamor, closing her

mind. "What can a handful of Whelm do against the might of the Aachim, that has endured for millennia?"

"Then how will you free yourself?" he asked, not caring, hoping that they would smash her, smash everything, yet wondering.

"I have a power over them," she replied. "They cannot hold me." Not much is needed to convince you, my friend, she thought contemptuously. You are so rotten that any excuse will suffice, even if you betray your own. No wonder you Aachim gave up your world so easily. No Faellem would ever betray her world or her people.

"How can I make this link?" he asked, and Faelamor knew she had him.

"Do you have some thing of hers that I can use? Something that she has held close about her? Something perhaps that you have secreted away?"

His sour face brightened briefly and he went away without speaking, only nodding to the guards at the outer cell. When he returned he had in one thick hand a fine silver chain. A small jade amulet hung from it.

"This was hers?" asked Faelamor. "You are sure of it?"

"Yes. I took it from her room when she was in Shazmak last, only weeks ago. I tried it already but could not make it work. Perhaps she has an immunity to such charms."

She examined it. "There is a residuum here, a puerile, common thing," she said. "Little wonder."

He cringed, but said nothing. He could wait.

"Give it to me, then go. Return in the morning."

The next morning Emmant was there before dawn. Faelamor was already awake. She handed the chain back to him.

"When you find her, give this to her and bid her put it on. I laid a certain wile within it during the night. Follow the instructions that I give you. A link will be formed between her and you, and she will be unable to break it. She will bow to your will."

"And she will love me? I have your word?" A whine had crept into his voice.

"Would you trust *my* word? If so, I give it to you freely." Then, in a low voice, she told him exactly what he must do.

Still Emmant hesitated. "How will I find her?"

"Go to Narne and seek her friend, one called Maigraith. You are sensitive, I can tell." She linked to Emmant and showed him Maigraith, so that he could not mistake her. "She will lead you to Karan. If that fails, look for her in Thurkad. Already Yggur sweeps on Iagador and there is nowhere but Thurkad that can resist him. Do what you must, then keep the Mirror safe for me. I will come to Thurkad for it."

"I must give Maigraith a reason for seeking Karan, else she will be suspicious."

"Tell her that you bear a message from Tensor, a message of conciliation. She will know that Tensor was like a father to Karan once. She will believe that he could forgive her. And tell Maigraith that I am held in Shazmak, but not to come here, for I will free myself. Tell her that we must speak, and to seek me at Tolryme, in Bannador. Go now and go in disguise; Maigraith may have heard of you."

Ten days passed while Faelamor clung to the bars of her cell and waited, hoping that she had judged Maigraith right. She will come. Already she will be regretting what she said to me, and she will be guilty and confused. She needs me—she will always need me, and her duty will call her back. It must. But will she come?

In the early morning she was awakened by cries and battle, then all at once the Sentinels failed and she walked free of her cell. She took upon herself a disguise and watched, appalled by what she had done; sickened by the ferocity of the Whelm. Their power over the Aachim was manifest. Where had they come from, and so many?

Then a dreadful realization dawned. These were not Whelm, no longer Whelm. More than Whelm—Ghâshâd! *He* stirred; the Mirror was loose; a wild triune at large. *He* would know what to do with her.

32

THE TRIUMPH
OF THE WHELM

When he had wept until he could weep no more Llian rose, his heart an icy fist of rage, and submerged his grief in the searching of the campsite. He put his hand in the ashes but they were cold. They must have come soon after he had fled, Llian thought bitterly. Karan knew they were coming. Why did she demand that promise? Why did she drive him away? Why had he gone?

It was mid-morning now, two hours after Maigraith and Faelamor found the campsite, and as long again before Faelamor returned alone. Searching by the stream he found bootprints—heavy folk with long narrow feet—and nearby a smaller print, though larger than Karan's foot. There might have been five, or even more.

Karan's belongings made a pitiful bundle when he finished collecting them: the cooking pot still lay where he had washed it the previous night but her mug and plates were trodden on and bent. The food bag was undamaged though the contents were scattered on the ground. He picked the food up mechanically and put it back. Her boots were slashed apart, even the heels wrenched off in their frantic search, though her other clothing, with the exception of the heavy cloak, which was gone, had not been damaged. Hairbrush, socks, knife, all bloody; rope, the soapstone jar of ointment, the lightglass, all scattered or trodden into the mud. He found her little journal under the tent, covered in mud, somehow missed in the dark. The hatchet was half-buried in the ground. He picked up what was not ruined and put it into the food bag.

Could she be alive? He allowed himself a little hope. It might not be her blood. This attack seemed too vicious, too vindictive to be the Aachim. But then, what did he know of them? How would they treat an outcast, a betrayer? No, it had the mark of the Whelm, especially the nightmares.

And she knew they were coming, yet had not tried to get away. She had seemed resigned to it, as though they had done something to strip her will from her. If that was so, why had they not used that power before? She'd had just enough strength to send him away. Oh, Karan!

At the end of his search Llian saw something white behind a log at the edge of the clearing. It turned out to be half of the plaster cast, rudely hacked down its length during the search for the Mirror. He carried it out into the clearing and sat down with it on his knee.

A wave of desolation swept over him. Everything that made Karan what she was, gone to nothing. He traced the curves of her arm printed on the plaster. How slender her wrists, how small and delicate her hands. How he missed her. *How he loved her!* The realization was quite shocking. He had never felt this way before, not at all. Why had she been taken away from him? Where was justice?

There he sat, head bowed, the drizzle making little beads on his hair and trickling down his face. His thoughts turned at last to the Mirror. "I will not speak of it, tonight of all nights," she had said. Even at the time he'd wondered what she meant. Even then she had known. She would not give the Mirror away that easily. Where had she hidden it, so that even the Aachim could not find it?

Looking down, he realized that he still held the plaster cast on his knee. No, it could not have been that simple. They'd searched beneath the cast; they said so at the trial. And not inside it, either, for he'd watched Rael mix the plaster and spread it over her arm, over and around the splint. He weighed the cast in his hand, looked at it more closely. The cut edge was jagged. There were a few spots of blood on it. Her blood! Abruptly he flung the stained thing from him. It struck a rock and cracked, exposing the end of one of the hollow metal rods. That reminded Llian of the whole sorry business back in Shazmak. How he had searched Karan's room and been caught—embarrassing to think about, even now.

Llian bent down and picked up the piece of plaster. He broke the plaster off the rod, rubbing it on his trousers until the beautifully worked surface was clean. He found the other piece, half-hidden in the leaves and cleaned it off as well, working without even thinking about it. He idly tried to screw the two rods back together, but they wouldn't go. There was something inside this one. He eased it out with a twig—a tightly coiled scroll of dark metal. It unrolled by itself and hardened into a sheet of black metal the size of a leaf from a book, with a reflecting material like mercury set within the black frame. His face—dirty, unkempt, whiskery—stared back at him from the brilliant surface.

Llian gazed at the Mirror in astonishment. It had not occurred to him that it would be coiled up—why would it?

Rael and he had both known those rods were there, but did not even think of them, once the cast was made. And the Whelm had searched hastily, in darkness. Karan must have put it inside when he went to fetch Rael for the plaster.

How desperate he had been to see it. He didn't want it now—it didn't belong to him. Then he came suddenly to his senses. What was he doing, sitting here in the open with it in his hands? Anyone could be out there, watching and waiting.

Suppressing the urge to look over his shoulder he slid the Mirror into a deep inside pocket of his cloak and buttoned the flap down, reminding himself to sew it in later, so that it couldn't possibly be lost. It coiled tightly in the darkness. He tossed the plaster cast casually back on the ground.

If I were a passing vagabond or a treacherous friend I would take all this, he thought, checking Karan's remaining possessions. At least I look the part. He cut off the unstained portion of a blanket and made a bundle of the items, slinging the swag over his shoulder on a piece of rope.

It was late morning now. Which way had they gone? Searching downstream he found the imprint of a long boot. Further downhill, on the other side of the path, there were more footprints, heavy nailed boots, broad and long. Llian examined them closely. One set was particularly deep. The others were fainter: just the impress of a nail-studded heel here, the crescent edge of a sole there. Was that a splash of blood on the moss? He touched one of the rusty spots with a fingertip, sniffed it. Blood, but whose? Hope welled. They must keep her alive, since they hadn't found the Mirror.

Llian followed the stream down toward the Garr. Twice he saw other prints, smaller and lighter, that he wondered at, but no more blood. They were the marks left by Maigraith and Faelamor but a few hours earlier, though of course he did not know it. The drizzle turned to misty rain. Suddenly a horse whinnied right in front of him. Two horses, tethered on long ropes, and the ropes already tangled. Without even thinking, Llian cut them free and kept on.

The gentle valley grew steeper and more rocky, the rivulet deeper and faster and more overgrown. Vines scrambled through the tall trees; ferns grew profusely underfoot and hung from every branch. The air was thick with moisture. Around midday he stopped to gnaw a piece of dark bread, for once having thought of food he realized that he was famished. The rain began to fall heavily.

All day he searched. Before the sun set the forest was covered in a gray mist and there was no further trace of them. Down nearer the river the going was so tangled that he made less than a thousand paces in an hour, and knew that there was almost no hope of finding her. Should he wait for dawn? Their tracks would be lost anyway, with the rain. But they must be making for the river and a secret boat, else they would have taken the path.

He went on, picking his way along the edge of the stream until it grew dangerously steep. There he was forced to turn away into the forest. It was more open along the ridge line. He made good progress and soon emerged on a rind of steeply sloping cleared land. Beyond lay the river, below a rocky bank three or four spans high. Llian followed the clearing upstream. Five minutes' walk and he found the rivulet again as it cascaded into the Garr over a stepped waterfall, thrice his own height. The rain had cleared but in the dim starlight no tracks were visible. He sat down on a rock to think.

Why come this way unless there was a boat waiting? Were they gone already, or did they wait for the night? He curled up on the damp soil beneath a bush to wait.

*   *   *

Llian woke suddenly from a troubled sleep. The pale radiance of the Chain of the Tychid filtered through the foliage. He rolled out of his cloak and peered through the vines that screened his camp from the river bank. The starlight gleamed from every leaf and blade, almost bright enough to read by.

Llian stood up and made as if to step out of the forest when he was arrested by a hollow thump: the noise, he realized, that had wakened him. It was followed by a metallic tapping, as against stone; distant, as though it came from the river. Without thinking he slipped out of the forest and crept on his belly to the river bank. There he concealed himself in the bushes that grew along the edge and looked down.

A boat was tied up fore and aft, some fifty paces away. It was long and narrow, with a projection at the front. A shadowy figure, tall and bulky, stood there looking up. Another figure had just begun to scale the rocky upper bank. It reached the top and crouched on the edge, looking this way and that, then, apparently satisfied, slipped across the verge and into the forest. Had Llian not turned aside he would have walked right into them. He worked his way back to the forest and crept closer.

When he was only a few paces from where the figure had disappeared, he wormed his way inside a straggly bush with long, drooping leaves and a faint odor of camphor. There was not long to wait. A sudden crunch of twigs and five tall figures emerged, clad alike in hoods and cloaks of dark cloth, belted at the waist. One came, then two carrying a stretcher between them, then another two with a similar burden.

The first paused at the edge of the forest, looked around, then beckoned to the others. As they passed, starlight fell upon them through a gap in the trees. A wisp of long gray hair escaped from beneath the hood of the leader: Llian saw a woman of middle age with a strong sharp face and a long chin. The faces of the others were not clearly visible. Llian's eyes turned to the first stretcher. It bore a man, Whelm, of middle age, tall and heavily built. Long dark hair fell over the stained bandage around his forehead. His chest was bandaged as well, the bandage dark with blood. His eyes were closed and he was tied to the stretcher.

On the second stretcher, wrapped in her tattered cloak, feet bare, her hair tangled, eyes wide open, staring unblinkingly at the place where he stood, was Karan. She, too, was bound to the stretcher. Llian stood, shocked into immobility. Before his sluggish mind could formulate a plan to rescue her the first stretcher had disappeared over the edge of the river bank and the woman was shepherding the second down the steep slope close behind.

Llian wrenched out his knife and for a mad instant contemplated throwing himself after them, but the opportunity had passed before he was really aware of it and he crouched in his bushes in impotent fury as the last bearer disappeared from view.

Crouching low, Llian dashed across the open space to his previous vantage point. The two stretchers were laid side by side, the first gently, the second less so, in the front of the boat. Each of the five took up an oar while the woman untied the bow rope, then the stern, and sat down at the rudder. The vessel began to drift, eased away from the bank with an oar. Directly below Llian it passed, the starlight picking out the projection at the bow, a figurehead in the shape of a chacalot, a voracious water reptile, all teeth and serrated tail. He saw one last time Karan's staring eyes, then the oarsmen took to their oars, the boat shot out into the full strength of the current and soon was a speck disappearing into the night.

Later, much later, he roused himself. The Chain of the Tychid had sunk behind the forest and the sky was lit only by a bright planet climbing over the eastern horizon beyond Narne. The sky in that direction was streaked with veil-like banners and the rising orb alternately dimmed and shone out brightly as it crept from one gauzy strip to another. Now it was above and in the open, touching patches of foam on the river to an opaline translucency, now skipping little reflections off the ripples caught up by the breeze that had begun to blow from the south. He watched dreamily, the self-reproach that had plagued him washed away in the wind. A curious lassitude took Llian, an acceptance of what had happened. What else could he have done? If things were reversed, would she have done more? But there was no comfort in that thought.

They were Whelm, no doubt of it, though not the ones that had followed them from Tullin. How had they found Karan so quickly? Not by any potency of the Mirror, else they would have found it too.

The questions were unanswerable. Several things were certain though, he mused, ticking them off on his fingers. One: the Aachim were near. Two: the Whelm must hope to keep her capture a secret, at least until they could find where the Mirror was hidden. Three: he had left sign of himself back at the campsite. Soon the attention of both must turn to him. He shivered, trying to avoid the inescapable, but it was forced upon him—it was up to him now. He, alone, unarmed, unskilled, must free Karan and get her away. But how? He had no strength to resist them, and where was there to hide? Nowhere nearer than Thurkad, many days, perhaps weeks away, through lands he hardly knew.

Where had they taken her? Fiz Gorgo was also a journey of weeks. Surely for Yggur, revenge on the thief would come a poor second to getting the Mirror back, as quickly as possible. That meant an answer now. They would go no further than Narne.

Llian made his way back along the river bank in the darkness. At first it was easy going in the undulating, cleared land along the shoreline. Then he came on a series of steep gullies, bare and rocky at the top, covered with almost impenetrable wet forest at the bottom. After struggling down into two of these and back up again, and being confronted by a third, Llian realized that it was useless. The night was wearing away; he was tired beyond belief. The way was too dark, too steep and too slippery, and he recalled that this gullied country extended downstream almost to the ferry, for he had looked down on it the previous morning from the high ridge.

While he was walking a thick overcast had blown down from the south and now light rain began falling again. He suddenly lost the will to go further. He huddled in his cloak against the steep edge of the gully, cold, wet and miserable, dozing fitfully until the dawn.

On waking, Llian found himself in a thicket halfway up a ridge. Earlier it had been raining heavily but the rain ceased with the dawn, replaced by a cold mist that crept imperceptibly out of the river. He ate a miserable breakfast standing up, then set out up the ridge. The crest was steep and slippery but the going was easier than in the thick forest, and he realized that he had but to continue along the ridge and he must come on the path to the ferry.

The sun rose at last but the fog only thickened. Llian trudged on up the slope, the mist condensing in small beads on his hair and eyebrows and trickling down his face. The damp had seeped into his bones: however vigorously he stamped his feet and waved his arms it did not warm him. Hours later he came to a narrow path and stood there, hesitating, unable to tell if it was the way to Narne or not.

He walked slowly on. In the fog the path was hard to follow and he strayed continually, one time walking for half an hour on a track that petered out against a moss-covered outcrop. Back he trudged. Now his imagination began to trouble him. Each group of bushes that loomed out of the fog became a squad of the enemy. Llian turned and a dark figure stood silently beside him. He sprang out of reach, but it was only a small tree with one branch thrust out over the path.

The fog grew thicker, so that he could see only one or two paces, and now he realized that he had wandered off the path and had no idea where it was. A fragment of the *Lay of Larne* came into his mind, the ballad that told of treachery, the slaughter of the innocents, and the princess heir carried into exile across the sea. It was on a day such as this, with fog in the forest, that the massacre had occurred. The back of his neck crawled.

Llian began to hear noises: rustling and tapping sounds like the wind in the branches—only there was no wind. A sound like footsteps came from behind. He whirled, eyes straining to pierce the fog. There was nothing to be seen, but still the noise continued for a few seconds before dying away. Then a groan, a deep, creaking groan such as an ancient tree might make when twisted by a high wind. Was it only his imagination, or were they trying to make him reveal himself?

He forced himself to calmness, seeking around for a place to hide, to think. It began to rain again and the leaf mold gave off a rich earthy smell. Before him was a large old tree, long dead and broken off halfway up. At the base it was cracked and hollow, the opening screened by a straggling bush. He crawled inside gratefully, onto a mound of decaying wood. The space was cramped and home to many crawling things, but it was dry.

He ate some bread and tried to work out a plan. Impossible to find his way in this fog. Anyway, they would be hunting him by now. How hard it all was without Karan; she always seemed to know what to do. He was too tired to decide, even to think, and in the end, after dozing, waking, dozing again, and the fog as thick as ever, the daylight began to fade.

Only then did he think of the Mirror. So long had he dreamed about it, puzzled over it, longed to look at it and touch it. Now all day it had lain neglected in his pocket. He took it out, staring at it in the gloom, tracing the silvery glyphs around the border with his fingers. The symbol in the top right corner was like three spheres grown together, surrounded by red crescent moons. Was there some meaning in that? Such a fine thing, so perfectly made. Did it hold the answer to his questions? If only he could make it speak.

He touched the symbol in various ways, but nothing happened. Many ways of unlocking were recorded in the Histories, and he spoke all that he could remember, but the Mirror showed only his face.

That night the fog disappeared with a shift in the wind, and as soon as it began to grow light, the fifth day since their escape from the tunnels, Llian made his way to the ferry landing. There he collected his pack, concealed himself in the trees and waited.

As the sun rose from a sea of mist the ferry emerged silently from the gloom, disgorging a crowd: farm laborers, travelers, a pedlar and others whose purpose seemed innocent enough. The laborers shouldered their tools and headed up the path at once. The others waited on the jetty while an assortment of boxes, bags, trunks and other packages was unloaded. Then the group that had been waiting silently to board the ferry pushed forward, only to be beaten back by the crewman who stood astride the single gangplank. Eventually order was established and the passengers began to file in.

It was at this point that Llian noticed a tall, lean, sharp-faced fellow standing beside the ferry, watching. Finally the embarkation was complete, the plank was drawn on board and the ferry slipped away. The watcher stood on the wharf until the vessel disappeared into the mist that still hung about the middle of the river, then walked slowly back to the shore and stood looking around idly.

Llian retreated into his cover. Several hours went by. Every so often the watcher walked a little way along the path, first upstream, then downstream, then came back and resumed his station. After the last such walk he returned hurriedly, slipping into the trees on the downstream side of the path. The next ferry was coming.

The sentry made his way past. Llian reached down and picked up a knobbly stick. A mutter came from the road. Several clots of people were making their way down the path.

Taking advantage of the moment, Llian picked up a thin dry stick and snapped it with a crack. The man turned sharply, looked around, then back to the people moving down the path. Llian flicked the broken stick so that it landed a few paces to his left with a soft rustle—the oldest trick in the world, but his quarry was taken in. He crept toward the sound, dagger in hand. Llian could hear his breathing. From his features he could have been one of the stretcher-bearers of the previous night.

He parted the bushes to one side of Llian with his knife. Llian gripped his stick, hesitated, then the sentry reached out to the bush that separated them. Suddenly there came a shout from the wharf and running feet. The ferry had arrived. The sentry slipped his knife back into its sheath and turned away.

Now! thought Llian. He slid out between the bush and the tree and dealt the sentry a clumsy blow to the side of the head. The man fell to his hands and knees, tried to get up, then Llian leapt on his back and knocked him down. He tied him up with strips cut from the sentry's shirt, gagged him with a piece of his shirt, threw his weapons and money in the river and raced up the plank just as the ferry was leaving. He paid the fare with coppers and sat down inside, head down and hood low over his face.

The journey of half a league across the great river took the best part of an hour as the ferry slowly ground its way along the cable. On the other side Llian made his way unhurriedly along the wharf in the midst of a crowd of travelers and so out into the streets of Narne.

Narne was the largest town in the area, and a trading port of some importance. It was a place of perhaps ten thousand people, but had been greater in the past, and now many of the buildings were empty and ruinous. The waterfront was covered in wharves, boat yards and warehouses. In the middle of the town was an oval-shaped park, with large old trees and a moss-covered stone temple in the center. Surrounding the park the old public buildings were of stone, but away from the center the plan failed and Narne quickly degenerated into a tangle of narrow, unpaved streets crammed with tall wooden apartment buildings, terraced houses and ruins.

Llian made his way to a grimy part of town near the river and there found an inn. He paid extra for a room all to himself, extra for hot water, and lay in the bath until the mud of the past days was washed away. Then he barricaded the door and slept until dark.

That evening he spent in the taverns of Narne, cautiously listening to the conversations of drinkers, occasionally asking an oblique question, but he gleaned nothing. It was clear that he was not the only one asking questions in Narne, though; people spoke of prying strangers that could only have been Aachim, and Llian realized how conspicuous he was, with his shaggy brown hair, among these close-cropped, black-haired people. When shortly the looks of the townsfolk became unfriendly he walked out into the night and strolled down toward the waterfront. He was not made to be a spy; he would have to find another way.

At the river Llian turned right and walked slowly downstream. Beside the ferry landing was a series of wharves, built out into the river on timber piles that were tarry, rotting and encrusted with weed and small black mussels. The warehouses, like most buildings in Narne, were long rectangular structures built of unpainted planks. Most were raised above flood level on poles. The roofs were shingled. The waterfront was quiet, except at the second warehouse, where through the open doorway a group of laborers was manhandling a bale from a tall stack onto a trolley.

He stood outside for a while, watching the operation. The bale was large and heavy, and at the crucial moment one of the laborers slipped. He lost his grip, the bale plummeted to the ground and burst open like a fan, sending raw wool across the floor and scattering the workers. An overseer snatched his lamp out of the way, cursing the offender roundly. Llian moved hastily away from the doorway, as though he might be blamed for the incident.

Beyond the last of the warehouses was a straggle of dingy cottages, also made of planks, several with small boats drawn up on the bank beside them. He examined each carefully then walked back the other way. At the wool warehouse the mess had been cleaned away and the workers were busy with another bale. Past the ferry jetty the warehouses extended just as far in the other direction. Llian came to a set of slipways, on the farthest of which a man was hauling up a boat, similar in design to the one Llian had seen the previous night, with a winch. Many other boats were tethered fore and aft to piles driven into the river.

He walked the length of the boat-mooring area, then back again slowly, examining each boat. He did not see the vessel he was looking for. He turned upstream once more and there it was, near the end of the row, partly covered in a canvas sheet: the figurehead of a chacalot. Llian stared at the boat, sure that it was the one, wondering what to do now that he had found it.

Abruptly a voice from behind him growled, "What're you doing, sneaking round my boat, eh?"

Llian turned. The speaker was a plump man who spoke with a nasal accent. His face was in darkness. Llian had his story ready.

"My name is Garntor," he said boldly, using the family name of his grandmother. "I'm looking for a friend, a young woman with red hair. I saw her in your boat, one night past. Do you know where she is?" Then he said softly, "I'll pay well if you can help me."

The man took a step backwards. The light from a street lamp fell on his unshaven face. He appeared taken aback.

"Don't know what you're talking about," he muttered. The accent made everything he said into a whine. "Boat's been here this last week. No work for me, that's what. Kids're starving, eh!"

You certainly aren't, you fat pig, Llian thought. "Look," he said, "I don't want any trouble. I just want to find my friend. I'll pay well," he repeated, jingling the coins in his pocket.

Fear and avarice fought each other on the man's face. Avarice won. "Hardly paid nothing," he whined. "Promised a lot, but paid nothing. Few coppers, that's all, and took me boat for two nights. And expect me to say nothing, eh!"

Llian found the man's habit of ending his sentences with a nasal "eh!" irritating, but he merely smiled and jingled the coins in his pocket again. The man licked his lips.

"I'll give you a silver tar if you will tell me who hired your boat, and where I can find them," said Llian.

The man's eyes gleamed in the lamplight; he licked his lips again and said, "Not enough. They'll come for me. Have to go away, won't I? Five silver tars, that's what it'll take, no less."

Llian frowned, then turned away, making a play of counting the money in his pocket. He turned back.

"Three silver tars and two coppers, that's all I have."

The other held out his hand, but Llian took a step backwards. "First the story."

But he took Llian's shoulder and hissed, "Not out here. Come behind the boat." Llian removed the grubby hand but did not budge.

"There's no one coming. Tell me here."

The man grew agitated. "Not here. Keep your tars!" he said, and turned away.

"All right," said Llian, and reluctantly allowed himself to be drawn behind the boat. The darkness was intense.

"Seven there were," the man began. "Two women and five men. The tall woman was the leader, eh! 'I want your boat,' she said. 'One night, maybe two. I pay good money. No one must know. You must not come near.'"

"When was this?" asked Llian.

"Rode in, in a great hurry, three nights ago. All seven went in the boat. Back before dawn, just her and two others. Upriver they'd been. Night before last they go again, eight o'clock. Hard pull for two, eh! Back after midnight: three in the morning maybe. Six of them, the other on a stretcher. And a girl with red hair. Dead, she looked. Can't hide from old Pender. Too late; in with the worms by now she'll be, eh! Pity."

He held out his hand. "There, that's worth three tars."

"Where did they take her," Llian demanded coldly, ignoring the hand.

"Don't know," mumbled Pender.

"Of course you do," said Llian, following his intuition. "You followed them. They were easy to follow, for one as clever as you, and they took the girl somewhere nearby, did they not?"

"Not nearby," Pender said, then stopped, flustered. "Well, course I followed them. Had to know what they did," he continued, with ill humor. "Took her to a big house in the old town, three from the end of Mill Street. Has a spire at the front, falling down. That's all I know. Give me my money," he said surlily.

Llian counted three silver tars and two coppers into the hand. Pender slipped the money into a rear pocket and waddled off. Llian stood looking after him, unsure that he had done the right thing. He pulled out his knife. "Pender!" he called. Pender came back reluctantly.

"I trust that I can rely on your silence," he said, holding the knife up so that it caught the light. Pender stopped dead. Llian stepped forward and grasped him by the shirt. He squirmed; stitching popped. "You've already betrayed them. Give me a reason why you won't me."

Pender's eyes bulged. "Choking me, master," he gurgled. "I know I look bad, but I give service when paid. The woman, she promised, but she still hasn't paid. I owe her nothing."

Llian looked at Pender, wondering. "I think I can trust you," he said. "Prove it and you shall have another five tars. Betray me and I will surely kill you and throw your woman and children into the river."

The man became so abject that Llian almost began to regret his threats. "Master, master," he wept. "Trust me. Keep your tars, only leave us be. Narne is a cruel place for foreigners. Trust me, eh! You paid well. I won't betray you."

"Very well," said Llian. "See that you don't. Be off now."

Pender disappeared into the darkness. Llian stood there for a moment, then followed. A door crashed nearby. He crept across a yard, bare save for an aged tree and a straggle of flowers beside the step. The yellow light of an oil lamp shone out through a window of little panes. Within, Llian saw a room shabbily furnished and the fat man sitting on the bed with his head hanging, while two children clung to a small woman with dark hair. He turned away, guiltily, thinking: What should I have done? Pender didn't look as though he could be trusted. Still, if he were to meet me in daylight I doubt that he'd be so frightened.

33

MAIGRAITH'S STORY

Maigraith watched Faelamor until she disappeared in the forest, then she continued down the stream. It was mid-morning; they had been searching for more than two hours, but without success. Now it began to rain; only a misting rain at first, but enough to hinder her. It was ages since the last footmarks, and they had been far upstream. Perhaps they hadn't followed the stream any further—they might have gone in any direction. How tired she was. Though her escape from Fiz Gorgo was over a month ago, she had still not fully recovered. How could she have, always hurrying, never enough sleep, afraid of what lay behind her and what might be ahead?

She leaned against a tree, its rough bark pressing into her shoulder, while she tried to think. They were probably going to Narne, but might have taken any way, and how could she find them except by chance? They were strong—they might even go openly. Better to go straight there and watch the waterfront.

Maigraith turned away from the stream and headed through the forest toward the ferry wharf. Had she delayed she would have encountered Llian as he followed the stream down toward the Garr, and the whole future of the Three Worlds might have been different, but by a bare half hour they did not meet. She was reproaching herself for rejecting Faelamor. The confrontation, so long in the making, had at first elated Maigraith, but that had passed leaving a bitter residue of duty neglected. No, wilfully cast aside, and with nothing to replace it.

Maigraith suddenly remembered the horses. She headed back to where they had been left, but the ropes had been cut and the mounts were gone. She turned around again and fought her way through the forest between the river and the path. That was a long weary trip in the rain, and it was nearly dark by the time she reached the wharf, but for once her fortune held: the ferry was still standing alongside the jetty.

When she came closer she saw the reason for the delay. One of the thick iron wheels by which the ferry tracked its cable was broken, the rim sheared completely away. This was clearly not an infrequent occurrence, for the deckhands had already unbolted it and were replacing it with another from their store. Now they struggled with levers and bars against the tension of the cable to force it over the rim of the new wheel. Many times they nearly had it, the cable balancing on the highest point of the rim, working awkwardly above their heads in the semi-darkness, rain sizzling on the hot lamps, then a lever would slip through cold fingers, the cable fly back and the workers scatter, tools clattering to the deck.

At last they forced it home, the trampers took up their positions at the spokes of the huge windlass and the ferry moved out into the flow.

The new wheel was evidently somewhat out of round, for the cable kept snagging then springing free with a thrunngg, the ferry slowing right down then starting again with a tooth-cracking jerk. As they got out into the full force of the current the upstream gunwale was forced down until it was within a hand's breadth of the water, and just a blow from a floating log would have swamped them. Maigraith looked up at the device that held them, and though she had traveled on the ferry before, she marveled that the mechanism did not suddenly snap and fling them all beneath the water to their deaths.

The windlass creaked, the cable ground through the pulleys; the dark water hurled itself past the boat, then at last the roar of the current grew less and the main jetty of Narne appeared, the street lamps shining on the wet decking. Maigraith crept off gratefully and into the town.

After some little searching she found an unobstructed vantage point, an open space at the top of a derelict warehouse where she could watch both the ferry jetty and most of the waterfront, though the street lamps gave barely enough light to see by. But though she watched all night, almost fainting from weariness, she saw nothing, for the Whelm had left Pender's boat concealed almost half a league upstream of Narne, out of sight even in the daylight.

All the next day Maigraith watched but at last she could watch no more, for she had barely slept for three nights now. She closed her eyes and dozed where she sat, and did not wake until the following day. Then she rushed down, sure that she had missed them in the night, and stood at the wharf watching the passengers get off each ferry, and questioned all the hands on the waterfront, but none could tell her what she sought. She began to doubt that Karan had ever come to Narne, and though the Whelm had clearly been there she could find no one to speak of them.

Another day she remained but learned no more, and suddenly fearing that Karan was far away she crossed back over the Garr on the ferry and went by the western path as far as Gilte, a day's walk downstream, questioning everyone that she met, but not until she was returning did she find any news, and that only a puzzling scrap.

As she trudged back toward the ferry, footsore and weary of heart, she came upon a group of rustics hoeing weeds in a field near the path. She leaned over the low hedge and called one to her, a scrawny old man. His leathery arms and legs were bare and his hands coarse and cracked, the joints swollen and twisted. He peered at her from beneath his broad hat of woven reeds, and his eyes were moist but keen.

"I'm looking for a young woman," said Maigraith, for what seemed the hundredth time. "She has curly red hair and green eyes, and she's about this tall."

"Can't say I've seen her, miz," said the old man, leaning on his hoe. He looked carefully into her face, then added, "Though you're not the first to ask."

At last, thought Maigraith. "Who else asked you?"

"Well, no one asked *me*, like. But a young fellow spoke to Creeny over there."

The old man had a curious way of talking. After each sentence he paused, in a reflecting kind of way, before going on slowly, speaking clearly as though he cherished each word.

"Didn't do him any good, of course. Creeny's mad as a pot, and simple as well."

Maigraith's gaze followed his gesture. The tall, loose-limbed figure was hoeing in a desultory way.

"Good way to be, I suppose, with what's about to come down on us. But I was walking with him, and I heard it all. Curious, it was. We was coming over on the ferry, and he running down the hill, like to break his neck. Ferry was away again by the time he got there, though he shouted foolishly at it. They never go back. Then he came and asked Creeny. We hadn't seen her though. Let's see now." He pondered for a moment. "That would be six days ago, and in the early morning, for we was off the first ferry."

Maigraith calculated. If the rustic was right, that was the very morning that Faelamor and she had reached Karan's campsite; almost the same time, in fact. The old man carried on, answering her next question before she had time to ask it.

"A youngish man, he was. About your height or a little taller. Straight brown hair, worn long. Unusual round here. Brown eyes too. Hadn't shaved in a while. Very anxious. Curious voice; trained in the Lore, I'd say." Then, noticing Maigraith's stare, "I traveled, you know, before I came to this. I've heard the Histories told."

He stood there for a while longer, reflecting, then slowly resumed his hoeing.

Maigraith gave him a wave of thanks but he did not look up, and she walked back up the road toward the ferry wharf. Who was he, who sought Karan so desperately? *I saw him myself*, she realized slowly. *Twice I saw him in Narne. It was the second morning after I came. He got off the ferry in the morning. I noticed him especially, for the people of Narne, of this whole region for that matter, mostly have black hair and they wear it close-shorn. Then I saw him again that night. He was walking along the waterfront, and back again. But that was not remarkable. Did he find her?*

She hurried back to Narne but the trail was cold, and though she spent several days there she learned nothing. The next morning she caught the ferry again, turned along the northward path and, sometime after midday, reached the clearing where Karan had camped, many days ago now.

The site was deserted, trampled, and it was clear that people had fought and died there, for the ground was littered with arrows and there were broken weapons rusting among the leaves. On the western side of the clearing five mounds lay together, and they had been fashioned with neatness and care. Back in the forest a little way she came on two others: the stench led her to them. Mere heaps of earth they were, and the body in one was already exposed. She walked over to look at it, but she could not get near: the smell was so overpowering that she was almost sick. The corpse was partly eaten by the scavengers that slunk only a little way off as she came closer, though enough remained for it to be identifiable as Whelm.

Maigraith turned away and hurried back to the campsite. There was little to be seen there. All of Karan's things were gone, save for the few that were broken and useless—a scrap of bloody blanket, shreds of the tent. Even the ruined boots had been taken. The clearing had a cold and mournful air and the trees all around seemed to have drawn back, as if in horror at what had been done there.

The Mirror brought them all here, she thought. Even after Karan was gone they were still here, fighting over it; dying uselessly. Whose were these other graves, so carefully made beside the forest; so unlike the shallow, careless mounds of the Whelm? But the thought of digging one up with her hands was beyond her.

Another place caught her attention, the grass trampled into mud by many feet, and walking across she saw something white lying among the leaves. Pieces of plaster from a cast. They were soft, slowly dissolving and crumbling in the rain. Nearby lay two hollow metal rods.

She picked up one rod, touching the delicately engraved metal. A shivery tingle ran up her arm, and a momentary vision of another embossed cylinder came to her, of her pulling the Mirror from it in Yggur's library at Fiz Gorgo. The Mirror had been here, not long ago. The cylinder was just a piece of metal, but a work of art nonetheless, and she slid it into a pouch in her cloak. The other tube seemed a dull, lifeless thing and she left it where it had been.

She went over to where Karan's shelter had been and sat down on a log that still lay where she had pulled it up to sit before the fire. There Maigraith stayed for the rest of the afternoon, possessed by a sweet, lethargic melancholy. All her works and strivings had turned to nothing. She had failed Faelamor. The Whelm had Karan; she was lost beyond recovery. And now the Mirror was gone as well, despite all that Karan had done to prevent it. Most likely the Whelm had tortured its hiding place from her. And where was Faelamor?

Maigraith had never loved Faelamor, but still she longed for her approval, for she had no other. Her duty was to serve, but she had cast Faelamor off and now there was nothing. She had gone away from Yggur too; another part of her life ended before it had ever begun.

As the light faded a gentle rain began to fall, and then a wind sprang up, driving the rain across the clearing at her and clashing the branches of the trees together. And it was raining in her heart, the rain even colder there and more lonely, and eventually it washed her spirit away and left her barren.

It was dark now. The dark came up quickly with the rain, and though she was empty inside the cold still struck at her. Mechanically she got up and took from her pack the fine, strong oiled cloth that Faelamor had bought for her in Preddle. She unfolded it; staked and tied it to make a tiny shelter. She took herself inside and hunched there, staring out into the darkness and the rain. She took something from her food bag and ate it, not noticing what it was, and not caring.

The night passed slowly and eventually her weariness dulled her misery, her self-disgust, even her guilt, and she slipped into sleep, though it was scarcely more restful than waking. For the whole night she watched powerless as her companions were pursued by phantoms, the corpses of the Whelm, with faces and limbs eaten away, and everything she did led only to greater torment.

At last the morning came, and with it a calming, gentle sleep. Maigraith lay basking in the morning sun, warm and at peace, and in her dream a cool hand stroking her brow. She was relaxed as she had not been for months, empty, concerned about nothing, all her troubles receded. She woke smiling and the sun was warm on her face, slanting into the shelter.

She yawned, stretched, opened her eyes, and looked up— straight into the deranged black eyes of Emmant! She twisted around and leapt to her feet, the shelter falling in a heap behind her.

"Who are you? What do you want with me?" she demanded, her hand upraised.

Emmant stepped back a pace, holding out open palms. The light faded from his eyes and he looked now like any other man, save that his skin was sagging and blotchy, the deep creases around his mouth hinting at the progress of his corruption. But there was nothing of that in his carefully schooled deep voice. "I did not mean to startle you," he said politely. "My name is Flacq. I seek one called Maigraith. You are like the one I seek."

"I am Maigraith," she said. "What is the message?"

"I bear secret word from Faelamor. She is taken by the Aachim and held in Shazmak. She will free herself and asks you to meet her at Tolryme, in Bannador."

Faelamor held? "Is there more?"

"Not from Faelamor." He appeared to hesitate. "But there is another thing."

"What is that?"

"I believe you are the friend of Karan of Bannador. Tensor seeks her."

"For what purpose?"

"Ah! You would not know. Karan came to Shazmak, and she and Tensor fought over the Mirror most bitterly; but she took it with her. Now Tensor wishes to make amends. They were very close."

"That I know. She has often spoken of him. But I cannot help you. It is nine days since Faelamor and I came here; even then the Whelm had her. The Mirror is lost as well. I have sought her in Narne and on both sides of the river but she is gone without trace."

Emmant turned away. "I will go to Narne; I will find her. If you see her, tell her to head for Thurkad; war is coming and nowhere else is safe now." He disappeared into the forest.

Maigraith watched him go, then she got up mechanically and lit the fire and made a brew of tea. With the bowl warm in her hands she sat down on the log and tried to decide what to do. She wanted to find Karan, but she knew not where to look. Her own feelings called her south, but even if Yggur wanted her, not even beside him would she face the Whelm again. So, her choice was really no choice, and it all came back to duty. Her little rebellion had failed; she had no worth save how Faelamor measured it.

A good while had passed by the time Maigraith reached Tolryme, a small town in northern Bannador near Gothryme manor. She feared that Faelamor would be gone, but she was not, and Maigraith found her as soon as she entered the market square. She was sitting at a table beneath a spreading fig on the sunny side of the square, a bowl of fruit in front of her.

"You have come then," she said as Maigraith approached. "I hoped you would. Do you have it?"

Maigraith confessed her failure. To her surprise Faelamor showed no anger, no expression at all.

"I've puzzled long about Karan since you told me of her talents. Where did they come from, such talents? I was struck by a remembrance, so I searched the archives of Fyrn here. My guess was right. Long ago, a male of the Faellem did dwell here briefly. A secret union with a girl of the Fyrn family produced a girl child. The matter was a shameful one, and concealed, though it was recorded. The deed was many generations back but the name, Melluselde, has been carried down, as they do in these parts, through daughter or son, whichever is the fitter. The blending brings the talent. But it was what I learned in Shazmak that terrified me."

She stopped then, glaring ferociously at Maigraith.

Maigraith was nonplussed. "Yes," she said at last, her cheeks pink, "she has Aachim blood, from her grandmother. I did not tell you before because of your bitterness to her. What of it?"

Faelamor controlled herself with an effort. "That makes her triune," she said, her lips a white line. "Descended from three human species, Three Worlds. When first I met her I saw a threat to me; now I know why." And she mused on the irony—that she had taken such pains to create such a one, then out of the grass should spring another, fully formed but wild, unbroken, and treacherous. Perhaps it was the balance trying to restore itself. This new one had subtlety but no power. Hers was the better.

"I have come back to you," Maigraith said, "but do not press me too far. If Karan hinders your plans you must find a way round her. Harm Karan and you will never see me again."

"*I will* not harm her," Faelamor replied, turning away to

her pack. She sat up with a pair of glasses in her hand. "Wear these! They will disguise the color of your eyes." Maigraith put them on. "Now, about the Mirror."

"I found how she carried it," and Maigraith showed the metal tube.

"Then where is it now?" cried Faelamor. "That cast was not in the clearing when first we went to the campsite. But when I returned, four hours later, it lay broken. Someone came, neither Aachim nor Whelm, and took the Mirror away. Ah! The one you mentioned. I heard of him in Shazmak. Her companion, Llian. He must have it. And he is Zain! This is a sorry mess. What will he do with it?

"He will go to Thurkad," she said thoughtfully after a while. "There's nowhere else to go. We must go there too. A critical moment in time draws near, and I am afraid and unready. Come, I must recast my plans yet again."

34

FIRE IN THE NIGHT

The old part of Narne lay on a flat section of the ridge overlooking the river. It was surrounded by a stone wall, broken in many places, and was old in name only, for most of the original stone buildings had long been torn down. In their place stood a curious mixture of squalid shacks, terraces and ornate but decaying mansions.

Mill Street ran from the market square back toward the river, ending in a blank wall behind a wool warehouse. All the houses in the street were built of roughly sawn boards and were quite irregular; rooms, verandas and patios jutted from each building in every possible arrangement, and seemingly in total indifference to the principles of construction. Most were raised on piles because of the floods.

The house that Pender had mentioned was near the wall, an area where the dwellings were mostly derelict and the streets empty. It was large and rambling, distinguished from its neighbors by a tall conical turret at the front, like a witch's hat, only leaning somewhat and with the shingles coming off. Even in the darkness the house had a forlorn, decayed appearance, with its sagging roofline and roughly boarded windows.

Llian strolled up the street, stopping two doors away in deep shadow. There was no sign of anyone at the house, although light showed through cracks in the boards. Once a youth walked unsteadily up the street, a wineskin dangling from one hand. Sometime later, in a house behind him, there was screaming and the sound of glass breaking, then silence. The night was cool.

Llian flexed his fingers and wriggled his toes. As he did so he saw a movement at the front of the house. Someone stood guard there in the darkness. The figure was outlined against the lighted interior for a moment, then disappeared, leaving only a thin line of light from the partly open door.

Bending low, Llian crept the distance to the house, slid down the side passage and ducked under the veranda. The house was a warren underneath, the front part raised on piles about half a span, the older rear part lower and set on foundations of crumbling brick or stone. The ground was littered with the forgotten things of other years: broken pots, rotten bags spilling sand, decaying timber, rusting iron.

Llian spent the tedious hours of the night exploring the underneath of the house, exquisitely cautious lest he send an ancient hoard crashing down in the absolute darkness and stillness. Sometimes he just lay there, ear pressed to the floorboards to catch whatever sounds were made above. There were few: the sentry at the front occasionally paced back and forth or went inside the house; doors were closed and opened; footsteps; low voices. Nothing to indicate that the occupants were Whelm or that Karan was inside. Finally he made himself as comfortable as possible in his cramped position and slept for what remained of the night.

He was awakened in the morning by the sound of feet running across the front veranda and a pounding at the front door. The door was opened and the ensuing conversation, in its low, urgent tones, came clearly through the floorboards.

"I was attacked from behind. Two at least, maybe three. They bound me," the man gasped out.

"Compose yourself, Tarlag," came a chill woman's voice. "Do not draw attention to yourself or this house. Tell what happened."

"I was standing guard. At the ferry landing. As you ordered. The late-morning ferry was coming. I heard a noise in the trees nearby. I went to investigate. They hit me from behind, tied me and left me there. I got free only last night. There was no ferry until this morning."

"How many were there? What do you know of them?"

"Nothing. They left no trace that I could see in the dark."

"Could it have been her companion, L-lian," she hesitated over the name, "that Idlis spoke of? The one who met her near Tullin and helped her to escape?"

Tarlag was scornful. "How could that be? All reports say that he is a fool and a coward. No, it must have been those skretza," he pronounced the word in a vulgar way, "those Aachim. We should destroy them, Vartila."

Beneath the house Llian smiled grimly, pleased to be underestimated. His actions would prove his worth.

"Perhaps you are right, Tarlag. The guard must be doubled, we are close to breaking her. Soon we will have it. We must: the need is great. Go now."

Llian heard a heavy set of footsteps going toward the rear of the house. When they died away Vartila said softly, "Watch him, Gend. Tarlag is careless, and there is a wrongness in his story. Pay off the boatman, and watch him too. I do not wish for more killing, but do it if there is no other way. Now, what news of the rest of our band?"

"They went up the river, following the Aachim." Gend's voice whirred like a flat stick swung though the air. "Would you really break her mind, Vartila?"

"Of course not. Such a talent we might never find again. I would keep her whole as long as possible. But she can suffer: that will keep the talent focused."

Footsteps went in two directions. Distantly came the sound of Vartila issuing orders, though Llian could not make out the words. But at least he knew that Karan was here.

The morning light seeped under the house; he resumed his vigil. Finally it was rewarded. In a room at the rear he found her. Vartila was talking in her rasping voice about Maigraith. She spoke of torture and cruelty such that Llian could not bear to hear, and of what they would do to her next, but Karan only sneered.

"I know you lie," she said. "Maigraith is free; even now she searches for me."

Silence, then the voice again.

"One last time I will ask you, what have you done with the *pash-lar,* the Mirror? I have no wish to destroy your mind, but I must have the Mirror." Her voice took on what she imagined to be a cajoling tone. "It is no dishonor to tell me now, for I will have it anyway."

A shred of a voice, Karan's voice still, replied haltingly: "You can break my mind but you won't get it, for it's gone beyond your reach. Llian has taken it down the river. He will be in Sith in two days, and the Mirror will be in safe hands. Go back to your master and tell him that."

Vartila laughed, like grit rubbing between metal plates. "You are lying, Karan of Bannador. The Great Betrayer, the Aachim call you. What is left of them. This Llian of yours attacked one of my men at the ferry yesterday. Already he is in Narne, seeking you."

It was Karan's turn to laugh, a lifeless, squeaking, horrible sound. "It was to Rulke that they gave the name: the Great Betrayer—even you bog swimmers should know that. By comparison I am the merest pinprick. As for Llian, he has not the strength, nor the courage. He ran away from you that night. He would not come here; he has no love for me. It was the Mirror he came for. Mendark sent him, even you must know that." There was the hiss of a sharply taken breath. "Yes, Mendark! The Magister will know what to do with the Mirror. But it is Tensor you must worry about now. He is in Narne too, and he never forgets."

"Enough," cried Vartila, her voice rising. "Do not play your games with me. Tell me where the Mirror is hid."

Karan must have spat at her. Vartila's reply was a meaty thump. Karan gave a short cry. Llian, beneath the floor-boards, ground his fists against his forehead.

Twice more that day Vartila came to Karan's room; twice the wisp of a voice defied her; twice she went away again. It was late afternoon now and the house was quiet. Again Llian explored the underside, until from the layout of the foundations and the sounds from above he knew where every room and corridor lay. The beginnings of a plan came to him. From the voices it appeared that there were at least six people in the house: Vartila, Tarlag, Gend, and three others who took watches at front or rear. The guard was rotated every two hours, changed every six. He would wait until after the midnight change—no, until two in the morning—the guards would be tired then, and the others, with luck, asleep.

The day faded. When it was fully dark Llian crept out and made his way down the street. The chimneys on both sides of the house were smoking. He bought food, a skin of nut oil used for cooking, a large sack and clothes and boots for Karan. The boots were the hardest to find; he wanted them to be as comfortable and as strong as the ones she'd lost.

In his previous wanderings he had passed a sawmill. He filled his sack with sawdust from a pile near the waterwheel, and staggered back up the street with the bag on his back. Being but one of many human beasts of burden, he excited no attention. In the dark he thrust the bag of clothes under an overgrown hedge and regained his refuge beneath the house.

At last it was midnight. There was a murmur of conversation from the front of the house, then the door closed with a soft click. The cane chair on the front veranda squeaked. There was no sound from the rear. Under the house the darkness was absolute. Llian dragged his sack to a place where the floorboards were cracked and gappy, and scooped out the sawdust until there was a pile knee-high and an arm's length across on the ground. He made a depression in the center of the pile and poured the contents of the skin into it. Then he waited.

At two in the morning the guards rotated. He almost missed it. An intermittent squeak told him that the sentry at the front was in his chair. The guard at the rear paced around the house several times, then Llian heard him no more. He struck sparks into the sawdust.

The oil-soaked pile caught with a yellow flame that burned up brightly for a minute then died down to an orange glow. When the fire was established he pushed sawdust on to it, and it began to smolder and give out thick belching smoke that hopefully would continue for hours. If his plan worked they would be overcome in their sleep. That would leave only the two guards.

If only he could link with Karan and warn her. He cupped his hands to his temples and squeezed, willing her to wake and know he was there, but in his mind's eye there was nothing but fog and soon the smoke broke his concentration.

He crawled out from beneath the house, took a piece of

cord from his pocket and stretched it between the fence and a pier of the house at ankle height. Then he positioned himself behind a water tank made of wooden staves bound with iron, and waited. It was only a few minutes before the sentry came, though it seemed longer. The man tripped, stumbled and fell to his knees cursing, then Llian clapped him across the ear with a length of wood and he lay still. He tied the man as well as he could in the darkness and rolled him with an effort, for he was heavy, against the fence. Smoke was beginning to billow out from under the house.

Llian crept along the side of the house, the frosty grass crackling beneath his feet. At the front, the other sentry was sitting with his feet on the rail, staring across the street. He did not look around as Llian raised his stick.

I can't do it, Llian thought suddenly, not like this; then the sentry turned, saw the shape with stick upraised and leapt out of his chair. The club came down on his head, cutting off the shout bursting from his lips, and he flopped onto the veranda, moaning softly.

Llian stared at his work for a moment, then walked through the front door, his sleeve over his nose. The room was full of choking smoke and lit only by an oil lamp turned low. He threw the bolt of the front door and took the lamp in his left hand. Smoke was belching up through the gappy floorboards. Down the hall he went on tiptoe. The layout of the house was engraved on his mind; he could have found his way around with his eyes closed.

Llian was halfway down the hall when there came a furious banging and rattling at the front door, followed by a thump as though someone had put a shoulder to it. He looked in the open doorway of the room he was passing. Dimly through the reek he saw a figure lying on the floor, overcome by smoke. The thumping continued from behind him.

The door opposite was abruptly flung open and the tall woman he had seen two nights ago—Vartila no doubt—appeared in the doorway, fully dressed but with feet bare, bent low in a coughing fit.

Looking up she caught sight of Llian through the smoke and said hoarsely, "Gend, is that you? What is happening? Are we afire?" Then, realizing that she was speaking to an intruder, her face became a mask.

She threw out an arm at him, her mouth working silently. Llian leapt at her with his shoulder and knocked her backwards into the room. She disappeared in the smoke and there was a crash as though she had brought down a cupboard. Syllables hissed out of the dark: alien, incomprehensible. A tingle ran up the back of his legs.

He jumped backwards through the door and slammed it shut, cutting off the sound in his ears, though it continued inside his head, growing deeper and slower until it resembled the croak of an old frog. A figure appeared in the hall in front of him; Llian struck the man in the throat with his fist and ran past.

The croak in his mind had grown to a dull rumble, the tingle in his legs became a sharp, spreading ache. Each footstep was a shock of pain. He was dimly aware of a dull glow seeping through the cracks in the hot floorboards. The hall ended in a closed door. Beyond was the windowless back room where Karan was held.

Someone shouted behind him. He turned, a jolt of agony shot up his spine and his legs and arms went numb for a second. Vartila appeared out of the smoke, arm still outstretched.

Llian smashed the oil lamp down on the floor in front of her. *Whoooomph!* A curtain of fire seared across the hall. He unbolted Karan's door and leapt through into the dim room, slammed the door and in a frenzy piled the shabby furniture in a heap behind it—wooden table, chests, washstand. The air was much clearer inside.

A harsh chuckle came from the far corner of the room. Karan was sitting half-upright on the wooden bed, supporting herself on an elbow. Her eyes were hollow, luminous; one cheek bore an irregular purple bruise. She was laughing. She held out her hand to him.

"Dear Llian. I knew that it was you. You should say, 'I've come to rescue you.'"

Llian leapt across the room and fell to his knees beside her. They embraced awkwardly. Flames roared outside the door. There was shouting, but it died away. The numbness began to disappear from his legs.

"I was sure you were dead. There was so much blood."

"Little of it mine, fortunately."

Karan sat there for a moment, her chin resting on Llian's shoulder, then disengaged herself and said, still smiling, "I *do not* wish to appear ungrateful, particularly since you've come all this way for me, but you *have* set fire to the house and barricaded the door, and if you look around you'll see that the room has no window. Do you have a plan?"

"Through the floor," said Llian. "The boards are old and rotten. We can escape under the house while they are saving themselves. They won't even know." He pulled out his knife, inserted the blade between two boards at the corner of the room and prised. The blade snapped off at the hilt. Llian hurled the useless thing away, looking around wildly for a tool.

"The washstand," Karan whispered urgently. "It's iron."

Llian regarded it doubtfully. Karan hobbled over to the piled furniture and dragged the washstand awkwardly to the middle of the floor. "Here, this board is already split. You'll have to do it," she croaked. "I can't use this hand." Her wrist was red and swollen. She saw him looking at it.

"They did not bother to bandage it after," she said.

A chill went over Llian at her words, and he saw that the laughter was just a glaze over her terrible hurts. He turned away, staring vacantly at the barricaded door, full of urges to smash and maim. Smoke was beginning to ooze around the edges and a dark scorch was growing in the center of the door.

"Llian," she called again.

The washstand had a thick iron base. Llian heaved it above his head and brought it down on the nearest floorboard with great force. The board shattered into splinters. He smashed the next one in the same way, cast the washstand to one side and kicked the broken pieces down the hole. Smoke gushed into the room. The hole was nearly a pace long and twice as wide as his head. He worked his way down into it.

"Hold on to my cloak and follow me."

Karan looked dubiously at the belching hole, then back at the door, which had begun to smolder. She took a deep breath, then nodded.

Beneath the house the air was stiflingly hot and smoky, and toward the front the smoke glowed red. As they crawled away from the hole a crash came from behind. The door or perhaps the wall had fallen in. In an instant the whole room was ablaze. A blast of heat came through the hole behind them, searing Karan's bare toes. She clung to Llian's cloak in a daze, jerking herself forward each time he moved, eyes running, lungs burning, head throbbing where once she crashed into a projecting brick. Above them the floor was now too hot to touch.

Finally they emerged at the back of the house. Llian had chosen a place where a thorny bush, neglected, had grown tall, and into it they crept gratefully, Karan so weary and weak that Llian had to support her.

He peered out. The whole right side of the house was ablaze and flames were leaping from the roof, but the back of the yard was yet in darkness. There was no one about, although shouts could be heard from the front. He took Karan under the arms and, half-carrying, half-dragging her, made his way across the back of the yard, through a tumbledown fence and up the far side of the house next door. They found shelter in a hedge. He wrapped his cloak around her and Karan sank down among the leaf litter, while Llian went out on to the street and mingled with the crowd that had gathered to watch the burning.

There were three people in the front yard of the house, and as Llian watched two more leapt through the front door, dragging a third between them. One was Vartila. The crowd murmured but made no offer of help.

That's all accounted for, Llian thought, turning back, save the one they had carried onto the boat. By the time he returned Karan was standing up. He retrieved the bag of clothing from beneath the hedge, gave her his arm and they walked slowly back through the narrow streets of Narne to the waterfront. They were out of sight of the house when they heard a crash, and flame leapt briefly above the rooftops. The roof had fallen in.

"With luck they won't discover our absence until the morning," said Llian. "We must be gone from Narne by then."

Karan gave him an enquiring look.

"I found the fellow that she got the boat from. He will take us."

It was still well short of dawn when they reached Pender's hovel. Llian pounded on the door. After a minute they saw a light moving about inside, and a woman's voice called. "Who's there? What do you want?"

"Wake Pender! Open the door! We need his boat!"

The light disappeared. A minute passed. The light returned. Pender's voice, a mixture of fear and defiance, came through the door. "Go away! Come back in the morning!"

"Pender! I am Garntor," said Llian. "Remember our bargain. Open the door at once. Hurry! You are in danger too."

Silence.

"Hurry!" Llian called again. "The Whelm are coming. We must flee at once."

The bar scraped against the door and it was opened a crack, then fully. Pender stood there, bare-legged, unshaven, his stomach straining at the waist of his nightgown.

Llian pushed through the doorway. Pender fell back in alarm, his hands upraised.

"Don't be afraid," said Llian, pulling silver tars from the pouch that Wistan had given him so long ago. "I keep *my* bargains."

Pender took the coins, the look of relief on his face almost comical.

"Now I need your help once more. You must take us down the river to Sith right away."

At the mention of Sith, Karan, who had been standing behind him, moved out into the light and began to speak. Llian laid his hand on her arm and squeezed; she stopped at once. Pender stared at the pale and filthy pair. Karan, bruised, blistered and barefoot, holding a badly swollen wrist. Llian's face was covered in soot and dust and on one side his hair was singed back almost to the scalp.

Pender pointed at Karan. "She was dead. I saw her," he quavered. "What are you? Necroturges? Mancers? You don't need my help. Go away!"

"You must; already you are in trouble. You must flee at once."

Pender turned and went heavily into the other room. A

woman appeared in the doorway. She was small and thin with glossy black hair to her shoulders, a narrow arching nose and gray eyes. She wore a faded shift with blue flowers embroidered across the shoulders. Her feet were bare on the earth floor of the hut. Llian strode over to her. She looked anxiously up at him but did not draw back.

"What do you want of us?" she asked, in a sibilant accent.

"We are all in danger from these Whelm—the ones who hired your boat three nights past. They are hunting us, and neither are *you* safe, now."

The woman looked around the hut. "We have nothing here anyway!" She considered for a moment. "Narne is a cold, unfriendly place and I won't miss it. We will take you. The fee is five silver tars: two for the journey and three for the trouble you have caused us."

Llian gave her the money. She walked into the other room.

"Get the boat," they heard her say to Pender. "We leave in half an hour."

She came back out again, smiled and held out a hand. "My name is Hassien." Her accent made it sound like *Hassssien*.

She disappeared back into the other room. Pender came sullenly by and went out the front door.

"We have to talk," Karan said in his ear. "To go to Sith may not be best, now. Besides, there is the matter of the Mirror."

Llian regarded her complacently. "Then let us talk, but later. We must be away before dawn. First let me bind your wrist again."

By the time the job was done and Karan had dressed herself, Pender was running the boat down the slips in the darkness. Karan waited in the shadows by the river bank, shadows that were broken only by the light of a distant street lamp. It was a dark, cloudy night. Llian went back to the house and found Hassien coming down the path with two small children.

"Is there else to fetch?" he asked her.

Hassien shook her head, the light from the window behind glistering on her hair. "We have little and it is all in the boat." He turned and walked with her.

"Get in," said Pender in a sour tone. Hassien laid the children down on a blanket at the bow and sat beside them. Even in the faint light Karan looked wan. She stumbled and fell against Llian as she tried to climb in, clinging to his arm for a moment to steady herself.

Pender untied the rope; Hassien pushed the boat away from the shore with an oar and slowly they drifted into the current. Pender dropped the steering oar into place, spat over the side in the direction of Narne and directed the vessel away from the projecting wharves toward the flow. The street lamps along the waterfront drifted backwards, developed haloes, disappeared. The skiff entered the fog lying in midstream and vanished.

Dawn came, a cold gray light creeping across the sky. The fog broke into patches and suddenly it was gone. Karan stirred, pulling the cloak up around her neck. Llian was staring straight down the river, lost in his thoughts. His brown hair was frizzy on one side from the fire, gray with ash and dust; his pale brown eyes were bloodshot; his face, hands and clothes smudged with soot. Karan elbowed him. He turned to her with a smile.

"Ah, yes, you wanted to talk about something."

She put her lips to his ear. "The Mirror!" she hissed.

Llian pretended not to understand.

"The Mirror!" she repeated.

Llian grinned smugly. He looked at her, then reached into the inner pocket of his coat. The smooth lining was cold to the touch. The Mirror was not there.

He frowned. He searched carefully through his pockets, then frantically, over and over again. Uncertainty, consternation, finally a sick despair washed over him as he scrabbled through his pack, through the bag he had carried, his pockets again, knowing that he had never taken it out of the secure, deep inner pocket, realizing that the Mirror was gone and he had no idea when he had lost it.

"It's gone," he said, crushed.

Karan frowned. "What's gone?

Llian looked at her. "The Mirror!" he groaned. "I went back to the campsite and found it. And now it's gone!"

Karan stared at him. "You found it, and you've lost it already?" her voice rising.

Llian sank his head in his hands. "I had it in my cloak and now it's gone. It must have fallen out under the house." He felt like leaping over the side.

Llian was so relieved that he felt all dizzy. He put his head in her lap and she repeated, yes, and felt no need to say

35

THE SIEGE OF SITH

"Oh, Llian, you're such a fool," said Karan, suddenly realizing what had happened.

Llian looked up sharply. Karan could not control herself; her face dissolved in a gale of laughter. "Such an absent-minded fool," she repeated, kissing him all over his face, laughing until the tears ran down her dirty cheeks. Hassien looked across at the noise.

"What have you done?" he gritted, wanting to shake her.

His furious, uncomprehending face set her off in another peal of laughter. "I haven't done anything. You gave me your cloak just after the fire, remember. You looked in your *coat* pocket." She patted the cloak, located a bulge, put her hand inside and pulled the coil out just far enough to be sure that it was the Mirror.

Llian was so relieved that he felt all dizzy. He put his head in her lap and closed his eyes, and felt no need to say anymore. Karan stroked his cheek and the frizzy stubble on the side of his head.

"I can never thank you enough," she said. "I'm sorry for teasing you." She could no longer hide her feelings toward him. Indeed she no longer wanted to. When Hassien looked back a few minutes later they had their arms around each other and were fast asleep. She smiled and looked away again.

"I tried to use it," he said later, when the high sun woke them. "I still feel a little ashamed about that."

"So you should be," Karan replied with a smile. "Did you see anything?"

"Nothing at all."

"Nor I."

"Another time," he said hesitantly, "I even thought about making a bargain with Tensor."

"You would dare? What for?"

"The Mirror in exchange for you. And a look at the secrets of the Forbidding."

She frowned.

"Have I angered you?"

Karan took his hand. "Of course not. I don't expect you to take on my burdens. I may be making a terrible mistake with this Mirror."

"You knew I had it," he said shortly. "I heard you say so to Vartila. How did you know?"

"I didn't know at all," she replied. "I was merely shooting out ideas in all directions, like sparks from a firework, hoping that one would catch in her mind and turn her attention elsewhere. But I knew you were in Narne. I knew you would try some ridiculous scheme, the kind that only you would think of. Like burning the house down while we were still in it."

"You mock me."

"Indeed I do not. You saved me, and doubly. For I was in despair, my quest in ruins, you gone I knew not where. I had plenty of time to think about my failings, in between her torments. The one was scarcely worse than the other.

"At first I thought Maigraith would come. Once I was sure that she was nearby, but she never found me and I couldn't call her. I'm afraid to use my talent." Her voice became melancholy. "And they tormented me with what they had done to her."

"I heard that," murmured Llian. "For some reason your talent is very precious to them. You must guard yourself."

"But they didn't know that I knew Maigraith was free, for at the moment I was taken my will cried out for a friend, and moving of its own volition, found one. I sensed her searching for me, not far away."

Llian was touched by the story, and saddened as well. He had not been there.

"But in the end I was ready to tell them everything, even knowing that they would kill me afterwards. Then I sensed you, creeping about in your foolish way, and I was hard pressed to contain my joy. You gave me the strength to resist."

"Then why did you send me away, back there at the campsite? I could have helped you then."

"Formidable you may be when roused, but you are a long time in the rousing," she teased.

"Yes, how I have been tormented by my cravenness."

"What nonsense! You swore that you would do whatever I told you, remember? Even then it took you long enough. There was nothing you could have done. If you'd stayed you would have been dead in the first minute, and I would have attacked them with such fury that they would have killed me too."

"Then why did you just wait for them?"

Karan closed her eyes, back in that nightmare, trying to make sense of it. "They did something to me. They had some power over me," she said haltingly. "Something happened. You saw the first of it, and then they reached me—my dream. I had will enough only to send you away. I was paralyzed in a way. It's not easy to recall."

And how could she tell him about her subsequent abuse? How she had been the link between the Whelm and their long-lost master. She had cut herself off from her talent now, too afraid to use it for fear of what might come next time. She dug a hole and buried the memories in it.

The river ran straight for several leagues but the banks were high on both sides and little could be seen save a white smear of mountains to the left and the smooth brown water ahead. Presently there came the sound of children's voices from the bow and the two, almost identical apart from their height and with a striking likeness to their mother, appeared.

The girl was about six years old; she shook both their hands gravely. The boy was younger. He turned his head away and would not look at them.

"I will make my Atonement," said Hassien, "then we take breakfast." She conducted an exercise of bowing, murmuring and delicate hand movements. Llian had not seen anything like it before.

Karan put her lips to his ear. "The people of the land of Ogur, far to the south near the Black Sea, have similar rituals, I am told, though if Hassien is from that country she is far from home indeed."

Hassien looked up and saw her whispering. She completed her ordinance then rose and came down to where they sat together, perhaps feeling a need to explain.

"Our lives are just a fragment in the great design—we cannot hope to understand or influence it, only to keep the shadows away from our door. The crimes of the past draw them to us. So I make my Atonement."

She fetched a large wooden bowl. The boat rocked slightly as she moved. "Will you share food with us?" she asked, looking first at Karan then at Llian. She did not even glance at Pender, who was still glowering at the tiller.

Karan smiled. "Your gift of food will lighten our journey, *halima nassa ak-tullipu mas,*" she said. "Gladly and with thanks." Hassien's face lit briefly.

The bowl contained a variety of dried fruits, even the wonderful gellon that Shand was so fond of. Llian had not tasted dried gellon before. There was dark bread, a strong yellow cheese and a pile of red triangular nuts. Karan took a piece of bread and offered it to Hassien, according to her custom, but she merely smiled, showing small white teeth, and shook her head.

They ate. When each had taken what they wanted, and the children had eaten, Hassien picked up the bowl again and offered it to Pender with an ironic bow. He sat there, holding the tiller with his right hand, staring forward while with his left he conveyed the remainder of the food to his mouth. When he had finished Hassien bowed again, even lower than before, and repaired to the bow. Now she looked at the two passengers, wondering. They sat close together, touching at shoulder and hip and knee, and did not move from each other all the day.

"How long is the journey to Sith?" Karan called out to Hassien, a long time later.

"Once we leave the hills the river is slow and winding. Traveling only in daylight, five or six days would be required."

"And traveling all day and all night?"

"A little more than two days. Do you wish it?"

"We must."

"Pender has no equal on the river," said Hassien, without pride or affection. "They will not catch us."

Karan, who knew something of the handling of boats, could see that this was no boast. Pender, for all his surliness, handled the big craft with such grace and subtlety that it seemed as though he was flesh with the boat and the boat one with the river.

"How is it that the best boatman on the river has no work?" asked Llian.

"We are foreigners. The folk of Narne are cold, hateful and suspicious. We may do only what no one else will."

All that day they traveled, and all night, and all the next day and night. The sun rose late and set early, its slanting attenuated rays giving little warmth. Each night a mist rose from the river and hung there until scattered by the morning breeze, but it influenced not their course or their speed in the slightest. At times it appeared that Pender drove the boat by sense alone, or perhaps some subtle variation in the sounds of the river from place to place. As the day wasted away the mountains and the tall forested hills gave way to the gentlest of hillocks, and then, when the river was joined by another of almost equal size arising in the peaks of northern Bannador, it transected the western edge of the Plain of Iagador. The high banks shrank down. Now they could see to their right a grassy plain that stretched treeless to the horizon, save where the meandering course of the river was marked by a ribbon of forest. On their left the mountains had receded, the westering sun reflecting off their snow-covered flanks. Here and there the river passed through patches of woodland, though mostly the banks were grassy or covered with the stubble of autumn crops.

On the afternoon of the second day the grasslands were

succeeded by a dry land of low ridges, steep and rocky on the northern side, gently sloping and covered in heath on the other, through which the great river had cut its meandering path.

"That is the land of Crayde," said Hassien, indicating the barren hills on their left.

Llian looked at the country without interest—its unfortunate, impoverished peoples featured little in the Histories. There was no trace of habitation to be seen, neither fortification, village nor road, just the drab foothills and the mountains of Fildorion towering behind. They passed on.

Karan did not talk further of her ordeal with the Whelm, and Llian, who could imagine it too well, did not question her. She was weak at first but recovered quickly, and cheerful now that they neared Sith and the end of her mission. But still she would not say who she would give the Mirror to, though it was plain that she hoped Maigraith would already be there. She often spoke of her, with longing.

It was near to noon on the third day when the river turned sharply east and ahead, running off the river in a gentle curve, was a steep-sided canal about a hundred spans across.

What a monumental labor that must have been, thought Llian as the current swept them past. Then they drifted down a long straight stretch where the cliffed banks towered above to left and right, and around another sweeping bend to the south. The cliffs fell away and ahead was the ancient stone bridge with its mighty central arch of iron over which the High Way passed, and on their left the waterfront of Sith, impossibly crowded with boats of all types. Behind the waterfront the city covered all the slopes of the island.

Karan gave a vast sigh. "Sith at last. If I must be in a city, this is where I would be. It is such a beautiful place. And the people are warm and generous."

"You don't like Thurkad?"

"*Thurkad!* Filthy, horrible place, like Narne grown a thousand times bigger, more squalid and more vile. Don't bring *that* up again."

Sith *was* a beautiful place too, what Llian could see of it from the boat. It was all built of yellow sandstone, the towers gleaming in the afternoon sun, the sun turning their slate roofs to silver. Even the wharves were clean and orderly, though very busy.

"After Sith, will you still do as you said before?"

The low sun shone through her hair so that it glowed like bronze poured from a crucible. She did not hesitate, or even need to think.

"Of course. I am going home to Gothryme. How I long for home. And it will need me, especially if the war comes that far."

"Perhaps you will have a further duty here."

"I owe no duty save to my own. Bannador is a free state and we are a free people. Not even if Maigraith begs on her knees will I have more to do with this business. What about you?"

Llian was silent. Gothryme was not where this would be resolved, or his tale completed. The Mirror would move on and he would not be able to follow it. And there was his debt to Mendark. Sooner or later he would be called to pay it— later, he hoped, after his failure with the Mirror. He felt quite afraid about that. Llian too wanted peace and rest, and not to carry his world on his back each day. And how could he part from Karan now?

"I am told that Gothryme is the most perfect place in the world," he said. "That's where I plan to spend the winter."

"And after the winter?"

"I don't know. I'll wait for a sign."

The free city of Sith was set upon hilly land enclosed on

all sides but the south by a loop of the river. On that side, in the distant past, the founders of the city had dug a canal, wide and deep, from one arm of the loop to the other. In this way they formed an island about two leagues across, and one and a half the other way. On this rocky hill, defended by the great expanse of the river and its steep banks, grew that great trading nation.

Pender unshipped the oars and directed the boat into the still waters of the harbor. Drawing up in a backwater, he leaned on his oars while Hassien scanned the harbor for a berth. Shortly she pointed and he pulled away to an old jetty made of unbarked logs, though even there the boats were tied up three deep, and they had to clamber from one to another with their few possessions to reach the wharf.

They climbed the short ladder and Llian stared around him. A maze of wharves stretched in every direction, and everywhere the activity was furious. Nearby a group of laborers were unloading sacks of grain from a small ship with triangular sails, staggering under the huge bags, while an overseer with a red face shouted at them from the wharf. A little further a girl was trying to coax a flock of goats one by one up a narrow plank. The lead beast had its foot on the plank but refused to go another step, and the rest of the flock milled around bleating on the deck.

They followed Pender across the wharves to the Customs House. As they reached it a man hurrying out the door bumped into him. The two stepped back, then the man's face creased in a delighted grin.

"Pender, my old friend," he shouted, his arms outstretched. "How good it is to see you. It must have been two years!" He stepped back and looked at his friend. "But what a time to be on the river." Then he caught sight of Hassien and the children standing quietly to one side and his face registered shock and dismay.

"Hassien," he cried. "What brings you here in these foul times?"

Hassien had smiled and stepped forward when he began to speak, but now she stopped uncertainly, her eyes searching his face.

"Dirhan," she said. "What is wrong? We have abandoned Narne and come to live in Sith. There is something the matter?"

"How is it that you have not heard? A great army has come out of the south, out of Orist. The whole of Iagador south of the Garr has fallen, Vilikshathûr is besieged, and already Yggur marches on Sith. The vanguard will reach the canal bridge in a few days. You have chosen an unhappy hour to come here. You did not know?"

"We are in trouble. We fled Narne two and a half days ago, neither stopping nor speaking with anyone. We brought these two. They are hunted by the terror-guard of Yggur, who pursue us as well. We must have a hiding place."

She introduced Karan and Llian to Dirhan, a small, dark-skinned man with a thin face and a beak of a nose. "It's lucky that you came when you did," said Dirhan. "By nightfall the port will be closed and not even I would be able to get you in. In the morning no one may enter, certainly not Yggur's spies from Orist, though if their need is great they might come across the water at night and climb the cliffs. Come with me; I'll have your boat attended to."

"Their need is great," said Karan, as they picked up their packs.

Dirhan looked at her curiously for a moment, then shouted and gestured with an arm. Two laborers came running. He gave them instructions and they rowed the boat out of sight. Pender stood looking after it for a moment, as though an inward struggle was taking place, then his face

went blank. He picked up the small chest that remained and
followed Dirhan.

"You'll find Sith at war a very different place," said
Dirhan to Hassien as he took them into the Customs House,
a long low building of yellow stone on the very edge of the
quay. "You must have a pass now to enter and to stay in the
city. I'll make the arrangements for you."

On the way out, behind the Customs House they passed
by a four-sided basalt obelisk carved with small writing
from top to base. Dirhan noted Llian's interest.

"The laws of Sith," he said. "You will have ample opportunity to study them while you are here. Indeed for your
pass you must sign a paper that you will observe them to the
smallest degree. We put great importance on the rule of law
here in Sith."

"It'll take hours just to read them," Llian grumbled.

"They are on every street corner," said Karan. "Sign and
we can go."

"That is correct," said Dirhan courteously, "but to have
your pass validated you must go to the Wall of Records and
make your own personal rubbing, and carry it with you at all
times. Come."

Half an hour later, clutching their passes and their copies of
the laws, they took farewell of Dirhan and turned toward the
city.

"There is a hut near Dirhan's quarters that we will use for
the time," said Hassien, in response to Karan's question.

They said their goodbyes there, and as soon as they had
departed Karan led them away at a great pace by the meanest of alleys and back streets, so that by the time they
reached their destination—a nondescript doorway running
off a blind alley—Llian was thoroughly lost.

Karan knocked sharply at the door. Eventually it opened a crack and a wrinkled face looked out at them.

"I am Karan; I must see Maigraith at once. Is she here?"

"Not seen in months," said the occupant in gravelly tones.

Karan's shoulders slumped and there was a high edge to her voice when she went on. "I would speak with Faichand then."

"I don't know of such a one."

"Then is any friend of Maigraith's here?"

"Gistel is away too. You say your name is Karan? I haven't heard of you."

"I am Maigraith's friend. Please let us in."

The crack widened a little. The face became that of an old woman with downy cheeks, a pointed chin and a straggle of gray hair. Bright blue eyes surveyed them. "Who is *he*?"

"A friend. His name is Llian. He has done me great service. Let us in. Maigraith would not like us to discuss her affairs on the step."

Karan looked anxiously up and down the alley. It was empty at the moment, though a stream of people was passing along the street beyond. A chain rattled and the door swung open. They entered. The old woman refastened the door behind them, then led the way along a dimly lit corridor and up a flight of stairs to a cold, smoky and windowless chamber. In the far corner of the room a fire glowed in a tiny grate, but gave out little heat.

"Wait here," said the old woman. "I'll bring food." She went out quickly.

Llian dropped his pack on the floor and sat down with his back to the wall. There was a threadbare carpet on the floor, with a swirling pattern of reds and blues that he could barely make out in the gloom. The carpet was pitted with black spots around the fireplace. The walls were paneled in dark timber, with a small tapestry on the wall above the fire, greatly begrimed with soot, and an oil lamp on a bracket beside the door.

Karan stood beside the fire, looking down at the coals. She stirred them idly with the toe of her boot and a small cluster of sparks leapt up.

"Now I'm worried. Where is Maigraith? And she said she knows nothing of Faichand. She must be lying. Why is no one here?" She kicked the fire again, angrily.

"We've come very quickly from Narne. A normal boat trip takes four or five days," said Llian reasonably. "No one knew you were coming today, or any day."

"I'm exhausted, Llian. I can't drive myself any further. The thought that sustained me all the way was that I could give up the Mirror here. To have to take it further is more than I can bear, and where is there to go?" And without the support of my talent, she added to herself. She had closed it off after Narne.

The old woman came back with food, plain fare, apologizing for it, blaming the war. Though she was courteous, she watched them warily, and when she went out she locked the door after her.

"She doesn't know what to do with us," said Llian. "Something has gone wrong. She is beyond her instructions, and afraid. Oh, and who is Faichand?"

"She is the one to whom I must give the Mirror. She is Maigraith's liege. I cannot speak of her."

"I'm afraid," said Karan, after they had eaten. "Sith is strong, but how can it resist such an army? The river will hold them only a few days. Even if Sith does resist, the lands around will fall and we'll be trapped here."

"How long will you wait for her?"

"Not long. Oh, why did I come? This place is as bad as

Shazmak. Worse, for there at least I knew they loved me. My heart tells me that there is something terribly wrong, but where can I go? The burden of this thing has grown too heavy for me."

Then at last there is no conflict, thought Llian. There is only one safe place left. Mendark will help and I can rid myself of this debt at the same time. "Come north to Thurkad. Mendark will take you in."

"Ah, yes. Mendark! I knew you'd come back to your plan when I had no one else to turn to. What conditions will he put upon his protection, I wonder? No, I'll take the chance that Faichand will come back. Thurkad shall be my last resort."

Days went by; miserable, cramped days in that little room. Karan was moody, capricious and fearful. On the fifth day after their arrival Yggur's armies drew up on the southern shore and Sith was besieged. The old woman came twice a day with food and drink, but the rations were much reduced. Llian spent most of his time writing his Histories. He carried his journal with him everywhere in a small satchel tied to his belt, for fear of losing his notes for his *Tale of the Mirror.*

Now it was late at night. Llian was sitting on the floor wrapped in a blanket, trying to read a book he had found in the cupboard, by the dim light of the fire. Karan lay asleep on the other side of the room. Heavy footsteps came down the hall, boards squeaked and there was a muffled exchange outside the door.

The door opened and a man entered. He wore a long hide coat with the wool on the inside. Snow lay thickly on his shoulders and brown hair and beard; he was Llian's height but far heavier, and though young, already thickening around the middle. The man looked at Llian, began to speak, then caught sight of the blanket-wrapped bundle on the other side of the room and went across to her.

He bent down and shook Karan roughly by the shoulder. She woke with a start and sat up, knocking his hand away. She pushed her hair from her face and stood up.

"Who are you?"

"I am Gistel. What is your business here?"

"My business?" she shouted. "Where is Faichand? I must see her urgently, on Maigraith's business."

"She has not been here for many weeks," said Gistel angrily. "Explain yourself! Who are you? You say you bring a message from Maigraith, yet we know that Maigraith is held in Fiz Gorgo, and that she went alone."

"I accompanied her there. I escaped, and she has since freed herself. I promised to come to Faichand here, and I have done so at great cost."

"Faichand left here a long time ago," said Gistel grudgingly. "She grew anxious about the mission. Perhaps she went to free Maigraith. I don't know, for she didn't confide in me, and there has been no news since. And who is this disgusting Zain? How dare you bring him here!"

Karan sprang to her feet and brought her knee up toward his groin. Gistel jumped backwards, stumbled and fell against the mantelpiece, discharging a clot of soot down on his head. Llian guffawed.

"Never say that again." Karan's voice was deadly quiet. "He has helped me greatly; so has he also done *her* service."

Gistel wiped the soot off his face and got up. His eyes glittered with malice, but he saw that Karan's hand was on her knife.

"And where is she?" she repeated. "If the cursed Mirror is so important why is she not here to take it? I never wanted it!" Abruptly she pulled the Mirror from her pocket and flung it at Gistel's feet. "There! Take it wherever you like; guard it until she comes for it. My duty is done."

The Mirror chimed, rolled across the floor, then slowly uncoiled and snapped into a shimmering sheet. Gistel's face was a study in lust for the precious thing. A very long time passed. Slowly he bent down to pick it up. Karan's hand crept back to her knife handle. His fingers touched the Mirror, then drew back. He looked up, saw the expression on her face, then slowly rose to his feet, stepped cautiously around it and went out, closing the door behind him quietly.

Karan came over to Llian, her eyes bright with tears, and sank her head on his shoulder. He put his arms around the middle of her back.

"I'm not cut out for this work either," he said to the top of her head. "What would I not give to be back in Chanthed now, sitting quietly in a tavern with a drink at my elbow, or telling by the fire this rainy night, while the wind howled harmlessly outside. Mendark has much to answer for as well."

36

REFUGEES

Next morning Karan woke feeling abandoned in a malign and yet indifferent world. It was raining, windy and cold. Strong winds during the night had blown some of the tiles off the roof and water had been pouring in for hours, running down the walls and pooling on the floor, so that when they woke the threadbare carpet was saturated and the room smelled like an old wet dog. Karan roused suddenly at dawn, jerked awake by one persistent aspect of her current nightmare.

"Something terrible has happened in Shazmak," she said in a dreary voice. "I dreamed it."

Llian, who was curled up in his blankets beside the fire, groaned and pulled the covers over his head. He wanted another two hours of sleep. Then, realizing that he'd had all he was going to get, he levered himself upright and tried to focus on what she was saying.

"I dreamed of the Whelm last night. They seemed to

come in a great destroying swarm, but they were different from the Whelm I knew, and the Aachim were powerless against them; just as I was powerless that night." And I am helpless now, she thought: I have no will left, and there is nowhere to go, and I dread to use my talent. Without it, it is as though I am going blind as well as mad.

While she was speaking the ceiling had begun to sag in the middle, under the weight of water. Now it cracked and a filthy flood poured down on Karan's bed. This was too much! The world seemed to have turned upside down in the night. She began to cry, then jumped out of bed and squelched across the carpet in her singlet and crept under Llian's blankets. Llian held her to him, noticing how thin she had become. But with the touch a fragment of her dream came across and he cried out, realizing who the Whelm really were.

"Ghâshâd! They are Ghâshâd!"

Karan whimpered and clung more tightly. Naming them set off an explosion in Llian's brain. The Histories listed the Ghâshâd. In ancient times Rulke had quickened them with knowledge after the Zain had failed him. They had been merciless enemies of the Aachim.

"Where did Yggur find the Whelm in the first place?" Llian thought aloud. "There has been no mention of Ghâshâd in the Histories these past thousand years—not since Rulke was imprisoned in the Nightland."

"We cannot even remember our true master, so long is he gone," said Karan from under the bedclothes.

"What?"

"Idlis said that to me long ago. He said they came from the icy south."

When Karan slept again Llian rose, looking down from the narrow window into the alley and the fog and rain. In this weather Yggur could land boats anywhere along the eastern side of the island and no one would know of it until his troops came ashore. If it kept up he could be in the city by nightfall.

Downstairs the old woman was sitting in a frayed cane chair by the kitchen fire, squinting at a small book bound in green.

"What news?" Llian greeted her. She pointed to a battered pot on the stove and only when Llian sat down beside her with a steaming mug in his lap did she begin. She was more cordial now that Gistel seemed to have taken responsibility for them.

"It's very bad. The city is in chaos. A great fear has come over us: it was everywhere I went this morning. What can there be in life for me to fear now, save the way it ends? I have no fear of death, yet today I am afraid. Even the water carriers have gone into hiding."

Pages rustled. Llian sipped the bitter, overburnt coffee. Outside the rain seemed to have stopped.

"There is one thing though," she mused. "The terror-guard of Yggur, the Whelm, were everywhere across the river yesterday, directing the war. Yet today they are gone, not one to be seen in the hours before the fog closed in. Perhaps they are not needed anymore, and go forward to torment others."

"Perhaps," said Llian, swallowing the last of the coffee. The mug was solid silver and very heavy. It seemed out of place in this shabby house. A shiver went down his back. Whelm. Ghâshâd. *Ghâshâd!* Perhaps Karan's dream was true. Perhaps they *had* gone to Shazmak. But the present was more urgent. "We've got to get away. Faichand will never come now, nor Maigraith. Where can we go? Would Gistel help us?"

The old woman looked around the empty kitchen. "Gistel!" she said to herself. "Perhaps, though I never liked him much. Now I wonder about him too. He was away for a long time. Where did he go?" She looked up from her book, peering at Llian as though weighing him as well. "I think it's too late. Still, what does it matter whether you go or stay? If you want to go, then go. But there is nowhere to go save Thurkad, and you'll have to walk."

As she was speaking Karan came into the kitchen. "I am afraid to go to Thurkad," Karan muttered.

"I fear to stay here," said the old woman, "but I'm too old to flee. You should have taken a boat down to the sea, but you've waited too long. The enemy holds the whole of Iagador south of the river. No boatman could take you there now."

"I know one who might," said Llian thoughtfully.

By eleven that night, the fog was so thick that they could not see from one end of the skiff to the other. They huddled together in the middle, waiting. Karan was apathetic, Llian anxious. Behind them Pender was swearing the same word over and over again, "Farsh, farsh, farsh!" A cold breeze blew momentarily.

"Where's Gistel?" said Pender, angrily. "He should have been here an hour ago. Already the wind comes up; the fog will disappear. Your guide is a traitor, eh!" He started to get out of the boat.

Llian was struck by the same fear but he could not allow Pender to go. "Wait," he called out.

"No longer. They're coming!"

It was so. Behind them, from further up the island, they could hear the sounds of battle, the shouts and screams of people. The breeze came again. The fog began to thin and disappear frighteningly quickly, the shiny roofs of the towers appearing first, then the towers themselves, though mist still lay on the river. The cold moonlight shone on Sith. Llian grabbed Pender's arm and forced him back roughly into his seat.

"Stay!" he said. "We go—with Gistel or without him."

"Five minutes then. No more."

They waited anxiously. The shouting grew louder. A fire broke out among the buildings behind the wharves, spreading quickly across the hill. Another blaze sprang up, this time near the waterfront. People began to stream out of the narrow streets onto the open wharf area. A man appeared, walking quickly along the edge of the wharves, looking down.

"There he is," said Llian, standing up on the side of the boat and holding on to the edge of the wharf. "Hoy, over here," he called, waving.

Pender climbed up as well. Gistel was running toward them now. "*Farsh!*" Pender swore, jumping down and sending the boat rocking. He tore at the rope. Llian looked around, not understanding, then he saw the two cloaked figures behind, also running. Pender pushed the boat away from the wharf with a huge thrust of his oar, unbalancing Llian and sending him flailing backwards against the bow.

Now the wind was breaking up the fog on the river into banks and billows. Pender heaved on the oars, expertly directed the boat toward the nearest fog bank. Three more figures converged on the spot from which they had fled, outlined against the burning warehouses. One of them pointed with a long arm, another kneeled. A bolt buried itself in the side of the boat, not far from Pender's hand. He swore again, dug the oars; the boat spun and disappeared into the fog.

At almost the same time a tiny, waterlogged dinghy, plastered with mud and twigs, grounded silently against the rocky southern side of the island. A bulky shadow scrambled from it and clung to the wet rock while the dinghy slowly spun off into the darkness. The shadow scaled the cliffs in the blackness and the fog and crept into Sith. There it scurried about, searching, and even in the violence of that terrible night the fleeing people stopped to stare at the tormented, dreadful creature. The black-bearded face showed nothing, but the glow of the flames highlighted the twin curving scars across Emmant's cheek.

"What do you want me to do, eh?" asked Pender, as they huddled among the reed beds on the northern side of the river, a league or more downstream.

For the past three hours they had dodged the patrols of the enemy, darting from one fog patch to another, then when the fog was gone, creeping along in the myriad channels and backwaters of the lower Garr, hiding under the overhanging trees. Sometimes they had to wade through the fringing marshes, dragging the skiff. In the bright moonlight there was no hiding place on the river.

Llian was wracked by indecision. He did not know the land and had no confidence that he could bring them to Thurkad, especially as the armies would be keeping a lookout for them. He had expected that Gistel would take them there. Karan knew the country well, but the proud, confident Karan was gone; in her place a stranger, withdrawn and miserable. When Llian spoke to her she only repeated, "I dread to go to Thurkad."

"We couldn't stay in Sith."

"I know that. I feared even more to stay."

"What about Bannador?"

"I should have gone there at once, from Shazmak, even leaving you behind. I once considered it. Now it is too late; they will already be there, waiting for me."

"Across the sea?" he asked doubtfully.

"They've followed all this way. I can't hide on the plains of Almadin."

"What can we do?" Llian pleaded, looking to Pender.

Pender found the experience a novel one but for the moment he said nothing. He was transformed—as capable and commanding on his boat as he had been surly and ill-at-ease off it.

"I wonder about the whole mission now," said Karan. "What right has *she* to this Mirror anyway? Her name rings in my mind, a jarring sound. I begin to think that to give it to her would be as bad as giving it to Tensor. I can't say what is right anymore; my judgment fails me, and my confidence, and all seems futile."

"I know something of running and hiding," said Pender in his nasal voice. "I would hide in Thurkad. A most wicked place, eh! Places there even *your* enemies wouldn't go. And much stronger than Sith."

"There is nowhere else to go, Karan. We must go to Thurkad."

Karan turned away, staring across the water. She shivered, and though she squeezed her eyes tightly closed, two small tears escaped.

Pender saw the tears and the entreaty. You are kind, he thought. I would do it for you, if you asked it.

"I don't know the country between here and Thurkad," he said, with the reluctance of the sailor for any form of travel requiring the use of his legs. "And not even I can take you downriver in daylight, now. But there are many channels in the marshes; beyond, the river has many mouths, eh! I can take you to the sea on a dark night. Then you go your own way to Thurkad."

But that night was clear and bright, with no fog and the moon nearly full, and so was the next, so they spent the two days among the reeds; dreary cold days. The third night was cloudy, foggy and dark and they set out as soon as the sun set.

Karan hardly spoke during that journey—she was overcome by feelings of helplessness and resignation. She had nothing more to give. If only Maigraith had come; but she would never find her now. Karan could feel the strength of Yggur all around her, and the Whelm. Beyond Yggur, dreams of those eyes grew: greater, more malevolent, and closer to her. *He* wanted her—she was part of his purpose. Day and night blurred together into one hideous dream. Beyond even that, a nameless, personal dread pursued her. She began to fear that she was losing her mind, though she took some comfort from Llian's presence. Even the mercenary solidity of Pender provided a kind of bulwark against her fears.

Pender took them down into the shifting channels through the marshes and by the morning, when the wind blew from the east, they could smell the salt of the sea. At Pender's insistence they hid in the bogs during the day, and it was well that they did so, for in the morning the enemy was about in small boats, combing all the channels, and later they heard the creak of timbers and the rattle of oars as a fleet rowed past upstream.

A wistful look came across Pender's fat, pocked face when first they smelled the salt sea on the wind. "How I long for the sea," he said forlornly.

This struck a spark of interest in Karan, for the first time in days. "What happened to you?"

"Had my own little ship, taking cargo along the sea; and beyond, sometimes. Too many enemies—always enemies," he said with resentment. "They did not want me. Took away their profit, eh! They joined against me, hounded me, fired my boat. Everything burned. I could not pay, had to run. I was the best sailor on the Sea of Thurkad. Now I paddle this stinking river, and can't even get enough for food and drink."

In the evening they evaded the patrols without difficulty and by midnight had reached the sea through the northernmost channel of the delta. The wind was blowing strongly from the north and a big swell was breaking over the sandbar offshore. Each swell struck the little boat side on, making it wallow and sending a shower of spray over the side that the wind caught and flung in their faces. Within minutes they were drenched. Pender clawed the boat around to the north and the spray eased, though now the bow rose up sharply with each wave and crashed down into the following trough.

"You're safe now, safe as anywhere," he shouted over the wind. "I'll put you on the beach; not a long walk to the village, eh! You can buy a boat, or steal one. Thurkad is two or three days north. I must get back to my children."

He pulled the boat through the surf to the beach and sat there. Karan stepped carefully from the bow onto the sand. She stood patiently, holding the rope, staring across the water. The stern rose and fell with each wave and the bow crunched against the beach.

Llian sat there, hopelessly afraid. He knew that even if he could steal a boat he could never sail it to Thurkad in that sea. He would sooner have walked that perilous path into Shazmak again.

"I can't do it," he said in a pale voice. "I've never sailed a boat before."

Pender looked at him in disgust. "What a pathetic thing you are," he said after a while. "To think I feared you once. Why should I help you? Not even for money would I do it." Then his gaze lit on Karan, vacantly staring, and their eyes crossed.

"Would you do it *for me*?" she asked, and for once Pender's mercenary heart was stirred. He considered, then his hand, perhaps by accident, brushed his purse and it chimed faintly. Llian put several thick pieces of silver into the leathery hand. Pender weighed them, left his hand outstretched a moment longer, until Llian grudgingly dropped another there. The money disappeared.

"Get in," said Pender.

"What about your children?" said Llian.

Pender sighed heavily. "I suppose they are as safe in Sith as anywhere," he said.

Mechanically, as though she had done it a hundred times before, Karan pushed the boat away from the shore and leapt nimbly onto the bow, without even wetting her boots. She climbed in and sat down, staring out to sea again.

I don't think she even realizes we were here, Llian thought. Pender unlashed the mast, stepped it, and put up the little sail. The wind still blew from the north. They headed out to sea on the first tack.

That night Karan cried out again in her sleep. Llian took her hand and for a while she was calm, but later she began to scream and thrash about, crying out in a dialect of Bannador, which he scarcely knew. He held her tightly, stroking her tangled hair and her salty cheeks, and they both slept.

Suddenly the link she had forged between them in Shazmak was alive again and a deluge poured across. A nightmare of faces: the face of Vartila; the face of Idlis; the face of Yggur; another face. Llian half-woke, remembering the dream he had had in Tullin, long ago. It was the same face that he'd dreamed about at the campsite. That figure, dwarfing its stone chair, flinging off its chains, reaching out.

Rulke! How had he not realized? Rulke! But why did she dream of *him*? Abruptly, Llian sprang from his half-sleep back into her dream.

Yggur he saw then, and Tensor. Llian even saw himself—the faces spinning, twisting, now blending into one another, now stark, alone. He saw again the Nightland, that intangible prison made to contain Rulke. He saw Rulke in it too, only this time he was not chained in that stone seat—he was working in a vast chamber, putting what appeared to be the final touches to a construct, an engine of unhuman proportions but unmistakable potential. This time Rulke did not look up, though he knew they had seen him, for he had drawn their gaze to him. Somehow this was more frightening than before.

Karan whimpered. The dream changed and Llian was looking up at the face of Emmant. He experienced once more the terror that he had felt before in Shazmak, until he realized, with the slow separation of his memory and Karan's dream, that *she* was the one Emmant gloated over, and that it was *him* she feared the most. He reached out, and Llian saw again the brutal, murderous lust of the outcast whom she had spurned and humiliated.

Karan screamed, the nightmarish yellowed sound of one driven to the brink of madness. Then with an awful laugh she wrenched herself free of Llian's arms and flung herself into the sea.

For a moment she was visible in the trough of the wave behind them, the moonlight shining on her pale face. Llian stood up at once, unbalancing the boat so that the next wave nearly swamped them. He scrabbled around for a line but couldn't find one, just stood looking despairingly after her as the distance grew swiftly.

Pender had reacted at once, heaving on the steering oar, spilling the wind from the sail, hauling the sail down, but still they drifted away. Llian was hopping up and down, screaming at Karan, the boat rocking dangerously. Pender grew suddenly angry, swung his hooked arm at Llian's midriff and with surprising ease knocked him over the side.

"A more worthless fool I've never met," he muttered, then shouted, "That way!" as Llian's head emerged from the water, his eyes like saucers.

Llian struck out strongly in the direction that Pender pointed, the waves lifting him and letting him fall again, though only occasionally did he catch a glimpse of her, lying unmoving in the water. When he reached the place where he had seen her last she was not there and he had to stand as high as he could in the sea, treading water furiously, before he found her nearby. She was pale and cold as death, though when he put his hand on her throat a faint pulse still ticked there.

Llian turned her on her back, holding her shoulders until she was upright in the water. She sank down to her chin, kept sinking, and he wrapped his arms around her back and squeezed her against his chest. Water rushed out of her mouth and nose, warm water ran down his back. Tucking her chin over his shoulder he squeezed again and again. More water rushed out, then he felt her take a shuddering, gurgling breath and she vomited over his shoulder into the water.

He scooped water and washed her face with it. Her head lolled in his hands, her eyes opened and closed again. Llian pushed her head back on his shoulder, holding her tightly, then looked around for the boat. It was nowhere to be seen.

He kicked himself higher in the water but there was no sign of the boat in the darkness. It was too tiring, holding them both so high, and he sank back down. A wave broke in his face; he wiped the water awkwardly from his eyes. What a fool I am, he thought miserably. Even Pender has more presence of mind. If it wasn't for him . . .

But where is he? In the darkness Pender might never find them. He might just abandon them. Llian searched for the shoreline, but he was no longer certain which direction to look. Even if he had known the direction, he was too low to have seen it, this far away, in the dark. The water was so cold that the feeling was already going from his feet. It would not take long to die.

37

THE OLD CITY

Llian kept himself and Karan afloat for what seemed like hours, though it was not really long at all. There was just a little spark of warmth between them where they touched, and cold water everywhere else. Then the oars rattled and the skiff appeared suddenly from upwind, gliding toward them under Pender's expert hand so close that Llian had only to reach up and grasp the side. Pender shipped the oars, heaved Karan into the boat, then Llian. He wrapped them both in a piece of canvas, though the wind still chilled them.

"She needs fire and a hot drink," said Pender. "We go ashore."

Llian huddled in the wrapping and looked at Pender's fat, ugly face with a great deal of respect.

A little way down the coast they found a tiny beach between two rocky headlands. Thick forest covered the land behind the beach; there was heath on the headlands. The north end of the beach was sheltered from the waves and there, just at the end of the rock platform, Pender drove the skiff onto the sand. They lit two large fires and put Karan between them, feeding her with thin soup and sweet tea. After that she slept, but the nightmares came again. Twice she ran away into the night. The second time they found her poised at the edge of a low cliff, and this time they took her back and bound her.

In the morning she seemed better, though she was weak. The wind had swung around to the south, offering hope of a faster passage. They set sail straight as an arrow for Thurkad.

Dawn came, the eighth since they had fled Sith, and the whole of the western sky was covered in a pall of smoke as the skiff rounded the cliffed headland and passed into the deep protected waters of Port Cardasson, the finest harbor in all Meldorin, the harbor of the most ancient city of Thurkad. The port was thick with vessels: from the huge ships, festooned with yellow sail, that came all the way from Crandor, laden with spices and silken cloth, jewelry and precious woods, to the tiny *kules,* with their single triangular rig, that fished the estuaries for jellyfish. Tree-covered ridges ran down to enclose a myriad of narrow, deep inlets. The harbor was dotted with tiny islands, some bearing slender light-towers to mark the channel.

The channel took a dog-leg to the left. Half a league away, partly hidden by a trio of rocky islands, was the city, a multicolored smudge against the rugged hills that squeezed it into the water. They passed between the islands, turned west again and crossed from the deep blue water of Port Cardasson into the shallow muddy expanse of Thurkad Cove.

Llian gaped. "In all my travels I've never seen such a city. They must have cut down a forest to build it."

"Nor smelt one, eh!" said Pender, covering his nose. The wind from the north carried an intense odor of rotting fish, and other things besides.

Karan, who seemed almost back to normal today, said, "It has always been an unhappy place for me."

Thurkad was not the greatest city in Meldorin, but it was by far the oldest, an old city even by the time of Shuthdar. The shore was covered in a vast concretion of wharves, warehouses and jetties that were built out over the water on mighty piles, blackened and tarry, three and four and even five storeys high. The structures extended out into the water for as much as a thousand paces, and ran the best part of a league around the cove. Some parts were upright, some leaning, and some had floors tilted and awash; braced crossways with beams the size of tree trunks or bound with black iron bands. The whole great structure was slowly subsiding into the mud and peat, yet each part had its precariously perched higher storeys. This was the wharf city of the Hlune, the robed folk who controlled all seaborne commerce in and out of Thurkad.

"The sea rises," said Karan, "and the land subsides. They forever build on top of the old. The ancient part of the city is like an iceberg; most of it now lies below the water."

The bay was busy with water traffic—rafts of logs brought down the River Saboth all the way from the mountains; barges bearing sacks of grain, barrels of salted fish, pickled vegetables, wine or oil; ferries running to the villages on the south side of the port and the roads beyond. They skipped in and out of the streaming traffic and drew up to a massive wharf platform. The water had an oily gleam. Patches of yellow scum clung to the piles.

They climbed a series of ladders built for giants and

stood on the black decking. The wharf city was vast and in ruinous condition—warped, rotting and pocked with jagged holes where part of the understructure had collapsed. Some of these voids were partly covered with loose planking but the majority yawned open, a trap for anyone who walked inattentively.

Pender found an official, paid the handover fee and checked the receipt carefully. Without it his boat would have disappeared in a moment.

Karan hesitated at the edge of the wharf until Llian, who was walking slightly ahead, came back and took her hand. Halfway across they passed by one of the holes in the deck, a long, narrow tear like a crevasse, evidently where one of the foundation piles had rotted away and carried everything with it. Within the crater the maze of crazily tilted timber made a honeycomb of black, slimy cells. The sullen water could be seen far below, and a stale odor of seaweed and decay drifted up.

A movement caught Llian's eye, then another. A thin, grimy face was staring up at him. Lots of faces. There were people living down there, crawling along beams, hauling on green ropes that trailed down into the water. He pointed them out to Karan.

"There are too many people here, and not enough land," she responded with a shudder. "No space is wasted. Let us get out of this damnable place; it gives me nightmares to feel it beneath me."

Karan shouldered her pack and hurried toward the western hills and the towers of the old city. At last they reached the shore, stepping off the age-stained deck onto the steep streets. They were narrow and paved with bricks of dark blue, flecked with black. The buildings were grimy stone. They settled themselves in one of the many inns that lined the edge of the wharf. Pender saw them to their door and disappeared.

Karan called for tea and, after it came, sat down on the floor in front of Llian.

"We should not have come here," she said, pouring the tea from a brazen urn with a compartment at the base containing heated stones.

"There was nowhere else to go."

"We haven't left my enemies behind; we've caught up to them."

"Who then? Who are you afraid of? Is it Mendark?"

"I don't know," she wailed. "I'm afraid to use my talent." She looked around her as though the walls were closing in.

Llian inspected his tea. It was rich red in the white bowl, but with globules of liquid butter on the surface which he spooned out carefully. It wasn't that he minded butter in the tea; many places in the north had that custom. This butter was more gray than yellow though, and it smelled rancid.

Karan clasped her hands around her bowl and put her head down so that the steam drifted over her face. The fragrant vapor seemed to give her some heart.

"It seems I must rely on your *friend,* Mendark. You'd better go and fetch him."

The melancholy and submissiveness in her voice grieved Llian. "I wouldn't call him a friend," he said. He was almost as apprehensive as she was about the meeting. "All right, I'll go. Will you be safe here?"

"I'll bar the door and sleep," she said. "Go. Hurry!"

It was after noon when he emerged on the street below. The wind carried the stench of the wharves to him. He looked around. A narrow promenade, cluttered with the tables of many outdoor cafés, stretched along the wharfside. Uphill the streets of the city formed a maze in all directions.

But Mendark was Magister; anyone would know where the Magister dwelt.

The first two people he spoke to brushed by without answering, but the third, an urchin of the streets, a grubby, thin child who looked about nine or ten, with scabs on both her knees, directed him to the citadel. The few coppers he put in her tiny hand were evidently a vast overpayment, for she gave him the most beaming white smile, looked around to be sure that no one was watching—no one was, as far as Llian could tell—palmed the fortune and skipped away. The citadel was a complex of towers on the hill above. Llian had noted them earlier from the boat.

He took a street that seemed to wander in the right direction, but in the labyrinthine alleys and roofed passages of the old city he continually lost his way. Once or twice he had noticed the child behind him. Now, just when he decided to hire her to be his guide, she was no longer there.

The gates of the citadel turned out to be almost an hour away. They stood open but four guards, arrayed in scarlet and blue, belts and boots shining, stood in a slanting spray of sunlight at the entrance. They moved to bar his way with their pikes.

"What is your business in the citadel, ruffian?" asked the foremost, and Llian wished he'd had the foresight to buy clean clothes, to wash, to shave.

He caught the gaze of the fellow and said determinedly, "I am Llian of Chanthed. I bear a message from Wistan, Master of Chanthed, to Mendark, Magister of the High Council of Thurkad. I beg admittance at once."

One of the guardsmen standing behind smirked and said something to his fellow, whereupon they both brayed with laughter. Their leader frowned and cautioned them in a low voice. They fell silent, but the broad smiles remained on their faces. He turned back to Llian.

"You will, of course, bear a token from Lord Wistan in earnest of your trust?"

Llian raised his hands, palm upwards. "Alas, I was beset by robbers; the token was taken," he lied.

The man's expression changed. "I know of no Magister bearing the name of Mendark," he said with a sly grin, rubbing his jaw. There came another burst of laughter, muffled this time, from behind. "Are you sure you have the right name, or even the right city? The bog dwellers of Chanthed are slow of wit, I am told."

Llian flushed. "It is you who are fools," he said angrily. "My errand is urgent. I will not be kept waiting by idiots. Admit me at once."

The smiles disappeared and the pikes swung upwards. "If you are who you say, which I doubt," sneered the captain, prodding him in the chest with the tip of his pike, "I warn you to step carefully. The name of Mendark is no longer a passport into the citadel. The traitor has been cast out and banished from old Thurkad."

Llian fell back a pace. "But . . . When? How? I've h-heard nothing of this," he stammered.

"The news is old. The whole of the civilized world knows of it. Soon it may even reach Chanthed." There was another burst of raucous laughter.

"Where can he be found? Mendark is still alive?"

"It is said that he dwells in Masande, by the water. That place has always had an uncanny stench to it. It is time we put it to the torch, and its vermin. Take care that you aren't there when we come for him."

Masande! Llian had no idea where that was, or even if it was a part of Thurkad. He walked down the hill a little way, until he was out of sight of the guards, and sat down on a stone wall beside the road. Each time someone came past he stood up and in his politest tones asked the way to Masande, to the dwelling of Mendark. No one answered him. The mere mention of Mendark's name was enough to turn them away. He walked slowly back down the hill, wondering what to do. Suddenly the child was beside him again, though he had not seen her coming. He supposed such skills were necessary for survival on the streets of Thurkad.

"Where does you want to go?" she asked in a squeaky voice as thin as her grubby legs. Her accent made "where" sound like "wir" and "want" as "warnt". "I can guide you."

"Masande."

"You want to go Masarnde?" She said something unintelligible, then, "Why does you want to go there?"

"That is my business. Do you know where it is? I will pay well." As soon as he said that he realized his mistake. Now he would pay ten times the price. Well, he still had coin, and it wasn't important enough to argue about.

"I know it. I will take you." She looked over her shoulder. "But not from here. Go down the hill. I will find you." She disappeared again.

Llian presumed that by "down the hill" she meant the wharf-front promenade where they had met before. For want of any other alternative he did as she said, and the moment he stepped onto the paving she appeared out of an alley crowded with stalls selling the meanest, weediest, moldiest and most diseased vegetables possible. He looked at her more carefully this time; such children were often in the employ of rogues.

She was one of the shabbiest little urchins that he had ever seen. She wore a dun coat, a scruffy, ragged thing with the pockets torn off, all moth-eaten and rotten as though it had spent the summer drifting in the harbor. Through the holes in the coat could be seen a ragged shirt, so large that it must have been cast off by an adult, and loose trousers of the same color torn off above the knee. None of the garments looked as if they had ever been washed. Her pale hair was relatively clean, though it had been hacked off at shoulder height with a knife. She had a long narrow face for a child, a long sharp nose and a pointed chin. The hazel eyes were large and a little too guileless for someone who lived on the street. Her legs and bare feet were spattered with mud but her hands were clean enough. Such was the somewhat contradictory picture before him.

He had to think. It would be dark in a few hours. He sat down at a café table on the promenade and shouted for tea. The girl stood watching. "What is your name, child?"

"Lilis."

"Lilis. What would you like to drink, Lilis. Are you hungry?"

She looked very wary. Why would anyone buy *her* lunch? She checked him over in much the same way as he had examined her. He seemed worried, and tired, and there were deep shadows under his eyes. His clothes were worn, travel-stained and crusted with salt. But he did not look like someone she need be afraid of, and his voice was so warm and kind she could not but like him. She was also very hungry. She'd not eaten today, though the three coppers would each buy scraps enough for a week, if she could keep them secret.

"Yes," she said hoarsely, "I'm hungry."

She sat down as far from him as possible.

What did children like? Llian had no idea, but it was cold and windy, so he ordered bowls of thick soup and when that was gone, and she had wiped the bowl clean with the bread, and he was sipping his buttery herb tea, he bought her a mug of sickeningly sweet hot chocolate. That was a delight that she had never experienced. She sipped the chocolate, lin-

gering over every tiny mouthful, alternately looking down at
the cup and up at him.

"Now, we go to Masande."

She jumped up at once, bowed her thanks and led him
quickly, though by a roundabout route, and with much looking behind them, to a southern suburb on a rocky promontory running down to the sea.

She asked him, "What does you do?" and on the way he
told her about being a teller, and the library at Chanthed, and
even a minor tale fit for a child, and so the journey went
quickly and pleasantly enough. Lilis listened in silence the
whole way, looking up at him and down at the street, and before them and behind, that being the responsibility of the
guide. Once, in a dark place, when his story was at its most
tense, and the heroine in the most grave peril, her cold hand
clutched his and held it until they came out of the alley
under a bright street lamp.

It was fully dark and light rain was falling by then.
Masande turned out to be an old quarter of the city, though
grown up outside the original walls, and made of two
parts—the old stone town on the ridge, and the new town
built against the edge of the great wharf.

Mendark's refuge was a villa set on a rocky knob that fell
steeply to the harbor. The villa was surrounded by a high
wall of gray basalt that was broken in places. There were
piles of cut stone on the ground and signs of hasty repairs. A
tall iron gate stood ajar. Llian pushed and it gave with a
rusty squeal. The guard post was empty, though a fire burned
there. A large, squat house stood in the middle of an untidy
lawn starred with small white and blue flowers. In an angle
of the wall, seven slender stone towers overlooked the harbor, some little taller than the house, others soaring more
than twenty spans into the air, and each surmounted by a

dome of metal leaves from which the lights of the city further up the hill glinted.

Llian pulled his hood down against the rain, walked quickly toward the door of the house and pounded on it. An answering shout came from inside, and shortly the door was opened by a tall woman who regarded him coolly.

"I'm Llian of Chanthed. I've come seeking aid. Is Mendark within?" The words tumbled out all in a rush, his composure giving way under her impassive gaze.

The woman looked him over carefully, glanced at Lilis waiting in the background, then held out her hand.

"I bid you welcome. Long have we sought you. Come within," she said. "My name is Tallia."

Llian gestured Lilis over, suddenly realizing that he should have agreed her fee beforehand. He took a silver tar out of his pocket and held it out with a smile. "Thank you, Lilis."

The light from the doorway was full on her face. She did not smile. How she lusted for that coin, more than anything she had ever wanted. She shook her head, and her eyes shone.

"You have paid already," she squeaked, and though he continued to hold out the coin, and she to covet it, she walked away.

Llian watched until she disappeared, then he turned back to Tallia.

Tallia had been observing in some amazement. She was thinking back to her conversation with Shand about Llian, in Tullin months ago. Indeed Llian must have had something special, to so charm a street urchin that she would refuse a tar. You could buy a life for that in Thurkad. And the thought reminded her of something else. Shand too had been coming to Thurkad. He had not yet appeared.

"The price of a guide such as her is a quarter grint by the

day, and you must watch your back. It seems you've found the only honest one in Thurkad. You will never be rid of her."

"I could use an honest friend," said Llian, shaking Tallia's warm, strong hand. She led the way down a bare hall and up a flight of stairs, holding the lantern aloft. "Mendark will be glad of your news, if it is good. We have had many setbacks."

They came at last to an open doorway at the end of another long corridor and passed through into a large rectangular room lit by three oil lamps suspended from the high ceiling. A hearty fire blazed in the far end of the room. The dark paneled walls were empty, save for a threadbare tapestry of a hunting scene in a forest—a hunter about to be gored by a boar. Two leather armchairs were drawn up in front of the fire.

"It is Llian," announced Tallia from the doorway. There was a rustle of papers from the chair nearest the fire, then Mendark stood up and advanced toward him, arms outstretched and a smile on his face. They embraced, then Mendark stepped back a pace, his hand still on Llian's shoulder.

"Llian! What a delight it is to see you. It must be five years since we traveled to Zile together. It might have been yesterday, for all the difference there is in you."

The greeting was rather more fulsome than Llian had expected. Mendark had been spying on him five years ago, he recollected. Don't rely on what he says, but watch everything he does.

Llian examined his sponsor. He saw a man seemingly of late middle age, with straight brown hair cut directly across at shoulder length, a thick nose, deep blue eyes and a full mouth with laughter wrinkles at the corners. Mendark's eyebrows and beard were almost black, flecked with gray. His face and hands were weatherbeaten and he wore heavy cream-colored woolen trousers, over high boots, and a brown wool shirt.

"The years have touched you lightly as well," said Llian, though he saw that the hair was thin and lank, the laughter wrinkles overlaid by a downcurling of the mouth, and there was a wary, weary look in the eyes, as though Mendark had expended almost all there was of himself.

"Come and warm yourself," said Tallia, who had gone over to the fire and was leaning on the chimneypiece. "He will question you for hours with no thought for your comfort.

"Oh," she said then, "there's no one in the guardhouse. They'll be in the inn on the corner. Shall I put the fear into them?"

Mendark scowled and nodded and she went out. He took Llian by the arm and led him to a chair by the fire. "Have you eaten?" he enquired, indicating a side table spread with bread, fruits and a platter bearing roast meat and vegetables, now cold.

"Not much," said Llian, eyeing the repast.

"We've already dined," Mendark said. "Take what you wish."

Llian filled a plate with food and sat down. He felt uncomfortable, conscious of his debt and wondering how Mendark would approach it. They did not speak further until he had finished eating, when Tallia came back in. Mendark poured each of them a bowl of dark wine from the pottery bottle that lay to hand.

"What trouble you've given us," he said, though yet he smiled.

"What do you mean?"

"Tallia spent weeks in the mountains, searching for you. We thought you were dead. Now, what is your news? What of the Mirror?"

Llian began his long tale.

"And after the Whelm took her?" Mendark asked, when he paused for breath.

Llian continued on to Shazmak, as far as the trial and his interrogation of Tensor. Mendark chuckled.

"You have courage, Llian, or incredible stupidity. Whatever possessed you to question him so arrogantly?"

"He treated Karan very badly."

"Not as he sees it. No matter. There is something else I wanted to ask you. What was it? Oh yes, this new *Tale of the Forbidding* that you told in Chanthed. I can't seem to find out anything about it."

"That's because Wistan suppressed it; and threw me out of the college when I wouldn't cooperate."

"Is that so? Well, it was time for you to go anyway."

"I was going to ask you about that," Llian said tentatively. "What do you require from me?"

"Plenty, but we'll come to that later. For the moment, just answers! What was so different about your tale?"

Llian told of the crippled girl's murder. "So someone must have entered the tower secretly," he concluded.

"Interesting! What's that, Llian? The privy? Down the hall and to your left."

Llian went out.

"What do you think, Tallia?"

"It looks as though he may have uncovered something."

"Perhaps, and then again it may come to nothing, like so many of these hints from the past. Did Tensor speak true, I wonder, when he said that whoever went first into the burning tower was a Charon, one of the three? Better follow it up."

"Tell me, Mendark, why *did* you sponsor Llian?"

"It was obvious that he was brilliant but needed the very best training. As did you before him! But I need someone with his talents too. Our past and our future are all tangled up, and who better to sort it out than a chronicler?"

"I thought you wanted him to sing your glories in a Great Tale after you were dead."

Mendark chuckled. He was not embarrassed at all. "That too."

Llian came back and finished the story of his travels. "So today we arrived here, and after much searching I've found you," he concluded. Though he had never ceased to think about the dream he'd had in Shazmak after reading *Tales of the Aachim,* and the fabled Renderer's Tablet, he said nothing of it to Mendark. That secret was his alone. But some day, when the debt was paid and Mendark was in a good humor, he would press him about the Forbidding. His need to know who had killed the crippled girl was not diminished by all that had happened since.

"Karan is here in Thurkad now with the Mirror?" cried Mendark, leaping to his feet. "Oaf! Why did you not bring it here? Need I remind you how much you owe me?"

"She would not come. She is afraid. And she will give up the Mirror only to someone called Faichand."

"Faichand!" said Mendark. "I've heard of her; a minor mancer, surely. Why her?"

"I don't know," Llian said. "And there's another thing. Karan often dreams of Rulke rising up and flinging off his chains."

"Rulke," said Mendark. "He is securely held."

"Is a watch maintained on the Nightland?"

"Indeed it is, and I maintain it still. But the defenses are in place and secure. Perhaps her trials have driven her mad."

Llian looked shocked, but it was the shock of hearing aloud what he was afraid to face. He closed his eyes and lay back in his chair.

"Where is Karan now?" asked Tallia sharply, bringing them back to the present. "Is she alone?"

"Yes."

"We'd better go," said Mendark, shrugging a cloak over his shoulders. "She is in terrible danger. The whole world has taken refuge in Thurkad, evil as well as good, and Yggur is only days away. Can she use the Mirror?"

"She said not, and I certainly can't," said Llian, recalling the day he had huddled in a hollow tree in the forests above Narne. "I had it for several days, and tried everything I knew or had read of, but I saw only my own face."

"What did you expect?" said Mendark mildly. "You more than most should know that there is a craft to the use of such things, and it is long in the learning."

They went out through the guard post, which was now occupied by the surliest guards that Llian had ever encountered, and onto the street.

"What news of the war? Does Sith still stand?"

Tallia shook her head. "It fell days ago, and all the lands to the south are overrun. You saw the smoke. Yggur is burning as he comes. His armies will be here in a few short days."

"What happened to you, Mendark?"

"I have been cast down. Perhaps I deserved to be. It seems I look too much to the past. All the more need to call in my debts. But we will talk of that later."

They hurried through the darkness. The drizzle had turned to steady rain and driven almost everyone off the streets. Once Llian thought he saw Lilis behind them, but when he looked again there was no one there. In an hour or so they reached the inn. Llian knocked on the door. It was nearly midnight, but Karan's voice called out instantly, "Who's there?"

Llian responded: the bar was drawn back cautiously.

Karan's knife was in her hand and she did not put it away when she saw him.

"Llian, where have you been?" she began; then, seeing the shadowed figures behind him, her face went white and she turned as though to flee.

"Karan, I have brought Mendark, as we agreed," Llian said urgently.

She turned back with an effort. "Who is the other one?" she demanded in a high voice that trembled. "I know her from somewhere."

Karan had changed into clean clothes, the dark-green loose trousers and blouse that she favored, and had evidently bathed recently for her feet were bare and her hair hung in red, lime-scented ringlets about her ears. The lantern she held in one hand accentuated the shadows beneath her eyes. She held it up to Tallia's face. "You!" she said, relaxing a little.

Llian introduced Mendark and Tallia. Karan shook hands with them, warily.

Karan walked slowly back from the door, eyeing the man who stood so confidently by her fire, inspecting her. So this was Mendark, whose legend stretched as far into the past as Yggur himself. He looks like those I see in every tavern, drinking wine and spinning lies, she thought contemptuously.

Mendark said something to Tallia and all three laughed. Then he saw Karan's small figure hesitating in the middle of the room and, by some trick of the light, he seemed to become smaller, less threatening, and his pensive manner took her fear away.

That was clever; he is sensitive at least, Karan thought grudgingly. She offered them tea.

Tallia leaned casually on the mantelpiece, sipping her tea

and talking quietly to Llian. She gave out the same calm authority that she had shown in Preddle, after Karan's ordeal in the stables.

Karan scowled at Tallia, resenting the glossy black hair hanging below her shoulders, her glorious chocolate skin, her dark-brown eyes flecked with gold, her long oval face. Tallia's garments were of finest lamb's wool; a scarlet scarf of silk was at her throat. Llian murmured something to her and she laughed, a rich deep sound, revealing beautiful teeth. They were laughing and talking together so freely that they might have been friends for years, and Karan felt as though Llian had abandoned her. Faithless friend, how can you laugh and joke with *her*? *She* could not understand what I've endured. Karan turned back to Mendark, who was leaning back in his chair, staring at the ceiling.

"What do you want with me?"

Tallia answered. "Remember our meeting in Preddle. I was spying for Mendark, and I reported back to him what I had learned about the Mirror and about you. You fled north while I waited for instructions. Perhaps if I'd followed you at once you might have had less trouble."

"Perhaps," scowled Karan, "though I do not trust easily, and your looks are against you."

"By the time Mendark's reply came, with orders to find you, you were far away. All I could do was send word that you fled toward Hetchet."

"Many messages went back and forth to find you and bring you here. So Llian came, in a roundabout way, though he would not have been my choice," said Mendark.

"Nor mine," said Karan, "though I would not be here without him."

Tallia continued. "I spoke to old Shand in Tullin and he told me where you'd gone. I almost caught you, south of the mountain, but the Whelm were between us. I drew them off to the west, but when it was safe to return you had disappeared. I thought you must have died in the snowstorms."

Karan inspected Tallia minutely, seeming to weigh all that she said, so that even Tallia felt self-conscious. "The balance falls in your favor," Karan said eventually. "But can I trust *him*?" she said rudely, glaring at Mendark.

Llian looked embarrassed. Tallia turned away, hiding a smile. Mendark returned her stare blandly.

"May I see it?" he said after a moment.

A refusal sprang automatically to her lips, then something in his face made her reconsider, and she slipped her hand into a concealed pocket and handed the Mirror to him without a word.

He held it gently between his fingertips. Why did I give it to him? she agonized. Has he placed a compulsion on me so easily?

Llian was astonished. She quelled him with a glare.

Mendark said a word under his breath and the tight coil of metal snapped open and lay upon his palm. He touched the scarlet and silver symbol with his fingertip. A picture grew on the Mirror: a black desolate landscape, a plain dotted with steely-gray masses, structures like a cluster of bubbles. The plain was cut by an icy rift, dark and deep; an iron tower leaned from a hill to one side. There were jagged mountains in the background. A small red sun peeped fitfully through rushing storm clouds. There was no living thing in sight.

"That is Aachan—the world of the Aachim and the Charon. I've seen its likeness often enough in Shazmak," said Karan.

Llian pushed closer, staring at the Mirror with bright eyes. "It's like looking through a window."

Mendark nodded absently. "But where does the window start, and where does it lead? Is this just a memory cast up by the stirrings of the Mirror? Is it Aachan as it once was; as it is now; as it will be? Why this place, and not another? Is there a message or a meaning?"

Karan shrugged. "I've never seen anything on it before," she lied. "In Shazmak they never talked about it."

Mendark touched the symbol again. The image vanished. He spoke another word, but nothing further appeared. He examined the Mirror closely but, discovering nothing more, handed it back to Karan. She looked surprised, then slipped it back in her pocket.

"You will come with me now," Mendark said to Karan. "Thurkad is a lawless place now that Thyllan is Magister. I am not completely beaten but I can defend you better on my own lands."

Karan had almost been ready to go with him, but something in the tone of his offer offended her and, without even thinking, she refused.

"I too can defend myself, and I have much experience with enemies. I will stay here. You may go or stay, as you wish," she said curtly to Llian. "My thanks for the assistance you have rendered me, though not for bringing me here."

"I will stay," said Llian, though not without a sigh for the comforts of Mendark's villa.

Mendark stopped dead. Karan was sitting on her cushion, hugging her knees with her arms. With a swift movement he sat down in front of her on the hearth. She turned her head away.

"Karan," he began. She did not stir.

"Karan, these are desperate times. Thurkad is besieged from without and within. Yggur's army has come on so quickly that he has outstripped our spies. It was not chance that cast me down from the Council. There are alliances building in Thurkad as much to be feared as the enemy outside. We must stand together or we will fall together. You are friendless and cannot stand alone. You must place your trust somewhere. Come with me."

"No!" she said angrily. "My enemies have hunted me for months. You look the same to me."

Mendark rose slowly to his feet. "Wretched girl," he said, looking down at her defiant form. "The old world is failing, the world of the Council, that has endured since the Forbidding. This opportunity will never come again."

Karan sensed his mood so strongly that it was almost as if she could read his mind. *How can she resist? Yes, why not! I will take it.*

Without warning Karan leapt to her feet, scattering the cushions, backing away, the small knife glittering in her upraised hand. Mendark made as though to raise up his arm. Karan tensed.

"Do so, mancer, and my point will be in your eye before you can utter a syllable," she breathed.

Llian watched, powerless to act, the hairs on the back of his neck erect. Any chance thing, a movement, a sudden noise, might set her off.

Then Tallia reached across from the mantelpiece and put her hand on Mendark's arm, saying softly, "Stay, Mendark."

The three stood frozen for a moment, then all at once the tension was gone. Mendark shook his head as though to clear it, then turned and went out without glancing back.

Tallia looked as though she wanted to speak with Karan, then changed her mind and followed Mendark.

Karan crouched there still, with staring eyes. Llian gently disengaged the knife from her cold fingers, led her back to the fire and sat her down on the cushions. She closed her eyes. A tremor ran through her; she looked up, giving Llian a wan smile, and gripped his hand tightly.

"For a moment I heard the music of the shades; it was calling to me," she said in a melancholy way.

"Too loudly," said Llian with a shudder. "Do not do that again, I beg you. Mendark is not to be trifled with."

"I will defend what was given me in trust."

On the street the rain had stopped. Mendark's hair billowed out behind him in the breeze as Tallia caught him up. They walked together back to the villa without speaking.

"That was foolish," she said as they mounted the front stairs. "She was near to coming with us. Now she never will. You chose a poor subject to try your tricks on, my friend. She knew what you were going to do before *you* did."

"I was sure she would give it up, if I pressed her."

Tallia glowered at him, part sympathetic, part pitying. "How *could* you have thought that, after hearing all that she has done?"

"I don't know," he said, and in the light he looked old and haggard. "I have just made a great, grave mistake. We must go back and put it right."

"Not now. Did you not see her desperation? I will speak to her in a day or two. Perhaps something can be retrieved."

"That is too long."

"Tomorrow then."

"Even that is too late. How long before Thyllan finds her? He has a thousand spies in this city, and he will not be as scrupulous as I am. It terrifies me to think of the Mirror in his hands." Mendark shook his head. "Never have I seen anyone move so quickly. She knew what I was going to do before I knew it myself. Karan is a powerful sensitive—perhaps even stronger than I am. She could be most useful to me, given proper training. What a fool I am."

38

A VISIT FROM THE MAGISTER

Though it was late in the morning, Karan was still in bed. She had had a fight with Llian and sent him away, and was immediately angry that he had gone. There came a tap on the door. Karan did not stir. Another, louder tap. She raised her head wearily. Would they never leave her be?

"Who is it?" she called through the door.

"Karan, are you there?" came a familiar voice from the other side.

Karan was overcome with joy. "Maigraith! Is it really you?" She thrust back the bolts and flung open the door. Maigraith stood there. There were tears in her eyes.

"Oh, Maigraith, you have come at last. I didn't even dare to hope. How did you get away? This thing has been too much for me. Let me give it to you." She fumbled in her robes.

"Leave it for the bye, Karan. It is you that I want to see. Oh, what have they done to you? You look at the point of death."

"I've been there more than once since you put upon me the burden of the Mirror. Now the doom of my family is coming on me. I am losing my mind." She spoke in a flat, passionless voice, so unlike the Karan that Maigraith had known. "I never thought to have enemies once. Now it surprises me to find that I still have a friend. They are closing in all around me, they hunt me, they never stop."

"It is over now. They will not touch you here. You have done your part, and no one could have asked more of you. I will take back the Mirror, if you wish it, and safeguard it until . . . Faichand comes. Oh, Karan, there is so much to talk about! First I must see to an errand, then I will return. I am on my way out of the city, to a secret meeting."

Karan paled. "Oh, be careful," she cried. "Yggur approaches."

"I know," Maigraith responded dreamily, a girlish eagerness on her face.

"You're going away again," said Karan, her voice suddenly dreary. "This time you won't return at all. Please don't go. My enemies are all about me."

"Do not talk like that, Karan. You are safe now. I will come back tonight."

"Please take it with you. Remember how you were fascinated by it in Fiz Gorgo?"

"No more. I learned that it is a twisted, deceitful, entrapping thing. I never want to look at it again. Hold it for me for just a few more hours. I cannot take it where I am going. Once I return I will know what to do with it."

"Please," begged Karan, her voice cracking. It was too late, Maigraith was already at the door. Then she turned back, remembering.

"There was an Aachim seeking you, from Shazmak."

Karan leapt up, terrified. "No!" she cried out. "No!"

Maigraith came back from the door and took her hands.

"There is nothing to fear. He comes on an errand from Tensor, with a message of conciliation."

"It must be a trick. He comes to trap me, to take me back to Shazmak. I will not see him. Do not tell him that I am here."

"I did not. But Tensor would not trick you. He would come and take you himself."

"That is true," said Karan. "But I still fear this man. Who is he?"

"His name is Flacq."

"I don't know him," said Karan, slightly relieved. "He must be newly come to Shazmak. Bring him tonight, if you must. I will see him if you are here with me. Promise that you will be here when he comes."

"If you wish it. Until the evening then."

Evening came and then the night, but Maigraith did not return. Neither had Llian come back. It was nearly midnight and Karan lay on her bed, dozing. There was a gentle tap on the door. She sought out with her mind, but she had been afraid to use her talent for so long that now it told her nothing. It had never been completely reliable anyway. She opened the door a crack. A man stood there; in the darkness she could not see his face.

"Good evening," he said. "My name is Flacq. I come from Shazmak, bearing a message of conciliation from Tensor."

The disguised voice meant nothing to her, though a slight familiarity of mannerism disturbed Karan, and she hesitated. The Aachim held out his hand; something glittered there. "I also bring you this. I believe it is yours. It was found in your room in Shazmak after you went away."

Karan took it from his hand, puzzled now. It was a fine silver chain with a jade pendant. Then she recognized it. It was Llian's, of course. She'd taken it from him the night before her trial, to help send the dream to him. He would be glad of it. She slipped it over her head and tucked it beneath her shirt. It was cool against her breast.

The Aachim moved toward her, into the doorway.

I know you! she realized. She tried to slam the door but her arm would not obey; suddenly she was terribly afraid. This is a nightmare, she thought desperately. I've had this nightmare before and I don't want it. Something was draining all will from her. Then the man slid through the door. The light shone on his face; the twin scars gleamed through his beard. *Emmant!* She wanted to scream but could not make a sound.

"Now you will be mine," he said. "In life and in death."

He moved slowly toward her. His face was changed almost beyond recognition, as though he had rotted inside. His breath stank like a dead thing by the roadside, and his once brown skin was yellow, rubbery and sagging off the bones. The flesh seemed to have melted away so that the scars stuck out like ridges across his cheek. His black eyes had retreated into his skull till they were like pellets in the bottom of a bowl. That dangerous grace was gone too; now he moved with a shambling, slubbering step.

Karan was almost sick with fear, and loathing. This was far worse than the Whelm; worse even than her chronic nightmare. A sick horror paralyzed her. She was alone. Her friends had deserted her. Even Maigraith had betrayed her, sent the beast to destroy her. She had promised, but she did not come.

Where was Llian? I thought you loved me, but where are you now? Away somewhere, plotting with your friend Mendark, another of my enemies. Enemy? she thought, confused now. You offered to help me. But you only wanted *it*. Even you, Llian, only wanted the Mirror.

Love, what love? The only one who loved me was this beast who now advances. There is no love in him now, he is as mad as I am. Abuse and death is all he offers. Oh, Llian, Llian, Maigraith, Hassien, Pender, the faces whirling in front of her, Pender, Pender, you saved me once, where are you now? "No!" she screamed.

She picked herself up, feeling her cheek swelling from the blows, licking a trickle of blood from her lip. She felt herself dwindling with each successive blow. How can you hate so much? What did I do to make you hate so much? At least speak to me. But the figure, broad, bearded and still immensely strong, said not a word.

Her wrist pained her. What a trouble that wrist has been to me, she thought wryly. No longer. It doesn't matter anymore. Nothing matters now. She backed away. Emmant followed in a crouch.

Strangely, she could feel his will within her, as though they were *linked*. How could he link with me unless I willed it?

Come to me, he called over the link. *You cannot resist me now. Come to me. Do you love me yet? You will. I can make you love me, you know.*

She burst out laughing at that, the laughter cutting through her madness like a knife, breaking the flimsy link.

"Love you," she screeched. "I could sooner love the maggot that crawls in the dung on the street than you. I was right to do what I did before. I will do it again." She pulled out the little knife and held it up before her.

He was bewildered. "I command you to love me. Faelamor promised that you would. I have betrayed Shazmak to the Whelm for you. All the days since, I have sought you: in Narne, in Sith, everywhere. Thinking of you always, of possessing you. Nothing else have I thought of but you. You must love me, you will."

Betrayed Shazmak? Faelamor? Was she back in her nightmare? She advanced on him, her eyes glittering.

"What madness is this?"

The look in her eyes chilled Emmant. He hesitated, backed away.

"Faelamor came to Shazmak," he stuttered, and his voice, that was always so deep, became shrill and cracked. "Tensor sent her there, a prisoner. She was desperate to escape. She promised you to me if I would help her. I taught the Whelm the secret way into Shazmak and instructed them in the disabling of the Sentinels. She said that they would free her. She enchanted the necklace for me. She promised that you would do my will, once I gave it to you. She has betrayed me."

Karan laughed, an empty, ugly sound. "Indeed, I think she has betrayed everyone *but* you. The chain is enchanted, but she made the charm for the owner, and that was not me. It is Llian's."

She held out the necklace, the little jade pendant dangling between her fingers, taunting him. "Here, give it to him. I'm sure that *he* will love you. His mind is very weak."

Emmant dashed the chain from her hand and launched himself at her. She backed toward the door, fell heavily on her side, tried to scrabble away. Emmant flung himself on her, crushing her. The scars on his face were absolutely white and his grimace had twisted them into the shape of sickles. His hands reached out for her throat, gripping, squeezing, then the little knife was in her good hand and she struck again and again.

At last they came, long after midnight: Llian, Tallia and Mendark. They stood in the doorway, surveying the wreckage of the dark room. There were two bodies on the floor, covered in blood.

Llian wept until his heart would burst. Mendark took him outside while Tallia turned the man over. His twisted, scarred face was unknown to her. She hauled his legs off Karan and dragged him to a corner of the room. Who are you, she wondered, and how came you here? Whatever you hoped to gain from the Mirror it was surely not this.

"I dreamed that we were bound together through all eternity, my love. Yet hardly a second of eternity has passed and already your embrace grows cold."

The cold clear voice came from behind her, and Tallia whirled around.

Karan still lay on her back, her clothes drenched with brown blood. She was reaching up with her arms and there was a smile on her face, but her eyes were closed.

"Where have you gone, my love? Indeed you are a most feeble lover to have tired so soon. Do not leave me. Come back, come back. Put your loving hands on my soft white throat," her voice became venomous, "and let me plunge this sliver into your black heart." Karan stabbed in a frenzy at the air above her, then went still.

Tallia came closer, looking down at her.

The smile broke across Karan's face again. "Where do you go, my love? I hear you creeping, afraid to wake me. Have you tired already of my embrace?"

Tallia did not wait to hear it again. She hurried out of the room and found Llian and Mendark in a parlor nearby.

"She is alive." Llian leapt up at once. "But I caution you, do not go near her. She is quite mad, and dangerous."

Llian pushed past her and ran back to the room, crying Karan's name. Then he yelped and as they ran into the room they saw him backing away, holding one hand in the other. Blood was dripping through his fingers. He looked quite bewildered. Karan was on her feet, the knife in her hand, her face an ugly mask. "I called you but you did not come," she said. "You promised."

Mendark pushed the others to one side, advancing slowly on Karan. She moved the knife in front of her, smiling now. "This is a game more to my liking," she said. "We have played before, you and I."

Mendark froze. As he did so, Maigraith appeared in the

doorway. She stepped across the threshold and stopped dead, bewildered by what she saw—Karan, demented and covered in blood, waving her knife; the corpse in one corner, three strangers, no, it was the young man she had seen in Narne—bailed up in the other. She was so shocked that she could not tell what to do. She called out, her voice soft with anguish, "Karan!"

Karan whirled, faster than thought, and slashed the air in front of Maigraith's face. Maigraith was wearing a long loose concealing cloak and a dark shapeless hood that cast her face in shadow, so that the others could not tell if it were man or woman there. But Karan knew.

"You promised to come back, and you did not. You promised you would not send him, yet he came. Emmant came! I cried out for you, I begged you, but you did not come. What does it take to drag you from the bed of your lover?"

She slashed again at Maigraith viciously. Maigraith fell back in confusion and distress, tears falling in the shadow of her hood.

"Not so," she said softly. She put her hands up but made no attempt to defend herself. Karan lowered the knife and a slow horror crept over her face, a self-loathing that so twisted her that it made Llian's skin crawl.

"I killed him," she said. "How easy it was, in the end. Help me, father."

"Now will you come with me?" Mendark asked Karan gently.

"I don't care anymore. Nothing matters."

But before they could move there was a racket in the corridor and a troop of guardsmen rushed in, followed by a tall man in black robes, with receding hair, pale eyes and a nose like a club. It was Thyllan, the man who had overthrown Mendark as Magister of the High Council. Karan stared at the intruder, trying to see his purpose through the fog in her mind. The guardsmen took in the situation at once, and though Karan struck at them she was no match for their pikes. Soon one cracked her on the side of the head and she fell to the floor.

Thyllan searched Karan and with a cry of triumph removed the Mirror from her secret pocket. Mendark moved forward, but the pikes came instantly up against his chest, and the captain of the guards looked enquiringly at the Magister.

Thyllan shook his head. "I can afford to be merciful now," he said, "but I warn you: look to your own security. Guards, bring her and everything that is hers."

The guards bound Karan's hands, hoisted her up and took her in the direction of the citadel.

The four stared at each other for a long minute, then Maigraith whirled and rushed out of the room. Llian picked up his amulet and chain and stumbled out the door.

It was morning now. Mendark and Llian sat by the fire in Mendark's villa, waiting for Tallia to come back with whatever news she could glean. They had been up all night. Neither had spoken in hours. Llian's agony had struck him dumb.

The door opened and Tallia came in. She looked exhausted.

"What have you found out?" cried Llian, leaping up.

"She is held in the citadel," Tallia said. "And that is all I learned."

"What about the other woman? Did you find out who she was?"

"No! Only Karan can say."

Mendark stared into the fire with his head sunk on his hands. The events of the past days had further diminished him; he felt that he had lost control of his destiny.

Just then there was a movement outside and the door was thrust open. A woman stepped noiselessly in. There was mud on her high boots and her blue cloak was dripping. She took her hat off and shook free the pale hair, her eyes coming straight to Mendark's. Suddenly he felt weak in the stomach.

"Mendark!" she said. "I am Faelamor. I have come for the Mirror."

Mendark slowly let out the breath that he had been holding. "I haven't forgotten you. How long has it been? Six hundred years?"

Faelamor shrugged, indifferent.

"So," he went on, "*You* were Faichand?"

"I was, but the secret is out."

"Then I need not ask how you came by the guards. You're too late. Thyllan has it, and he is Magister. In time of war he is all-powerful. There is nothing I can do to get it back."

Her face went cold. "Then what of the girl?"

"He has her too, but she's no good to anyone now; her mind is completely gone."

Faelamor's mask cracked. It might have been worse. "Tell it."

Mendark told her, briefly, of the events leading up to that scene in the room, and the dead man, Emmant. Faelamor's face melted a little more. All had gone well, save this matter of Thyllan, and that could be remedied. Soon they would all be here.

Llian stared at the ageless face, hating and distrusting her, but fascinated too. To meet one of the Faellem was a rare experience these days, and no chronicler would have met Faelamor in many a hundred years. He noted her distinguishing features for his tale, especially the golden, feline eyes and the remarkable translucent skin.

"So this is the miserable Zain," Faelamor said, staring back. "The line fails, it would appear."

"What does Thyllan want the Mirror for?" Tallia interjected.

"He wants it for the making of gates, portals," said Mendark, "as, no doubt, did Yggur. Imagine the power he would hold if he could instantly transport his armies, or his spies, anywhere on Santhenar. The Mirror is thought to contain the secret: how to make such devices."

Llian, who had been sitting at the table listening to the conversation go back and forth, could no longer contain himself and burst out in fury, "Damn the Mirror! You must free Karan."

"I don't see how I can," said Mendark.

"I heard that Thyllan has her in chains," said Tallia. "That she needs be restrained."

"Chains!" cried Llian in grief and fury. "Karan in *chains*! You must do something."

"While she's up there, I'm helpless."

"The citadel is *barred* to Mendark," Tallia explained. "He can enter neither openly nor secretly. Our position is precarious; doubly so now that the enemy is at our gates. Thyllan could have us taken, killed even, and there is nothing anyone could do, now that we are at war. As long as he keeps her in the citadel, we're powerless."

"There is a way," said Faelamor, who had been sitting quietly by, "and Mendark alone has the means of it. You must call a Great Conclave. That will force them down from the citadel. Then there will be a chance to get the Mirror back, and her too if you wish it, though she is vicious and treacherous."

"Of course," said Mendark. "What cloud was over me that I did not recall that way?"

But why is Maigraith not here? said Faelamor to herself. She *must* attend the Conclave. And she turned and went as silently as she had come.

"We have just looked upon a very evil one," said Llian. "Did you see the hate on her face? Do not trust her; do not call this Conclave."

"Not evil," said Mendark, "though she might do it. Desperate, driven. To lead the Faellem is to be the Faellem. Of course I do not trust her, but I will call the Conclave. He *must* come; he *must* bring the Mirror and submit it to the Just. At last I can see an advantage and I will take it . . ."

Llian frowned, puzzled.

"A Great Conclave is held only when Thurkad is in a dire extreme," Mendark explained. "Sometimes it throws up a new way, or a new leader. Because I was Magister before him, even at such a dire time as this, Thyllan cannot refuse me. He must bring Karan and the Mirror to the Conclave, which will be held in the city, not in the citadel."

"How will that help to free her?"

"I don't know," Mendark responded brusquely, "but at least she'll be within our reach if we find a way."

"He might refuse."

"He cannot: he's not *that* secure in his strength."

Days went by. The armies of Yggur were drawn up on the plain south of Thurkad. Embassies were sent, returned. The walls of Thurkad were not suited for defense, so the army prepared to do battle outside the southern gate. Then news came of another army advancing swiftly on Thurkad from the north-west, spreading out, encircling the city. There was uproar, panic; the only way out was by sea. The harbor was jammed; every craft capable of floating was packed to the waterline. Attackers and defenders faced each other, and the waiting began.

39

THE PRISONER

S ome days later Mendark called Llian in.

"Shut the door," he said. "Go through that business about the Forbidding again. The ending to your tale, and what you learned from Tensor. I'm really worried now, what with Yggur marching to war, Faelamor turning up, Karan's dreams of Rulke—it's too much of a coincidence."

Llian told the story again. "I don't even know where to begin," he said at the end.

"I don't know either." Mendark rubbed a hairy cheek. "Well, Rulke's archives are here in the Magister's scriptoria."

"And you never looked at them?"

"Remember who you are speaking to," Mendark growled. "His records fill many rooms, but most are undecipherable. I've looked at everything that could be read. But then, not having your new evidence, no one was looking for this. Better take a fresh look."

"You said the citadel was *barred*."

"It is, to me and those in my employ. A barrier that we cannot cross. But he cannot bar everyone in Thurkad. Do you dare attempt it?"

So! thought Llian, there *is* a way inside, and still Karan lies in chains. "How would you get me in?"

"I have ways."

"Then why can't you get Karan out?"

Mendark sighed. "Leave me to do my business. She will be well guarded, by human guards and by wards like the Sentinels in Shazmak. Besides, Thyllan must bring her to the Conclave in three days. And don't get any clever ideas—you're going in for one reason only."

He *doesn't* care, thought Llian. Well, if I get the chance . . .

"I will do it," he said.

"Good. Come back in a couple of hours, and I'll have the maps and catalogs for you to study."

"Do you think this is a good idea?" Tallia asked after Llian had gone. "Breaking the truce of the Conclave? If he's found out, Thyllan can refuse to come."

"It's a risk, but nowhere near the risk of not finding out. I've *got* to know!"

It was three in the morning. Carrying food and water for two days and a night, a map and catalog, a lantern and two skins of oil under his cloak, for as usual it was raining, Llian set out with Tallia through the back streets to a nondescript building. He wore anonymous servant's garb: dark-blue pantaloons, blouse and cap, a short cape, sandals.

At the back Tallia raised a trapdoor, climbed down into a cellar, did something that Llian didn't see, bits of earth-stained plaster fell and part of the wall swung out with a groan.

"This hasn't been used for a very long time," Tallia said,

holding the lantern out before her and stepping through into an earthy passage.

Llian followed her through the darkness, feeling claustrophic. There was nothing to see save earth and rock or, in places, stonework weeping damp. The tunnel undulated, but more up than down, which made sense, since the citadel was near the top of a hill. A few curves, sharp and shallow, a right-angle bend, a long up-sloping straight, then Tallia stopped suddenly.

"What's the matter?"

"I thought I felt something. No, it's nothing." She went on more slowly, then stopped as though she had run into an invisible barrier. "Aah!"

"Are you all right?"

"I ran right into the ward. It hurt. This is as far as I can go, but it's probably safe for you. See if you feel anything."

He crept forward a pace, then another. "Nothing!"

"Good luck, chronicler." She held out her hand, drew it back smartly as though stung, then saluted him.

Llian waved an arm at her; then, feeling most uneasy, he made his way up the passage. When he looked back a minute later Tallia's lantern was lost to sight. He was utterly alone, under the ground.

A few minutes later he came, after a series of right-angle bends and a steep up-slope, to a blank wall. Tallia had told him what to do—find three separate depressions in the wall, and press a finger into each at the same time. That took a lot of trial and error for the walls were quite uneven. After twenty or thirty tries he got it right and a slab rotated without a sound, leaving a space large enough to wriggle through. As soon as he had done so it closed again, just as silently. He was in the cellars of the citadel!

It was all rather easier than he had hoped. The tunnel

brought him out close to his destination. Llian was outside the door in less than ten minutes, without seeing a soul.

He had been given a key, a flat strip of metal. He simply pushed it in the slit in the door and waited. After a full minute the door clicked. Llian slipped inside, shut the door and shot the bolt.

He had expected a low-roofed, moldy crypt, a wider version of the tunnel, but the room Llian found himself in was more like a library—huge, high-ceilinged and dry. Obviously designed to protect important documents. There were rows and rows of bookshelves and scroll racks, and, down the far end, cupboards from floor to ceiling. The place was vast—thousands of files and volumes that no chronicler had ever seen.

Llian consulted the catalog that Mendark had annotated for him. He walked up and down the shelves, seeing how they were organised, taking down a book here, a scroll there, dipping into each then putting it back, trying to catch the flavor of the archives. Where to start? To read the contents of the room would take months.

He began on the most interesting category, documents from the time of the Forbidding. Hours later he realized what a hopeless task it was. The heading actually covered hundreds of years, thousands of documents, but none was relevant. He had his lunch, topped up the lantern and tried to work out a better approach. The whole business now seemed pointless. What fool had made the catalog? An apprentice chronicler would have done better.

He searched files on Shuthdar, on the flute—these were the earliest of all; on the Clysm; the Faellem and the Aachim. By the end of it he could have filled in many missing gaps in the Histories, but had found nothing that helped him with his quest.

He looked through the catalog again. Something stood

out this time. A section entitled *Correspondence—other Charon*. Subheadings included Kandor, Yalkara, as well as other names, some of which he knew to be blendings, interbreeds between Charon and Aachim, or Charon and other races. What would they write about? Llian spent more tedious hours going through letters, treaties, reports on agriculture, mining, weather, roads and a thousand other mundane issues. Each of the Charon had an empire, and the amount of correspondence generated was prodigious.

Now the lamp began to flutter yellow. It was nearly out of oil. Already the first skin was used up. How long had he been here? Had Tallia said twelve hours from one skin of oil, or eighteen? Surely the latter, for he was worn out. Llian laid an armload of ledgers on the floor for a mattress. He had slept badly ever since Karan had been taken. He snuffed the lamp and slept.

The second day passed in much the same way as the first. The work was tedious and frustrating. There was far too much to look through, and the catalog entries usually contained shelves full of records under a single heading. His last skin of oil was running low, and some must be saved for Karan, and to get back out again.

He went back to the correspondence files. Anything explicit would probably have been destroyed, but there could be a hint in letters or dispatches that would mean nothing to anyone but him. Here was a sheaf of letters between Rulke and Kandor. Llian riffled through them. There were hundreds, many hours of reading. On impulse he stuffed them in his bag. What else? Letters between Rulke and Yalkara, not as many. The first crime made the next easier. He took these as well.

He unfolded the map, tracing the way out with his finger to imprint it on his mind. He had never been good with maps. Now, where would Karan be? He examined the plans of the floors above. There were nine levels, marked in tiny writing. Kitchens, pantries, halls—seemingly dozens of them—libraries, map room, servants' quarters, dormitories, hundreds upon hundreds of rooms. Further down, store-rooms, armories, guardrooms, cellars, *cells*!

Be calm! he told himself. Karan need not be in the cells at all—she could be locked in any room of the citadel. And even if she was down there, she would surely be guarded.

But the thought of finding her was lodged immovably in Llian's mind. No matter what misgivings arose, and there were many—of being caught, of Thyllan finding out what he was looking for, of interfering in whatever plans Mendark had made—he cast them all aside. Mendark could go to blazes!

The cells were right across the other side of the citadel. How could he get down there without being discovered? Llian worked out a route on the map and memorized it. After a few minutes he came into lighted ways, extinguished his lantern, clutched a sheaf of papers in one hand and tried to make himself look like any messenger boy. It must have been very late for he saw only two people on the way, and neither showed any interest in him.

Here was the stair he was looking for, running steeply down to the lower level. Llian crept down and stuck his head round the corner. He saw a gloomy corridor with only one or two lamps along it, but there was enough light to see that there were cells both to the left and right. He eased his way along the wall, keeping away from the light. Further down was an open room like a cell without bars, closed off from the corridor by a long bench. It looked like a guardhouse, and it was empty. Where was the guard?

Just then he heard a gurgling snore and, peering over the bench, he saw the guard flat out on a long stool. The room stank of stale beer. Llian marched past and was not challenged.

Beyond were many cells both small and large, most occupied by sleeping prisoners, probably retainers loyal to Mendark. He had to light his lamp again to see whether Karan was among them. She wasn't, and one or two stirred irritably under his light. He continued past more cells and came to another guard post. This one was unmanned. All of the cells here were empty, save the one with the lamp outside.

"Karan!" he whispered, gripping the bars.

She lay on a heap of straw on the floor, a dingy blanket clutched about her shoulders, red hair at one end, bare feet at the other. She did not move.

"Karan," he said more loudly.

She stirred, shivered, and ever so slowly raised her head, looking at him without recognition.

"Karan! It's me, Llian. Come quickly!"

She got up, dripping straw, and shambled across to the door. She stared up into his face, then turned and went the same indifferent way to her bed. Her cheek was badly bruised. The look on her face made his heart break.

He called her back again, and again she ambled up to the bars as though he was of no significance. Llian took her hand. She looked down, then up at his face. A spark lit in her eyes, but it went out again.

He reached through the bars and caught her in his arms. Again she almost recognized him, then her eyes went blank. She came unresistingly, as though she had no will of her own, but on touching the bars she shrank away. Llian let her go and shook the door. It didn't even rattle. He scooted across to the empty guardhouse. No keys there! Back at the other, the guard still slept secure in the knowledge that the whole citadel was warded. Where were the keys?

Ah! A bunch dangled from a peg on the wall. Llian crept in. The guard stirred, belched beery fumes and put his head back down on his arms. Llian reached around behind him and grabbed the keys. Not carefully enough—they rang together. The guard groaned, rolled over and almost fell off the stool. Llian held his breath but soon the man was snoring as before.

Back at Karan's cell he tried the first key in the lock. It didn't work. Neither did the second, nor the third, nor any of the others. Karan walked across and watched what he was doing with an expressionless face. He tried each key again, three or four times; he wiggled the door, but to no avail.

"Wrong keys," said Karan and went back to her straw.

How would she know? Llian ran back to the guardhouse. The guard was still snoring, his hand groping around blindly for something. The beer jug stood on the floor just out of reach. Eventually he gave up and slumped back again, making a whistling snore through his teeth. Where could the keys be? The guardhouse was spartan, just a few pegs in the wall, one holding up a threadbare cloak, empty shelves below, more shelves under the bench. Llian got down on hands and knees. It was hard to make anything out in the gloom. He crawled under the bench, groping around in the dark, but could find nothing. Then the guard turned over and Llian heard an unmistakable jingle.

The man was now sitting slumped over, breathing noisily. Yes, there they were, half-covered by a belly as big as the barrel he'd got it from. Llian reached his hand up into the doughy sack but at the first pressure the guard groaned and leaned further forward. Llian had to whip his hand out of the way before it was trapped. Now the hand was groping again. Llian put the jug within reach and the guard lifted it to his lips and took a great swig with his eyes closed. Beer ran down his chin, he gasped, belched and slumped sideways, exposing the keys. In a flash Llian had them off his belt and scuttled out into the corridor.

The second key snapped Karan's lock and he was inside. He ran across and folded her in his arms. She hung there like a rag doll. She was terribly thin.

"Come on!"

She followed him to the door, then stopped and would go no further, just kept pointing out into the corridor. Llian was about to sling her across his shoulder when he heard a voice raised up in drunken song. Something smashed, the guard cursed, flat feet flapping on the stone, then the song began again.

Llian almost panicked. "It's the guard." He ran back and forth, unable to decide what to do.

Karan, who had shown no signs of intelligence all this time, suddenly jerked as though she had been stabbed with a red-hot needle. Indifferent to her own fate, the danger to Llian had roused her. Her eyes rolled back and forwards, her pinpoint pupils dilated.

"*Llian!*" she whispered, a gaunt version of her old self again. "Oh, Llian, you came for me." She flung her arms around his neck and kissed his face. Just as quickly she let him go. The guard was now bawling out his sentimental dirge.

"Get out, before you're locked in too. Oh, Llian," she said, staring at him as though he was the most precious thing in her life. "Please go. He'll kill you."

Llian tugged at her hand. "Come on! There's still time to get away. He's drunk!"

"I can't. Quick, into my bed. Under the straw."

How could anyone hide in that miserable pile? Nonetheless he ran over, lay down and Karan piled rank, moldy straw over him. She lay down in front, flung the blanket over them both and snuggled in. A cold hand wormed its way down into the straw and gripped his hand.

None too soon. The guard lurched into view, shining his lantern into the cells on the other side of the corridor.

"Twelve . . . thirteen . . ." He skipped the empty cells opposite, continued down to the end, then they heard him shuffling up this side. He appeared before Karan's cell, swaying, trying to remember what number he was up to.

"Fourteen!" he cried triumphantly, raised the jug to his mouth to celebrate, realized that it was broken and cast it aside with a crash. He swayed, grabbed the cell door to hold himself up and it swung open, scraping the skin off his toes.

The guard cursed and banged it shut, trying to sober up, trying to remember. Had he locked the door or not? Of course he had. He never forgot a thing like that, even though this cell, in any case, was warded. He looked down at the squat black Sentinel, rather like a witch's hat but with fluted sides, that stood against the wall just beyond the bars. Through a slit a yellow light glared watchfully. It was comforting to see it. He had been warned about this prisoner. Clever, they said.

He held up his lantern. The red-haired woman lay listlessly on the straw, as she had for most of the time she had been here. She didn't look so clever. Still, better lock her in at once, before anyone found out. If she did escape, Thyllan would have his ears, and he'd be in the front line by lunchtime tomorrow. He put the lantern down and felt on his belt for the keys. They weren't there! Now that was strange. He never took those keys off, save to give them to his relief.

The guard ran off in a panic, sandals flapping. Karan stood up, kissed Llian's mold-smelling cheek, brushed straw off his shoulders, squeezed his hands. Llian flinched.

"What's the matter?" She examined his hand, which had an angry red gash across the palm. "Who did this to you?"

Llian hesitated. "You did. Don't you remember? After Emmant . . ."

Karan looked as though she had been struck. "I knifed you? *Emmant*?" She moaned, her eyes crossed and Llian thought she was going to relapse. But his peril dragged her out of it. "Oh, Llian, forgive me. I don't remember."

"Later! We've got to go. The guard will be back in a minute."

"Yes. Go quickly. Even drunk he's more than a match for you."

"You're coming with me," he said. "I'm not going to leave you behind this time."

She pointed to the Sentinel. "It's set to me; I can't get past it."

"Maybe we can break through it," said Llian, opening the door. Karan looked doubtful. He took her hand. "Now, fast as you can!"

He took off and she ran too. Llian passed straight through. Free! he exulted, then the hand that held Karan's encountered sudden resistance, a jerk that almost pulled his arm out of its socket, and a numbing shock like the one Vartila had struck him with in the house in Narne. He crashed on his back and heard a tinkle from his pack, the lamp breaking. At the same moment the corridor was seared by a yellow glare from the Sentinel that flared up the spectrum to blue and to violet. It began to clang furiously, a racket like standing underneath a temple bell.

Llian picked himself up. Karan lay on the floor, wringing her hand, which was swelling visibly as though it had been stung. She looked at him blankly for an instant, then she was herself again.

"I didn't think we could," she said, ghastly in the violet glare. "Please go. They have to bring me to the Conclave tomorrow, but they don't even have to keep you alive."

Llian looked around wildly. Nothing he ever did seemed to go right. The guard appeared, staggering out of his guard-house with sword in hand. What could he do? Was there any way of breaking this Sentinel? He tried to pick it up but it wouldn't move, as though something was holding it down. He kicked it, hurting his toes. It was unharmed.

Suddenly inspired, Llian whipped out the oilskin and squeezed the contents in through the slit. The clanging grew muddy but the violet glare was as baleful as ever. The guard pounded toward him. Llian ripped the lamp off the wall, smashed the glass and touched the wick to the Sentinel. A small yellow flame grew there. Just in time, for the guard was almost on him, swinging his sword in unsteady arcs. Llian hurled the broken lamp at his head, missed, turned to run and slipped on a patch of oil.

He fell right into the path of the guard, who took a tremendous swipe with his sword. Had it connected it would have taken his head clean off, but Llian fell flat on his face and it whirred above him. The guard overbalanced and fell, landing on Llian's back, knocking the breath out of him and cracking his jaw against the floor. The sword clattered across the flagstones. Llian lay still, winded and stunned.

The guard clouted Llian over the head. Then, as Karan stood with her hands out, straining against the Sentinel but helpless to do anything, he kicked Llian in the ribs, three times, and staggered across to his sword. Llian groaned and pushed himself to hands and knees, spitting blood.

Karan screamed, a terrible ululation. The guard looked over his shoulder, then hefted the sword. At the same moment flames burst out of the top of the Sentinel, something tinkled inside, the clanging wheezed to a stop and the violet glare went out, leaving the corridor lit only by the guard's lantern, which lay on its side on the floor. The guard did not even look around, so intent was he on bloody murder. The sword reached its apex. Llian tried to scramble backwards but, like a cat on ice, kept slipping on the oil.

Karan came out of the cell like a bullet, leapt high and her knees struck the guard in the back of the neck. Her outstretched hand caught his sword arm and knocked it sideways. He smashed into the floor and did not move. Karan heaved Llian to his feet, snatched up the sword and yelled, "Which way?"

Llian pointed back up the corridor toward the guardhouse.

"No, that's the way they'll come. Quick, grab that lamp!"

Llian did as he was told, Karan took his hand and they ran down the corridor into the dark. Already they could hear distant shouting. Around another corner, another corridor junction, up a little staircase. Karan suddenly stopped, out of breath but laughing.

"Firebug! Can't you think of any other way to rescue me! And don't think I invite any old errand boy to my bed. Now, where are we going?"

Llian was delighted to see the old Karan back again, even if it was just a shadow of her normal self. "A secret tunnel, but it's a long way away—right on the other side of the citadel. I don't see how we can get there from here, with the whole place alerted."

"Well, most of the guards have gone to the war. Give me the map. Stick your head around the corner and see if you can see any lights."

"Nothing!"

"We're here, right?"

He laboriously worked out their position and nodded.

"Where's the tunnel?"

Llian traced out his route.

"That far?" She frowned. "Well, we'd better get as far away from here as possible. Let's take these stairs, right up to the top. It's a bit further, but maybe they won't expect us to go that way."

The stairs were narrow and very steep, a service way, nothing like the grand affairs in the main parts of the citadel. They wound their way up six or seven floors, stopped for a breather, then up the remaining two to the top floor of the citadel.

At the top she stopped, panting, trying not to make a noise. "I'm so weak," she cried in frustration. "I'll just have to sit down for a minute."

Llian was glad of the excuse. He kept watch while Karan unshuttered the lamp and consulted the map again. "This place is a warren," he said. "A dozen staircases, a hundred corridors. They can't search them all at once."

"Anyone in sight?"

"No!"

"Then we'll go right across this floor to the other side, then all the way down. That should bring us out quite close to your secret tunnel. What do you think?"

They scampered along, turning the corner into a much wider corridor that was carpeted, hung with tapestries and portraits. Some of the doors were open, revealing opulent, empty rooms. Halfway along, passing a massive set of double doors, someone said, "Right away!" and the door was flung open.

"Don't look back!" Karan muttered, gripping Llian's arm. "Just walk normally, as though you are any other servant."

Faint hope! thought Llian, considering the state of your rags.

"Hoy! You there!" The call echoed along the corridor.

"It's Thyllan," said Karan. "Run!"

They fled.

"After them!" Thyllan boomed. "Guards, to the east stairs!"

They reached the end of the corridor, skidding on the carpet, and hurtled down the first flight. Llian stopped on the landing, holding his ribs.

"Are you all right?"

"I'll manage."

Halfway down the second flight they heard their pursuers reach the top of the stairs. They ran until Llian could run no more, until Karan felt like a limp rag.

"This is the last," she panted. "Do you remember where to go now?"

"I think this way," gasped Llian. He hobbled ten or twelve paces along the corridor, then back. "No, it's that way." He ran a bit further, then stopped. "I'm not sure."

Karan had the map out. A horde was clattering down the stairs. "Follow me," she cried, running past him and folding the map up as she ran. She took a left turn into a wider corridor.

"Yes, I'm sure I remember this way," said Llian. Behind them the pursuing guards appeared, only a spear-cast away. Now another group poured around the corner before them. Trapped!

"Down here!" Karan darted into a side passage, then right, left, and left again into an even narrower one. They'd temporarily lost their pursuers, gained perhaps a minute. Suddenly they burst into an unfurnished room that had no other door. "Is this it?"

"Yes! Yes it is! I took note of those marks on the wall."

"Then find the way out! I'll try to stop them." She held out the guard's short sword.

The instructions for opening this door were different. Four separate bumps on the wall had to be touched in sequence. Llian tried a set that looked right. Nothing. Another set, but the wall remained a wall: cold, grimy and damp. A third set. A fourth, his fingers dancing over every bump, every knob on the wall.

Clang! The sound of sword on sword. He looked back. Karan was waving the blade around in what looked like a professional manner, and in the narrow hall only one guard could get at her at a time. But he was head and shoulders above her, and his weapon much longer. It could only end one way. It would have ended already save that they had orders to keep her alive.

"Give up," cried Llian, knowing that one slip of the blade and she would be dead.

"Be damned!" she cried. "Find it, you fool!"

Llian kept at it. Then, when he was beginning to think that he was in the wrong place, even the wrong room, the wall gave a groan and started to revolve.

"Karan," he screamed. "I've got it!"

At the same moment the fellow slipped his sword under Karan's guard and sent her weapon flying. She jumped backwards, but he was desperately fast. In three strides he had her by the arm, a grip that was unshakeable. Behind him were a dozen others, and Thyllan too. There was no escape.

"Go, Llian," she said softly to his mesmerized face. "I'll be all right. I'll see you tomorrow."

"Don't count on it," grated Thyllan.

Llian realized that she spoke sense. They had no reason to treat him kindly. He waved, jumped through the doorway and slapped the other side of it. It began to close.

The big man who was holding Karan let her go and raced forward. Immediately she flung herself free of the other guard and darted across the room, making a diversion so Llian could get away. The big guard jammed his foot in the door, then looked back to see what she was doing. The door closed, grinding away as though there was no resistance.

The guard screamed and tried to pull his foot out but it was too late. Bones cracked; he screamed again, trapped by his mangled pulp of a foot. The door slammed shut.

Llian shuddered. He lit the lamp. Better get on his way—they'd soon force the door, or break it. He squeezed the dribble that remained in his oilskin into the lamp and began the journey back.

"You're a fool, Llian! No wonder they threw you out of the College. What on earth were you thinking?" Mendark had been in a black rage even before Llian came staggering in to report his fruitless journey.

"How could I leave her there once I had seen her? You did nothing for her."

"*Nothing?*" Mendark was beside himself. "I've been working day and night for a week on this Conclave, and now you've mucked it all up. You had no business being anywhere near there. Do you realize what you've done? Thyllan doesn't have to come to the Conclave now. And what if you were caught and he learned what you were after? He's no fool. He would have a hundred scribes in there by now, in spite of the war, and if there was anything to be found, he would have found it. And you found nothing at all!"

"The records were obviously cataloged by an idiot," said Llian. "There wasn't time."

"I cataloged them myself," said Mendark coldly. "Never make excuses to me!"

"Well, I found nothing that seemed useful. Maybe when I've—"

"Aaarrgh! Get out of my sight. Tallia? *Tallia!*"

Llian made himself scarce. He hadn't been game to tell Mendark about the stolen letters.

*   *   *

That night he couldn't sleep for thinking about his folly, and how Karan would suffer for it. In the middle of the night he started going through the letters. A sleety dawn rain was spattering on his window by the time he found the next clue. It was in a letter from Kandor to Rulke, written over a thousand years ago, when the Clysm, the devastating war between Charon and Aachim, was at its height.

                                                    17 Mard, 4201

My dear Rulke,

I am so weary of war, and this world, that I would do anything to end it. The loss of Perion [*he referred to the ruin of his empire after the Sea of Perion dried up*] has eaten the heart out of me. Once more I beg you—share what you know with me. Say the word and everything I have is yours. I will even bend the knee to you. You know how much that takes, but I am beaten.

Something happened at the time of the Forbidding. I have spent a fortune trying to find out what it was. Was it you? Let us come together on this—we are both Charon. I think you forget that sometimes. I beg you, by the one thing that you cannot refuse, that tops all other considerations: the survival of our species.

I have written to Yalkara as well. I will gladly bring what I have to Alcifer, if you will it. I wait upon your reply.

    Kandor

At last, vindication!

There was no record of a reply from Rulke. Llian knew that Kandor had been killed about a thousand years ago. Had any meeting, any exchange ever taken place? If not, might Kandor's papers still be in his abandoned stronghold, Katazza?

What was the date of his death? Learning dates was childhood stuff, done in the first year of Llian's sojourn at the college, nearly sixteen years ago. Kandor's death was quite easy to remember—Galend 22, 2092, measured in years after the Forbidding. One thousand and six years ago, almost to the day. But Kandor's letter used the Charon calendar, dating from their conquest of Aachan.

Llian converted the dates. The letter had been written more than a year before Kandor was killed. Time enough for the two, and Yalkara as well, to have met. But if so, Llian had seen nothing in the files. He'd have to get back into the archives to be sure. If there was nothing there, the next step was a journey to Katazza. Either way, he would need the money and resources that only Mendark had.

Llian tried several times to see him, to put this proposal to him, but Mendark was frantically busy and would not admit him. It would have to wait until after the Conclave.

40

THE GREAT CONCLAVE

It was the night before the Great Conclave, long past midnight. Mendark and Tallia stood before Mendark's desk, which was piled high with maps and papers and scrolls partly unrolled. They had been reviewing the protocols for the Conclave and discussing strategies all day. Llian, still exiled, was hunched up in a chair by a downstairs fire.

Suddenly there was an altercation. A bell rang in the hall. Tallia went to the window that looked down on the gate and pushed it open. The intruders were clearly visible in the light from the guardhouse. "It is Tensor," she called over her shoulder, "and there are Aachim with him, eight or nine of them. Shall I allow them?"

Mendark nodded and she called out to the guards to let them through, her voice pealing like a bell in the night silence. She went down to open the door.

"*Tensor!*" Llian cried when she told him on the way down. He ran toward the back door. Tallia caught his wrist.

"Quiet! Do you think he concerns himself with pawns at a time like this? Go upstairs."

Shortly she came up and Tensor followed, mud-spattered and weary. He refused all offers of refreshment.

"There is a Conclave tomorrow," he said. "To what purpose?" He looked around the room, his eyes piercing Llian. "Karan is here?"

Mendark told Karan's story again, briefly, wearily.

Tensor reproached himself bitterly. "Emmant! That was my doing. I should have foreseen this, after the Syndics cast him out. He was a very unhappy man. So Karan is taken, and the Mirror too. What can a Conclave do?"

"It was to bring them out of the citadel, though after Llian's stupidity yesterday, maybe not." He related what Llian had done.

Tensor inspected Llian as though he was a maggot in the dinner.

"The Zain has neither ethics nor honor, nor, it seems, much intelligence," he said. "Well, that later. Here is my news. We sought Karan for weeks, after Shazmak, but fruitlessly, and, until recently, harried by the Whelm. Then they vanished—they have learned to fear us! We searched as far south as Sith, though we could not get into the city, and in Bannador before the burning, but she was not there. Even to get here was an ordeal—Thurkad is ringed by great armies and must fall. After this there will be no power in Meldorin but Yggur—and the Aachim. Even as I left Shazmak my people were readying themselves."

"Then you have not been back since Karan fled?"

"So I said. But we are ready. Long have we guarded our strength for this time."

He turned to go, then stopped at the door. "I have not forgotten you, Llian of Chanthed. We will yet have our reckoning." Then he was gone.

"Mendark!" said Llian. "I need to talk to you."

"Go away. We will also have a reckoning, you and I, but not tonight."

The Conclave began in the late morning, in the Great Hall of old Thurkad. That was a long, high hall, very plain, the walls and vaulted roof paneled in dark ironwood. It was very ancient, a remnant of the earliest city, and had a special place in the hearts of the people of Thurkad. The hall was austerely furnished, with only a large table at one end and thirteen chairs, at which sat the arbitrators, the Just, and a dais beyond for witnesses and claimants. For the audience there were fixed benches with high wooden backs. Above, a high balcony looked down on the table.

Tallia led Mendark and Llian into the Great Hall and sat down at the bench behind the table of the Just. Tensor was already there.

"What if Thyllan refuses to come?" Llian asked Tallia.

"Then we must think of something else."

"You still haven't explained the purpose of this Conclave," Llian whispered to Tallia. "How can it help Karan?"

"In time of peace her case would be dealt with by the lesser Conclave, but in war it is suspended. The purpose of the Great Conclave is to deal with the danger to Thurkad, but Mendark has drawn the protocol so that the Just must resolve the ownership of the Mirror first. Everyone who has an interest in the Mirror must declare it, and plead their case; and Mendark first, because he called the Conclave."

"And if Thyllan does not abide by their arbitration? What will happen then?"

Tallia turned a shocked face to him. "The decree of the Just will not be challenged."

*   *   *

Llian sat musing on his hard bench. It was only a week to endre, mid-winter week. A week and a half to hythe, mid-winter day, an ill-omened date. And today was Galend 22, 3098; the anniversary of Kandor's death. Another coincidence?

The clock on the wall struck eleven. Thyllan had still not come. Nonetheless the Prime Just, a frail old woman with white hair and sunken cheeks, signed to Mendark to begin his address. He walked across to the dais. It was open at the front, with a semicircular wooden railing level with his chest, and behind an arched hood flared to twice his height.

"I thank you, Nelissa," he said, bowing in her direction, and beginning in his ponderous way. "I have called this Great Conclave, as is my right and duty as the longtime Magister of the Council of Santhenar, that we might find a path through the peril . . ."

The doors banged open. Thyllan had come after all, with a retinue of guards and attendants, and Karan hobbled beside him. Thyllan scowled at Mendark. There was a long swollen gash on his face, Karan's work no doubt.

Back at the dais, Mendark was completing the formalities of his entreaty. ". . . but a few days ago, unlooked for, Karan of Bannador came to us, bearing an artifact known as the Mirror of Aachan, stolen from Yggur. These last months I have spent trying to bring this device to Thurkad, for our glory as well as our defense. But Thyllan the usurper stole it, and the woman as well. This act challenges our ancient codes and threatens the safety of Thurkad itself. Will the Conclave permit it?"

"Do not waste our time with posturing, Mendark," said the Prime Just through shrunken lips. She looked old, sour and fearful. "Yours is the right, and we are hearing it, though to call a Great Conclave at this time shows only contempt for our ancient traditions. Just this morning I heard Thyllan's complaint that you broke the truce. Make your case well, or you too may be charged."

"First I would tell you of Yggur, and the foundations of his grievance against us in the Proscribed Experiments that went so wrong."

"We know it," said Nelissa, "and we also know your dubious part in it, and your penchant for rewriting history. Make your point."

"Of his taking ruined Fiz Gorgo," continued Mendark, though now he seemed to have lost the thread of his argument. "The slow . . . building of his forces, the excursions against his neighbors, until the whole of Orist was his, from the River Fiery to the Birquâsh Mountains, and all the peoples of Meldorin waited in dread. But here in Thurkad, protected by the mountains, we have laughed at him until this day. And why does he march? He blames the Council for all his troubles, though we did but . . ."

"Leave history to the plodding chroniclers," Nelissa interrupted again, "or we will still be in Conclave when he batters down the doors. Get to the root of the problem. What help can the Mirror be to us? Why did Thyllan act as he did? Was he right to do so? Karan of Bannador, you are central to this. Give us your story. No, come down here," she said, gesturing to the dais where Mendark still stood, as Karan began in an almost inaudible voice.

Karan began to rattle down the steps in her chains.

"Release her!" cried Mendark. "None may be shackled in the Great Conclave."

Thyllan gestured to his armorer, who came down with a thick key in his hand and released the chains. They rattled onto the floor, then Karan limped down to the Just, her bare feet making no sound on the stone. There were red welts about her slender ankles, and her cheek was bruised purple and black. At the dais, within its dark, flaring hood, she looked terrified and lost.

None of those present, save Llian and Tensor, had heard the story of her escape from Fiz Gorgo as she told it then. Though she spoke woodenly, looking neither to right nor left, and in a distant voice, as if it had happened to someone else, none failed to be moved by her courage. The light gradually faded from the high windows as she told of the nightmare journey. She did not tell them about the waking of the Ghâshâd though; the memories of that night at the camp near Narne were hidden too deep.

The Just listened carefully to her tale. There was a long silence when she was finished.

Tensor shook his head. "So brave, so clever and resourceful. How came you to betray us?" he said sadly.

"I betrayed the Aachim to save them from you. You are Pitlis come again."

Tensor rocked on his feet. Then he cried, "You are mad, like your mother," and dismissed everything she had said with a flick of his wrist.

"Is there not more?" Mendark asked gently. "Tell the Conclave what happened when Emmant came to your room."

"Came here? I don't remember that," she said, looking confused. She had wiped it from her memory again. Mendark filled in the details, then Karan was released, but only to the front bench where the other witnesses sat.

Servants appeared with platters of food. When it was eaten and the empty trays borne away, and they sat with their bowls of red buttery tea steaming in front of them, Mendark rose again.

"The Conclave does not know the history of the Mirror." He gave Nelissa a defiant stare. Her mouth seemed frozen, a down-hooking slash, but she signed to him to continue.

What he said was similar to what Karan had told Llian a long time ago, before Shazmak, though Mendark took rather longer to tell it.

"The Council's purpose," he continued, "has always been to study the sciences of the enemy and make defenses against him. Many battles we have fought, many defeats suffered. Few victories, save for putting Rulke into the Nightland, and keeping him there. I believed the Mirror might advance our great project (his final banishment), and sent Llian of Chanthed to find Karan and bring her to Thurkad. I have no false hopes for the Mirror: it is like a book of a million pages, each torn to pieces and cast into a barrel. We may never learn to decipher it." Mendark paused, but Nelissa merely waved tiredly.

"Thus we come to the essence. Thyllan threw me down from the citadel and seized the Mirror for himself. For himself," he repeated. "My long service in the Council is known to all, but Thyllan is an upstart, an adventurer, a self-seeker. Are you fools, to trust the fate of Thurkad to one such as he?"

"Mendark twists the truth to suit his own case," Tallia said in Llian's ear. "Thyllan and he have long been warring."

Thyllan leapt to his feet. "Mendark calls you fools because that is how he thinks of you. But you know the truth of the matter," he boomed, looking at each of them in turn. "He plays games with words. The project is obsolete— Rulke dwindles. Each time we check him he is weaker, duller. Soon he will be so feeble that we can reach into the Nightland and crush him: then Santhenar will be free. May that day come while I am Magister. Do not be swayed by the sneers of Mendark. He shows how little he values your counsel."

"No," cried Karan wildly, "for Rulke touches me in my dreams. He is cruel, and strong."

Thyllan looked at her pityingly. "Always it is the mad ones who are touched by the finger of the gods. You may have your dreams, but leave the affairs of Thurkad to those who dream only of its glory."

"That is a deadly folly," shouted Mendark. "Thyllan tells you what you want to hear, as Rulke shows you what you want to see." But Mendark seemed to speak without conviction, and beside Thyllan he looked old and weak, and the Conclave began to turn away from him.

"The fool is old," Thyllan roared, "trapped in the past! Santhenar is being refashioned and so must the Council be. The Mirror shows us the way. The secret of making portals lies within it—instant travel anywhere in the world. What power will Thurkad have then?"

Thyllan was magnificent, his hair wild and his eyes glowing, and he awoke in the breasts of all who listened a lust for power, a longing for great leadership, and a greed for the glory that would be Thurkad. "Under Mendark we declined, while he diverted himself with trifles. And where is the wealth of the Council now? The treasury is bankrupt, yet he idles away his dotage in luxury." He flung out his arm at Mendark. "The result—Yggur is at our gate! We must meet him, destroy the threat and make Thurkad strong again, a great, proud city, the first city of Meldorin, even of Santhenar. Already our armies have hurt the enemy. We will cast him back into the stinking swamps of Orist where he belongs."

Now he spoke quietly, cajolingly, as one who was not required to explain but did so anyway, out of his great regard for his subjects. "I expelled Mendark, it is true, but only for the good of Thurkad. He has so little honor that he broke the truce of the Conclave yesterday, sending his chronicler to steal into the citadel. *Why was he really there?* Not to set free this girl, as he pretended. He broke into Rulke's archives. *What was it he sought so urgently?* Mendark has kept that from the Conclave. Something to his advantage, you can be sure."

Mendark glared at Llian through bushy eyebrows, as though to say, *see what you've done, you fool!*

"Why, Mendark?" cried Nelissa. "What was Llian looking for?"

"I cannot tell the Conclave that," Mendark said. "I will say it only to the Arbitrator, in private."

"One rule for Mendark, a different one for everyone else," Thyllan said with venom.

Nelissa held up her hand. "I cannot force you, but it weakens your case immeasurably, Mendark." And from that moment the mood of the room shifted perceptibly to Thyllan's side.

"Who would you trust?" Thyllan roared. "Mendark broke the truce, showing the contempt he feels for me and for the traditions of Thurkad. But still I came to his Conclave to explain what I have done. Yes, I took the Mirror. I am proud to admit it. It will be the foundation of our new project, and we will have the powers of the Charon. No longer will we struggle just to keep watch on Rulke; we will destroy him. His strength will be Thurkad's. Would you give up such a destiny?"

A great sigh of yearning went through the Conclave.

Then the moment was shattered. "You know nothing of the Mirror," came a high, cold voice from the balcony above. "You will never learn its secrets."

The whole Conclave looked up. Standing at the railing was a small woman dressed in dusty traveling clothes, her long silver hair plaited and bound up at the nape of her neck.

There was such a puissance, a strength of purpose about her that even the Prime Just quavered when she asked her name.

"I am Faelamor," the woman said. "I did not die; I hid myself from the world. It was I who trained Maigraith to creep into Fiz Gorgo and take the Mirror. It is mine, *and I will have it!*"

Tensor was on his feet, staring at her with such intensity that scarcely could he restrain himself from crying out.

Faelamor turned back to the Just. "You are wrong about the Mirror. It was only ever used by the Aachim as a seeing device, a trivial thing. In the Clysm Yalkara took the Mirror, that the Aachim laid aside, *that they no longer dared to use,* and bent it to her will, using it for seeing and spying. In her last years we fought many battles, she and I, but at last I was defeated, for she knew too many secrets. She found a warp in the Forbidding, made a gateway and fled, leaving the Mirror behind.

"So it is mine, the spoils of war. But I lay at the point of death for many years, and in that time the Mirror was hidden. When at last I regained my strength, I put it about that I was dead. I sought the Mirror, and learned that Yggur had found it."

Her voice was cold and even and strong. She had no need of rhetoric. "The Mirror has no power, none at all. What it has, if you can read it, is knowledge, and many, many secrets, not least the one that you mention, the way that Yalkara made her gate. But none *here* can render it. Yalkara locked it, and there is only one key. *I have that key.*"

Tensor stood up. He raised his hand, and a still expectancy came over the room. He looked toward the Prime Just.

"Arbitrator, attend your office. There is no dispute that the Mirror is ours; we made it in Aachan in the depths of time and brought it here to Santhenar. No dispute that it was stolen from us by Yalkara. No other has the right to it."

"What do you say to this?" asked Nelissa, turning to Faelamor.

"Mad Karan was right! Tensor would use it against Rulke and drag the whole world into war. The Aachim have declined to nothing and will not see it. They have forfeited their right."

"We care for this world and will do nothing to harm it," Tensor said vehemently. "Faelamor would smash the Forbidding, break open the Way between the Worlds and bare Santhenar to the violence of the void. Give the Mirror back. Our enemy is your enemy. We have a weapon against him that cannot fail."

Tensor drew himself up, his dark eyes flashing, and he was glorious—his pride in the renascence of the Aachim was unshakable. Then he looked to Faelamor. "*How came you here?*" he said, in a great voice. "How did you get out of Shazmak?"

"Did I not say to you that you could not hold me?" she replied. "That your folly would set in motion the doom of the Aachim? So it proved to be, for the Whelm have found the secret way into Shazmak and it lies in ruins."

"Ruins!" cried Tensor, in a voice that curdled the breath of those that watched. "What of my people?"

"I know of none who lived."

"All dead?" said Tensor. "*All dead!*" His voice sank to a whisper. He stood for a moment, his head bowed, then suddenly he snapped erect, letting out a cry of agony that tore at Llian's heart. Even Faelamor swayed back from the railing. He struggled with himself, staring into the empty air until the whole room quivered with his grief.

At last he mastered himself, and his deep voice was soft, but pregnant with menace. "How came the Whelm to Shazmak? Who showed them the way? Why would they do this?"

Faelamor's voice was equally soft, and so low that the watchers could scarce hear it. "Why? Do you not know who the Whelm are, you who just boasted so loudly of the strength of the Aachim? They are Ghâshâd, your ancient enemies that Rulke twisted to his own purpose, long ago."

"*Ghâshâd!*" Tensor looked as though he would burst with rage and terror. "Ghâshâd! This cannot be borne."

Karan cried out and squeezed her head between her hands.

"And who showed them the way?" Faelamor went on. "Who but the confessed betrayer of the Aachim? The one who was with the Whelm in Narne before they went straight to Shazmak. The one who now pretends madness that she might escape punishment for her crimes. Never was one so young so treacherous." She pointed an accusing finger.

"Karan! Karan of Bannador. *She* is the betrayer. See how she cries out in her guilt and shame. *She* showed them into Shazmak!"

"Never," Karan said, weeping and trembling. "Never."

Llian was on his feet, shouting, "No! No! It is not possible," but Tallia gripped his shoulder tightly and pressed him back in his seat.

"That is not the way of the Conclave," she said. "She will have her chance."

Llian turned a bewildered face to her, terrified for Karan. "This is no Conclave, it is a trial, a farce, and she has no one to defend her."

Karan faced her accuser, but it was clear to Llian that the madness was coming on her again. "Not I," she wept, shaking and shivering. "I did not betray Shazmak, even under the torture of the Whelm." The suppressed memory burst into her brain. "*She* it was who showed them," she said. "Faelamor did it! She promised me to Emmant. She gave him a charm to bind me. In return he showed the Whelm the secret path into Shazmak, and taught them to disable the Sentinels. He told me so, before I killed him." Her face showed her horror. "Killed him . . ." Her voice trailed away.

Tensor looked at Faelamor.

"The girl is confessed to be a liar, a betrayer, a murderer," said Faelamor. "To escape her crimes she pretends madness. Nothing she says can be believed."

"It cannot be denied," said Tensor heavily.

Karan's eyes went wildly around the room. Mendark she saw, and Tallia, Tensor, Thyllan, others that she knew; but none would meet her eye. None believed her. Then she looked on Llian, through a mist, and there were tears running down his cheeks. Her only friend now.

There came a commotion outside. Nelissa had been speaking quietly with the other Just. Now she used her thin arms to push herself to her feet and stood at the end of the table, leaning on her stick, swaying.

She is weak and confused, thought Llian in horror. She will condemn Karan unheard. He looked up at Faelamor. She too was on her feet, gripping the railing.

Outside, even through the closed doors, they heard the pounding feet, the shouts, the cries, the hammering at the door. A guard drew it open and a tall man in the garb of a messenger crashed into the room. He fell to his knees, gasping for breath. His uniform was splattered with blood. He forced himself to his feet, staring around the room until his eyes lit on Thyllan.

"The war . . ." he croaked.

Thyllan clambered over the benches in his haste. "How goes the war, messenger? There is a setback?"

"The war is over," the messenger said limply. "The army

is utterly destroyed. Yggur is at the southern gate. There are too few to defend it. Thurkad is done."

The shouting died away. The rain, which had been falling heavily all day, eased suddenly. Faelamor had come down from the balcony and stood near the Prime Just, but she seemed anxious and kept looking up. Tensor watched her with narrowed eyes. Now every eye turned to Nelissa, who still stood.

She spoke with effort, her voice rasping. "This is our Arbitration.

"Tensor, your claim is valid. The Mirror is yours by right, but how can we give it back? The Aachim are destroyed and our need is dire. Your warnings and the warnings of Faelamor are heeded, yet we know our enemy, and he is Yggur. We will keep the Mirror until the war is over and the enemy defeated. Thyllan, you acted improperly and we reprimand you. Yet we know you acted only for Thurkad. There is no penalty."

The silence was absolute. No one moved or spoke. All eyes were on Tensor. The despair on his face drained away, replaced by an absent, lost look, but his jaw was set and his lips moved.

Mendark started, then leapt up onto the dais.

"There is power enough in this room," he cried out, "to hold back even the might of Yggur. Our weakness is his strength. Let us put aside our differences and unite against him. When he is defeated will be time to consider the Mirror."

A murmur of assent went round the room. All eyes were on Tensor now. Faelamor edged closer; a tremor shook her small frame. Tensor's shoulders slumped; he strained his lips into a broken smile, at last dipping his head in acquiescence. A little sigh came from Tallia. The tension eased.

"Karan of Bannador," Nelissa said, without a trace of pity, "at another time you would be put away. But we are at war now, in great peril, and treachery breeds treachery. We can show no humanity to traitors. Take her outside," she said, making a slashing motion to the guards. "Do it quickly."

Mendark leapt up again. "This is not the will of the Conclave!" he shouted. "The charges have not been proven. She cannot be touched."

"The Arbitration will not be challenged, *citizen* Mendark," said Nelissa coldly. "And you are charged with contumely against the Great Conclave. Take him as well; hold *him* below. The Conclave is ended. Go now, salvage what you can."

Faelamor stared at Karan, knowing she had won but taking no joy in it.

Karan looked up at Llian and a chaos of images flooded him: falling down the steps at her feet in the ruins; her frozen face as she sailed the Garr after the death of Rael; sharing food and wine in Shazmak, that night when she had been happy as a child; teasing him in the boat as they fled from Narne . . . The images slowly blended into one another, became her now. "Do not be sad," she seemed to be saying. "They were good times we had together, but now it is time to go." She gave him such a tender, loving smile that it broke his heart.

The guards stepped forward. Tensor bowed his head in grief. "Goodbye, little one. I am truly sorry."

They took her, one gripping each arm, and began to lead her away, and Mendark too.

A berserk rage grew in Llian. The man beside him, a high official of the city, wore a ceremonial sword, and though Llian had never used such a weapon in his life, he reached out for it, preparing to violate the Conclave and die beside Karan.

Tallia gripped his arm, saying "No!" in an urgent whisper, but he thrust her away so hard that she went backwards over the bench.

"I spit upon the ancient traditions of Thurkad," Llian said between his teeth. The sword came easily to his hand and he tensed, preparing to spring out among the guards to certain death.

Then there was a noise on the balcony above, and Faelamor called out in a high voice, "Maigraith! At last! Come forth."

Every face in the room looked up. Maigraith came to the rail and threw back her hood. The glossy dark hair cascaded over her shoulders like bundles of chestnut silk. She was not wearing her glasses. She leaned out over the railing and the lights, suddenly bright, caught her wine-dark eyes so that they gleamed like rubies.

She was looking directly at Faelamor, and there was an expression of fearful resolve on her face. She made as though to speak, but she never spoke.

Tensor stared at her with shocked intensity and sudden recognition. "Do the Charon spring up again from the earth?" he cried. "*Never more!*" He raised his hand toward Maigraith; then, as if his courage had failed him, lowered it again. Faelamor was even closer to Nelissa now. Tensor bowed his head, shaking it slowly, then jerked up at a furtive movement by Nelissa.

Karan gave a low moan that made Llian's blood congeal. The guards let go her arms, staring at her. Llian stared too, and the sword slipped from his fingers and clattered to the floor. Her thick red hair was standing up, making a halo around her head, and her eyes had rolled back until only the whites could be seen. She shook her head and beat slowly at the air with her open palms. A sick horror gripped Llian.

He heard Maigraith's voice clear from above, "No, you cannot. You must not. *No!*"

Tensor put out his hand, quite gently, toward Nelissa. There came a flash, the color of old blood, and a dull boom that echoed in Llian's ears long after the sound had died away.

Pain flared in his temples, as though his head was being ground between two boulders. His eyes seemed to boil, he was blind, then a gate closed in his brain, another opened, the pain eased and he could see again. He saw Nelissa, who still held the Mirror in her left hand. The dark cave of her mouth gaped in a scream that had no sound. Her stringy muscles spasmed violently and flung her backwards against the wall with a crack like an egg being broken. The Just were scattered like grain. The whole room went black.

Llian picked himself up from the floor. People lay prostrate everywhere. Thyllan was frozen on his knees, unable to rise, a trickle of blood running from the wound on his cheek. Tallia sat on the floor, her hands folded in her lap, her lips moving though she made no sound. Mendark lay twitching next to the dais. Faelamor was crawling slowly down the room, away from the dais, blindly bumping into fallen chairs and table legs. Maigraith could not be seen, though a slim hand hung through the iron of the balcony.

Tensor stepped forward and plucked the Mirror from Nelissa's lifeless fingers. Llian looked frantically around the room. Why had he been spared? His courage wavered. What could he do when the powerful had failed?

Then his gaze fell on Karan, crumpled on the floor between her guards, blood pooling on the floor beside her, her hair gone limp, the bruise livid on her pale face. A great anger grew in him, a fury at Tensor, at Mendark, at Thyllan and Faelamor and Nelissa; no, no longer at Nelissa, she was gone. At Tensor, especially at Tensor. Then he was on his toes and running silently across the room, picking up the stick that Nelissa had used to support herself, there where it lay beside the table, lifting it high and bringing it down with a crack on the back of Tensor's head.

Tensor stopped, then slowly turned around. The potency had hurt even him. His face and hands were ghastly white. He swayed. There was red on his lip and chin. His bloody eyes transfixed Llian and held him.

"You alone are unaffected," he breathed. "I have need of one such as you. Come to your reckoning, chronicler."

"I will not go with you," said Llian, hating and fearing him, but though his will was as iron his legs would not obey.

Tensor took him by the hand and led him, without even a struggle, from the Great Hall and out of Thurkad by a secret way, to the north.

GLOSSARY

of Characters, Names and Places

Aachan: One of the Three Worlds, the world of the Aachim and, after its conquest, the Charon.

Aachim: The human species native to Aachan, who were conquered by the Charon. The Aachim are a clever people, great artisans and engineers, but melancholy and prone to hubris. After they were brought to Santhenar the Aachim flourished, but were betrayed and ruined in the Clysm, and withdrew from the world to their vast mountain fortress cities.

Aachimning: A friend of the Aachim.

Aftersickness: Sickness that most people suffer after using the Secret Art, or even after using a native talent. Sensitives are very prone to it.

Alcifer: The last and greatest of Rulke's cities, designed by Pitlis the Aachim.

Almadin: A dry land across the sea from Thurkad.

Alyz: Llian's little sister.

Assembly: The ruling committee of Thurkad. A body that is ineffectual in a crisis.

Bannador: A long, narrow and hilly land on the western side of Iagador. Karan's homeland.

Benbow: A ruined village in the mountains between Chanthed and Tullin.

Blase: One of Tensor's Aachim band.

Blending: A child of the union between two different human species. Blendings are rare, and often deranged, but can have remarkable talents.

Booreah Ngurle: The burning mountain, or fiery mountain, a volcanic peak in the forests east of Almadin. The Charon once had a stronghold there.

Callam: Llian's older sister.

Carstain: Nearest town to Fiz Gorgo.

Chacalot: A large water-dwelling reptile, somewhat resembling a crocodile.

Chain of the Tychid: A ribbon of seven very bright stars, and many fainter ones, visible in the winter sky at southern latitudes.

Chanthed: A town in northern Meldorin, in the foothills of the mountains. The College of the Histories is there.

Chard: A kind of tea.

Charon: One of the four human species, the master people of the world of Aachan. They fled out of the void to take Aachan from the Aachim, and took their name from a frigid moonlet at the furthest extremity of the void. They have strange eyes, indigo or carmine, or sometimes both together, depending on the light.

Chronicler: A historian; a graduate in the art and science of recording and maintaining the Histories.

Cloak, Cloaked: To disguise oneself by means of illusion.

Clysm: A series of wars between the Charon and the Aachim more than a thousand years ago, resulting in the almost total devastation of Santhenar.

College of the Histories: The oldest of the colleges for the instruction of those who would be chroniclers or tellers of the Histories, or even lowly bards or king's singers. It was set up at Chanthed soon after the time of the Forbidding.

Compulsion: A form of the Secret Art; a way of forcing someone to do something against their will.

Construct: A machine partly powered by the Secret Art.

Council; also Council of Iagador, Council of Santhenar, Great Council, High Council: An alliance of the powerful. With the Aachim it made the Nightland and cast Rulke into it. After that it had two purposes—to continue the great project (q.v.) and to maintain the watch upon Rulke.

Crayde: A town in Iagador.

Darsh: An untranslatable Aachim epithet (very offensive).

Dirhan: Customs officer in Sith and friend to Pender and Hassien.

Dolodha: A messenger girl; one of Yggur's servants.

Droik: Idlis's dog.

Elienor: A great heroine of the Aachim from the time when the Charon invaded Aachan.

Emmant: A half-Aachim, librarian at Shazmak. He also traveled in disguise as Flacq.

Faelamor: Leader of the Faellem species who came to Santhenar soon after Rulke, to keep watch on the Charon and maintain the balance between the worlds. Maigraith's liege.

Faellem: The human species who are the original inhabitants of the world of Tallallame. They are a small, dour people who, by long custom, are forbidden to use machines and particularly magical devices, but are masters of disguise and illusion. Faelamor's band were trapped on Santh by the Forbidding, and constantly search for a way home.

Faichand: The name that Faelamor went by when she hid herself from the world.

Farsh: A mild obscenity.

Festival of Chanthed: An annual festival held in Chanthed, at which the Histories are told by the masters and students of the College.

Fiz Gorgo: A fortress city in Orist, flooded in ancient times, now restored; the stronghold of Yggur.

Flute; also golden flute: A device made in Aachan at the behest of Rulke, by the genius smith Shuthdar, stolen by him and taken back to Santhenar. When used by one who is sensitive, it could be used to open the Way between the Worlds. It was destroyed by Shuthdar at the time of the Forbidding.

Folc: A flat dry country north of Chanthed.

Forbidding: See *Tale of the Forbidding*.

Fyrn: The family name of Karan of Bannador, from her mother's side.

Galardil: A forested land east of Orist.

Galliad: Karan's father, who was half-Aachim.

Garr: The largest river in Meldorin. It arises to the west of Shazmak and runs to the Sea of Thurkad east of Sith.

Gellon: A fruit, tasting something like a mango and something like a peach.

Ghâshâd: The ancient, mortal enemies of the Aachim. They were corrupted and swore allegiance to Rulke after the Zain rebelled, but when Rulke was put in the Nightland they forgot themselves and took a new name, Whelm.

Gift of Rulke; also Curse of Rulke: Knowledge given by Rulke to the Zain, enhancing their resistance to the mind-breaking potencies of the Aachim. It left stigmata that identified them as Zain.

Gistel: A servant of Faelamor in Sith.

Gothryme: Karan's impoverished manor, near Tolryme in Bannador.

Great Betrayer: Rulke.

Great Conclave: A forum which may be called in Thurkad to resolve some great crisis afflicting the city.

Great Library: Founded at Zile by the Zain in the time of the Empire of Zur. The library was sacked when the Zain were exiled, but was subsequently re-established.

Great Mountains: The largest and highest belt of mountains on Santhenar, enclosing the south-eastern part of the continent of Lauralin.

Great Project: A way sought by the Council to banish the Charon from Santh forever.

Great River: see Garr.

Great Tales: The greatest stories from the Histories of Santhenar; traditionally told at the Festival of Chanthed, and everywhere on important ceremonial occasions. There are twenty-two of these.

Grint: A copper coin of small value.

Hassien: A woman living with Pender in Narne.

Hennia: A Zain. She is a member of the Council of Iagador.

Hetchet, Gate of Hetchet: A town to the west of Chanthed; once a great city.

Histories: The vast collection of records which tell more than four thousand years of recorded history on Santhenar. The Histories consist of historical documents written by the chroniclers, as well as the tales, songs, legends and lore of the peoples of Santhenar and the invading peoples from the other worlds, told by the tellers. The culture of Santhenar is interwoven with and inseparable from the Histories, and the most vital longing anyone can have is to be mentioned there.

High Way: A north-south road on the eastern side of the island of Meldorin.

Hirthway: The main north-south road running through the center of Meldorin.

Hythe: Mid-winter's day. It is the fourth day of endre, midwinter's week. Hythe is a day of ill-omen.

Iagador: The land that lies between the mountains and the Sea of Thurkad.

Idlis: The least of the Whelm, long-time hunter of Karan. Also a healer.

Jark-un: The leader of a band of the Whelm.

Jepperand: A province on the western side of the mountains of Crandor. Home to the Zain; Llian's birthplace.

Just: The arbitrators in a Great Conclave of Thurkad. They are also responsible for the administration of justice.

Kalash: A drug given by Faelamor to Maigraith to disguise the color of her eyes.

Kandor: One of the three Charon who came to Santhenar. He was killed sometime after the end of the Clysm, the only Charon to die on Santh.

Karan, Karan of Bannador: A woman of the house of Fyrn, but with blood of the Aachim from her father Galliad. She is a sensitive and lives at Gothryme.

Lake Neid: A lake in the swamp forest near Fiz Gorgo, where the half-submerged ruins of the town of Neid are found.

Lasee: A pale yellow brewed drink, mildly intoxicating, and ubiquitous in Orist; fermented from the sweet sap of the sard tree.

Lauralin: The continent east of the Sea of Thurkad.

Lay of the Silver Lake: An epic romance that tells of the subjection of the tiny state of Saludith.

League: About 5000 paces, three miles or five kilometers.

Library of the Histories: The famous library at the College of the Histories in Chanthed.

Lightglass: A device of crystal and metal that emits a soft light when touched.

Lilis: A street urchin in Thurkad.

Link, Linking; also **Talent of Linking:** A joining of minds, by which sensitives' thoughts and feelings can be shared, and support given. Sometimes used for domination.

Llayis: Llian's father, a scribe.

Llian: A Zain, and a master chronicler and a teller. A great student of the Histories.

Magister: A mancer and chief of the High Council of Iagador. Mendark has been Magister for a thousand years.

Maigraith: An orphan brought up and trained by Faelamor for some unknown purpose. A master of the Secret Art.

Mancer: A wizard or sorcerer; someone who is a master of the Secret Art.

Mantille: An Aachim; Karan's paternal grandmother.

Master Chronicler: One who has mastered the study of the Histories, and graduated with highest honor from the College.

Master of Chanthed: Currently Wistan. The Master of the College of the Histories is also nominal leader of Chanthed.

Meldorin: The large island that lies to the immediate west of the Sea of Thurkad and the continent of Lauralin.

Mendark: Magister of the Council of Iagador, until thrown down by Thyllan. A mancer of strength and subtlety, though lately insecure due to the rise of his long-time enemy, Yggur.

Mirror of Aachan: A device made by the Aachim in Aachan, for seeing things at a distance. In Santhenar it changed and twisted reality, and so the Aachim hid it away. The Mirror also developed a memory, retaining the imprints of things it had seen. It was stolen by Yalkara and used to find a warp in the Forbidding and to escape back to Aachan.

Nadiril: The head of the Great Library in Zile. Nadiril the Sage is also a member of the Council of Iagador.

Narcies: Tragic heroine of the *Lay of the Silver Lake*.

Narne: A town and port at the navigable extremity of the Garr.

Necroturge: One who has communion with the dead.

Neid: see Lake Neid.

Nelissa: A member of the Council of Iagador and Prime Just of the Great Conclave.

Nightland: A place, distant from the world of reality, wherein Rulke is kept prisoner.

Old human: The original human species on Santhenar, and still by far the most numerous.

Orist: A land of swamps and forests on the south-west side of Meldorin; the land of Yggur. Fiz Gorgo is there.

Orstand: A justice and member of the Council. Mendark's oldest friend.

Pash-lar: Whelm word for the Mirror of Aachan.

Pellban: Fifth master of Chanthed and author of the *Lay of the Silver Lake*.

Pender: A boatman who has fallen on hard times.

Perion, Empire of: The Great Empire of Kandor. It collapsed after the Sea of Perion dried up.

Pitlis: A great Aachim of the distant past, whose folly betrayed the great city of Tar Gaarn to Rulke and broke the power of the Aachim. He was the architect who designed Tar Gaarn and Alcifer. He was slain by Rulke.

Port Cardasson: The port of Thurkad.

Proscribed Experiments: Sorcerous procedures designed to find a flaw in the Forbidding which could be used to banish Rulke forever. Hazardous because of the risk of Rulke taking control of the experimenter.

Preddle: A walled city on the Hirthway.

Quilsin: A land to the south of Orist.

Qwelt: A badly scarred man who worked in a stable in Preddle.

Rael: An Aachim, half-cousin to Karan.

Read: Truth-reading. A way of forcing someone to tell the whole truth.

Recorder: The unknown person who set down the tales of the four great battles of Faelamor and Yalkara, among many other tales. He is thought to have taken the Mirror (after Yalkara finally defeated Faelamor and fled Santh) and hidden it against some future need.

Rulke: A Charon of Aachan, known also as the Great Betrayer. He enticed Shuthdar to Aachan to make the golden flute, and so began all the troubles. After the Clysm he was imprisoned in the Nightland until a way could be found to banish him back to Aachan.

Santhenar, Santh: The least of the Three Worlds, occupied by the old human peoples.

Sard tree: A tall tree that dominates the swamp forests of

Orist. Its papery bark is used for writing scrolls and its sweet sap for brewing lasee.

Sea of Thurkad: The long sea that divides Meldorin from the continent of Lauralin.

Secret Art: The use of magical or sorcerous powers.

Secret of the Charon: The method of making and using the flute.

Sending: A message, thoughts or feelings sent from one mind to another.

Sentinels: Devices that keep watch and sound an alarm.

Shand: An old man who works at the inn at Tullin, and is more than he seems.

Shazmak: The forgotten city of the Aachim, in the mountains west of Bannador.

Shuthdar: An old human of Santhenar, the maker of the golden flute. After he destroyed the flute and himself, the Forbidding came down, closing off the Way between the Worlds.

Sith: A free city and trading nation built on an island in the River Garr, in southern Iagador.

Skeet: A carrier bird, gray or blue-gray. Large, ugly and ill-tempered.

Skretza: An untranslatable word of offense.

Slukk: A Whelm epithet (very offensive).

Span: The distance spanned by the stretched arms of a tall man. About six feet, or slightly less than two meters.

Stassor: A city of the Aachim, in eastern Lauralin.

Sundor: Once a proud city in central Meldorin, now just a village.

Sweetcake: A thin round biscuit, between a bread and a teacake, but hard; sweetened with honey and flavored with petal water.

Syndics: A ruling Council of the Aachim, sometimes a panel of judges. None can lie to them in formal trial.

Szdorny: An Aachim term for one who is cunning and clever. It denotes both admiration and disapproval.

Tale of the Forbidding: Greatest of the Great Tales, it tells of the final destruction of the flute by Shuthdar. The Forbidding sealed Santhenar from the other two worlds.

Talent: A native skill or gift, usually honed by extensive training.

Tales of the Aachim: An ancient summary history of the Aachim, prepared soon after the founding of Shazmak.

Tallallame: One of the Three Worlds, the world of the Faellem. A beautiful, mountainous world covered in forest.

Tallia: A trusted lieutenant of Mendark. She is a mancer and a master of combat with and without weapons.

Tar: A silver coin widely used in Meldorin. Enough to keep a family for several weeks.

Tar Gaarn: Principal city of the Aachim in the time before the Clysm; it lay east of Crandor.

Tell: A gold coin to the value of twenty silver tars.

Teller: One who has mastered the ritual telling of the tales that form part of the Histories of Santhenar.

Tensor: The leader of the Aachim. He sees his destiny as to restore the Aachim and finally take their revenge on Rulke, who betrayed and ruined them. He is proud to the point of folly.

Terror-guard: The Whelm.

Three Worlds: Santhenar, Aachan and Tallallame.

Thurkad: The timeless city, the most ancient in all of Santhenar, and the wickedest. A very populous city on the River Saboth and the Sea of Thurkad. Seat of the Council and the Magister.

Thyllan: Warlord of Iagador and member of the Council.

He intrigues against Mendark and overthrows him as Magister.

Tiltilluin and **Tintilluin:** Twin mountains guarding the high pass from Tullin to Bannador.

Tintinnuin: A volcanic peak south of Tullin.

Tiriel: Lover of Narcies, tragic heroine of the *Lay of the Silver Lake*.

Tirthrax: The principal city of the Aachim, in the Great Mountains.

Tolryme: A town in northern Bannador, close to Karan's family seat, Gothryme.

Triune: A double blending—one with the blood of all Three Worlds, three different human species. They are extremely rare and may have remarkable abilities.

Trusco: The captain of the college guard and Wistan's only friend.

Tullin: A tiny village in the mountains south of Chanthed. Shand lives there.

Turlew: A bitter, failed chronicler, now Seneschal to Wistan.

Twisted Mirror: The Mirror of Aachan. So called because it does not always show true.

Vartila: The leader of a band of the Whelm, and rival to Jarkun.

Voice: The ability of great tellers to move their audience to any emotion they choose by the sheer power of their words.

Vuula: Karan's mother, who killed herself after the death of Galliad.

Wahn Barre: The Crow Mountains. Yalkara, the Mistress of Deceits, had a stronghold there, Havissard. A place of ill-omen.

Walf: A smuggler who guided Maigraith and Karan to Fiz Gorgo.

Way Between the Worlds: The secret, forever-changing and ethereal paths that permit the difficult passage between the Three Worlds. Closed off by the Forbidding.

Whelm: Presently servants of Yggur, his terror-guard; formerly Ghâshâd.

Wistan: The seventy-fourth Master of the College of the Histories and of Chanthed.

Yalkara: The Demon Queen, the "Mistress of Deceits." The last of the three Charon who came to Santhenar to find the flute and return it to Aachan. She took the Mirror and used it to find a warp in the Forbidding, then fled Santh leaving the Mirror behind.

Yggur: A great and powerful mancer. Formerly a member of the Council, now a renegade, living in Fiz Gorgo. His armies have overrun most of southern Meldorin.

Zain: A scholarly race who once dwelt in Zile and founded the Great Library. They made a pact with Rulke and after his fall were slaughtered, the remnant exiled. They now dwell in Jepperand and make no alliances.

Zile: A city in the northwest of the island of Meldorin. Once capital of the Empire of Zur. Now chiefly famous for the Great Library.

Zophy: Llian's mother, an illuminator.

Zurean Empire: An ancient empire in the north of Meldorin. Its capital was Zile.

GUIDE TO PRONUNCIATION

There are no silent letters, and double consonants are generally pronounced as two separate letters; for example, *Yggur* is pronounced *Yg-ger*, and *Faellem* as *Fael-lem*. The letter *c* is usually pronounced as *k*, except in *mancer* and *Alcifer*, where it is pronounced as *s*, as in *manser, Alsifer*. The combination *ch* is generally pronounced as in *church*, except in *Aachim* and *Charon*, where it is pronounced as *k*.

Aachim	Ar'-kim	**Chanthed**	Chan-thed'
Charon	Kar'-on	**Faelamor**	Fay-el'-amor
Fyrn	Firn	**Ghâshâd**	G-harsh'-ard
Iagador	Eye-aga'-dor	**Karan**	Ka-ran'
Lasee	Lar'-say	**Llian**	Lee'-an
Maigraith	May'-gray-ith	**Neid**	Nee'-id
Rael	Ray'-il	**Shuthdar**	Shoo'-th-dar'
Whelm	H'-welm	**Yggur**	Ig'-ger

VISIT WARNER ASPECT ONLINE!

THE WARNER ASPECT HOMEPAGE
You'll find us at: www.twbookmark.com then by clicking on Science Fiction and Fantasy.

NEW AND UPCOMING TITLES
Each month we feature our new titles and reader favorites.

AUTHOR INFO
Author bios, bibliographies and links to personal websites.

CONTESTS AND OTHER FUN STUFF
Advance galley giveaways, autographed copies, and more.

THE ASPECT BUZZ
What's new, hot and upcoming from Warner Aspect: awards news, bestsellers, movie tie-in information . . .